Every Bride NEEDS A GROOM

Also by Janice Thompson and available from Center Point Large Print:

The Icing on the Cake
The Dream Dress
A Bouquet of Love

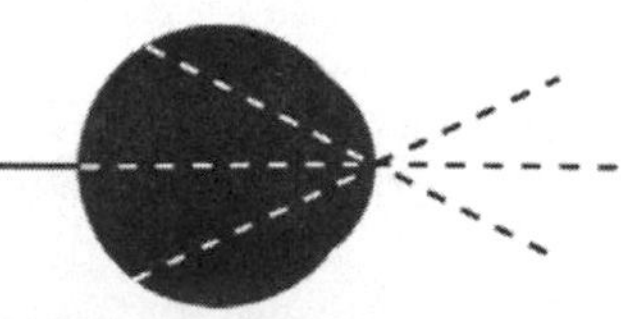

This Large Print Book carries the Seal of Approval of N.A.V.H.

BRIDES WITH STYLE • 1

Every Bride NEEDS A GROOM

Janice Thompson

CENTER POINT LARGE PRINT
THORNDIKE, MAINE

This Center Point Large Print edition is published
in the year 2015 by arrangement with Revell,
a division of Baker Publishing Group.

This book is a work of fiction. Names, characters, places, and incidents are the product of the author's imagination or are used fictitiously. Any resemblance to actual events, locales, or persons, living or dead, is coincidental.

The text of this Large Print edition is unabridged.
In other aspects, this book may vary
from the original edition.
Printed in the United States of America
on permanent paper.
Set in 16-point Times New Roman type.

ISBN: 978-1-62899-619-7

Library of Congress Cataloging-in-Publication Data

Thompson, Janice A.
Every bride needs a groom / Janice Thompson. —
Center Point Large Print edition.
pages cm
Summary: "Katie Fisher wins a designer wedding dress on the same day her boyfriend breaks up with her. In order to use the dress, she'll have to find a groom"— Provided by publisher.
ISBN 978-1-62899-619-7 (library binding : alk. paper)
1. Dating (Social customs)—Fiction. 2. Large type books. I. Title.
PS3620.H6824E94 2015b
813′.6—dc23

2015011746

To the real matriarch of Fairfield, Texas:
Eleanor Clark.
You have inspired me, reshaped my view
of the golden years, and given me hope
that I can continue to share my gift
all of my days, no matter my age.

And to the queen of country music,
the amazing Loretta Lynn.
What fun to name my chapters
after your song titles!

Every Bride NEEDS A GROOM

1

God's Country

> It was very much like Norman Rockwell: small town America. We walked to school or rode our bikes, stopped at the penny candy store on the way home from school, skated on the pond.
>
> Dorothy Hamill

That whole thing about being a big fish in a small pond is more than just a saying, at least in my neck of the woods. When you grow up in a sweeter-than-peaches town like Fairfield, Texas, you find yourself captivated by the love of family, friends, and neighbors. And don't even get me started on the church folks. They'll swallow you up with their bosomy hugs and convince you that you're the greatest thing since sliced bread.

If you're not careful, you'll start believing it too, especially if you're fortunate enough to be named Peach Queen like I was my senior year at Fairfield High. And why not? Why shouldn't a small-town girl like me allow a little lovin' from the locals to go to her head? Being a somebody in a small setting is a sure sight better than being a nobody in a big one.

Not that us small-town girls are unaware of the goings-on beyond our quaint borders, mind you. Oh no. I've had glimpses of life beyond the confines of my little town—say, on one of those housewives reality shows. But I can't picture it. Not really. I mean, who in their right mind would treat their friends and family members like that? And the language! If I ever took to swearin' like those potty-mouthed gals, my mama would stick a bar of soap so far down my throat I'd be gargling bubbles for days to come. No thank you. I may be twenty-four years old, but respect for my elders has been pounded into me. If I ever lost sight of it, my grandmother would be happy to remind me with a swift kick to my backside.

We small-towners aren't just taught respect, we genuinely care about our neighbors. It's not unusual for folks to linger in the checkout line at Brookshire Brothers grocery store to chat about the weather or discuss plans for the upcoming peach festival. And the investment at our local churches is stronger still. The big news there most often revolves around the various prayer lists, where the Pentecostals are interceding for Brother Sanderson, who has undergone a much-needed hip replacement, and the Baptists are shocked to hear that Bessie May Jenson, the congregation's oldest member, has recently suffered a gall bladder attack. This sort of news is always followed by a rousing chorus of "God bless 'em!"

and "Don't stop praying!" from the prayer warriors.

And boy howdy, do those prayer warriors take their work seriously. The Fairfield Women of Prayer—known to the locals as the WOP-pers—have pulled many a wandering soul back from the abyss. Take Levi Nash, for instance. Fairfield High's best-loved football hero tried to get involved with drugs his freshman year of college. Stress *tried*. Party-lovin' Levi never stood a chance, not with the WOP-pers beating down heaven's door on his behalf. Before he knew it, the dear boy, as they called him, had seen the error of his ways. He'd also transferred to a Bible college in the Dallas area, where he planned to major in theology. Go figure. No doubt the WOP-pers would pray in a godly wife for Levi and a couple of precocious kids to boot.

Yep, those prayer warriors clearly had an inside track straight to the Almighty. My grandmother—known to the locals as Queenie Fisher—insisted this had something to do with the fact that the WOP-pers didn't discriminate. They invited women from all of the local denominations to pray in one accord. Even the Presbyterians. Whatever that meant.

"There's something to be said for praying in unity, Katie," Queenie would say as she wagged an arthritic finger at me. "When you're out of unity with your fellow believers, you're prone to wandering."

And heaven forbid any of us should wander. Not that the temptation rose very often. Most of us wouldn't trade our small-town living for any amount of money. Okay, so my oldest brother, Jasper, talked incessantly about moving away to Houston, but Pop always managed to reel him back in by reminding him that he would one day manage our family's hardware store. That seemed to pacify Jasper, at least for now. And Dewey, my middle brother, had talked loosely about going to A&M but ended up at the local junior college, closer to home. This, after Queenie insisted she might just have a heart attack if a family member ever moved away. My grandmother had nothing to worry about where my youngest brother, Beau, was concerned. The way Mama coddled that boy, he would never leave home. Or learn to do his own laundry. Or get a job.

With the exception of my older cousin Lori-Lou Linder, no one in my circle had ever moved away to the big city. Who would want to leave paradise, after all? Certainly not me. Not now. Not ever. In my perfect small-town world, Daddy coached Little League, Mama directed the choir at our local Baptist church on Thursday nights, and Queenie sat enthroned as Fairfield's most revered matriarch. And that was precisely how I liked it.

I pondered my idyllic life as I drove to the local Dairy Queen on the last Thursday in April. After a full day's work at our family's hardware store, I was due a break, and what better place than my favorite local hangout? Besides, Casey would be waiting on me in our special booth, the second one on the left. If I knew him well enough—and I did—he would have my Oreo Blizzard waiting for me.

Waiting.

Casey.

Hmm. Seemed a little ironic that my boyfriend would be waiting on me for a change. How many months—okay, years—had I spent waiting on him to ask me to marry him? Seemed like forever. Oh well. Something as great as a marriage proposal to an amazing fella like Casey was worth the wait. Besides, I had every reason to believe it wouldn't be long before he popped the question. The signs were all there.

Any moment now I'd have a wedding to plan. Not that the lack of a proposal had slowed down my hoping and dreaming. I'd started mapping out my wedding at the age of six, when I'd first served as a flower girl. In the years since, I'd turned wedding planning into an art form.

A delicious shiver ran down my spine as I thought about how wonderful my big day would be. I'd planned out every single detail, right down to the music, the colors of the bridesmaid dresses, and even the flavor of the cake. Of course, all of it hinged on one thing: Casey's proposal.

Which, I felt sure, would arrive any day now.

Just as I pulled into a parking spot at the DQ, my cell phone rang. I recognized my cousin's number. After turning off the car, I climbed out and took the call. "Hey, Lori-Lou!"

Her usual cheerful voice sounded from the other end of the line with a hearty, "Hey yourself! What are you up to today? Working?"

"Hmm? What?" I waved at Casey through the big plate-glass window at the front of the DQ, then pointed at my phone to let him know I'd be a minute. "Oh, yeah." I turned my attention back to my cousin. "Just wrapped up at the hardware store. We've been swapping out the window displays for the upcoming summer season. Now I'm meeting Casey at Dairy Queen for an Oreo Blizzard."

A lingering sigh erupted from Lori-Lou's end of the line. "I'm so jealous."

"Of what?" I leaned against my car but found myself distracted by the pensive expression on Casey's face. Weird.

"A Blizzard sounds great in this heat." She sighed again. "It's sweltering outside and it's not even summer yet."

"Ah. It is hot."

"Our AC is on the fritz and we don't have the money right now to fix it. That's not helping things. But honestly? I'm most jealous because I can't remember the last time I had a minute to do anything fun with Josh like hang out at Dairy Queen."

"Aw, I'm sorry." And I was. Sort of. I mean, how bad could it be? The girl had a great husband and three adorable—albeit rowdy—children.

"You have no idea what it's like to be married, Katie," she said.

Gee, thanks.

"Well, married with kids, anyway. We never have date nights anymore. These three kiddos of ours are so—" The intensity of Lori-Lou's voice grew as she hollered out, "Mariela, stop eating your sister's gummy worms! Do you want to end up in time-out again?"

I giggled. "Nope. Don't want to end up in time-out again. And give that ornery little girl a hug from me. I miss her."

"Sure you do."

"No, really. I miss all of your kiddos."

"Stop it, Gilly!" Lori-Lou hollered. "If you smack your sister one more time, you're going to spend the rest of the day in your room." The shrill tone of her voice intensified further. "*Why* are you kids so out of control? You. Need. To. Calm. Down! You're going to wake up your baby brother!" This led to a lengthy period of time where I lost my cousin altogether. I could hear cries coming from the baby moments later. Lori-Lou finally returned, sounding a little breathless. "Sorry about that . . . You know how it is."

Actually, I didn't. But she happened to be offering me a living illustration. "Oh, no problem."

"Hey, not to change the subject, but has Casey popped the question yet?"

Ugh. She would have to go there. Again. And how had we transitioned from ornery kids to marriage proposals? I couldn't help the rush of breath that escaped. "Not yet, Lori-Lou. I tell you that every time you ask."

My gaze shifted back through the window to my boyfriend, who gave me a little wave. My heart soared with hope as I waved back. I could almost see it now—me walking down the aisle in a fabulous dress, Casey standing at the front of the church with his groomsmen at his side. Six of them, to match my six bridesmaids. Okay, maybe seven.

"Right, I know." My cousin's voice startled me back to reality. "But do you think it's going to happen soon? I have a special reason for asking this time, I promise."

"Oh? Well, he *has* been acting a little suspicious." I glanced through the DQ window once again and noticed that Casey had engaged the elderly store manager in conversation. "I didn't see him at all yesterday. He just sort of . . . disappeared."

"Very odd."

"That's what I was thinking. I have a sneaking suspicion he went into Dallas to pick out my ring." The very idea made my heart flutter. For years I'd worn my grandmother's antique wedding ring on my left ring finger. She's always called it my purity ring—a reminder to stay chaste until marriage. The idea of replacing it with a modern ring from Casey made me giddy with anticipation. *Where* would he propose? *How* would he propose? *When* would he propose? My imagination nearly ran away with me as I pondered the possibilities.

"Ooh, you think it's going to happen soon?" Lori-Lou giggled. "Well now, that's perfect."

I nodded, which was dumb, because Lori-Lou couldn't see me over the phone. "Yeah. Why else would he be gone all day? Casey never leaves Fairfield unless it's important."

"Good, because I wanted to talk to you about something that involves him. You read *Texas Bride* magazine, right?"

"Usually." I released a lingering sigh. "To be honest, I've been trying to lay off of bridal magazines for the past couple months. I guess you could call it a self-imposed fast. Since the proposal hasn't actually taken place yet, I decided not to get too caught up in the wedding stuff just yet, for my own sake and my family's. They're getting tired of hearing all of my plans, I think."

"Ah. Well, I wondered why you hadn't said anything about the contest."

"Contest?" That certainly piqued my interest.

"Yeah. They announced it a couple of issues back." Lori-Lou hollered at one of the kids, then stopped a toddler tantrum in the background. "The magazine is linking up with Cosmopolitan Bridal in Dallas. You know about that shop, right?"

"Of course. They have the most exclusive bridal gowns in the state."

"In the country," Lori-Lou said. "And here's the great part. *Texas Bride* announced that they're teaming up with Cosmopolitan Bridal to sponsor a contest. An essay contest. Deadline is May 1."

"May 1, as in tomorrow?"

"Right. By midnight. Then one month later, on June 1, they're going to announce the winner."

"Okay." I tried to figure out what this had to do with me. "What does this winner get, anyway?"

"Cosmopolitan Bridal is going to give away a couture gown to one lucky bride-to-be. And—drum roll—she also gets to be on the October cover of *Texas Bride*! Can. You. Believe. It?"

Whoa. No wonder Lori-Lou was so excited. "Sounds like the opportunity of a lifetime."

"Right? And I totally think you should enter. You would stand a great chance, since it's an essay contest. Your writing skills are amazing."

"You think?" I sucked in an excited breath and considered her words. In my wildest dreams I couldn't imagine winning a dress from Cosmopolitan. "Oh, Lori-Lou, this is . . ."

"The best news ever?" She giggled, then called

out, "Gilly, if you hit your sister one more time, you will never eat another gummy worm as long as you live!"

I did my best to ignore the ranting going on from the kids in the background as I thought this through. Every wedding dress at Cosmopolitan was a one-of-a-kind. Brides came from all over the country to have specialty gowns crafted for their big day, and they paid for it . . . to the tune of multiple thousands of dollars per gown. All of this per *Texas Bride* magazine.

"They're going to tailor a special gown for the winner," Lori-Lou added. "Can you even imagine?"

Oh, I could imagine, all right. The idea of walking down the aisle in an original Cosmopolitan gown made my head spin . . . in a good way.

"So, I have to write an essay? About what, specifically?" I glanced through the window of Dairy Queen once more and gave Casey a thumbs-up to let him know I was okay. He nodded and turned his attention back to the restaurant's manager. "By midnight tomorrow night? Do I email it or something?"

"Yes, there's an email address. Just write five hundred words about your dream dress and your dream day," Lori-Lou explained. "Easy-breezy, right? All of the essays are going to be read by Nadia James, and she's going to choose the one that she feels the strongest about. Or, as the contest entry says, 'the most compelling.' "

"Nadia James?" Whoa. Texas's most touted dress designer would read my essay? The very idea made my palms sweat. The woman was revered among brides across the continent, not just in Texas. "I'm sure hundreds—maybe thousands—of girls will enter," I argued. "And most of them will actually be engaged. You know?"

"I read the rules, even the fine print. There's nothing in there that says you have to have a date set or anything like that. It just refers to the entrant as the 'potential bride' and leaves it at that. You're a potential bride. I mean, c'mon. All single women are, right?"

Ugh.

"So, I think you're okay to enter," she said. "I honestly do."

"You really think I stand a chance?"

"Yep. It won't hurt anything to try. You can write a compelling essay. Give it a title. Call it 'Small-Town Wedding, Big-Town Dreams.' "

" 'Small-Town Wedding, Big-Town Dreams,' " I echoed. Sounded about right, though I certainly had no aspirations of becoming a big-town girl.

"What have you got to lose?" Lori-Lou asked. "Wouldn't you like to win a gown from Cosmopolitan Bridal?"

The idea of wearing a designer gown on my big

day seemed like something out of a fairy tale, not something likely to happen to a girl like me. Still, what would it hurt to write an essay? Maybe I could play around with the idea a little.

After having an Oreo Blizzard with my sweetie. I waved at Casey and then said my goodbyes to Lori-Lou, promising her that I would at the very least pray about it. No harm in that. Surely the good Lord would show me what to do. And maybe, just maybe, I could throw in a "please let Casey pop the question soon" prayer while I was at it.

After all, what was a potential bride . . . without a groom?

2

Don't Mess Up a Good Thing

Everybody wants you to do good things, but in a small town you pretty much graduate and get married. Mostly you marry, have children, and go to their football games.

Faith Hill

In the Fisher family, we celebrated traditions that went back dozens, if not hundreds, of years. Springtime tea at Queenie's house, Christmas Eve service at the Baptist church, reinventing the front window display at our family's hardware store with the change of every season, and canning local peaches from Cooper Farms. These were the things I'd grown to appreciate.

The tradition I loved most took place every Friday night when the whole Fisher clan gathered at Sam's Buffet, the best place in town for good home-style cooking—outside of Mama's kitchen, anyway. I'd never known a finer location for barbecue, salad, home-style foods like macaroni and cheese, chicken-fried steak, mashed potatoes, gravy, and more. And the pies! Coconut meringue, milk chocolate, deep-dish apple, lemon meringue

. . . Sam's always had an assortment guaranteed to make your mouth water. In the South, grazing around a buffet was something of a religious experience, and we Fishers were devout in our passion for yummy food.

Our weekly dinner routine usually kicked off with Queenie and Pop arguing over who's going to treat who—or would that be whom?—to dinner. Queenie always won. Pop, never one to offend his mother, sighed and conceded, then proceeded to order the buffet. We all ordered the buffet. Well, all but Mama, who, under doctor's orders to lower her cholesterol, ordered the salad bar. That happened one time, and one time only. From that point on she ordered the buffet and made healthier choices. Mostly. There was that one time when, stressed over losing her top soprano from the choir, Mama ate her weight in lemon pound cake. But we rarely spoke of that anymore. In front of her, anyway.

Not that anyone blamed my mother for giving in to temptation. Who could go to Sam's and nibble on rabbit food with so many other flavorful offerings staring you in the face? Not me, and certainly not my three brothers, who all chowed down like linebackers after a big game. The poor employees at Sam's probably cringed when Jasper, Dewey, and Beau came through the door, but they never let it show. Instead, they greeted our family with broad smiles and a hearty

"Welcome!" then told us all about the special of the day.

As much as I loved Sam's, it wasn't the first thing on my mind when I awoke on Friday morning. I'd tossed and turned all night as I pondered Lori-Lou's suggestion that I enter the contest. Should I allow the lack of a groom-to-be to stop me from writing an essay? I needed to check out the fine print myself, just to put my mind at ease. And if I decided to go through with it, I'd have to get my act together . . . quickly!

I stopped by Brookshire Brothers and was relieved to find several copies of *Texas Bride* on the rack. The rules seemed simple enough and, just as Lori-Lou had said, only referred to the "potential bride," not an engaged woman. Still, I wondered if—or when—I would find time to write my essay, what with family dinner plans and all. An evening at Sam's with the family meant I wouldn't have time to carefully construct my entry until later that night. Hopefully I could press the Send button before midnight.

I read and reread the rules while I worked at the hardware store that afternoon. Pop never seemed to notice, thank goodness. I would get the usual ribbing about needing a fiancé if he saw me with a bridal magazine. I didn't need to hear that again. Besides, Casey would propose. Soon I would have a fiancé. But what would it hurt to give this contest thing a try in the interim?

Carrying the magazine to the restaurant that evening seemed a little over the top, but my mother and brothers were used to me daydreaming with a bridal magazine in my hand, so they probably wouldn't mind. Queenie would likely take it as a hopeful sign. And with Casey out of town—again—I was safe to browse the pages without putting him on the spot.

I pulled into the parking lot of Sam's Buffet in my '97 Cadillac DeVille—a hand-me-down from Queenie after she purchased the 2001 model—and noticed that my parents had just arrived. Mama bounded from her Jeep, nearly stepping into a pothole as she headed my way. I noticed her new hairdo at once and gave a little whistle.

"Mama! It's beautiful."

"Do you think?" She fussed with her hair and grinned. "There's a new girl at Do or Dye and she doesn't know a thing about my usual cut, so she just went at it like a yard guy with a weed whacker. Said this style was all the rage in Dallas right now. I guess that's where she's from." Mama ran her fingers over her hair. "I've never considered myself trendy."

Boy, you could say that twice and mean it. Mama's usual style was reminiscent of the early eighties. But this new do suited her. In fact, she looked downright beautiful.

My father approached, his expression a bit sour as his gaze traveled to my mother's hair.

“You okay over there, Pop?” I asked.

He shook his head. “Not sure yet. What do you think of Mama’s hairdo?”

“I think it’s gorgeous.” I offered an encouraging smile. “She looks like Diane Keaton in that one movie, you know . . .”

“Oh, that one with Nicolas Cage?” Mama fumbled around in her purse, obviously looking for something. “I always loved that movie. So funny. Well, except that one part where I had to fast-forward because it was so, well, you know.”

“It was Jack Nicholson,” Pop said.

“Nicolas Cage, Jack Nicholson . . .” Mama pulled out a tiny compact, popped it open, and gave herself a look. “What’s the difference?”

“Trust me, there’s a world of difference.” My father dove into a passionate dissertation about Jack Nicholson’s performance in *One Flew Over the Cuckoo’s Nest*.

“I don’t know what that has to do with anything, Herb,” my mother said. “Katie wasn’t even talking about that movie at all. Were you, Katie?”

“Oh, no ma’am. I—”

“And this conversation about cuckoos has nothing whatsoever to do with my hair.” She snapped her compact closed and shoved it back into her purse.

I bit my tongue to keep from saying something I shouldn’t. I’d better get this train back on track.

"Pop, I mentioned Diane Keaton because she wears her hair just like this." I pointed to Mama's new do. "And she's gorgeous, just like Mama."

"Humph." My father's nose wrinkled, and I could almost read his mind: *It's not your mother's usual style.*

And heaven forbid anything should change. Consistency was key in his life, after all. To my father, staying regular had less to do with the bottle of fiber on the kitchen counter and more to do with the day-to-day routine of everyday life.

"I think it's kind of nice to try something new." Mama looked at her reflection once more and giggled. "Would you believe that stylist tried to talk me into going blonde?"

"B-blonde?" My father's eyes widened. "Glad you didn't bow to the pressure."

"Hey, what's wrong with blondes?" I pointed to my long mane. "It's worked for me."

"And for your mama, back in the day." Daddy slipped his arm over her shoulder and pulled her close. "Your mother was quite a looker." He kissed her forehead.

"Back in the day?" My mother shrugged off his arm. "*Was* quite a looker? For those remarks, I might just have to go platinum to spite you." Her gaze narrowed and I thought for a minute she might throw her purse at him. Wouldn't be the first time she'd used the oversized bag as a weapon.

"Well, if you ever did I'd love you anyway. You were beautiful then, but you're even lovelier now, Marie. Or should I call you Ms. Keaton?" My father pulled her into his arms and planted kisses on her cheeks.

My mother's expression softened like a chocolate bar left sitting out in the sun. "Call me whatever you like," she said, her face now lighting into a smile. "Just call me."

Mama gave him a playful wink, and before I could look the other way, she kissed him square on the mouth. In front of God and everyone. Well, not that anyone happened to be looking. Our early arrival at Sam's always put us here ahead of the dinner crowd. This to help Queenie, who struggled to get around on her cane.

Queenie.

Strange that she hadn't arrived yet. I glanced around, curious. "Have either of you heard from Queenie?"

"Now that you mention it, no." Mama turned to look at the handicapped parking spaces, which were all empty. "Odd. She always beats us here."

"Oh, she probably stopped off at Brookshire Brothers on the way." Pop waved his hand as if to dismiss any concerns. "It's double coupon day. You know how careful she is with her money."

Mama didn't look convinced. "Maybe, but I'm still concerned. If she doesn't show up in a few minutes I'll call her."

Pop laughed and led the way toward the door of the restaurant. "You'll be wasting your time. She's having the hardest time getting used to that newfangled smartphone of hers. Says it's smarter than she is."

"Nothing is smarter than she is," I countered.

"True." Both of my parents nodded. Queenie wasn't just smart by the world's standards, she had the wisdom of the ages wrapped up in that eighty-one-year-old brain of hers.

Just as we got to the door, my brothers rolled up in Jasper's new Dodge Ram. His tires squealed as he whipped into the parking lot from the feeder road. I knew Mama would give him what for the minute he joined us.

"Jasper Fisher!" She hit him on the arm with her overloaded purse as soon as he was within reach. "What if there had been a small child or elderly person in your path?"

"Mama, really." He pulled his baseball cap off and raked his fingers through his messy blond hair. "Ain't never run over anyone yet." He slipped his arm over her shoulder and gave her a kiss on the cheek. "But don't worry. There's still plenty of time to remedy that. Give me awhile."

Her eyes narrowed to slits. "Good thing your grandmother wasn't here to witness your driving skills or to hear you smart off to your mama like that. She would tan your hide."

"Wait, Queenie's not here yet?" Dewey yanked

off his cap and looked around the parking lot. "That's weird."

"Very." Beau shrugged. "It just won't be the same if she doesn't show up. Who's gonna talk about hernias and hemorrhoids and stuff?"

"I volunteer." Dewey raised his hand. "I've become an expert after hearing her stories."

For a minute I thought Mama might smack him with her purse too, but she refrained.

"Are you sure Queenie's coming?" Jasper asked.

"Sure she's coming?" Mama, Pop, and I responded in unison. We'd never had Friday night dinner at Sam's without her—unless you counted that one time when she was hospitalized after having an allergic reaction to her titanium knee implant. And nothing had seemed right that night.

Mama glanced out at the feeder road. "I sure hope that old car of hers is working. I've been telling her for years that she needs a newer vehicle, but you know how she is about spending money."

I knew, all right. My grandmother was ultra-cautious when it came to the financial, unless she happened to be springing for dinner at Sam's. I also had my suspicions she planned to pay for my wedding dress when the day came. If I entered that contest and won, it would potentially save her a bundle. Just one more reason to write that essay.

"I doubt she's running late because of her car,"

Pop said. "That Cadillac of hers is in tip-top shape. Fred Jenkins up at the mechanic shop keeps it running smoothly."

"She's always been one to get folks to work hard," Mama said. "And Fred Jenkins tops the list."

"Think we could get her to light a fire under Beau here?" Pop slapped my youngest brother on the back, nearly knocking him off his feet.

"I'm hungry," Beau grumbled. "We gonna stand out here all night talking or get inside and eat?"

Minutes later we were seated at our usual table, eating our usual slices of yummy bread and fighting one another for our usual place in the buffet line. I'd just filled my plate with thick slices of barbecue beef and mashed potatoes when Queenie showed up, looking none too happy. She shuffled toward our table, her cane providing just the right balance to get her there.

"Well, thanks for waiting, everyone. Don't I feel special."

She might not feel special, but she certainly looked it. Soft white curls framed her perfectly made-up face, evidence that she'd made it to her usual Friday morning beauty parlor appointment. And the outfit! I thought I'd seen most of her ensembles, but this one surprised me. The blouse and slacks had a colorful springtime look—all flowery and pink. Beautiful, especially against her pale skin. Well, mostly pale. If I looked hard enough, I could see bits of foundation between the teensy-tiny wrinkly folds.

Unfortunately, one thing dampened her overall look—the sour expression on her face. And trust me, if Queenie wasn't happy, well, no one in the Fisher family was happy.

"We waited like pigs at a trough, Mama." Pop forced a smile, clearly trying to make her laugh. When she did not respond in kind, he rose and pulled out her chair.

"I raised you better than that." Queenie lifted her cane and pointed it at him as if to use it as a weapon.

He took it out of her hand and hung it over the back of her chair. "Well, we're happy to see you now, Mama. We're already prayed up, so grab a plate and dive in."

"Hmm." She eased herself down into the seat, which happened to be to the right of mine.

"You look fabulous, Queenie," I said. "Like something straight out of a magazine."

"Thank you, child." She offered a warm smile, the first sign that she might have forgiven us for starting without her. As the edges of her lips turned up, the wrinkles in her soft cheeks disappeared for a moment. Then her expression shifted and the wrinkles became visible once again. Fascinating. Who knew the human skin had that much elasticity?

"So glad you made it." I wiped my hands on my

napkin and then reached to pat her arm. "We were getting worried."

"Blame it on the Methodists." She unfolded her napkin and draped it over her lap.

Mama looked perplexed. "The Methodists made you late?"

"Yes." Queenie gestured to the waitress, then turned back to Mama. "The Methodists are having their annual craft fair tomorrow. The whole church is flipped upside down. The WOP-pers had no place to pray, and there's nothing more annoying to a group of prayer warriors than missing out on an opportunity to pound on heaven's door."

"But that was all taken care of in advance," Mama said. "You ladies were supposed to meet at the Presbyterian church this week. Bessie May told me that—"

"Nope." Queenie put her hand up as if to bring the conversation to a halt. "Decided to stay put at the Methodist church, even under the circumstances. I do not believe the Presbyterian church is an appropriate place to meet for prayer."

She turned her attention to the waitress long enough to ask for a glass of tea, no sugar. Queenie was the only one in the family who didn't take sugar in her tea. Her concerns about type 2 diabetes kept the sugar at bay.

I found myself distracted by what she'd just said. "So, the Presbyterians can join your prayer group, but you can't pray at their church?" I asked.

"Exactly." Queenie nodded and reached for a piece of bread from the basket in the center of the table. "Discussion ended, please and thank you."

"Probably best to change the subject." Pop gave me a "can it!" look, sticking a piece of sliced beef in his mouth.

"I do hope you've saved some of that barbecue for me, son. You know how I love it." Queenie took her fork and stabbed a piece of meat on his plate, then took a bite. "Mmm. That fixes everything."

"Even the brouhaha with the Presbyterians?" I asked.

She gave me a "let it go, Katie" look, but I couldn't get past her earlier comments. I wanted to ask, "What's your beef with the Presbyterians?" so we could get to the bottom of this once and for all. From the look on my father's face, though, I knew this wasn't the time or place to press the issue.

"Wait. I thought it was the Methodists we were mad at." Jasper looked up from his plate, his brow wrinkled.

"We're not *mad* at anyone. I'm just irritated because the Methodists made it difficult to pray." Queenie slapped his hand as he reached across her to grab a slice of bread from the basket in the middle of the table. "Discussion over. Now, let's all just get busy doing what we came here to do."

"Gossip about folks from other denominations?" Dewey asked.

Queenie scowled at him. "We don't gossip. We share our concerns. And if I can't share them with my own family, who can I share them with?"

"She has a point there, you must admit." Pop snagged a piece of bread and tossed it to Dewey, who caught it in midair. Queenie let out an unladylike grunt and shook her head.

The conversation shifted to baseball, and that inevitably led to Mama asking me why Casey hadn't shown up yet. "Where is that boy, anyway?" She glanced toward the door as if expecting my boyfriend to materialize. He usually joined us on Friday nights, as did Dewey's on-again, off-again girlfriend, Mary Anne. These days, Mary Anne was more off than on. I was secretly grateful for that. I'd never thought she was good enough for my brother, to be honest.

"He can't come tonight," I said. "I think he's working or something."

"I sure hope he's able to take some time off when you two . . ." Mama's voice lingered off, and she patted my knee as if she felt sorry for me. "I mean, *if* you two . . ." She shook her head and took a bite of her salad. "Isn't this the yummiest new dressing? I'll have to ask Gretel Ann what she puts in it. Mmm."

And that pretty much ended her conversation about Casey. Not that I minded. She hadn't hurt my feelings, anyway. Folks were surely wondering why he seemed to be taking his time. But I didn't need to focus on Casey tonight. I had to whip together an essay guaranteed to catch the eye—and heart—of Nadia James, the dress designer from Cosmopolitan Bridal.

What could I say to win her over? Would I tell her about my small-town life? Convince her that the dress had to be perfect for a small-town-girl-goes-uptown-for-her-wedding-day event? Would I share the story of how Casey and I had grown up together and were destined to be man and wife from the time we were children?

Man and wife. Hmm. I caught a glimpse of my parents, who gazed at each other with genuine sweetness. One day that would be Casey and me. We'd sit next to each other at Sam's, elderly parents at our side, gabbing with our children about hernias and hemorrhoids. We'd talk about baseball and reminisce about Queenie's obsession with the Presbyterians.

One day.

In the meantime, I'd better wrap up this meal so I could get home to write an award-winning essay before the clock struck midnight.

3

For the Good Times

Listen to advice, but follow your heart.
Conway Twitty

I made it through the meal without overeating, something that rarely happened at Sam's. My thoughts were elsewhere this evening, firmly fixed on the essay I needed to write when I arrived home. My distraction must've raised a red flag with family members. Several times Mama glanced my way as if to ask, "What's up with you, girl?" I just smiled and opened my bridal magazine, scouring the pictures of dress designs. Oh, the dreaming a girl could do with so many options at her disposal!

About halfway into the dessert round, Jasper tossed a chunk of bread at me. It hit me on the forehead. "You okay over there, Katie?"

I picked up the piece of bread and popped it into my mouth. "Hmm?"

"Readin' that magazine again?" Dewey rolled his eyes.

"Mm-hmm." I didn't look up for long because a shabby chic gown on page 67 had caught my eye. Lovely. I could almost picture myself wearing something similar on my wedding day. Simple. Small-town. Country-ish, even. Add a nice pair of cowgirl boots and the ensemble would be complete. If I opted to go that route, anyway. I'd have to ask Casey's opinion on the whole shabby chic thing. He might not be keen on it.

Jasper stuck a huge chunk of dinner roll in his mouth, then spoke around it. "Want my opinion?"

"What's that?" I closed the magazine and looked at him.

"Run." He nodded. "As fast and as far as you can."

I pressed the magazine into my oversized purse and took a sip of my tea. "Puh-leeze. That's your plan, not mine."

"Yep, it's my plan, all right." He took another bite of bread. "But you would be wise to follow my lead, Katie." His expression grew more serious. "Live your life. Don't fret about getting married right now. Have fun. That's what I'm doing."

"You'll settle down someday, Jasper." Mama wiped her lips with her napkin, which smeared her lipstick all around her mouth. "Hopefully sooner rather than later." She glanced at me. "And don't you be discouraging Katie here. She needs a good man in her life."

Weird, the way she'd phrased that. Casey was a good man.

My grandmother nodded. “Yes, Katie should get married and settle down.”

“Settle down?” Seriously? Could I get any more settled?

Queenie pointed at Jasper. “And you, young man, need a swift kick in the backside for driving like a maniac in the parking lot. I heard all about it from Missy Frasier, who pulled in right behind you. You scared the poor girl to death. She got so worked up telling me about it that she had to take a pill.”

“But I . . .” Jasper hung his head and went back to eating.

Queenie turned to Beau. “You stay as sweet as you are, honey bun. You hear me? Don’t ever break Queenie’s heart by falling off the straight and narrow.”

“Oh, no ma’am. I won’t fall, I promise.” Beau dropped some crumbs from his fork as he scooped another piece of cake into his mouth.

“Stick close to the family and you’ll do just fine.” My grandmother gave him a tender smile as she passed him a napkin. “There’s no place like home, after all.”

“Why would he want to move away?” Pop glanced up from his food long enough to pose the question. “His mama waits on him hand and foot. Does everything for him.”

“Beau’s my baby.” Mama’s face lit into the loveliest smile. “Can’t help spoiling the baby.”

This garnered a snort from Jasper.

And me. "He's twenty-two, Mama," I argued. "Twenty-*two*."

"Wouldn't matter if he was fifty-two. He'd still be my baby boy." She turned her attention to Beau. "Want Mama to slice up another piece of bread for you, honey?"

He nodded. "Yes, thank you, Mama."

She went to work carving out a large chunk of bread, which led to a loud groan from the others at the table. Beau was too busy staring at the bread to notice.

"Want me to butter this for you too, baby?" she asked him.

"Yep. Thanks. You're the best, Mama."

"Bless you for that, son. A mother needs to feel needed." Mama slathered his bread with butter, then addressed the rest of us. "See? Beau will never leave me. He's gonna stay put right here in Fairfield . . . forever."

"Not sure if that's a blessing or a curse," Pop whispered and then gave me a wink.

"Why would anyone want to leave? Small-town living is good for the soul." Queenie took a sip of her tea and leaned back in her chair, knocking her cane off in the process.

"Don't I know it." Pop rose and fetched my grandmother's cane, then hung it back on its perch. "Give me a small town any day. No rushing through traffic. No running late to catch the subway to work. No fighting the crowds on downtown streets."

"No stress." Mama passed Beau's slice of bread to him. "Well, other than the stoplight going out at Main and Elm, but we don't get a lot of cars through that intersection anyway, and Mayor Luchenbacher promised to fix it soon."

"I want to get the heck out of Dodge," Jasper said. "There's only so much of this good clean air I can stand. I still want to go to Houston and look for work there. It's the best place on the planet to find a job, and the cost of living is better than most anywhere else."

"Houston?" Mama paled as if she was hearing all of this for the first time. Which she wasn't. "Oh, but it's not safe in the city, honey." Her brow wrinkled. "So much crime."

"We have crime here too," Jasper said. "Didn't you hear that Bobby Jo Henderson got arrested for tipping cows in Doc Henderson's field?"

"He wasn't arrested. The sheriff gave him a warning. And that was just in fun."

"Try telling that to the cows." My father jabbed me with his arm, which sent my fork flying out of my hand, across the table, and onto the floor next to Widow Harrison at the next table. I hollered out a quick apology, but before I could remedy the problem myself, the waitress showed up.

"Saw the whole thing," she said. She passed a

clean fork to me and made her way to a nearby table to clear it for the next guests.

"I could never live in the city," Mama said. "You can't leave your doors and windows open."

"Oh, that reminds me." Dewey dove into an animated story about a skunk wandering into Reverend Bradford's house through the doggie door.

"Well, that's not commonplace," Mama argued. "And I'd rather have a skunk in my house any day than a burglar."

"I might rather have the burglar." Pop laughed. "Less mess to clean up afterward."

Mama rolled her eyes and muttered something under her breath.

"Hey, doesn't Aunt Alva still live in Dallas?" Beau licked the butter off of his fingers as he glanced Queenie's way.

You could've heard a pin drop at that question. My grandmother glared at him. "We don't talk about Aunt Alva." Queenie dabbed at her lips, smearing her lipstick in the process.

"Why not?" Beau looked perplexed.

I gave him a "shush" look. I'd never figured out the story about Queenie's older sister, but this clearly wasn't the time to ask.

"So, we can't talk about the Presbyterians and we can't talk about Aunt Alva." Dewey chuckled. "I guess that limits the conversation to Doc

Henderson's cows and the criminal element taking over the city of Fairfield."

"Criminal element, pooh." Mama shook her head. "Such an exaggeration."

The expression on Queenie's face showed her relief that we'd switched gears from talking about Alva. "I still say it's safer here," she said. "You couldn't pay me enough to live in the city. We might have a problem with skunks, but those city folks have to worry about snakes."

"Snakes in the city?" I asked.

"Yes." My grandmother's eyes widened. "They're small. They get in tiny spaces. City dwellers have snakes in their homes and don't even know it."

"Only the kind you need to unstop your toilet," Pop said. "I can sell you one of those at the hardware store."

"Speaking of toilets . . ." Mama took a teensy-tiny bite of her lemon pound cake. "When you live in the city, you can't even flush your toilet without the folks downstairs knowing about it. Folks live on top of one another in condos and such."

"Kind of like we do at our house right now?" Dewey asked.

"Oh, that reminds me, I need to put a new handle on that upstairs toilet," Pop said. "It's been acting finicky."

Queenie rolled her eyes. "My point is, people

are pressed in like sardines in the city. No space to move around or have privacy."

"Privacy?" Jasper snorted. "We have that here?"

"In theory," Pop said. "In theory."

"Good luck finding a Dairy Queen in the city," Mama added. "I hear they're not building them in metropolitan areas anymore."

This led to a lengthy discussion about ice cream, which caused Pop to say that he needed a piece of coconut pie. He returned moments later with a slice of chocolate pie in his right hand and a slice of coconut in his left. "Couldn't make up my mind," he said. "Oh, and Marie, they just brought out fresh lemon pound cake. You should have another piece."

"Oh, I shouldn't. I really shouldn't." Mama remained in her seat for a moment and then bounded to the dessert table.

"There she goes again," Queenie said. "Marie and her pound cake."

The conversation carried on long after Mama returned to the table, but my thoughts were elsewhere. I couldn't stop thinking about the contest and the essay I needed to write. What should I say? Should I mention our quaint little town? The church sanctuary where I planned to say my "I dos"? Should I talk about Casey and how we met at the ballpark when I was running for cheerleader of the Little League team?

"You okay over there, Katie?" Queenie asked.

"Oh, yes ma'am. I'm just . . ." *Strategizing. Writing a letter in my head.*

"Thinking about that new window display at the hardware store, I'll bet." Pop winked. "I know how much you love that."

"Oh, I do." Changing out the displays was my very favorite part of working at the store. Well, that and the customers. But my mind was definitely on other things.

By the time I arrived home from Sam's, I'd sketched out the whole letter in my mind. I knew just what to say. I waited until the whole family was tucked away for the night before grabbing my laptop and composing the essay. It didn't take long to lay out my plea for the dream dress. After all, I'd been planning for my big day all of my life. I knew just how I wanted things to go.

The essay—all five hundred words—came together seamlessly. I pushed the Send button at exactly 11:17, just forty-three minutes shy of the midnight deadline. Whew! Talk about cutting it close.

I couldn't help but smile as I reread my essay after sending it in. It sounded pretty good. No, really good. If I didn't know any better, I'd say it was God-inspired.

God-inspired.

Just like my relationship with Casey. I smiled again as I thought about my fiancé. Well, soon-to-be-fiancé. If he knew I'd penned this essay, would it hurry him up? Would he tickle my ears with the question meant to make my heart sing? Would our happily ever after start sooner rather than later?

For the first time all evening it occurred to me that Casey hadn't called. I'd received a text early in the afternoon, but nothing tonight. Nothing whatsoever, not even our usual "Love you, sleep tight" text. I double-checked my phone, just to be sure. Nope. Nothing.

Oh well. He was probably at his house this very minute, scheming up a way to propose. And wouldn't he be thrilled to receive the news that I'd saved a bundle by winning the perfect gown?

If I won.

Oh, but I would. I knew it in my heart of hearts. This was my answer, my solution. I would win the dress, walk the aisle, and live out my forever with my small-town sweetheart. We'd raise our kiddos in Fairfield. Casey would coach Little League alongside Pop. I'd take over the choir at the Baptist church when Mama retired. And we'd all live happily ever after.

I hoped.

4

I've Got a Picture of Us on My Mind

The way I see it, if you want the rainbow, you gotta put up with the rain.

Dolly Parton

I spent the next couple weeks with my stomach in knots. Barely a day went by when I didn't wish I could un-press the Send button. Ugh. Every day I prayed Casey would propose. Every day he didn't. In fact, he seemed to be acting a little odd—evasive, even—whenever I dropped hints about our relationship, which really bugged me. But I couldn't beg the guy to marry me, now could I?

Instead, I went about my business, working at the hardware store, hanging out with Casey and my friends at Dairy Queen, and listening to my brothers ramble on about the goings-on in our little town.

Until Thursday evening, May 14, when I received a call from Queenie.

"Katie, I want you to come by my place in the morning for breakfast." Her words sounded more like an order than an invitation.

"But we're going to dinner tomorrow night at Sam's, Queenie."

"I know, but I need some time with you . . . privately."

Hmm. Seemed suspicious. Still, I knew better than to turn her down. "What time?"

"Seven thirty should be good for me. That way we can visit before you have to go to work. Sound agreeable?"

Sounded more like a business meeting, but I didn't argue.

I tossed and turned all night, unable to sleep. Worries consumed me. Had Lori-Lou told Queenie about the contest? Maybe that was why I'd been summoned into her royal chambers—for a lecture about how I'd overstepped my bounds. What if she told my parents? Then what? I'd look like an idiot.

I already felt like one.

When I did sleep, crazy dreams consumed me. In one of them, I wore a zebra-striped wedding gown, a wacky avant-garde number with huge, puffy sleeves. I walked the aisle toward Casey, who turned and ran in the opposite direction. I'd run too if someone walked toward me looking like a caged animal.

I woke up earlier than usual on Friday morning, determined to put the weird dreams behind me, though I couldn't get Queenie's breakfast invitation off my mind. No doubt she had ulterior motives.

I pulled up to her house at 7:30 on the dot and got out of my car. The front walkway was surrounded by the loveliest flowers, all pinks and yellows. Queenie had quite an eye for color. She had quite an eye for everything.

I didn't have to knock. She stood in the open doorway, arms extended. "Glad you could come, Katie-girl."

That made me feel a little better. I relaxed and did my best to give a genuine smile. "G'morning, Queenie." I slipped into her warm embrace and received several kisses on my cheeks. As her soft skin brushed against mine, I thought it felt a bit like velvet.

She took me by the hand and led me inside her spacious, comfortable home—the same one I'd grown up loving. We passed by the photographs of our various family members—including the second cousins twice removed—to the breakfast table, where a spread of foods awaited. Pancakes. Bacon. Orange juice. Yum. I settled into a chair and she blessed the food, then we dove right in.

I had a feeling this visit wasn't really about the food, at least not completely. We made small talk and nibbled for a while, but I could sense something coming around the bend.

After she finished up her first cup of coffee, Queenie rose—slowly, using her cane—and walked to the coffeepot for a refill. "You want more, honey?" she asked.

I shook my head. “Nah. Better not. I’ll take one to go when I get ready to leave for the store.”

With a shaky hand she refilled her cup, then turned to face me. “I do hope you can give me a few more minutes before you leave. There’s something I want to talk to you about.”

Ah. I knew it.

I rose and helped her with her coffee cup. She hobbled back to the table and took her seat, then lifted the hot coffee, her hand still trembling. “Let’s talk about that boyfriend of yours, Katie.”

“Casey?”

She gave me a knowing look. “Well, yes, Casey. Unless there’s some other boyfriend out there I need to know about.”

“Nope. No one.” I smiled and tried to look confident.

“Honey, I get the sense that you’re itching for a proposal. Am I right?”

“Well, I’m not sure *itching* is the right word, Queenie, but yes. Isn’t that the idea?”

The long gap in conversation made me a little nervous. Queenie stirred her coffee, which was weird, since it didn’t have any sugar or cream in it.

Maybe I’d better build her confidence with another speech. “I’m pretty sure he’s going to propose any day now. I think he went to Dallas to order my ring a couple weeks ago, then went back yesterday to pick it up. Maybe it had to be sized or something like that.”

"You sound pretty sure of yourself. And of him. Has he given you any clues, other than his disappearing act?" She put the spoon down and stared at me intently. Too intently, really. Made me nervous. I could never keep my emotions hidden from Queenie. She could read me like a book. No doubt she was scanning a few pages now.

"Just a few suspicious comments about plans. And the future. He's always talking about his future. Career stuff. The kind of house he'd like to one day live in. Pretty sure those comments are meant to tease me."

"Could be." She sipped her coffee. "Some men are just a little slow to bat, honey." Her nose wrinkled, and I wondered if maybe her coffee was too hot. "Not sure why he's taking his time, but I suppose that's a good thing. Kind of reminds me of that Loretta Lynn song 'You Wouldn't Know an Angel if You Saw One.' I sometimes wonder if he sees what's right in front of him."

"Yeah, I wonder too." I couldn't help but smile as she mentioned one of my favorite songbirds. "I love Loretta Lynn."

"Me too." Queenie sighed. "Always have, from the time I was young. We have a lot in common."

"Oh?"

"Well, sure. We're both small-town girls. She's from Butcher Holler, I'm from Fairfield."

"What else? Is there something you're not telling me? You own a guitar? Write songs when no one's around?" I took another nibble of my food and leaned back in my chair.

"Hardly." Queenie shrugged. "But we do have one key thing in common. Loretta and her husband Doo married impulsively." As soon as she'd spoken the words, my grandmother clamped a hand over her mouth. "I'm sorry, honey. I didn't mean to say that. Not out loud, anyway."

"Are you insinuating that you and Grandpa married impulsively?" I asked.

She brushed some crumbs off the edge of the table. "I loved your grandpa. He was truly one of the best men I've ever known. But yes, I guess you could say I did marry him impulsively. And things weren't always a bed of roses, if you know what I mean. We had our share of obstacles."

"Like Loretta and Doo."

"Yep." My grandmother took another sip of her coffee, and for a moment I thought I'd lost her to her memories. She put the cup down and smiled. "You remember that story about Loretta? The one where she accidentally put salt in the pie instead of sugar?"

"Of course. The pie was for some sort of contest, right?"

"Yep. She worked so hard to bake the best pie to impress the fellas. Her sweetie bought the pie and took a big bite. Only, it tasted like salt, not sugar."

"I remember." What this had to do with Queenie's comment that she'd married impulsively, I could not say. "What are you getting at, Queenie?"

"If it's meant to be, it'll be, whether you put salt in the pie or sugar. If he loves you—if he really, really loves you—any obstacle can be overcome. That's how it was with Grandpa and me. We got past the salt. And if it's meant to be with you and Casey, you'll get past the salt too, and the rest'll be sugar."

"You think?"

"I really don't know for sure, but I know someone who does." She pointed heavenward. "Only he knows who we're supposed to end up with. But that's part of the adventure—finding out his will, then getting in the stream."

"Hmm." I didn't feel very adventurous at the moment. And for whatever reason, Queenie's story about the pie left the weirdest salty taste in my mouth. "So, do I just come out and ask him if he's going to marry me?"

"No." She picked up her cup and nearly dropped it. "Don't even bring yourself into it. Whenever he gets to talking about his career, the home he'd like to live in, just listen. Let him talk. Ask for details about *his* plans. *His* future. Ask where he sees him-self in five years. Or ten years. Or whatever. Might be hard, but leave yourself out of it for now." She took another swig of coffee and adjusted her position in her chair. "He needs to know that you care as much about his plans as your own. You see?"

“Yes, I get it. Sort of a nonthreatening way to bring up the subject of our life together.” I grinned in spite of myself. “Makes sense.”

“I suppose you could look at it that way.” Queenie’s furrowed brow didn’t bring me much comfort, but I managed to remain positive anyway. “Point is, the conversation might just add a wee bit of sugar to the pie, if you catch my drift. And I have it on good authority that Casey likes pie.”

I rose and gave her a kiss on the cheek. “You’re always loaded with great advice, Queenie. Thanks so much.”

“Mm-hmm.” She nodded and attempted to stand. I reached to help her. After a few moments of awkward silence, she glanced my way, her eyes glistening with tears.

My heart skipped a beat as I analyzed the pain in her expression. “Queenie? You okay?”

She reached for my hand and squeezed it so tight that it hurt. “Just promise me something, honey.”

“Anything.”

“Promise me you’ll make the best possible decision for your future happiness. And pray. Ask God’s opinion. Don’t just jump willy-nilly into something because it feels right in the moment. Really, truly seek the Lord and ask his opinion. If you think that Casey’s approach is too calculated, think again. It’s better to think things through from start to finish before jumping in."

"Well, of course. Do you think I'd do something without thinking it through? I'm more levelheaded than that." *I think.*

"I want you to pray it through. Look for answers, not just in your heart but in your head. If you ask the Lord's opinion, he'll be happy to give it. Problem is, most of us just move along with our emotions leading the way and live to regret it later."

The sadness in her eyes made me curious. "Queenie, is there something you're not telling me? Do you think Casey and I shouldn't . . . well, get married?"

"I didn't say that, honey. I just want God's best for you. If you ask him, he'll tell you what to do."

Her words lingered in my thoughts long after we parted ways. Did my own grandmother really think I shouldn't marry the man of my dreams? What was up with the hesitations?

I pondered all of these things as I drove to the hardware store. Once I arrived, Pop put me to work, sorting through a new shipment of door hinges. Exciting stuff. I dove right in, my focus still on Queenie's words. Perhaps she had a point. If I focused on Casey, if I cared more about his plans than my own, then perhaps God would open the door for those plans to include a happily-ever-after for me too.

5

Ten Little Reasons

> You do sing about what you know about. And I grew up in a small town, and I grew up in a place where your whole world revolved around friends, family, school, and church, and sports.
>
> Kenny Chesney

In the weeks leading up to the June 1st contest announcement, I could barely sleep. Most nights I tossed and turned, designing wedding gowns in my head. Every second or third day I'd go into a panic, wondering what I'd do if I actually won the dress. On the in-between days I convinced myself there was no way I'd win, not with thousands of entries. By the time I received my proposal, which seemed to be taking longer than I'd imagined, the whole contest thing would be behind me, just an elusive dream.

On Monday morning, June 1, I drove to the hardware store and found it teeming with customers. Mrs. Raddison needed a new faucet for her kitchen sink. Reverend Bradford browsed the lawn and garden aisle, looking for a connector for his water hoses. And Brother Mitchell, my favorite Sunday school teacher from early childhood, had finally decided to spend "the big bucks," as he called it, on a new power drill. Pop was busy unloading a new shipment of fertilizer, so I waited on the customers and then headed to the front window to continue my work on the summer window display.

I'd just hung up a banner advertising the sale on fertilizer when my cell phone rang. I pulled it out of my pocket, stared at the unfamiliar number, and answered with, "H-hello?"

"May I speak to Katie Fisher?" a female voice said from the other end of the line.

"Th-this is she."

"Katie, this is Madge Hamilton, assistant to Nadia James, from Cosmopolitan Bridal."

My heart sailed directly into my throat, making it impossible to respond. I finally managed a shaky, "Yes?" Maybe they called every losing entrant as a courtesy. Right?

"I am delighted to inform you that you've won our *Texas Bride* contest." Her voice sounded chipper. Light. "Your essay was chosen from over four hundred entries."

For a minute I thought I might faint. I'd pictured this call a hundred times but hadn't really believed it would take place. In my imagination, sure. But in real life?

"W-what?" I nearly lost my balance.

Pop meandered down the aisle nearby, his eyes

wide as he saw me bump into the window. "You okay over there, Katie-girl?"

I nodded, then eased my way down into a seated position. "I'm sorry. What did you say again?"

Pop must've thought I was talking to him. He hollered out, "I said, 'You okay over there, Katie-girl?' "

The woman on the other end of the phone laughed. "I said you've won the contest. But I can tell you're in shock, and I don't blame you. It's a lot to take in, I'm sure."

"That's putting it mildly," I managed.

"Putting *what* mildly?" Pop asked as he took a few steps in my direction. I pointed to the phone.

He shook his head and whispered, "I've told you not to talk on that thing at work, Katie Sue. Very unprofessional."

I turned my gaze out the window to avoid his glare.

"This is quite an honor," Madge said. "Trust me. Hundreds of girls would love to be in your place right now."

She went on to say something about how my essay had touched Nadia James's heart to the deepest level, but I only heard about half of it.

"I . . . I'm sorry," I said when I finally found my voice again. "Did you just say that I"—my voice squeaked—"w-won?"

"You did. What a compelling essay, Katie. Small-town girl with cosmopolitan wedding plans. We all read it and loved it. You have some serious writing skills, by the way. Are you a writer by trade?"

"Oh, no ma'am. I work at a hardware store."

"Oh yes, that's right. I remember reading that now. Well, you have quite a way with words. And the way you described your fiancé, well, it just swept Nadia off her feet. You two must really be in love."

"Yes ma'am." I swallowed hard as I realized she'd called him my fiancé. "Only, Casey isn't actually—"

"We can't wait to hear the details of the proposal. It'll make a terrific addition to the *Texas Bride* article."

Ack. "I, well . . ."

"So, we have a dress to design," she said. "And fittings will need to start soon because Nadia will be leaving for an internship in Paris."

"She won't be in Dallas anymore?"

"Only for the next week or so. Then she'll leave for an exciting year in Paris. Her son Brady is taking over the shop in her absence. He—well, he'll be here to supervise as our seamstresses work on your gown." Why the woman sounded hesitant, I could not say. "Anyway, the point is, this will be a rushed job because Nadia is leaving soon. When can you come to the shop for your first fitting?"

"Oh, I . . ." Hmm. Go to Dallas? Wasn't it more

important to talk Casey into marrying me first so that I could show up with a ring on my finger?

"It's important to get going on your dress design before Nadia leaves. And we have to think of the time frame for your big day. What date have you set for the wedding, honey? I don't remember that part from the essay."

That's because I didn't mention a date.

Should I fess up? Tell her that I wasn't exactly engaged—only almost engaged?

"Oh, never mind. I can hear that you've got something going on in the background there. We can talk about your wedding plans later."

I didn't have a chance to get a word in edgewise because she continued to fill my ears with instructions. She buzzed through a list of details that included an interview and photo shoot with *Texas Bride* and several dress fittings.

"I see that you live in Fairfield. Hmm. You're an hour and a half from our shop. I'm not sure that's practical."

I'd do anything to have the dress of my dreams. But how could I manage going back and forth to Dallas for fittings? Pop would flip if I left in the middle of a shift at the hardware store, and Mama would have a conniption if I missed choir practice, but maybe I could work around those things. Bessie May drowned out the rest of us altos, anyway. I'd never be missed.

"We really need to go ahead and set up an

appointment for your first fitting," Madge said. "Ideally, we would need to get your measurements as quickly as possible—say, by next Monday?"

"Next Monday?"

"Yes. If you come sooner rather than later, it would give Nadia time to draw the sketches before she leaves. Then we'll need you to come and go while the dress is being made. Is that doable?"

"How long will it take?" I asked.

"At least a month or so. Maybe longer. But we need to get the ball rolling. Let's just say one week from today at noon for the consult, shall we? Does that work for you?"

"Well, I'll do my best—"

"Great. We look forward to getting to know you and making the dress for your big day."

She ended the call in a hurry, but I was grateful for the reprieve. I needed time to think. To plan. To get my heart beating normally again.

For a good ten minutes after the call ended, I stared at the phone in total silence. Maybe I'd just dreamed this whole thing. Surely I hadn't won the contest.

I headed to the stockroom at the back of our store and began pacing, my emotions shifting from disbelief to an undeniable sense of excitement. Surely God had just opened a door for me. This was all a sign that Casey was going to pop the question. Hopefully soon.

My roller coaster of emotions continued as I began to pray about all of this, thanking God from the bottom of my heart for giving me such an amazing opportunity. Then I lit into one of my favorite worship songs, which must've alerted my father. He stuck his head in the door, eyes wide.

"Someone having a church service in here?"

"Yep. Just having a little praise and worship."

"Next time invite me to join you. Mama says I have the best baritone voice in town." He lit into an off-key rendition of "What a Friend We Have in Jesus," and I giggled as he disappeared back out into the store.

After a while I calmed down a bit. I couldn't share my news with Pop, but I did feel the need to tell someone. Only one person made sense. I picked up my cell phone and pushed the button to call Lori-Lou.

After three rings I half expected it to go to voicemail, but she answered, breathless. "Katie? That you?"

"Yes. I have such exciting news. I—"

"I'm in the bathroom. Hiding. From the kids."

"W-what?"

"It's the only privacy I can get around here. Hold on a minute. One of the girls is beating on the door." Her voice grew shriller as she hollered out, "Mariela, if you bang on that door one more time, so help me, you're going to be grounded from now until you leave for college." The noise level escalated and then she returned. "Okay, what were you saying?"

I could barely remember. The image of her hiding in the bathroom served as a deterrent and affected my ability to think clearly for a moment. "Girl, you're not going to believe the call I just got."

"Ooh, tell me!"

I'd just started to when I heard a loud flush, followed by water running. "Speak up, Katie. It's loud on this end."

Ew.

"I won the dress!" A nervous laugh surfaced, though I tried to press it down.

"I'm sorry, what did you say? The water was running. I thought you said you won the dress."

"I did! I won the dress!"

The squeal from her end of the line nearly deafened me. I had to move the phone away from my ear.

"Oh, Katie, that's the best news ever!" She lit into a lengthy conversation about the style of the gown, asking me a thousand questions along the way. Finally she paused. "So, um, I hate to bring up the obvious, but does this bride have a groom yet?"

"Well, not officially, but I'm 99 percent sure Casey's going to pop the question soon. He's been back and forth, going out of town and then returning. The boy has a ring in his pocket. I know he does. He even asked me some weird questions the other day about the cost of apartments. Isn't that odd?"

"Perfect sign. Well, hurry him along. You know those people at the bridal shop are going to be asking a lot of questions."

"They already are. But just so you know, no one else has a clue about any of this. Not my family. Not anyone. I mean, Queenie knows that I'm hoping for a proposal, but she . . ." I hesitated, unsure of how much to share with Lori-Lou. "She wants me to be 100 percent sure. She doesn't want me to jump into something."

"Jump into it?" Lori-Lou laughed. "How many years have you and Casey been dating again? A dozen?"

"No. I'm only twenty-four. That would mean we started dating at age twelve. We only made it official when we were seventeen."

"Well, that's almost eight years, girl. Besides, you've known him since you were twelve. No one will think you're jumping into anything. Besides, someone needs to make a move. The people at Cosmopolitan Bridal are going to announce it to the world in just a few months, Katie Sue."

"Trust me when I say that no one in my inner circle reads *Texas Bride*, so I think we're safe there. And other than you, I don't have any friends or family in the Dallas area, so no one will hear those radio announcements anyway."

“Wait . . . doesn’t Queenie have a sister who lives here?”

Ack. I’d almost forgotten about Alva—the family’s black sheep.

“Well, yes. Alva’s there. But what are the chances she would find out and say something to Queenie? They don’t even speak.”

“True, that.” A shriek followed. “Mariela! How did you get that door unlocked? Mama needs her privacy!” This escalated into an argument between mother and daughter. I could tell I’d lost my cousin altogether, so I said my goodbyes.

After I ended the call with Lori-Lou, I went back to work on the summer window display and pondered my situation with Casey. He needed to know about the dress. If I showed up at the bridal shop next Monday without an engagement ring, I’d have a tough time answering questions about how my wonderful fiancé had proposed, now wouldn’t I?

I had to talk to Casey about our future together as a couple. And I had to somehow get him to pop the question.

6

A Dear John Letter

Of emotions, of love, of breakup, of love and hate and death and dying, mama, apple pie, and the whole thing. It covers a lot of territory, country music does.

Johnny Cash

After a stressful afternoon of trying to balance work with my frazzled emotions, I managed to talk Pop into letting me off early. By four thirty I was in my car, driving through the heart of town to Casey's house. If I knew my guy—and I did—he was just arriving home from work. Changing into his jeans and cowboy boots, no doubt, then heading out to work in the yard for his mama. Such a great son. Such a great guy.

Underneath the brilliant late-afternoon sun, the whole town seemed brighter, happier than ever. Banners hung along Main Street, advertising next month's Fourth of July parade. Folks strolled from building to building, store to store, chatting and hugging like the old friends they were.

What a blissful place to live. What a fantastic place to marry and raise a family. No wonder my parents had opted to stay here all these years. We lived in paradise.

When I turned right at the next corner, I saw Reverend Bradford shopping at the local bookstore. He waved as I drove by and I returned the gesture. He turned his attention to Mr. Finkle, the store owner, who patted him on the back and gestured for him to step inside the store.

As I drove past Tu-Tu-Sweet, our local bakery/ballet studio, I caught a glimpse of a faux wedding cake in the front window, one I'd never seen before. I made a mental note to stop by tomorrow to check it out. I'd have to start shopping for wedding items soon. Well, as soon as I had a date set. To my left, flags flew over the courthouse, the sunshine causing the white stripes to shimmer in the breeze. All in all, a picture-perfect day to broach the happily-ever-after question with my sweetheart.

Mayor Luchenbacher stood in front of the courthouse, gazing up at the American flag. He gave me a frantic wave, and I rolled down the window to holler, "Good afternoon!" I didn't dare slow down for a conversation. He'd have me signing up to coordinate the Fourth of July parade again. Hopefully I'd be too busy planning for my big day to head up the festivities this year.

The radio station blared out a familiar worship song, and I leaned back against the seat as I drove, the words sliding off my tongue. Words of joy.

Hope. Faith. They made my heart sing all the way to Casey's homestead.

When I pulled up to the Lawson home, I sighed with pure joy. I'd always loved this expansive property with its traditional picket fence. Gorgeous. I could see myself living in a place like this someday. Our children would run and play in the yard. Our dog—probably a Lab—would romp around with the kids and then take a dip in the pond out back. Someday. Then again, from what Casey had shared, he might be more interested in getting something new. Maybe we'd build a small house on the back acreage. That might be nice. We could have our own space and still be close to the family.

Before getting out of the car, I checked my appearance in the rearview mirror. A quick lipstick touch-up was called for, and then I climbed out of the car, adjusted my twisted blouse, and headed to the front door, where Casey's mother greeted me with tilted head and wrinkled brow.

"Well, Katie Sue. Didn't know you were coming over."

"Neither does Casey." I giggled. "Just wanted to surprise him. Is he here?"

"Yes. He's . . ." Her words drifted off. "Well, let me get him for you, honey. C'mon in." She gestured for me to come inside. "You want a glass of sweet tea? There's a fresh pitcher in the fridge. Help yourself."

"Oh, yes ma'am." I followed her down the

front hallway of the house, taking in the country-chic décor. Some might consider it outdated, but I was enamored by the simple, rustic environment. Homey. That was the word. And nothing made a girl feel more at home than homey. The wood paneling in the living room put me in mind of the eighties, but even that brought comfort. Familiarity.

I made myself at home in the kitchen until Casey joined me a couple minutes later. My honey walked into the room looking as handsome as ever. His dark hair was a bit more tousled than usual, and those gorgeous blue eyes flashed with intrigue when he saw me standing in the middle of his kitchen, swigging a giant glass of sweet tea. I couldn't help but wonder about the basketball shorts and faded T-shirt, though. He usually wore jeans and button-ups around the house, even on the most casual day.

I let out a whistle. "Hello, handsome. Love seeing you like this."

"Thanks. Different, right?" The edges of his lips curled up in a smile. "And hello yourself. Didn't know you were coming."

"Exactly." I snuggled into his arms and gave him a kiss on the cheek. "That's what makes it so fun. Thought I'd surprise you by stopping by. That okay?"

"Sure. But you look like you have something on your mind."

"O-oh?"

"Yep. I'd know that look anywhere." He gave me an inquisitive look. "Is your mama trying to get you to talk me into singing that bass solo next Sunday morning? I tried to tell her it's out of my range."

"Nope. She never said a word about it."

Casey looked half relieved, half perplexed. "Ah. So, is it your dad?"

"Oh no. Not that. I—"

"Does he need me to come and move that shelf unit to the back of the store? I've been promising to do that for weeks now but haven't had time."

"Nothing like that." I tried to figure out where to start this delicate conversation. "I, um, just have a lot on my mind today. I just wanted to ask you—"

"Something big going on at the store? Or is Queenie still upset with the Methodists?"

"Presbyterians. But I really came by to—"

"She's mad at the Presbyterians too?" he asked. "Wonder how she feels about the Lutherans. And the Charismatics."

"Pretty sure she's okay with the Lutherans, but I wouldn't place any bets on the Charismatics. Anyway, that's not why I came by, I can assure you."

"Dewey in trouble again? Mary Anne break his heart?"

"Well, yes, but that's not it either." I took a seat at the breakfast table and he sat down in the chair next to me. I gazed at him, wishing I could work up the courage to come out and ask him about his intentions. Still, a girl could hardly pop the "are you ever going to propose?" question.

"You've got something on your mind, Katie." He poured himself a glass of tea, then leaned back in his chair. "Might as well spit it out. No offense, but you've never been very good at hiding your emotions, especially when you're upset."

"Well, I just woke up this morning thinking about . . ." *Marrying you. Duh.* "Thinking about the future."

"The future?" He took a swig from his glass. "Like, years-from-now future or tomorrow future?"

"Both, actually." *And thanks for playing along.* Maybe this would be easier than I'd guessed. "Casey, I just wondered if maybe *you've* given any thought to, well, the future." I mustered a smile and prayed he would take the hint.

An odd expression overtook him and a moment later he nodded. "Katie, I think about the future every day."

"Really?" A hopeful spark ignited within. "Me too. So let's compare notes, okay?"

"O-okay."

"Where do you see yourself in five years?"

"In five years?" He rolled his eyes. "Out of this town, for sure."

"W-what?" In all the years I'd known him, I hadn't heard him talk about leaving. "You mean, like, the outskirts of town? In a different house? Different property?"

"No. I mean, like, *way* out of town. Another state, even. If a man's gonna have a career—a real career—it's going to be in someplace bigger than Fairfield, Texas."

"But I thought you planned to live here someday. On this land, I mean."

"That's my parents' plan for me. They've said it a thousand times. And I've done my best to play along because I didn't want to hurt their feelings. Heck, I even thought I could talk myself into it. But I'm not really into all of that, Katie. I thought you knew that. Sometimes I think my father loaded me up with ideas that were really his, not mine. I want something bigger than a few acres of land and a garden. You know?"

No, I didn't know. My response was stuck in my throat, however, and refused to dislodge itself.

He rose and paced the kitchen, finally coming to a stop in front of the refrigerator, where he turned back to face me. "Katie, I'm glad you asked me about the future, because there's something I need to talk to you about. I've been praying about this for days. Just didn't know how to come out and say it, but you've given me the perfect segue."

"Oh? Have I now?" I tried not to let the little giggle in my heart escape. Oh, hallelujah! He was going to propose right here, in his kitchen! Perfection! I'd always joked about getting engaged on a random weekday. What a story to tell our kiddos: "Mama got her proposal on a Monday afternoon over a glass of sweet tea at your grandma's kitchen table, the one that was passed down from one generation to another." Lovely!

"Just say it, Casey." I smiled. "Won't hurt a bit, I promise."

He nodded, walked over, and stopped right in front of me, taking my hand. My left hand. With his free hand he reached into his back pocket. My heart skip-skip-skipped, and I wanted to sing a funny little ditty just to celebrate this glorious moment. He pulled out a small box, just the right size for a ring.

Praise the Lord! Thank you, Queenie! Your suggestion worked like a charm. We're talking about the future now, aren't we?

"Katie, you're the sweetest girl I know. So understanding."

"Th-thank you. I feel the same about you." *But this would be better if you dropped to one knee. That would make for a better story.*

My sweetie's smile lit the room, and I stared into his handsome face, a face lit with joy as he spoke. "You asked about my future, and I honestly believe it's going to be great. Better than great, actually."

"Me too!" This time the giggle escaped. "I can see it now."

"I can too." A contented look came over him. "And I like what I see. A lot."

A delicious sigh wriggled its way up inside of me as I whispered, "So do I."

"And because I'm so sure the future's going to be bright, I need to show you something that might come as a bit of a surprise."

Maybe not as much of a surprise as you think. I've been prepping for this for years!

His hands trembled as he opened the box, revealing . . .

Huh?

Instead of a ring, the box held a strange-looking pin. Weird. Casey pulled it out and held it up in front of me. "Can you read the inscription on this?" he asked.

I squinted to get a better look. "Chesterfield Oil and Gas?"

Weirdest. Proposal. Ever.

"Yes." He nodded and gazed at the little pin in his palm. "Chesterfield Oil and Gas. In Tulsa."

"O-okay."

He paced the kitchen and finally came to a stop in front of me once again. "Katie, I don't know any way to tell you this other than just coming out and saying it. I've been offered a job in Tulsa at Chesterfield Oil and Gas. They want me to start next month. I've been trying to figure out a way to tell you for ages now, but there just didn't seem to be the right opportunity . . . until now."

"W-what?" My heart felt like a stone. "What are you saying? You're . . . you're leaving?" How had we jumped from proposal to rejection in less than a minute? Surely I'd misunderstood.

"It doesn't have to be forever," he said. "But a great company with potential for financial advancement? I can't get that here in Fairfield. You have to admit it. This is a dead-end town."

"A dead-end town?" My heart felt as if it had been personally attacked. How could he say that about the place I loved so much? "I've never heard you say anything like that before. *I'm* here. In Fairfield, I mean."

"I know. And I'm not asking you for a long-distance relationship here, Katie. I've given this a lot of thought, and I know that's not what's best for the two of us."

Ooh, got it! He planned to propose but wanted to give me a heads-up first that we would be living elsewhere. Likely wanting to gauge my reaction. Well, I'd offer a brave smile and face the "do we really have to move away?" question later. Surely he would change his mind. Maybe the Texas heat was getting to him. He would come to his senses soon.

"So, you don't want a long-distance relationship?" I asked.

"No." He opened his hand and looked at the

Chesterfield Oil and Gas pin. "I know it wouldn't work for either of us." He rolled the pin around in his hand, then looked my way, his nose wrinkled. "To be honest, Katie, I . . ." His voice lowered to a hoarse whisper. "I . . ."

"You . . . ?" *What?*

Any bit of lingering hope withered as I saw the somber expression in his eyes.

"I just feel like I need to focus on my work right now. My future with the new company is hanging in the balance. I need to play it safe. Be fully on board. That way they won't question my loyalty. You understand, right? You are, as I said, the sweetest, most understanding girl in Fairfield."

"Wait." In that moment, I had the strangest out-of-body experience, the one where you feel like you're dreaming. The one where you hope—no, pray—you're dreaming. "Are you breaking up with me?"

His expression contorted and his eyes filled with remorse. "We don't really have to say it like that. I know this is hard to hear, but I think we should step back for a few months. Maybe reassess at Thanksgiving when I come home for a visit."

"Thanksgiving? That's months from now."

"Yeah. Mama said she'd kill me if I didn't come home for the holidays."

"So your parents know? They've known you're moving away?"

He nodded.

"Great. Everyone knows but me." Only, I knew now, didn't I? And now . . . well, it pretty much changed everything.

I couldn't say what happened next because I found myself in a somewhat catatonic state. I vaguely remember knocking over the glass of sweet tea and leaving it to run down the edge of the table. I sort of remember stubbing my toe on the leg of the kitchen table as I fled from the room. And I'm pretty sure I remember nearly tripping down the steps as I bolted from the front porch.

Still, when I reached the car, as I stared back at the large ranch-style home, I had to believe the whole thing had been a terrible dream. I'd wake up soon, and Casey and I would laugh at how real it had all seemed.

Or not.

I couldn't stop the tears as they flowed down my cheeks. I didn't want to. My entire world had just come crumbling down around me. Every fantasy, every plan . . . vanished.

Thank you very much, Chesterfield Oil and Gas.

A humming noise from inside my purse got my attention. I glanced down at my phone as it buzzed and realized I'd missed another call from Cosmopolitan Bridal. I listened to the message, recognizing Madge's voice right away.

"Something I forgot to mention," she said, her

voice sailing along in the same chipper fashion as before. "We'll be counting on you to be available not just for fittings but for press engagements, radio interviews, and that sort of thing. Hope this isn't too much of a distraction from your wedding plans."

Wedding plans?

What wedding plans?

As I pushed the button on my phone to end the message, I leaned back against the seat and dissolved into a haze of tears.

I had the gown. I had the church. I had the guests. The only thing missing from this wedding . . . was the groom.

7

Somewhere Between

> I would rather wake up in the middle of nowhere than in any city on earth.
>
> Steve McQueen

Just two days after I learned that I'd won the dress of my dreams, my would-be fiancé packed his bags and headed north to Oklahoma to look for an apartment. He might not be leaving for good just yet, but it sure felt like it. Looked like he was eager to get his new big-city life started.

I received the news through the grapevine—i.e., the WOP-pers—who made it their mission to pray the dear boy back home again. No doubt they would do it too, though frankly, I didn't care if I ever saw him again.

Okay, I did care. A lot. But how could I live with what he'd done to me? Talk about humiliating.

I went back and forth in my thinking—from wanting him to come home to wishing I'd never see him again. Mama seemed the most perturbed of all. On Thursday morning as we wrapped up breakfast, she stormed around the kitchen, her temper evident to all.

"I'm just so shocked." She shoved some dirty

cups into the sink. "Did anyone see this coming?"

Dewey and Beau shook their heads, but Jasper gave her a knowing look. "No, but it's inevitable, Mama."

"Inevitable?" I put my hands on my hips and glared at my brother. "Explain what you mean by that."

"Not inevitable that he would leave you," Jasper said. "It's just inevitable that folks would want out of this town. I've tried to say it for years, but no one listens to me. Maybe now they will."

"But why?" Mama looked flabbergasted. "I just don't get it. I had no clue he wanted to leave."

"Me either." Dewey shoveled cereal into his mouth. "Weird."

"It's not weird that he wants to earn a decent living," Jasper countered. "There's no money in Fairfield, you know. No real money, anyway."

"Sure there is." My father reached for his wallet and opened it, revealing a couple of twenties and a five-dollar bill. "You just have to work hard to earn it, like any other respectable town. Money doesn't grow on trees, you know."

"Unless you happen to work for an oil and gas firm in Oklahoma," Jasper said. "In which case it grows on trees, under oil rigs, and in the air around you." He leaned my way and muttered, "Which is precisely why I've got to get out of this town and find a real job."

I pondered my brother's "get out of this town"

comment all day. Maybe, all things considered, that was my answer. I needed to, as Jasper would say, get the heck out of Dodge. If I left Fairfield for a week or two, I could put this whole ugly breakup with Casey out of my mind. And maybe, if those WOP-pers were worth their weight in salt, Casey would be here waiting on me when I returned. I hoped.

As if operating under heavenly orders, Lori-Lou called me that very moment. I hated to share the news with her but had no choice. I couldn't muster up any enthusiasm, answering with a somber "Hey."

"Hey yourself." Lori-Lou sounded like her usual chipper self. "You doing okay, Katie?" Before I could answer, she plowed ahead, her voice more animated. "Your mama called Queenie, who told all of the WOP-pers, so naturally my mama found out. She called me this morning and said that Casey, well . . ."

"Yeah." I sighed. "It's true. I should've told you but didn't know how."

"Oh, Katie. My heart is broken for you." She turned to fuss at one of the kids, then returned. "I want you to come here. Stay with me. It'll do you a world of good."

"Ironic. I was thinking the same thing. Getting away from Fairfield for a while might be just the thing to get me over this hurdle."

"Yes, I really think it'll be relaxing and—

Mariela! How many times have I told you not to run around the house naked? Put your clothes back on this very moment!"

Hmm. Maybe staying with Lori-Lou wouldn't be very relaxing after all. But it would provide a break from my current plight.

"Please come," she implored. "Stay at my place. We're getting the AC fixed this afternoon, so wait until the morning to come, but plan to stay with me a couple of weeks. It'll do you good to get away from Fairfield, and maybe we can figure out what to do about the dress while you're here."

"The dress. Ugh. I'm supposed to be at Cosmopolitan Bridal on Monday for my first fitting. They called about two minutes after I got my heart broken."

Lori-Lou groaned. "Well, I know it's probably the last thing you want to deal with, but what are you going to do about the dress? Have you given it any thought?"

I had, of course. In fact, I'd thought about that contest dozens of times over the past three days. Shame washed over me every time. No way could I go to the bridal shop now, not with my would-be fiancé leaving me in the lurch. What would I say? How could I face them?

Lori-Lou interrupted my ponderings. "Remember that scene in *Coal Miner's Daughter* where Doo got jealous because Loretta was more successful than he was?"

I sighed. “Lori-Lou, you’ve been spending entirely too much time with Queenie. She’s rubbing off on you. And I don’t know what this has to do with me coming to Dallas.”

“Oh, everything! I’ve been thinking . . . maybe that’s what’s happened with Casey.”

“Wait . . . what? Are you saying that Casey is jealous of me? I’m not successful by any stretch of the imagination.”

“But don’t you see? You’re everyone’s little darling. You’ve won every award that Fairfield has to offer, right down to Peach Queen. You’re golden.”

“Golden?”

“Everything you touch turns to gold.”

“Puh-leeze. I work at a hardware store.”

“And everyone adores you. Don’t you see? You’re a big fish in a small pond. Casey looks at how loved you are, how you’ve won over so many people just by being you, and he feels like he can’t compete with that.”

“So I should stop being lovable?”

“Of course not. That’s not my point.”

I didn’t have time to ask her what her point was because the kids interrupted once again and she had to end the call. Still, I couldn’t stop fretting over her words all afternoon. Was Casey really jealous of me? If so, why? I’d certainly never done anything—deliberately, anyway—to provoke that.

Casey.

My heart grew heavy as I thought about him. With Casey in Oklahoma, I didn't know how I could keep up appearances in Fairfield. Folks were already questioning . . . everything. Clearly everyone in Fairfield had heard about his leaving. If I ever doubted that, my questions were answered when I worked the cash register at the store that afternoon.

Mrs. Jamison patted my hand as she paid for her toilet handle. She leaned in to whisper, "Sweet girl. Don't give up. I'm sure there's a fella out there for you someplace." Then she patted my hand again. Lovely.

Mr. Anderson was loaded with sage advice as he paid for his door hinges. "I say give the guy time to figure out who he's gonna be when he grows up. It's just a phase. Went through something myself before I married Mrs. Anderson. He'll come back . . . eventually."

Mrs. Keller had the best advice of all. "Don't focus on what you've lost," she said as she hefted a huge bag of fertilizer onto the counter so I could scan in the price. "Focus on what you didn't know you had."

"What I didn't know I had?" I scanned the fertilizer and then lifted it to my shoulder to carry it out for her.

"Sure. You've heard the old saying, 'If God closes a door, somewhere he opens a window'?

There's a whole future out there for you that you haven't even discovered yet. Don't worry about what hasn't happened. Set your sights on what's gonna happen. It's an adventure, you know." She gave me a little wink and then held out her arms. "Now, give me that bag. Do I look like a lightweight to you?"

She didn't, actually. I just couldn't think clearly because of what she'd said.

An adventure? In Fairfield? With 99 percent of the population reminding me every few minutes of my heartbreak? Who had time—or energy—for that type of excitement?

By the time I'd ended my shift at the store, I knew what I had to do. A phone call to Cosmopolitan Bridal was in order, right this very minute. I made my way to the restroom so that I could have some privacy, then called Madge's number. Her voicemail kicked in after the fourth ring. When I heard her businesslike voice, it stopped me in my tracks. I couldn't leave a message. No, news like this had to be delivered in person.

I'd drive to Lori-Lou's tomorrow, get settled in, then head to the bridal shop first thing Saturday morning. I'd cancel all plans for the dress. It was the least I could do, all things considered. If I let them know quickly, then some other lucky bride could walk the aisle wearing her Nadia James couture gown. My heart ached at the idea of losing the dress, but doing the right thing was definitely more important. I'd come clean. Tell them every-thing. Afterward I'd settle in at Lori-Lou's place for a few weeks so that God could mend my broken heart.

When I arrived home from work that afternoon, I gathered the courage to tell Mama—not about the gown, but about visiting Lori-Lou. I found her in the kitchen making our usual Thursday night dinner, meatloaf. I explained my plan of action, doing my best to hold back the tears as I thought about leaving.

"Wait, you're going where?" Mama looked up from mixing the meatloaf, her brow furrowed.

"To Dallas to visit Lori-Lou."

"But Pop needs you at the store. You can't leave, honey."

The moment I heard those words, my heart twisted inside of me. As much as I loved being part of a tight-knit community, the words "you can't leave" made me want to. Leave. Soon.

"Mama, I work harder than anyone I know, and I never take a vacation. Well, unless you count those four days I worked at church camp as a counselor, but that was hardly a vacation, especially when you consider the fact that I spent a full day in the ER with one of the campers who broke her ankle. I'm due a little time off, and under the circumstances . . ." My words drifted off as I pondered my recent breakup with Casey.

"Say no more." Mama's eyes misted over. "You need to get away to deal with your heartbreak."

Something like that. I also needed to rehearse my "I can't go through with this" speech for the fine folks at Cosmopolitan Bridal. But I couldn't tell Mama any of that. In some ways, that relieved me a little. If I didn't go through with the wedding gown thing, my parents would never have to know I'd entered that stupid contest in the first place. That fact brought me some degree of comfort.

"Well, I have a perfectly lovely idea," Mama said after a moment of quiet reflection. "While you're in Dallas, why don't you go on over to Dallas Baptist University and see Levi Nash? He'll be tickled pink to see a familiar face."

"Mama, surely you're not suggesting anything by that."

"Well, heavens, no. He's a good boy, though, that Levi. And his faith is stronger than ever, thanks to the prayers of the WOP-pers."

"What does that have to do with me?"

"Oh, nothing. Only, he's a great catch. That's all."

"Mama!"

"Just saying, just saying! There are other fish in the sea besides Casey." She gave me a look and then walked into the other room, muttering something about how she'd learned that lesson personally. Weird. Had my very own mother just suggested that I date someone else right after having my heart broken? Crazy.

Pop didn't take the news about my leaving as well as Mama. When I told him that I planned to go to Lori-Lou's for a few weeks, he went into a panic. Well, not exactly a panic, but his version of it. Mama told him about halfway into our family's usual Thursday night dessert—chocolate pudding. I held my breath. My brothers all stopped eating—my first sign they were taking this seriously—and stared at Pop.

"That's impossible." My father pushed his pudding dish away and gave me a pensive look. Clearly he didn't believe Mama's words.

"She needs to get away for a while, Herb," Mama argued. "Katie is twenty-four years old. If she wants to go to Dallas for a couple of weeks to stay with family, we can't stop her. Besides, it'll do her a world of good."

"Weeks?" He groaned. "I can't believe you're saying this, Marie. Wasn't it just a month ago you sat at Sam's Buffet, listing all of the reasons why folks are better off in a small town? Now you want our daughter to go to the city—where they have snakes in the kitchens and neighbors living on top of one another? Where folks share their plumbing with total strangers? That's okay with you now?"

"Oh, Herb, get over it." Mama rolled her eyes. "It's just a couple of weeks. What are the chances Katie would have to deal with snakes in that length of time? Besides, she's already dealt with one far worse than the reptilian variety."

Pop looked genuinely confused. I felt a little confused myself.

"That Casey Lawson is a snake of the worst kind." Mama's jaw clenched. "Getting my girl's hopes up and then dashing them with his impulsive move to Oklahoma." She mumbled something under her breath that I couldn't quite make out.

"Now, Marie, we've known Casey since he was a boy," Pop countered. "He's a good kid, and his parents are pillars in the community."

"Even if they are Presbyterians." Jasper slapped the table and laughed.

I couldn't help the little sigh that erupted. As mad and disappointed as I was with him, I knew Casey was a good kid. Er, man. He would make things right eventually. I knew he would.

Just like I would make things right with the folks at Cosmopolitan Bridal.

"I can fill in at the store for Katie while she's gone." Mama's words interrupted my train of thought. "It'll be fine."

In that moment, I truly believed it would be. That same feeling lingered as I packed my bags later that evening. It stuck with me as I drove to Dallas the following morning. My feelings of hope didn't dissipate until I entered the messy three-bedroom condo that Lori-Lou and her husband shared with their children. At that point, with rambunctious kiddos swarming me, their shrill voices echoing off the Sheetrock in the small space, I wondered if perhaps I'd made a mistake.

"Aunt Katie, Aunt Katie!" Four-year-old Mariela jumped up and down, then wrapped her arms around my right thigh.

The youngest, Joshie, wrapped himself around my left ankle and tried to ride it like a pony. This left little room for Gilly, the two-and-a-half-year-old, but that didn't stop her. She attempted to propel herself into my arms, nearly knocking me over in the process.

"Well, hello, strangers." I laughed and then knelt down to give them all hugs. "I'm going to be your roomie for the next couple of weeks."

"What's a roomie?" Gilly asked.

"It means she's going to stay with us." Mariela put chubby hands on her hips and spoke to her younger sister in a know-it-all voice. "Maybe forever!"

"Yes, I'm staying with you," I said. "But not forever." When Mariela pouted I added, "But Aunt Katie is going to have a lot of fun with her babies. Pinkie promise!" I held out my pinkie and she grabbed it with hers.

"I hope so." Lori-Lou chuckled. "Let me start by apologizing. I'm so sorry you have to share a room with the baby." My cousin's nose wrinkled. "But he's the quietest of the three, if that makes you feel any better. And I'm pretty sure these two girls would drive you crazy if you bunked with them."

"I'll do just fine," I said. My words were meant to convince myself as well as Lori-Lou. "And I'm sure the blow-up mattress will be comfortable." *I hope.*

I couldn't help but smile at the kids. Mariela looked adorable with her cute little pigtails and freckled nose. She had that impish look that rotten children often have, the one that says, "I'm secretly up to no good." Still, no one could deny her outward beauty. Gilly, on the other hand, made me laugh just looking at her. For one thing, her shirt was inside out. And her socks didn't match.

"Please ignore the way she looks." Lori-Lou gestured to Gilly. "She didn't start out the day looking like this. She's changed clothes four times already."

"She looks cute," I countered.

"Hmm." Lori-Lou pointed at her daughter's feet. "See those socks she has on?"

I glanced down and nodded.

"One of them is mine," Lori-Lou said. "The other one is the baby's. And you don't even want to know whose underwear she's wearing. Worst part is, she's not potty trained, so she won't be wearing the underwear for long. They'll be sopping wet in a matter of minutes. I've never seen a kid go through as many panties as this one."

Okay then. Welcome to the big city, Katie Sue. This is what you've been missing.

Still, baby Joshie was adorable. I swept the little one into my arms and held him close . . . until I realized he had on a stinky diaper. Then I passed him right back to his mother.

Lori-Lou bounced him on her hip as if he didn't smell at all. "Josh has a couple of vacation days coming. He says he'll watch the kids so we can have some girl time." My cousin's eyes flooded. "I love that man. He's so great."

Terrific. True love. Nothing like a little salt in an open wound.

Lori-Lou must've realized she'd struck a nerve. "I'm sorry, Katie. But if it makes you feel any better, we spend about half the time arguing about, well, everything. The man drives me out of my ever-lovin' mind, but I love him. I really do."

Well, wonderful. While I wasn't pining away for Casey, I'd enjoy listening to my cousin and her husband argue. And then watch them kiss and make up. Perfect way to get over a breakup.

She shifted the baby to her other hip, and the stench from his diaper permeated the room. "Anyway, I hate to bring up a sore subject, but what did you decide to do about the wedding gown?"

Was she kidding? What else could I do? "I can't go through with it. Not now."

"You're going to tell them?"

I sighed and nodded. "Don't have any choice. I was hoping you'd go with me tomorrow. What do you think?"

"Tomorrow?" She hesitated. "I think I'd better make sure Josh can watch the kids. Otherwise we'll have a fiasco on our hands if we have to take these three into the swankiest bridal shop in town."

"In the state," I corrected her.

"In the country." She laughed. "Which is precisely why I can never, under any circumstances, take any of these three—Mariela! Don't you dare use those markers on my new coffee table! We've talked about this a hundred times." She raced across the room and grabbed the markers from the four-year-old, who burst into tears. About three minutes into the emotional tirade, Lori-Lou glanced my way. "Sorry!" she hollered above the din. "Welcome to my world, Katie."

Some welcome. And some world. But this would be my home for the next two weeks, and I'd better learn to love it. At least here no one would break my heart.

8

Who Was That Stranger

A city is not gauged by its length and width, but by the broadness of its vision and the height of its dreams.

Herb Caen

Spending the night on an air mattress turned out to be quite the adventure. Add to the discomfort a crying child just three feet away, and it made for a sleepless night. Mostly sleepless, anyway. I did doze off a couple of times. One of those times I dreamed about Casey. Sad, sobering dreams. Bittersweet. I also thought about the fact that I'd missed the family's Friday night gathering at Sam's Buffet. Bummer. As much as I needed to be away from things, I still felt homesick, especially when I thought about the coconut meringue pie.

I awoke on Saturday morning with that horrible feeling you always get just before doing something you don't want to do. The sound of the children's voices rang out from the kitchen, but they paled in comparison to the argument going on between Josh and Lori-Lou over the AC repair bill. I didn't mean to eavesdrop on their conversation, but in such a confined space I didn't have any choice. Lovely.

A few feet away from my air mattress, baby Joshie slept in his crib. I would've let him continue to doze, but the smell leaking from his diaper was enough to prompt me to wake him. Ick.

After I rose and slipped on my robe, I picked up the baby from his crib and made my way out to the kitchen, holding him at arm's length.

"Well, good morning, sunshine." Lori-Lou laughed when she saw me.

Mariela lunged at my legs, almost knocking me over in the process. Lori-Lou reached for the baby and said something about taking him for a quick bath before breakfast. The two of them disappeared from the room before I could say, "Hey, who's watching the other two?"

I spent the next fifteen minutes debating the finer points of cereal eating with Mariela and trying to figure out some strategic way to get a Cheerio out of Gilly's left nostril. I'd never seen anyone stick cereal up their nose before, so this caught me totally off guard.

My cousin's husband came into the kitchen a few minutes later, matter-of-factly tugged the Cheerio out of Gilly's nose, yawned, and poured himself a cup of coffee.

"Welcome to reality, Katie."

His version of it, maybe, but definitely not mine.

"One day"—Josh gestured around the messy kitchen—"this could all be yours."

"Once she finds the right man, anyway." Lori-Lou's voice sounded from the hallway. She stepped into the kitchen with the baby, wrapped in a towel, in her arms.

"So, let me get this straight." Josh leaned against the counter and took a swig of his coffee. "You two are spending the morning at a bridal shop where Katie has won a multi-thousand-dollar dress that she's not going to be wearing?"

"Something like that," I said. And then sighed. "I'm not keeping the dress."

"She's keeping the dress." Lori-Lou gave me a "we're going to talk about this" look.

"No. I'm not." I shook my head and sipped some of my now-cold coffee. "This is a moral decision. What would Jesus do?"

"Jesus wouldn't need a wedding dress, but I suppose that's irrelevant." Josh seemed to drift off in his thoughts for a moment, then added, "He wouldn't keep the dress. No way."

"But she'll never have another opportunity to have a dress from Cosmopolitan," Lori-Lou argued. "And she won the contest fair and square. Nadia James loved her essay. That was the determining factor, not the wedding date."

"Or the need for a groom?" Josh's right eyebrow elevated.

"There will be a groom." Lori-Lou glared at her husband. "Someday."

I groaned at that comment. Right now I didn't care if I ever found a groom. Weddings were highly overrated, after all.

"Might even be Casey. He'll come to his senses." My cousin passed the baby off to her husband and then poured herself a cup of coffee. "Wait and see."

"Could we end this conversation right here?" I stepped toward the door leading into the hallway. "I'm not taking the dress. Conversation over. I don't care how much it's worth—it's not worth it to me to do anything deceptive."

"Amen. Preach it, girl." Josh shifted the baby to one arm so he could continue drinking his coffee. "I'll be here taking care of the kids while you two swank it up at the froufrou wedding place."

"Swank it up? Froufrou?" Lori-Lou smacked herself in the head. "You've been watching those wedding dress shows, haven't you, babe?"

"Maybe." He crossed his arms at his chest. "What's it to you?" This was followed by a belly laugh. "Anyway, do the right thing, Katie. Don't take the dress."

Lori-Lou grumbled about this as we headed down the hallway to our respective rooms to get dressed. She continued to fuss several minutes later when we got into my car.

"I get Josh's point," she said. "But I totally disagree."

"Lori-Lou, I don't have any choice."

"Sure you do." She pointed to the stop sign ahead. "Turn right up here. Then left at the next light. We're about ten miles away from the store."

"Remember that scene in *Coal Miner's Daughter* where Doo takes Loretta out to a big piece of property and shows her the house he plans to build for her?" I made the right-hand turn and kept my eyes on the road.

"Of course. Turn left up here." Lori-Lou gestured and I eased my way over to the left lane.

"In that scene Loretta and Doo have been married awhile and she's had some measure of success, and he takes her up to this piece of property where he's already laid out a plan for a house."

"I remember, Katie."

"Point is, he doesn't consult with her, just goes off on his own and makes the plans without involving her."

"Right. She got mad."

"Very. I mean, she was thrilled that he wanted to build a house, but mad that he set out on his own to do it without her input."

"I can't imagine Josh going out and doing something like that without asking me." Lori-Lou grunted. "For one thing, our bank account isn't quite big enough for a down payment. We've been saving, but it's so hard with kids."

She carried on about their poor financial state, but I didn't hear half of it.

Lori-Lou let out a squeal and pointed to my right. "Oh, slow down. I think we're coming up on Frazier."

I slowed down and she gestured for me to get into the right lane. "I didn't mean to get you all worked up about that," I said. "I guess my point was, sometimes we get ahead of ourselves. And that's what I did with Casey."

"You wanted to build a house but forgot to ask Casey if he wanted to live there?" she asked.

"Something like that. Not a literal house, but—"

"Stop! It's right up here. See the sign?"

In the distance I saw the beautifully scripted sign reading COSMOPOLITAN BRIDAL. My heart quickened and then felt like it had turned to lead. I could avoid the inevitable no longer. What I wanted—what I needed—was to get this visit to Cosmopolitan Bridal over with.

We pulled up to the store's parking lot, and Lori-Lou's cell phone rang. She spent the next ten minutes bickering with Josh about how to discipline Mariela for coloring on her younger sister's arm with a marker. I spent those ten minutes praying for the courage to tell Nadia James that I could not—would not—allow her to make me a wedding dress.

Lori-Lou ended the call and glanced at me with an exaggerated sigh. "He's so totally hopeless."

"What do you mean?"

"He's clueless when it comes to dealing with the kids."

"He's on a learning curve, Lori-Lou."

She snorted. "Hey, he's had those three kids the same length of time I have, and I've figured it out."

I didn't want to argue with her, but she clearly didn't have it all figured out. Did any parent ever?

"Okay, you ready to go inside?" she asked. "This is about as close to heaven as we're gonna get in this lifetime."

"I . . . I guess." Right now, it felt a little more like purgatory. If I could just get past this "tell them what happened" part, my stomach could stop churning.

We got out of the car and crossed the parking lot to the gorgeous double doors. Lori-Lou pulled open the one on the right, and we stepped inside Cosmopolitan Bridal for the first time. The place was teeming with customers, many of whom wore expensive clothes and carried designer purses.

I stared up, up, up at the chandeliers hanging from the high ceilings above. Wow. Candelabras graced the walls to our left, and the tapestries on the windows were crafted from the most gorgeous fabrics I'd ever seen.

"Whoa," Lori-Lou said. "Check out this place, will you?"

"Welcome to Cosmopolitan Bridal," an older woman behind the counter called out to us. "I'll be with you shortly." She turned her attention back to an existing customer and I turned back to examine the room. Man, what a place!

I couldn't help but notice the intoxicating scent of some sort of air freshener wafting around us. It certainly wasn't the Lysol spray Mama used to mask the odor of the kitty litter box in our upstairs bathroom.

Lori-Lou let out a soft whistle. "We're not in Kansas anymore, Toto."

"You can say that twice and mean it."

"We're not in Kansas anymore." She giggled. "Check out that display. Do you think those are real diamonds on those branches?"

"Surely not." They looked like diamonds, though. Everything in the place looked expensive. Right away I felt overwhelmed, and not just because of the mission set before me. I'd always been intimidated by folks with lots of money, although I'd never really voiced that thought aloud. The kind of people who came into this shop had money. Lots and lots of money. I had no money. Well, not much, anyway.

"Chin up," Lori-Lou whispered. "You have every right to be here."

I glanced at her, wondering how she'd known my feelings.

"You're an open book, Katie." She nudged me

with her arm. "Always have been. Just enjoy being here, okay? Who knows when we'll ever see a place like this again."

"True."

I took a few steps toward a row of white gowns, my head high, my shoulders back, with the most confident expression I could muster.

Distracted by a mannequin to my right, I paused. The wedding dress on it made me forget all about being intimidated. The gown drew me in and made my knees all rubbery, in a good way. Well, until I saw the price tag. "This dress is $6,700," I whispered to Lori-Lou.

"Wow." Her eyes grew large as she reached over to look at the tag for herself. "That's more than we paid for the used van we're driving. If I bought that dress I'd never come up with the money for a down payment for a house."

"No kidding." I made my way from aisle to aisle in the shop, completely mesmerized. I'd never seen so much white in all of my life. White taffeta, white silk, white tulle. Oceans and oceans of white. The mannequins, taller and slimmer than most I'd seen in department stores, were adorned in the gowns Nadia James had become famous for. Each was patterned after a female great from days gone by. I stopped to look at the Audrey Hepburn, then shifted my attention to the Grace Kelly. Wow. I couldn't believe the detail in both.

On and on I went, looking at the various gowns.

The Doris Day caught my eye, as did the Ann-Margret. The one that puzzled me most was the Petula Clark. I'd never heard of her. Neither had Lori-Lou, apparently. She stared at the dress and shrugged.

Off in the distance a gorgeous blonde—probably a couple years older than me—walked to the cash register to talk to the older woman. I stared at the tall, stately woman with her fashionable hairdo, expensive clothes, and over-the-top heels.

"Look, Katie." Lori-Lou jabbed me with her elbow. "A real live Barbie doll." She giggled and leaned over to whisper, "I wonder if there's a Ken doll around here someplace."

Yep. There was a Ken, all right. He appeared from behind the row of gowns to our left. A handsome specimen of a man—tall with dark hair and just enough of a five o'clock shadow to make him gorgeous. I stared into the most beautiful eyes—after I got past the solidly built Adonis-like physique. The guy had to be at least six feet three. Okay, six four. Except for a slight limp, he moved with confidence and a bit too much speed for his delicate surroundings. The phrase "bull in a china shop" came to mind at once.

As he rounded the corner, a swatch of wavy dark hair fell casually on his forehead. He brushed it back with his hand. Something in his handsome face felt familiar, like I'd seen him before. Then again, he had that familiar Greek god look—firm features, confident set of his shoulders, perfectly placed smile. And it didn't hurt anything that the guy's skin was bronzed, as if he'd spent the last few days on the Riviera, not holed up in a bridal shop. But judging from the fact that he ended up behind the counter talking to the older woman, he worked here. Fascinating. I couldn't take my eyes off of him. Didn't want to.

He glanced at me, his beautiful blue eyes sparkling as he gave me a nod and said, "Welcome to Cosmopolitan Bridal."

Lori-Lou stopped cold and grabbed my arm, moving us back a few feet. "Y-you know who that is, right?" Her words came out as a hoarse whisper.

"He looks vaguely familiar." I gave the guy another look. Yep. Familiar. But why? "Do you know him or something?"

"Know him?" Lori-Lou clamped a hand over her mouth and then pulled it back down. "Katie, don't you ever get out? That's Brady James, point guard for the Dallas Mavericks."

"Ah. Basketball." That explained it. "I remember now. He's one of Casey's favorite players. I think I've watched him play a time or two."

"*Was* one of Casey's favorite players. He blew out his knee four months ago. Happened on live TV, right in the middle of a playoff game. I feel really bad for the guy." Lori-Lou shrugged.

"Wonder what he's doing in a bridal shop. Weird, don't you think?"

Suddenly something Madge had said made perfect sense. "Oh, wait. I get it now."

"Get what?" Lori-Lou asked.

"Madge told me that Nadia's son was taking over the shop when she left for Paris."

"Seems a little weird that a pro basketball player is in the wedding biz, though. He's definitely not the type. I once knew a guy who liked taffeta but always suspected there was more to that story."

I gave Brady James a second look and tried to analyze him through that filter. Nope. No way. This guy was all guy, all six feet five of him. Or six six. He seemed to be growing taller the more I stared at him. Or maybe I just felt small in his presence. He certainly commanded the room.

Stop staring, Katie. It's not polite.

But how could a girl help herself? A specimen like this didn't come along every day, especially not in a bridal salon. Staring up into that handsome face, I almost forgot why I'd come to Cosmopolitan Bridal in the first place.

Almost, but not quite.

9

You're Lookin' at Country

When you take a flower in your hand and really look at it, it's your world for the moment. I want to give that world to someone else. Most people in the city rush around so, they have no time to look at a flower. I want them to see it whether they want to or not.

Georgia O'Keeffe

Brady James looked at us again, and a welcoming smile lit his face. I felt my cheeks grow hot. Had he noticed me staring? He headed right for us, but I wanted to run for the door.

"Oh. No. You. Don't." Lori-Lou spoke through clenched teeth. "Don't take a step. You're going to face this like a man."

"Face this like a man?" Brady asked as he drew near. "Well, if I must." When he chuckled, his eyes sparkled with merriment, which only made him more handsome and forced me to stare even more. "What am I facing?"

"Oh, I was talking to Katie Sue here." Lori-Lou nudged me with her arm, then looked at him with a smile too broad for comfort. “This is Katie. She needs to face life’s situations like a man.”

Brady gave me an inquisitive look. “Not exactly your usual opening line, but I’m thinking this has something to do with a wedding? Or a wedding dress?”

“Yes. A wedding dress. I’ve come to talk to you about a dress,” I managed.

A boyish smile turned up the edges of his lips. “Well then, you’ve come to the right place. I’m Brady. What can I help you with?”

Get it together, Katie. You look like a goober standing here.

“I, um, spoke to a woman named Madge. On the phone, I mean. Yesterday. No, maybe the day before. I can’t remember.” *I’ve been busy getting my heart crushed, so the days are getting mixed up.* “Anyway, she doesn’t know I’m coming today. She’s expecting me on Monday. Maybe it would be better if I talked to her alone? Would that be okay?” My sentences came out sounding rushed. Staccato. Breathy.

“Of course. I’ll get Madge for you. If anyone knows how to take things like a man, she does.” He leaned so close I could smell his yummy cologne. “Brace yourselves, ladies.”

Oh, I needed to brace myself, all right. My heart felt more vulnerable than ever as his arm brushed against mine. When he pointed at the middle-aged woman with dark red hair, I drew in a deep breath and willed my erratic heartbeat to slow down. I had to jump this hurdle so I could get back to the business of recovering from my heartbreak.

Just. Get. This. Over. With.

"Madge is one tough cookie." Brady waggled his brows.

"Ooh, cookies." Lori-Lou licked her lips. "When we're done with all this, let's go grab some lunch, Katie. I never get to have lunch without my kids."

"How did we transition from wedding dresses to cookies to lunch?" I asked.

Brady shrugged. "Not sure, but cookies do sound good. I'm pretty sure one of the girls brought in some homemade chocolate chip cookies just this morning. They're in the workroom out back." He grinned and then walked across the room toward Madge. I couldn't help but notice that he favored his left knee. Poor guy.

I gave the older woman another look to see if she really looked as tough as he'd described her. Broad shoulders. Button-up blouse over black slacks. Sturdy. Plain. Completely different attire from the glitzy blonde chick. Yes, Madge looked somewhat out of place in this swanky joint, but she barked out orders from behind the cash register like she owned the place. Well, until Brady approached her, then she appeared to melt like butter. A smile lit her face, replacing the stern expression.

"There's a little song I sing with the kids," Lori-Lou whispered as she gestured to the woman. " 'One of these things is not like the other.' " My cousin shook her head. "That's what comes to mind when I see that Madge lady working here. She just doesn't seem to fit the place. Looks like she'd be more at home working at Fanny's Fine Fashions in Fairfield."

"Oh, I don't know. I think there's room for every kind of person in the wedding biz," I said.

Madge walked our way and my heart rate picked up.

Here goes nothing.

"Can I help you ladies?" she asked.

I offered a slight smile. "Yes. You're Madge?"

"Last time I checked." She put her hands on her hips. "What can I do for you?"

"Oh, I'm Katie Fisher. You called me the other day, remember? I'm the one who—"

"You won the contest!" The woman let out a squeal and grabbed my arm. "Well, why in the world didn't you just say so? You're early, kid! Didn't expect to see you until Monday. What brings you here today?"

"Well, see, that's the thing. I came today because I happened to be in Dallas with my cousin Lori-Lou here."

"Good to meet you." Madge grabbed Lori-Lou's hand and shook it. "Member of the wedding party? I know a maid of honor when I see one!"

"Actually, Lori-Lou is married."

My cousin grinned. "So, I guess that would technically make me—"

"Matron of honor!" Madge clasped her hands together. "Well, no time to waste. C'mon in and meet the crew. We've got a lot of work ahead of us. Nadia's in her office behind the shop, so I'll let her know you're here. She'll be thrilled you're early! That'll give her a couple of extra days for the design."

So much for thinking the woman was as tough as nails. Looked like she had a soft spot for contest winners, which only made my plight more pitiable. Or terrifying.

At this point, a couple of other girls came out of a back room, joining the blonde. After Madge introduced me as the contest winner, all three started applauding. Oh. Dear. Then they took to chattering. One of them appeared to be speaking another language, but I couldn't quite make it out, what with so many voices overlapping. Beyond them, Brady James glanced at me with intrigue in his eyes.

Madge continued to gush over me, and seconds later Brady joined us.

"Wait . . . you're the one who won the contest? Why didn't you tell me? I would've introduced you to Madge and made a big deal over you being here. She's been so excited to meet you. We all have."

"Well, thank you, but that's the thing. I don't really want to—"

"And my mom. She's in back," Brady said. He reached to straighten a veil on the mannequin to my right. "She's going over some paperwork in her office right now, but I'm sure she'll be thrilled you're here. Did she know you were coming?"

"No. I didn't tell anyone." And I certainly hadn't planned on a reception like this. How could I tell them now that I wouldn't be taking the dress? They were treating me like the queen of Sheba.

"Shame on you for not warning us that you were coming in early." Madge patted my arm in a motherly fashion. "We would've called the press. At the very least, I would've brought my camera."

"Ooh, I have a great camera on my phone." The blonde grabbed her phone and started snapping photos of me. "Do you mind?"

"Well, actually . . ." Ugh. I could just see it now: *Jilted Fairfield bride-to-be shows up at Cosmopolitan Bridal to make a fool of herself in front of pro basketball player and his . . . mother?*

Not that I was ever really a bride-to-be. And that reminded me that I had to tell Madge I wouldn't need a wedding gown.

"I'm sure Madge and the girls would love to show you around while you're waiting on my mom." Brady gestured to the three young women standing nearby and introduced them as Twiggy—

Really? Twiggy?—Crystal, and Dahlia, the one I'd seen earlier with Madge.

Dahlia had one of those rich accents from . . . maybe Russia? No, Sweden. Hmm. I couldn't really tell, but she definitely wasn't from Fairfield. Her platinum blonde hair reminded me of one of those gals from the older Hollywood housewives show. Her face was a perfect oval. Her cheekbones high and exotic. Not a wrinkle around those beautifully made-up eyes. I'd be willing to bet she'd had work done, but no telling where. Every feature was picture perfect.

Twiggy, thin with a short reddish-blonde pixie cut, seemed really nice and bubbly. She held herself with confidence. And judging from the way she sashayed when she walked, she'd done some time as a runway model before taking on this job at the bridal shop. Maybe that's where the name had come from. A stage name, perhaps? And the dress she wore showed she knew her stuff when it came to fashion.

Then there was Crystal, who drew me in at once. Her freckled nose and dirty blonde hair put me in mind of someone I knew quite well—myself. And when she opened her mouth to speak, the thickest Southern accent tumbled out. If I had to guess, I'd say Crystal was from South Carolina. Or Alabama. Or Georgia.

Turned out I was right on the last count. She hailed from Georgia. Looked like we had another thing in common: peaches. All of this I learned in only a couple minutes of knowing her. And the fact that she had a passion for fashion, as she put it.

The three girls seemed giddy and fun as they took photos of me and then shared about their various jobs at the shop, but Madge was all business. "I'll show you around until Nadia is free." She turned her attention to Brady and smiled. "Sound agreeable?"

"Sure." He shrugged. "Not sure it'll take very long."

"Are you kidding?" I glanced at the racks on my right. "I live, eat, sleep, and breathe wedding gowns. This is like heaven to me." I glanced around the room. "Everything is so . . . white."

"Just how you pictured heaven, then?"

"Well, close." I released a happy sigh. "Just waiting for the angel choir to chime in."

"My pitch is terrible," Madge said. "So don't count on me for any angel action."

Brady laughed and gave her a hug. "Well, enjoy yourselves, ladies. I'll let Mom know you're here. If anyone needs me after that, I'll be in my office."

I still couldn't quite figure out what a pro basketball player was doing with an office at a bridal shop, even a shop owned by a family member. Had he traded in his running shoes for gowns and veils? Very odd. I tried to picture the look on Casey's face should he see his favorite player seated behind a desk at a bridal salon, but I couldn't. No doubt he would cringe at the very idea. Then again, what did it matter what Casey thought?

Madge's words interrupted my own thoughts. "We'll start with existing gowns so you can see Nadia's work," she said. "It should inspire you. She's going to be creating yours from scratch, you know, based on your favorite movie or TV star."

"Or singer," Twiggy chimed in.

"Yes, or singer." Madge nodded. "Point is, you get to choose the person who inspires you, and Nadia will take it from there."

"She does such a spectacular job of capturing the look and feel of that person in the gown," Crystal said. "Have you seen the Katharine Hepburn gown? It's like you've stepped back in time."

"I'm sure they're all great," I said. "But I really need to tell you that . . ." My words trailed off. I couldn't seem to spit out the rest.

"Oh, it's okay, honey," Madge said. "No need to spill the whole story right off. You need time to think it through, I suppose."

"Time to choose the best parts of the story for the *Texas Bride* interview," Crystal added.

"In the meantime, I'll show you the inner sanctum. Nadia's design studio." Madge leaned close to whisper, "Almost no one gets to go in there, so you have to promise not to share what you see until that reporter from *Texas Bride* comes to interview you. It's all top-secret information until then. Got it?"

"Got it," I echoed. "But that's really why I've come. I have something I need to tell you that's kind of a secret too."

"Ooh, inquiring minds want to know." Madge laughed.

"Katie's *great* at keeping secrets." Lori-Lou gave me a "please don't spill the beans until after she's shown us around the shop" look, and I obliged by closing my mouth and trailing on Madge's heels.

I elbowed my ornery cousin and mouthed the words, "I *have* to tell them."

She gave me a bemused smile, followed by a wink. Goofy girl. Did she not understand that I couldn't go through with this?

We saw thc gowns, many of which took my breath away. I'd never seen so many designs in my life—everything from frilly to simple to over the top. Many were Nadia's, but the shop featured designs by a host of well-known designers, including one of my favorites from the Galveston area, Gabi Delgado.

After touring the gowns, Madge took us to the studio in the back where Nadia designed her line of wedding dresses. Long tables stretched the expanse of the room, with sewing machines and fabrics in abundance. I'd never seen so many bolts of satin and tulle in my life. And the trims! I could've spent hours just looking through the shimmery bolts of loveliness. They took my breath away. I wanted to finger each one and dream of the possibilities for where they might end up. Brides from all over the globe would likely find these lovely bits attached to their gowns.

"Want to see the fitting rooms?" Madge's words interrupted my ponderings.

"Hmm?" I couldn't imagine why fitting rooms deserved a stop on the tour, but why not?

She led the way to a row of closed doors and opened the first one to reveal a spacious changing area unlike any I'd ever seen before.

"W-wow." I'd been in a few fitting rooms in my life, of course. Department stores at the mall in Dallas, for instance. And Fanny's Fine Fashions in Fairfield. The one and only fitting room at Fanny's was spacious—well, spacious enough for Fanny, who'd been aptly named, to fit inside. The curtain in front of it offered a wee bit of privacy. Stress *wee bit*.

This room, however, outdid anything I'd ever seen. I stared in awe and muttered "Wow!" once again. It was octagon shaped, mirrors covering every side but one. A cushioned round bench sat in the center of the room. All in all, this room was the ideal place to don a wedding gown. And speaking of gowns, a beautiful ruffled one hung on the hook near the door. Brilliant. Shimmering. Luscious. I could almost see myself walking the aisle in something like that.

Only, I wouldn't be walking the aisle anytime soon, and I needed to let these fine people know right away. I had to speak my mind, no matter how difficult. This seemed like as good a place as any. I swallowed hard, ready to dive in.

Lori-Lou must've figured out my plan to spill the beans—probably my wrinkled brow and strained silence. At any rate, she headed off to the ladies' room. Coward.

Alone in the changing room with Madge, I finally worked up the courage to share my story. "Ms. . . . Madge, I need to let you know something. I didn't come today to start the fitting, or even to talk to Nadia about the dress."

Madge fussed with the ruffled gown, straightening the hem. "Oh, but you must talk to her today. She's leaving town soon."

"Well, I came to tell you that . . ." *Suck it up, Katie. Say the words.* "I cannot, under any circumstances . . ." *Deep breath! Forge ahead!* "Go through with this."

The woman's broad smile faded in an instant as she turned her attention away from the dress and to me. "I-I'm sorry. What did you say? You can't go through with the initial consult *today,* you mean? Or not at all?"

"Not at all. But more than that—I can't go

through with any of it. Not just the consult, but the whole thing. No dress. No . . . wedding." I shook my head and glanced in the mirror, noticing the dress on the hook in the background had created an optical illusion. Almost looked like I was wearing it. Weird.

Okay, what was I supposed to be saying again? Oh yes. I faced Madge head-on and tried to calm my shaky voice. "I've just gone through a, well, a . . . a breakup."

"A breakup?" Madge's eyes widened. "With your fiancé?"

"Well, sort of. I mean, I . . . we . . ."

At this point Lori-Lou pressed her way back inside the changing room. "What she's *trying* to say is, the wedding's off."

"The wedding's off?" Madge repeated.

"Actually . . ." I released a painful sigh. "It was never really on."

10

I'm Living in Two Worlds

> I was from a small town, and nobody really expects you to leave, especially before you graduate. That doesn't happen.
>
> Taylor Swift

"Did you say the wedding's off?" Madge's eyes widened as she dropped down onto the cushioned round bench. "The wedding's *off?*"

Good grief. Did she have to keep saying it aloud? Wasn't I hurting enough already? "What I'm trying to say is, it wasn't really on to begin with." I plopped down onto the bench next to her. "I mean, I *thought* Casey and I were getting married. I would never have entered the contest otherwise. But it wasn't official. And now it's . . . impossible."

"Impossible?" Madge echoed. She leaned forward and put her head in her hands. "Impossible. The wedding's impossible."

Do you have to keep repeating everything?

"At least impossible for now," Lori-Lou interjected. "Casey is moving to Oklahoma."

"Well, that's no reason to break up. I hear

Oklahoma is nice." Madge lifted her head. "Maybe you'll still marry him and move there? You think?"

"Oh, no ma'am." I shook my head. "I'll never live anywhere but Fairfield. Can't picture it. And to be honest, I really think it's over with Casey." As soon as I spoke the words, my heart twisted inside of me. In all the years I'd known and loved Casey, I'd never pictured myself saying that. Or thinking it. Yet something about voicing the words felt strangely freeing.

"Are there any other guys in Fairfield you could marry?" A hopeful look sparked in Madge's eyes. "Anyone special come to mind?"

"W-what? No." I shook my head. Was she kidding?

"Guess I'm grasping at straws." Madge groaned. "It's just that Nadia's only got a narrow window to take care of all this before leaving for Paris. This is so important to her. It's a chance for her gown to be featured on the cover of *Texas Bride*. That's such an honor. If I have to tell her that she's not making the dress for you . . ." Madge shook her head. "It will crush her. Your name has already been announced, after all, and the reporter has set the date for the interview and photo shoot. This is a huge deal to her. Really, to all of us."

"Surely some other bride could take my place."

"No." Madge rose and paced the room. She

hesitated at the dress and fingered the lace around the neckline. "The contest is over. You have no idea how complicated it was to put together. We can't possibly start again."

We sighed. All three of us. I happened to catch a glimpse of our trio of expressions in one of the full-length mirrors. Somber. Pitiful.

Then Madge turned away from the gown and snapped her fingers. "Perfect solution. Here's what we're going to do, Katie. You're going to let Nadia make you the wedding dress of your dreams. You'll appear on the cover of *Texas Bride*, the October edition. And I'll work double time to run interference so that no one around here is any the wiser."

"I just can't do it, Madge." I rose and took a couple of steps in her direction. "I can't lie to Nadia. It's not right."

"I'm not asking you to lie, and I won't either. We just won't mention that you're not getting married. Yet." With a wave of her hand she appeared to dismiss the matter. "I'm sure you'll get married someday."

I sighed again.

"Technically, it doesn't matter anyway, don't you see? There was nothing specific in the rules about a wedding date or even an engagement. So let's just let it go, okay? Skip the wedding part. Just take the dress."

"I . . . I . . ."

She gave me one of those stern looks that I often got from my mother. "I'm simply asking you to let Nadia James make you a wedding dress. That's all. I'm not saying you have to wear it this year. Or next. Or ever. Maybe you'll get old like me and give up on the idea of a wedding altogether."

Gee, thanks.

"But if you do find the right fella, you'll have the perfect dress hanging in your closet. Nadia will get her moment in the sun when the dress appears on the cover of *Texas Bride*, and you'll have the dress of your dreams."

"Or when Casey comes to his senses." Lori-Lou reached for her phone, which beeped four or five times in a row. "Still thinking that could happen."

Ugh.

Her phone beeped again, and she groaned.

"What in the world is going on with that phone?" Madge asked. "Some sort of emergency?"

"I'm sorry. It's just that my husband doesn't know how much water to mix into the baby's formula. And I think my oldest daughter locked herself in the bathroom and can't get out." Lori-Lou responded to the text, then shoved the phone in her purse. "Sorry for the interruption, but the man is hopeless. Completely and totally hopeless. But I love him anyway."

I had just opened my mouth to continue the debate with Madge when I heard Brady's voice from outside the dressing room. "You ladies okay in there?"

Madge opened the door a crack and waved her hand. "Yep. Now go away, Brady. We're talking business in here. Besides, I thought you were going to your office."

"Haven't made it that far yet." He leaned against the door frame, his towering presence a little intimidating. "Just wanted to let you know that I talked to Mom. She's ready to see Katie now."

"Perfect." Madge nodded.

"If you ladies are talking business, don't you think it involves me? I am managing the store now, remember?" His words sounded a little strained, as if he'd had this conversation with Madge before.

"Sure, sure, kid." She waved him away. "Whatever you say. Just give me a minute with the ladies and then we'll head back to your mom's office." Madge closed the door in his face. "Poor guy. I know this isn't the life he would've chosen for himself." She took a seat on the bench once more and sighed. "It took Nadia weeks to convince Brady that he should take over the shop while she's in Paris. He agreed to do it, and he's settling in well. But I daresay he would rather be back out on the court. When his leg is ready, I mean. Until then, he's on our team."

Lori-Lou glanced toward the closed door. "I'd say he's a great team player. That's what they do. They stick around and pick up the slack. They don't care about the glory. If there's a need, they meet it, injured or not."

"That's Brady, all right. The boy's a real gem." Madge lowered her voice. "And it's not like he can play right now anyway. He's only three months out from his knee surgery, and the doctor says he might need another one because it's not healing properly."

I felt for him. Taking over his mother's wedding dress shop was probably the last thing he wanted to do. And here we were, excluding him from a conversation that involved the shop.

"He's the one in charge once his mom leaves for Paris." She chuckled. "Well, in theory, anyway." She leaned against the door, her voice growing louder. "If you ask anyone who works here, I run this shop."

"I heard that, Madge." Brady's voice sounded once more from outside the door.

"We have to tell him," I whispered. "That I don't need the dress, I mean."

"No way." Madge shook her head and lowered her voice to a hoarse whisper. "We'll go out there and smile and meet with Nadia. And we will not —under any circumstances—say a word to Brady. Not yet. The boy's nervous enough already. Let's don't rock the boat."

I agreed to keep my mouth shut, at least for now. When we exited the dressing room, I found Brady standing in the hallway. His blue eyes pierced the distance between us. "I was getting worried about you ladies."

"Nothing to worry about." Madge patted him on the back. "Now, you take it from here, Brady. Introduce Katie to your mom. I've got to get back up to the counter." She headed to the front of the store, mumbling under her breath something about how her work was never done.

Brady seemed to have resigned himself to the fact that he was now my tour guide. He looked at me. "So, you saw everything?"

"Yeah. All but your mom's studio, of course."

"She's going to meet us there in a couple minutes." He looked around as if trying to figure out what we should do next. The poor guy really looked lost. I could picture him shooting hoops, but not trimming out wedding dresses or talking brides into petticoats for their gowns.

He led the way to the back of the shop and turned to face me. "Do you know anything about my mom?"

"Do I?" I couldn't help the smile that followed. "Are you kidding? I've been following her designs for years. She's famous, you know."

"So they tell me."

"You goober." Lori-Lou jabbed me with her elbow. "Brady is famous too."

"Oh, I've heard all about you from Casey," I said. "I think he was watching the game when you . . ." I pointed to his knee. "Anyway, he was watching that night. Everyone in town talked about it."

"Which town?"

"Fairfield."

"So I'm famous in Fairfield, eh?" He led us through the workroom at the back of the store to a door that read STUDIO. "Well, that's good to know. But my mom's reach is a little farther than that. She's headed to Paris, which is why I'm here managing the shop."

"Working for Madge." Lori-Lou gave him a funny smile.

I expected Brady to smirk, but he actually grinned. "Madge definitely calls the shots around here, but don't ever tell her I told you that. We couldn't manage without her. I don't mind admitting she's the boss of, well, everything."

"She seems really . . . businesslike."

"All business, but she's really a marshmallow on the inside," Brady said. "Anyway, Mom's doing an internship in Paris for a year. That's why I'm at the shop. I'm—"

"You're filling in for your mom?" Lori-Lou asked. "Must be quite a gig after basketball, right?" She laughed. "From dribbling to walking the aisle. Quite a shift."

"Yeah." His gaze shifted to the carpet and then

back to us. "Look, this isn't my idea of a dream job. In fact, it's not a job at all. It's a family business and one that someone has to run while she's away."

"I'm sorry, Brady." Lori-Lou's voice softened. "I was just kidding with you. I guess I don't really know you well enough to do that. Yet."

"Nah, it's okay." He shrugged. "It's just all new to me." His face lit into a smile. "Everyone's excited about the contest, which makes the transition easier. It's been months in the making, and Mom couldn't wait to meet the winner. Brace yourself, okay? I'm sure she'll ask you a million questions about your wedding plans."

"O-oh?"

"Yes. At some point she'll want to know your theme and color choices. Also your fiancé's tuxedo preferences."

"My fiancé?" The words stuck on the roof of my mouth, kind of like peanut butter. *Madge, I'm going to blow this! I have to tell him.*

"Sure. She wants to provide the tuxedo too," Brady said. "Didn't you know that? I thought Madge would've told you."

"She didn't. We, um, didn't really have a chance to talk about all of that."

"It was all spelled out in the contest entry form," Brady explained. "He'll have to come for a fitting in a few weeks. And the bridesmaids too."

"Bridesmaids?"

"Ooh, yes, yes!" Lori-Lou raised her hand. "I get to be in the wedding party, right? Matron of honor? Isn't that what you said out there?"

I glared at her.

"I've always dreamed of being a matron of honor. This will be quite a privilege, let me tell you." Her nose wrinkled. "But my figure's not what it used to be. You can thank three ornery kids for that."

Brady turned his attention to her. "Do you think you'll be able to find something off the rack? We have more choices than most bridal stores, so I'm hoping the bridesmaids can find something that will work with the overall theme." He turned back to me. "You did say you had a theme, right? Most brides do these days."

"Well, I've always loved shabby chic," I said. "But honestly, I think I should tell you that—"

"That we'll definitely be able to pick something off the rack." Lori-Lou smiled. "You've got oodles of options."

"Oodles of options. That's a new one." He grinned, and for a moment that handsome face of his looked magazine-cover ready. Yummy. If I told him the truth about my wedding—or lack thereof—I'd wipe that gorgeous smile right off his face. Maybe I'd better wait awhile to do that. Besides, what would Madge say? I'd only known the woman a few minutes, but I had a feeling she could take me down in a hurry.

"This is your special day, Katie." Brady gave me a warm smile. "My mother wants to do everything she can to make it the best it can be." He reached to take hold of the handle on the studio door. "It doesn't hurt that the press will be there, you know. Great advertisement for the shop and for her designs."

"Wait, press? At my wedding?"

"Sure. Didn't you read the entry form at all?" His brow wrinkled in concern.

"Katie's just distracted," Lori-Lou said as she glanced down at her phone once again. "You know how hectic things can be during times like this."

Times like this? I glared at her again.

"Well, the point is, my mom wants all of this to be perfect for everyone, and not just because of the press. She loves what she does and wants everyone to be happy."

He opened the door and gestured for us to enter. I took a couple of steps inside Nadia's studio and fell in love with the place all over again. Seeing the dresses done up in the store was nothing in comparison to this. The fabrics, lace, and embellishments still took my breath away.

"Wow." I couldn't seem to manage much else.

"Wow, wow!" Lori-Lou echoed as she stood frozen in place. Except for the incessant beeping from her phone, the whole room was silent.

"Mom's pretty fixated with fashions from

days gone by," Brady explained as he led us to the sewing area.

"I read all about it in *Texas Bride*," Lori-Lou said. "The article said her work has prompted a revival in the industry."

"That's true." Brady nodded, and I could see the look of pride in his eyes as we talked about his mother.

"I just know that brides can't get enough of her gowns," I added.

"They're coming from out of the woodwork." He laughed. "Not just from Texas, but all over the US and beyond."

"Vintage is in." Lori-Lou stopped at the cutting table to run her hand over a swatch of satin. "Wow. Wow."

"You ladies give me a minute to let Mom know you're here. She's anxious to meet you, Katie." Brady smiled and headed off to a room marked OFFICE.

Moments later Nadia James entered the sewing room. I couldn't help but gasp as the lovely woman moved in our direction. She had to be about Mama's age, but talk about polar opposites. Where Mama was short and slightly round, Nadia was tall and thin. Mama's short gray hair was naturally curly. Nadia had obviously taken hours to perfect her platinum locks.

Lori-Lou nudged me with her elbow and mouthed "Wow" once more. I felt like echoing the word myself. Nadia was the sort of woman who looked as if she belonged on the cover of a magazine. Gorgeous. Other than on television, I'd never seen anyone so well put together. And well preserved to boot. Her perfectly bobbed platinum hair held my attention, but the perfection didn't end there. High cheekbones. Excellent skin. And the makeup! Man, talk about flawless.

We didn't get a lot of women like this in Fairfield. Well, unless you counted Frenchie at Do or Dye. She'd gone away to beauty school a duckling and come back a swan. Rumor had it she'd gone under the knife, but the supposed plastic surgery had only changed her appearance—in particular, her nose. Her sparkling personality remained the same.

Speaking of sparkling, the older woman now standing in front of me sparkled with glitz and glam. No wonder folks gravitated to Nadia for her vintage gowns. She shimmered to the core. Well, maybe it had a little something to do with the crystals on her blouse. And that necklace! Were those real diamonds? Surely not.

Brady gestured to her with a broad smile on his face. "Ladies, let me introduce you to my mother, Nadia James. Mama, this is Katie Fisher, our contest winner."

I gave her a closer look and saw the family resemblance. Both were tall. Both had sparkling blue eyes. Both had that "just been in the sun" bronzed look about them. Most of all, they both seemed confident and kind. Approachable. All it took was one look at the sincerity in this amazing woman's eyes for me to know I had to come clean about my non-wedding, no matter what Madge had insisted.

"I . . . I . . ." I swallowed hard, knowing I was about to wipe that sparkle right out of her eyes with my terrible news.

Courage, Katie. Courage.

11

For Heaven's Sake

> You aren't wealthy until you have something money can't buy.
>
> Garth Brooks

Nadia extended her hand with a warm smile. "Katie, I'm so glad to meet you," she said. "I've looked forward to this day for ages."

I took hold of her hand—wow, soft—and shook it. "Nice to meet you." The intoxicating aroma of expensive perfume wafted in the air between us. I didn't know much about such things, but I could tell money when I smelled it.

"For some reason, I thought you were coming Monday, not today." Nadia tucked her hair behind her right ear.

"Her plans have been a little . . . loose." Lori-Lou typed something into her phone, then glanced up at our hostess with a whimsical smile.

Nadia glanced at my cousin, her thinly plucked brows elevating slightly. "And who have we here?"

"Oh, this is Lori-Lou," I said.

"Katie's matron of honor," Brady explained.

"Yes, matron of honor. Because I'm married

with children." Lori-Lou giggled. "Otherwise I'd be a maid of honor. I mean, you know . . ." Her words drifted off as I glared at her once again.

"Wonderful to meet you!" Nadia fussed with her hair. "Well, as I said, I wish I'd known you were coming this morning, ladies. I would've called the news stations. They could've sent a camera crew to greet you. Hope you don't mind that it's just me."

My heart quickened. "Oh, I'm relieved, actually. Can't imagine being greeted by the press. You see, I don't want my parents to know about this."

"Don't want your parents to know?" Nadia's face contorted, then she snapped her fingers. "Oh, I get it! You want to surprise your parents with the gown? This is even better! We'll let them know at the last minute, when your photo appears on the cover of *Texas Bride* magazine. How's that? I'll be flying back in from Paris for a charity event that week prior, so it's the perfect time for the big reveal. I don't mind holding off with the media. Makes perfect sense, actually. We'll stir up excite-ment in the week leading up to the reveal. Create a sense of anticipation."

Anticipation. Now there was a word I knew well.

"My parents live in Fairfield," I explained. "They rarely pay attention to Dallas news, especially wedding stuff. It's the furthest thing from their minds."

"Don't folks get married in Fairfield?" Nadia asked. "Weddings aren't a big deal?"

"Well, sure, they're a big deal. But in Fairfield we all get married in our local church or at the civic center. There's a gazebo at the park that we sometimes use for photos. Most of the girls I know got married in gowns that they bought at Fanny's or online."

"Fanny's?" Nadia looked confused.

"Online?" Brady echoed.

"You're in the big city now, Katie." Lori-Lou laughed and shoved her phone in her purse once again.

Nadia took me by the arm and patted it as she led me to her work area. "Yes, here in Dallas we do it a bit differently, especially at Cosmopolitan. Weddings are all about the gown. And the veil. But mostly about the gown." Nadia released a girlish giggle. "We are dedicated—and I do mean completely dedicated—to giving the bride the experience of a lifetime. A girl only gets married once, you know." A sad look came over her. "Well, in theory, anyway."

"Oh, I know Cosmopolitan is the best."

"It's wonderful to make brides feel . . . wonderful." Nadia glanced at her watch. "I wish I had time to visit with you awhile, Katie—to hear your story—but I have an appointment with another bride in less than an hour. Would you mind if we went ahead and took your measurements right away, instead of waiting until Monday? That way I can spend the weekend thinking through a plan. It'll give me a head start, which is always nice."

I shook my head. "No. I mean, no, please don't." I felt my face grow warm as I looked at Brady.

"Oh, right, right." She glanced at her son. "Do you mind, honey? We need some privacy. And would you mind fetching Madge for me? And Dahlia too. I'll need her help with my sketches."

Brady shot out of the room quicker than a player making a three-point shot in the fourth quarter of the game. I turned to face my benefactor, determined to tell her the truth before Madge arrived. "Nadia, I'm so grateful for this. You have no idea."

"Oh, sweetie, I do." Her eyes filled with tears. "I was a young bride once too." In that moment, the strong features in her face softened. "I married young and had nothing. Absolutely nothing. It would've meant the world to me to win a dress like this, so I understand."

"Well, thank you, but what I meant to say was—"

"Ooh, your ring!" She reached for my left hand and lifted it. "It's gorgeous! Antique?"

"Yes. It was my grandmother's."

"I love it. Keeping things in the family is so nice. I'm sure your fiancé was thrilled for the opportunity to slip it on your finger."

"Well, actually, he—"

"Nadia!" Madge's voice sounded from the open doorway. "You need me?"

"I do." Nadia released her grip on my hand. "And Dahlia too."

"She's with a customer right now." Madge walked our way. "Princess Bride."

"Ah." Nadia nodded as she looped the measuring tape around my hips. "Got it."

"Princess Bride?" I glanced up as Nadia reached around me to measure my bust. *Awkward!* "An actual princess?"

"No." Madge rolled her eyes. "In this case she happens to be the daughter of some oil sheik in the Middle East. Spoiled rich kid. Princess attitude, but none of the grace. We get a lot of 'em in the store, trust me."

"Ooh, this I've gotta see." Without any other warning, Lori-Lou shot out of the workroom door and back into the shop. I felt sure she'd return with some whopper stories.

"These Princess Brides are accustomed to getting what they want when they want it, with never a thought for cost. Daddy has deep pockets." Madge smirked and reached for a notepad.

Nadia glanced over at her and flashed a warning look.

Madge clamped her mouth shut. "Anyway, how can I help?"

"I'm taking measurements. You write everything down." Nadia glanced up at me with a smile. "Hips are thirty-four inches."

I did my best not to groan aloud.

"Now, while I measure, let's talk styles," Nadia said. "What sort of design are you looking at? French bustle? Trumpet skirt?"

"Hmm?"

"I was thinking with your figure, maybe a modified sweetheart neckline? What do you think?"

"Sweetheart?"

"Something light. With an airy feel. Maybe a dropped waist? Ruffles?"

"I . . . it sounds wonderful."

Nadia appeared to be thinking. "Maybe I should have asked what famous person we're patterning this gown after. You have someone special that you like from days gone by?"

"Oh, lots of famous movie stars." In that moment, however, I couldn't think of a single one. Nadia began a lengthy discussion about the various movie stars she'd patterned dresses after in the past. Her favorite, it turned out, was Grace Kelly.

Several minutes into the conversation, Dahlia entered with Lori-Lou on her heels.

"Wow, Katie! You should've seen that bride out there. She was . . . wow." Lori-Lou gave Dahlia an admiring look. "Great job reining her in, girl. Impressive."

"Thank you." Dahlia giggled. "I left her in Twiggy's capable hands. She's great with the Princess Brides."

"So you get that a lot?" Lori-Lou sat in a chair across from me and watched as Nadia measured the circumference of my neck.

"Girl, we see all sorts." Madge looked up from her tablet to join in the conversation. "You wouldn't believe what we go through with the various brides that come in."

"What do you mean?" Lori-Lou looked confused.

"Well, there's the organized bride who knows what she wants, down to the style of dress and type of fabric," Nadia said. She looked at Madge. "Neck size is 13.5 inches."

"Got it." Madge wrote down the number.

"There's the spoiled rich girl bride who just wants a designer gown because it's going to make her friends jealous," Dahlia added. "You just saw one of those for yourself."

"There's the 'I'm so clueless I don't know what I want' bride," Madge said. "And then . . ." She shuddered. "Then there are the really tough cases."

"Tough cases?" I couldn't help myself. I had to ask.

Nadia stopped measuring me long enough to explain. "Sure. Brides whose parents just went through a divorce. Brides who've just lost a family member. Brides who want to be happy about their upcoming wedding, but just can't seem to focus because of what they're going through on the perimeter. Those poor girls can't help that they're going through trauma, so I do my best to wrap my arms around them and talk them through."

"We have other tough cases too." Madge chuckled. "You gonna tell her about the double Gs, Nadia?"

"Double Gs?" I asked.

Nadia's cheeks turned a lovely crimson shade. "The double Gs are the large-chested brides. Hard to fit, but just as deserving as every other bride-to-be. We get them in every shape and size around here, trust me. Short, tall, curvy, rail-thin . . . and we somehow manage to fit every one. But you . . ." She gave me a reassuring smile. "You are the ideal shape. Perfect for a magazine cover in every conceivable way." She pulled the tape taut and then turned to Madge. "Bust size thirty-five inches."

I suddenly felt more than a little intimidated. "I'm sorry. I hope you'll forgive me, but I feel so out of place right now."

Nadia put the measuring tape down. "Why, honey? Have I done something to make you feel uncomfortable? I sure hope not. Maybe we've rushed into this? Perhaps I should've waited until Monday after all. I just thought that it would be nice to get this part over with, but I didn't mean to make you feel uncomfortable or rushed."

"I'm just not used to . . ." I gestured around the room filled with hundreds of thousands of dollars' worth of materials. "This."

Nadia followed my gaze. "Being fitted for a couture gown, you mean?" she asked.

"Well, that, and all of this. I'm just a small-town girl. This is very . . . new to me."

"You'll get used to being pampered." Nadia gave me a motherly smile. "We want to make you feel like a real princess."

"Accept it, Katie." Lori-Lou glared at me. "It's a gift."

"Sounds nice, but . . ." I said the only thing that came to mind. "Mrs. James, do you happen to know anything about Loretta Lynn?"

"The country-western singer? Sure."

"Well, if you recall, she left her little hometown of Butcher Holler for the first time with her new husband, Doo. They drove all over creation trying to get radio stations to play her song and eventually ended up in Nashville. Remember?"

"It's been a long time since I saw the movie about her life, but I think I vaguely remember what you're talking about. They took a road trip?"

"Yes. They left Butcher Holler and set out for new places," I explained.

"An adventure," Lori-Lou added. She reached for her phone as it beeped again.

"Wait. Butcher Holler?" Dahlia looked back and forth between us. "Is that a place?"

"Of course it's a place." Madge clucked her tongue. "You don't know Loretta Lynn's real-life story?"

Dahlia shook her head.

"Quite the tale," Madge said.

"Well, anyway, I feel kind of like Loretta Lynn right about now," I said. "A fish out of water. That was my point."

"Dallas is your Nashville, in other words. Got it." Madge slipped an arm over my shoulders. "You'll be okay, kid. And we promise not to make you sing, if that makes you feel any better."

As she released her hold on me, I shrugged. "Dallas is still close enough to home to feel familiar, but big enough to intimidate me. And this shop . . ." I gestured to the room. "All of this pretty stuff—it's way outside my norm. We don't get a lot of niceties like this where I come from. It's out of my element."

"But Loretta Lynn eventually felt at home in Nashville, especially on the stage at the Grand Ole Opry." Madge gave me a knowing look. "It could happen to you too. Like Nadia said, we'll turn you into a real princess."

"Yes." Nadia clasped her hands together at her chest. "You'll be a couture bride in no time."

I put my hand up in protest. "No thank you. Don't want to fit in. Just call me a misfit and send me back home where I belong. When the dress is finished, I mean."

"Oh, but like I said, you've got the perfect physique for one of my gowns," Nadia said. "And look at that gorgeous face of yours. I love everything about it, right down to the freckles and blonde hair. Between you and the dress, this is going to be the prettiest cover *Texas Bride* has ever seen. I can't wait."

I sighed, unsure of what to say next.

"Now, you've given me such a lovely idea." A thoughtful look settled on Nadia's face. "When you mentioned Loretta Lynn, actually. It occurred to me I've never patterned a dress after her."

"Ooh, perfect choice," Madge said. "Frilly but simple. Small-town girl goes to the big city."

"I can see it now." Nadia dropped her measuring tape and reached for a sketchpad. "What do you think, Katie? Would you like the idea of having a Loretta Lynn–inspired gown?"

"Well, Queenie would sure love it. She's always quoting Loretta Lynn."

"Queenie?" Nadia, Madge, and Dahlia spoke the word in unison.

"My grandmother. The matriarch of our family. She's nuts about Loretta. She'd be tickled pink." *Of course, she has no idea I'm here and no idea I'm getting a gown at all, but she would be thrilled. After killing me.* Okay, Queenie wouldn't really kill me—I hoped—but this whole thing would certainly be enough to send her into a tizzy.

"Glad you like the idea," Nadia said. "I guess we'll dive right in. Let me tell you how I work. First, the bride chooses her inspiration—in this case, Loretta Lynn. Then I craft a look specifically for her, with all of her inspiration's elements. We're going for something that says Katie and Loretta, all at the same time. Make sense?"

"Well, sure, but . . ." Did I actually *say* I wanted a Loretta Lynn gown?

"A bride has to trust her designer." On and on Nadia went, talking about her plan for my life. My soon-to-be-married life, anyway. Not that I was soon to be married. Should I mention that? Just about the time I'd worked up the courage, she slipped the measuring tape around my waist and pulled it snug.

"Oh, I'm sure anything you do will be brilliant," I managed as I sucked in a breath to make myself as small as possible.

"Twenty-six-inch waist," she said.

"I remember when I had a twenty-six-inch waist." Lori-Lou sighed. "I think I was twelve at the time."

That got a laugh out of Dahlia.

"We'll start with sketching some designs," Nadia said as she slipped the measuring tape around my upper arm. "I hope you can come back Monday to look over the final sketches before I have to get on the plane to Paris. I'll leave Dahlia here to work on the sewing. That okay with you?"

"Oh, whatever you think," I said. "I'm easy."

"Come around eleven on Monday, if you can. At that time I'll give you my suggestions for fabrics, trims, and so on. The fabric, I always say, is as much the inspiration for the gown as anything else. People underestimate the role that a good satin or crepe plays."

I was underestimating it even now. Then again, with a measuring tape looped around my arm, who had time to think of satin or crepe?

"We'll have to sign a contract for the gown at that point."

"A contract?" I felt panic well up inside of me.

"Oh, no money will change hands, so don't fret over that. Just a standard contract to say that you'll give Cosmopolitan Bridal credit for the gown when you wear it." The measuring tape slipped out of her hand. "When did you say your wedding was again, Katie? I can't remember the date."

"Oh, I . . ."

Madge threw a warning look my way. "Katie hasn't settled on a date yet, Nadia, which gives us plenty of time. Isn't that wonderful?"

"It helps." Nadia looked relieved at this news. She picked up the measuring tape from the floor. "But we do have the impending deadline of the photo shoot on July 15, so we'll have to move quickly. Just five weeks to design this dress and get it made. I don't usually work this fast, but I feel sure I can do it with Dahlia's help." She gave her assistant an admiring smile.

"Happy to be of service. This one's going to be fun." Dahlia's rich Swedish accent laced her words.

"Can we do it?" Nadia asked.

"Even if I have to stay and work nights." Dahlia gave her a confident look. "You can count on me."

"Thank you, sweet girl. I know I can. And I know this one means as much to you as it does to me."

"Oh, it does." Dahlia's eyes misted over. "I'm so excited I can barely think straight."

Yippy skippy. One more person who would hate me if I backed out.

"The article is set to go live in *Texas Bride* the first week of October." Nadia slipped the tape around my arm once more, then adjusted it. "I'll trust that the finished product will be exactly what you had in mind, Katie." She turned to Madge and said, "Upper arm is nine and three-quarter inches."

Lovely.

"I remember when my arm was nine and three-quarter inches." Madge made a funny face as she wrote down the number. "I was in kindergarten."

That got a laugh out of everyone in the room, especially Lori-Lou, who snorted.

“I think we’re going to be good friends, you and me.” Madge nodded at my cousin.

The ladies carried on and on, talking about the idea of using Loretta Lynn as an inspiration for my so-called wedding gown. I could tell that Nadia was growing more excited by the moment. How could I possibly burst her bubble? Clearly my news would crush the woman. And Dahlia too.

No, I’d better keep my lips sealed for now and pray about how to open them later, at a more opportune time. Maybe I could send Nadia an email once she went to Paris. Perhaps that would be for the best. Until then, I’d sit here and listen to them ramble about fabrics, ruffles, and lace.

After wrapping up the measurements, Nadia took a seat and started making some initial sketches. “This is just for fun, you understand. The finished work will come later. Initially, we just consult, gab, dream dreams, come up with ideas.”

Only, I wasn’t really coming up with any ideas. Not that she happened to notice. Nadia kept sketching and gabbing.

“It takes at least five or six fittings before we’re done. While I’m in Paris, Dahlia will be your go-to girl. And you can always talk to Brady. He’s . . .” The edges of Nadia’s lips turned up in a smile. “He’s been a great asset to the store.”

This time Madge snorted.

“Anyway, he’ll be here to help you with . . .”

Nadia's nose wrinkled. "Actually, he's not much help with the design part."

"Or the sewing part," Dahlia added.

"Or the management part," Madge threw in.

"But he's great with public relations." Nadia put her index finger up in the air. "And he'll be in charge of coordinating things with the people from *Texas Bride*, so he's your go-to guy, Katie."

"Got it. Brady's my go-to guy." I could almost picture the tall basketball player as my go-to guy now. I'd go straight to him and share the news that my wedding was nothing but a farce. Then he could go to his mother and share the news with her. Perfect.

"At any point, we'll get this done." Nadia continued to sketch out her ideas. The simplistic design drew me in at once. Apparently Lori-Lou loved it too. The two of us stood over Nadia's shoulder, watching the magic take place.

"Wow, that's great, Nadia," I found myself saying. "I love the sweetheart neckline. And the ruffles are just right."

"Very Loretta Lynn, but not over the top," Lori-Lou chimed in.

"Thanks." Nadia looked up from her sketchpad, her eyes brimming with tears. "Have I mentioned how excited I am about this one, Katie?" She reached out to grab my hand. "This is really a dream come true, for all of us. Your happily ever after is playing a role in *my* happily ever after. I'm going to have a dress on the cover of *Texas Bride*, and you're going to get the gown of your dreams. It's all so . . . perfect." Her voice quivered.

Yes, indeed. It was all so perfect. Unless you counted the part where the whole thing was based on a half-truth.

"It's an answer to prayer," Nadia whispered. "Truly."

Lori-Lou nudged me with her elbow and I glared at her, then settled my gaze on the sketch once again. Wow, this woman really knew her stuff. Watching the design come together made me think, if only for a moment, that maybe, just maybe, I would really get to wear this dress. Someday. Yes, perhaps after all I'd get to have my happily ever after. Until then, however, I'd have to wait for the perfect opportunity for my go-to guy to get to work fixing all of this for me.

12

Somebody's Back in Town

A city is a state of mind, of taste, of opportunity. A city is a marketplace where ideas are traded, opinions clash, and eternal conflict may produce eternal truths.

Herb Caen

I somehow managed to make it through the rest of the weekend. Sunday morning was spent at Lori-Lou and Josh's church, a place unlike any I'd ever visited. They called the large metal building with its massive parking lot and drum-infused music a megachurch. No doubt Mama would've called it a rock and roll concert and would've scheduled an appointment with the pastor forthwith to change the structure of the service to include more hymns and fewer flashing lights.

Still, I found myself clapping along and connecting with the lyrics of the songs, particularly the third one, which had a resounding faith theme. Even the sermon seemed to fit my situation. The pastor took his text from Proverbs, specifically focusing on lying. Ironic, since I'd agreed not to come clean with Brady or his mother about my wedding . . . or lack thereof.

I hardly slept on Sunday night, what with the baby fussing for hours due to teething issues. Monday morning came far too soon. Josh took off for work, and Lori-Lou spent the morning on the phone with several of her friends, trying to find a sitter, but to no avail. With no other choice but to take the kids with us, we headed back to Cosmopolitan to meet with Nadia one last time before she left for Paris. I still felt a little guilty about agreeing to Madge's plan. I'd rather just come clean before Nadia left the country, but what could I do? Madge intimidated me—perhaps as much as Queenie.

Queenie.

I sighed as I thought about my grandmother. I wondered if she was still mad at the Presbyterians. Boy howdy, she would've had a field day with the megachurch folks.

Lori-Lou didn't seem to notice my concerns as she drove us to the bridal shop. She gabbed on and on about a rental house Josh had found online while the kids hollered at each other in the backseat.

"It's going to be perfect for us, Katie," she said above the noise from the children. "With an extra bedroom we can use as a playroom." She pursed her lips. "I remember the days when we would've killed for an extra room to use as an office. Now every square inch of the house is covered in toys. Getting married and having kids changes everything."

Gee, thanks. Another crushing reminder of my current state of singleness.

As we pulled into the parking lot of Cosmopolitan Bridal, the most horrifying odor emanated from the backseat. Mariela let out several squeals in a row. "Ew, Mama! The baby's stinky!"

"Baby's stinky!" Gilly repeated.

"My nose isn't broken, thank you very much. I plan to change him in a minute, right after I call your daddy about the house." Lori-Lou rolled her eyes.

Me? I rolled down the window.

My cousin shook her head as she glanced my way. "You have a lot to get used to, Katie."

"Don't think I'll ever get used to that."

The minute she put the car in park, I bolted. She hollered, "Chicken!" out of the open window. I didn't hear the rest of what she said, though, because I barreled through the front door of the bridal salon lickety-split.

Brady greeted me with a huge smile as I entered the store. In fact, I very nearly ran him down. Not that a five-foot-two girl could run down a six-foot-something basketball player, but I did manage to startle him a little. As I landed against him, I felt his muscles ripple underneath his white shirt. I did my best to still my quickening pulse but found it difficult.

"Well, hello there," he said as I took a step backwards.

Hello there, Mr. Go-to Guy.

"Mom said you were coming back today. Good to see you." He reached to steady me as I lost my balance and nearly toppled into him again. From the twinkle in his eye, I got the feeling he really was happy to see me. But he wouldn't be if I told him my news, would he? He'd be booting me out the door.

"Hi. Good morning. Is your mom ready for me?"

"Almost. She told me to offer you a cup of coffee when you got here to stall a few minutes. I think she's made some progress on the design since Saturday, but probably won't have the final details until she's had more time to pick your brain. She wants you to be happy."

"Oh, I'm sure I will be." *If I can just get past feeling so guilty.* "I'd love a cup of coffee." I stifled a yawn. "Long night. The baby kept me up. Teething."

"Baby?"

"Oh!" I clamped a hand over my mouth. "Not *my* baby. My cousin's."

Brady nodded. "Ah. The gal with the cell phone?"

"That's the one."

"She's not with you today?" He glanced toward the door as if expecting her to materialize.

"She is, actually." I gestured to the parking lot. "She just needed to . . . well . . . get some last-minute work done while she was still in the car."

"All work and no play, eh? Sounds a lot like my mom. And me too, for that matter." As if to prove the point, he readjusted the mannequin with the $6,700 dress on it.

I stifled another yawn.

Brady laughed. "C'mon, sleepyhead. I'll lead you to the coffee machine. That way you'll be fully awake when you approve your wedding dress design. Otherwise you might okay something you don't really care for."

As Brady took his first few steps, I couldn't help but notice that he still favored his left knee. I followed behind him as he led the way to the workroom at the back of the store. All the while I wrestled with guilt, the pastor's sermon on lying replaying in my head. A guy this sweet didn't need a fake bride stringing him along. Wouldn't it be better to go ahead and tell him now? Why oh why had I agreed to go along with Madge's plan?

After filling a cup for me, he offered me cream and sugar. I took both. "That's what I like," he said. "A girl who's not afraid to dump a few calories into her coffee."

"Hey, what's coffee without the good stuff?" I gave it a good stir and took a little sip. "Ooh, hot." I stirred it again. "I work long hours, so I need my caffeine."

"I'm a workaholic myself, so I get it," he said.

"Looks like we have a lot of things in common then." I took another little sip of my coffee. Mmm. Sweet.

"Oh? We have a lot in common?" He quirked a brow as he reached for another cup to fill. "You play basketball too?"

"Ha. Very funny." I looked up at him. Way up. Of course, I had to get past the strong athletic physique first. Not that I minded the side trip before settling my gaze on those gorgeous blue eyes. "I work for my parents too. We own a family-run business. So there's one thing we have in common. Besides liking sugar and cream in our coffee, I mean."

"What kind of family business?" He filled his cup and then dumped in three packets of sugar and a ton of creamer.

"Hardware store."

"Oh, that's right. I remember reading it in your essay. I feel like I learned a lot about you. Great writing, by the way. You should think about adding 'professional writer' to your résumé." He stirred his coffee and then tried to take a drink. He pulled the cup away from his lips at once. "Gets me every time."

I laughed. "You okay?"

"Yeah. I've had worse injuries, trust me." He glanced down at his left knee and winced.

Poor guy. I decided to change the subject.

"Anyway, working for the family is . . . different. There's no way out, though. If I ever left the hardware store, I don't know how my dad would survive without me. He depends on me for so much."

"Totally get that." A wistful look came over Brady. Just as quickly, his sadness seemed to lift. "So, what does one do in a hardware store? Besides waiting on customers, I mean."

I thought through my answer. How could I make the hardware store sound glamorous? "I, um . . . sometimes I do the window dressings. And I rearranged the lawn and garden section last week. I like putting things in order. Well, in the order that makes sense to my mind."

"I like to put things in order too. I guess you could say I'm calculated in my approach. Did you happen to notice the shoe display at the front of the store?"

"Of course. I saw at least five or six pairs that I'd love to own."

"You just proved my point. See, they weren't selling. It occurred to me that brides don't come into a bridal salon looking for shoes. They're an afterthought. Brides come in looking for a gown, but if we're savvy, we put the other things they'll need in strategic places so they'll have to trip over them on the way out. That's how I decided to put the shoes where you saw them."

"Right." I'd hardly given any thought to

wedding shoes until seeing the display. Not that I needed wedding shoes. "Wise move on your part."

He shrugged. "Just trying to think like a bride." A grin followed. "Not that I'm good at that part, but you get the idea. I'm giving it the old college try."

Madge walked into the workroom at that very moment. She grinned as she listened in. "Brady's going to make a lovely bride someday. And he'll know just where to find the perfect heels to make his ensemble complete." She patted him on the back and then looked at me. "Good to see you again, Katie. Nadia will be with you shortly."

"Oh, I know. Brady told me."

"Brady. Right. Keep forgetting he's the manager now." Madge elbowed him and smirked. "He'll always be Nadia's little boy to me. All six feet four of him."

Well, that answered the question about his height, anyway.

Madge took a couple of swigs from a cup of coffee, then tossed the rest in the trash and left the room.

"Working for family is a dream come true." Brady rolled his eyes. "Anyway, that's my take on it. What about you? What do you love about the hardware store?"

"I love the customers. Love 'em."

"What else?" He took another sip of his coffee.

I thought about it for a moment before

answering. “Honestly? I love the designing aspects. Laying out the specials. Decorating for holidays. Making sure people are . . . I don’t know . . . entertained?”

“Entertained by a store?”

“Well, I like to make sure the window displays are entertaining. Eye-catching. And I guess you’re right about the writing. I write most of the copy for the store. Put together ads for the local paper. That sort of thing.” I glanced down at my watch.

“Getting anxious?” Brady asked. “I could see if Mom is ready for you now.”

“No, I’m actually just wondering about Lori-Lou. She’s been in the car a long time.”

“On the phone.” We spoke in unison and then laughed.

“It’s part of her anatomy,” I added.

“Let’s go back to the front of the store then,” Brady said. “Maybe she’s already come inside and is looking for us. But we’ll have to finish the coffee first. No food or drinks in the store. Too dangerous.”

“Oh, I’m sure.” I did my best to take a few more sips of the coffee, but it was still too hot for comfort. I ended up tossing what was left in the trash can by the door. Brady did the same. What a waste of good cups of coffee. Still, I understood his point about not having food or drinks around the dresses. I could only imagine the possibilities for disaster.

He led the way out of the workroom, glancing back at me as we made our way into the shop. "Hey, speaking of phone calls, I had one this morning from the *Texas Bride* reporter, Jordan Singer. He was just double-checking the date for the interview."

"July 15, right?"

Brady looked concerned. "Well, that's the photo shoot part. We need five weeks to pull the gown together. But the interview will come first. Didn't Mom mention that he's going to be here next Monday—June 15—to interview you?"

"Next Monday?" *Oy vey.* "No. Pretty sure I would've remembered that. I thought he would interview me at the photo shoot. And that brings up something very important I need to talk to you about. Do you mind if we speak privately, Brady?"

To my left, Madge cleared her throat. We looked at her, and she put her hand on her neck and mumbled something about having a cold. Then she flashed me a "don't you dare" look.

At that very moment, the front door of the shop flew open and Lori-Lou stumbled inside, baby in her arms and two squabbling kids at her side. The wind must've done a number on her hair. She looked a fright. Not that anyone could make out her face underneath the mass of windblown locks, in any case.

As soon as Crystal, Twiggy, and Dahlia saw her enter, they all gasped.

"Oh no!" Crystal put her hands over her eyes. "Anything but that!"

"What?" I asked.

"Incoming Mama Mia!" Twiggy whispered.

"Cleanup on aisle four!" Madge threw in. She reached into her pocket and came out with a walkie-talkie, which she raised to her lips.

"Mama Mia? What's that?" I tried to follow her gaze but only saw my cousin and the kids. "Code word for the mother of the bride?"

"No." Dahlia shook her head. "A testy mother of the bride is called a Mama Bear. Sometimes known as a Drama Mama if she's making the bride overemotional during the fitting."

"But . . . Mama Mia?" I asked.

"A bride with small children. In this case, three. And she's bringing them with her."

"Oh, that's no bride-to-be." I laughed. "That's my cousin Lori-Lou. You met her on Saturday, remember? She tried all morning to get a sitter but couldn't."

"That's Lori-Lou?" Dahlia seemed stumped by this. Well, until my cousin brushed the unruly hair out of her face and stopped hollering at Mariela.

"She might not be an incoming bride, but she's still a Mama Mia," Twiggy whispered. "You can't deny that she's a mama."

Crystal nodded. "Every time we get one of those, we feel like pulling our hair out by the time they're gone."

"Code pink and blue," Madge said into the walkie-talkie. "Code pink and blue."

Brady flew into gear, moving the mannequin wearing the $6,700 gown and other merchandise up out of reach. Madge went to the jewelry case and closed the glass panel on the front, then got on her walkie-talkie again and radioed the news to a teenage boy in the back of the store, who headed our way and started pulling the shoe rack up out of reach.

Lori-Lou didn't seem to notice any of this. She'd decided to pacify her children with some M&Ms. Perfect. Just the solution in an ocean of white satin and crepe.

Twiggy sighed as she looked my way. "We get at least two of these a day. I adore kids—in theory, anyway—but they wreak havoc on the place."

"You wouldn't believe the thousands of dollars small children have cost us over the years." Madge shuddered. She shoved the walkie-talkie into her pocket.

I'd have to remember to tell Lori-Lou later. Right now she was busy giving Gilly a juice box. Grape. Lovely. I could see it now—all over the ivory silk gown directly to the child's right.

"What is it about mamas?" Madge asked. "So many are preoccupied."

"They don't pay attention to their little *dah*-lings." Crystal's Southern accent thickened. "So those precious children just run a-*mock*."

“That’s amuck, Crystal,” Dahlia said.

“Amock. Amuck. It’s all the same thing. They *tay*-uh the place up and Mama Mia is ob-*liv*-ious. Then when she’s gone, we all have to work double time to put the place back ta-*gay*-thuh.”

“Remember the kid with the chocolate bar?” Twiggy visibly shivered. “I’ll never forget that.”

“Four hundred dollars just to get the stains out of that taffeta dress.” Dahlia’s eyes moistened. “I worked for weeks on that dress, only to see it covered in chocolate like a kid’s T-shirt after a day at the circus. Horrible, horrible.” A lone tear trickled down her left cheek.

“If Nadia sees the kids with the M&Ms, we’ll have to call in a therapist,” Twiggy said. “Someone needs to talk to Lori-Lou before any damage is done.”

I raised my hand. “I’ll do it. She’s my cousin, after all.” I’d just gathered the courage to say something to Lori-Lou when the door of the shop swung open and an older fellow, mostly bald, stepped inside. Tall and thin, he seemed especially out of place in a bridal gown shop. And judging from the expression in his eyes after he pulled off his sunglasses, he felt a little out of place too.

“Ugh.” Madge slapped herself on the forehead. “Just when I thought it couldn’t possibly get any worse, the devil himself has to show up.”

“The devil?”

“Well, a distant cousin, anyway.” Madge turned

to the others, eyes wide as she said, "Alley-oop!"

Brady, who'd been hyper-focused on Lori-Lou and the messy kids, startled to attention. "Shoot." He raked his fingers through his hair and groaned. "Here we go again."

I watched as the older man took a few steps in our direction, his focus on Brady. Unfortunately, he didn't happen to see that Gilly had taken up residence on the floor directly in front of him. The poor guy tripped right over her. This led to bloodcurdling screams from the toddler and a look of hatred from my cousin, who'd only seen enough of what had happened to think the man had deliberately hurt her child.

Gilly continued to wail, the older fellow groaned and grabbed his foot, and Lori-Lou carried on like a Mama Bear. Or would that be Drama Mama?

Then Mariela burst into tears. The baby started crying too, probably scared by all the noise.

I started to rush toward them, but Madge took hold of my arm. "Let it be, girl."

"But—"

"Let it be. That old guy's got it coming to him. A little time on the floor will do him good."

"Really? What did he do?"

"He won't leave our Brady alone, that's what. Tries to wear him down. Get him back in the game before it's time. He's a barracuda."

"Leave him alone? Huh?"

I watched as Brady helped the older man to his feet, then went over and comforted the children.

"I really wish that old fart would give our boy some space. Brady doesn't need to be rushing back onto the court, no matter how popular he is with the fans. He needs time to recover, physically and emotionally. The doctors agree, which is why they've placed him on medical leave."

"Is that . . ."

"Stan is Brady's agent. And he's all business, trust me. Never gives Brady a minute just to . . . be."

Stan now stood aright, but I could tell from the way he favored his foot that he'd been injured. Madge and Dahlia headed over to Lori-Lou and offered to take the kids in the workroom to have their snacks. With the wailing behind us, I was finally able to focus on Stan and Brady as an agent-player duo. The older man reminded me of a fellow back in Fairfield—Mr. Harkins, who worked at the bank. I couldn't help but stare at Stan's shiny bald head and his somewhat crooked nose. What really got me, though, was his voice. He might look scrawny, but he came across as authoritative and strong.

"See there, boy?" The fellow slung his arm over Brady's shoulder. "You're in fine shape. You came to my rescue, just like you've done a thousand times for the team."

"You were on the floor, Stan." Brady chuckled. "Taken down by a three-year-old."

"Two-year-old," I added as I took a few steps in their direction.

"Taken down by a two-year-old."

"Still, you're missing my point." Stan pulled a hankie out of his pocket and swiped it over his sweaty head. "Point is your knee must be healed or you couldn't have moved so fast. I'd say you're nearly ready to get back in the game."

"I'm in the game, Stan." He gestured to the shop.

The older fellow swiped his head again, then shoved the handkerchief in his pocket. "I refuse to believe you've traded in your Mavericks jersey for a wedding gown. Please tell me it ain't so."

"Well, when you put it like that, no. Of course not. But I'm where I'm supposed to be for now. I've tried to tell you that before." Brady gave him a pensive look and I suddenly felt like an intruder. I stepped aside and pretended to look at one of the wedding gowns.

"It takes time to heal." Brady spoke in a hoarse whisper.

"Well, sure, but remember, my boy, men who take their time come in second. You've never come in second. Besides, the fans are clamoring for you. You wouldn't believe the calls I'm getting. And the owner of the team wants to make sure you'll be back next season." Stan gave

Brady an imploring look. “You are coming back, right? I mean, this wedding biz thing is just a temporary assignment while the knee heals. Right?”

“My mother’s going to be in Paris for a year, Stan.”

The older man paled. “But you’re under contract.”

“I know.” Brady’s face contorted. “But I’m also on medical leave.”

I wanted to interfere at this point but knew better. How dare this old coot come in here and start shoving Brady around? Not that anyone could shove a six-foot-four fella around, but still . . .

“Look, Stan, I’d love to stand here and chat all day, but Katie here has an appointment with my mom soon.” Brady nodded toward me, and I took a step in his direction.

“Katie?” Stan’s gaze narrowed as he looked me over. “Great. Another distraction.”

I had no idea what he meant by that but didn’t comment.

“If you’ll forgive me, I need to help a customer,” Brady said.

I watched from a distance as Brady dealt with a bride whose temper had gotten the better of her. Someone had obviously taught the boy some serious negotiation skills on the court, and they transferred over nicely to the bridal shop. Stan muttered something about needing a cup of coffee and disappeared into the back room.

I turned my attention to the wedding veils while watching Brady in action out of the corner of my eye. A few minutes later, the bride left with a smile on her face and a discount on her dress.

Stan reappeared, coffee cup in hand, at the very moment Brady headed my way. "Sorry I can't stay and chat, Stan." Brady narrowed his gaze as he saw the open coffee cup. "But Mom's waiting and her time is limited. Excuse us." He pushed past his agent and gestured for me to join him. As we headed to the back of the store, I glanced one last time at the bald-headed man, who'd pulled out his hankie once again.

"What just happened out there?" I asked.

Brady shook his head. "Don't worry about it. It's mine to deal with."

"Hmm." The older guy clearly had him rattled, but I'd better not say anything else. For that matter, I'd better not come clean about my issues anytime soon. Looked like Brady James had enough on his plate for one day. Right now I'd be better off just following along behind him and keeping my mouth shut.

13

I Keep Forgetting That I Forgot about You

The nice part about living in a small town is that when you don't know what you're doing, someone else does.

Immanuel Kant

My visit with Nadia went better than expected. I got so drawn into her design, so overwhelmed by her kindness and love toward me, that I totally forgot I wasn't getting married. We talked for nearly an hour and I gave her idea after idea, all of which she took to heart.

We went back and forth by email until Thursday morning, at which time she presented me with a rough draft of my gown, one that simply took my breath away. I could see myself—really see myself—walking down the aisle in that. Obviously she could see it too. After promising to email me the final design before passing it off to seamstresses, she hopped on a plane for Paris and left me in Dahlia's capable hands.

The following morning I headed home to spend time with the family. My parents' thirtieth anniversary party was scheduled for the next day, and I needed to be there for them.

Mama thought I was coming back for good. Pop likely did too. But I had to return to Dallas so I could figure out how to deal with the guy from *Texas Bride*. With a Monday morning interview scheduled, I had to think quickly.

I couldn't tell my parents that, however, so I prepped myself to tell them that I needed more time with Lori-Lou and the kids. I arrived in Fairfield on Friday evening just in time to have dinner at Sam's. I ate my fill of coconut cream pie and shared funny stories about my time in Dallas, excluding all of the parts about the bridal salon, of course.

I couldn't help but notice Jasper giving me odd looks. He managed to catch me alone at the dessert bar and leaned in close to whisper a very unexpected question. "What's this I hear about you hanging out with Brady James?"

"W-what?" I stared at him, completely stunned. "Who told you that?"

"Josh. Queenie emailed him to check up on you, and he said you and Lori-Lou were all gallivanting with a pro ball player."

"Oh no." I dropped my pie plate and Jasper caught it on the way down. "Does Mama know?"

"No way. Queenie only told me because she wanted to know who Brady James was," Jasper said. "I think she was hoping he was some sort of secret love interest."

"No way!" I shook my head. "I barely know the guy."

"Well, maybe you should take a minute to tell her how you came to spend time with him. Josh said it had something to do with wedding gowns? Didn't make a lick of sense to me." Jasper grabbed an extra slice of pie and headed back to the table.

I couldn't get past what he'd said. So Queenie knew I'd been at a bridal salon, and she knew about Brady? Why oh why had Josh told her all of that?

I made my way back to the table and did my best to make it through the meal. I could feel my grandmother's eyes on me and knew a conversation would follow. Sure enough, it came in the parking lot, after everyone else had left for the night.

"Something you want to tell me, Katie?" she asked. "About a certain fella you've been seen with in Dallas?"

"It's nothing like what you think, Queenie."

"You've been spending a lot of time in a bridal shop, Josh says. Is there a reason for that?" She gave me a pensive look. "Still holding out hope that Casey will change his mind?"

"No, it's not that at all." To be honest, I hadn't spent as much time thinking about Casey as she might've thought. All of the hustle and bustle of the past week had pretty much taken precedence. That, and a houseful of unruly toddlers.

My grandmother reached to take hold of my hand, and her eyes moistened. "Can I ask you a question, Katie, and answer me honestly."

"Sure, Queenie." *Oh. Help.*

She gave me a thoughtful look, her soft skin wrinkling in concern. "Do you think maybe you're not really in love with Casey?"

"W-what?"

She squeezed my hand. "I'm going to venture a guess that you've been so excited thinking about your wedding that you haven't really had adequate time to think about the groom. Is that why you're still shopping for wedding items, even though he's gone?"

"Queenie! Of course I've thought about the groom. I . . . I love Casey."

"You hesitated."

"No, I do. I've loved him since we were kids. Everyone knows it. Mama knows it. His mama knows it. You know it."

"But do you know it? I mean, do you really think you're in love with Casey, or are you just in love with the idea of a big wedding with all the trimmings? Is that why you won't give up on this idea?"

I clamped my lips shut before saying something I might regret. How dare she suggest such a thing? Sure, I wanted a big church wedding. And yes, I'd collected enough issues of *Texas Bride* to paper our house. But did that mean I didn't love Casey? Of course not.

"I'm just asking you to pray about it, honey." Queenie attempted to shift her weight, but her arthritis must've gotten the better of her. She almost tumbled right into me.

"I-I have. I've had plenty of time to pray. And to think."

"And?"

"And . . ." I sighed. "I have to confess, I've always wanted a big church wedding. That part is right. But I was in love with Casey."

"Was?"

"Am. I am."

"You hesitated again." She pulled me into her arms and planted a kiss in my hair. "Remember what I said that day at my house. Be methodical. Don't dive in headfirst. Take your time. God has big things for you, sweetheart. Maybe even bigger than you dreamed for yourself."

"Yes ma'am." I returned her hug, then thought about her words as I drove home. I pondered them as I climbed into my bed—ah, how wonderful to sleep in my own bed! And I even dreamed about weddings that night. Oddly, I didn't see Casey in my dream. He was nowhere to be found.

When I awoke Saturday morning, the whole Fisher clan was in an uproar, preparing for my parents' anniversary party at the church. I'd never seen Mama so frazzled. Or Pop, for that matter. He'd actually closed down the hardware store for the day. This probably wouldn't be a good time to tell them I planned to go back to Dallas for another week. I'd have to do that after the party.

We ran into a situation when we prepared to leave the house. "Katie Sue, there's something you need to know." Mama stood next to my car with a concerned look on her face. "The party has been moved to the Presbyterian church, which has raised all sorts of problems with Queenie."

"Wait. Why isn't it at our church?" I asked.

"There was a flood three days ago. Well, not technically a flood. A toilet overflowed in the women's restroom and leaked under the wall into the carpet of the fellowship hall. The whole place smells like a sewer."

"Ew."

"Yeah. We tried to get the Methodist church at the last minute, but they're doing a community outreach today and have over a hundred elementary school children on the premises."

"That might be a problem."

"Right. So obviously, that left us with the Charismatics and the Presbyterians." Mama's gaze narrowed. "I weighed my options. I really did. But in the end, I went with the Presbyterians."

"Mama, are you saying Queenie won't come to

her own son's anniversary party just because of where it's located?"

"She'll come, if Bessie May has to drag her kicking and screaming. But she's not happy."

"But this isn't about her. It's about you and Pop."

"Right. Your father tried to tell her that, but would she listen?"

"I talked to Queenie last night. She never mentioned any of this."

"He didn't call her until this morning. If we'd given her time to think about it, she would've left town."

"I just don't understand her issues with the Presbyterians. It's the strangest thing."

I pondered this dilemma as we drove to the church. The fellowship hall at Fairfield Presbyterian was a lovely room, even larger than what we boasted at the Baptist church. And with the WOP-pers doing the decorating, the whole place was festive and bright, just perfect for an anniversary celebration. Still, 10:00 a.m. came and went and the guests arrived in droves, but no Queenie.

For whatever reason, the WOP-pers took it upon themselves to spend the first forty-three minutes of the party focused on my love life, or lack thereof. They somehow involved my mother in the conversation, which only made things more awkward.

The women gathered around me like chicks around a mother hen. Bessie May slipped her arm through mine and patted me like a small child. "Have you been enjoying your time in Dallas, sweet girl?"

"I have."

"Have you had a chance to visit with a certain handsome young man while there?" Bessie May giggled.

My heart lurched as an image of Brady James flitted through my mind. Had Queenie told my mother that I'd met the handsome ball player?

"We've been sending up prayer after prayer that the Lord would send him a godly wife," an older woman named Ophelia said with a wink. "And it's occurred to us that perhaps you are it!"

"Wait . . . who?" I asked.

"Why, Levi Nash, of course." A faint humor lit Bessie May's eyes. "You haven't figured that out yet?"

"Levi Nash?" I shook my head, unable to process her words. "Are you serious?"

"I believe she is serious, Katie," Mama said. "The WOP-pers have been praying for Levi for quite some time, as you know. He's walking the straight and narrow now."

"And you all"—I gestured to the group of women—"believe Levi is the perfect fella for me?" When they nodded, I turned to face my mother. "Mama! I can't believe you of all people really think that. Levi and I have nothing in common."

"You both love the Lord."

"Well, yes, but if that's grounds for matrimony, then I could marry millions of single men across the continent."

"Ooh, that reminds me of a show I watched on television where a fella married seventeen wives." Bessie May fanned herself with her hand. "I can't believe he got away with that. I do believe he went to jail in the end, if that counts for anything."

"That wasn't my point, Bessie May," I said. "And I guess I should go ahead and say that I plan to go back to Dallas for the next week or so to spend more time with Lori-Lou."

"Poor thing." Ophelia patted me on the arm. "That Casey Lawson really did break your heart, didn't he?"

"That snake." Mama's eyes narrowed.

"That scoundrel." Bessie May shook her head.

"A wolf in sheep's clothing," Ophelia chimed in.

Before I could come to my almost-fiancé's defense, Mama clasped her hands together at her chest. "Well, forget about him, honey! I happen to know that Levi is back for the summer, serving as an intern at the church. Maybe you can connect with him while you're home. He's heading up the youth department now, you know."

"Interning?" I asked. Crazy to think that the guy who'd once wreaked havoc in the youth group was now heading up the whole thing, but whatever.

"Yes. And if you're in Dallas too long, you won't get to connect with him. Do you really have to go back?"

I thought about the interview with the reporter and made up my mind in a hurry. I'd have to go back, if for no other reason than to let Brady know the truth. In fact, I should probably call him today just to put him on alert so that the reporter wouldn't show up.

I didn't have time to say anything else, though, because Queenie arrived. Turned out she'd been in the parking lot for a good fifteen minutes, unwilling to come in the door. Go figure. Reverend Bradford, the Presbyterian pastor, greeted her with a smile, but she huffed right past him and went straight to the food table.

After filling her plate, she took a seat at a table on the perimeter of the room. I walked over and sat beside her, ready to get to the bottom of this.

"Okay, Queenie, enough already. What's your beef with the Presbyterians?"

"Hmm? What?" She glanced my way, the soft wrinkles in her brow deepening.

"You know what I mean. Whenever you talk about how the WOP-pers allow all denominations in their group, you always add the words 'even the Presbyterians,' as if they're somehow different from the rest."

Her cheeks blazed pink. "Do I? I didn't realize."

"Mm-hmm. And Mama said that you had every intention of coming to the party today until you found out it was going to be held here, at the Presbyterian church. Why should that make any difference?"

"Well, the Presbyterians are godly folks, just like all the rest. I suppose . . ."

"You have a problem with their doctrine?" I asked.

"Oh my goodness, no. Nothing like that. I don't claim to be a theologian. Denominational doctrines aren't my specialty. To be honest, I always get a little confused where all of that is concerned. If they're Jesus-lovin' people, well then, they're all right with me."

"Okay, then what is it? Why do you always hesitate when it comes to the Presbyterians?" I glanced up and noticed that Reverend Bradford was waving at us from across the room. I responded with a little wave, but my grandmother ignored him. "Don't you like Reverend Bradford?" I whispered. "Is that it?"

"L-like him?" Her face grew redder still and she reached for a napkin, which she used to fan her face. "Who said anything about liking or disliking Paul Bradford?"

Very. Odd.

"So you don't like him?" *And why did you call him by his first name?*

"I never said that either." She attempted to stand, but her arthritis kicked in. "I've been told he's a fine pastor. Just fine. I'm sure he's very good at what he does." She glanced up at him and her cheeks flamed again. "Whatever that is. Now, if you don't mind, I have more important things to do, please and thank you."

"Queenie . . ." I stood and helped her up but didn't release my hold on her arm. "There's something you're not saying. What is it?"

"I believe they need to adjust the thermostat in here," she said. "It's so hot I could fry an egg on this table. Don't these Presbyterians know anything about how to cool a building?"

"No, it's perfectly comfortable. Now, let's talk about Reverend Bradford. Why did you say—"

"You two are talking about Paul Bradford?" Bessie May sidled up next to us and gave Queenie a funny look. "I thought you gave up talking about him fifty-some-odd years ago, Queenie."

"W-what?" I looked at my grandmother, stunned. "Gave up on him?"

"You're a silly old fool, Bessie May." Queenie's eyes narrowed to slits. "And if you know what's good for you, you'll . . . Stop. It. Right. There."

"Just saying, it's not good to hold a grudge. Even against the Presbyterians." Bessie May leaned toward me and cupped her hand next to my ear. "It's not really the denomination as a whole, you see. It's just one very ornery fella who broke her heart back in the day."

A little gasp escaped as I turned to my grandmother. "Queenie?"

She put her hand up. "I forbid you to discuss this further. Let it go."

Bessie May giggled and then moved toward the food table. "Aptly put, my friend! Let it go. Let it go."

My grandmother released a groan. "Honestly! That woman is filled with enough hot air to fill the *Hindenburg* and is equally as dangerous. Maybe more so."

"But Queenie—"

"No." She glared at me. "This conversation has ended. You just forget you heard any of that, all right?"

I doubted I could ever forget it but offered a lame nod. I couldn't say which bothered me more—the fact that this conversation centered on a man other than my grandfather, God rest his soul, or the fact that my grandmother seemed to hold a grudge against an entire denomination because of one man. The idea of my grandmother having her heart broken by any fella really set my nerves on edge, but . . . a reverend? No one messed with Queenie Fisher, even a man of the cloth.

I scurried over to the food table to chat with my father, who was filling his plate. "Pop, I have a question."

"Sure, kiddo. What's up?"

I lowered my voice to a whisper. "What in the world happened between Queenie and Reverend Bradford?"

My father nearly dropped his plate. I had to reach out to help him steady his hand. "Who told you about Reverend Bradford?"

"Bessie May."

My father shook his head. "That's one story best left untold, Katie."

"But Pop—"

"Your grandfather was an amazing man. Best dad I could've asked for. I sincerely doubt Reverend Bradford"—my father spit out the words—"would've made my mama half as happy. So let's just let sleeping dogs lie, Katie."

Okay, I had no idea what dogs had to do with this. And all that stuff about making my grandmother happy? Maybe I was reading too much into this. Still, I couldn't seem to let go of the fact that my grandmother had some sort of secret from her past. And a broken heart to boot.

I decided to bypass my dad and go straight to the one person who could—and probably would—give me the gritty details. I found Bessie May at the dessert table, reaching for a slice of my parents' anniversary cake.

"Okay, Bessie May," I said. "Fess up. What happened between Queenie and Reverend Bradford?"

"E-excuse me?"

"I have to know the truth. It's not fair that I only have bits and pieces of the story."

The fork in her hand began to tremble. "Well now, Katie Sue, we're talking about a tangled web here. And I'm not sure I'm the right one to be telling this tale."

"You're exactly the right one. Please, Bessie May. I want to know."

She set her plate down on the edge of the table. "Did you ever see *Coal Miner's Daughter*, Katie?"

"Is this a trick question?"

"Alrighty then. Remember that scene where Doo cheated on Loretta?"

"Which time?"

"Good point." Bessie May paused. "Well, anyway, after one of the many times, Loretta went back to the tour bus and wrote that song, 'You Ain't Woman Enough to Take My Man.' "

"I remember it clearly."

"Loretta was angry. Very, very angry."

"Right." I stopped to think through what I'd just heard. "Are you saying that Reverend Bradford *cheated* on Queenie?"

Bessie May reached to clasp her plate with her left hand, but her right hand went straight up in the air. "I didn't say that. If anyone asks . . . I. Did. Not. Say. That." She lost her grip on the cake plate and down it went, straight to the floor.

I leaned over to pick it up, but Reverend Bradford came straight for me. Oh dear.

"I'll take care of that, Katie," he said with a smile. "You just help Bessie May get another plate, okay?"

"O-okay."

I went to work doing just that but leaned in to whisper to Bessie May, "When you say cheat . . ."

"I did not say cheat. You did."

"Okay, but when you say cheat, do you mean, like . . ." This time I almost dropped the plate.

"Heavens, no. He's a reverend. A man of the cloth. But his heart was all twisted up with two different gals at once. One of them, Queenie, pretty much climbed on the proverbial tour bus and wrote 'You Ain't Woman Enough to Take My Man' so the other gal would know to back off. But the other gal didn't back off." Bessie May glanced at Reverend Bradford as he drew near with a rag in one hand and a mop in the other. "You get my drift?"

I wanted to say yes but still felt confused. Very, very confused.

"The, um, man in question . . . married the other gal—er, girl?" I whispered as I glanced down at the good reverend, who now worked cleaning up Bessie May's mess.

"Nope." Bessie May grabbed me by the arm and pulled me over to a nearby table. "In the end, he didn't marry either of them." She chuckled.

"Ain't life strange? Just when you think you've got everything figured out."

Right now I couldn't figure anything out. Mostly this conversation. One thing I did understand: Queenie's heart had been broken by Reverend Bradford years ago. And her broken heart had obviously never mended—thus her beef with the Presbyterians. Thank goodness Reverend Bradford wasn't Baptist. Queenie's bitterness might've changed our entire family's denominational leanings.

Still, it seemed really, really odd that my grandmother had all of these skeletons in her closet. She'd done a fine job of keeping her emotions to herself.

Or maybe she hadn't. I glanced across the room and watched as she sat alone at her table, eyes fixed on Reverend Bradford as he worked. He glanced up and caught her gaze, then gave her a little wink.

Alrighty then. Maybe the skeletons in Queenie's closet had a little life left in them after all. And maybe, just maybe, I would get to watch them make their way out into the open.

14

Why Can't He Be You

> I grew up in a small town where everyone wanted to be the same or look the same and was afraid to be different.
>
> Kate Bosworth

I spent the rest of the weekend in Fairfield, then headed back to Lori-Lou's on Sunday night. I arrived just in time to learn that she and Josh had put an offer on a house.

"Oh, Katie, it's perfect." Lori-Lou clasped her hands together in obvious delight. "Very little money down because it's one of those . . ." She looked to Josh for help.

"Repo," he said. "Thc bank repossessed the house from thc owners when they got behind on the mortgage."

"They're letting it go for a song. And the very best part?" She released a squeal. "The mortgage will actually be less than our rent here. And we'll have double the space. Isn't God good?"

"We haven't exactly been approved for the loan yet," Josh was quick to add. "And we'll have to count every penny to come up with the down payment. But I think we can make it." He gave her a kiss on the forehead and before long the two of them were smooching. Ugh.

I'd wanted to give Josh a piece of my mind for telling Queenie about my trip to Cosmopolitan Bridal, but he seemed so happy about the house possibilities that I decided I'd better wait. Besides, who could blame him for not standing up to Queenie? From what I'd been told, the only person who'd ever tried and succeeded was Aunt Alva, and none of us had seen her for years.

One particular conversation couldn't wait any longer. I had to let the people at the bridal shop know about my lack of wedding plans before the reporter arrived. Madge would be upset, but I had to risk that. I called Brady's direct line at the store but got his voicemail. Great. I'd have no choice but to wait until morning. Maybe I could catch him in time, before the reporter arrived.

Lori-Lou wasn't able to go with me Monday morning because she and Josh had an appointment with their Realtor, so I drove myself to Cosmopolitan. Pulling up in the '97 Cadillac was a wee bit embarrassing. Hopefully no one would see the old girl. She sputtered to a stop and I got out, straightened my twisted blouse, and then drew in a deep breath, ready to get this over with. I walked inside the store and found it strangely quiet.

Madge saw me right away and headed toward me. "Katie, I'm glad you're here. Dahlia has put together a pattern for your gown and wants to show it to you after your interview."

"Well, actually, about the interview . . ." I shook my head. "Don't you see, Madge? I can't go through with it. This whole thing has reached a ridiculous point."

"No it hasn't. You're overthinking it."

"I'm not overthinking it. I'm being realistic. If I don't tell Brady, it could come back to hurt him and the shop, and ultimately his mom. I don't want to be responsible for that."

"I'm telling you, you're overthinking this. There's nothing in the contract about a wedding. And I'm begging you to let Nadia have her moment in the sun. Please don't ruin this for her."

My heart softened toward Madge as I noticed the tears in her eyes. "Why is her career so important to you, Madge?"

Madge swiped at her eyes with the back of her hand. "She's like a sister to me, a sister that I never had. We're as opposite as two people can be—kind of like you and Lori-Lou. But I'll go to my grave looking out for her."

"Don't you think—and this might just be a guess—that she can handle whatever fallout occurs if I tell her?"

"Probably. But I don't want anything to mess up her time in Paris. She's worked too hard for this. Let's just let it ride, shall we? You won the contest fair and square and you got the dress. It also won't change the fact that Nadia James is a woman of her word. She gave you what you won."

"Talking about Mom?" Brady's voice rang out from behind us. "Are you having some concerns about the design of the dress, Katie?"

"About the design?" I turned to face him. "No. Not at all."

"Good." A boyish smile lit his handsome face. "Because Jordan Singer will be here in half an hour. I'm glad you came when you did. I wanted to go over some of the interview questions with you before he arrives. Do you mind?"

I would've responded, but his gorgeous eyes and broad smile held me captive and I forgot what we were talking about. One thing was clear—for a guy who didn't want to be in the wedding gown biz, Brady James was starting to look at home at Cosmopolitan Bridal. Peaceful, even.

Well, peaceful until the door to the shop opened and his agent walked in.

"Roll out the red carpet, folks." The familiar bald-headed fellow took a deep bow at the waist. "It's Stan the Man, showing up for round sixty-three of his never-ending pep talk with his favorite player. Maybe this time I'll be able to pound some sense into that thick head of his."

"Oh, joy." Madge groaned. "Stan the Man. Just what I needed to make my morning complete."

"Hey, I heard that, Madge." Stan gave her a

playful wink. "And I'll take it as a compliment, thank you very much. One of these days you're going to see that it's me and greet me with the respect I deserve."

"Or not," she said.

"Admit it, Madge-girl. You love this crusty old soul."

"You've got the crusty part right," Madge muttered under her breath. "And the old part too."

"I heard that. And I'd be willing to bet we're the same age, so guard what you say. If I don't show up to annoy Brady, he'll settle into his life here at the bridal whatchamacallit and end up pushing petticoats for a living. We can't have that."

"Stan, really? Petticoats?" Brady shook his head.

"Someone's gotta keep your career afloat, my boy. Anything I can do to convince you that you should get back to the business of playing ball."

"Well, maybe we can talk later. Katie and I need to go over the Q&A for her interview."

"Ah yes, the infamous Katie." Stan sighed as he looked at me standing next to Brady. "The distraction."

"Stop it, Stan." Brady gave him a "cut it out" look and I did my best to ignore him. "She's practically a married woman."

Oh boy. Now what?

"Well, that makes me feel a little better, as long

as you're not the groom. Gotta keep you focused on my game, son."

"Katie's our contest winner. She's getting married . . ." He looked at me. "When did you say the wedding is going to take place?"

Before I could say, "Never," Stan groaned. "Marriage is an institution, I tell ya. And it's one I was happy to escape from."

"You need to get married and settle down, you old coot." Madge gave him the evil eye. "Finding a good wife would do you a world of good."

"I found a wife once. Lost her a couple years later in the shoe department at Macy's. She never turned up again. Last thing I heard, she was draining some other sucker's pocketbook dry. Good riddance, I say."

"Nothing like true love." Brady chuckled. He glanced at his watch. "I hate to interrupt this inspiring conversation, but Katie and I really need to—"

"Don't ever get married, son." Stan nudged him with his elbow. "You'll be in a lot better shape if you stay single and free, like me."

Brady's smile shifted to a more thoughtful look, and he seemed to forget all about the upcoming interview. "No, I want a wife and family someday. I've been praying for the right person to come along." He shrugged. "Just haven't found her yet. But she's out there."

"Well, stop looking," Stan said. "You're still

young. Live your life. There's plenty of time to be tied down later."

Interesting. Stan's little speech reminded me of what Jasper had said that night at Sam's.

"Tied down?" Fine wrinkles appeared on Brady's forehead. "Huh?"

"Yeah, you know." Stan rolled his eyes. "The old ball and chain." He nudged Brady again and gave him a knowing look.

"Puh-leeze. How would you know?" Madge balled up her fists and planted them on her hips. "Doesn't sound like you were tied to your wife long enough to know anything about it."

"I've been a confirmed bachelor ever since she took off. Er, ever since I ditched her at Macy's. Nothing wrong with the free and easy life."

"Nothing except for years of heartache, loneliness, and pain." Madge grimaced. "But who am I to say?"

"Point is, I can do what I want when I want, and no one is any the wiser." Stan scowled at Madge.

She pursed her lips and crossed her arms. "Whatever you say, oh wise one."

"That's more like it. Now, don't you worry about me, and don't you dare put any ideas into this boy's head. I'm married to the game, and Brady here is too." Stan slapped Brady on the back, but I could tell that move didn't go over very well.

"Basketball makes for a lonely bedfellow in

the long term." Madge wagged her finger in Stan's face. "You can't cuddle with a basketball, you know."

"I beg to differ." Stan chuckled. "I've done it many a time. Besides, a basketball doesn't argue with you or spend your money on expensive shoes. And doesn't keep you up nights talking about nonsensical things like hot flashes."

"My mama has hot flashes," I chimed in. "She takes special vitamins for them. They help a lot."

Stan looked at me. "Great news, kid. If I ever find my ex, I'll tell her."

Okay then. No more getting involved in this conversation.

"I'm not sure I'd agree that basketball is the be-all, end-all," Brady said. "It's just a game."

At that statement, you could've heard a pin drop. Stan turned almost in slow motion to face his favorite player. His eyes narrowed as the punctuated words, "What are you saying, Brady?" came out.

"Saying it's just a game. Like any other game. It plays itself out. As my mama would say, it's non-eternal."

"Are you saying there's no basketball in heaven?" Stan stood as stoic as a Greek statue. " 'Cause if you are, I might just have to reconsider where I'm going when the final quarter is over."

"Good grief." Madge slapped herself on the forehead. "Of course there's no basketball in heaven. And no women in high-heeled shoes from Macy's."

"But there is a Clinique counter, right?" Dahlia popped out from behind the rack of gowns where she'd been working. " 'Cause I can't imagine going for all eternity without my makeup."

"Not sure how we got from basketball to makeup," Stan said. "But that's the problem with women."

"What's the problem with women?" Madge glared at him.

"First they're spending your money on heels, next they're headed to the makeup counter. It's a never-ending financial dilemma."

"Enough, folks. Enough." Brady shook his head. "But going back to the earlier conversation, I do plan to get married someday. Looking forward to it. Now, if you don't mind, Katie and I really need to—"

"He just hasn't found the right girl yet," Madge interjected. "Some people get so distracted that they don't see what's right in front of them." Her words were directed at Brady, but I had the weirdest feeling she was also trying to get some sort of subliminal message through to Stan. Odd.

He didn't seem to notice. The old coot mumbled something about basketball, and minutes later he and Brady were embroiled in a dispute over a recent game. Go figure.

"Men." Madge shook her head. "You can't live

with 'em and you can't live without 'em."

Stan paused from his conversation with Brady to look at Madge. "Strange. That's what I've always said about women."

"And there you go." Dahlia went back to work straightening the row of white gowns. "The battle between the sexes rages on, and no one comes out a winner."

"Some folks must," I said. "I mean, this is a bridal shop. You see plenty of brides come through here. People must be getting married and settling down. So surely there are still some people interested in marriage, right?"

Everyone in the room turned to stare at me, their silence deafening.

Oh boy. Why did I have to go and say that?

"Well, duh, Katie." Dahlia gave me a perplexed look. "You're one of them."

"Sure, sure." Stan patted me on the arm in fatherly fashion. "You're about to enter a life of marital bliss. We all have a lot to learn from you. Right?"

Yeah. Like how to ditch a would-be fiancé in a hurry. I could certainly teach lessons on that.

"Katie's a great teacher," Madge said. "I've learned so much from her already." She gave me a penetrating look, one meant to shut me up.

"I'm sure you're going to be one of the lucky ones, Katie." Dahlia sighed. "You're going to marry . . . what's his name again? . . . and live happily ever after."

"Casey," Brady said. "Her fiancé is named Casey Lawson. It's in the essay."

Dahlia's eyes took on a dreamy look. "Well, you and Casey are going to have a blissful life in Fairfield and raise 2.5 children and live in a house with a white picket fence."

"I'd pay money to see the 2.5 children." Stan elbowed Madge.

Madge, God bless her, managed to turn the conversation around, and before long we were talking about basketball once again. She gave me a "whew!" look, but I could read the warning in her eyes. No point in upsetting the apple cart, as Mama would say. I didn't want to spoil things for Nadia, after all. And with the reporter from *Texas Bride* coming soon, I'd better mind my p's and q's. Looked like I couldn't get out of the interview, no matter how hard I tried. Not with all of these people surrounding me, any-way.

A couple of minutes later, Twiggy and Crystal entered thc shop from the workroom. Crystal glanced up as an elderly woman came barreling through the front door, fussing and fuming about the weather.

"Incoming tornado," Dahlia whispered. "Brace yourselves for a storm, ladies."

I was bracing myself for a storm, all right, but not the kind she had in mind. My storm involved a hurricane of emotions that had whirled out of control when Brady mentioned Casey's name. I bit back the tears, but Brady must've noticed. His compassionate look calmed me down at once. He mouthed the words, "You okay?" and I nodded, forcing a smile.

"Let's get back to work, shall we?" Madge gestured to the woman at the front of the store. "Someone needs to greet our guest."

Twiggy and Crystal headed off to do just that. I brushed the tears from my eyes and, for the first time, could see the woman more clearly.

"Oh no."

I didn't mean to speak the words aloud, but what else could I do? The woman who fussed and fumed as she crossed from the door to the shoe counter was none other than Aunt Alva, black sheep of the family. She hadn't yet noticed me, so I ducked behind a mannequin and tried to steady my breathing.

Madge gave me the oddest look. "Um, you okay back there?"

"Someone you know, kid?" Stan added.

I whispered, "It's my great-aunt Alva."

Brady smiled. "That's great, Katie. Do you think she'll stay long enough to add a few thoughts to the interview? She knows your fiancé, right?"

"Well, she knew Casey when he was a boy." I felt the tops of my ears grow hot. "But we haven't exactly . . . I mean, she doesn't know him these days."

Madge glared at me.

Brady leaned in close, his breath soft against my cheek as he whispered, "Are you telling me that your aunt doesn't know you're engaged?"

"Um, something like that. Remember, I told you and your mom that all of this is top-secret information."

"Well, you said your parents didn't know, that you planned to surprise them. It's the whole family? No one knows you're getting the gown?"

Another glare from Madge put my nerves on edge.

"Gonna surprise 'em, eh?" Stan laughed. "That's one way to tell the family. Land yourself on the cover of a national magazine wearing a Nadia James original and see their heads roll."

"Keeping it from the extended family complicates things, for sure." Brady released a slow breath. "Guess that means we can't include your aunt in the interview." He scratched his head. "Or even tell her about the dress?"

"I don't know if she knows about that. If Lori-Lou told her, I'm going to . . . going to . . ." I groaned. "It's complicated."

"Sounds like it. But why not tell them? Your parents will probably be thrilled to save the money, right? I mean, wedding gowns are expensive."

"Right. I'm just, well . . ."

"So you're scared?" Brady's brow wrinkled in obvious confusion. "Scared of your family's reaction to the dress? Or to the engagement? That's why you're keeping it all a secret?"

"I'm just terrified . . . period."

Boy, if that didn't sum it up, nothing did.

Brady shook his head. "I'm. So. Confused."

"Me too, and I don't even know any of these people." Stan shrugged and peeked out at my aunt. "Why are we hiding behind a mannequin again?"

Madge squinted her eyes. "Get over it, girl. You don't have to tell your aunt about the interview. Just make nice and maybe she'll go away. Then again, that's been my approach with old Stan the Man here, but he doesn't seem to be going anywhere."

"I heard that," Stan said.

The two of them headed off to the counter, bickering all the way.

Brady glanced at me. "Katie, I'm just trying to make sense of this. You don't have a wedding date. Your family doesn't know you've won the contest. And the interview is supposed to be a secret. Is there anything else I should know?"

"Yes, actually, there is."

I'd just opened my mouth to add, "My fiancé isn't even my fiancé," when something—er, some*one*—interrupted me.

Aunt Alva let out an unladylike whoop and then hollered, "Katie Sue Fisher! *There* you are! I had a feeling I just might find you here."

15

Girl That I Am Now

A city is more than a place in space, it is a drama in time.

Patrick Geddes

Nothing—and I do mean *nothing*—could've prepared me for running into my great-aunt at Cosmopolitan Bridal. I hadn't seen the woman in years, after all. Why here, of all places? And why now?

Surely Lori-Lou was behind this. Or Josh. Only, Josh didn't really know Alva, did he? And Lori-Lou hadn't spoken to her in years.

So. Odd.

I sucked in a deep breath and worked up the courage to "face this like a man," as Lori-Lou had said. Looked like I was doing a lot of that these days. Brady and Stan disappeared into the workroom, and I headed toward my aunt.

"Aunt Alva!" I tried to steady my voice. "What in the world brings you here?"

"Katie Sue Fisher, as I live and breathe!" She extended her arms, and a broad smile lit her chubby face. "That's a fine how-do-you-do when we haven't see one another in years. I'd say a handshake is in order if you're not the hugging sort."

"Oh, I'm definitely the hugging sort."

She swept me into her arms, which totally threw me. Queenie's description of Alva was a cold, mean woman, not one who grabbed near strangers and pulled them into bear hugs. I had a lot to process during the thirty seconds that her sagging bosoms held me in their grip. Nothing about this seemed remotely normal. Or expected. Or within the realm of possibility.

She finally released me, and I did my best not to let the relief show on my face as I took a giant step backwards.

"Now I'll answer your question, Katie Sue." My aunt brushed a loose hair off my cheek with her index finger, a gesture I knew well from Queenie. Weird. "You wanted to know how I came to find you here?"

"Yes ma'am."

"Can we sit down someplace so we can chat?"

Madge must've overheard that last part because she suggested the spacious fitting room, the one with the cozy padded bench in the center. A couple minutes later I found myself closed inside with my aunt, who eased her ample frame down onto the bench.

"There, that's more like it. Now, where were we?"

"You were telling me how you knew to look for me here," I said.

"Right, right. Well, it's the strangest thing. I got this new smartphone. Tried to figure it out looking through the contacts list, and I accidentally telephoned someone."

"Oh?"

"Lori-Lou. Haven't talked to her in years, but there she was on the other end of my phone. Now, don't be mad, Katie . . . I'm sure she didn't mean to let it slip, but she said something about you being in town. I was floored. Thought you'd stay rooted in Fairfield forever."

"Well, I haven't moved here, Aunt Alva. I'm just here for . . ." I released a sigh, unable—er, unwilling—to complete the sentence.

"I know why you're here. She told me all about that contest. So, you're engaged?"

Ack. "She told you I'm engaged?"

"Well, she let it slip that you were in town to be fitted for a wedding gown. What else could I deduce?"

"I see."

"She refused to tell me which bridal shop, but you know me . . ."

Actually, I don't.

"I'm not the sort to give up easily. I'm like a dog following a skunk down a hole. Or would that be up a tree? I'm not really sure where skunks go when they're running from dogs."

I cleared my throat.

"Anyway, I called every shop in town. When I

tried this one, I talked to some woman named Twiggy—do you suppose that's her real name? When I told her I was family, she clued me in that you were being fitted for a gown here."

"I see." I'd have to remember to talk to Twiggy later. So much for keeping things a secret.

"I couldn't come right away, what with my knee giving me fits and all," Alva said. "But once I got past all that, I got in my car and came on up here to have a little chat with that Twiggy gal and ask when you might be coming in next. Just happened in on a day you were here, which is just peachy." She clasped her hands together, a gleeful look on her face. "So tell me about this fella of yours. I vaguely remember hearing you were dating the Lawson boy."

"Oh?" How in the world could she have known that? Was Aunt Alva spying on us? "Casey's a great guy. He's really sweet." *When he isn't breaking my heart.*

"When's the wedding? I don't suppose I'll be invited, but it's good to know what's going on in the family anyway. Keeping up from a distance is a sure sight better than not keeping up at all, at least that's my philosophy."

"Well, I'm afraid you won't be the only one who doesn't get to go to the wedding, Aunt Alva." I took a seat on the bench next to her.

"Figured you wouldn't want me there." She let out a little humph.

“Oh, it’s not that. Not at all.”

My aunt gave me a pensive look. “Is it because he’s Presbyterian?”

“W-what? How did you know that Casey is Presbyterian?”

“I have my sources. I still know folks in Fairfield, you know. Bessie May and I talk every now and again.”

“You do?” But she was Queenie’s best friend. How in the world . . . ?

“Is that why I can’t come to the wedding?” Alva asked. “Because it’s at the Presbyterian church?”

“No.” I shook my head. “If there was going to be a wedding, it would be at our church.”

“What do you mean, *if?* Are you saying there’s no wedding at all?”

I lowered my voice, just in case anyone happened to be standing on the other side of the door. “The whole thing is a giant fiasco, trust me.”

“But you won a contest. That Twiggy girl said you’re getting a free wedding dress. Isn’t that right?”

“Well, yes. In theory.”

“Here you are in the bridal shop. You must be here for a reason.” She paused. “Do you mind if I ask why you’re getting this gown made up if you don’t plan on wearing it?”

“I’m going to wear it for the photo shoot one month from today, and then one day I’ll wear it at my for-real wedding.”

"Which isn't taking place at the Presbyterian church. But at least there is a for-real wedding, right?"

"Not really." I rose and paced the little room. "It's complicated. And why in the world is everyone so hung up on the Presbyterians?"

"Define *everyone*."

"You. Queenie." I hesitated. "Though I guess I've finally figured out why she is. But why you?"

"Humph. This conversation just took an interesting twist. And for the record, I've always had a special place in my heart for the Presbyterians, so if you do decide to get married, feel free to invite me if you have the service there."

Ironic. Alva would come, but Queenie wouldn't.

Not that I was getting married. I needed to make that very, very clear.

I sat down and reached for her hand. "Alva, I'm sorry to tell you the wedding is off." I sighed. "I'm not marrying Casey."

"You're not marrying him? For real?"

"For real."

"Do the folks back home know?"

"They know that Casey and I have parted ways. He moved away to Oklahoma."

"You poor thing. I understand what it's like to be alone. I truly do." Her eyes flooded with tears.

Interesting.

"But the big question is, do the folks back in

Fairfield know you're here at this bridal shop, getting a wedding dress, even though you're not marrying the Lawson boy?" She crossed her arms.

"No. That part they don't know."

Crazy. I'd only been with my long-lost aunt five minutes and had already told her the very thing I hadn't yet been able to share with Brady.

Ironically, Brady rapped on the door of the fitting room at that very moment. "You ladies okay in there?"

I opened the door and saw him standing there with Stan at his side.

"Aunt Alva, this is—"

"Brady James." My aunt took one look at the ball player and almost hyperventilated. Her eyes practically bugged out of her head. "I-I-I know who he is."

"You're a basketball fan?" Stan stepped inside the fitting room.

"A fan?" She unzipped her sweater to reveal a Mavericks T-shirt underneath. "You never met such a fan! I would have season tickets if I could afford them. But at least I can watch the games on TV. Wouldn't miss a one!"

"See there, Brady?" Stan gave him a knowing look. "Told you the fans were clamoring for you."

"We're clamoring, all right." Alva's girlish giggle filled the room. "Come over here, young fella. I want to ask you a few questions about that game with the Spurs. Then we'll talk about your knee. But first, let me show you something I think you'll be very, very interested in."

Brady hesitantly stepped into the fitting room. The four of us fit easily in the large space, but it felt more like eight or twelve, what with all of the mirrors reflecting our images every which way.

My aunt rolled up the hem of her slacks, showing off mismatched trouser socks. She kept rolling until we saw a whiter-than-snow kneecap. "I've got a titanium knee myself." She patted it and laughed. "Got it six months ago."

"Really?" I said. "Weird. That's the very thing Queenie has."

A deafening silence rose up between us. Alva turned to face me. "If you don't mind, I would like to avoid that subject altogether."

"Titanium?" Brady asked.

"Knees?" Stan chimed in.

"Queenie." Alva glared at me. "Now, with that behind us, let's talk shop. That Spurs game was a complete fiasco, but I guess I'm not telling you anything you don't already know. So let's skip right on over to your injury. I want to know every detail about your surgery, Brady James. And most importantly, when will you be back on the court? I don't think I can last a season without you. My heart's not strong enough for that."

"Amen!" Stan said. "Preach it, woman."

She stood without rolling down her pants leg. Wagging a bony finger in Brady's face, she took to preaching, all right. "Things just won't be the same next season if you're not there to raise my blood pressure." Her cheeks flushed red. "Well, you know what I mean. With your plays." She shook her head. "Anyway, it won't be the same without you."

"Told you." Stan nudged him.

"The orthopedist did the best he could, under the circumstances," Brady said. "And the goal is to get me back on the court by the time the season kicks off." He must've caught his image in the mirror, because I saw him glance down at the reflection of his bad knee. "Honestly? It still bugs me . . . a lot. I feel like it could go right out from under me sometimes."

"A feeling I know well." She took a step, nearly losing her balance. Brady helped her take a seat once more, and she started rolling down her pants leg.

"I heard on the news that you were running some sort of shop. This is it?" She stopped fussing with her pants and stared at him. "My favorite player plays around with wedding gowns on the side? That's kind of . . . odd."

"My point exactly." Stan put his hand on Alva's shoulder. "Thank you for putting words to what I've been trying to say for weeks." He faced Brady. "See? Do you get it now? The fans are having a hard time and folks in the media are having a field day with your transition from the court to the . . .” He waved his arms around. “Fitting room.”

“Can’t say I blame ’em!” Alva laughed and slapped her titanium knee. “Ouch.”

“They can’t get over the fact that my boy Brady here is in the wedding gown business.”

“So what?” I offered Brady what I hoped would look like an encouraging smile. “He’s multifaceted.”

“He’s multifaceted, for sure.” Madge appeared in the open doorway. She stepped inside the fitting room with the rest of us. “You should see him behind a sewing machine. The boy can whipstitch like nobody’s business. And he’s becoming quite the expert with veils.”

Stan put his fingers in his ears. “Make it stop! I can’t take it anymore. I’ve gotta get this boy back out on the court before he slips off to a place where he’s irretrievable.”

That got a laugh out of Madge. “Don’t worry about him, Stan. He’s still got the love of the game in him. I think he dreams about basketball.”

“Praise the Lord.” Alva attempted to stand again. “Thought for a minute there I was going to lose my favorite player.” She poked a finger in Brady’s chest. “I’ve heard of fellas falling in love with girly things. Never dreamed you were one of those.”

“Well, for pity’s sake.” Madge laughed. “It’s not like that.”

"No, it's nothing like that." Brady sat on the bench. Alone. Poor guy.

No doubt he missed basketball. With so many people hounding him, it had to be tougher still. Didn't anyone hear him say that the knee still gave him fits?

"I'd be heartbroken if you quit for good." Alva's downcast expression confirmed what she'd just said. "Please promise you won't."

Brady stood and flinched as his knee buckled. "I'm not quitting, I promise."

"Can I get that in writing?" Stan asked.

Brady groaned.

Alva's gaze narrowed. She looked back and forth between us. "I'm trying to get all of this straight in my head. Brady is here, in a dress shop, because of his knee." She turned to face me. "And you're here, in a dress shop, because you won a contest."

"That's right," Brady and I said in unison.

"Well now, I have a suspicion there's more to this story. Much more." Alva nudged me. "And the answer is staring me in the face. Well, technically, he's so tall he's staring at the top of my head." She looked back and forth between us. "I see now why everyone around here is being so secretive about everything and why it's all so hush-hush."

"Wait . . . secretive?" Brady looked confused.

"Of course." My aunt clasped her hands

together and squealed. "It's so obvious when I see the two of you together. I've put the puzzle pieces together. Katie told me all about the fiasco with the fella from Fairfield."

"Fiasco?" Brady looked at me, wrinkles forming between his brows.

I felt the blood drain out of my face but couldn't muster up a word. Not a word.

"And now it's as plain as the nose on your handsome face. My sweet niece is really secretly engaged . . . to you!" Alva pointed at Brady. "Do I have it right? Is that why it's all so top secret?"

"W-what?" Stan paled and I thought he might have to be revived. He sat and put his head into his hands. "I knew it. I *knew* she was a distraction."

"W-wait, what? No!" Brady shook his head. "I'm so confused."

"I might just have to reconnect with the Fisher family if Brady James is a member." Alva's face lit into a smile. "Those ladies up at Curves are going to be green with envy once they hear that the Mavericks' point guard is my nephew by marriage." She giggled. "I can't wait to tell them."

Brady glanced my way, and I could read the panic in his expression. Still, to his credit, he said nothing else.

I felt panic rise up inside of me as well. "Aunt Alva, you can't tell them that!"

"Okay, okay, I won't rush to tell anyone right

away. You two want your privacy. I get that." She poked her finger in Brady's chest again. "But you'd better take good care of this girl. I've known many a man who said he'd love and cherish a woman, only to drop her like a ball dribbling down the court. If I hear you've done anything to break Katie's heart, I'm coming after you faster than a long shot in the last two seconds of the game. You hear me?"

"I, um . . ." Brady looked at me, concern in his eyes. "I wouldn't deliberately hurt anyone. But honestly—"

"Good. Because I've known far too many women who were mortally wounded over a love spat." Her eyes clouded over, and she used the back of her hand to swipe at them. "Well, you two didn't come to talk about all of that, though I'm glad you've let me in on your little secret."

"Aunt Alva, we don't have any secrets. Honestly."

"Well then, it makes me feel very special that you've included me. It's been years since anyone in the Fisher family"—she spat the words—"felt the need to include me in anything."

An awkward pause followed, and I tried to gauge Brady's reaction. Oh boy, were we going to have a lot to talk about after this.

"I, um, think we'd better get out to the front of the store," Brady said. "I'm guessing Jordan Singer is here by now."

"Jordan Singer?" Alva's nose wrinkled. "Who's that?"

"He's the reporter for *Texas Bride*, and he's about to interview Katie, since she won the dress."

"The one she's going to wear when the two of you get married." My aunt giggled. "Oh, this is perfect. Absolutely perfect!"

Brady took off so fast it made my head spin. Stan turned and glared at me. If I hadn't been so dumbstruck, I would've hollered, "It's not true! None of this is true!" but I couldn't seem to get my brain and my tongue working in unison.

Madge stood in total silence, eyes wide as saucers.

Aunt Alva slipped her arm through mine, and we followed the men back into the store. She chatted all the way, going on and on about how wonderful it would be to have a pro basketball player in the family.

And Brady? Well, I could tell that he had located the reporter by the businesslike tone in his voice when he addressed the man standing near the counter. "Perfect timing, Jordan," Brady called out. "C'mon over and meet our bride, Katie Fisher."

"*Our* bride." Aunt Alva elbowed me. "*Our* bride. I get it now, Katie. I get it." She said something about how her life would be complete once I married the pro ball player, but I missed most of it. I pretty much missed the interaction between Brady and Jordan Singer too.

Right now, one thing and one thing only held me captive—the sight of my three brothers sauntering through the front door of Cosmopolitan Bridal.

16

Holding On to Nothin'

I think growing up in a small town, the kind of people I met in my small town, they still haunt me. I find myself writing about them over and over again.

Annie Baker

If someone had asked me, "Where's the last place on earth you'd ever imagine seeing your brothers?" I might've gone with "a high-end bridal shop in Dallas." I'd seen them in a variety of places over the years: on the ball field, chugging Mountain Dew in front of the Exxon station, swallowing down barbecue at Sam's, giving themselves brain freezes at Dairy Queen . . . but never, ever in an ocean of white taffeta and tulle. And certainly not surrounded by experts in the wedding business.

And yet, I couldn't deny the fact that Jasper, Dewey, and Beau stood at the front door of Cosmopolitan Bridal looking like small-town deer caught in the headlights of a big-city BMW.

"Ooh, incoming country boys." Crystal giggled.

"*Handsome* country boys," Twiggy echoed.

"What have we here?" Dahlia stared at my three

brothers. “Not sure what we ever did to deserve these three, but I pray they’re not grooms-to-be.”

“They’re not.” I swallowed hard. “They’re my brothers.”

“Your brothers?” The ladies spoke the words in unison.

“Yep. My brothers.”

“Well now.” Alva rubbed her hands together. “Plot twist.”

It was a plot twist, all right. I tried to envision Jasper, Dewey, and Beau through the eyes of the bridal shop staff. Three burly boys in jeans, plaid shirts, cowboy boots, and baseball caps. They looked as out of place as fish out of water.

Just when I thought the day couldn’t possibly get any more interesting, Beau gave me a friendly wave and called out my name. “Yoo-hoo! Katie Sue!”

Dahlia looked at me, eyes wide. “You should’ve warned a girl.”

“I had no clue they were coming.”

“I just can’t believe I’m looking at Jasper, Dewey, and Beau.” Aunt Alva shook her head. “They look nothing like the little snot-nosed boys I remember. Last time I saw them was in a photograph your mama sent me years ago. They were hanging upside down from a tree in your side yard. I do believe one of them was hiding from your father because he was in trouble.”

“Not much has changed then.” I returned

Beau's wave and tried to figure out what they were doing here.

"Well, I'll be." Alva chuckled. "I knew they'd be all grown up, but those fellas look like men, not boys."

"Oh, they're men, all right." Dahlia fussed with her hair as my brothers drew near.

I watched as the girls greeted my brothers and welcomed them to the shop. Dewey, known to our locals in Fairfield as a bit of a player, took one look at Dahlia and froze in place. Now here was a side to my middle brother that I'd never seen before. Player, yes. Womanizer, yes. Frozen in place by a gal he'd just met? Never. She greeted him with that thick Swedish accent of hers, and it appeared to hold him spellbound.

Behind Dewey, Jasper stood in a similar statuesque pose. I'd seen my oldest brother smitten before, but when he clapped eyes on Crystal, he couldn't seem to see straight. Or walk straight.

The one who surprised me most, however, was Beau. He might be twenty-two, but all of Mama's babying had pretty much kept him away from the dating scene. I'd secretly wondered if he would ever take any serious interest in the opposite sex. But unlike the older boys, he didn't seem frozen at all. In fact, his fluid movements in Twiggy's direction caught me completely off guard. And when he sidled up next to her with a twangy

"How do you do?" the shock was apparently enough to de-ice Jasper and Dewey. They startled to attention and greeted the ladies.

I did my best to make proper introductions, but no one seemed to notice I was even there. Well, no one but Aunt Alva, who whispered, "Do the boys know you're engaged to Brady James?" in my left ear. I shook my head so hard that I almost gave myself whiplash.

I'd just started to respond when I noticed Brady still standing by the counter with the reporter. He signaled for me and Madge to join them. My brothers must've thought they were invited too. They looked at Brady and Jasper gasped.

"Doggone it, it's true!" Jasper took several steps toward the ball player. "You're Brady James."

"I am." Brady gave him a warm smile. "And you are . . . ?"

"My brother Jasper," I said.

"Oh, family." The reporter grabbed his tablet and turned it on. "It'll be great to have additional input for the article."

"Article?" Jasper looked perplexed by this. He turned his attention back to Brady. "See now, Josh said you were workin' at the bridal shop, but I didn't believe it. Had to see it for myself."

From behind the counter Stan let out a groan. "See, Brady? No one can believe it."

"Let me get my brothers in on this action." Jasper called for Dewey and Beau, who turned their attention from the girls long enough to acknowledge Brady. Before long all three of my brothers had engaged him in an intense conversation about that infamous game with the Spurs.

When Jasper stopped for a breath, I tapped his arm. "Are you saying you guys drove all the way to Dallas just to meet Brady?" I asked.

"I would've driven twice as far," Alva interjected. She stuck out her hand to Jasper. "Howdy, boy. I'm your aunt Alva."

"Aunt Alva?" My brother stopped in his tracks and looked her over. "Whoa."

"Whoa is right. Wouldn't have recognized you for anything," she said.

"That's strange, because I definitely would've recognized you. You look just like Queenie, so I'm pretty sure I would've figured it out in a hurry."

"Just like her," Dewey agreed.

"Spittin' image," Beau added.

"I'd appreciate it if you'd stop bringing up her name." Alva's expression soured. "But listen here, boys, your timing stinks. Your sister here's got a big interview with this reporter." Her nose wrinkled. " 'Course, I probably wasn't supposed to say that out loud, with everything top secret and all, but she's gonna talk to him about that wedding dress she's getting."

Jasper looked at me. "You're getting a wedding

dress? But why? I thought you and Casey were . . .”

“Tsk, tsk. Don’t go there.” Alva gave me a wink. “It’s all top secret.” She laughed and slapped Jasper on the back. “Only, now you boys are in on it. And I don’t mind saying I’m relieved I’m not the only one who knows. Having a ball player in the family is going to be the best thing that ever happened to any of us, don’t you think?”

“Wait.” Dewey pulled off his baseball hat. “Having a ball player in the family?”

Madge coughed. “There’s been a huge misunderstanding. Fellas, let me offer you some homemade peanut butter cookies, baked by Crystal this very morning. They’re in the workroom. Alva, why don’t you come with us so you and the boys can catch up on old times?”

I cringed as my aunt left with my brothers. No telling what she’d say to them. I’d be dead in the water before this day ended. Jasper, Dewey, and Beau would tell my parents everything. And Queenie . . . I shuddered as I thought about how she would respond if she heard any of this.

“Katie? You ready for the interview?”

“Hmm?” I looked at the reporter.

“I’m assuming from what I’ve just overheard that your fiancé is a ball player?” Jordan asked. “Is that right? Casey plays ball?”

“Oh yes. Casey has always played ball.” At least

I didn't have to fabricate that. "Baseball. From the time he was a kid."

"Got it." Jordan looked around the shop as he shifted his tablet under his arm. "Well, let's find a place where I can interview you. Would you mind if Brady stayed with us? I have some questions about the shop's role in the contest, if you don't mind."

"I don't mind a bit." In fact, having Brady there felt strangely comforting. We would have a lot to talk about when this day ended, no doubt, but at least he kept silent for now. Still, he gave me the strangest look as we walked back to the studio. Poor guy. He probably wondered how—or why—he'd gotten stuck in the middle of my family drama. He was probably also wondering why my aunt assumed we were a couple. I couldn't figure that part out myself.

Right now I just wanted to run straight out the front door. Instead, I tagged along behind the guys, through the workroom, where I saw my brothers eating peanut butter cookies and flirting with the girls. I gave Aunt Alva a warning look as I passed through the room, and she waved in response and gave me another wink. I followed behind Brady and Jordan until we reached the studio, where I took a seat at Dahlia's work table.

I glanced down at the sketch of the Loretta Lynn dress and sighed. Off to my right I saw the fabrics for my gown, already cut, with the ruffles started. "Oh, look!" I grabbed one of the pieces and examined it. "Dahlia's been working."

"She's moving fast on this one," Brady said. "The photo shoot is just a month away."

"To the day," Jordan added. "July 15."

"It's going to be the prettiest dress ever." No sooner had I said the words than my eyes filled with tears. I didn't deserve a dress like this. And I certainly didn't need a dress like this, what with being single and all.

"I can tell you're emotional." Jordan reached for his camera. "Do you mind if I get a quick shot of you as you hold the fabric? And the sketch too? The passion in your eyes will translate better to the page if I can capture it on film first."

I didn't have time to say, "Please don't," before he started snapping pictures.

Afterward he took a seat and reached for his tablet. I did my best not to let my nerves get the best of me, but I couldn't stop thinking about Aunt Alva, couldn't stop wondering what she might be telling my brothers right about now.

"I have quite a few questions for you, Katie," Jordan said. "Do you mind if I record our conversation?"

When I shook my head, he pressed a button on his cell phone and set it on the table between us. Then he reached for his tablet once again and turned it on. "Okay, first question: what is it about the wedding dress that matters so much?"

"Oh, wow." I stared at the reporter and tried to put it into words. "It's so hard to explain, but it's a magical thing." My gaze shifted back over to the fabrics and ruffles near the sketch of my gown. "Kind of like Cinderella getting her ball gown from her fairy godmother. When you've got just the right dress, you believe that anything could—and will—happen. Happily ever afters. The perfect ceremony. Anything. Everything."

"It all comes down to a dress?"

"Not the dress specifically, but the feeling you get when you're in the right one."

Brady smiled. "My mom always says when a girl has the right dress, she's capable of just about anything."

"Well, I happen to be married to a dress designer myself," Jordan said. "Have you heard of Gabi Delgado Designs?"

I gasped as the realization hit. "Of course! You guys live in Galveston, right?"

"Right."

"She's done a lot of great gowns, but I especially loved the one for the bride who was having twins."

"Bride having twins?" Brady looked perplexed.

"Technically, she was already married." Jordan laughed. "Bella Neeley and her husband D.J. recently renewed their wedding vows, and Bella was almost eight months pregnant at the time. They're good friends of ours."

"Well, that dress was amazing. I'll never forget it." I gazed at Jordan. "If you're married to a dress designer, then you get it, right? The right dress is like . . . like . . ."

"Finding the right person?" he tried.

"Well, finding the right guy is a lot more important than finding the right dress." I swallowed hard at that statement. A wave of guilt slithered over me.

"Sorry to interrupt." Madge's voice sounded from the doorway. "Your aunt wants to know if you want to meet her for lunch when you're done. She and the boys are going to a Mexican restaurant around the corner."

"I have to get back to Lori-Lou's to watch the kids," I said. "She and Josh are getting a new house."

"Gotcha." Madge nodded and then looked at Jordan. "Just for the record, I heard that last question. I've met many a bride who'd found the right dress but had the wrong guy. Even the best dress in the world can't fix that."

"Some of them get married to Mr. Wrong anyway?" Jordan asked. "Just so they can wear the dream dress?"

Madge shrugged. "Just saying I've witnessed it firsthand. Once that dress is tucked away and preserved, the bride's still stuck with the wrong fella." She gave me a knowing look. "Nothing worse than that. Don't ask me how I know."

Some sort of subliminal message, maybe? Or did Madge have a story?

"Anyway, I'll tell your aunt that she and the boys should go on to lunch. Just hope the girls don't decide to take off with them." Madge turned away from us, muttering something under her breath, then added, "Gotta get back to the front of the store. Someone's gotta keep this place running while everyone else is busy flirting."

"Flirting?" Jordan looked back and forth between Brady and me.

"Just ignore her," Brady said. "Next question?"

"Well, let's get back to you, Katie." Jordan tapped the front of his tablet and it sprang to life again. "Tell me what you like most about the Loretta Lynn gown, then tell me how it makes you feel when you see yourself in the gown that Nadia made just for you."

"My favorite things about the gown? That's easy. It's not as fussy as some of the wedding dresses I've seen. I mean, if you think about Loretta Lynn, she comes from a simple background in Butcher Holler. I'm from a simple background in Fairfield. So having a fussy dress would've been too much. On the other hand, Loretta Lynn's style has always been ruffly and sweet. Look at the dresses she performed in during the eighties. Everyone wanted to look like her because she was so delicate and pretty. But in a nonthreatening way."

"A nonthreatening beauty?" He laughed. "You'll have to explain that one."

"Just saying she never had to try too hard. So many women—even brides—try too hard. They don't look like themselves on the wedding day. They're so overly made-up, so fussy, that people don't recognize them when they walk down the aisle. I want people to know me, to know that I'm the real deal. Genuine."

The moment those words were spoken, I had a revelation. I wanted people to know me. Me. Not the dress, but the girl inside the dress. Simple. Unpretentious. Genuine.

Only, I hadn't been very genuine, had I? I'd made this all about the dress. The day. The event. Really, I needed to make it about me. And the groom.

Not that I had a groom, but if I did . . .

Jordan continued to pepper me with questions, but I couldn't get past what I'd said. Nothing about me had been genuine, at least not since my arrival in Dallas. And now look at the mess I'd caused—Aunt Alva thought I was marrying Brady, my brothers couldn't figure out why I was hanging out with a pro basketball player, Stan thought I was a distraction to Brady's career, and Mama and the WOP-pers were likely praying I'd come to my senses and marry Levi Nash and have a houseful of babies.

Eventually Jordan shifted gears to get Brady's

input. I sat like a schoolgirl with a crush as I listened to the handsome basketball player answer each question with confidence and poise. This guy might not be a pro in the wedding world, but he certainly knew how to handle the press. I had the feeling he knew how to handle a great many things. And his obvious love of the Lord came through with every answer. I found myself completely drawn in as he spoke, hanging on every word, every syllable. When he glanced my way I felt my cheeks grow warm.

Careful, girl.

I cautioned my heart to steady itself. The idea that it had fluttered in the first place alarmed me a little. But who could resist someone with this sort of charm and grace? I had a feeling the WOP-pers would change the direction of their prayers if they could meet this guy face-to-face. In the meantime, I'd just sit here and listen to his heartfelt words and allow my heart to flutter all it liked.

17

You Lay So Easy on My Mind

If you don't like the road you're walking, start paving another one.

Dolly Parton

When I arrived back at Lori-Lou's condo, I found her awash in tears. The baby had screamed all afternoon due to teething pain, Gilly had overflowed the toilet in the hall bathroom by shoving dirty panties down it, and Mariela had colored on the kitchen wall with Lori-Lou's new craft markers.

My cousin was on her knees on the floor, scrubbing the wall, tears streaming down her face. "We'll never get our deposit back now. We need that money to put down on the new house." She leaned her head against the wall and cried some more. "How are we ever going to make a fresh start if we can't move to a place with a lower payment?"

"I'm sorry, Mama!" Mariela started wailing too. After a while I felt like crying myself.

My cousin finally dried her eyes and looked up

at me with a sigh. "I'm sorry, Katie. I know this isn't much fun for you."

"Don't worry about it. Please."

A strained smile turned up the edges of her mouth. "How did it go at the bridal shop? Did you have your interview?"

"I did. It went okay. Oh, and Aunt Alva was there. And my brothers."

"Aunt Alva?" Lori-Lou paled. "Oh, yikes."

I gave my cousin a pensive look. "Anything you want to tell me?"

She threw the rag into the sink. "Look, it wasn't my fault. She caught me at a vulnerable moment. One minute we were talking about her new phone, the next she was wheedling family information out of me." A sheepish look followed. "Will you forgive me?"

I couldn't help the feelings of emotion that escaped as I said, "I already have. But you're not going to believe what happened. For whatever reason, she thinks I'm engaged to Brady James."

"Engaged to Brady James?" Lori-Lou quirked a brow. "Now there's a thought."

"It was the biggest mix-up ever. But just for the record, it turns out Aunt Alva's pretty great. A lot like Queenie, actually. It's so sad that they don't speak because they'd have a lot to talk about. It's weird how much they have in common."

"Okay, but let's go back. Did you say your *brothers* turned up at the shop too?"

"Yes. And we can blame your husband for that. Josh is the one who told Jasper about Brady James, so he came to see for himself."

"To meet his favorite player."

"Turned out Brady wasn't the one who ended up captivating the boys," I said. "I think they're twitterpated."

"Twitterpated?" She took a seat at the breakfast table and reached for her coffee cup.

"Dahlia, Twiggy, and Crystal."

"Ooh. Wow, that was fast."

"No kidding. And get this—the last thing I heard, Aunt Alva took all six of them out to lunch at a Mexican restaurant. Weirdest thing ever."

"Going out to lunch sounds wonderful." Lori-Lou sighed. "Doing anything grown-up sounds wonderful. Shoot, I'd give my right eye just to go grocery shopping by myself." Her eyes flooded with tears.

"I'll make you a deal, Lori-Lou. Tomorrow morning I'll watch the kids and you can go to the grocery store alone. Take all the time you need."

"Seriously?"

"You bet. As long as you promise to buy some of those kiddy yogurt things I loved so much."

"You know those are for toddlers, right?"

"Who cares? I loved 'em."

This got a smile out of my cousin, one of the first I'd seen all day. We ended up having a great conversation after that, but it was interrupted by a phone call, this time on my cell. I glanced down and saw *Cosmopolitan Bridal* on the screen, so I answered it right away, thinking Dahlia must be calling about my dress. A male voice greeted me instead.

"Hey, Katie, this is Brady James."

For whatever reason, my heart skipped a beat when I heard his name. "Brady." I released a slow breath and tried to figure out what to say next. I needed to address what had happened today at the shop, after all. "Hey, listen, about what my aunt Alva said today . . . I hope you don't think I told her any of that? She's just . . . confused."

"Well, she's getting up there in years. It happens."

"True."

"I won't lie, it kind of threw me that she thought we were a couple, but my grandmother got like that in her golden years too. If she ever says it again, should I just play along? That's what people say you should do with folks who have memory loss. It stirs up trouble to argue with them."

"I don't really know what to tell you about that," I said. "To be honest, I don't know her well enough to speculate."

"Well, I'm calling with an idea. After you left today, Jordan and I went to lunch. He thinks you're really great, by the way, and he loved your answers to his questions about the dress."

"Aw, really?"

Out of the corner of my eye I caught a glimpse of Lori-Lou staring at me. Nosy poke! I turned away from her to focus on Brady.

"Yeah, and he suggested we go ahead and scope out a place for the photo shoot. Someplace that jives with the theme of the dress, so definitely country-western. I was just trying to put together some ideas for places when my mom called, asking how the interview went. She's been a little anxious, since she's so far away."

"Oh?" My heart quickened as soon as he started talking about her. Maybe Madge had told her the truth about me.

"I told her it went great and she was thrilled. But she loved the idea of settling on a place for the photo shoot. She suggested some practice shots."

"Do we really have to do that?" I asked. "I've never been very photogenic."

"Are you kidding me? That gorgeous hair? Those freckles? That great smile?" He cleared his throat. "Sorry. Anyway, I'm guessing you're very photogenic. Why are you so hard on yourself?"

"I . . ." I couldn't find the words to explain. If I told him about the rejection I was currently facing, he'd know everything. And if he knew everything . . . Hmm.

Maybe that would be a good thing. Maybe I'd be off the hook and wouldn't have to go through with the photo shoot after all.

"I was thinking of the stockyard," Brady said. "Ever been there?"

"Once, several years ago. They have a cattle drive?"

"Every day at eleven. My mother thought it might be fun to photograph you there, since your wedding is going to be country chic. That's the theme you said, right?"

"Well, it's what I like, sure. And it matches the Loretta Lynn dress."

"Perfect. What about your fiancé?"

I felt sick as Brady spoke those words. "What about my fiancé?" I asked.

"Doesn't he like the country chic thing?"

I sighed. "I kind of think Casey is burnt out on country living. He's more of a big-city kind of guy at the moment." *Tulsa, to be precise.*

"Oh, interesting. Well, the stockyard is perfect for both of you then. It's in Fort Worth, right in the heart of the city, but it's still got that country flair. Do you think maybe Casey would like to join us there? It would be great to meet him in person before he comes in for his tux fitting. And who knows? Maybe Jordan will want to get him in the cover shot. You never know."

"N-no." I shook my head. "He, um, he's actually out of the state on business right now."

"Oh, bummer. Well, I guess I'll have to meet him later on."

"Guess so."

"So, back to my original idea. What are you doing tomorrow?"

"Tomorrow?" I looked at Lori-Lou. "Sorry, but I just volunteered to watch the kids in the morning."

"Ah. I was hoping to steal you away to find the perfect spot."

"Steal me away?"

"He wants to steal you away?" Lori-Lou's eyes widened. "Ooh, this is getting good."

I shook my head and put my finger to my lips, hoping she would shush before Brady heard.

He didn't seem to notice. "If you're free in the afternoon, that works for me. I'd like to take you up to the stockyard to see if we can find some spots for the photo shoot. Would that be okay?"

Lori-Lou mouthed, "Is. He. Asking. You. Out?"

I shook my head and responded with, "Of course not!"

"Of course not?" Brady sounded dejected. "You don't want to go?"

"Oh, I wasn't talking to you, sorry." I narrowed my gaze at Lori-Lou as she tried to interject something else. "Maybe I can work it out."

"You can!" Lori-Lou reached for my phone and turned on the speaker button so she could listen in. "You totally can."

"I'd love to go with you, Brady." I pulled the phone out of my cousin's hand.

Lori-Lou let out a squeal. "I know! Let's all go!

It sounds like the perfect way to spend the day."

"I'm sorry? Was that you?" Brady sounded confused.

"It's me, Lori-Lou," my cousin responded in a singsong voice. "I don't really need Katie to babysit. She was just being nice. I'd rather go with you guys to the stockyard. It's one of my favorite places."

"That's great," Brady said.

"The kids will love the stockyard. And I've got a great eye for photography. I'll help you two find the perfect spot, and I'll even snap the pictures."

"The kids?" Brady appeared to hesitate. "So, everyone's coming?"

"Sure! We'll make a day of it. And like I said, I'm great with the camera, so maybe we can do some practice shots. Maybe I can bring my wedding dress for Katie to wear. It'd swallow her alive, but oh well."

"No thank you." I shook my head. "Let's skip the dress."

"Whatever." Lori-Lou sounded hurt that I'd rejected her dress, but I couldn't picture myself showing up in public wearing someone else's gown.

"Brady, I'd love to go," I said. "And it sounds like we're bringing the whole crew. You okay with that?"

"Sure."

I couldn't tell if he was just being polite or

really wanted Lori-Lou and the kids there, but we went ahead and set our plans in motion, agreeing to meet in the back parking lot—wherever that was—at 10:15 the next day.

I could hardly sleep that night as I thought about meeting up with Brady. Doing so would finally give me the perfect opportunity—away from Madge—to tell him that I couldn't go through with the photo shoot or take the dress. He would be disappointed, sure, but maybe he would understand my situation if I presented it carefully.

The following morning Lori-Lou awoke not feeling well. On top of that, her car wouldn't start. I offered to drive, which meant we had to transfer car seats into my Cadillac. Mariela was particularly whiny and not thrilled with the idea of going to the stockyard. By the time we reached the parking lot, I realized why. The poor kid lost her cookies—er, breakfast—all over the backseat of my car. Minutes later, her mother joined her.

Just about the time Brady arrived, Lori-Lou had put in a call to Josh to come and take them all back home. She made profuse apologies to Brady. His response? Ever the gentleman, he offered to chauffeur them back to her place.

"No, you guys will miss the cattle drive." Lori-Lou leaned against my car, looking a little green around the gills. "We'll be fine."

"You sure?" he asked.

"Yeah. We always recover from these things quickly, trust me." She proved it by getting sick once more, right in front of us. Lovely.

Josh showed up about fifteen minutes later to cart his sick family home. Turned out he had the bug too. They left moments later, kids crying, Lori-Lou holding her stomach, and Josh looking like he needed to crawl under the covers.

This left Brady and me alone to clean out my car—ick!—and tour the stockyard without the others. I didn't mind that part one little bit. From the look of relief on his face, he didn't either. We started on the far end of the venue, near the parking lot. Just about the time we made it to the first row of shops, we realized the cattle drive was about to begin. People began to gather along the edge of the street to wait. A young man approached Brady and tapped him on the arm.

"Hey, you're Brady James!"

"The one and only." He flashed a welcoming smile.

"I've been praying for you, man. How's the knee?"

The two of them engaged in a conversation, which ended with the total stranger praying for Brady right then and there. Well, after he asked for Brady's autograph.

On and on the people came, each with a request to sign this or that. I couldn't help but admire Brady as I watched him in action with his fans, who approached him as if he were a long-lost friend.

Long-lost friend.

As I gazed up at Brady's kind face, as I took in the joy in his eyes while he talked to total strangers about his life, I realized I felt like I'd found that very thing . . . in him. And as he looked my way, offering a boyish smile, I had the feeling he'd found a friend in me too. Why that felt so good, I could not say. After all, I had lots of friends in the little town of Fairfield. But having one in the big city made me feel more at home than I would have dreamed possible.

In fact, I felt so at home that I might just have to stay for a while.

18

My Past Brought Me to You

You can be the moon and still be jealous of the stars.

Gary Allan

A familiar old-school country song blared from the overhead speakers as the crowd along Main Street thickened. Brady's fan club dissipated, likely overwhelmed by the noise and chaos. We were finally left to ourselves.

"You want to watch the cattle drive?" Brady asked. "I think you'll like it."

"Sounds like fun." We eased our way into a spot near the street. Unfortunately we landed right next to an overly romantic couple. They started out holding hands. A few minutes later they were smooching, right there in broad daylight. Awkward.

The crowd continued to press in around us, which pushed Brady a bit closer to me. I didn't mind. His yummy cologne tickled my nostrils. At least I thought it was his cologne. With people packed in like sardines, who could tell?

I glanced up at him to find that his gaze was

already on me. He looked away, his cheeks turning red. Of course, that might have something to do with the heat.

"Brady, I wanted to apologize for yesterday. I know it was all so . . . chaotic. You guys probably aren't used to that kind of family drama at the shop."

"Oh, we see our share of drama, trust me. That was a little different, though. Your brothers seem pretty nice."

I couldn't help but snort at that one.

"Having your family around is a real blessing, Katie. But I'm not telling you anything you don't already know."

I looked up at him and smiled. "My brothers are a pain in the neck, but I adore them. Even Jasper. He's a challenge because he's always wanting to leave home."

"Leave Fairfield?"

"Yeah. It's hard on my parents to hear him talk like that."

"So they don't think anyone will ever want to leave?"

I shrugged. "Most people adore our town. They get so rooted that the idea of going anyplace else seems ludicrous. You know?"

"I've only ever lived in the big city, so I guess I can't really relate to that part. But life is an adventure."

It was an adventure, all right, especially if you

happened to be a six-foot-four pro basketball player in a large crowd. Another round of folks wanting autographs showed up just then. Brady willingly obliged, and even answered a few too-personal-for-comfort questions about his knee. Man, did people get in his business, or what?

When the last of the autograph seekers turned away, I felt free to respond to what he'd said about life being an adventure. "My dad isn't all that adventurous," I explained. "He runs a hardware store. But what he lacks in adventure, he makes up for in loyalty."

"Loyalty to family is important." A thoughtful look settled into Brady's eyes. "If I ever understood that, it's now."

"True." I thought about my parents, my brothers, and Queenie. "But how will you ever know what you're truly called to do if you're only ever doing what family members tell you to do?"

I saw what could only be described as tenderness in his eyes as he responded, "I'm the only son my mom has. The only child at all. She needs me. And I'm going to be there for her, even if it hurts."

"Does it?" I asked. "Hurt, I mean."

"Wedding gowns aren't my first love," he said. "But they're growing on me." He gave me a little wink and my heart fluttered.

"Ha. Well, you're being more adventurous than you know because you've stepped outside

of the box. Outside of your comfort zone."
"True, that."
"The problem with my family is that they never step outside of their comfort zone. My dad is as regular as a clock. And he doesn't seem to be able to function without me." I pulled out my phone to prove my point. "I've had three texts from him just since we got here, asking random questions about where things are in the store. Sometimes I wonder who's the parent and who's the child. He depends on me for so much."
"Yep. I get it. Trust me."
Brady and I both grew quiet. Not that anyone around us would notice our silence. The music continued to blare, and at the end of the road I could see a flurry of activity.
A voice came over the loudspeaker announcing the start of the cattle drive. Seconds later, the whole atmosphere came alive with excitement as cowboys on horses led the cattle down the middle of Main Street.
"Just like something straight out of the Old West," Brady called out above the din of horses' hooves clip-clopping along the road and cows making that strange lowing noise.
I nodded, then turned my attention to the animals passing by. This would be the perfect place for a photo shoot. If I happened to be getting married. Which I wasn't. Still, I could see myself wearing the Loretta Lynn dress in this setting,

with cowboys on horses in the background and longhorns lumbering by. Obviously Brady could see it too. A couple of different times he leaned over to give me ideas for how and where we could get some great shots.

When the cattle drive ended we walked through an area with quaint shops, including a large old-fashioned candy store. We stopped inside and I squealed when I saw the taffies. "Ooh, I have to buy some of these. I love them."

"Here, let me get them for you, Katie. I love 'em too. We can share."

I felt my cheeks grow warm as he grabbed a bag and handed it to me. "Fill 'er up, kid."

I did. In fact, I put so many taffies in the bag that he ended up handing me a second one. When we reached the register, the clerk engaged Brady in a lengthy conversation about basketball while he paid for the candy. As they gabbed . . . and gabbed . . . and gabbed . . . I nibbled on taffy. Okay, more than nibbled. I ate four pieces. Brady didn't seem to mind.

When he wrapped up the conversation with the store clerk, Brady signed a couple more autographs for two little boys in the store, and then we walked back outside. He reached into the bag to grab a piece of taffy, unwrapped it, and popped it into his mouth.

I found myself mesmerized by him. "Okay, I just have one question, Brady James."

"Yeah?" He gave me a curious look. "What's that?"

"Are you always this nice?"

"Nice?" He gave me a funny look. "I'm just being myself."

A flood of emotions washed over me as I thought about how humble he was. "Well, don't ever stop. I mean it. You're a great guy, whether you're playing basketball or helping a girl find the perfect wedding dress."

"Right now I think I'd rather be helping the girl out than playing ball. Not sure my knee's ready just yet."

"Right." I sighed. "I feel for you. I really do. I wish your agent was more understanding. I know it's none of my business, but I wanted to give him a piece of my mind yesterday."

"Stan." Brady shook his head. "That guy wears me out, but I know he's got my best interest at heart. He's totally in my business, but then again, I pay him to be. That's what agents are for."

"I know what it's like to have people in your business, trust me. My family doesn't know the first thing about boundaries. Well, all but Aunt Alva. She puts the word *distant* in the phrase *distant relatives*."

"What do you mean?" He popped another piece of taffy in his mouth and gestured for me to sit on a nearby bench.

"I mean, until yesterday I hadn't seen the woman

in years." I took a seat on the bench and he settled into the spot next to me. "Since I was a kid."

"Wow. Well, she's definitely something, isn't she?" He grinned and tossed the taffy paper back into the bag. "I liked her, though."

"Me too. But I think she might be a little delusional. She's a big fan of yours, that's for sure."

"That's what makes her delusional?" Brady quirked a brow.

"No, silly." I jabbed him with my elbow. "I just think she's hoping you'll marry into the family so she can get season tickets to the games." I gave him a playful smile.

Goodness. Was this guy easy to flirt with, or what?

"Good to know I still have a few fans out there. But I guess the only way we can convince her I'm not your fiancé is to let her see you marry the real one. That ought to do the trick, right?"

"Right." Perfect opportunity to segue into the truth. "Since you brought up Casey, there's something I need to tell you about him."

"Oh, I already know. Madge told me."

"She—she did?"

"Yep. She told me that he's a ball player. Or at least he used to be. Baseball, right?" When I nodded, Brady lit into a lengthy story about how he'd played Little League as a kid. At some point along the way I got caught up in his story and gave up on trying to tell him the truth about Casey. On and on Brady went, talking about what it was like growing up with a dad who loved sports.

I wasn't sure how to broach the subject, but something he said made me curious, so I dared to ask. "What's your dad like now? Does he come to your games?"

"My dad . . ." Brady's words trailed off, and I could read the pain in his eyes. "He passed away when I was twelve. Killed in a car accident."

"Oh, Brady." My heart skipped a beat and I felt like a heel for bringing it up. "I'm so sorry. I had no idea."

"Please don't be sorry." He gave me a sympathetic look. "My memories of him are all good. He was a great dad. The kind of guy who laughed —in a good way—at everything. Positive, upbeat guy. And a dreamer too. Always reaching for the stars and telling me I could do the same."

"Sounds a lot like his son."

If I didn't know any better, I'd say Brady's eyes misted over as I spoke the words. "That's quite a compliment. Thank you."

"You're welcome." I grew silent for a couple of minutes as I pondered the depth of emotion I'd seen in his eyes. "Did your mom start her business while he was still alive?" I asked after a while.

"No." Brady shook his head. "She started about a year after he passed away. I think she did it to fill the time, but also to bring in income. Started with a couple of friends asking her to make their gowns, and it kind of went from there. Her big break came about ten years ago when a local designer saw one of her gowns and approached her about doing a show with him. Next thing you know she had her own line. Then she had a write-up in *Texas Bride*. Then Madge came to her and offered to help fund the shop."

"Whoa, whoa." I put my hand up. "Madge funded the shop?" No way. Simple, frumpy Madge?

"Yep." Brady chuckled. "You probably would never have guessed that, right? She doesn't come across as a woman with a lot of money. Not pretentious at all. But she's definitely the pocketbook behind the project."

"Wow."

"Trust me, the shop has done so well that Madge's investment has been paid back several times over. Both women have done very well for themselves."

"I'd say."

"And Mom has helped a lot of other people along the way. Dahlia was in a pretty low place when she came to us. Crystal too. Her parents had just passed away in a house fire, and she'd moved to Dallas to try to get past the pain. She had worked in retail but never a bridal shop, so hiring her was a bit of a stretch."

"Wow, Brady."

"Yeah, my mom has always known how to love people through hard times. It's a gift."

I paused to absorb everything I'd just learned. "I'm sure your dad would've been so proud of her."

Brady grew silent, and I could see his jaw tense as emotion took hold. "He was always the first to sing her praises. And I have no doubt he'd be crooning day and night if he could see all that she's accomplished."

"He'd be so proud of you too." I reached to put my hand on Brady's arm . . . his very, very muscular arm. "Was he a basketball fan?"

Brady's eyes took on a faraway look. "You have no idea. From the time I was a kid we shot hoops together. Every time I aim for that basket—whether I'm in front of a huge crowd or just on the court by myself—I picture him standing next to me, telling me I can do it." He grew silent. "Only, now I can't do it."

"Because of your knee?"

Brady nodded. "Yeah. I mean, the doctor says I can go back in time, but right now it just seems impossible."

"What would your dad say?"

He appeared to be thinking. "He would tell me to pray about it and then wait on God's timing. He'd remind me of the Scripture about how with God all things are possible."

"And that would be true," I said.

"Right. Point is, my dad was a great guy, and he would've been very proud of the fact that I've made a name for myself as a player." Brady's cheeks flushed and he quickly added, "A *basketball* player. Not a *player* player."

"Of course." I couldn't help the giggle that escaped.

Brady grew more serious. "But he would have been more proud that I've stepped in to help Mom here so that she can fulfill her dreams in Paris. He was so proud of her and wanted her to shine. I can't help but think he's smiling down on me as he watches me"—Brady shrugged—"get swallowed up by a world of taffeta and tulle."

"You're getting more and more comfortable in that world, and that's okay. Maybe he would want you to know that."

"Yep. I am feeling pretty comfortable." He slipped his arm across the back of the bench, and I fought the temptation to lean into him. Brady wasn't the only one who felt comfortable. Why I felt so at home around this guy, I couldn't say. He towered above me—my five-foot-two frame completely dwarfed by his six-foot-four one—but he always seemed to make me feel ten feet tall.

And right now, as we stuck our hands in the taffy bag at the exact same moment . . . as our fingers touched, sending tingles all the way down to my toes . . . ten feet tall felt just about right.

19

My Shoes Keep Walking Back to You

I'm a romantic, and we romantics are more sensitive to the way people feel. We love more, and we hurt more. When we're hurt, we hurt for a long time.

Freddy Fender

Our morning at the stockyard stretched across the lunch hour. Brady insisted on buying me lunch at a barbecue place that turned out to be almost as yummy as Sam's. The conversation went really well until the end of the meal when he brought up Casey.

Brady took a swig from his glass of tea and then leaned back in his chair. "Tell me about your fiancé, Katie. Where did you meet him?"

"Is this for the article?" I asked. "Because if it is, I'd rather not."

"No, not for the article." He gazed at me from across the table, a pained expression on his face. "I'm not all business, you know."

"I-I know." I gave a deep sigh. "I'm sorry, Brady. I have a lot on my mind today."

"Like what? Stressing over the photo shoot?"

"Not really so much that."

"Your wedding?" Brady grabbed the bill, then pulled out his wallet.

"No, trust me. Not that."

"It's coming together like you'd hoped, then?" He gave me an inquisitive look as he placed a credit card with the bill.

I shook my head. "I'm not saying that either."

"Is there anything I can do to help?"

"You and your mom are doing a lot already. Too much, really."

"Never too much for you, Katie." As Brady spoke these words, he reached across the table as if he wanted to take hold of my hands. He stopped just before touching me. "I-I'm sorry."

"Sorry for what you've done for me?" I asked.

"No. Not at all." He pulled his hands back and passed the bill off to the waiter, who'd appeared at his side. "You've been really easy to do for. And I'm glad—really, really glad—that you're the one who won the contest. We wouldn't have gotten to know you any other way. So I'm grateful."

There was a genuineness in his voice that touched me to the core. For whatever reason, his kindness stirred up emotions in me that I hadn't felt before. In that moment, I knew what I had to do.

"Brady, there's something I need to tell you. It's really important."

"Of course. What is it, Katie?" I could read the

concern in his eyes, which did little to squelch the gnawing in my gut.

"It's about my wedding."

He put his hand up. "I might work in a wedding shop, but I need to give a little disclaimer that I stink at wedding stuff. So if you're looking for my advice or my input, it's probably going to stink. I might just ruin your big day."

"Oh, trust me, you're not going to be the one to ruin my big day." I sighed. "It's too late anyway."

"Too late? What do you mean?"

The waiter returned with the check and Brady glanced at it, took his credit card, and signed the receipt.

"Brady, I just feel like I should tell you that—"

His cell phone rang, and he groaned as he glanced down at it. "I'm sorry, Katie. It's my mom. She knows we're out looking for the perfect site for photos, and I think she's anxious." He shrugged and answered the phone. Seconds later, the two were engaged in a lengthy conversation about various places at the stockyard that would be good for pictures.

A short time later Brady ended the call and then leaned my way. "I haven't been very good company, I'm afraid. And I guess that call doesn't really prove what I said earlier, that I'm not all business."

"It's okay," I said. "It really is."

We could talk later. Or not. Why I felt like

baring my soul to this handsome basketball player, I could not say. I barely knew the guy. Still, he deserved to know the truth. Maybe if I could get him to understand my situation, he could help me figure out a plan to let his mother know before the photo shoot.

"I promise not to ruin the rest of the afternoon with business stuff. Where would you like to go next?"

"You're not ruining my day at all, Brady. I've really enjoyed being with you." And I had. More than I'd imagined. "And I know the perfect place we can go. My country girl roots are about to be exposed."

"Oh?" He rose.

"Yep. It's the perfect place." I stood and faced him. "The petting zoo."

"The petting zoo?" He chuckled. "Now, that's a first."

"Do you mind? I'd love to."

"Don't mind a bit."

His leisurely manner continued as we walked down Main Street toward the pen where the animals were kept. At the entrance we bought some feed for the goats and then went inside the covered area.

"We're the only adults in here." Brady laughed as he looked around. "That's a telling sign, don't you think?"

"Maybe, but it doesn't matter. I love animals. I

miss them." I knelt down in front of the first cage and dumped some of the feed into my palm, then passed it off to a baby goat.

"Whatever you say." Brady followed my lead and tried to do the same, but a goat snatched the feed cup straight out of his hand.

"Ha. Looks like you're not as fast in the pen as you are on the court."

"Hey now."

"I'm serious. When you hang out with animals, you've got to think quick."

"Obviously." Brady stuck his hand inside my cup and grabbed some feed, then passed it off to a baby goat, which licked his hand clean. "See there? I'm a fast learner."

"You're good with animals." And people. No one could deny this guy was great with people.

I knelt down for some time, the weirdest emotions rippling over me as I tended to the goats. I was struck by feelings I hadn't experienced for a while—homesickness, and heartsickness too. A lump rose in my throat.

"Casey has goats," I whispered.

"Casey?" Brady tried to dump more of my feed into his hand but missed. It landed in a clump on a goat's nose. "Oh yeah. The fiancé."

I sighed. "The fiancé. Only . . . not."

"Not? He doesn't really have goats, you mean?"

"Oh, he has goats. Four of them." Tears sprang to my eyes. "I miss them."

"The goats or the fiancé?" Brady set the feed cup down on a post and stared at me.

"All of them." Being around these animals had stirred up far too many emotions. When I shut my eyes I could see myself standing on Casey's property. Running in the field. Playing hide-and-seek as kids. The scents, the noises of the animals in the background. All of it melded together in my memory, in my heart. And in that moment, though I could never have predicted it, tears flooded willy-nilly down my face.

"Let's get you out of here." Brady's voice startled me back to reality. "I think the scent of the goats is getting to you." He helped me stand and then slipped my arm through his to walk me out of the petting zoo, back to Main Street. I didn't say a word the whole time. I couldn't, not with all of the sniffling going on. We finally came to a stop at a lamppost near the parking lot. Brady reached into his pocket and came out with a handkerchief, which I used to blow my nose.

"I don't know what happened back there, Katie," he said. "But we're not coming back to the stockyard for the photo shoot. This place is obviously too emotional for you."

"I'm sorry. I really am. I just don't think I can do it, Brady."

"The photo shoot, you mean?"

"No. Well, yes. The whole thing. All of it. The dress, the photo shoot, the—" I stopped myself before saying anything else. “I tried to tell Madge, but she wouldn’t listen. This isn’t what you think it is. I’m not who you think I am.”

He stared into my eyes with the sweetest, kindest expression on his face. “I know exactly who you are. You’re Katie. From Fairfield.” A little wink followed as he added, “Enamored by goats.”

“Right. But the rest of it . . . it’s not what you think.”

“Katie, I’ve had the strangest feeling all along that you don’t like the wedding dress design. Is that it?”

“Oh, I totally love the design. It’s not that at all.”

“You’re not happy with the way the interview went yesterday?”

“The interview was a farce.”

“A farce?” He shook his head. “Explain.”

“It was a farce. I’m a farce. The wedding . . . is a farce. And the fiancé?” I pinched my eyes shut. “He’s the biggest farce of all.”

“Wait. Are you telling me that you’re not really engaged to Casey Lawson?”

My nerves really kicked in now. I shook my head. “I . . . I’m not engaged to Casey Lawson.”

“He broke your heart?” Brady’s jaw twitched. “If he did, I’ll hunt him down and—”

“It’s not like that.” I paced the sidewalk. “I mean, he did break my heart, but not today. It was a couple weeks ago. Before I ever met you.”

“Huh?” Brady’s confusion was evident by the

expression on his face. "What are you saying?"

"I'm saying that he broke up with me right after I found out I'd won the dress. The engagement was off—really, it didn't even exist at all. I was never going to marry Casey."

Brady scratched his head. "Of course you were going to marry him."

I put my hand up. "Let me rephrase that. In my imagination I had the whole thing planned out. The entire wedding was strategized from beginning to end. I could tell you anything you wanted to know about my big day, but I couldn't tell you anything about what my life would be like after that. I planned for one thing and one thing only . . . and it didn't happen."

"It's really not going to happen? Is that what you're saying? No wedding?" Brady's expression shifted from concern to frustration. "Please tell me this is some kind of sick joke so that I don't think you were just taking advantage of my mom."

"I never wanted to take advantage of her . . . or you. And I do hope to get married someday." I glanced at his face. The clenched jaw clued me in that he was angry. Who could blame him? "I'd love to wear the dress your mom designed for me. But it's not going to happen anytime soon. Casey . . ." The tears came in earnest now. "Casey took off for Oklahoma."

"Oklahoma?" Wrinkles formed between Brady's brows.

"Where the wind comes sweepin' down the plain." I gave a deep sigh. "And I'm just plain stuck being a wannabe bride with an MIA groom." My voice began to quiver again. "Only, I didn't know he was going to be MIA. I was sure Casey was the one. So sure that I made plans as if he'd already popped the question."

"Wait. You're saying he never did?" Brady raked his fingers through his hair.

"Not technically. But don't you see? The point is, I was so busy planning for my fairy-tale wedding that I overlooked my very real life." Tears came with abandon now as I felt the release of my words. "I'm an idiot. I wanted the wedding. I wanted it so bad that I entered the contest thinking it was inevitable. Only, it wasn't. And . . . he wasn't. And . . . we weren't. Nothing was inevitable except the part where I came out looking and feeling like a fool. I wanted the dress. I wanted the church. I wanted the invitations."

"Wanted it so much that you didn't mind putting my mom on the spot?" A flash of anger sparked in his eyes.

"Trust me, I never wanted to hurt her. I came that first Saturday just to tell her I couldn't go through with it. But something—someone—stopped me."

"Someone?" He gave me a knowing look. "Let me guess. Madge?"

"Yeah."

"So, no wedding and no groom . . . but she still wanted you to take the dress?"

"You've got the picture. She didn't want to get your mom worked up before leaving for Paris. She thought it would be better to let sleeping dogs lie."

"Do you mind if I ask what you planned to do with this dress if you weren't going to wear it?"

"I don't know." I squeezed my eyes shut and willed myself not to cry. "Sometimes I think the whole wedding thing was just a big fantasy, something I dreamed about but was never meant to have."

"You wanted the wedding, or you wanted the groom?"

A lump rose in my throat and I tried to speak around it. "I wanted him too."

"Wanted . . . as in past tense?" For whatever reason, the hopeful look in Brady's eyes gave me the courage to speak my mind.

"Wanted. Past tense." I paused. "Casey is a great guy. He would've looked great in the tux. And he would've been smashing in the wedding pictures. And if you want the truth, I'm sure he would've made a great dad to our kids, even if he is a Presbyterian."

"Wait. What does being Presbyterian have to do with anything?"

"I have no idea, really, but it factors in. Ask Queenie."

"Well, if I ever meet her, I will."

"Point is, he wasn't the right guy for me. The wedding was never supposed to happen. It's so obvious now. I had to come all the way to Dallas to see what I couldn't see in Fairfield. I was just blinded by . . ."

"The idea?"

I sighed. "Too many years reading bridal magazines."

"Don't let Jordan Singer hear you say that!" Brady rested his hand on my shoulder and smiled.

"Jordan Singer." I hesitated. "The photo shoot. I-I can't do it. You see what I mean? How can I go on the cover of a bridal magazine wearing a dress that was never meant for me?"

Brady didn't respond for a moment. Instead, he started pacing. And pacing. And pacing some more. His expression shifted several times—from confusion to frustration to resignation. Finally he came to a stop in front of me, a more peaceful look on his face.

"Okay, it's clear we've got some things to figure out. But maybe Madge was right. Maybe you should still take the dress." Brady shrugged. "Just because the fiancé wasn't the perfect fit doesn't mean the dress won't be. And just because the wedding isn't pending doesn't mean you're not going to someday be a beautiful bride. I say you put on the wedding dress, hold your head up high, and march into that photo shoot with a smile."

"You sound just like Madge."

"Well, for once I agree with her."

"You do?"

"I do. So what if the timing isn't right? Take the dress anyway. It's yours. We want you to have it. I want you to have it."

"You've been too good to me, Brady. You've gone above and beyond." I tried to swallow the ever-growing lump in my throat. "This has nothing to do with Cosmopolitan Bridal. Or your mom. Or you." I put my hand on his arm. "You've all been nothing but wonderful. But I can't take this dress, Brady. I can't."

"You can and you will. Jordan is coming back with a photographer on July 15. Dahlia's working like crazy on the dress to meet that deadline. Don't let her work be in vain, okay? You're going to put on that dress and look like a million bucks."

"But that's the point. I might look like a million bucks in a dress that I don't deserve, but I'll feel like a loser. If Casey saw me standing there, dressed in that gorgeous Loretta Lynn gown, he'd—"

"He'd feel like an idiot for letting you go."

Brady's words threw me for a loop. They also gave me the first bit of encouragement I'd felt in quite some time.

"You think?" I whispered.

"No, Katie." Brady grabbed my hand and gave it a comforting squeeze. "I don't think. I *know*."

20

Miss Being Mrs.

As a remedy to life in society I would suggest the big city. Nowadays, it is the only desert within our means.

Albert Camus

Two weeks after our trip to the stockyard, I learned that Dahlia had made enough progress on the dress for me to come in for my first official fitting. When I tried to argue the point with Brady, he reminded me that I'd won the contest fair and square and had every right to try on the dress because it was meant for me. So I showed up on the last Tuesday in June to take a peek at the Loretta Lynn gown in its earliest stage of production.

Dahlia brought it to the front of the store, where she placed it on a hanger for all to see. She hadn't added any of the ruffles or embellishments yet, but from what I could see, it was shaping up to be the prettiest gown in the place. Exactly my taste. Was it really meant for me? My heart said yes, but my conscience debated the issue.

"You want to try it on for me, Katie?" Dahlia asked. "It's going to look great on you."

Before I had a chance to respond, however, Dahlia was distracted with a customer. "Ooh, incoming Barbie Bride," she whispered.

"Barbie Bride?" I glanced up at the front of the store and saw a gorgeous brunette entering. She looked like a runway model. By now I should be used to all of these labels that Dahlia and the others placed on their customers, but I was not.

"Check out the hair, the makeup." Dahlia whistled. "She's practically perfect in every way."

"Practically perfect in every way is Mary Poppins, not Barbie," I argued.

"Well, physically perfect. You know the type I'm talking about." She gestured to her chest. "Curvaceous. Buxom."

"Buxom?" Crystal giggled. "Is that a re-ul word?"

"Of course it's real." Twiggy rolled her eyes. "Don't you see any buxom women in Atlanta?"

"Duh." Crystal pointed to her own chest and we all laughed. She headed off to wait on the new customer, who'd come into the shop for a tiara. Ironic.

"I'm sure you see a lot of Barbie doll types come through the bridal shop," I said after she left.

"Maybe not as many as you think," Madge said. "Mostly we just get normal-shaped girls. With hips. And bellies. And saggy boobs. But you know the interesting part? Put those girls in a wedding gown and they look perfect."

"Speaking of perfect, let's get you in that gown,

Katie. Okay?" Dahlia clasped her hands together and grinned. "I can't wait to see it. And we have to take pictures to send Nadia. She called this morning and gave me specific instructions on the angles of the photos. She wants to see my seam work. Do you mind?"

"As long as no one else sees the pictures, I guess it would be okay." I would flip out if anyone from home saw me in the gown.

The thought had no sooner flitted through my mind than the front door of the shop opened and who should walk in but my brother Jasper. Again. He took one look at Crystal, who was working at the front counter, and headed her way. I stood transfixed, watching all of this take place. He clearly hadn't noticed me or, if he had, was ignoring me.

"There's one of those handsome brothers of yours," Dahlia said. "Come back for another visit, I see."

"Looks like it. Give me a minute, Dahlia. I want to talk to him before I try on the dress, okay?"

"Sure."

I walked up to the counter and stood next to Jasper. He continued to gab with Crystal but didn't seem to notice me. I cleared my throat. Nothing. I coughed. When Crystal headed off to tend to a customer, he finally looked my way.

"Hey, Katie. What are you doing here?"

"I could ask you the same thing. Jasper, you do

realize this is a bridal shop, right? A place where women come to buy their wedding dresses?"

"Well, yeah. I can see that." He glanced around with a horrified look on his face. "Promise you won't tell Mama I was here?"

"Only if you make the same promise."

"Trust me, mum's the word."

Mum—er, Mom—was the word, all right.

"And if you happen to see me in a wedding gown, you won't ask any questions?"

"Wedding gown? Are you getting married? To Casey?" My brother's expression hardened.

"I didn't say that."

"Then what Alva said is true? About you and Brady being engaged?" He leaned against the counter.

"Definitely not. He's a great guy, but I'm just getting to know him."

"Then I'm confused. You're going to wear a wedding dress?"

"Yes. I'm going to be modeling it for a magazine cover."

"Oh, okay. Why didn't you say so? They're paying you to model gowns now?"

"Um, no. But close." I decided to change the subject. "Isn't Pop missing you at the store?"

"Told him I was coming into Dallas to pick up some supplies. Nothing unusual about that. I come to Dallas all the time to get supplies for the business. You know that."

"Well, yes, but—"

"Beau is holding down the fort until I get back."

"Beau?" I laughed. "Beau? Working?"

Jasper nodded. "I know, it's hard to believe. But something's grabbed ahold of him over the past several days. He's a changed man. I've never seen him act so . . . responsible."

"Um, Jasper?" I pointed to the door, where Beau and Dewey stood side by side. "Looks like you might want to rephrase all of that."

"No way." Jasper slapped himself on the forehead. "He promised he'd cover for me at the store. Pop's gonna flip."

I took a few steps toward my brothers but didn't get to them fast enough. Twiggy beat me. She offered to show Beau the latest order of tuxedos, fresh in from Paris. Like Beau gave a rip about tuxedos. Still, my youngest brother trotted off behind her.

Jasper had been right about one thing—something had definitely grabbed ahold of Beau. Her name was Twiggy.

And Dewey? He'd come to Dallas for one reason and one reason only . . . and she happened to be standing next to me. I watched as Dahlia's face turned the prettiest shade of crimson when Dewey talked to her. Good grief. I needed to get this train back on track, and quick.

"Dewey, I hate to be the bearer of bad news,

but Dahlia and I have to take care of something in the back."

"You do?" Dewey looked perplexed by this. "Like what?"

"Oh, don't worry about us," Dahlia said. "You just look around the shop and I'll be back out in a few minutes. Don't go anywhere, okay?"

"Oh, I won't." Dewey gave her a little wink and she giggled.

We had just turned to walk back to the studio when the door to the shop opened again. Dahlia stopped in her tracks, eyes widening in obvious terror.

"What is it?" I asked.

"Sybil. Incoming." Madge's voice sounded from behind us. She reached for her walkie-talkie and whispered the words again: "Sybil. Incoming."

"Sybil?" I asked. "Her name's Sybil?"

"Um, no." Madge shook her head. "Her name's Francine Dubois. But she's definitely a Sybil."

"I don't get it."

Dahlia pulled me behind a rack of gowns, her voice lowering to a hoarse whisper. "Did you ever see the old movie *Sybil*? The one about the girl with all of those personalities?"

"Don't think so."

"You never knew what she was going to do. She was . . . c-c-crazy." Dahlia could barely get the word out.

"Crazy as a loon," Madge added. "The crazy ones are harder than all the Drama Mamas and Princess Brides put together. They . . . well, you'll see."

"Not sure I want to stick around to see," I said.

"Too late." Dahlia turned me around to face the door. A fairly normal-looking woman stood near the entrance of the store. She pulled off her dark sunglasses to reveal finely plucked brows and heavily painted eyes. Crystal headed her way, offering assistance.

I shrugged. "Seems okay to me."

"Just. Wait," Dahlia whispered as she gestured for me to move out from behind the rack. "Give it ten minutes."

Fortunately—or unfortunately—it didn't take ten minutes. Judging from the minute hand on my watch, it took exactly four. Miss Sweet as Sugar flipped out on Crystal at the four-minute mark, completely changing personalities. At the five-minute mark, she began to weep uncontrollably. At the seven-minute mark, she'd dried her tears and was inviting all of us to her ceremony. At the nine-minute mark, she threatened Madge with a lawsuit.

"Oh. My. Goodness." I wanted to run for the door, afraid of what might come next.

Fortunately, Madge appeared to have a special anointing for dealing with the Sybil bride. She not only managed to talk the emotional nightmare down from the ledge but also gave her a discount on a pair of shoes. But the one who really seemed to know how to handle her best, ironically, was Brady. He somehow got her redirected when she lost it, and had her smiling by the time she left the store.

Wow.

When the Sybil incident ended, Dahlia and I were finally free to head back to the fitting room. Even as she helped me into the Loretta Lynn gown—what there was of it so far, anyway—I could tell that Dahlia would rather be out in the store, visiting with Dewey. Thankfully, my oohs and aahs must've brought her back to reality.

"You like?" she asked.

"Mm-hmm." I stared at my reflection in the mirror. Even without the embellishments—the lace, the crystals, the ruffles—the gown looked amazing. Dahlia still had a bit of work to do to get the bust to fit, but she assured me that would not be an issue. She reached for her phone and snapped several photos of me in the gown, which she planned to send to Nadia right away.

I gave a little twirl and examined myself in the mirror. The length of the train was just perfect—not too short, not too long. I could see myself walking down the aisle in this dress. Someday. If I ever found a groom.

Stop it, Katie. Just smile and say thank you. That's what Madge would want.

So I smiled. And said thank you.

Dahlia looked as if she was about to respond when Madge showed up at the fitting room door. “I hate to bother you, but we have an incoming 9-1-1.”

“Oh dear.” Dahlia looked my way, her eyes wide. “Do you mind, Katie?”

“Well, no, but what in the world—”

Dahlia took off in a hurry, with no explanation whatsoever.

“9-1-1?” I turned to Madge. “Are you calling for an ambulance?”

“Oh, no, honey. That’s not what I meant at all. A 9-1-1 is an overly emotional bride. In this case it’s a sweet girl whose father passed away just a couple of months ago. He won’t be there to walk her down the aisle, so the dress fitting is going to be an emotional roller coaster for the bride and her mother. Dahlia knows just how to handle it, trust me. She’s been through this dozens of times. One of the services we provide is counseling. It’s not on the résumé, but we do it.”

“Wow, Madge.” Tears sprang to my eyes as I thought about that poor bride and her situation.

“People think the wedding gown biz is all glitz and glam, but they don’t see the hard parts.” Madge took a seat on the cushioned bench. “We’re half counselor, half wedding gown expert, half BFF.”

"That's three halves," I said.

"Yep. Which is why it takes so many of us working together to accomplish anything. But you know what? I'm grateful for open doors."

"Open doors?"

"Sure." Her eyes filled with tears. "I never married. Never had kids to pour myself into. When these brides come in, the Lord opens a door for conversation, and sometimes—if I'm not feeling like a sourpuss—he uses me to offer a bit of encouragement."

"Oh, Madge." I slipped my arm over her shoulder. "You're a softie inside of that hard shell, aren't you?"

"Shh." She put her finger to her lips. "Don't give away my secret. Around here, folks think I'm a drill sergeant."

"One with the sweetest disposition in town." Brady's voice sounded from the hallway outside the open fitting room door.

"Better get back to work, boss." She rose and saluted him. Brady pulled her into an embrace and planted a kiss on her forehead.

"I should be the one saluting you, you know. You've got that drill sergeant act down pat."

"It's just an illusion, my boy. Just an illusion."

She headed to the front of the store, which left me alone with Brady. It felt a little odd to be standing here in a wedding gown now that the other ladies had ditched me. I couldn't even figure out how to get out of the crazy thing without their help. Not that I wanted to. I felt like a princess, and all the more when I saw the admiring look in Brady's eyes.

"You look amazing, Katie. Gorgeous."

His flattery tickled my ears and made me feel a little giddy. Just as quickly, I felt like a traitor. I pictured myself standing in Casey Lawson's kitchen as he broke up with me. The emotions of that moment flooded over me even now, and I felt the sting of tears in my eyes.

"You okay, Katie?" Brady's voice shook me out of my reverie.

"I . . . I think I'm just emotional. Hearing about that 9-1-1 bride really got to me. You guys are a lot more than a bridal shop, Brady."

"Agreed." He nodded.

"I think Madge opened my eyes. This is a ministry for all of you. It's a place to reach out to people who are going through stuff."

"That's my prayer every single day, that God will bring exactly the right people here so that we can bless them. Most of the time they end up blessing us too. Like you, Katie."

"Me?"

"Sure. Everyone has loved having you here, and you've definitely brought out the softer side of Madge." He gave me a knowing look. "Maybe you should be in the wedding business."

"You think?"

"I do!" Madge's voice sounded from outside the door. "You'd be great at it, Katie."

"See what I mean?" Brady chuckled. "Underneath that crusty exterior is a marshmallow." He leaned so close that the scent of his yummy aftershave caused my nostrils to flare. "But don't get her worked up or you'll see a completely different side of her."

"Oh, trust me, I've seen that side too. She's a tough cookie. But she reminds me of Queenie. The image she puts out there is one tough mama. On the inside, though, she's like a flower, unfolding one petal at a time."

"Madge? A flower?" Twiggy entered the room, all giggles and smiles. "That's a good one, Katie."

"Hey, I heard that." Madge popped her head in the door. "And just so you're aware, folks, I come in this place every morning smelling like a rose. A tea rose, I mean. It's my perfume." She stepped inside the room and started fussing with the laces on the back of my dress.

"How do you guys do it?" I asked.

"Do what?" Madge, Twiggy, and Brady said in unison.

"The people part. Working in the wedding business isn't just about dresses, is it?"

"It's about people," Brady said.

"And there are people of every sort who come through that door," Madge added.

"True," Twiggy said. "There's the Dollar Store Bride—that's the one who doesn't have the money but really wants the dress."

"And the Ninja Bride—ready to take out anyone in her way," Madge chimed in.

"The Flighty Bride," Twiggy continued. "She can't make up her mind about anything."

"The Dieting Bride." Madge groaned. "She's the one who really wears a size 14 but insists she'll be a 10 by the time the wedding arrives, so she refuses to order a dress in the proper size."

"And then there's the Not-Quite-a-Bride Bride." Twiggy sighed. "Those are the worst."

"Not-Quite-a-Bride Bride?" I asked.

"Yes. It's always the same. They come into the shop looking for a dress, but when we press them for a wedding date, they fumble around."

My heart jolted.

Twiggy giggled. "Can you imagine? Shopping for a wedding dress with no groom? These girls are so desperate to get married that they show up alone—or with a friend, even—to try on gowns that they hope they'll one day wear. If they find the right guy. I feel a little sorry for them, really."

The compassionate look Madge gave me drew Twiggy's attention my way.

"Huh?" Twiggy gave me a curious look.

I glanced at my reflection in the mirror and suddenly felt ill.

“Katie?” Twiggy looked concerned. “Are you okay?”

I shook my head. “I . . . I think I should’ve eaten some breakfast. I’m just a little woozy.”

“She needs some air.” Madge began to fan me using one of the store’s brochures.

“Maybe Dahlia tied the laces too tight,” Twiggy said. “You’ve got such a tiny waist. I’m sure she just wanted to emphasize it.”

“Don’t.” I put my hand up. “Don’t emphasize anything.”

“O-okay.” She stepped toward me and loosened the laces. “Sorry about that.”

“No, you’ve done nothing to be sorry about. It’s all me. Every bit of it.” I couldn’t stop the sudden rush of tears.

Brady took one look at me and ushered the other ladies out of the room. Once we were alone, he turned my way. “Katie? What’s happening?”

I stared at my reflection in the mirror. With Brady standing next to me, we looked like a wedding cake topper. The image was more than I could bear.

“I have to get out of here. I. Need. To. Get. Out. Of. This. Dress.”

“I thought we agreed you were going to keep it. Don’t you like it?”

“Yes.” I turned to him, feeling heartsick. “I love it. That’s the problem. I love the dress. I love this store. I love these people. I love everything. But it's not right, Brady."

"Not the right fit?" he tried.

I shook my head. This guy just didn't get it, did he? "The only thing that's not a good fit here is me. I don't belong here. This isn't the right time. Or place. Or situation. You know that. I told you—Casey's gone. The wedding isn't happening. And the last thing I want to do is hurt your mom when she finds out."

"Then let's tell her." He shrugged. "Let's go ahead and get it over with. She'll probably take a day or so to get over it, but she'll figure out a plan that we can all live with. And then you can relax and just enjoy the dress."

"You think she'll want me to keep it if she knows the truth?"

"I do." He smiled. "That dress was meant for you. I believe it with everything that's in me. And if you don't take it, nothing will be the same. Don't you see that?"

Yes. The dress was meant for me. And it fit beautifully. Only, I didn't deserve it. Right now I just wanted to get out of it, put back on my jeans and T-shirt, and run from this place once and for all.

21

I Don't Wanna Play House

> I love my small town, and I love going back there and supporting the community. But I could not have stayed there. No way.
>
> Jeremy Renner

I somehow managed to stay put in the fitting room but couldn't seem to control my emotions. I could read the concern in Brady's eyes and felt com-pelled to say something. Anything.

"I'm the Not-Quite-a-Bride Bride. That's what Twiggy called me."

Brady shook his head. "No. Technically she didn't call you that. Not you personally, anyway. But I might need to talk to the girls about using code names like that. I don't suppose it's very flattering."

"Tell them I've come up with a new one for girls like me." I yanked off my veil and handed it to him. "The Phony Baloney Bride."

"Phony baloney?" He gently laid the veil on the bench. "There's nothing phony about you, Katie. In fact, you're more real than most of the girls I've known put together. You look like the real deal in this gown, and you will be, in God's timing. That's all I've been trying to say. The dress was meant for you, no matter when you wear it."

I sighed. "I'll pray about that, Brady. I will. If you think I should do the photo shoot, I'll do it for you. And for your mom. And Madge. And all of the wonderful people I've met here in the city."

An awkward silence followed after I said the word *city*. In spite of what Mama had told me that night at Sam's, I hadn't seen one snake since I moved here. Weird.

"So . . . question." My hands began to tremble as I worked up the courage to broach the subject on my heart. "Have you told your mom yet? About my situation, I mean."

He shook his head. "I started to, but Madge reminded me this is fashion week in Paris. I'm going to give it a day or two and then give her a call."

"Ah."

"Don't fret, Katie. It's going to be fine. I know my mother better than anyone. She's going to agree that you should keep the dress, so stop worrying. Promise?"

"I guess. You don't think she'll be mad?"

"No. All that matters to her is a lovely young woman on the cover of *Texas Bride* wearing her gown."

"Lovely?" I didn't mean to say the word aloud, but there it was.

"Yep." Brady smiled. "I don't mean to sound biased, but I see a lot of brides come through this place, and you're going to be the most beautiful one yet. Not just on the outside either."

"O-oh?" His compliment caught me off guard.

"You're always thinking of others. That's a beautiful trait, Katie. We don't see as much of that here as you might think. Most brides are pretty self-focused. Sorry to be so blunt, but they are. You're not like them . . . and I like that." He grinned. "Anyway, I'm going to get out of here and let you get changed."

"Yeah, I need to go soon anyway. Aunt Alva is expecting me for dinner tonight."

"Are your brothers going too?"

"No. They have to get back to Fairfield. Pop is waiting on them at the store, I'm sure."

"Well, have fun. Tell Aunt Alva I said hello."

"I will. And by the way, I plan to tell her that we're not really engaged, so you're off the hook. You don't have to marry me after all."

"Well, that's a relief." He gave me a playful wink. "Might be awkward, marrying someone I just met."

"I know, right?" My heart fluttered a bit as I took in his whimsical smile.

With Dahlia's help, I spent the next several minutes getting back into my jeans and T-shirt. I said my goodbyes to my brothers, who seemed sad to leave. I thanked Dahlia for her work on my dress and then waved goodbye to my new friends—even Stan, who'd just arrived for his daily pep talk with Brady. I walked out of the store to the parking lot, deep in thought about the day.

When I climbed inside my car and tried to start it, nothing happened. I tried again. Nothing. I rested my head against the steering wheel and ushered up a prayer for mercy. My day had been hard enough already. Still, the car didn't start. As much as I hated to go back inside, I had no choice.

Brady met me at the front of the store and I explained my predicament.

"I don't mind giving it a look," he said.

"Betcha he can figure it out," Madge added. "He's always loved stuff like that. From the time he was a boy."

"Tinkering with things makes me happy." Brady shrugged. "What can I say?"

"Say you'll get back to the business of tinkering with a basketball." Stan raked his hand over his bald head. "Did I really just use the word *tinker?*"

"You did." Madge laughed. "And I'd pay money to hear you say it again."

"Tinker." Stan busted out with a belly laugh, and before long we were all laughing. It felt really good, especially after the emotions from earlier.

Brady followed me outside to my car, making small talk all the way. I found his conversation comforting. It felt good to know I had someone to call on, what with my brothers being gone and all, and Brady didn't look as if he minded a bit. In fact, if one could gauge from the expression on his face, he wasn't upset at all.

"Pop the hood for me, Katie."

Brady opened it and then spent the next ten minutes oohing and aahing over a variety of meaningless things underneath. I stood next to him and listened as he carried on, but couldn't make sense of half of it.

"Looks like you've got a loose belt here." He pointed down at it. "And these hoses are shot. In this heat you'll need to make sure you replace them. They're cracked."

"I have a cracked hose?"

"More than one. Can't believe this old thing is still running."

"It's not at the moment. Remember?"

"Right. I'm also guessing your battery's dead. How many miles did you say this car has on it?"

"Two hundred and fourteen thousand. But trust me, it comes from a long line of people who keep going even when they should give up."

Brady gave me a curious look at that one.

"So, I guess I need a new battery." I sighed. "And some hoses. Where do I find all of that?"

"Do you have AAA?"

I shook my head.

Brady glanced over as a customer pulled into the spot next to my car. "Well, let's start with the battery. That's the most critical thing right now. I'll take it out and we'll go to the store and get another one, then I'll put the new one in for you. Madge won't mind keeping an eye on things. We'll be closing soon anyway."

"You would do all of that for me?" I could hardly believe it.

"Well, of course."

"Do you think it will take long? I'm supposed to be at Aunt Alva's house in less than an hour."

"Can you call her?"

I nodded and fumbled around for my phone. Less than a minute later her voicemail kicked in. "Weird. Maybe she didn't hear the phone ringing?" I left a message and then ended the call and pressed the phone back in my purse.

"Hmm." Brady appeared to be thinking. "Well, here's another idea. We'll just load up your stuff in my truck and I'll take you over there. Then I'll come back here and take care of the battery after we close up shop for the night."

"That's too much to ask, Brady."

"It's not." He closed the hood. "I want to help you, Katie. Please. Just let me tell Madge I'll be gone for the rest of the day."

I offered a lame nod, and before I could say, "What sort of movie hero are you?" we were in his truck, headed to Aunt Alva's house. I had a doozy of a time finding the place. Her directions, it turned out, were a bit skewed. Brady was a good sport about it, though. He didn't complain once, even though we had to turn around several times. Instead, he made light of it and we ended up laughing.

By the time we arrived at Alva's house, she was standing on the front porch waiting for me. When she saw us pull up in Brady's truck, she started waving. Brady got out and came around to my side to open my door for me.

My aunt approached with a smile as bright as sunshine. "Now, that's what I like to see. A true gentleman. Your skills on the court are great, Brady, but I'm more impressed by the fact that you're a Southern gentleman."

"Why, thank you, ma'am." He gave a deep bow at the waist and then laughed.

"I hope you're staying for supper," Aunt Alva said. "I've made lasagna."

"Oh, I wouldn't want to impose. Just brought Katie over because her car broke down."

"Yes, I left a message on your phone, Aunt Alva."

"My phone?" She fished around in her pockets but came up empty. "I can never for the life of me remember where I put that goofy thing."

"Well, anyway, he came to my rescue." I couldn't help but smile as I said those words aloud. "So he really is a gentleman."

"Well then, I insist you stay for dinner as a thank-you for rescuing my niece. My cooking skills aren't what they used to be—mostly because of my vision going south—but I gave it the old college try. So c'mon inside and you can tell me all about how you rescued this niece of mine."

I felt my cheeks grow warm as I glanced at Brady.

"Are you sure?" he asked.

"As sure as you were in the final ten seconds of that game with the Rockets. Remember that? You took a long shot from the opposite end of the court, and what happened?"

He grinned. "I can't believe you remember that."

"As if anyone could forget!" My aunt recounted all of the details of the game and then paused for breath. "What were we talking about again? Oh yes, dinner. I do hope you'll stay, Brady. Please? You're practically a member of the family now. Not that being a member of this family means much, but I guess that's not the point."

"About that, Aunt Alva," I said. "Brady and I aren't engaged. I think you misunderstood."

"You're . . . you're not?" Her smile faded. "Well, cut off my legs and call me shorty. I felt sure you two were getting hitched."

"No. It's kind of a long story," I said.

"Well, we'll have plenty of time over supper to talk. Maybe by dessert we can get this boy to pop the question." She slapped him on the back. "So c'mon in, Brady."

As if he'd want to stay now.

Still, he offered a genuine smile. "I just hate to impose."

My aunt put her hands on her hips as she glared at him. "You ready to bolt just 'cause I said my cooking's not what it used to be?"

"Oh, it's not that at all. Just didn't know if you really wanted me to stay or if you were just being polite." He directed his words to her but looked at me. "And I need to work on Katie's car tonight."

"I can probably take care of my car in the morning," I said. "Maybe you could just take me to Lori-Lou's tonight after dinner?"

"Sure." He nodded. "Happy to spend more time with two of the sweetest ladies in town."

"Why, thank you very much." Alva ushered us through the front door. She led the way into the dining room and we took our seats. "I made a homemade lasagna. Got the recipe from my favorite show on the Food Network, *The Italian Kitchen*. Have you ever seen it?"

"Oh, sure. The one with the elderly Italian couple?" Brady nodded. "It's one of my favorites. I love the way they argue with each other while they cook. Lots of fun."

"I don't get a lot of company around here, so it's fun to cook for other people."

We spent the next hour and a half eating,

laughing, and basically having the best time I'd had in ages. I couldn't believe how well Brady and my aunt got along. More than that, though, I couldn't believe how kind Alva turned out to be. From all of Queenie's stories, I would've pictured her as an ogre, not a sweet, lonely woman with a penchant for pro basketball.

As I nibbled on my dessert—a yummy tiramisu she'd made just for me—I gazed tenderly at my aunt.

"What's up, sweet girl?" she asked. "Do I have something in my teeth?"

"No, nothing like that." I giggled. "I just wanted to thank you for the dinner. It's been such a great night."

"Really great." Brady grinned and sipped from his coffee cup. "I've loved every minute."

"Me too," I said. "Aunt Alva, it's been so great to have time with you. I didn't realize how much I missed you until I started spending time with you again."

"That's the way of it, I suppose." She leaned back in her chair and took a sip of her coffee.

I knew my next words were risky but felt they were necessary all the same. "You know, everyone in the family misses you." I drew in a deep breath. "Especially Queenie."

"She'll go right on missing me then."

Ouch. Maybe I'd overstepped my bounds. Brady glanced my way and I could read the concern in his eyes, but I felt I needed to keep going. "Alva, you know that my grandpa Joe passed away four years ago, don't you? Queenie has been living alone ever since. It's been a hard time for her, especially since her surgery."

"I . . . I heard. I still pick up a few things through the grapevine. Bessie—"

"May." We spoke the word together and I smiled. "Well, I guess it's a good thing that she's kept in touch. Is that how you knew about Casey and me dating?"

She nodded and her gaze shifted to the ground.

"Aunt Alva, I'm glad you're staying connected to the goings-on back home."

"This is home now." Alva's jaw clenched.

"But Fairfield will always be—"

"The place where no one needed the likes of me. But never mind all that. If you've come to give me what for, I guess I can take it, but I don't have to like it."

"Not at all. Like I said, I just came because I've missed you and I truly enjoy being with you."

Her expression softened. "Well, thank you." She dabbed at her lips. "Please forgive me, Katie. There are some topics that are still hard to discuss."

Brady finished his coffee and glanced at his watch.

"It's late," I said. "I suppose we should be getting back."

"I'll walk you out." Alva led the way out of the dining room and into the living room. I noticed a black-and-white photograph on the end table. "Alva, is this you and Queenie?"

"I don't know why she expects everyone to call her that." Alva rolled her eyes. "She always thought she was the queen, but I was the oldest sister, you know."

"You still are," I said. "Her sister, I mean." I picked up the picture frame and gazed into the faces of the two girls. "How old were you when this was taken?"

"I don't know. I think maybe I was seven, she was five? Something like that."

"Well, it's darling. You were both so precious."

"Humph. I've never been precious a day in my life."

I couldn't help myself. I threw my arms around her neck and gave her a kiss on the cheek. "You *are* precious," I said. "And don't ever forget it."

Her eyes flooded with tears. She extended her arm for Brady to join the circle, and moments later the three of us stood in an embrace. My heart did that strange pitter-pat thing as he slipped his arm over my shoulders and pulled me close. For a moment I could hardly breathe. Then again, Alva had pretty much swallowed me up in her bosom, just like that first day at the bridal shop.

When the hug ended, Alva clasped her hands together. "Ooh, I have the most wonderful idea.

You should stay here with me tonight, Katie."

"Stay here?"

Brady glanced at me. "I think this is the perfect solution, Katie. Stay here with your aunt, and I'll fix your car in the morning and bring it to you."

"Perfect!" Alva gave a little squeal. "We'll have a slumber party. I've got a lovely spare bedroom. It's just sitting there, as empty as can be. I'll loan you a nightgown, if you need. Even have a spare toothbrush."

"Well, there you go." Brady laughed. "The house comes equipped with a spare toothbrush."

Aunt Alva gave me a wink. "If you enjoy your time, maybe we could extend things a little."

"Extend things a little?"

"Sure. What would you think about coming here to stay for a week or two? However long you're in Dallas? Just rest your heart and your head on the pillow in that guest room of mine. No noise. Just quiet. I'll leave you to yourself as much as you need."

"Oh, Aunt Alva." I reached over and gave her another hug. "That sounds wonderful."

"You think Lori-Lou will mind?"

"I think she's preoccupied with the kids and moving plans. She's got to be tired of me. The air mattress is taking up precious space in the baby's tiny bedroom. She trips over it just to get to his crib."

"Then it's settled. Can you call and tell her?"

"I guess I'd better let her know I'm not coming back to her place tonight anyway." I glanced at Brady. "Want to hang around until I've told her, just in case the plan changes?"

"Sure." He took a seat on the sofa and offered a smile so sweet that it convinced me he didn't mind sticking around one little bit. And judging from the warmth that filled me as I gazed at him, I didn't mind it either.

22

Shoe Goes on the Other Foot Tonight

Some of God's greatest gifts are unanswered prayers.

Garth Brooks

I gave Brady a warm smile as I punched Lori-Lou's number into my cell phone.

"H-hello?" She sounded a little breathless. Odd.

"Am I interrupting something?" I asked.

"Um, no. Nope. No." She giggled. "Nothing. Nothing at all. Stop that, Josh! Not now."

Ew!

"I'll make this fast. I'm calling to let you know that I'm staying overnight with Aunt Alva."

"Okay. Weird, but okay." She giggled again. "Josh, stop it."

"Lori-Lou, I love you. You know that."

"Of course I know that. But I have a feeling you're about to challenge that notion in some way. What's happening?"

"Your house. It's so . . ."

"Chaotic?"

"Well, yes."

"Loud?"

"That too."

"Impossible to navigate because of the toys?"

"Boy, if that ain't the truth." Josh's voice sounded from the other end of the line.

"I'm not saying that I'm not grateful for the time I've spent with you," I added. "But Alva has asked if I would stay with her. She's got a great guest bedroom."

"And a spare toothbrush," Brady called out.

"Wait," Lori-Lou said. "Was that Brady James I heard?"

"Yes."

"He's at Aunt Alva's with you?"

"Yes. Long story."

"Mm-hmm." She chuckled. "Well, it's a story you're going to share when we do see each other again. You'll have to come get your stuff, right?"

"Right. I'll come by tomorrow morning after Brady fixes my car."

"He's fixing your car?" She laughed. "Katie, I turn my back on you for five minutes and you have a thousand adventures without me."

"Not deliberately."

"Right, right." She dissolved into giggles again and then ended the call. Probably for the best.

I turned to Brady and smiled. "Well, that's behind me. Looks like you're free to go now. If you want, I mean."

"Wish I could stay, but I'd better get back so I can figure out the car thing." He stood and gave

Alva another hug before turning to me. “Walk me out?”

“S-sure.” For whatever reason, my heart started that little pitter-pat thing again.

“I’ll be clearing the table,” Alva called out as she headed out of the living room. “Take your time, you two. Take your time.” A little wink followed. For pity’s sake. Did she think I needed to be spending time alone with Brady James?

Hmm. The idea wasn’t altogether unappealing.

I followed him outside to his truck. “Brady, I can’t thank you enough for everything you’ve done for me.”

“Happy to be of service.” His warm smile convinced me that his words were genuine.

“Your kindness to me has proven Mama wrong. She said that people in the big city are impersonal and rude. You’ve been anything but.”

“I can’t speak for all the people in Dallas.” He reached out and slipped his arm over my shoulders. “But spending time with someone like you makes it easy to be friendly. You bring out the best in people.” He gave me a hug and then stepped back. “Anyway, you and Alva have a great time at your slumber party. I’ll call you tomorrow morning when the car’s ready. Then I’ll come and fetch you.”

I nodded, realizing for the first time just how much I wanted to be “fetched” by this sweet guy.

"And while we're talking about making calls, I think I'll go ahead and call my mom in the morning before I come. I'll fill her in."

"Ugh. She's going to hate me."

"Pretty sure she could never hate you. I can't imagine anyone feeling that way about you, Katie. Don't worry, she's pretty clever. She'll come up with a new slant for the *Texas Bride* article, I'd be willing to bet. It'll all work out."

"I hope so."

"I know so."

As he spoke those last words, I had no doubt whatsoever. If Brady knew so, I could know so too.

I watched as he got into the big, manly crew cab of his truck—the one with the extended bed and huge black tires—and drove away. My heart didn't slow down until I was back inside Aunt Alva's house again. I walked through the living room and dining room and into the kitchen, where I found her washing dishes by hand and singing a funny little song. She looked up as I entered and then tossed me a dishrag.

"Might as well join in, Katie Sue."

I stepped into the spot beside her, feeling completely at home in this kitchen. Out of the corner of my eye I gave her a closer look. I saw soft, wrinkly folds of skin on her face, which was the same ivory color as Queenie's but with the addition of some minuscule age spots. The wrinkles traveled like tiny ripples down to her throat, and when I let my gaze wander down her arms, I found them there too. Her soft hands played with the bubbles in the sink, in much the same way I'd seen Queenie do. The two ladies even shared the same style in clothes—floral tops and solid-colored slacks. Even Alva's shoe style felt reminiscent of home.

So many things about this woman reminded me of Queenie. The flashing eyes that spoke of stubbornness and authority. The pursed lips. The strong, charismatic voice. The authority in her stance, despite the stooped shoulders. If I didn't know any better, I'd almost think that Alva and Queenie were twins. The similarities were mind-boggling, to say the least.

My aunt stopped and gave me a closer look. "Something's happened to you, Katie Sue."

"What do you mean?"

"I mean you look . . . different." She waggled her brows.

"Do I?" I sighed and then dried a plate that she passed to me. "I have no idea what you mean by that."

"Sure you don't." She laughed. "Girl, I wouldn't blame you. No one would. There's nothing like a handsome man to knock a girl off her feet." For whatever reason, her smile faded in a hurry, and she got right back to the business of doing dishes.

“Aunt Alva . . .” I looked up. “Have you ever felt . . . confused?”

“Yep. During the playoffs last season. I was rooting for the Mavericks, but then midseason my loyalties shifted to the Spurs.” She glanced my way with an imploring look. “Please don’t tell Brady, okay?”

Maybe there was some comparison there. Not that I really knew or cared much about basketball. Still, with my heartstrings suddenly twisted up in a knot around Brady James, maybe I’d better start caring about basketball.

Aunt Alva started humming as she turned her attention back to the dishes. Eventually she looked at me again. “I like having you here, Katie, and not just because of your help with the dishes.”

“Aw, thank you. I like being with you too.”

“I know it’s not like Fairfield.”

“I can’t believe I’m admitting this, but I’m glad it’s not. I came to Dallas to clear my head. You know?”

“I do. More than you know. That’s the same reason I came to Dallas—to clear my head. I’ve been here ever since.”

“I get that. I’m not saying I’m ready to move here, but it’s been nice to get away from things for a while. It’s a whole new world in the big city.”

“One with handsome basketball players.” She winked. “Hey, speaking of Brady James . . .”

"Were we talking about Brady James?" I felt my face heat up, and that weird heart-racing thing started again.

"Yes, speaking of Brady, I wanted to tell you my theory on why he's scared to get back to the business of playing ball."

"Oh, it's because of his knee," I said.

"It's true, his knee needs more time. But there's more going on than that. People think that guys don't get scared, but they do." Alva gave me a knowing look. "Brady's scared."

"Of?"

"Letting his team down, plain and simple. He's scared to get back in the game because he's afraid he won't be able to play like he used to. So he'd rather risk not playing at all. When you don't play, you don't fail."

"You're right."

"Of course I'm right. Remember that scene in *Coal Miner's Daughter* where Loretta had to stand in front of a crowd and sing for the very first time? She was terrified. It takes courage to do the one thing you're most terrified to do, but it's always worth it in the end."

"I understand being afraid," I said. "I've been a little scared of letting my family down."

"Letting your family down?" Alva pursed her lips. "Why let them control your destiny, kid?"

"Oh, I'm not saying it's like that. Just saying that I hate to disappoint them. So I totally get what you're saying about Brady being afraid of disappointing his fans."

"Ah." A cloud seemed to settle over her. "Well, maybe we all need to get over this feeling of being a disappointment to others and just get on with the business of living."

I thought through her words. "You're a smart cookie, Aunt Alva."

"Ooh, cookies." She nearly dropped the dish in her hands, but the most delightful look came into her eyes. "I was thinking of making some oatmeal raisin cookies in the morning. Do you like those?"

"They're my favorite. Queenie's too. She makes the best in town." I bit my lip, knowing there would be a reaction from my aunt. Why had I mentioned Queenie again? Somehow I just couldn't help myself when I was around Alva.

An awkward silence grew up between us. She wiped her hands on her apron and leaned against the counter. Her thoughtful expression caught me off guard. "Katie Sue, let's get one thing out in the open, if you don't mind."

"Sure, Aunt Alva."

"Despite what you might be thinking, I really don't hate my little sister," my aunt said. "You need to know that."

Relief flooded over me as I realized she wasn't upset with me. "You don't seem the sort to hate anyone, Aunt Alva. I just don't know what to think about the situation between you and Queenie. It's so . . . odd. I'm looking at it from the outside in, and you know the story from the inside out, so our perspectives are different."

"It's kind of a long story, too long for your first night here. But it all goes back many, many years, long before you were even born."

"I see."

"I wonder, Katie . . . do you happen to know a man named Paul Bradford?" My aunt's eyes misted over as she mentioned his name.

"*Reverend* Bradford? At the Presbyterian church?"

Her gaze narrowed as she shifted her attention to the dishes once more. "Yes, do you know him?"

"Of course. I've grown up knowing him. In fact, I saw him recently at my parents' anniversary party. Great guy." But what did he have to do with Aunt Alva and Queenie?

I gasped as the realization hit me.

Oh. My. Goodness.

Queenie's heart had been broken when Reverend Bradford showed an interest in another woman. Now I knew *who* that other woman was. She was standing next to me, washing dishes.

"Do you want to tell me the story?" I asked.

She sighed and passed me another plate. "Not yet. Maybe one day I'll explain it all. Or write it all down in a letter. You can read it after I'm dead. It'll be less painful that way."

"I have to wait until you're dead to know the details of what happened between the two of you? Er, the *three* of you?"

"Maybe." Her eyes filled with tears. "I'll think on it. Perhaps there's a way to get things out in the open without hurting folks all over again. I'll have to pray about that. In the meantime, let's just have a good time, you and me. It's wonderful to have someone from the family spend time with me. That's all. Wonderful."

I had to admit, it felt pretty wonderful from my perspective too. In fact, only one thing had felt more wonderful tonight . . . that awesome moment when my heart skipped to double time as Brady James pulled me into his arms.

23

Two Steps Forward

Everyone feels like family and I am back in the city that I love.

Chris Noth

I got the best night's sleep I'd had in ages in Aunt Alva's guest bedroom. I didn't even mind the 1970s paintings on the wall or the harvest gold carpeting. And the silk nightgown she loaned me—circa 1968—made me smile. But the room felt just right for me, including the down comforter on the bed. Since she kept the house as cold as a refrigerator, the comforter came in handy. I loved snuggling under the covers when chilly.

When I woke up the following morning, the smell of bacon gave me more than enough reason to get out of bed. I found one of Alva's robes hanging on the hook at the top of the bedroom door. I donned it and headed to the kitchen, where I found my aunt in a floral dressing gown. She stood at the stove, cooking up a storm.

"Good morning, sunshine." Alva gestured with her head to the refrigerator. "There's milk in the icebox."

Icebox?

"Might as well pull out the butter too. It needs to soften a bit before we can use it. We're gonna need it for the flapjacks. They'll be done in a few minutes."

"Wow, you're cooking for an army over there."

This whole breakfast reminded me of another one several weeks ago. I'd sat at Queenie's table on a random weekday morning, talking about my relationship with Casey.

Casey.

Hmm.

For whatever reason, thinking about him didn't bring as much pain as it had that day. Maybe my heart really was starting to heal. At any rate, a plate of pancakes smothered in butter and yummy syrup would certainly help.

Our conversation shifted, and Aunt Alva went off on a tangent about how she was a week behind getting her hair done. How we'd transitioned from flapjacks to hair, I could not say.

"Just wanted to make you aware of my schedule, honey bun," Alva said. "I've got my weekly appointment at the hair salon a couple of days from now, on Friday."

Interesting. Queenie always went to Do or Dye on Fridays to get her hair done. The similarities between the two women grew stranger and stranger.

"Why Friday?" I asked.

Alva gave me a "surely you jest" look. "Silly

girl. So it'll still look fresh for church on Sunday. Wouldn't want to show up for Sunday service with bed head, you know. Gotta put my best foot—er, curl—forward." This led to a lengthy conversation about what her schedule looked like the rest of the week. "I come and go from the house quite a bit," she said. "I might be in my golden years, but I'm still very active. And a good driver too. Those people at the DPS might've questioned it last time around, but I proved 'em wrong. Sure did."

Just like Queenie.

"Now, let's eat." She lifted the platter of flapjacks, nearly dropping it. "I'm starving."

"Me too."

I'd just taken my seat at the table when my cell phone rang in the living room. I sprinted to find it and answered when I saw my mother's number. I could tell from the sound of her voice that something was troubling her.

"Mama, you okay?" I asked.

"Well, I suppose I'm all right physically, but if you're asking about my mental and emotional state, I've been better. Things have been rough at the store without you, honey."

"Ah. I'm sorry, Mom."

"I don't mind admitting we're getting worried about you, Katie Sue."

"Worried? Why?"

"Well, for one thing, your brothers came home

with the strangest story yesterday. Something about some girls they've met at a store in Dallas, thanks to you. Didn't make a lick of sense. Why in the world are the boys meeting girls at some sort of store? Have you been shopping a lot while you're there?"

"Well, not really. I—"

"I know some girls like to go on shopping sprees when they get their heart broken, but it only leads to ruin in the end. You'll run up credit card debt and end up in debtors' prison."

"Mama, I don't have any credit cards. And I haven't been shopping." Not really.

"Well, color me confused."

I didn't know what to say, but it didn't really matter anyway, because Mama did all the talking.

"Your brothers insist you've been spending time with a ball player. A pro ball player, no less. Now, I know my girl really well. She's never kept any secrets from me. So I told them it couldn't possibly be true or she would've told me."

Oh dear.

"Actually, Mama, I have met someone who plays for the Mavericks. Brady James. Have you heard of him? We've struck up a friendship."

"A . . . friendship?" She grew silent.

"He's very nice. I think you would like him."

"Well, I must say I'm a little surprised. Your brothers aren't giving me much information, and I for one am feeling a little left out. I don't know what in the world you're up to in Dallas, but Pop and I want you to come home now. He needs your help at the hardware store, and the choir's just not the same without your voice. I had to give Bessie May the solo in last Sunday's special, and you know she can't hold a candle to you when it comes to singing."

"Mama, that's not true. She has a lovely voice." Shaky, but lovely.

"It's just not the same." Mama sighed. "Nothing's the same since you went away."

"I've only been gone three and a half weeks."

"Seems like three months. I just don't understand why you need to spend so much time with Lori-Lou. Aren't those children about to drive you bonkers?"

"Actually, I spent the night with Aunt Alva last night. I'm in her living room now." I lowered my voice so as not to be heard.

"Aunt Alva?" Now Mama sounded interested. "Seriously?"

"Yes. We had a slumber party."

"Well, if that doesn't beat all." I could almost hear the wheels turning in her head. "Queenie's liable to have a conniption."

"Only if she knows, Mama." *So please don't tell her.*

"Well, what in the world are you and Alva doing? Can't you stay connected through the internet or something? Come back home and send her emails. Ask her to friend you on Facebook. There are plenty of ways to stay connected to people these days without actually having a slumber party. We need you here. Nothing's the same."

Hmm. If I didn't know any better, I'd say Mama was a tad bit jealous of my blossoming friendship with Alva. And Lori-Lou.

"I told you, Mama. I'm getting away for a while. Since Casey left, well, I just needed to think things through." I couldn't mention the upcoming photo shoot, obviously, but it weighed heavy on my mind. I couldn't go back to Fairfield for good until the dress was finished and the photo shoot was behind me. Now that Brady knew about my situation, I owed it to him. I would carry through with this, if for no other reason than to make things easier on him.

Mama cleared her throat. "I'm pretty sure I've got this figured out, Katie Sue. I know a little something about broken hearts."

"Huh?"

"I know why you're staying away so long. It's a tactic, isn't it?"

"A tactic?" Okay, now she really had my attention. I took a seat on Alva's paisley sofa. "What sort of tactic?"

"It's a ploy to bring Casey back home. Stay away and make him wonder what you're up to."

"That makes no sense at all, Mama."

"Are you thinking that he'll come back because he's worried about you being gone? I'm not sure that's the best strategy."

"Strategy? You really think I'm doing this to draw attention to myself? To make Casey come looking for me? That's . . . crazy."

"I'm clueless, if you want the truth of it." Mama's voice shook. "Honestly? I don't care if we ever see Casey Lawson again."

"What? Really?"

"Really." Her voice continued to tremble with emotion. "He can move away to Tulsa and stay there, for all I care. I'd rather see you end up with someone who deserves you, someone who won't leave you dangling for years on end. Someone who makes you feel the way your father makes me feel." Her words grew more animated by the moment. "Someone who'll go the distance with you. Someone who cares about family and sees your potential. That's the kind of guy I see you with." She released a long breath. "There. I got it out in the open."

I half expected her to leap into a sermonette about Levi Nash, but she refrained, thank goodness.

"You know what, Mama? That's exactly the kind of guy I see for me too." I rose and paced Alva's spacious living room, my gaze landing once again on the photograph of Queenie and Alva as young girls. "And you're right . . . that guy isn't Casey. Giving me time away in Dallas has put all of that into perspective. I've needed to completely step away to see that. You know what I mean?"

"I guess. But you've picked a doozy of a place to go. If you knew the story about Queenie and Alva, you'd understand."

"Oh, I think I'm beginning to understand." I lowered my voice. "We, um, had a little conversation last night. I'm starting to see what happened . . . from both sides."

"Did she tell you that she's the one who broke up the relationship between Reverend Bradford and Queenie?"

"Well, it wasn't phrased exactly like that, but I sort of figured it out on my own."

"Alva was behind it. She instigated the whole thing. Flirted with the poor fellow and got him all confused. Totally ruined any chance Queenie had. I don't think the good reverend was really interested in Alva, but she wouldn't give up on the idea. You want my opinion?"

I had a feeling Mama was about to give it, regardless of my answer.

"I think Alva didn't care about Paul Bradford. She just didn't want him to marry her sister."

"Why?"

"Because she didn't think he was good enough for her."

Whoa. I lowered my voice to a hoarse whisper.

"You're telling me she arranged for Queenie to have a broken heart . . . to somehow protect her?"

"She didn't want her sister to end up with a man who didn't deserve her. That's the long and short of it," Mama said. "But Queenie went on to meet your grandpa Joe when his family moved into town. They had a whirlwind courtship and —on the heels of Reverend Bradford's wedding— she decided to marry him. From what I was told, Alva wouldn't even come to her wedding."

"No way."

"It's true. Bessie May spilled the beans. And it wasn't much longer before Alva moved away to Dallas."

And Alva had never married. Sad.

I felt like a real heel talking about the woman behind her back in her own home. Not that I'd brought up the subject, but I needed to put a cap on it before it got out of hand.

"Mama, I really don't think we should be—"

"The worst part is, she could've been surrounded by family all of these years if Queenie had been willing to forgive and forget. I think Alva pulled away to keep the peace. This ridiculous separation has affected the whole family. You can call it whatever you like, but in the end, bitterness has grown up between them, and the devil thrives on bitterness."

At that very moment, Aunt Alva popped her

head in the living room door and gave me a cute little wave. "Yoo-hoo, kiddo! Your pancakes are getting cold. Better come and eat while the eatin's good! And I haven't forgotten about those oatmeal raisin cookies. I've already got the dough started."

"Okay, I heard that." Mama sighed. "She actually sounds pretty chipper."

"You're right." I waved at Aunt Alva and gave her a thumbs-up.

"Go eat your pancakes," Mama said. "But promise you'll come back two weeks from Friday for Queenie's birthday party. She'll never forgive you if you're not here."

"What date is that?"

"The seventeenth."

Perfect. Two days after the photo shoot. "I'll be there. Where is it?"

"At Sam's, of course. The whole family will be there."

Not the whole family. Alva wouldn't be there, would she?

Or maybe she would. Maybe I could begin to work on her now, to see if I could talk her into going with me.

I said goodbye to Mama and ended the call. I thought about her words all morning long as I ate my breakfast, then dressed in the same clothes from the day before. In spite of my blossoming friendship with Brady, I still held some bitterness in my heart toward Casey. I didn't mean to. But in the quiet moments, usually before getting out of bed in the morning, I still seethed on the inside over his decision to leave me behind.

All right, so his decision to leave had forced me to move on.

And yes, being forced to move on had led me to Cosmopolitan Bridal.

And okay, my decision to move forward with the wedding gown had led me to Brady James.

And sure, my heart fluttered whenever he glanced my way.

When I saw it all in perspective, the bitterness faded away. In that very moment.

Brady showed up around eleven in his truck. Alva greeted him with as much enthusiasm as she had the first day she'd met him and offered to feed him a late breakfast. Brady thanked her but declined.

"Sorry, Alva," he said. "I've got to get back to the shop. I've left Jasper and Dewey working on Katie's car."

"Wait." I put my hand up. "My brothers are back in Dallas . . . again?"

Brady nodded. "Yeah, Jasper said something about needing to shop for supplies for the store."

"He did that yesterday."

"I think maybe he got distracted yesterday and forgot? Anyway, he and Dewey are working on the car. Putting in a new battery. You'll never believe what Beau is doing."

"Try me."

"Last time I saw him, he was working the cash register at the store."

"Are you serious? We couldn't get the boy to work at the cash register at the hardware store if we tried all day."

"Yep. Twiggy was busy with a customer and they needed the help. He stepped right up."

"Whoa. I think we're witnessing a real live miracle, folks."

Brady and I talked about the changes in my brothers all the way back to the bridal shop while we nibbled on some of my aunt's oatmeal cookies. I also opened up and spilled the whole story of Alva and Queenie. Why I felt so comfortable talking to Brady James, I could not say. But he had great insight, particularly when it came to my grandmother and aunt.

"Time has passed, Katie," he said. "And hearts change. Some grow harder. Some soften. But God can still mend relationships, even after all this time."

"Would you pray about that? I'd love to invite Alva to Queenie's birthday party."

"When is it?"

"Two weeks from Friday. In Fairfield."

"I'll pray, I promise." He gave me a thoughtful smile. "The way you talk about Fairfield makes it sound so great. One of these days I'll have to go there myself. Meet Queenie in person."

"I'd like that." I found myself smiling as the words came out. "A lot."

I snuck a peek at him out of the corner of my eye. He gave me a little wink and my heart did that fluttering thing again. Gracious. If this kept up, I'd have to go find a cardiologist.

Right in the middle of my heart palpitations, Brady switched gears, talking about the one thing I'd avoided all morning: his call to his mother.

"I think she was surprised," Brady said. "But I explained the whole thing and told her that Madge didn't want you to say anything."

"We can totally cancel the dress order, Brady. I don't mind."

"No, it would break her heart. She loves that design. And she still wants to go through with the photo shoot. She's just trying to come up with a new angle for Jordan's article. She said something about calling you the Someday Bride."

"The Someday Bride?"

"Yes, the bride who's been dreaming of her big day all her life. The one who plans everything in advance."

"That would be me."

"Yep. You and thousands of other women. She thinks it'll make the article more interesting that the girl who won the dress doesn't have a fixed date. Or a fixed groom."

"Or a fixed *anything*." I sighed.

"Oh, I don't know about that. I think you've got a fixed attitude. You're a hopeless romantic." His convincing smile won me over.

"Well, true. And I guess there are a lot of other hopeless romantics out there," I said.

"Yep. And they're not all women either." A playful smile tugged at the corners of his mouth.

Gracious. Was this sweet guy flirting with me, or what?

Before long we were engrossed in a lengthy conversation about the photo shoot.

"Because Mom can't come back for the shoot, she wants me to go along and represent the bridal shop," Brady said. "You okay with that?"

"Of course. Sounds like fun."

"Dahlia will come too. She'll take care of the dress and make sure it looks great. And I'm sure Madge will be there. We'll make a party out of it."

"Dahlia?" My thoughts reeled backwards in time to the conversation I'd overheard in the fitting room, the one where Twiggy said she felt sorry for the poor, pathetic brides who didn't yet have a groom. "Do . . . do Dahlia and the others know? About my situation, I mean?"

"They do." He gave me a tender look. "But you won't be hearing a word about it. Mom made a point of telling them to handle it like the pros they are."

"Do you think it changes their opinion about me?"

"Not a bit. Now stop fretting, okay?" He started talking about the various photo op places we'd seen at the stockyard. That conversation somehow shifted to goats, then to horses. This provided the perfect segue to talk about my life back in Fairfield, which I did with abandon. Brady seemed to hang on my every word, genuinely interested in what I had to say.

When we arrived back at the bridal shop, I found Dewey and Dahlia in the parking lot working on my car. Now, I'd seen Dahlia at work behind the sewing machine. I'd watched her pin and tuck hems. But I'd never seen her under the hood before. With my brother speaking so enthusiastically about all things mechanical, the girl practically swooned. Go figure.

We joined them, but only for a moment. I could tell from my brother's crooked smile that he wanted to be left alone with the Swedish beauty. Okay then. I'd give him some space, especially if it meant he would fix my car.

"See now why I left it in his capable hands?" Brady said as we walked toward the store. "I think he's trying to impress Dahlia."

"No joke. Well, if he keeps on impressing her, I might just get an oil change and tire rotation out of it, so don't bother him."

Brady laughed and opened the door to the

shop. True to his word, Beau was behind the counter, working the cash register. He punched a few keys and then spoke to the young woman standing on the other side of the counter. "That will be $695.14, ma'am." His Texas drawl sounded even thicker today.

"My goodness, with such a handsome fella waiting on me, I'll happily spend that much and more." The girl smiled. "Thanks for the recommendation about the shoes to go with my bridesmaid dress. I think they're a perfect match."

"Yer welcome, ma'am." He took her credit card and rang up the transaction, then closed the drawer and handed her a receipt. "Have a great day."

"Oh, I have already." She winked.

This didn't appear to go over well with Twiggy, who approached at just that moment. She glared at the young woman and showed her to the door. Wow. Looked like things were really stirring at the bridal shop today.

Beau looked my way and his cheeks flushed. "Well, hey, Katie. Didn't see you come in."

"Mm-hmm."

"I, um, well, I'm helping out."

"So I see."

"He's had a hankerin' to work in a bridal shop for years." Jasper's voice sounded from behind me. "I guess it's been a secret desire none of us knew about."

Beau gave him a warning look. Just as quickly, his expression softened. I noticed his gaze shifting to Twiggy, who greeted an incoming customer at the door. "I have secret desires, all right." He sighed and took a few steps toward us, away from the counter. His next words came out sounding a bit strained. "Houston, we have a problem."

"What's the problem, little brother?" Jasper elbowed him in the ribs. "Can't choose between the satin and crepe for your gown?"

"It's Mama."

"Mama's never been a problem for you, little brother," I said. "She thinks you hung the moon. You're her baby."

"Mama's *always* been a problem for him," Jasper argued. "He just never saw it till now. The apron strings are choking the life out of him."

"I'm not really saying Mama's the problem," Beau said. "I guess I'm the problem because I've let her pretty much rule my life. I'm just saying there's going to be a problem with Mama when she finds out that, well . . ."

"You've fallen and you can't get up?" Jasper gave him a look.

He nodded. "Yeah." A broad smile lit his boyish face. "And I don't wanna, either. Get up, I mean." Another lingering gaze at Twiggy followed. From across the room she turned away from the customer and gave him a little nod.

Jasper whacked Beau on the back. "Don't you worry about Mama. She wants her boy to be happy. She always has. It'll be hard to hear that you've developed an interest in a girl, but she'll get over it."

"She wants me happy, sure, but she also wants me close to home. Now that I . . ." He scratched his head. "I'm just confused."

"When she meets Twiggy, she'll love her." Something occurred to me in that moment. "Hey, I have an idea." I snapped my fingers. "You guys should invite the girls to Queenie's birthday party. Seriously. It's two weeks from Friday, at Sam's. That's the perfect opportunity to introduce them in a friendly setting. Everyone will be in a celebratory mood."

"Take Twiggy to Fairfield?" Beau looked more than a little concerned.

"I'm trying to picture Crystal hanging out at Dairy Queen." Jasper shook his head. "Nope. Just ain't happening."

"Well, how do you know unless you take them there? At the very least, you can introduce them to Mama and Pop. It's the right thing to do."

"Kind of like you introduced them to Brady?" Jasper gave me a knowing look. "Like that? I mean, you two are an item, right? I'm not blind."

"We're not an item, Jasper, and you're completely changing the subject." I swallowed. Hard. "Anyway, I think it's a good idea."

“For you to introduce Brady to the folks?”

“No, for you guys to introduce the girls to the folks.”

He shrugged and we ended the conversation, but I couldn’t stop thinking about what he’d said. Sooner or later we would all have to cross the great divide between Fairfield and Dallas. Between now and then, however, I’d have to figure out a way to invite Alva to go with me to Queenie’s party. And I might—just might—work up the courage to invite a certain basketball player to join us too.

24

Tomorrow Never Comes

Hope is a gift we give ourselves, and it remains when all else is gone.

Naomi Judd

Just two days before Queenie's birthday party, I tried on my finished dress in preparation for the photo shoot. I could hardly believe how wonderful I felt with it on. Dahlia got so excited that she decided to Skype the whole event with Nadia.

"Turn around, Katie." Nadia's voice sounded from the speaker on Dahlia's laptop.

I complied, showing off the mid-length train on the back of the dress.

"Great job, Dahlia." Nadia sounded impressed, but she didn't gush. Maybe it wasn't in her nature to gush. "It's going to be perfect for the photo shoot. Now, Katie, I don't want to tell you how to pose for the photos, but do your best to show off the dress if you can, okay?"

"I will."

"Since we're billing you as the Someday Bride, I thought it would be nice to give you a stand-in groom. You okay with Brady playing that role? I think his basketball fans would eat it up, and it would certainly increase the sales for the magazine."

"Brady?" I felt my cheeks grow hot.

"Sure." Nadia's businesslike voice clipped along at a steady pace. "Ask him to put on a tuxedo and go along for the ride, okay? If the photographer asks for a groom, he'll be ready to go."

"You don't think that'll confuse his fans?" I asked.

"We can explain that he's a good sport." She grinned. "Get it? Good sport? It'll show that he's a team player, and that should make Stan happy."

"I doubt it," Madge called out. "That old coot's never happy."

Nadia laughed. "True. But let's just play out this day like the fairy tale it is. And remember, Katie, you represent every someday bride. I ran the idea by Jordan Singer and he thought it was perfect. His readers will eat it up. You've spent your whole life dreaming of the perfect dress, the perfect wedding . . ."

"The perfect groom." Madge elbowed me but I shushed her.

"Well, do your best not to get the dress too wrinkled on the ride over there, okay? Are you riding in Brady's truck?"

"Yes ma'am. My car would never make it."

"You don't have to call me *ma'am,* Katie. Just Nadia will do."

"Yes ma'am." I put my hand over my mouth and giggled. "Sorry!"

"Dahlia, go ahead and bustle the gown now," Nadia said. "When you all get to the stockyard, keep the dress bustled until the last minute. God forbid you should drag that train in the mud or" —she shuddered—"anything else. There are animals everywhere, after all." She paused, but before anyone could get a word in edgewise, she added another thought. "When you're ready for the first shot, unhook the bustle and let down the train, but be very careful."

"Will do, Nadia," Dahlia said. She went to work bustling the back of my gown, carrying on all the while about the embellishments on the bodice and the gorgeous ruffles on the skirt. "I daresay even Ms. Loretta Lynn herself would be happy to wear this dress."

"We might just have to ask her that question," Nadia said. "I'll ask Jordan to try to contact her."

Wow. I could hardly believe it. Maybe Queenie's favorite singer would put her stamp of approval on my wedding dress. The one I wasn't getting married in . . . at least not anytime soon.

When we ended the Skype session with Nadia, Crystal and Twiggy went to work doing my hair and makeup in preparation for the event.

I noticed Crystal's silence while the other ladies gabbed. "Are you okay?" I asked.

"Hmm?" She shrugged. "I guess. Days like this are hard."

"Why?"

She sighed. "I sometimes wonder if I'm ever going to get married. I guess I'm just one of those someday brides that Nadia talked about."

"Aren't we all?" Dahlia asked.

"Count me in," Twiggy said. "I'm a someday bride too."

"Looks like we're all in the same boat," I said.

Crystal took a seat on the bench. "By the time I'm engaged, I'll be an old woman."

"Like me?" Madge's voice sounded from behind us.

"You're not old, Madge." Dahlia walked over and gave Madge a kiss on the cheek. "You're forever young."

"And you're still a someday bride too." Crystal gave Madge a knowing look and then giggled.

"With hips like mine, I'll never fit into an A-line gown," Madge said.

"When the time comes, you're going to be a beautiful bride, Madge," Dahlia said. "I'll make your dress myself and you'll look like a million bucks."

"Whatever. I was never meant to be a beauty queen. And the only thing polished about me is my wit. No one can argue that point." Madge winked. "Truth is, I'm doing the best I can. All women my age are. And if we don't look the part—if our makeup isn't perfect, if our figure isn't the same as it was when we were teens—then the world will just have to go on spinning anyway. I have it on good authority that we all age. Our bodies change. Don't believe me? Look at Robert Redford."

"True." Crystal's nose wrinkled.

"And Jamie Lee Curtis. She's never been one to disguise her age."

"I'm going to age like Dolly Parton," Crystal said. "That woman is per-*pet*-ually thirty-nine."

This led to an interesting discussion about country music, which led them back to talking about my gown. I swished and swayed, checking out the dress from every angle, and gave a blissful sigh. I caught a glimpse of Madge in the mirror, staring at me like a proud mama hen. I couldn't help but smile.

Several minutes later, Brady appeared at the fitting room door. I hardly recognized him in the sleek tuxedo, but he took my breath away. Literally. "Whoa." I didn't mean to say the word aloud, but who could blame me?

"Wowza." Madge whistled. "You clean up nice, boss."

"You can say that twice and mean it." I bit my lip to keep from saying anything that might embarrass either one of us. "You really do look great, Brady."

"I look like a cake topper." He checked his

appearance in the mirror and groaned. "Don't I?"

That got me tickled. Before long I was laughing so hard the girls had to stop working on my makeup. I promised Crystal that I'd double-check my appearance before the shoot began and take care of any necessary touch-ups.

"Trust me, you're the prettiest bride to ever grace the cover of a magazine." Brady gave me an admiring look. "You won't need to change a thing."

"Aw," all of the females said in unison.

"Thank you, Brady." I gave him a smile and then tried to look as if his words hadn't affected me. The heat in my face gave me away, though.

Dahlia's eyes narrowed. "Boss, are you flirting?"

"Me? Flirting?" He cleared his throat.

"Well, it's time to get this show on the road." Madge put her hand on Brady's back and nudged him out the door. "We've got a full day ahead of us. C'mon, folks."

Brady extended his arm. "Are you ready, Katie?"

"As ready as I'll ever be."

I held tight to his arm as we walked through the shop, so as not to get tangled up in the cumbersome ruffled skirt. Several people stopped me to comment on my gown. I felt like a princess wearing it.

Just before we reached the door, a young woman entered. Madge reached for her walkie-talkie and whispered, "Incoming Joie de Vivre."

“Joie de Vivre?” I stopped in my tracks, intrigued by this one.

“Rediscovering life after a recent catastrophe,” Madge explained. She gestured to the woman, who stood off in the distance, examining a gown. “Her name is Penny Jones. And she’s our most recent Joie de Vivre Bride.”

“I’m not sure I understand,” I said.

“Notice the smile on her face? It’s as broad as the sun up above. But the mist of tears in her eyes? They tell a different story. This is a young woman whose first husband passed away in Afghanistan. She didn’t think she would ever remarry. But then she met her current fiancé, and hope, once dead, sprang to life.”

“Joie de vivre. Hope springs to life.” I whispered the words, realizing how closely they matched my situation, then threw my arms around Madge’s neck. “Madge, you’re a remarkable woman. So intuitive.”

Brady let out a snort. “You mean nosy?”

“No, I mean intuitive.” My heart flooded with joy for her. “She sees things that the rest of us don’t see. She even notices the little things.”

“In spite of all my flaws?” She quirked a brow.

“I see no flaws in you. In fact, you’re the most beautiful woman here,” I said. “And I really mean that. Your heart makes it so.”

“I might have to argue that point.” She leaned over and kissed me on the forehead. “I would argue that you're the most beautiful. I haven't known you long, kid, but I can say in all honesty that they grow 'em sweeter in Fairfield."

"And I might just have to agree." Brady placed his hand on my back and smiled.

"Yep." Madge nodded. "Now listen up, you two. Once we get to that photo shoot, I'm counting on you to knock 'em dead. Take the best possible pictures for *Texas Bride* and show the world that Cosmopolitan Bridal is the best place on earth to buy a wedding gown." She glanced at the Joie de Vivre Bride. "I've got a customer to take care of, but Dahlia and I will meet you there in a few minutes, after I make sure the other girls are okay to manage the store without us. Now scoot."

Brady kept his hand on my back, gently guiding me out the door. In that moment, with the eyes of everyone in the store on the two of us, I felt like a bride. I felt lovely. It had nothing to do with the makeup or the hair, though those things certainly didn't hurt. No, what I felt came from a deeper place than that. Madge had touched a nerve with her joie de vivre comment. With those words, hope sprang to life. I would one day wear this dress for real. It would be more than just a pipe dream. In the meantime, Brady and I would play the role of cake toppers, giving the photographer all of the pictures he needed for the magazine, even if we had to playact to do it.

25

Hello Darlin'

I have an affection for a great city. I feel safe in the neighborhood of man, and enjoy the sweet security of the streets.
Henry Wadsworth Longfellow

Perched in the passenger seat of Brady's truck, all adorned in white, I felt like a bride. Well, a pretend bride on her way to a stockyard for a photo shoot, anyway. My tuxedo-adorned groom glanced at me and laughed. "I'm sorry, but something about the way you're sitting cracks me up. You're like a stone. A white stone."

"I'm terrified to move."

"Because of the dress?" He tugged at his collar. "Afraid you'll ruin it?"

"I'm just a klutz. Knowing me, I'll spill coffee all over it." I sat perfectly still, afraid to breathe.

"There's no coffee in my truck."

"Right. Well, maybe motor oil."

"I don't think you'll be touching any of that." He grinned and then eased on the brake to stop at a light. He gave me a comforting look. "Just rest easy, Katie. And if you do run into any problems, don't worry. Dahlia will have an emergency kit with her."

"Emergency kit? Huh?"

"Yep. Instant stain remover. Needle and thread. Mini scissors. You name it, she'll have it."

"Good." I nodded and did my best to relax. "Is it hot in here?" Ribbons of sweat trickled down my back.

"I'll adjust the AC." He turned the fan directly on me and increased the flow of air. I tried to settle against the seat, but my sweaty back made it impossible. Instead, I closed my eyes and tried to imagine what Queenie would do if she saw me like this. She'd call for the WOP-pers to pray, naturally. And if Alva saw me sitting here in a wedding dress next to Brady? Well, she'd go on assuming the two of us were a couple.

Out of the corner of my eye I watched Brady drive the truck. He talked about nonsensical things, everything from the weather to the photo shoot. Something about his voice—that soothing, comforting voice—calmed my soul. It also gave me the tingles. Or maybe the dress gave me the tingles. The taffeta parts were a little itchy, after all. Still, being here with him, all six feet four of him, made me happier—no, giddier—than I'd been in ages. I couldn't help myself as the giggles bubbled up.

Brady looked my way and grinned. "You okay over there?"

"Peachy. Just peachy." Saying the word *peachy* reminded me of the night I'd been crowned Peach Queen back home in Fairfield. As wonderful as I'd felt that night, sitting here with Brady, dressed in wedding duds, felt even better.

We arrived at the stockyard at exactly five minutes till three, just in time to meet with Jordan and the photographer, who'd wanted to capture the shots mid-afternoon due to the setting of the sun. Brady pulled the truck into the parking lot and tried to strategize the best place to park.

"I don't want you to have to walk far in that dress." His nose wrinkled. "On the other hand, I don't want to be near the front of the parking lot because the ground is still wet from the rain we had yesterday. No point in getting muddy."

No, indeed. If I got this gorgeous Loretta Lynn gown muddy, Nadia would never forgive me.

He parked in the middle, in a spot with enough open space on either side to accommodate my full skirt. Then he placed a call to Madge, who had gotten tied up at the shop with a bride.

"Looks like Madge and Dahlia are going to be a little late," he said. "Think you can make it to the shoot without them?"

"I'll do my best, boss." I laughed. "Sorry, I think I've just heard the others call you that so many times it stuck."

Brady came around to my side to help me out.

When he took hold of my hand, it felt perfectly natural. I couldn't help but smile.

"You ready to do this?" he asked.

"As ready as I'll ever be."

The moment we stepped out of the truck, we drew a crowd. I'd worried about how people would respond to seeing a bride walking down the main street of Fort Worth, and I prayed that they wouldn't get the wrong idea about Brady. With someone as well known as Brady James, the risk of media showing up was very real. Why hadn't I thought of that?

"Oh, Brady." I shook my head and took a few steps away from the crowd. "We can't do this. People are going to think . . ."

"Don't worry about the fallout, Katie. I've already put Stan to work on a story for the media so people don't get the wrong idea. If I know him—and I do—he'll come up with some slant to get me back on the court."

"No doubt." I giggled.

He leaned over to whisper, "If anyone asks, we'll explain that I'm just a prop."

"You could never be just a prop." My words came out sounding a little too passionate.

He smiled. "Well, thank you for that." He held out his arm and I slipped mine through his. "We're going to march down Main Street like we belong here. Let the chips fall where they may."

“Speaking of chips . . .” I pointed down to the road, where the cattle drive had taken place a few hours prior. “Watch your step, cowboy.”

He laughed.

And off we went, the happy bride and groom, arm in arm. A crowd continued to gather around us, and people pulled out their phones to take pictures.

“Hey, Brady!” an older fellow called out. “You gettin’ hitched?”

“Nope,” he called out. “I’m just a prop, folks. Just a prop.”

“You look like a cake topper,” another man hollered.

“Told you.” Brady looked my way and rolled his eyes.

“A very handsome cake topper.” I gave his arm a little squeeze. “Chin up, Brady. We’ll get through this.”

“No wonder your head hasn’t been in the game,” the older fellow added. “You’re distracted.”

Great. Someone else who thought I was a distraction in Brady’s life.

Thank goodness Brady didn’t feel the need to respond to that last comment. He just held his head up and guided us through the crowd to the spot near the museum where the photo shoot would take place.

Jordan met us there, a broad smile on his face as he saw us coming toward him.

"Well now, I get two for the price of one—a bride and a groom."

"We aim to please." Brady grinned and released my arm. "Hope you don't mind that I'm playing the role of groom."

"Don't mind a bit, if the Someday Bride doesn't."

"The Someday Bride doesn't." I giggled.

"Show him your dress, Katie," Brady said with a smile.

I did a little twirl and showed off the ruffles in the skirt.

"Looks great." Jordan smiled. "And it's going to photograph well, I'm sure. We've got a spot all set up for the first shot." He pointed at the area, which had been taped off to keep the crowd away. "Perfect background, right?"

Perfect was right. Underneath the mid-afternoon sun, the area felt like a scene from the Old West. In a few hours, if this photo shoot lasted that long, Brady and I would be riding off into the sunset. For some reason that got me tickled. That, and I couldn't stop thinking about the fact that he'd called himself a prop.

Jordan introduced us to the photographers—a married couple, Hannah and Drew Kincaid from Galveston. Turned out they had done a lot of photo shoots involving brides, so they knew just how to ask me to pose. Good thing too, because I froze up the minute I stepped into the spot they'd prepped for me. The first couple of shots were rough at best. And it didn't help that total strangers were watching, whooping and hollering, and asking Brady about the big day.

Madge and Dahlia finally showed up, but their presence didn't serve to calm my nerves, especially with Dahlia fussing over the wrinkles in the dress. Only when the photographers decided that Brady should join me in the photos did I begin to calm down.

He stepped into place next to me and slid his hand on my back. "The prop has arrived."

"You're no prop," I whispered. "And I'm no model."

"Oh, I don't know. You're prettier than a picture, that's for sure." He gave me a little smile and I calmed down immediately.

"Okay, you two." Hannah gestured with her hand. "I hope this doesn't make you feel too awkward, but you're going to have to give us some up-close and personal poses. Can you do your best to get cozy?"

Oh, I could definitely get cozy with this guy. On the other hand, he was a full head taller than me. Maybe more so. Hannah saw my plight right away and brought me a wooden crate to stand on.

"Try this." She put it in place and gestured for me to make use of it.

With Brady's help I climbed up onto the crate, nearly falling in the process. He caught me around the waist, and the cameras started snapping. I settled into place and gave them a funny pose, one that sent me toppling right into my groom. The cameras kept snapping. Brady, in an impulsive move, grabbed me around the waist and lifted me into the air. The crowd roared with delight.

"Three-point shot!" someone hollered.

He laughed and set me back down on the crate.

"Let's try some sweet poses now," Hannah instructed. "Cheek to cheek. That sort of thing."

"Happy to oblige." Brady gave me a little nod.

"Face each other and put your palms together," she instructed. "And then lean in."

"Lean in, eh?" Brady quirked a brow as he placed his palms against mine. "Don't mind if I do."

My heart skip-skip-skipped as I leaned against his cheek for several photos. I felt his breath warm against my face. Hannah and Drew took several shots from a variety of angles while the crowd continued to whoop and holler.

"Okay." Drew put his camera down and walked toward us. "We'll do a few shots of Katie with Brady looking at her."

"Adoringly," Hannah added. "Can you look at her adoringly, Brady?"

"Won't take much effort." He gave me a little wink.

Madge let out a whistle and the crowd responded with another whoop.

“Katie, we’ll do a bunch of different poses,” Hannah said.

And we did. I loved the ones with my back to the camera as I looked over my shoulder. I even loved the ones where I sat on the crate, sort of hunched over, like an exhausted bride after a long day. My favorite, however, was the one where I caught a glimpse of Brady looking at me from a distance, his eyes brimming with affection.

Wow, could this guy act, or what?

Hmm.

Hannah and Drew instructed us to take a break while they readjusted the sun deflectors, and Brady walked my way. He slipped his arm around my waist, and I gave him a curious look.

“They’re not shooting right now,” I whispered.

“I know,” he whispered back. He stared into my eyes and I felt myself melting, kind of like the Wicked Witch after being hit with a bucket of water. I couldn’t seem to control the emotions that washed over me as he pulled me closer still. “Can I be honest here?” he whispered.

I nodded. “Honesty is good. Take it from someone who’s been afraid to be honest—with herself and with you.”

“I’m going to be perfectly honest.” He brushed a loose hair out of my face, and I thought I heard the click of a camera but ignored it, too drawn in by this handsome prop of mine. “This news of yours, about not being engaged?”

"Made you want to jump off a bridge?" I tried.

He shook his head. "No. Not even close."

"Made you wonder how you were going to handle the press once the word got out?"

"Well, there is that. But that's not what I was referring to." He gazed into my eyes with such tenderness that I felt like swooning. Not that I'd ever swooned a day in my life, but I suddenly understood what the term meant. The cameras continued to click, but I found myself completely ignoring them, enraptured by this awesome man in front of me.

I sighed. "Made you wish you'd never met me?"

"Good try." He reached for my hand and gave it a squeeze. "But you're 100 percent wrong on that count." He laced his fingers through mine. "Your news about the wedding being off is actually the best news I've heard in a long, long time."

"It . . . it is?"

To my left, the cameras continued to click.

"Mm-hmm." He leaned in close to whisper in my ear, "Because I don't mind saying I can't stand Casey what's-his-name."

"Lawson."

"Lawson," he echoed. "Never met the guy, but I can't stand him."

"Oh?" My knees went weak as Brady pulled me into his arms.

"Yep," he whispered. "I'm not like other guys I

know—playing the field. I've been hanging on for the ride, waiting for God to zap me with someone who made my head spin."

"O-oh?"

"And you?" He brushed his cheek against mine, words soft in my ear. "You made my head spin."

I couldn't help but giggle. "And that's a good thing? Or are you saying I make you dizzy?"

"You make me dizzy, all right." In a typical impulsive move, he grabbed me by the waist and spun me around. The cameras continued to click, click, click.

"Whoa." I laughed so hard and so long that the crowd joined in. Before long they were all cheering.

Brady put me back down and took hold of my hands. "I don't mind admitting that I was half crazed, thinking of you marrying that Casey guy."

"The one you hate." I bit back the smile.

"Well, *hate* is a strong word. I strongly disliked him."

"Because . . ."

"He had what I wanted."

"What. You. Wanted." I repeated the words but didn't have time to think them through before Brady's soft kiss on my forehead caught me off guard.

Oh. My. Goodness.

I stood there melting in his arms. Okay, maybe the ninety-degree heat had a little something to do with the melting, but still, I felt myself lost in a haze—a wonderful, romantic haze, one that included a crowd of onlookers and a couple of photographers who seemed to be enjoying this.

Oh boy, you make a great prop.

I gazed into his eyes and whispered, "Are you saying all of this so we'll get a great shot?"

He shook his head. "I couldn't care less about the photos, Katie."

Jordan held his hand up and cleared his throat. He took a couple of steps in our direction. "Sorry to interrupt, but we're nearly ready to wrap up. Just a couple of shots left."

"Give her a kiss, Brady!" someone in the crowd hollered out.

"Yeah, every bride needs a kiss from her groom," Madge said with a wink.

"A kiss, eh?" Brady grinned that boyish grin of his. "I'd be pleased. If the lady doesn't mind."

I giggled and my heart started that crazy skittering thing again. "The lady doesn't mind."

Nope. She didn't mind one little bit. And she had a feeling—call it a bride's intuition, call it whatever—this would be the first of many, many kisses yet to come.

Brady lifted me back onto the crate so we could stand face-to-face, and then, with cameras clicking all around us, he gave me a kiss sweeter than all of the peaches of Fairfield combined—one worthy of a magazine cover.

26

Before I'm Over You

> A city is a place where there is no need to wait for next week to get the answer to a question, to taste the food of any country, to find new voices to listen to and familiar ones to listen to again.
>
> Margaret Mead

By the time the sun had fully gone down, Brady and I had finally managed to sneak away from the crowd and have some alone time. With Madge and Dahlia's help, I managed to change out of my wedding gown in the restroom and back into my jeans. Dahlia went on and on about the photo shoot, then helped me get my dress onto a hanger and back into a zipper bag.

"Can I ask you a question?" She looped the bag over her arm, fussed with it for a moment, and then passed it to me.

"Sure." I did my best to juggle the bag so as not to harm the gown inside.

"You two weren't acting out there, were you? I mean, I've known Brady for years and I've never seen this side of him before."

I shook my head and draped the bag over my

left arm. "I honestly don't know how to answer that question." Little giggles followed.

"Oh, girl . . ." Madge shook her head. "You can't deny the obvious. And maybe it's not as complicated as you've made it. Maybe it's very, very simple." She walked out of the restroom, carrying on about how life was just like that—full of surprises.

It was full of surprises, for sure. I couldn't help but smile all the way back to the store, where I left the dress so that it could be cleaned. Brady and I said our goodbyes—very generic, since we happened to be in front of the ladies at the shop—and I headed off to Aunt Alva's house. She peppered me with questions. When I couldn't answer them without blushing, she pursed her lips and smiled.

"I see how it is."

Yep. She saw, all right.

I hated to ruin anyone's good mood, but I needed to talk to her about Queenie's party. After I explained that I would be leaving for Fairfield on Friday afternoon, she wrinkled her nose.

"I'll miss you, girlie. I'm getting used to having you around."

"Well, that's the thing," I said. "You don't have to miss me at all, Aunt Alva. Come with me."

"To Fairfield?" Her eyes widened in obvious surprise. "Over my dead body."

"It's time, Alva. You should come. It's Queenie's birthday."

"I know when my own sister's birthday is." She released a sigh. "But no thank you. You go on and have a good time. I'll be here waiting when you get back. Maybe I'll paint the guest room while you're gone." She went off on a tangent about how she'd been thinking of painting that room a lovely shade of rose, but I knew she was just avoiding the obvious. Maybe I'd been wrong. Maybe this wasn't God's perfect timing to take Alva home again. Oh well.

I tumbled into bed that night, the scenes from the photo shoot still fresh on my mind and the scent of Brady's cologne lingering in my imagination. I replayed that awesome moment when he'd given me such a sweet little kiss on the forehead, then that lovely point where his lips had touched mine. Who would have guessed the day would go the way it had, and yet . . .

I slept, dreaming of Brady, then awoke all smiles. I thought of him all day Thursday, though I didn't see him once, since Alva and I spent the day resting. I replayed the moment of our kiss over and over as I slept Thursday night and awoke Friday morning in a joyous mood. In fact, I kept on smiling until noon, when Lori-Lou called to tell me that she and Josh had been approved for the house and had a lot of packing to do.

"You sound out of breath, Katie," she said.

"Oh, I'm just putting my suitcase into my car. Going home for Queenie's party. You coming?"

"No." Lori-Lou sighed. "Josh is working extra hours, so I'd be by myself with the kids."

"I could help."

"You're sweet, but it's too much to handle if he's not with me. Besides, we're down to one car right now. Mine still isn't working. Before you go, though, I need to talk to you about something."

"What's that?" I hefted my suitcase into the backseat.

"Did you know that Casey's back home?"

That stopped me dead in my tracks. "Casey's back home?"

"Yeah. Beau called Josh yesterday."

"Casey's in Fairfield?"

"I think maybe he didn't like the job in Tulsa? Or maybe it wasn't a good fit? I don't know. I just know he's back home. Beau said that everyone's walking on eggshells around him."

Casey. Back home. Crazy.

My heart flip-flopped all over the place at this news. I vacillated between anger, hopefulness, and a variety of other emotions that ping-ponged around my heart. Most of all I wondered why he hadn't called me.

Then again, why would he? We weren't a couple anymore, after all.

Lori-Lou went on to ask about the photo shoot, and I told her about the shot of Brady kissing me.

"Wow." She giggled. "Wow, wow. Now there's a plot twist. What are you going to do if they choose that one for the cover? Your family is bound to see it. And Casey too, right?"

"He doesn't read bridal magazines, but I suppose it's inevitable. Who knows, maybe the people at *Texas Bride* won't choose that picture for the cover, right?"

"True. They might want one of you in the dress. By yourself, I mean. But still . . ." Lori-Lou started scolding Mariela for coloring on the walls. She returned breathless. "Sorry about that."

"Don't ever be sorry about your life, Lori-Lou," I said. "You've got a great life. Great husband. Wonderful children."

"If you don't put those colors down right this minute, you'll never use them again, young lady!" Lori-Lou's voice faded and then she returned again. "What were you saying?"

"Just saying that life is good. It's full of twists and turns, but it's good. And I'm not really worried about the magazine cover. My parents—and Casey—will find out in a couple of months, but I'll have to cross that bridge when we come to it."

"In the meantime, don't do anything rash."

"Like appearing on the cover of a national magazine kissing a pro basketball player?"

"I thought you said he was kissing you?"

"Right. I think I kissed him back, though."

"Hey, no one would blame you. The guy's great. Tall, handsome, suave, but kind too. And he's a Christian."

"And he's been waiting on the perfect-for-him girl. I heard all about it."

"Does he realize the perfect-for-him girl still hasn't quite let go of the not-so-perfect-for-her guy back in Fairfield?"

"I've let go of him, trust me." The truth of those words settled over me. "So, Casey's really back in Fairfield?"

"Mm-hmm. Just try to avoid him this weekend."

"Oh, I will."

I thought about my cousin's words as I headed back inside. Before leaving, I gave Aunt Alva a hug and tried one last time to talk her into going with me. She shook her head and told me to have a good time.

"But we're having the party at Sam's," I said. "That's your favorite restaurant, right?"

"You'll have to eat a double portion of barbecue for me," she said. "I just can't do it, honey. Not yet, anyway."

I wondered when—if ever—she would work up the courage to go back home again. Still, it wasn't my business.

I made the drive back to Fairfield, a thousand different thoughts flying through my head. Brady. Kissing. Photos. Casey. Newspaper. Mama. WOP-pers. Queenie. Birthday. Alva.

It all rolled together in my brain.

I arrived at Sam's about twenty minutes early and checked my email on my phone. My heart jumped when I realized Jordan Singer had sent me a link to the photos from Wednesday's shoot. I clicked the link, and picture after picture greeted me in living Technicolor.

Oh. My. Goodness.

I rolled the window down on my car to keep from getting overheated, then flipped through the pictures, mesmerized by how great the shots were. Hannah and Drew had done a spectacular job of capturing not just the ambience of the setting, not just the amazing Loretta Lynn gown, but the emotions on my face.

And Brady . . .

Whoa. My heart quickened as I saw picture after picture of Brady gazing at me with pure adoration in his eyes. Either the guy was a terrific actor, or . . .

"Katie?"

Mama's voice came from outside the open window. I minimized the photo on the screen and turned to face her. "Yes?" I did my best to steady my voice. "You scared me."

"Katie, what was that?" She pointed at my phone. "What were you looking at?"

"Oh, some pictures. Wedding gowns. You know how I am."

"Well, yes, I know you like wedding dress

photos, but that almost looked like . . ." She shook her head. "I could've sworn I was looking at a picture of you in that wedding dress. Pull it up again so I can see it. Strangest thing ever."

Thank goodness I didn't have time to do that. Queenie pulled into the spot next to us and needed help getting out of her car.

"Why in the world they don't have more handicapped spots is beyond me. There are never any available, no matter what time of day I come."

Like she had ever come at a different time.

I noticed that my grandmother was having more trouble with her knee than usual and asked her about it. "Oh, this old thing?" She pointed down. "It gives me fits, but I keep going. I'm still a spring chicken, you know."

"Well, happy birthday, spring chicken." I gave her a kiss on the cheek.

"You back for good?" Queenie asked. "Or just home for the weekend?"

"I came home to spend time with you, but I might go back for another week or two." Or longer. Somehow the thought of spending more time with Brady held me in its grip.

"Guess you heard that you-know-who is back." Queenie gave me a pensive look.

"Yeah, I heard he was home." I sighed. "That might be a good reason for me to stay put in Dallas a little longer, if you want the truth of it."

"You can't avoid the inevitable forever," she

said. “And I don’t know how in the world you’re handling staying with Lori-Lou. All of those kids would drive me bonkers. How are you managing?”

Oy vey. There it was. The dreaded question. “Well, actually, it’s pretty crowded at Lori-Lou’s place, so I found someone else to stay with.”

“Someone else?” Queenie’s gaze narrowed. “You have other friends in the city?”

“Not friends exactly, Queenie,” I said. “More like . . . family.”

“Family?” She tilted her head and I could read the confusion in her expression. Until the light bulb went on. Then, in an instant, confusion morphed to anger. “Oh no. Tell me you haven’t made amends with Alva.”

“Made amends? Queenie, I never had a falling-out with her. In fact, I’ve never had much of anything to do with her, good or bad.”

“How in the world did you end up at her place, anyway? Did she track you down?”

The timing certainly wasn’t right to tell Queenie the whole story.

“Well, I think it’s time to change the subject.” Queenie squared her shoulders. “We gonna stand out here in the heat or go inside? Where is everyone, anyway?”

Mama gave me a wink. “They’re inside.”

They were inside, all right. The whole Fisher clan was seated at the usual table holding signs that read “Happy birthday, Queenie!”

She shook her head and grumbled that we shouldn't have gone to so much trouble, but her attention was quickly diverted to the three strangers at the table. I was a little diverted too. Looked like my brothers had talked Dahlia, Crystal, and Twiggy into coming to the party.

Oh boy.

Was this going to be fun, or what?

27

You Wouldn't Know an Angel (if You Saw One)

Change is the one thing we can be sure of.
Naomi Judd

Mama stared at the girls, her eyes narrowing as she noticed Twiggy sitting next to Beau. And Crystal sitting next to Jasper. And Dahlia sitting next to Dewey.

"Well, who do we have here?" My mother took a seat and looked all around the table, her brow knitted.

"Mama, this is Dahlia." Dewey looked a little scared, but Dahlia didn't seem to notice.

She offered Mama a broad smile. "Nice to meet you, Mrs. Fisher. I've heard so much about you. And Queenie . . ." She looked at my grandmother, who took her usual seat at the head of the table. "My goodness, I feel as if I already know you, I've heard so many fun stories."

"All good, I hope." Queenie gave my brother a concerned look.

"All good." Dahlia smiled.

Mama seemed to be having a hard time with

our guests. She narrowed her gaze as she looked at Dewey and his guest. "Dahlia?" Mama spoke the word, then repeated it slowly, as if trying to make sense of it. "Dah-li-a."

"It's Swedish," Dahlia explained, her accent sounding even heavier here in Fairfield than it had in Dallas. "It means *valley*."

"Well, my goodness." Mama fanned herself with her hand. "Down in the valley, the valley so low."

Dahlia's countenance fell at once.

"Mama!" Dewey groaned. "It's a beautiful name for a beautiful girl."

"Well, she is lovely, isn't she?" Mama pointed at Dahlia's hair. "Is that real?"

"Mama!" I gave her a scolding look.

Dahlia didn't seem bothered by my mother's hair question. "Actually, they're extensions. I got them at a salon in Dallas a few months ago. I think they work for my face shape, don't you?"

"Did she say *salon* or *saloon?*" Mama whispered.

I gave her a warning look.

"I need to take you to meet Nancy Jo at Do or Dye." Mama turned her attention back to Dahlia. "She's new in town and is really hip. Like you. I'd bet you two would be terrific friends. What did you say those things in your hair are called again?"

"Extensions."

"Extensions." Mama mulled over the word and

shrugged. "Need to get me some of those, I think. This current Diane Keaton 'do' is turning out to be more of a 'don't,' don'tcha think?" She fussed with her hair.

Jasper, perhaps nervous by our mother's odd welcome to Dahlia, decided this would be the perfect time to introduce Crystal.

"Mama, I want you to meet someone. This is Crystal. She's from Georgia. Where they have peaches."

Like that would help.

The petite blonde flashed Mama a broad smile. "Oh, Miz Fisher, I've heard so much about you!" Her Southern drawl seemed more pronounced today. "Jasper here tells me you're the *purr*-fect mama, and that's just *purr*-fect with me, because my mama and daddy are singing with the angels right about now. I miss 'em *so* much." She rose and walked to my mother's chair, then wrapped her in a big hug. "I hope we'll be *free*-unds. Can we?"

"Well, shore, honey." Mama's own accent thickened. "I have a feeling we're two peas in a pod."

"Mmm, peas." Crystal giggled. "I haven't had a good bowl of black-eyed peas since I left Georgia."

"Then you have to come to our house when we're done. I made a big pot of black-eyed peas just yesterday."

"Ooh, I'd love that. Yum." Crystal gave Mama

another hug, told her that she felt sure they'd be best friends, and then headed back to her chair.

Beau, perhaps encouraged by this scene, cleared his throat. Mama shifted her attention his way, her gaze landing on Twiggy, who sat beside him in complete silence.

"Beau? Who have we here?"

The whole table grew silent. You could've cut through the tension with a knife.

Beau took a swallow of his sweet tea, then released a slow breath. "Mama, I'd like you to meet Twiggy."

"Twiggy?" Mama's brows scrunched. "Like the model from the sixties?"

A delightful smile lit Twiggy's delicate face. "Yes, that's right."

"Is she your mama or something?" Before Twiggy could respond, my mother gave the young woman a closer look. "I do think I see a family resemblance, especially in the calorie department. You look as if you could stand some padding, girlie. We'll have to load you up with carbs. It'll do you a world of good."

Twiggy paled. "Oh, no thank you. I'm off of carbs. In fact, I'm gluten-free. Well, mostly."

"Gluten-free?" My mother's eyebrows shot up so high I thought they might take leave of her face. "Well now."

Oh. Dear.

Mama couldn't abide anyone who hated bread.

Bread was a staple in our world, kind of like air or water. Or lemon pound cake.

Beau's sweetie lit into a dissertation about some diet plan she'd found online. Before long she and Dahlia were engaged in a conversation about it. Mama, on the other hand, refused to play along.

"The only diet I've been able to stick to is the one where you cut back at the buffet."

"Or eat your weight in lemon pound cake," Beau whispered to me.

"I heard that." Mama gave him a sour look. She pointed at Twiggy's short bob. "Now that's a haircut! I think I saw this once on a TV show. Did you pay money to have that done or cut it yourself?"

"I-I paid money." Twiggy squared her shoulders. "I've never cut my own hair. Well, not since I was three, anyway."

"I've cut Herb's hair for years," Mama said. "And my boys' too, though frankly, most of the time they just shaved it all off in the summertime, due to the heat. I always say a woman who can cut her man's hair is of great value. She saves him the $6.99 at the barber shop."

"Oh, I *ahl*-ways cut my brothers' *hay*-er too," Crystal said. "I'm *real*-ly good at it."

Mama turned her gaze to Crystal and smiled. "Good to know. Why don't you and I go have a look at the buffet, Crystal? In fact, I'll show you around the restaurant so you'll feel right at home."

"Oh, yes ma'am." Crystal rose and joined my mother. "I'd love that."

"When we're done, I'll come back and feed that skinny one some bread." She pointed at Twiggy, who sat in stony silence, glaring at Beau.

Mama and Crystal headed off arm in arm to take a little tour of the restaurant. Dahlia engaged my grandmother in some conversation about the weather. And Twiggy—God bless her—reached for a slice of bread from the basket in the center of the table.

Beau offered a little shrug, then passed her the butter. "And there you have it," he said with a smile. "That's our mama."

Yep. That was our mama, all right. Nothing we could do about that, at least at the moment. Queenie switched the conversation to the recent drought, and Pop joined in, talking about how he'd seen an upswing in the sale of garden hoses.

Less than five minutes later Mama and Crystal returned to the table, all smiles. I couldn't help but notice my mother was carrying a large slice of lemon pound cake. Strange, since we hadn't eaten any real food yet.

"You'll never guess, Katie. Crystal's from Georgia." Mama took her seat once again and set the pound cake down.

"Well, yes, I know. She's—"

"From Atlanta. She was Miss Peaches two years in a row. Isn't that a fun coincidence? I told her that you were Fairfield's Peach Queen your senior year and she can totally relate." Mama gave Crystal an admiring look. "She even loves peach cobbler, my all-time favorite."

"Well, Mama, you didn't think I'd bring home a gal who didn't like peaches, did you?" Jasper looked offended. "I know a good girl when I see one."

"I believe you do." Mama shook her head and looked at all of the girls. "I still can't get over the fact that all of you met in a bridal shop. Doesn't make a lick of sense to me."

"Well, that's kind of a long story," I said.

"No time for that now." Mama shifted her gaze to Twiggy. "I daresay we get busy feeding this one something before she wilts away to nothing. Oh my goodness. Why, you're eating the bread."

"I am." Twiggy took another bite. "It's good."

"Well, for pity's sake. I hope we don't have to call 9-1-1," Queenie said. "I once heard of a gal who had to be hospitalized after eating bread."

"It's a very real problem," I said. "People who are overly sensitive blow up like balloons when they eat bread."

"Good thing I'm not overly sensitive then." Queenie gave me a wink.

"It's not really like that, anyway," Twiggy said and then took another nibble. "I'm not hyper-sensitive to gluten or anything like that. Mostly I just don't like the carbs, so the gluten-free diet works for me. Really, it's more Paleo, if you want the truth of it." She took another big bite of the bread.

"Paleo?" Mama's nose wrinkled. "Are you an archaeologist or something?"

"No. It's a kind of diet."

"Well, I understand. The doctor put me on a diet once too. Didn't really take, but I gave it the old college try." Mama took a nibble of her lemon pound cake. "I think mine was called the California diet. No, maybe it was the Arizona diet. Anyway, it was named after some state. Never heard of the Paleo thing. I'll have to look it up on the internet."

Queenie sighed. "I'm terrible on the computer. Things are whirling so fast on that machine, I just can't keep up. To be honest with you, I'd be just as happy if there was no such thing as the internet. I liked things the way they were before we were all in each others' business on those crazy social media sites."

"Oh, but if we didn't have internet, our whole business would collapse," Pop said. "We're dependent on networking, you know."

"Well, all this talk about bread has me hungry," Queenie said. "Does anyone mind if I get some food? It is my birthday, after all."

"Yes, we wouldn't want the birthday girl to starve." Pop chuckled.

Everyone rose and made their way to the buffet.

Mama caught me in front of the salad bar and leaned down to whisper in my ear, "Dewey's got his eye on that tall girl with the platinum hair, does he?"

I nodded. "Dahlia's very nice."

"I don't trust anyone whose name I can't pronounce."

"Like Mayor Luchenbacher?" I asked.

"Well, of course I can pronounce Luchenbacher. I grew up with Karl Luchenbacher. That's not foreign to me. Delilah is foreign."

"Dahlia."

"Exactly. Foreign. And I can't understand half of what she says. Do you think she's trying to impress us with that accent of hers?" Mama's eyes flashed with suspicion. "Maybe she's really from California or someplace like that, and she's just acting. Putting on a show so people think she's all hoity-toity when she's just a regular small-town girl like us."

"I don't think there's much that's regular about us," I said.

"I'm definitely not regular," Pop said as he stepped into the spot next to me. "Haven't been for the past four years, but I think it's got something to do with male menopause."

This led to yet another bizarre conversation with my parents.

"That Twiggy girl is the last person on earth I'd picture with my Beau." Mama reached to fill her plate with lettuce. "Such a skinny little thing."

"Mama, why do you care if Beau has a girl?"

Mama turned back to look at me. "I don't expect you to understand, Katie. You're not a mama."

"But even if I was, I'd want my kids to be happy. It's obvious Beau is very happy with Twiggy."

"He can be happy with someone closer to home. When the time is right."

I pulled her off to the side, away from the others. Time for a heart-to-heart with Mama. "What if the time is right now?" I asked. "And what if the place really is Dallas? Would that be so awful?"

A painful silence followed my words.

"What if this is God's answer to Beau's prayers for someone to love?" I continued. "Would you argue with him? The Lord, I mean."

"She lives in *Dallas*."

"If we could put that part aside and focus on the look of happiness on Beau's face, then wouldn't you agree this is for the best?"

Mama said nothing. She shifted her salad plate from one hand to the other.

"Point is, she brings out the best in him," I said.

"In Dallas."

"That's where her work is, sure. But Dallas isn't exactly Timbuktu, Mama. It's only an hour or so away."

"Conversation over." Mama headed back to the salad bar. "My goodness, it's crowded in here tonight. We have to fight for food."

Among other things.

We filled our plates and headed back to the table. Before long everyone but Mama settled into comfortable conversation. We even had Queenie laughing on more than one occasion. When it came time to open gifts, she turned her attention to the packages, obviously intrigued. She had just ripped the paper off of a gift from Mama when something—or rather, someone—caught my attention from the other side of the room.

Walking toward us, albeit hobbling a bit, was Aunt Alva . . . on Brady James's arm.

28

Who's Gonna Take the Garbage Out

My plan is to have a theatre in some small town or something and I'll be manager. I'll be the crazy old movie guy.

Quentin Tarantino

I couldn't say which shocked me more—seeing Aunt Alva or seeing Brady. Not that I was unhappy to see either, mind you. Just stunned.

The moment Queenie laid eyes on her sister, she stopped unwrapping the gift and froze in place, eyes wide.

Pop rose and moved toward his aunt, then swept her into his arms. "Well, as I live and breathe. So good to see you, Alva. Wonderful of you to come. God bless you for that."

This got a "humph" from Queenie, who went back to her gift.

"I'd know this face anywhere." Pop gestured to Brady. "One of my favorite basketball players ever."

"Thank you, sir." Brady smiled, but I could tell he was a little nervous.

I rose and made introductions. Pop seemed

pretty flabbergasted to find one of his favorite Mavericks players standing next to him at Sam's. Across the room, a couple of other customers whispered to one another as they stared at Brady.

"It's so nice to meet you, sir." Brady extended his hand.

My father shook it and then looked at me. Then back at Brady. "I'm sorry . . . where did you say you two met?"

"My mom owns a store in Dallas," Brady said. "Katie is . . ." He gazed at me with tenderness in his eyes. "A customer."

"A customer." Pop looked at Brady. "Our family owns a store too. Hardware. What sort do you have?" Brady had just opened his mouth to respond when Pop interrupted him. "Let's pull up a couple of chairs. You two hungry?"

"Starving." Alva nodded. "Haven't had Sam's barbecue in years."

Pop, God bless him, put Alva and Brady on the far side of the table from Queenie.

Alva shifted her gaze to the table, where Queenie continued to work on the gift from Mama. "Hope you don't mind that we've come without an invitation."

"Oh, they had an invitation." I flashed a warm smile. "From me."

Another "humph" followed from Queenie.

When my aunt lit into a lively conversation

with Twiggy, Dahlia, and Crystal, Mama looked aghast.

"You know these gals, Alva?" she asked.

"Well, sure. We're all friends. People in the city are very friendly, you know. Not like here."

This garnered another grunt from Queenie, who'd managed to get the gift from Mama opened at last. It turned out to be a devotional about the power of positive speaking. Ironic.

From across the table Brady looked my way and shrugged. I did my best not to let the joy on my face show, but Mama must've picked up on it. She gave me one of those "we're going to talk about this later" looks.

He offered to fix Alva's plate and disappeared to the buffet. I caught up with him in front of the barbecue.

"I can't believe you're here," I said.

"Me either. Alva called me right after you left. Said she'd had a change of heart. But she knew she couldn't drive all this way, so she asked me to play the role of chauffeur."

"You've been doing a lot of role-playing lately."

"No." He smiled. "Not role-playing at all. It's the real deal, every bit of it. And I'm glad to be here."

He might not have been so glad a minute or so later when the locals swarmed him, asking for autographs. After delivering my aunt's plate to the table, he graciously signed all sorts of things—

from menus to church bulletins. By the time he arrived at the table with his own food, my aunt was nearly done eating.

Brady took a seat and gave me a little wink. Alva must've picked up on this and smiled at me. Then she looked at my mother. "Marie, you look even younger than the last time I saw you."

Mama looked stunned by this, but a smile turned up the edges of her lips. "Well, thank you, Alva. That's very sweet."

"It's the hair. Why, you look just like Diane Keaton in that movie she did with Jack Nicholson."

"That's what Katie said when she saw my new do." Mama fussed with her hair and then reached into her purse for her lipstick compact. "Maybe I'll keep this hairdo after all."

"Katie's a smart girl." Alva winked at me. "Pretty sure it runs in the family."

"Lots of great things run in the family," Pop said. "Right, Mama?"

He looked at Queenie, who never lifted her gaze from the pile of presents in front of her. She'd opened them all and looked as if she wanted to bolt.

I had a flashback to a particular Friday night when I'd gathered around the table with my family at Sam's. This very table, in fact. My brother had joked about hernias and hemorrhoids that evening. I'd dreamed of a day when I'd grow old with a fella who didn't mind such bizarre conversations around the dinner table. Now here we sat—Brady James and the whole Fisher clan. Strange.

A few minutes later we wrapped up the party—if one could call it a party—and my brothers headed out with the girls. Mama had somehow coerced them all into going back to our house for coffee and birthday cake. Pop carried Queenie's gifts out to her car and she followed on his heels, still not speaking to her sister. I found myself alone with Alva and Brady.

"Well, that was awkward." Alva's nose wrinkled. "Sorry, kiddo. I thought maybe the timing was right."

"No, it's my fault. I'm the one who encouraged you to come. Queenie is just so . . ."

"Stubborn. Always has been." Alva shrugged. "Runs in the family."

We walked out to the parking lot, where Pop was still loading presents in the back of Queenie's car.

I looked at Alva and released a breath. "What do you say we nip this in the bud, once and for all?"

"You think?" She looked nervous.

"This is as good a place as any." I looked up at Brady for some encouragement, and he gave me a confident smile.

"You ladies do the talking. I'll do the praying."

"He's closer to heaven all the way up there." Alva gave a slight chuckle. "Okay. Let's get this over with."

We walked over to Queenie's car just as Pop opened the front door for her. My grandmother glared at me as we drew near, as if to say, "Back off, people."

I didn't back off. Neither did Alva, who stood to my left.

"Queenie, we need to talk, and I think it's better done before we get to the house."

"No talking necessary," she said.

"Queenie, please . . ." Alva's voice sounded shaky. "Can't we just say a few words?"

"Nothing to say."

"But you two used to be really close." I posed this more as a question than a statement, but I could tell Alva was a nervous wreck.

"We were." Alva nodded. "Very close."

"And then?" I asked.

My aunt's eyes misted over. "And then . . . life happened."

"Life happened?" Queenie finally looked at us. She rolled her eyes. "*You* happened. Life didn't happen."

"Queenie . . ." A lone tear trickled down my aunt's wrinkly cheek.

"Conversation ended, please and thank you." Queenie turned the car on.

"Oh no you don't." My father, never one to

argue with his mother, reached inside the car and turned it off. "We're going to deal with this right now, Mama, whether you want to or not."

"Humph."

"Jealousies are jealousies," he said, "but sisterly love lasts forever."

"Sisterly love?" Queenie huffed. "Don't talk to me about sisterly love." She looked over at Alva, her eyes brimming with tears. "All these years, and you come back now? Why?"

"Because I love you."

"Love? Where was your love five years ago when I had my gallbladder out? I was sick in the hospital and you didn't come see me."

"I had surgery on my knee six months ago and you didn't even pick up the phone," Alva countered.

"I lost my husband and you didn't so much as send me a note or card."

A painful silence hung over us at that proclamation.

"I . . . I didn't know what to say." Alva's gaze shifted downward.

"Wait." I put my hand up. "This could go on for hours. Point is, you two haven't spoken in years. We get that. What I want to know is, why? Can you just get to the root of the problem, deal with it, and move on?"

"She. Knows. Why." Queenie's jaw clenched.

"And I told you back then that I was sorry.

You wouldn't have it. You've never had it." Alva pointed an arthritic finger at her younger sister. "You've never forgiven me, and it's eaten you alive all these years."

"Time to get things out in the open," I said.

My grandmother gave me a warning look, but I wouldn't be shushed. We'd spent too many years in this family keeping things under wraps.

"Confession is good for the soul," I said. "So c'mon, Queenie. Why can't you let go of what happened all those years ago?"

She shook her head. "If Alva wants to tell you, she can. I . . . I just . . . can't." My grandmother paled and looked as if she might be sick.

"Queenie?"

She leaned forward and gripped the steering wheel, her breathing unsteady.

"Mama? You okay?" Pop leaned in the car. "Are you getting overheated?" He reached around her and put the key in the ignition.

"I'm . . . I'm not feeling well."

"Queenie, I'm so sorry," Alva said. "Really, truly sorry."

My grandmother nodded and then slumped over the steering wheel. My heart rate doubled as I called out her name and then turned to Brady.

"Call 9-1-1!"

I tossed him my phone. Queenie lay completely still. Alva crouched over her, tears flowing.

"Sister!" she called out. "Sister, look at me. You wake up right this minute!"

"I don't think she can, Alva." My father checked his mother's pulse. "Everyone back away. She needs air."

"But she needs me," Alva said. "I've never been here for her." Her voice elevated. "But I'm here now, Queenie. I'm here now."

"She's got a pulse. I think she just passed out." Pop pointed the air vents at her. "I pray that's all it is."

Several minutes passed, but they felt more like hours. The wail of a siren in the background eventually alerted me to the fact that the ambulance had arrived. Less than a minute later a young paramedic was working on my grandmother. Pop made a quick call to Mama, who turned her car around and headed back to Sam's with my brothers and the girls right behind her.

"What happened?" the paramedic asked as he checked her pulse.

"She was in the middle of an argument with me," Alva said.

"Next thing you know, she was having trouble breathing," Pop said. "Then she passed out."

"Was she in pain?" The paramedic listened with his stethoscope to Queenie's chest.

"I . . . I don't know." Pop shook his head.

About the time Mama and the others arrived, the paramedics had Queenie loaded up on a stretcher. We all gathered around her in a circle. If there was one thing we Baptists knew how to do, it was pray.

Turned out the Presbyterians were pretty good at praying too. Reverend Bradford showed up at that very moment. He rushed to my grandmother's side. "Queenie? Queenie, I'm here. Hang on now, you hear me? Hang on."

She seemed to rally at the sound of his voice and gave a slight nod. Still, her eyes never opened.

"What happened here?" He looked at Alva and his eyes widened.

"It's my fault." Alva began to cry in earnest now. "Everything is always my fault."

"No. No one is pointing fingers," Reverend Bradford said. "Right now, the only one we need to be focusing on is Queenie. So let's pray."

The Presbyterians and Baptists all joined hands in a circle and prayed the house down. Er, the parking lot. Reverend Bradford apparently had a slightly charismatic edge to his praying that seemed to get Mama more emotional than ever. Her tears flowed as he interceded on my grandmother's behalf.

And when Brother Kennedy, a local Pentecostal deacon, joined in, we really had a prayer meeting. We didn't get a lot of "Amen!" and "Hallelujah!" action in the Baptist church, but I certainly didn't mind it today, not with my grandmother's life hanging in the balance.

By the time we finished, I had no doubt in my mind the Lord had heard our multi-denominational prayer. I had a feeling Queenie had heard it too, based on the half smile that appeared on her lips as they lifted the stretcher into the ambulance.

"Is she coming to?" Mama asked.

The paramedic nodded. "I think so, but let's keep her calm, okay? Not saying you folks shouldn't pray, but that was a little loud."

I watched as my grandmother disappeared into the ambulance, then I felt Brady's arms slip around me. Nestling into his comforting embrace, I wept.

"She's going to be okay, Katie. I just know it."

I nodded and gazed up into his eyes filled with compassion. In that moment, I knew he was right. She was going to be okay. In fact, everything was going to be okay.

29

If Teardrops Were Pennies

There are things about growing up in a small town that you can't necessarily quantify.

Brandon Routh

The whole incident with Queenie shook me up so badly that Brady offered to drive me to the hospital. My parents and Alva followed behind us. Then came the various boys and their respective girls, who'd all decided to stay until we knew for sure that Queenie was okay.

Turned out she was.

It took Doc Henderson a few hours to come to his conclusion, but he shared the news sometime around midnight. "It wasn't a heart attack, folks. Just a case of angina, possibly brought on by stress. Has she gone through anything stressful today?"

"You could say that twice and mean it." Pop sighed. "Yes, she's had a stressful day."

"My fault," Alva whispered, her eyes flooding for the hundredth time. "Always my fault."

"*Not* your fault," Reverend Bradford said. He

turned to the doctor to ask if he could go into the room to visit with Queenie and was told to keep the visit short. Seconds later he disappeared.

Pop shook his head. "It'll be interesting to see how that one pans out."

"Well, we've got her on medication that will keep her very calm while she's here." The doctor turned to look at Brady. "Don't I know you?"

"This is Brady James." Pop squared his shoulders and made the introduction, clearly proud to be doing so.

"I thought so." Doc Henderson chuckled. "Hey, how's the knee?"

Brady shrugged. "It's on the mend. Had my first surgery four months ago. They're talking about a second one, but I'm not sure yet when that will be."

"Take it slow and easy," Doc Henderson said. "I've known many a knee surgery that didn't take because the patient tried to move too quickly. Tricky business, these knee problems."

"Try telling that to my agent." Brady rolled his eyes.

"Give me his number and I'll be glad to." The doctor nodded and then faced my dad. "Now, about your mom. I'll probably release her tomorrow afternoon. I like to give these things time—usually twenty-four hours or so. But when she goes home it'll have to be to a stress-free environment."

"Guess that means I'll be going back home," Alva said.

"No way." I rose and walked over to take the seat next to her. "You're coming back to our place, Aunt Alva."

"I insist," Mama added.

"But Brady . . ." She gave him a hesitant look. "He came all this way just for me."

"And I want to stay until I know for sure Queenie's okay." He glanced at me. "Is that all right?"

"Of course." Relief flooded over me at this declaration.

"I saw a hotel up near the freeway. I'll stay there."

"You'll do no such thing," Mama said. "You should come to our place."

"I don't think there's room, Marie," Pop said.

"Well, let's do this. I'll send all of the boys—you included, Brady—to Queenie's place. And the girls"—she glanced at Dahlia, Twiggy, and Crystal—"can stay with us."

Beau looked at her with widened eyes. Likely he thought our mother would murder Twiggy in her sleep. "You sure, Mama?"

"I'm sure, baby boy. We all need some rest, and it's too late for anyone to be driving back to Dallas tonight. The girls and I will get along just fine, I promise."

Everyone stood at the same time, several in attendance yawning.

"Madge is gonna have her hands full tomorrow if none of us show up for work." Dahlia slipped her arm around Dewey's waist. "But I'd hate to leave until I know for sure your grandmother is okay."

"I'm happy you're staying." He planted a kiss in her hair. Mama watched this from a distance and then announced that she was heading back home.

Brady took me back to my car, and I gave him instructions for how to get to Queenie's house. Before we parted ways, he pulled me close and gave me a little kiss on the cheek. "I'm praying for her, Katie."

"I'm grateful." The words were more than just a platitude. Knowing that he was praying for my grandmother meant everything to me.

When I got back to my house, I saw that Mama had already settled our guests in the various bedrooms and the boys were nowhere to be found. I tumbled into bed and slept like a rock. When I awoke the next morning I found Mama and Pop in the kitchen, visiting with Dahlia, Twiggy, and Crystal. Turned out Mama and Crystal both liked to cook. And when my mother plopped a huge stack of pancakes down in front of Twiggy, she never said a word about gluten. Instead, she just dove right in, a delirious smile on her face.

"We'll get 'er fattened up yet," Mama whispered. "Then just see if my baby boy finds her so beautiful."

I rolled my eyes but said nothing. What would be the point?

Afterward we headed up to the hospital, and the boys met us there. My heart did that usual pitter-pat thing that it always did when I saw Brady. He smiled and extended his arms. I gave him a warm hug.

The three girls said their hellos and goodbyes pretty quickly, then Dewey announced that he was driving them all back to Dallas. Jasper and Beau offered to go to Queenie's house to pick up a change of clothes. I had just stepped out of my grandmother's room to say goodbye to everyone when I saw a familiar face. Bessie May. She came tearing around the corner, fear in her eyes.

"Katie Sue! I'm so glad you're here. How's Queenie?"

"Better," I said.

She grabbed my hand. "Your father says there's a pro basketball player in Queenie's hospital room."

"That's right."

"*Why* is there a pro basketball player in her hospital room? Don't you find that odd? The woman never watched a basketball game in her life, other than the ones at the high school, and she wasn't terribly fond of those. In fact, she's not fond of sports at all."

"True. It's kind of a long story, Bessie May."

"I have plenty of time for a long story. I always get a little dizzy when I go into hospital rooms, so I'll just sit right here and you can tell me all about it."

"Isn't this Saturday? Don't you have a rummage sale at the church this morning?"

Her eyes widened and she gasped. "For pity's sake! Yes!" She rushed into the room to say hello to Queenie, then quickly tore out the door, headed to the church.

"She's very fast for someone her age," Brady observed as I came back into the room. "Was she a ball player in a former life?"

"Hardly. The woman knows nothing about sports, as was probably evidenced by the fact that she didn't know who you were. Er, are."

We visited with my grandmother for a while. She seemed genuinely embarrassed that people had created such a fuss. On and on she went, talking about what a goober she felt like. Until Mama happened to mention that Alva had spent the night at our place.

"O-oh?" Queenie sat up a little straighter in the bed. "Is she still there now?"

"Yes, she's resting up. I think last night was harder on her than she wanted to admit."

"Ah." Queenie shook her head. "Well, how's the weather out there?"

Nice diversion.

My father glanced at his watch a couple of times, and Queenie finally took the hint. "I know what you're fretting about, Herb. Just go open the store. It won't hurt my feelings in the slightest. I'm about ready for a nap anyway." She yawned to prove her point.

"Well, if you're sure, Mama." My father stood and walked over to his mother's bed and gave her a kiss on the cheek. "Glad you're going to be okay. You gave us quite a scare."

"Sure didn't mean to." My grandmother shrugged. "Now, get on out of here. You've got work to do. They're gonna spring me loose soon, so I'll call you when I need to hitch a ride."

My father nodded and then said his goodbyes. The rest of us decided to leave a short while later when Queenie dozed off. No point in sitting there staring at a sleeping woman.

"Want to go to Dairy Queen for lunch?" I asked Brady.

"Dairy Queen?" He stretched and glanced at his watch. "Haven't been to one of those in ages."

"Well, you don't know what you're missing. If we leave now, we can get there before the lunch crowd."

"Sounds great."

We stepped outside of my grandmother's room, and I gasped when I saw an old friend in the hallway. He was approaching with a concerned look on his face.

"Levi Nash."

His handsome face lit with recognition when he saw me. "Katie. I just stopped by to check on your grandmother. We've been praying for her. How's she doing?"

"Better, actually. I heard you were going to be coming back to Fairfield for the summer. It's good to see you."

Levi's attention shifted to Brady and he smiled. "Well, I guess the rumors are true. I heard there had been a sighting of Brady James." He stuck out his hand.

"In the flesh." Brady shook Levi's hand.

"Good to meet you." Levi turned back to me, which made me feel honored. Most folks made such a big deal about Brady that they hardly seemed to take notice of me. "To answer your question, I'll be back and forth from Dallas to Fairfield. I'm interning at the church, but I'm still leading a Bible study on campus in Dallas too."

"That's wonderful."

"I think my mom's glad to have me home, even if it is just for the summer."

"The WOP-pers are glad too."

"Those WOP-pers." He laughed. "They're something else. They sure prayed me back from a rough place. I'm thankful for that."

"You seem so happy, Levi," I observed. "Peaceful."

"Does it show?" He grinned. "Still can't believe I'm the same guy."

"You're not, actually."

"Guess you're right. My whole world has changed."

"It's obvious. This new life seems to really agree with you."

"Thanks. I'm just so grateful." He turned to give Brady a nod. "Great to meet you. Think I'll go in and visit Queenie now."

"She's asleep," I said. "So you might need to wait a bit."

"No I'm not." Queenie's voice rang out from inside the room. "All that chattering outside has me wide awake again."

I clamped a hand over my mouth. "Oops."

"Send that boy in here," she said. "I need some Levi time."

He laughed and stepped inside the room with a wave of his hand.

"He seems like a great guy." Brady slipped his arm over my shoulders as we walked down the hospital corridor together.

"My mother wanted me to marry him," I said.

Brady stopped and looked at me. "Wait . . . she wanted you to marry Levi? Or Casey?"

"Levi." I laughed. "It's complicated."

"Well, do me a favor and don't marry either one." He gave me a little wink and pulled me close.

I agreed, without any hesitation at all.

Less than five minutes later we pulled into the parking lot at Dairy Queen. As I stared through the plate-glass windows, I had a flashback to a day not so many weeks ago when I'd sat in this very same place, ready to go inside to meet Casey for an Oreo Blizzard. It felt like a million years ago.

Or not.

Brady and I stepped inside the restaurant, and I thought my heart was going to sail right out of my throat when I saw Casey sitting with a couple of his friends in our old booth.

Oh. Help.

"You ready to order?" Brady turned his attention to the menu. "I'm starving."

"Mm-hmm."

He ordered a burger and I got the chicken fingers basket, then we headed to a table near the back. As we passed by Casey, he glanced up at me, his eyes widening. They grew even wider when he saw Brady. I gave him a little nod and kept walking, but I felt like I might faint.

"You okay?" Brady asked. "You look like you're not feeling well all of a sudden."

"Yeah. I'll explain when we get to the table."

I didn't get a chance to explain. The other patrons at Dairy Queen gathered around us, gushing over Brady like a celebrity. He took it in stride, but I could tell he really wanted to just fade into the woodwork. Or eat a cheeseburger in peace.

We did manage to eat . . . finally. "You sure you're okay over there?" he asked after several moments of silence on my part.

"Yeah. I, um . . . there's someone here that . . . well . . ."

"Someone in Dairy Queen?" He looked around at the various booths, stopping when he got to Casey's. I didn't have to explain, because Casey was staring at us as if he wanted to take Brady down. I had the strangest feeling it would only be a matter of time before the Oreos hit the fan.

30

If You Were Mine to Lose

We cannot direct the wind, but we can adjust the sails.

Dolly Parton

Brady stared at Casey and then looked back at me. "I'm guessing that's the person you're talking about."

"Yeah. That's the one."

"Casey?"

"Yeah." I sighed. "Sorry."

"Don't be." Brady glanced his way once again, then reached for my hand. "Should I say something to him? Is he making you uncomfortable?"

I was uncomfortable, all right, but didn't want Brady to draw attention to the fact. I didn't have to fret over Casey for long because my former almost-fiancé and his friends left the restaurant a few moments later. No doubt all of the attention on Brady was more than Casey could take. I finally breathed a sigh of relief. Well, until Mama walked in with Aunt Alva. They waved and came straight toward our booth.

"Well, hello, you two." Mama plopped down

and fanned herself with a church bulletin. "We just stopped in for a bite. Didn't think you would be here."

"Your mama was kind enough to come back to the house to fetch me," Alva said. "I had a hankerin' for a burger and some ice cream."

At that moment, the manager of the restaurant showed up with two M&M Blizzards in his hand. "For our special guest." He smiled as he handed one of them to Brady and the other to me. "Welcome to the Fairfield Dairy Queen, Mr. James."

"Well, thanks." Brady took his Blizzard and swallowed down the first mouthful. "Mmm. If I keep eating like this, I'll never play ball again."

"Ooh, someone take that ice cream away from him!" Alva laughed. "It'd be a crime if Brady James stopped playing ball." She pointed her finger at him. "Ice cream is hard on the joints." She looked at the manager and said, "Can you bring me one too?"

"You a friend of his?" the manager asked.

"You betcha. We're practically family. If I have my way, we actually will be." She gave Brady a playful wink.

The manager nodded, then headed off to fix a Blizzard for Aunt Alva.

Ophelia Edwards, one of Mama's more trouble-some choir members, sat in the booth behind us. She joined in the conversation without invitation. "Marie, who is this handsome young man sitting with our Katie Sue?"

"Now, Ophelia, you know Brady James, surely." Mama continued to fan herself. "Everyone knows Brady."

"Can't say as I've seen him before." Ophelia took off her glasses and wiped them with her chocolate-smudged napkin, then put them back on, covered in streaks. "Nope. He doesn't look familiar."

Alva rolled her eyes. "Surely you've seen him on television."

"Oh, is he that new fella on *Guiding Light*?" Before any of us could answer, Ophelia slapped the table with her hand. "I can't believe I'm admitting right here in Dairy Queen that I watch that show. I've tried to give it up, but it just keeps hanging on. Like a bad cough."

"No, ma'am, I'm not on *Guiding Light*," Brady said. "In fact—"

"Well, I don't blame you for quitting. All of those nasty bedroom scenes." Her face reddened. "You're a good man to give it up."

"Oh, I'm not saying I gave it up. I'm saying—"

"Well, make up your mind. Either you're on *Guiding Light* or you're not."

"He's not, Ophelia." My mother made a "she's crazy" sign behind Ophelia's back. "*Guiding Light* hasn't been on since 2009. Please don't ask me how I know that."

"Well, for pity's sake. I could've sworn I watched it yesterday." Ophelia's nose wrinkled.

"This is Brady James," Alva said. "Point guard for the Mavericks and a good friend of the family."

"The Mavericks? Don't think I've seen that show. When does it come on?"

"It's not a show, Ophelia," Mama said. "It's a . . . never mind."

"Well, why did you say the boy was on television? I swear, people are so hard to follow sometimes." Ophelia took a bite of her chocolate-covered dip cone, which left a smudge of chocolate on her cheek. She then turned her attention to Alva. With narrowed gaze, she pointed to her and said, "You look familiar. Do I know you?"

The manager arrived just then with Alva's Blizzard. He passed it off to her and she took a bite, then gave Ophelia a knowing look. "Well, you should, Ophelia. We graduated from Fairfield High the same year. In fact, we were pretty good friends back in the day."

This apparently led to some confusion on Ophelia's part. She couldn't quite place Alva. Not that my aunt seemed to mind. She turned her attention to her ice cream.

Out of the corner of my eye, I watched Brady. Such a great sport. I couldn't picture him living here, in Fairfield. Couldn't see him having lunch at Dairy Queen every day. Still, he seemed to fit in just about every place he went.

When we finished our Blizzards, I asked Brady if he wanted to take a drive around Fairfield and he agreed. We said goodbye to Mama and Alva, then headed out of the restaurant. Getting out took awhile, what with all of the people stopping us along the way.

Finally cleared from the traffic, Brady reached for my hand and squeezed it. When we got to the door, I realized that Casey was sitting outside at one of the tables on the patio. He glanced up at Brady. And me.

Mostly me.

"You're Brady James." Casey's opening line wasn't very well thought out, apparently, since he wasn't actually looking at Brady when he spoke the words.

"Right." Brady slipped his arm over my shoulders.

Casey looked back and forth between Brady and me, and I could read the confusion in his eyes. Now he homed in on me, giving me a penetrating gaze. "Katie, we need to talk."

"Brady and I were just headed out for a drive. Can it wait?"

"I, well . . ."

Brady cleared his throat and then announced that he would be waiting in the truck. I nodded and told him I'd be right there. Once he disappeared from sight, Casey tried to take my hand, but I wouldn't let him.

"Katie, I'm confused."

Well, duh.

"I mean, I'm confused about what you're doing in Dallas. This is out of character for you to go away."

"Ah. I see. So, it's okay for you to go to Oklahoma, but I can't go see my cousin in Dallas? If we're not a couple anymore, then why do you care where I go?"

"It's just not like you to go away."

"I happen to like Dallas. I've met a lot of nice people there."

"Okay, I have to ask—what's the deal with Brady James? How in the world do you know him? When I talked to you about him during the playoff game, you didn't even know who he was. Now you're dating him?"

"Who said Brady and I are dating?"

"It's obvious you have feelings for him. And vice versa. You were holding hands."

"Brady and I are in the getting-to-know-you stage. And to answer your question, I met him at a store where he's working."

"Wait. A pro ball player works in a store? What kind of store?"

"It's kind of a long story, Casey, and I don't have time for a long story. That's what I was trying to say before. We're headed out for a sight-seeing trip and then back to my parents' place to have dinner. I'm leaving to go back to Dallas tomorrow after church, so you won't be seeing me around." I took a step away and then turned back. "So, what happened in Tulsa?"

"Nothing." He shrugged. "I'm going back. Just came home to pack up my stuff."

"Queenie thought you were back for good."

His eyes widened. "Oh, I see. Is that what you thought?"

"I didn't know what to think. I still haven't quite figured out the part where you left in the first place, so seeing you come back again is even more confusing. It's all so strange."

"Kind of like you staying in Dallas and buddying up with a pro basketball player at some store."

"We're changing. Both of us." *Obviously.* "We're not the same people when we're away from Fairfield."

He shrugged. "Guess not."

"And that's okay. Maybe we needed this to discover who we really are." I glanced toward Brady's truck and saw him standing next to the door on the passenger side. I wouldn't keep him waiting any longer. "Anyway, have a nice trip back to Tulsa, Casey. Give your mama my love before you go. Oh, and if you happen to see me on the front of a bridal magazine wearing a really awesome dress, don't panic."

"What?"

"Just don't read too much into it, okay? It's not a ploy to get you back. In fact, I seriously doubt you'll ever see me wear that dress in person. So rest easy."

"O-okay." He paused. "Have fun in Dallas."

"I will," I said. And I meant it. I gave him a little wave and walked toward Brady, all smiles.

"You okay?" he asked when I drew near.

"Oh yeah. Better than I've been in a long time. Feel like I've lost a hundred pounds."

"Katie, if you lost a hundred pounds, you'd be the size of a toddler."

That made me laugh. He pulled me into his arms and gave me a kiss on the forehead. "That's just a sampling of what's to come," he whispered.

"Mmm." Sounded good.

We spent the next few hours on a lengthy drive through the country. I showed Brady everything. The property my great-grandparents had owned. The high school. The lake. I took him by every place that had ever meant anything special to me while growing up, including the ballpark where my father coached Little League.

As we stood at the edge of the ball field, Brady pulled me close. "I can see why you love it here, Katie. This is very . . . quiet. Peaceful." After a moment's silence he added, "Quaint."

I couldn't tell from the way he used the word if

he really meant it as a compliment. "You mean small?" I asked.

"I think it's just right. There's enough of a town to offer the things you need, but not enough to overwhelm you. It's nice."

"Well, speaking of town, there's one place I haven't taken you yet. Would you like to see our family's hardware store?"

His eyes sparkled as he answered, "I thought you'd never ask."

"Pop's already gone home by now, I'm sure," I said. "But I have a key."

We drove to the store and found it empty, as I'd said. That turned out to be a very good thing.

I never thought I'd be kissed by a pro ball player in the lawn and garden section of my family's hardware store, but that was exactly what happened. Brady caught me somewhere between the fertilizer and the sprinklers and gave me a kiss so sweet that I almost tumbled straight into the insect repellent display. When we came up for air—and it took awhile—I felt a little woozy.

He caught me and grinned. "Easy now."

I giggled.

"I guess I should've asked your permission before doing that."

"Doing what? Kissing me? Who asks permission?" I gave him a wink. "I'm not sure I really got the full effect. Would you mind trying again?"

And so he did. He kissed me again in the lawn and garden section. And twice in housewares. And three times in hardware. By the time we reached the electrical department, I'd pretty much made up my mind that we had already generated enough electricity to light the city of Fairfield for a month. He must've realized it too, because he took a giant step backwards and mouthed, "Wow."

"Yes. Wow. That's—that's the word I was thinking." Wow. Wow to the moon and back. Most of all, wow to the idea that I'd waited until the age of twenty-four to really, truly have that sort of reaction to a kiss from a boy. Correction—a man. Yes, Brady James, all six feet four of him, was more than enough man to knock a girl off her feet in the hardware store.

"You're quite a kisser," I said.

"Well, I should be. I've had a lot of practice on *Guiding Light*. But don't tell Ophelia."

We both laughed until tears came.

Then, in an instant, I remembered something. "Brady, it's almost six thirty. Mama's expecting us home for dinner."

"What about Queenie? Should we go back up to see her before visiting hours are over?"

"I'm sure she's already been released, actually. I'm guessing Pop is there now, ready to drive her home. I'll stop by her house tomorrow after church. Besides, I have a sneaking suspicion she'd want the two of us to spend more time together. She's a romantic at heart, even though she doesn't always come across that way."

"You think?"

"Yes." I thought about what I'd just said. "I'm pretty sure Alva would too. You know, those two sisters are more alike than they are different. And I think they would both be tickled pink that you and I are . . ." A girlish giggle escaped. "Well, you know, that we just . . ."

"Kissed in the family hardware store?"

"Yes. Kissed in the family hardware store."

"Well, anything for the family," Brady said. He reached down and gave me a little kiss on the tip of my nose. "Anything for the family."

31

There Goes My Everything

Stand straight, walk proud, have a little faith.

Garth Brooks

On Sunday morning we all attended church together. Brady left immediately after the service so that he could call his mom and update her on the photo shoot.

I managed to talk Alva into staying in Fairfield and riding back to Dallas with me. If she'd known that I planned to take her to Queenie's house after church, she probably would've bolted. Still, with nowhere else to go, she reluctantly tagged along. My parents led the way in their car, and we followed behind them in mine, knowing we would have to leave for Dallas by four o'clock.

When we arrived at my grandmother's house, I could tell Alva was hesitant to go inside. In fact, I wondered if I would be able to talk her into getting out of the car at all.

"Couldn't I just wait here?" she asked.

I gave her a sympathetic look. "Alva. C'mon in. Let's get this over with."

She sighed and followed me to the door. My dad gave the usual three-rap greeting, then opened the door and led the way inside. Queenie was all smiles until she saw Alva. Then her smile quickly faded. She said nothing to her sister at all. Not "Thanks for coming." Not "Get out of my house." Nothing. It was as if Alva hadn't come at all.

Mama and Pop did their best to make small talk, asking Queenie how she was feeling.

"Oh, I'm fine," my grandmother responded with a wave of her hand. "Fit as a fiddle. Not sure what happened the other night. Just got worked up, I guess."

"Well, I'm glad you're okay now, Queenie," I said. "You scared us to death."

"Didn't mean to do that." Her nose wrinkled. "In fact, I didn't mean to draw attention to myself, period. That's the last thing I wanted to do, especially with all of the young folks showing up with dates."

"It was an interesting evening, for sure." Pop shrugged. "Not exactly our usual Friday night routine, but I kind of liked the changes."

"You liked seeing your mother passed out in a car in the parking lot of Sam's?" Queenie asked.

"Of course not, Mama," he said. "Just saying that I'm coming to the realization that breaking from the norm can be a good thing. And I'm really glad you're better now."

"Thank you. I'll be back up and running soon. Tell me what I missed at church this morning. Did Bessie May sing the solo again?"

Mama rolled her eyes. "Yes. And speaking of Bessie May, I'm not going to be able to stay very long. I have to be at the church at four o'clock for a meeting. We're getting new choir robes, and Pastor needs me to be there to settle a dispute between Bessie May and Ophelia about the color. Can you believe Ophelia wants to go with purple? I mean, seriously. Purple?"

"I like purple," I said. "It might shake things up a little."

"But . . . purple?" Mama looked aghast.

"Alva and I need to leave by four o'clock too," I said. "We've got a drive ahead of us."

"I still can't believe you're going back," Mama said. "Are you moving away for good, Katie?"

"Would it be so awful if I did?"

She paled. "What are you saying?"

"I don't know. I love it there, Mama. I really do. I mean, I love Fairfield too, but there's something about Dallas . . ."

"It's that boy."

I didn't know quite how to respond to that one. After a moment, I finally decided that I needed to come clean and tell my parents the whole story about the contest, the dress, the photo shoot . . . everything.

And so I did.

My father sat with his jaw hanging down as I relayed the story, and Mama . . . well, she looked as if she might be sick.

"You're telling me that you're about to be on the cover of a national magazine wearing a wedding dress that was made just for you?"

I nodded.

"So, those pictures I saw you looking at on your phone the other night . . . ?"

"Were from the photo shoot. Would . . . would you like to see them? They're really good."

It took her a minute, but she finally agreed. I pulled them up on my phone and then passed it her way. Though she refused to admit it aloud, I could tell she thought the pictures were beautiful. Pop certainly did. He whistled when he got to the picture of Brady kissing me.

"Guess it's a little clearer why you're set on going back to Dallas."

"Yeah." I sighed.

"So this is how it is." Mama gave me a pensive look. "One minute you're marrying Casey Lawson, the next you're kissing a baseball player."

"Basketball player," Pop, Alva, and I said in unison.

"And Mama, just for the record, you were ready

to marry me off to Levi Nash the minute you heard that Casey had left town."

"True." My mother fanned herself with her hand. "I never felt that Lawson boy was good enough for you, just so you know."

Her statement seemed to strike a chord with Alva, who squirmed in the seat next to me. "Is it getting warm in here?" she asked.

"No, it's just fine." Pop settled back in his chair.

"I for one think it's good for Katie to get away and experience new things," Alva said. "To have new adventures."

"You would." Queenie's first words to her sister were short and to the point. "Which is, I suppose, why you've convinced her to stay with you."

"W-what? You think that's why I asked her to stay with me—to separate her from her family?" Alva looked shocked by this.

"Well, isn't it?" Queenie placed her hands on the arms of her chair.

"Of course not." Alva shook her head. She glanced around the living room, and I could tell she wanted to get up and look at a photograph she kept eyeing on the mantel. I'd never noticed it before, but it was the same photo that she'd framed and put on display in her own living room. Ironic.

Queenie directed her next sermonette at me. "Well, I suppose there's nothing I can say to keep you here. It's not like this is the first time someone's taken off for Dallas and left me in the lurch."

As those words were spoken, I realized exactly why Queenie didn't want anyone to move away from Fairfield. Why she'd fought so hard to keep Jasper here when he'd wanted to move to Houston. Why she'd talked Dewey into going to the local junior college. Why she'd encouraged Mama to hold so tightly to Beau.

She'd already lost her sister to the big city. She didn't want to lose anyone else.

In that moment, the revelation came swift and sure. Queenie didn't hate Alva at all. She loved her so much that she kept a tight rein on everyone else so as not to lose them as well.

Alva cleared her throat and I turned to her, seeing the tears trickling down her cheeks. We had to put an end to this.

"You two need to talk, Queenie," I said. "Get things out in the open."

"Nothing to talk about."

"Sure there is, Mama." My father stood. "Marie and I will go in the kitchen and make some coffee."

"When you come back, bring me one of those little sandwiches Bessie May brought over last night," Queenie said. "I haven't had lunch."

"Sure," Pop said. He and Mama scurried from the room.

"You want me to stay or to leave?" I asked.

"Stay," Alva and Queenie said in unison.

"Okay, stay it is." I settled back against the cushions on the sofa. "Who wants to go first?"

I noticed that Alva's hands were trembling. "Queenie, I . . . I owe you an apology."

Queenie huffed but didn't say anything.

"All those years ago, I got in the middle of your relationship with Paul. I led you to believe that I had feelings for him, but it wasn't true."

"Wasn't true?" Anger flashed in my grandmother's eyes. "You're telling me now that you didn't try to break us up because you cared for him?"

"I liked him fine as a person, but I didn't think he was right for you. I didn't think he was good enough for you, if you want the truth of it." Alva sighed. "I was young and foolish. But I'm older and wiser now."

"Older, for sure." Queenie gave her a sideways glance. "But I'm not buying that story, Alva. Not one bit."

"Well, that's your loss, because it's the truth. I didn't want to give up my sister to just anyone. Paul was a fine boy—man—but I didn't think he deserved you. I didn't really consider what it would do to you if he broke your heart."

Queenie's eyes flooded with tears. "You don't know what you're talking about, Alva."

"Yes I do."

"No you don't. You think that Paul broke my heart?"

"Well, sure. You two broke up, didn't you? I assumed . . ."

"You assumed wrong. I turned him down." When Alva didn't respond, Queenie raised her voice. "Alva, do you hear me? Are you listening? I said that I turned him down."

"What do you mean?" Alva looked stunned.

Tears ran down my grandmother's face. "Paul Bradford proposed to me the summer after I graduated from college, but I turned him down."

Alva scooted to the edge of the sofa. "Why would you do a fool thing like that? If you loved him, why not marry him?"

Queenie swiped at her cheeks with the back of her hand. "Because as much as I cared about him, I cared about my sister even more. Even if she wouldn't speak to me all these years."

"Are you saying you turned the man down because of me?"

"Of course I did. I thought you had feelings for him, and I didn't want to hurt you. You were the last person on God's green earth I'd want to injure."

"Were?" Alva gave her a hopeful look.

Queenie sighed. "Are."

"All these years I didn't know what to think." Alva rose and paced the room. "I wondered why you didn't marry him. Wondered if he'd broken your heart."

"Well, you can rest easy on that count," Queenie said. "He didn't break my heart. I broke his. And I'm not sure he ever got over it."

At that, the room went silent.

"You're just plain crazy, you know." Alva stopped at the edge of the fireplace and looked at the photograph on the mantel. "You always have been, but this really takes the cake."

"Thanks a lot." Queenie squirmed in her chair.

"No, I mean it. Paul Bradford was in love with you and you let him slip through your fingers because you were more worried about me? I'd say that's the definition of crazy."

Queenie bit her lip. "You might be right."

"Maybe it's not too late, Queenie." I gave her a hopeful look.

"What do you mean?"

"I mean, he's a widower. You're a widow. Maybe you two should . . ." I left the sentence open-ended.

"Not. Going. To. Happen." Her jaw clenched.

"Because he's Presbyterian?"

"No." Pain flashed in her eyes. "Because too much time has passed. It's water under the bridge now."

"But I want you to be happy." Alva walked toward her sister and took a seat in the chair next to her. "You still can be."

My grandmother's eyes filled again, and she swiped at them with her hand. "Alva, I had the best husband a woman could ever ask for. Joe meant the world to me. I'm sorry you never really had the chance to know him. You would have loved everything about him. So don't worry about my happiness. God turned my broken heart into the most wonderful experience of my life."

"So why the tears?" I gazed tenderly at my grandmother. "Is it possible you're starting to have feelings for Reverend Bradford again?"

"I let go of those feelings years ago."

"But Queenie, no one would blame you if they . . . resurged. You know?"

"I'm too old for feelings."

I shook my head. "No one is too old for feelings."

"I am. I'm eighty-two. Eighty-two-year-olds should be more practical, less emotional."

"If anyone has earned the right to be emotional, it's someone your age. So don't apologize if you are smitten. And by the way, love knows no age limits. Is it possible—even a teensy-tiny bit possible—you've got some feelings for Reverend Bradford?"

"His name is Paul." Her words came out as a whisper.

"Paul." I gave her a bright smile. "He showed up at Sam's the night you collapsed. Did you know that?"

She shook her head. "No, but I'm not surprised."

"I'd venture to say he's in love with you now." I don't know where the words came from, but I'd obviously spoken them aloud, based on the look of shock on my grandmother's face. "Isn't he?"

Her gaze shifted downward and then back up to me. “Yes. He is.”

“Really?” I got it right!

“Yes, I have it on good authority he is crazy about me.” Queenie sighed. “Head-over-heels, can’t-sleep-nights, can’t-walk-straight, can’t-remember-if-he’s-fed-the-cat crazy.”

“How do you know that?” Mama asked as she walked back into the room with a tray of sandwiches in hand.

“Because he told me.” Queenie tried to stand, nearly stumbling in the process. “Yesterday. And the day before. And the day before that.” She finally managed to stand upright. “He’s told me every day for the past six months. Every single morning there’s a note on my front door that says, ‘You are loved.’ ”

“Are you serious?” I asked.

“Want the proof?” Queenie hobbled over to her desk and opened the drawer. She reached inside and came out with a folder stuffed full of handwritten love letters, which she pulled out and showed us. My father happened in at that very moment with several cups of coffee on a tray.

“This,” my grandmother said as she clutched the letters to her breast, “is all the proof anyone will ever need. Paul Bradford is head over heels in love with me.”

32

Let the World Keep On A-Turnin'

It's important to give it all you have while you have the chance.

Shania Twain

My father very nearly dropped the coffee tray when he heard his mother's impassioned speech about Reverend Bradford.

"W-what did you say, Mama?" The cups on the tray rattled this way and that.

"I said that Paul Bradford's head over heels in love with me. And if you need any proof, this is my July folder of love notes. Would you like to see June? May?"

"Are you serious?" My father set the tray down on the coffee table and stepped toward her.

"They go back for several months." She pointed at the drawer. "The man's been driving me out of my ever-lovin' mind telling me how much he adores me. I thought I'd go insane if I didn't tell someone."

I couldn't help the laughter that escaped. "Oh, but Queenie! This is the stuff romance novels are made of. Wow. Double wow. That's so cool. And so . . . romantic."

"I know." She sighed and took a seat once again, still holding on to the letters. "He's always been the romantic sort. Time hasn't changed that."

"Then why not put the poor man out of his misery once and for all and marry him?" Alva asked.

"I can't." Queenie shook her head. "I just can't."

"Why?" Mama asked.

"Ooh, let me guess." I put my hand up. "It's because he's Presbyterian?"

Queenie laughed. At first it came out as one of those lightweight chuckles, but eventually it morphed into a full-fledged belly laugh. "Oh, good grief, no. I have nothing against the Presbyterians. Nothing whatsoever. I never have."

"You don't?" Mama and I spoke in unison.

"No." Queenie's face turned the prettiest shade of pink. "I just stayed away from the Presbyterian church—especially for prayer meetings—because I knew he was there, slipping love notes into my purse when no one was looking. I couldn't think straight when I was around the man. I just wanted to toss caution to the wind and run straight into his arms." She fanned herself with one of the love notes.

"Then why didn't you?" I asked.

"Because I worried about what people would think." She looked at her sister. "I worried about what you would think. Even after all these years, your opinion matters most to me."

"I think you're nuts, but I've already said that." Alva slapped her hands down on her knees. "Listen, if I ever turn down a perfectly wonderful man, it won't be to save face with you or anyone else. It'll be because he's not the right fella for me. And by the way, I might've convinced you that I had an infatuation with Paul Bradford, but trust me, we would've been miserable together."

"Really?" A hopeful look crossed Queenie's face. "You mean that?"

"I do. For one thing, I can't abide a man in a robe."

"A bathrobe?" I asked.

"No." Alva shook her head. "That robe he preaches in. Reminds me of a woman in a dress. Seems kind of strange to me."

"Seriously?" Queenie said. "I think he looks perfectly wonderful in it. I feel closer to heaven when I see a reverend in a robe."

"And there you have it. He makes her feel closer to heaven." I laughed. "Write that down, Queenie. Leave it on his door tomorrow morning, and just see how he responds. I have no doubt in my mind you'll end up making his day. His week. His year. He's been waiting for this and deserves to hear it straight from the horse's mouth."

"Oh, I don't think I could. I just don't."

"Why?"

"Because . . ." She paused, and I could almost read her thoughts. They were the same thoughts Mama had expressed every time she feared one of us kids might be moving away.

"You're afraid of change," I said.

She nodded. "Everything is running smoothly right now. If I interrupt the flow of that, who knows what'll happen."

"So what?" Pop shook his head. "Seriously. So what? That's what I was saying before about Friday night at Sam's being a blessing in disguise. We're stuck in a rut and I'm tired of it."

Queenie looked startled, but Mama even more so.

"Stuck in a rut?" she said.

"Yes, Marie. Stuck, stuck, stuck." He paced the room, clearly agitated.

Mama shook her head. "But Herb, I like things to stay the same. I thought you did too."

"There was a time when I did, yes. But something's stirring inside of me and I can't seem to stop it. I'm . . . bored."

"Bored?" Mama paled. "But consistency is a good thing. I like to know that you're coming home from the store at 5:05 p.m. I like to know that Katie and the boys are tucked into their beds at night."

"You do know we're all in our twenties, right, Mama?" I said.

"Of course I know. I gave birth to you. But that

doesn't make the changes any less painful. In fact, it makes them worse." She sighed. "Is it really so awful to know that everything around here moves like clockwork? Friday nights at Sam's. Thursday evenings in choir. Sunday morning and evening at church."

"She likes routine," Pop said.

"And control," Mama said. "I like to be in control of it all. So when things happen that are out of my control—"

"Like Queenie being hospitalized or Beau falling for a sweet gal who lives in Dallas?" I offered.

"Yeah, like that. It rocks my boat."

"Your mother has never cared to have her boat rocked." Pop gave me a knowing look.

Ew.

"Point is, all of these changes of late have upset my apple cart, and it's really got me rattled."

"Peach cart might be a better choice of words," Pop said. "But you know what? Forget the apple cart."

"W-what?" Mama looked stunned. "What did you say?"

"I said forget the apple cart. Kick it over. Embrace change." He gave my mother a funny look. "I think I have the answer, Marie. It's been staring me in the face all along. You and I . . . we're going to do something different. Something totally unexpected."

"We . . . we are?"

"Well, sure. If the kids can all accept the changes that life has to offer, then so can we. I say we get on that big ship—the new one in Galveston—and go to the Cayman Islands."

"The Cayman Islands?" Mama's eyes widened. "Herb Fisher, we rarely leave Fairfield except to run to the mall in Dallas, and that's only a couple of times a year. How can we go to the Cayman Islands?"

"That's my point. That's exactly why we must go there. And Cozumel. I understand the ship makes a stop there. We'll go to one of those private islands and go snorkeling."

"Snorkeling?" Mama looked aghast. "I've never snorkeled a day in my life."

"Then you're long overdue."

Queenie rose from her chair and announced that she had to make a run to the bathroom. As if the woman could run. "My goodness, this is all so exciting," she said. "You've got me so worked up that I hope I make it to the powder room." She gave me a little wink and added, "Fill me in when I get back."

My father took a few steps in my mother's direction. "Don't you get the point, Marie? It's time to break with tradition. Do something new. Adventurous." A dreamy look came over him. "Shoot. Maybe I'll sell the hardware store."

"What?" Mama and I said in unison.

"Why not? A man can't work forever."

"But you're only fifty-seven," Alva said. "Too young to retire."

"So what?" He shrugged. "There's no law that says a man has to work until he's sixty-five. I've got some money put away. And if we sell the store, we'll be set for our golden years. Maybe we can jaunt around the country in an RV like my old friend Buster Haggard."

Mama leaned over to whisper, "You might recall that Mr. Haggard lost his marbles at about this same age. Bought an RV and hit the road. We haven't seen him or his wife Mabel since. Last I heard, they bought a little cabin in the mountains in New Mexico." She shivered. "Can you imagine?"

"I can!" Pop clasped his hands together. "Let's follow in Buster's footsteps."

"You want to hit the road and never come back?" Mama looked floored by this. "You want people to say we've lost our marbles?"

"No. But doggone it, Marie, I love the idea of doing something different. Let's skip Sam's this coming Friday night."

"Skip Sam's?"

"Sure. Let's drive to Dallas and eat a steak. A giant, juicy steak at one of those big, fancy steakhouses. And afterward we'll go to that cheesecake place and spend eight dollars on a slice of cheesecake."

"Surely you jest."

"Surely I don't." He waggled his thick brows. "Try me."

"But I can get lemon pound cake at Sam's for a fraction of the cost," Mama said.

"And you do. Every week. But when we're in Jamaica—"

"Wait." She put her hand up. "Who said anything about Jamaica?"

"The cruise I was talking about. It stops in Cozumel, Grand Cayman, and Jamaica."

"You've really been researching this?"

"For three months. Even talked to a travel agent."

"We know a travel agent?"

"My third cousin twice removed. She lives in Waco and I sent her an email. Anyway, when we're in Jamaica we'll eat jerk chicken and drink virgin piña coladas."

"I'll die of botulism."

"But what a way to go, Marie." He grinned. "Can you imagine the stories our kids—and grand-kids—would tell? Grandma and Grandpa went to Jamaica and breathed their last breath on a tropical island, drinking piña coladas and eating contaminated chicken. It'll be great."

"Herb, you've lost your mind."

"Maybe. But it's about time, I daresay."

Now Mama started pacing the room. "I don't think you understand. If I go on a vacation to

Jamaica, who's going to take over the choir while I'm gone? Everyone knows the choir is my domain."

I raised my hand. "I have a suggestion. Let Bessie May do it."

"Bessie May?" Mama's cheeks flushed pink.

"Sure. She's been dying to take over for as long as I can remember."

"But she has arthritis," she argued. "She couldn't possibly lift her arms to direct. Not long enough to get through three verses and a couple of choruses."

"Then let them sing one of those praise choruses the kids sing," Pop said. "They don't have a lot of words. Surely she could last that long, arthritic joints or not."

Mama looked as if she just might faint. "Herbert Fisher, are you actually suggesting that I let Bessie May lead a contemporary worship song while I'm gone?"

He nodded and looked as calm as if he'd just said, "Hey, let's eat grilled cheese for lunch."

"But Herb. Surely you don't mean that." Mama's eyes reflected her complete shock at this idea. "A praise chorus?"

"I do mean it. And if you feel like arguing with me, I'm up for it. I can think of all sorts of other suggestions to change things up. At the church. At the store. In our . . . private life." His eyes sparkled with mischief. "That reminds me, I've been thinking about changing the color of the paint in our bedroom. That tan color is so depressing. What about something in a great shade of red? Not a bright red, but more of a wine color. Doesn't that sound romantic?"

At that, Mama had to sit down.

My father took a seat next to her. "Marie, the point is, I'm ready to do something different. Unusual."

Mama turned to me, her hands trembling. "It's finally happened. Your father has snapped. I've heard of this in men his age but never dreamed it would happen to him. To us." She shook her head. "I don't know what to say. I'll miss you after they take you away to the padded room, Herbert."

"Don't be silly. Say you'll dance with me, Marie." He rose and grabbed her hand. "We might need to take salsa lessons before we get on the cruise ship. I hear they've got dance competitions, and I'll want to enter."

"He's running a fever." Mama rose and felt his head. "I'm sure of it. He's delirious. Someone needs to call 9-1-1."

"Delirious, yes." My father chuckled. "Feverish, no. Unless you mean feverish for you." He planted a huge kiss on her, dipping her à la *Dancing with the Stars*.

Mama came up from the kiss, her cheeks blazing red. "Well, if that doesn't beat all."

“What did I miss?” Queenie asked as she hobbled back into the room.

“Pop’s lost his marbles,” I said.

“They’re going on a cruise,” Aunt Alva added. “To Jamaica.”

“Does that mean they won’t be here to eat dinner at Sam’s Friday night?” Queenie asked.

“We’re not leaving that quickly,” Pop said. “But you people can expect some changes around here, that’s for sure.”

“Fine by me. I’d like to go to Lonestar Grill on Friday. I hear they’ve got great chicken-fried steak.”

“Or maybe you could come to Dallas for a few days and stay with Katie and me,” Alva suggested.

“I just might.” Queenie nodded. “I just might.”

“See there, Marie?” Pop plopped back down in his chair and leaned back, crossing his arms. “That’s what happens when you kick over the apple cart.”

“Apples, mmm.” Alva giggled. “Apple pie sounds really good right about now. Katie, do you have any interest in stopping by Sam’s for some pie on our way out of town? We can skip the meal and get right to the good stuff.”

“Skip dinner?” I said. “Go straight to dessert?”

“Sure. I do it all the time.”

“We don’t,” I said. “We eat at the same time. Same place. Same meals. Same . . . everything.”

“Did you not just hear my passionate speech

about kicking over the apple cart, kiddo?" My father laughed. "Go to Sam's. Eat pie. Skip the meal. Do a dance in the middle of the restaurant. Let the people talk."

"Amen!" Alva chuckled. "What he said. Let's get some pie. And maybe some ice cream too. A girl only lives once. She might as well enjoy herself, don't you think?"

"I do."

Before we left, Alva walked over to Queenie and the two embraced. Genuinely, truly embraced. I gave Queenie a kiss on the forehead, then walked over to her desk and pulled out her stationery and a pen. Without saying a word, I laid both on the desk in plain view. She looked up at me and I gave her a wink. No doubt she'd be writing Reverend Bradford a note shortly after we left. I hoped.

Alva and I landed in the parking lot at Sam's at 4:17 p.m. I'd never been to Sam's at 4:17 before. The hostess looked confused, but she walked us to our usual table.

"I don't want to sit here," Alva said. "Too sunny. Let's go in the front room."

That just about caused the waitress to call for backup. "O-okay."

Minutes later we were chowing down on huge slices of apple pie. Then I had a brownie. And just to top it all off, I ate a piece of lemon pound cake. No doubt the rumors would fly once Alva and I left. Gretel Ann would call Frenchie at Do or Dye. She'd tell her that "that Fisher girl" had gone crazy. Before long the whole town would be buzzing that I'd had my dessert before my dinner. They'd blame it on my breakup with Casey. They might even speculate that I was losing my marbles like Pop. But I didn't care. Maybe I was losing my marbles. Or maybe, as Mama said, my apple cart had tipped over.

Mmm, apples.

Just for fun, I headed back up to the buffet for a second slice of apple pie. If I was going to be the topic of conversation in Fairfield, Texas, I might as well go for the gold and really give 'em something to talk about.

33

Heart Don't Do This to Me

A city becomes a world when one loves one of its inhabitants.

Lawrence Durrell

The week before *Texas Bride* released their October issue, Nadia flew back to Dallas so that she could attend her charity event. We spent the next several days dealing with the media while preparing for the magazine to hit the newsstands. I'd never seen the folks at the bridal shop so excited.

I'd been nervous about seeing Nadia in person, ever since the day Brady told her about my broken engagement. Still, with my heart becoming more entangled with her son's every day since, I had no choice. I finally broached the subject the night before the magazine released. We all met up at Alva's house for dinner.

Over a yummy meal, we shared details about several upcoming press engagements and a visit from a high-end buyer from out of state. The rest of the meal was spent talking about the dress itself and how much Nadia loved the final product.

She used her napkin to dab at her lips, then pulled it down and looked at me. "Katie, I'm going to need to go soon. I really need some sleep. But before I do, I want to talk to you about something. Would you walk me out to my car?"

I nodded, feeling my heart slither up to my throat. "Sure. I've been wanting to talk to you too."

I followed her out of the house to her car, and she opened the driver-side door. Before she got inside, she faced me and placed her hand on my arm. "I need you to know something, Katie."

"Y-yes ma'am."

"Before I ever design a gown, I pray and ask the Lord to show me not just the design but the fabrics, the textures, everything."

"I think that's great."

"Sometimes I have a real sense about things. Other times, not so much. But in your case, I knew without a shadow of a doubt just what sort of dress would be perfect. I didn't know anything about your fiancé, nor did I need to. The dress I designed was for you. And it was heaven-inspired. I need you to know that in case you have any doubt in your heart about whether or not that Loretta Lynn gown was meant for you."

"Oh, Nadia." I threw my arms around her neck. "You aren't mad that I didn't let you know right away? I wanted to. I really did. But everyone seemed to think I should keep it to myself so that you wouldn't be hurt. Please forgive me."

"Well, of course I forgive you. I was never mad, just a little perplexed. I was sad that you didn't think you could tell me right off the bat, but I'm definitely not hurt that you're not marrying the wrong man. That would have been catastrophic."

I felt the edges of my lips curl up in a smile.

"I knew the minute Brady picked me up at the airport the other day and from the smile on his face every time he mentioned your name—he's fallen . . . again. Only, this time he didn't break anything." She grinned. "If you know what I mean."

I pressed back a giggle. "If anyone had told me I'd end up falling for a pro basketball player in Dallas, I would've said they were crazy."

"So you do have feelings for my sweet boy?"

"Do I? He makes it so easy. I've never met anyone like him. These last couple months have more than convinced me that my heart is tied to Dallas."

"Well, speaking of which, I wanted to talk to you about the dress, but something else too. Madge tells me that you've been a huge help around the shop. She's really impressed with your design skills."

"I've enjoyed helping rearrange the layout and the window displays. And I'm so grateful for the income. It's been a fun way to freelance."

"Well, we've seen an upswing in sales since

those displays have been redesigned. Not only that, she said that you're the one who came up with the national ad that's going in the *In Flight* magazine next month. Is that right?"

I nodded.

"From what I can tell, you've got a penchant for PR. You see what it takes to draw people in. That's why the windows go over so well with the customers."

"You think?"

"Well, sure." She smiled. "Katie, I want to make this official. I want to offer you a full-time position at the shop."

"Really?"

"Yes. Your dedication over these past several weeks has convinced me that you are more than just a customer. You have a natural talent, and I'd love to see it cultivated."

"Oh, Nadia. I'd be honored. You have no idea."

"I think I have some idea. I was young once too, and needed a break. I hope you enjoy being with us at Cosmopolitan." She reached over and gave me a motherly hug. "I know it's not the same, being in Dallas. But it's not really that far from Fairfield."

"I know. And my parents are going to be coming back and forth more often now. In fact, they're coming tomorrow so they can be here for the big day."

"So they know about the dress now?"

"Yes ma'am."

"Wonderful. I can't wait to meet them." She yawned and then slipped into the driver's seat. "Give that boy of mine a kiss from me and tell him not to stay out too late. We have a big day tomorrow."

"Will do." I gave her a little wave and watched as she pulled away. My heart was so full I could hardly stand it. When I turned around, I saw Brady standing in the open doorway of my aunt's house. I sprinted to him.

"What did she say?" he asked.

"She offered me a job."

He smiled. "I had a feeling that was coming. Madge has been singing your praises."

"Just Madge?"

"Well, the girls put in a good word for you too." He pulled me into his arms and gave me a little kiss on the forehead.

"Just the girls?" I gazed up at him and caught a glimpse of the moonlight above.

"Well, maybe someone else. But he's a little biased, so I'm sure the decision wasn't based on anything he had to say."

"Surely not." I gave Brady the sweetest kiss, and then we stood in a comfortable embrace.

After a few moments, Brady loosened his hold on me. I could tell he had something on his mind. "I, um . . . I saw the orthopedist this morning."

"You did?"

"Yeah. He wants to do another surgery on my knee."

"Why didn't you tell me, Brady?"

He shrugged. "I've been thinking about it. Praying about it. Hadn't really decided until tonight, so I didn't bring it up."

"Well, now I can pray too. Are you going to do it?"

"I am." He nodded. "It still bothers me . . . a lot. I know that Stan thinks I'm ready to play again, but I'm not. And my mom still needs me at the shop. And now that you're there, well . . ." He pulled me close again. "Just one more confirmation that it's okay not to return to the game just yet. I've got to be healed up before I get back on the court."

"Getting healed up is for the best." Alva's voice rang out from behind us. "Sorry to be a nosy poke, but I had to come out to, um, take out the trash."

"Sure you did." I laughed and then extended my arm so that she could join us in a hug.

After Brady left that night, I settled into bed but had a hard time sleeping. With so much stirring, the sense of anticipation kept me wound up tighter than a clock. When the alarm went off at 6:30 I'd only had three hours' sleep, but I had to put on my game face.

Game face. Ha. Those words made me think of Brady, and thinking of Brady made me want to get to the shop as quickly as I could. I had to wait on Aunt Alva, of course. She moved a lot slower than I did but still managed to be ready by eight.

We arrived to a flurry of activity. The girls were all dressed to the nines. Well, all but Crystal, who was noticeably absent. I asked about her, but Brady just shrugged. "I get the feeling she's going through a transition of some sort."

"Transition?"

"I'm not sure. Did you know that you have guests?"

He pointed to some customers on the far side of the shop who were busy looking at gowns with Nadia and Madge. Only when they turned to face me did I realize I was looking at my parents. Not that I would've recognized Mama. She'd had her hair colored, a lovely honey shade. And the makeup . . . wow. I'd never seen her look so polished and professional before.

I rushed to greet them and wrapped them in a warm embrace. "You've met Nadia?" I asked.

"Yes, and Madge too. They're even sweeter than you described them to be."

"She called me sweet?" Madge put her hands on her hips and laughed. "Go figure."

"We were just telling the ladies what a beautiful shop this is." Mama pointed to the gown on the mannequin near the front of the store. "And your dress! Katie, it's fabulous. Looks just like something Loretta Lynn would wear, but it also reminds me so much of you. It's perfect!"

Nadia beamed. "That's the idea. But we have Dahlia to thank for that. She's been a big help to me while I've been in Paris."

"That Dahlia is the sweetest thing," Mama said. "She was such a comfort to us on the weekend that Queenie was hospitalized. Oh, and speaking of Dahlia, did you know Dewey drove us here? He's been dying to come for a visit. And thank goodness too! If it hadn't been for him, we would've gotten lost."

"Not me," Pop said. "I've got that newfangled GPS thing on my phone. Now that we're out and about more, it's come in handy."

"Where is Beau?" I asked. "And Jasper? Are they both coming?"

"Well, it's the strangest thing." Mama wrinkled her nose. "Beau is coming in his own truck. But Jasper said he'd rather stay at the hardware store. Pop offered to shut it down for the day, but Jasper wouldn't hear of it."

"Very strange."

"You can say that twice and mean it," Mama said.

"Very strange," Pop and I said in unison.

That got a laugh out of Mama and Nadia. Mama stayed in good spirits until Beau arrived a few minutes later. When he entered the store, he went straight to the counter to visit with Twiggy, only giving the rest of us a little wave.

“Well now, that boy of mine.” Mama clucked her tongue and took a step in his direction.

“Marie.” Pop rested his hand on her arm. “Let it be.”

“Let it be? But I just want to say hello to my son.”

“Marie.”

Turned out Beau wanted to talk to Mama more than any of us knew. After saying a few words to Twiggy, he headed our way and announced that he’d loaded his truck with all of his belongings from home and planned to stay in Dallas, starting today.

“Wait, w-what?” Mama looked stunned.

Pop, on the other hand, looked relieved.

Dewey, who’d just joined us, didn’t say a word.

“I’ve got a new job, Mama,” Beau said. “Making good money too.”

“There is a God and he loves me!” Pop raised his hands to the sky.

Mama’s eyes narrowed to slits as she looked at Beau. “You took a job . . . where?”

“Well, it’s the craziest thing,” he said. “I think you’re going to laugh.”

“Try me.” Mama crossed her arms at her chest. “And please don’t tell me you’ve developed a penchant for dress design. I’m not sure my heart could take it.”

Dewey slung an arm around Beau’s shoulder. “Now there’s a brother I can be proud of.”

My father pinched his eyes shut and shook his head. "It's my fault. I should've been a more manly influence. I let your mother coddle you, and now look at what we've created . . . a wedding dress designer."

"No, Pop. It's nothing like that." Beau rolled his eyes. "It's something completely different. I'm going to get to use my God-given talent to help others. It's a great feeling."

"Talent?" My father looked stumped by this. "You have talent?"

"Easy, Pop." I gave him a stern look.

"Yes," Beau said. "It's a great opportunity, and I can say without any hesitation that I already love it."

"And what he really, really loves," Dewey interjected, "is a certain little gal who's no longer gluten intolerant."

"He's in love with her?" Mama turned and glared at Beau. Her tightened expression softened after a moment. "Well now, I have an idea. Why don't you work from home in Fairfield? People do that all the time these days. And if that little skinny gal is truly interested in you—and who wouldn't be interested in this handsome face?—she would come to Fairfield. She has to know that you live there, after all. And a woman's place is with the man she loves."

"Well now, maybe it's the other way around," Pop said.

We all stared at him.

"What do you mean, Herb?" Mama asked.

"Maybe, just maybe, a man's place is with the woman he loves."

You could've heard a pin drop at that statement.

"Don't you remember when we were dating?" he said. "I wanted to move away to Waco? I had a great job offer."

"I remember the job offer, but I thought you turned it down because you really wanted to stay put in Fairfield."

"No, you wanted that. And I loved you, Marie. Still do. So I stayed in Fairfield and took over my father's hardware store. I'm not saying I regretted that decision, but I will say that I just wanted to see the smile on your face every morning. Being where you wanted to be made my heart happy enough to stay put."

My mother put her hands on her hips and for a moment looked as if she might cry. "Herbert Fisher, why didn't you ever tell me this?"

He shrugged. "I got over it."

"Got over it?"

"Well, you know what I mean. I grew to love our life in Fairfield and hardly ever thought about that job again." He slipped his arm over Beau's shoulder and gazed at Mama. "But Marie, maybe our boys need the same consideration."

"Are you saying . . ." Mama flinched as she glanced at Beau. "Are you saying that my baby boy should really move far, far away from home, from those he loves, to enter into a relationship with a gal from someplace we don't even know?"

"Precisely." Pop nodded. "And I'm also saying that he's not a baby. He'll figure that out when he has to show up at work every day and pay rent on an apartment. In Dallas. Which, by the way, isn't far, far away from home."

"Technically it's a house," Beau said. "I'll be living in a house with a guy named Stan."

"What?" I said. Now here was an interesting piece of the puzzle.

"Yep. He's great. And that's what I was trying to say earlier. I'm going to be working for Stan, not the bridal shop. He's a sports agent and he needs someone to assist him. You won't believe the big-name players he represents. I've met so many cool people."

"Oh, thank the Lord." My father slapped Beau on the back. "I couldn't quite picture how I'd go about telling my friends that my son designed wedding gowns for a living."

Beau rolled his eyes. "Stan's been agenting for years, and he's going to teach me the ropes."

Stan chose that very moment to enter the front door.

"Oh, great," Madge said as she and Brady walked our way. "Look who's come for a visit."

"C'mon, admit it, Madge," Brady said. "He's growing on you."

"Like a fungus." She rolled her eyes.

The door opened again, and this time Lori-Lou entered with Josh and their girls. Alva followed behind them holding baby Joshie.

Madge flew into gear at once, reaching for her walkie-talkie. "Incoming Mama Mia!" she said. "Incoming Mama Mia!"

"Whatever does she mean?" my mother asked.

"It's code for . . . oh, never mind." I laughed and walked over to greet Lori-Lou, who fussed at Mariela.

Less than a minute later Lori-Lou looked as if she might be sick. She managed to say, "I-I don't feel so well," before bolting from the room.

Josh watched her leave and then turned back to me with a sigh. "It's always like this."

"Always like what?" Alva asked as she shifted Joshie in her arms. "She gets sick a lot?"

"Yes. When she's . . ." He pointed at the girls, who'd taken to crawling under one of the clothing racks.

"Josh? Are you saying that Lori-Lou is . . . expecting?" Alva let out a little squeal as he nodded. "Seriously?"

"Oh, it's serious, all right. And trust me, it was quite a shock. She's been in tears for weeks. I can't believe no one's noticed."

"So, that day at the stockyard," I said. "Lori-Lou was having morning sickness?"

"Right. I think she was actually relieved that you thought it was the stomach flu."

"This is a particular strain of the flu that lasts about nine months." Mama laughed. "Caught it a few times myself."

I wanted to run after Lori-Lou and apologize for not paying more attention, for being so distracted with my new life at the shop. But just as I turned to do so, the door opened again and the shop filled with reporters and photographers from all of the local news stations. I watched as Nadia greeted them, and then the real fun began.

Our copies of *Texas Bride* were hand-delivered by Jordan Singer, who arrived moments later. I couldn't believe my eyes when I saw the quote from the queen of country music herself—Loretta Lynn. Turned out she loved the dress and gave it her stamp of approval. I loved it too. And when I saw the photo that had been chosen for the cover, I couldn't help but laugh. There I sat, plopped down on a wooden crate, in that gorgeous Loretta Lynn gown. Its ruffled skirt spilled out beautifully around me, as if I'd somehow planned it that way, and the details on the bodice shimmered under-neath the afternoon sunlight. All in all, a perfectly wonderful photo.

Best of all? The handsome fellow in the tuxedo. He stood just a few feet away, gazing at me with a smile ten thousand times sweeter than all of the peaches in Fairfield.

Epilogue

Less than two weeks after the magazine cover went live, my parents left for their first-ever Caribbean cruise. Mama called me from the port in Galveston just as I arrived at the shop on a Saturday morning. We hadn't opened yet, so I had plenty of time to talk.

"Katie, can you hear me?" She spoke a little too loud for comfort.

"Sure, Mama." I pulled the phone away from my ear. "What's up?"

"Listen, we're leaving on this ridiculous cruise right in the middle of hurricane season, so if you never see us again, just know that I love you and I wanted the chance to see you walk the aisle in that beautiful Loretta Lynn gown."

"Mama, I'm not engaged."

"Well, I know, but someday you will be. If we're swept away by a hurricane, please bury me in my blue dress. You know the one, with the pretty collar?"

"Mama, if you're swept out to sea, we won't need to bury you."

"True." She sighed. "Well, don't miss me too much. Oh, and check on Jasper while we're gone. You do know what's happening back home, don't you?"

"What do you mean?"

"You're not going to believe it," Mama said. "You're just not."

"Oh, I don't know. These days I'd say my mind is opened to believing all sorts of new and interesting things. What's up?"

"Call him when we hang up. He'll tell you. But in the meantime I have some news about Queenie."

My heart skipped a beat as fear settled over me. "What happened to her? Is she sick?"

"No."

"She fell and hurt herself?"

"No. Not even close. Brace yourself, Katie."

"O-okay." I drew in a deep breath, unsure of what to expect.

"She's. Become. A. Presbyterian."

I couldn't say why those words struck me like they did, but I laughed so hard I almost dropped the phone. Then Mama started laughing. After a while we simply had to end the call because we couldn't get it under control. Brady heard me all the way from the workroom and came out to the front of the store, filled with questions. When I told him, he started laughing too.

I spent the next few minutes trying to picture my grandmother in the Presbyterian church. Watching the man she adored preach . . . in a bathrobe. Okay, not a bathrobe, but a robe. Feeling closer to heaven.

Funny how life turned out.

A quick glance at the clock let me know we still had fifteen minutes before opening, just enough time to call Jasper. He answered his cell phone on the second ring with a brusque "Hello?"

"Mama said I should call you. What's up?"

"She told you about Queenie?"

"Yep. I hear she's a Presbyterian now."

"Yes, but wait . . . there's more. There's been a sighting."

"A sighting?"

"Queenie. And Reverend Bradford. Sitting in your spot at Dairy Queen, eating Oreo Blizzards."

"Whoa. I thought Queenie was borderline diabetic."

"Katie, be serious. I'm trying to tell you they're a couple."

"Queenie and Reverend Bradford. Out in public. Eating ice cream." I thought about that and smiled. "Which explains why she's become a Presbyterian. But she really is borderline diabetic, Jasper. She's kept it under control with diet and medication. You didn't know that?"

"I guess I'd forgotten." He sighed. "It's true what they say . . . people will sacrifice just about anything for love."

"Even their health." I laughed, then grew more serious. "Or the desire to move to the big city."

"Yeah, and that's probably the real reason Mama told you to call me. Crystal has moved to Fairfield."

"What?"

"Yep. I, um . . . I'm going to ask her to marry me, Katie."

"Oh, Jasper." I felt the sting of happy tears in my eyes. "I'm so happy for you."

"I'm pretty happy for me too. And you know what? Now that Crystal's here helping out at the hardware store, I don't feel that same pressure to get out of town. In fact, Fairfield is looking better by the day."

"I'm so glad. I'll bet Pop was surprised, though."

"He was. Did you know he was actually talking about selling the store? Can you believe that?"

"Yeah, he mentioned it awhile ago."

"Well, I think I've talked him into letting me take over as manager instead. That way he and Mama are free to gallivant around the country."

"Now that they've lost their marbles," I said.

"Yep. And speaking of which . . ."

Off in the distance I heard the sound of a customer's voice. Sounded familiar.

"Is that Bessie May?" I asked.

"Yes." He chuckled. "Arguing with Crystal about the price of a garden hose. You know how she is. Always wanting to barter."

"Let me guess. She's offering her two jars of peach preserves in exchange for the hose."

"One jar. Her prices have gone up. But Crystal's taking the bait," Jasper said. "Sorry, but

I'm going to have to intervene before things get out of control. Gotta go, sis. Take care of yourself in the big city."

"And you take care of yourself in the small town."

We ended the call and I couldn't help but smile. I pictured it all—my brother in a small town with the woman of his dreams at his side, me in the big city. I sighed, thinking about how good God had been to us.

"You seem kind of dreamy over there." Madge's voice startled me back to reality. "If I didn't know any better, I'd say you were in love."

"Oh, I'm in love, all right." A giggle followed. "With this place. With my new life. With . . . all of it."

"All of it?" She jabbed me with her elbow and gestured to Brady, who fastened a veil loaded with Austrian crystals onto a mannequin.

"Well, it might be a little soon to say." I'd never admit my feelings aloud to Madge, but right now they had me smiling from the inside out. I continued to gaze at Brady, emotions overtaking me. I felt my cheeks grow warm as he looked my way and gave me a wink. In the process of flirting with me, he nearly tumbled from the ladder. Poor guy.

"See the effect you have on him, girl?" Madge groaned. "It's the only downfall to you working here. Now he'll never get any work done." She mumbled something about how he'd never worked very hard in the first place, but she lost me after a line or two. Brady James was the hardest-working man I'd ever met, and the most dedicated team player. No doubt about that.

He climbed down from the ladder, extended his arms, and gave me a "come hither" look.

I glanced up at the clock and took note of the time. Only two minutes until the store opened. Just enough time for one final play from my end of the court. With a spring in my step, I raced across the bridal shop and flew straight into the arms of the man I adored.

Acknowledgments

A huge thank-you to my agent, Chip MacGregor, who not only represented this story but also gave me the idea. I'll confess, I wasn't sure I could pull off a story about a guy running a bridal shop, but Brady ended up being the perfect hero!

As always, I'm grateful to my editor, Jennifer Leep, and to my awesome marketing team at Revell—Michele Misiak, Erin Bartels, Lanette Haskins, and many others.

I have come to depend on my line/copy editor, Jessica English, on every Revell story. I can't fathom publishing a novel without her. What a blessing she is in my life.

More than anything, I must give thanks to Eleanor Clark, one of the finest ladies I've ever known. I loosely patterned the character of Queenie after her, but only the good parts. She's truly one of the godliest women on the planet—an author, grandmother, mother, friend, and true patriot. What a blessing she's been in the lives of so many. She showed me her town—Fairfield—in all of its glory. Through her, I learned that quaint, small-town living is a lovely way to spend your life.

To the people of Fairfield, thanks for letting me poke fun at you. I haven't been to any of your churches and took quite a few liberties with the denominational jabs, but they were all in fun. I know that you are all working hard for the cause of Christ and celebrate your efforts. Even the Presbyterians.

To my wonderful proofreaders who read the book from cover to cover before I turned it in, bless you. I rarely see my own errors, so having your eyes on the story helped . . . a lot.

To my Lord and Savior Jesus Christ, thank you for one more opportunity to share a fun story with a faith message. I count it a privilege.

About the Author

Award-winning author **Janice Thompson** enjoys tickling the funny bone. She got her start in the industry writing screenplays and musical comedies for the stage, and she has published over one hundred books for the Christian market. She has played the role of mother of the bride four times now and particularly enjoys writing lighthearted, comedic, wedding-themed tales. Why? Because making readers laugh gives her great joy!

Janice was named the 2008 Mentor of the Year for American Christian Fiction Writers (ACFW). She is the incoming president of her local (Woodlands, Texas) chapter and is active in that group, teaching regularly on the craft of writing. In addition, she enjoys public speaking and mentoring young writers.

Janice is passionate about her faith and does all she can to share the joy of the Lord with others, which is why she particularly enjoys writing. Her tagline, "Love, Laughter, and Happy Ever Afters!" sums up her take on life.

She lives in Spring, Texas, where she leads a rich life with her family, a host of writing friends, and two mischievous dachshunds. She does her best to keep the Lord at the center of it all. You can find out more about Janice at:

www.janiceathompson.com
or www.freelancewritingcourses.com.

Center Point Large Print
600 Brooks Road / PO Box 1
Thorndike, ME 04986-0001 USA

(207) 568-3717

US & Canada:
1 800 929-9108
www.centerpointlargeprint.com

Lecture Notes in Mathematics

Edited by A. Dold, B. Eckmann and F. Takens

Subseries: USSR
Adviser: L. D. Faddeev, Leningrad

1412

V. V. Kalashnikov V. M. Zolotarev (Eds.)

Stability Problems for Stochastic Models

Proceedings of the 11th International Seminar held in Sukhumi (Abkhazian Autonomous Republic) USSR, Sept. 25–Oct. 1, 1987

Springer-Verlag
Berlin Heidelberg New York London Paris Tokyo Hong Kong

Editors

Vladimir V. Kalashnikov
Institute for System Studies
Academy of Sciences of the USSR
Prospekt 60 let Oktjabrja 9
117 312 Moscow, USSR

Vladimir M. Zolotarev
Steklov Mathematical Institute
Academy of Sciences of the USSR
Vavilov st. 42, 117 333 Moscow, USSR

Consulting Editor

Vladimir M. Zolotarev
Steklov Mathematical Institute
Academy of Sciences of the USSR
Vavilov st. 42, 117 333 Moscow, USSR

Mathematics Subject Classification (1980): 60B10, 60B99, 60E10, 60E99, 60F05, 60K25, 60K99, 62E10, 62F10, 62F35, 62H12, 62P99

ISBN 3-540-51948-3 Springer-Verlag Berlin Heidelberg New York
ISBN 0-387-51948-3 Springer-Verlag New York Berlin Heidelberg

Printed in Germany

Printing and binding: Druckhaus Beltz, Hemsbach/Bergstr.
2146/3140-543210 – Printed on acid-free paper

CONTENTS

Introduction

ARKHIPOV S.V. The density function's asymptotic representation in the case of multidimensional strictly stable distributions ... 1

AMS Classification 60E07. Key words: multidimensional stable distributions, asymptotic representations.

FACTOROVICH I. Limiting behaviour of the sum of i.i.d. random variables and its terms of greatest moduli in the case of logarithmic type tall function 22

AMS Classification 60F99, 60F05. Key words: limit behaviour of the sum of i.i.d. random variables, logarithmic type tall function.

HAHUBIA Ts.G. On the adaptive estimation of change points 33

AMS Classification 62F35, 62G05. Key words: change point, parametric and semiparametric models, adaptive estimation.

HANIN L.G., RACHEV S.T., GOOT R.E., YAKOVLEV A.Yu. Precise upper bounds for the functionals describing tumour treatment efficiency 50

AMS Classification 60E99, 92A07. Key words: survival probability, "hit and target" model, given marginals.

KAGAN A.M. A multivariate analog of the Cramér theorem on components of the Gaussian distributions 68

AMS Classification 60E10, 62E10. Key words: Cramér theorem,

multivariate Gaussian distribution, linear forms, Darmois-Skitovitch theorem.

KAGAN A.M. A refinement of Lukacs theorems 78
AMS Classification 62E10, 60E10. Key words: Gaussian distribution, Poissonian distribution, linearity of regression.

KALASHNIKOV V.V., VSEKHSVYATSKII S.Yu. On the connection of Renyi's theorem and renewal theory 83
AMS Classification 60K05, 60F99, 60E15. Key words: Sum of random number of random variables, rate of convergence, renewal function.

KLEBANOV L.B., MELAMED J.A., RACHEV S.T. On the products of a random number of random variables in connection with a problem from mathematical economics 103
AMS Classification 60F99, 62E10, 90A19. Key words: limit theorem, Pareto distribution, characterization, average annual sum of capital.

KOROLEV V.Yu. The asymptotic distributions of random sums 110
AMS Classification 60F99. Key words: limit theorem, random number of summands, convergence to Robbins mixtures.

KRUGLOV V.M. Normal and degenerate convergences of random sums 124
AMS Classification 60F99. Key words: random number of summands, normal convergences, degenerate convergences, Zolotarev's centers.

LEVIN V.L., RACHEV S.T. New duality theorems for marginal problems with some applications in stochastics 137
AMS Classification 46E27, 62B10. Key words: marginal problems, duality theorems, Kantorovich-Rubinstein distance,

approximation in maxima scheme.

LIBITSKY A.D. Stable random vectors in Hilbert space 172
AMS Classification 60E07. Key words: stable measure, representation of characteristic function.

MARKUS L. The mean's consistent estimation, in the case random processes, satisfying partial differential equations .. 183
AMS Classification 62M09. Key words: consistence of estimators, least squares method, random fields.

MELAMED J.A. Limit theorems in the set-up of summation of a random number of independent identically distributed random variables 194
AMS Classification 60F99, 60F05, 60F25, 60F10. Key words: random number of summands, quick convergence, local limit theorems, large deviations.

NAGAEV A.V., SHKOLNIK S.M. Some asymptotic properties of the stable laws 229
AMS Classification 60E07, 62F10. Key words: stable laws, Fisher information matrix.

NIKULIN M.S., VOINOV V.C. A chi-square goodness-of-fit test for exponential distributions of the first order 239
AMS Classification 62F10, 62G10. Key words: chi-square goodness-of-fit tests, exponential distributions of the first order, minimum variance unbiased estimators.

NUMMELIN E. A conditional weak law of large numbers 259
AMS Classification 60F10, 60F05. Key words: weak law of large numbers, large deviation limit, dominating point of a convex set.

OBRETENOV A. On the rate of convergence for the extreme value in the case of IFR-distributions 263

AMS Classification 60K10, 62N05. Key words: failure rate function, extrem value theory.

OMEY E. On the rate of convergence in extreme value theory ... 270

AMS Classification 60F99, 60K10. Key words: extremal value, rate of convergence, probability metric.

PLUCINSKA A. Some properties of stochastic processes with linear regression 280

AMS Classification 62E10, 62M99. Key words: linear regression, memory of stochastic processes.

PUCZ J. On characterization of generalized logistic and Pareto distributions 288

AMS Classification 62E10. Key words: characterization, Pareto distribution, logistic distribution.

ROSSBERG H.-J. Limit theorems for positive definite probability densities 296

AMS Classification 60E10, 10B10. Key words: positive definite densities, complete convergence, new CLT.

SENATOV V.V. On the estimate of the rate of convergence in the central limit theorem in Hilbert space 309

AMS Classification 60B12. Key words: central limit theorem in Hilbert space, rate of convergence, eigenvectors of covariance operator.

TRUKHINA I.P., CHISTYAKOV G.P. Stability of decomposition in semigroups of functions representable by series in the Jacobi polynomials 328

AMS Classification 60E10, 60E99. Key words: Jacobi polynomials, semigroup of functions, stability of decomposition.

WESOLOWSKI J. A regressional characterization of the Poisson distribution 349

AMS Classification 62E10. Key words: constancy of regression, Poisson distribution.

YAMAZATO M. Hitting times of single points for 1-dimensional generalized diffusion processes 352

AMS Classification 60F17. Key words: Brownian motion, hitting time distribution.

REBOLLEDO R. Pseudotrajectories and stability problems for stochastic dynamical systems 360

AMS Classification 58F11, 60H99. Key words: Stochastic dynamical systems, stability, Thermodynamics Formalism.

INTRODUCTION

An International Seminar on Stability Problems for Stochastic Models was held in Sukhumi (Abkhasian Autonomic Republic) from 25 September till 1 October 1987. This seminar was the eleventh since the Steklov Mathematical Institute USSR Acad.Sci. (SMI) launched them in 1974*) .

Traditionally other Institutes and Universities take part in organizing of the seminars too. Thus the Institute for Systems Studies (ISS) is a permanent co-organizer of these seminars. Essential help in the organizing and holding of the seminars (and, particularly in that of the Seminar-87) was received from International Research Institute for Management Sciences.

An active role in the organizing of the seminar in Sukhumi was played by the Abkhasian State University. The Rector of the University, Prof. Z.Avidzba, Vice-Rector Prof. O.Damenia and our colleagues from the University R.Absava, A.Gvaramia and L.Karba. All of them were members of Organizing Committee and we are grateful to them for their hospitality.

Participants of the seminar lived and worked on the Black Sea shore in the tourist hotel "XX s'ezd VLKCM". Remembering the good conditions which were created for us we especially thank the head of the Abkhasian tourist office, N.Akaba, and the director of the hotel, G.Meshveliani.

There were more than 100 participants at the seminar representing scientific centres and universities of 13 countries of Europe, Asia, Africa and America (both North and South). More than 60 reports were delivered during the 5 days.

The variety of topics of these reports can be explained by a

---

*) See LN in Math., volumes 982, 1155, 1233

tradition: the principal aim of the seminar is to publicise ideas and methods used in stability theory of stochastic models and it does not imply a rigid topic selection for the reports.

The reports delivered made up the basis for two volumes of Proceedings. One of them traditionally is published by ISS Publishers in Russian*) . The other is the present one.

The preparation of the manuscript of the Proceedings demanded a great deal of activity. Our sincere words of gratitude are addressed to active and permanent participants of the seminar L.B.Klebanov from Leningrad (for it was there that the final preparation of the manuscript took place) and I.A.Melamed from Tbilisi.

All the authors are indebted to Acad. L.D.Faddeev (adviser of the USSR Subseries of LNM) and Dr. A.P.Oskolkov for the possibility to meet again under the cover of a Lecture Notes volume.

V.M.Zolotarev

---

*) All of these Proceedings are being translated into English in the "Journal of Soviet Mathematics", published by Plenum Publishers.

THE DENSITY FUNCTION'S ASYMPTOTIC REPRESENTATION IN THE CASE OF MULTIDIMENSIONAL STRICTLY STABLE DISTRIBUTIONS

S.V.Arkhipov

Introduction

During the last few years a continually increasing attention was payed to a peculiar - the so called strictly stable-class of multidimensional distributions, and the interest has not stopped growing up to the present. One of the reasons may be that in a certain sense this class forms the most part of the stable distributions.

To describe the strictly stable laws it will be advantageous for us to observe their characteristic functions (ch.f.) in a form not considered previously (except the case of $\alpha = 1$):

$$f(t) = \exp(g(|t|\tau)), \quad t \in \mathbb{R}^n, \quad n \geq 2, \quad \tau = t/|t|,$$

$$g(t\tau) = \begin{cases} \Gamma(-\alpha)\, t^{\alpha} \int\limits_{S^{n-1}} (-i\tau, \xi)^{\alpha} \mathcal{M}(d\xi), & \alpha \in (0,1) \cup (1,2), \\ -\frac{\pi}{2}|t| \int\limits_{S^{n-1}} (\tau, \xi)\, \mathcal{M}(d\xi) + i(\tau, b), & \alpha = 1, \end{cases} \tag{1}$$

where $\mathcal{M}$ is a finite measure on the unit sphere $S^{n-1} = \{\xi : \xi = 1, \xi \in \mathbb{R}^n\}$, having for $\alpha = 1$ the supplementary property:

$$\int\limits_{S^{n-1}} \xi\, \mathcal{M}(d\xi) = 0.$$

The power of a complex number in (1) is interpreted with the aid of the principal value

$$(-iy)^{\alpha} = |y|^{\alpha} \exp\left(-\frac{\pi\alpha i}{2} \operatorname{sign} y\right), \quad y \in \mathbb{R}.$$

Except some particular cases there does not exist any clear expression for the density function of a stable law, consequently the investigation has to deal with different exact ot asymptotic representation of the density. The material, presented here, may be regarded as a further development of results, published in 12 . There was discussed the case $0 < \alpha < 2$, when the spectral density μ belonged to the special space $C^{\infty}(S^{n-1})$.

Further we change this requirement to a less restricting one supposing μ to be chosen from the famous Liouville space $L_2^{r}(S^{n-1})$. The spectral density μ belongs to $L_2^{r}(S^{n-1})$, $r > 0$, when $\mu \in L_2(S^{n-1})$ and in in addition it has r derivative (r can be a fraction).

A fundamental problem is to get an asymptotical expression for the density $p(x)$ when $|x| \to \infty$. Taking the case of $\mu \in C^{\infty}(S^{n-1})$, when the density function $p(x)$ has a complete asymptotical decomposition, the situation considered now has the peculiarity that depending on the smoothness one can get only a finite order asymptotical decomposition.

The embedding theorems enable us to transfer our results to spectral densities chosen from Hölder spaces.

The method we suggest constructing the asymptotical form of the density function gives the analogous result for the derivatives of the density without any difficulties.

2. The fundamental result

Let $\{Y_{l_j}(\xi)\}$ be an orthonormal system of spherical harmonics (sph.h.) in $L_2(S^{n-1})$. The linearly independent harmonics of order l are indexed by j, $j = 1, \ldots, d(l)$, where

$$d(l) = \frac{(2l+n-2)(l+n-3)!}{(n-2)!\, l!}$$

A survey of the theory of sph.h. can be found e.g. in [9] .

THEOREM. Let us suppose that the density μ of the spectral measure belongs to $L_2^r(S^{n-1})$, $\alpha \leq r < \infty$. The following asymptotical representation holds true $x \neq 0$:

$$p(|x|\xi) = \frac{\mu(\xi)}{|x|^{\alpha+n}} + \sum_{k=2}^{m-1} \frac{2^{\alpha k}}{\pi^{n/2}\,\Gamma(k+1)} \cdot \frac{\mu_k(\xi)}{|x|^{\alpha k+n}} + R_m(x), \tag{2}$$

where $\xi = x/x$ and the functions $\mu_k(\xi)$ are given on S^{n-1} by the following series, converging in the mean square sense

$$\mu_k(\xi) = \sum_{l=0}^{\infty} \sum_{j=1}^{d(l)} (-i)^l \frac{\Gamma((l+\alpha k+n)/2)}{\Gamma((l-\alpha k)/2)} g^k_{l_j} \mathcal{I}_{l_j}(\xi) \qquad \text{for } \alpha \neq 1,$$

$$\mu_k(\xi) = \sum_{l=L}^{\infty} \sum_{j=1}^{d(2l)} (-1)^l \frac{\Gamma(l+\frac{k+n}{2})}{\Gamma(l-\frac{k}{2})} g^k_{2l,j} \mathcal{I}_{2l,j}(\xi) \qquad \text{for } \alpha = 1.$$

$$L = \begin{cases} \frac{k}{2}+1 & \text{, when } k \text{ is even} \\ 0 & \text{, when } k \text{ is odd} \end{cases}$$

and where

$$g^k_{l_j} = \int_{S^{n-1}} g^k(\tau)\, \mathcal{I}_{l_j}(\tau)\, d\tau.$$

The remainder $R_m(x)$ can be estimated in the following way

$$\|R_m(x)\|_1 = \left\{ \int_{S^{n-1}} (R_m(|x|\xi))^2 d\xi \right\}^{1/2} \leq \frac{C_1(m)}{|x|^{\alpha m+n}}, \tag{3}$$

where $C_1(m)$ is a constant, depending on m, α and $\mu(\xi)$, furthermore on satisfies the condition

$$2 \leq m \leq [r/\alpha] + 1. \tag{4}$$

The upper bound for m shows the maximal possible number of the numbers in the representation (2).

COROLLARY 1. Assume that $\mu(\xi) \in L_2^r(S^{n-1})$, $r \geq \alpha + n/2$. So the functions $\mu_k(\xi)$ can be regarded as elements from the Hölder space of the sphere. More accurately $\mu_k(\xi) \in C_*^{r-\alpha(k-1)-n/2}(S^{n-1})$, if the exponent of smoothness is an integer, and $\mu_k(\xi) \in C^{r-\alpha(k-2)-n/2}(S^{n-1})$ otherwise. The representation (2) remains true, but the estimation (3) must be changed as follows:

$$\|R_m(x)\|_2 = \max\{|R_m(|x|\xi)| : \xi \in S^{n-1}\} \leq \frac{C_2(m)}{x^{\alpha m + n}},$$

where

$$2 \leq m \leq \left[\frac{r - n/2}{\alpha}\right] + 1.$$

COROLLARY 2. Let X be a strictly stable random vector in $\mathbb{R}^n$, and G a cone with its vertex at zero such that $g \in \operatorname{supp} \mu$, where $g \in S^{n-1} \cap G$. Denoting by

$$G(u(\xi)) = \{x = |x|\xi : |x| \geq |u(\xi)|, \ \xi \in g\}$$

we have

$$P\{X \in G(u(\xi))\} = (\alpha + n - 1)^{-1} \int_g \mu(\xi)(|u(\xi)|)^{-(\alpha+n-1)} d\xi +$$

$$+ \sum_{k=2}^{m-1} 2^{\alpha k} (\alpha k + n - 1)^{-1} \pi^{-n/2} (\Gamma(k+1))^{-1} \int_g \mu_k(\xi)(|u(\xi)|)^{-(\alpha k + n - 1)} d\xi +$$

$$+ \int_g R_m(|u(\xi)|\xi)\, d\xi.$$

This representation is asymptotical in the sense that the remainder tends to zero when

$$\min\{|u(\xi)| : \xi \in g\} \longrightarrow \infty.$$

3. Some preliminary results from the theory of functional spaces on the sphere

The system $\{\mathcal{I}_{l_j}(\xi)\}$ of sph.h. is complete in $L_2(S^{n-1})$ and every function $\theta(\xi) \in L_2(S^{n-1})$ can be expanded into series converging the the mean square sense in the following way (see [5] , § 31):

$$\theta(\xi) = \sum_{l,j} \theta_{l_j} \mathcal{I}_{l_j}(\xi),$$

where

$$\theta_{l_j} = \int_{S^{n-1}} \theta(\xi) \mathcal{I}_{l_j}(\xi)\, d\xi.$$

DEFINITION 1. The operator determined by the equation

$$T\theta(\xi) = \sum_{l,j} t_l \theta_{l_j} \mathcal{I}_{l_j}(\xi)$$

is called the multiplier operator, and its spectrum $\{t_l\}$ the multiplier by spherical harmonics.

Now let us turn to the multiplier operator $(E+\delta)^{r/2}$ with the multiplier $\{(1+l(l+n-2))^{r/2}\}$, where E is the unit operator and and δ is the spherical part of the Laplacian, or the Laplace-Beltram operator (cf [5], § 31).

DEFINITION 2. For $0 < r < \infty$ we call the space $L_2^r(S^{n-1})$ the sphere S^{n-1} , satisfying that

$$(E+\delta)^{r/2}\theta(\xi) \in L_2(S^{n-1}).$$

We note immediately that the spaces $L_2^r(S^{n-1})$ determined just now coincide in the the sets of their elements with the well-known Sobolev-Slo detzki spaces $W_2^r(S^{n-1})$. For the sake of better comparability of the he results we recall the definition used in the theory of singular integrals ([5] , § 31), and which differs from the one given regularly in the theory of partial differential equation.

Let θ be extended by constant (i.e. $\tilde{\theta}(x) = \theta(x/|x|)$) to the spherical segment Ω: $0 < \rho_1 \leq \rho \leq \rho_2 < \infty$. The space denoted by $W_2^r(S^{n-1})$ consists of those functions extended to Ω as mentioned above, they belong to the usual Sobolev-Slobodetzki space $W_2^r(\Omega)$ (cf. [10]).

REMARK 1. Usually in the theory of multivariate differentiable functions theorems are completely proved only for the classes of functions defined on the whole $\mathbb{R}^n$. With the aid of multiplication of the function $\theta(\xi) \in W_2^r(\Omega)$ by the function $\theta_0(\rho) \in C^\infty(\mathbb{R})$: $\theta_0(\rho) = 1$ on $[\rho_1, \rho_2]$ and $\theta_0(\rho) = 0$ outside the segment $[\rho_1/2, 2\rho_2]$ we get the needed extension to $\mathbb{R}^n$ saving the class. This gives the possibility to extend the theorems proved for $\mathbb{R}^n$ to arbitrary domain $\Omega \subset \mathbb{R}^n$ (cf. [6]).

The the results of [1] it follows that

i) $L_2^r(S^{n-1}) = W_2^r(S^{n-1})$, $r > 0$,

ii) for $r > 0$ the space $L_2^r(S^{n-1})$ consists of distributions.

LEMMA 1. If $\theta_1(\xi)$, $\theta_2(\xi) \in L_2^r(S^{n-1})$, $r > n/2$ then $\theta_1(\xi) \cdot \theta_2(\xi) \in L_2^r(S^{n-1})$.

PROOF. The statement of the theorem is the obvious consequence of the remark 1, the results of [11] on multipliers in $\mathbb{R}^n$ and i).

Now we define the Hölder spaces of functions on the sphere.

DEFINITION 3. We say that $\theta(\xi) \in C^\lambda(S^{n-1})$, $\lambda > 0$, when the function $\theta(x/|x|) \in C^{[\lambda]}(\mathbb{R}^n \setminus \{0\})$ ($[\lambda]$ is the integer part of λ), and in addition if $\lambda \neq [\lambda]$ then the derivatives of order $[\lambda]$: $u_k(x) = (D^k\theta)x$, $|k| = [\lambda]$ satisfy the following condition on the sphere:

$$|u_k(\xi_1) - u_k(\xi_2)| \leq C\,|\xi_1 - \xi_2|^{\lambda - [\lambda]}, \qquad \xi_1, \xi_2 \in S^{n-1}.$$

DEFINITION 4. We say that $\theta(\xi) \in C_*^{\lambda}(S^{n-1})$, $\lambda = 1,2,\ldots$, when $\theta(x/|x|) \in C^{\lambda-1}(\mathbb{R}^n \setminus \{0\})$, and the derivatives of order $\lambda-1$: $u_k(x) = (D^k\theta)(x)$, $|k| = \lambda - 1$ satisfy the following condition on the sphere:

$$|u(\xi_1) - u(\xi_2)| \leqslant C|\xi_1 - \xi_2| \ln 2(|\xi_1 - \xi_2|)^{-1}, \quad \xi_1, \xi_2 \in S^{n-1}.$$

LEMMA 2. If the function $\theta(\xi)$ belongs to the space $L_2^r(S^{n-1})$, $r > n/2$, then

$$\theta(\xi) \in C_*^{r-n/2}(S^{n-1}), \text{ when } r - n/2 \text{ is integer}$$

$$\theta(\xi) \in C^{r-n/2}(S^{n-1}) \text{ otherwise.}$$

The proof is based on the embedding theorems of the spaces $W_2^r(\mathbb{R}^n)$ into $H_\infty^{r-n/2}(\mathbb{R}^n)$ (see [6], p.229, [7], p.67), furthermore on the remark 1 and i).

LEMMA 3. Let $\{t_l\}$ be the spectrum of the multiplier operator T. T is a continuous operator from $L_2^r(S^{n-1})$ to $L_2^{r+u}(S^{n-1})$ iff $t_l = O(l^{-u})$.

PROOF. The lemmas statement directly follows from the proposition 6.1 of [1] and from ii).

The following lemma explains the connection between the order of smoothness of the functions $g(r)$ and $\mu(\xi)$ from (1).

LEMMA 4. If $\mu(\xi) \in L_2^r(S^{n-1})$, $r > 0$ then $g(r) \in L_2^{r+\frac{n}{2}+\alpha}(S^{n-1})$, $0 < \alpha < 2$ and we have the summation formulae:

$$g(r) = \pi^{n/2} 2^{-\alpha} \sum_{l,j} i^l \Gamma((l-\alpha)/2)(\Gamma((l+n+\alpha)/2))^{-1} \mu_{l_j} \mathcal{J}_{l_j}(r), \quad \alpha \neq 1, \tag{5}$$

$$g(r) = \frac{1}{2}\pi^{n/2} \sum_{l=0}^{\infty} \sum_{j=1}^{d(2l)} (-1)^l \Gamma(l - \tfrac{1}{2})(\Gamma(l-(n+1)/2))^{-1} \mu_{2l,j} \mathcal{J}_{2l,j}(r), \quad \alpha = 1. \tag{6}$$

PROOF. Applying (1.16), (1.19) in [1] to the right side of (1) we get (5) and (6). The assertion about the order of smoothness follows from the asymptotical relation

$$\frac{\Gamma(z+a)}{\Gamma(z-b)} \sim z^{a+b} \qquad \text{for} \qquad z \to \infty$$

and from the lemma 3.

4. Auxiliary statements

The densities of strictly stable distributions (s.s.d.) are determined by the inversion formula of characteristic functions that can be written with the aid of spherical coordinate system in the form

$$p(x) = (2\pi)^{-n} \int_0^\infty \int_{S^{n-1}} \exp(-i|t|(\tau,x) + |t|^\alpha g(\tau))|t|^{n-1}\, d\tau\, d|t|.$$

In order to get the decomposition of the density function it is necessary (similarly to the one-dimensional case):

a) to rotate the contour of the integration on the radial variable.

b) to decompose by Taylor formula the ch.f.

c) to calculate the inverse Fourier transforms of the homogeneous functions, having been got in b).

As the integral

$$\int_0^\infty \int_{S^{n-1}} \exp(-i|t|(\tau,x))\, \theta(\tau)\, |t|^{\gamma-1}\, d\tau\, d|t|$$

is conditionally convergent only for $0<\gamma<\frac{n+1}{2}$ even if the function $\theta(\tau)$ is smooth enough (cf. [8] , p.173), it is necessary to apply the Abelian summation method of integrals. So the original formula for the decompositions of the densities of s.s.d. has the form:

$$p(x) = (2\pi)^{-n} \lim_{\varepsilon\to 0} \left\{ \int_0^\infty \int_{S^{n-1}} \exp(-i|t|(\tau,x) + |t|^\alpha g(\tau) - \varepsilon|t|)|t|^{n-1}\, d\tau\, d|t| \right\}. \tag{7}$$

Now, taking into account (7) we turn to the more detailed consideration of the problems, stated in a) - c).

a) The possibility of rotation the contour of the integration is based on the lemma 5, which is the extension of the lemma 2.2.2 in [3] to the multidimensional case.

Further the logarithm of the ch.f. will be used in the form suggested in [3] , formula (B.34):

$$g(|t|\tau) = -|t|^{\alpha} \lambda(\tau) \exp(-i\pi \beta(\tau) K(\alpha)/2), \tag{8}$$

where $K(\alpha) = \alpha - 1 + \operatorname{sign}(1-\alpha)$, $\lambda(\tau)$ $\beta(\tau)$ functions and $|\beta(\tau)| \leqslant 1$.

REMARK 2. Similarly to [3] we shall equally use the representations (1) and (8) choosing the one of them which appears to be more advantageous in the given situation.

Let us denote

$$\omega(z,\tau,x) = \exp(-iz|x|(\tau,\xi) + z^{\alpha} g(\tau) - \varepsilon z)\, z^{n-1},$$

$$S_{\pm}^{n-1} = \{\xi : (\xi, x) \gtrless 0, \ |\xi| = 1, \ \xi \in \mathbb{R}^n\}.$$

LEMMA 5. The integrals

$$Q(C_{\varrho}^{+}) = \int_{S_{\pm}^{n-1}} \int_{C_{\varrho}^{\pm}(\tau)} \omega(z,\tau,x)\, dz\, d\tau \tag{9}$$

for every fixed $\varepsilon > 0$ tend to zero as $\varrho \to \infty$ or as $\varrho \to 0$ if the sequences of contours are chosen the following way:

$$C_{\varrho}^{+}(\tau) = \{ z : |z| = \varrho, \ (-\tfrac{\pi}{2}) \min(1, (1-\beta(\tau)K(\alpha))/\alpha < \varphi_1 < 0, \quad \tau \in S_{+}^{n-1} \},$$

$$C_{\varrho}^{-}(\tau) = \{ z : |z| = \varrho, \ 0 < \varphi_2 < \tfrac{\pi}{2} \min(1, (1+\beta(\tau)K(\alpha))/\alpha, \quad \tau \in S_{-}^{n-1} \},$$

where $\varphi_j = \arg z$, $0 < \alpha < 2$.

PROOF. We fix a direction τ on the sphere. Then the internal integral in (9) differs from the one-dimensional inversion formula only in the scalar product (τ, ξ), in the exponent $\exp(-\varepsilon z)$, and in the Jacibian z^{n-1}, and this fact does not change the arguing followed in the proof of the lemma 2,2.2 in [3].

Finally we remark, that the choice of the contours $C_\varsigma^{\pm}(\tau)$ ensures the powers in the exponent to be negative.

b) The decomposition we need can be achieved applying the Taylor formula with the integral remainder member to the function $\exp(ag(t)s)$, $a \in \mathbb{C}$ ($\mathbb{C}$ is the complex plane). Taking $s=1$ we have

$$\exp(ag(t)) = 1 + ag(t) + \ldots + \frac{(ag(t))^{m-1}}{(m-1)!} + \\ + \frac{(ag(t))^{m-1}}{(m-1)!} \int_0^1 (1-u)^{m-1} \exp(ag(t)u)\,du, \tag{10}$$

c) The following two lemmas show, how to calculate the inverse Fourier transform of homogeneous functions having support in the half-space.

LEMMA 6. Let $\theta(\tau)$ be an even of odd function $\theta(\tau) \in L_2(S^{n-1})$, $a \in \mathbb{C}$. The following representations hold with uniformly convergent series $(\lambda = (n-2)/2)$:

$$\int_{S_\pm^{n-1}} e^{a(\tau,\xi)} \theta(\tau)\,d\tau = \frac{1}{2}\pi^{n/2} \sum_{l,j} \theta_{2l,j} \mathcal{J}_{2l,j}(\xi) \times \\ \times \sum_{N=0}^{\infty} \left(\frac{a}{2}\right)^{2N+2l} \left(\Gamma(2l+N+\lambda+1)\Gamma(N+1)\right)^{-1}, \tag{11}$$

when $\theta(\tau)$ is even, and

$$\int_{S_\pm^{n-1}} e^{a(\tau,\xi)} \theta(\tau)\,d\tau = \frac{1}{2}\pi^{n/2} \sum_{l,j} \theta_{2l+1,j} \mathcal{J}_{2l+1,j}(\xi) \times$$

$$\times \sum_{N=0}^{\infty} \left(\frac{a}{2}\right)^{2N+2l+2} \left(\Gamma(2l+N+\lambda+2)\Gamma(N+1)\right)^{-1}, \tag{12}$$

when $\theta(\tau)$ is odd function.

PROOF. Since the parity property holds for $\theta(\tau)$, it is sufficient to prove the assertion only for one half-sphere, say for S_+^{n-1}. We show the equation (11) in the case of even function and $n \geq 3$, noting that in the other cases the proof can be carried out in the same way.

The left side of (11) is an integral operator with symmetric kernel. As the well-known Schmidt theorem (see e.g. [9], § 4, N 5) states, it can be expanded into the uniformly convergent series

$$\int_{S_+^{n-1}} e^{a(\tau,\xi)} \theta(\tau)\, d\tau = \sum_{l,j} C_{2l} \theta_{2l,j} Y_{2l,j}(\xi), \tag{13}$$

where $\theta_{2l,j}$ are the coefficients of the Fourier series by sph.h. of the function $\theta(\tau)$. We determine the eigenvalues C_{2l} from the Funk-Hecke formula (8 , p.162):

$$C_{2l} = (4\pi)^{\lambda} \Gamma(\lambda)\Gamma(2\lambda+1)/\Gamma(2l+n-2) \int_0^1 \exp(ay)\, (1-y^2)^{\lambda-\frac{1}{2}} C_{2l}^{\lambda}(y)\, dy.$$

Here $\lambda = (n-2)/2$ and $C_{2l}^{\lambda}(y)$ are the Gegenbauer polynomials.

REMARK 3. For $n=2$ the orthogonal polynomials in the Funk-Hecke formula are the Chebyshev polynomials: $\cos(l \arccos y)$.

Further, to reduce the problem to the known (given in tables) integrals, first we develop $\exp(ay)$ into series and then change the order of summation and integration

$$C_{2l} = (4\pi)^{\lambda} \Gamma(\lambda)\Gamma(2\lambda+1)/\Gamma(2l+n-2) \sum_{N=0}^{\infty} \frac{a^N}{N!} \int_0^1 y^N (1-y^2)^{\lambda-\frac{1}{2}} C_{2l}^{\lambda}(y)\, dy. \tag{14}$$

Let us calculate first sum on (14). Denote that the first ℓ integrals in this sum equal zero. This can be proved by the method suggested in [4] (p.247). Thus we have

$$c_{2\ell} = (4\pi)^{\lambda}\Gamma(\lambda)\Gamma(2\ell+1)/\Gamma(2\ell+n-2)\sum_{N=0}^{\infty} a^{2N+2\ell}/(2N+2\ell)! \times$$

$$\times \int_0^1 y^{2N+2\ell}(1-y^2)^{\lambda-\frac{1}{2}} C_{2\ell}^{\lambda}(y)\,dy. \tag{15}$$

Now transform (15) by the formula 7.311.2 of [2] . We obtain

$$c_{2\ell} = \pi^{\lambda+1}\sum_{N=0}^{\infty}\left(\frac{a}{2}\right)^{2N+2\ell}\left(\Gamma(2\ell+N+\lambda+1)\Gamma(N+1)\right)^{-1}. \tag{16}$$

Putting $c_{2\ell}^{(1)}$ and $c_{2\ell}^{(2)}$ in (13), we get (11).

LEMMA 7. Let the even function $u(\tau)$ and the odd function $v(\tau)$ belong to $L_2^{\tau}(S^{n-1})$, $\tau \geqslant \gamma + n/2$, $\gamma > 0$. Suppose they have the series developments on the half-spheres S_+^{n-1}, S_-^{n-1}:

$$u(\tau) = \sum_{\ell,j} u_{2\ell,j}\, \mathcal{J}_{2\ell,j}(\tau) \quad \text{and} \quad v(\tau) = \sum_{\ell,j} v_{2\ell+1,j}\, \mathcal{J}_{2\ell+1,j}(\tau)$$

respectively. Calculating for $x \neq 0$ the inverse Fourier transform - in the Abelian summation sense - on the half-space containing whether S_+^{n-1} or S_-^{n-1} we get for the function $|t|^{\gamma}\theta(\tau)$ the equation:

$$(2\pi)^{-n} a^{\gamma+n} \lim_{\varepsilon\to 0}\int_0^1\int_{S_{\pm}^{n-1}} \exp(-ia|t||x|(\tau,\xi) - \varepsilon b|t|)\theta(\tau)|t|^{\gamma+n-1} \times$$

$$\times\, d\tau\, d|t| = \lim_{\varepsilon\to 0}\left(J_\varepsilon(|x|,\xi,a,b) \pm K_\varepsilon(|x|,\xi,a,b)\right), \quad \xi\in S_{\pm}^{n-1}, \tag{17}$$

where formulas for J_ε and K_ε was get in proof of lemma. Note that

$$I_\xi = \lim_{\varepsilon \to 0} J_\varepsilon = 2^{\gamma-1} \pi^{-n/2} |x|^{-(\gamma+n)} \sum_{\ell,j} (-1)^\ell \Gamma(\ell + (\gamma+n)/2) \times$$

$$\times (\Gamma(\ell - \gamma/2))^{-1} u_{2\ell,j} \mathcal{Y}_{2\ell,j}(\xi) \in L_2^{\tau-\gamma-\frac{n}{2}}(S_\pm^{n-1}) \tag{17a}$$

if $\theta(\tau) = u(\tau)$ and

$$I_\xi = 2^{\gamma-1} \pi^{-n/2} |x|^{-(\gamma+n)} \sum_{\ell,j} (-i)^{2\ell+1} \Gamma(\ell + (\gamma+n+1)/2) \times$$

$$\times (\Gamma(\ell - (\gamma-1)/2) v_{2\ell+1,j} \mathcal{Y}_{2\ell+1,j}(\xi) \in L_2^{\tau-\gamma-\frac{n}{2}}(S_\pm^{n-1}) \tag{17b}$$

if $\theta(\tau) = v(\tau)$. Furhermore, $a, b \in \mathbb{C}$,

$$\operatorname{Re} b > 0, \quad \operatorname{Im} a \lessgtr 0 \quad \text{if} \quad \tau \in S_\pm^{n-1}. \tag{18}$$

PROOF. The conditions (18) are necessary to the convergence of the integral (17). Let $\theta(\tau) = u(\tau)$ and $\tau \in S_\pm^{n-1}$ (in other cases the formula can be derived similarly). Interchanging the summation and integration we have

$$I_\xi = a^{n+\gamma} 2^{-n} \pi^{-n/2} \lim_{\varepsilon \to 0} \{ \sum_{\ell,j} u_{2\ell,j} \mathcal{Y}_{2\ell,j}(\xi) \sum_{N=0}^{\infty} \int_0^{\infty} e^{-\varepsilon b|t|} |t|^{\gamma+n+2N+2\ell-1} \times$$

$$\times d|t| (-i|x|a/2)^{2N+2\ell} (\Gamma(2\ell + N + \lambda + 1) \Gamma(N+1))^{-1}.$$

On the basis of equations 8.312.2 and 8.335.1 in [2] we can write in the following form

$$I_\xi = 2^{\gamma-1} \pi^{-(n+1)/2} \lim_{\varepsilon \to 0} \{ (\tfrac{a}{\varepsilon b})^{\gamma+n} \sum_{\ell,j} u_{2\ell,j} \mathcal{Y}_{2\ell,j}(\xi) \sum_{N=0}^{\infty} \Gamma(N + \ell + (\gamma+n)/2) \times$$

$$\times \Gamma(N+\ell+(\gamma+n+1)/2)(\Gamma(N+1)\Gamma(N+2\ell+\lambda+1))^{-1}(-ia|x|/\varepsilon b)^{2N+2\ell}\}.$$

Here the sum by N differs from the hypergeometric function only in a constant, so we can transform the last equation in this way:

$$I_{\xi} = 2^{\gamma-1}\pi^{-(n+1)/2}\lim_{\varepsilon\to 0}\{(a/\varepsilon b)^{\gamma+n}\sum_{\ell,j} u_{2\ell,j}\,\mathcal{Y}_{2\ell,j}(\xi)(-ia|x|/\varepsilon b)^{2\ell}\times$$

$$\times\,\Gamma(\ell+(\gamma+n)/2)\Gamma(\ell+(\gamma+n+1)/2)(\Gamma(2\ell+n/2))^{-1}\,{}_2F_1(\ell+(\gamma+n+1)/2,\ \ell+$$

$$+(\gamma+n)/2;\ \ 2\ell+n/2;\ -(a|x|/\varepsilon b)^2)\}.$$

Respecting , that ([4] , p.105):

$${}_2F_1(\alpha,\ \beta;\gamma;z) = (1-z)^{-\beta}\,{}_2F_1(\gamma-\alpha,\ \beta;\ \gamma;\ z/(z-1)),$$

when $\arg(1-z)<\pi$, we derive a further expression of I :

$$I_{\xi} = 2^{\gamma-1}a^{1+n}\pi^{-(n+1)/2}\lim_{\varepsilon\to 0}\{\sum_{\ell,j} u_{2\ell,j}\,\mathcal{Y}_{2\ell,j}(\xi)(-i|x|a)((\varepsilon b)^2+(a\,x)^2$$

$$+(a|x|)^2)^{-(\ell+\gamma+n/2)}\Gamma(\ell+(\gamma+n)/2)\Gamma(\ell+(\gamma+n+1)/2)(\Gamma(2\ell+n/2))^{-1}\times$$

$$\times\,{}_2F_1(\ell-(\gamma+1)/2,\ \ell+(\gamma+n)/2;\ 2\ell+n/2;\ (a|x|)^2/((a|x|)^2+(\varepsilon b)^2))\}.$$

Let us find now I_{ξ}. From the asymptotical behaviour of the hypergeometric functions and from the fact that $u_{2\ell,j}=O(\ell^{-r})$ (see Lemma 3) follows the convergence of the series in $L^2(S^{n-1})$ for $r\geqslant\gamma+n/2$ and for every $\varepsilon\geqslant 0$. That's why we can get donn to the limit according to ε inside the sum. Further, taking into consideration the property (23) on p.112 of [4] we have (17a). From the asymptotical behaviour of the gamma function and from lemma 3 it follows that function of sphere, which is determined by (17a), belongs to $L_2^{r-\gamma-\frac{n}{2}}(S_+^{n-1})$.

Finally we note, that we don't step over the bounds of the functional spaces on sphere of ordinary functions because of the requirement: $r \geq \gamma + n/2$ (cf.ii)). The calculation of $\lim_{\varepsilon \to 0} K_\varepsilon (|x|, \xi, a, b)$ where

$$K_\varepsilon = \sum_{l,j} u_{2l,j} \mathcal{J}_{2l,j}(\xi)\, 2^{\Gamma-1} \pi^{-(n+1)/2} \sum_{N=0}^{\infty} \left(-\frac{ixa}{\varepsilon b}\right)^{2N+1} \left(\frac{a}{\varepsilon b}\right)^{\Gamma+n} \times$$

$$\times \Gamma(N+(\gamma+n+1)/2)\Gamma(N+(\gamma+n+2)/2)\left(\Gamma(N-l+\tfrac{3}{2})\Gamma(N+l+\lambda+\tfrac{3}{2})\right)^{-1}$$

is analogues.

5. The proof of theorem

We choose (7) as the starting point of our discussion. First we observe the function $g(\tau)$ in the form (8). We divide the integrals in (7) into two parts according to half-spaces containing S_+^{n-1}, S_-^{n-1} respectively. Applying now the lemma 5 in each summands we can rotate the contour of the integration with the angle $\pm\varphi$ respectively as $S_\pm^{n-1}$ where φ takes its value from the interval

$$0 < \varphi < \frac{\pi}{2} \min\left(1, \min\{(1-\beta(\tau)K(\alpha))/\alpha : \tau \in S_+^{n-1}\},\right.$$

$$\left.\min\{(1+\beta(\tau)K(\alpha))/\alpha : \tau \in S_-^{n-1}\}\right).$$

If $\tau \in S_\pm^{n-1}$, then after changing the variable $z = |t|\exp(\pm i\varphi)$ respectively, we get the following equation

$$p(x) = (2\pi)^{-n} \lim_{\varepsilon \to 0} \Big\{ \int_0^\infty \int_{S^{n-1}} \exp(-ie^{-i\varphi}|t||x|(\tau,\xi) - \varepsilon|t|e^{-i\varphi} +$$

$$+ |t|^\alpha e^{-i\varphi\alpha} g(\tau))\, |t|^{n-1} \exp(-i\varphi n)\, d\tau\, d|t| + \int_0^\infty \int_{S_-^{n-1}} \exp(-ie^{i\varphi} \times$$

$$\times |t||x|(\tau,\xi) - \varepsilon|t|e^{i\varphi} + |t|^\alpha e^{i\varphi\alpha} g(\tau))\, |t|^{n-1} \exp(i\varphi n)\, d\tau\, d|t| \Big\}.$$

Let us rewrite now the exponent, which is the ch.f. of a s.s.d. into the form (10). Now we divide the expression into three summands I_1, $I_2(x)$, $R_m(x)$ and calculate them in a different way.

The summand $I_2(x)$ consists of the $m-1$ middle members in the sum (10):

$$I_2(x) = (2\pi)^{-n} \sum_{k=1}^{m-1} \lim_{\varepsilon \to 0} \Big(\int_0^\infty \int_{S_+^{n-1}} \{\ldots\} t^{\alpha k+n-1} \overset{k}{g}(\tau)/(k!\exp(i\varphi \times$$
$$\times (\alpha k+n))) d\tau\, d|t| + \int_0^\infty \int_{S_-^{n-1}} \{\ldots\} t^{\alpha k+n-1} \overset{k}{g}(\tau)/(k!\exp(-i\varphi(\alpha k+n))) \times \qquad (19)$$
$$\times d\tau\, d|t| \Big).$$

Observing $g(\tau)$ in the form (1), one can consider the question upon the smoothness of the function $\overset{k}{g}(\tau)$. The lemmas 2 and 4 involve that $\overset{k}{g}(\tau) \in L_2^{r+\alpha+n/2}(S^{n-1})$. It is easy to see as well that $\overset{k}{g}(\tau)$ can be written in the form (see (8))

$$\overset{k}{g}(\tau) = u_k(\tau) + i v_k(\tau) \qquad \text{for } \alpha \neq 1 \quad \text{and}$$
$$\overset{k}{g}(\tau) = u_k(\tau) \qquad \text{for } \alpha = 1$$

where $u_k(\tau)$ and $v_k(\tau)$ are even and odd functions respectively. The further transformation of (19) is based on the formulae (17). Because of the limits on smoothness of the functions $\overset{k}{g}(\tau)$ stated by the lemma 7, it is required to satisfy the condition

$$r \geqslant \alpha(k-1), \qquad k = 1, \ldots, m-1. \qquad (20)$$

Applying (17) we unite the integration domains in S^{n-1}:

$$I_2(x) = \sum_{k=1}^{m-1} 2^{\alpha k} (\Gamma(k+1))^{-1} / (\pi^{n/2} |x|^{\alpha k+n}) \sum_{l,j} (-i)^l \Gamma((l+\alpha k+n)/2) \times$$

$$\times (\Gamma((l-\alpha k)/2))^{-1} \overset{k}{g}_{lj} \mathcal{J}_{lj}(\xi) \qquad \text{for } \alpha \neq 1, \qquad (21)$$

$$I_2(x) = \sum_{k=1}^{m-1} 2^k (\Gamma(k+1))^{-1} \pi^{-n/2} |x|^{-(\alpha k+n)} \sum_{l=0}^{\infty} \sum_{j=1}^{d(2l)} (-1)^l \times$$

$$\times \Gamma(l+(k+n)/2)(\Gamma(l-k/2))^{-1} g^k_{2l,j} \mathcal{Y}_{2l,j}(\xi) \qquad \text{for} \quad \alpha = 1. \tag{22}$$

In connection with (22) we note, that the summation by l in the case of even k begins at $k/2+1$, because for $l = 0, 1, \ldots, k$ in the denominator stands the gamma function of negative integer argument.

REMARK 4. Now it is more convenient to use the logarithm of the ch.f. in form (1). Then the first summand in $I_2(x)$ can be transformed. Taking g_{l_j} from (5) and (6) into (21) and (22) we find that it is equal to $\mu(\xi)/|x|^{\alpha+n}$.

$R_m(x)$ is sum of integrals. consisting of the remainder from (10) in the integral form. Now we estimate the modulus of $R_m(x)$:

$$|R_m(x)| \leqslant (2\pi\Gamma(m+1))^{-1} \lim_{\varepsilon\to 0} \Big\{ \int_0^\infty \int_{S_+^{n-1}} \exp(-\sin\varphi(\tau,\xi)|t||x| - \varepsilon \times$$

$$\times \cos\varphi|t|)|t|^{\alpha m+n-1}(\lambda(\tau))^{m-1} d\tau\, d|t| + \int_0^\infty \int_{S_-^{n-1}} \exp(\sin\varphi \times \tag{23}$$

$$\times (\tau,\xi)|t||x| - \varepsilon\cos\varphi|t|)|t|^{\alpha m+n-1}(\lambda(\tau))^{m-1} d\tau\, d|t| \Big\}.$$

Since the function $\lambda(\tau)$ is even, the integrals on S_+^{n-1} and S_-^{n-1} coincide. Thus it is sufficient to calculate one of them by using lemma 7. One can derive the following inequality from the restriction on the smoothness in the lemma 7 and from the fact that $\lambda(\tau) \in$ $\in L_2^{r+\alpha+n/2}(S^{n-1})$:

$$r + \alpha + n/2 \geqslant \alpha m + n/2.$$

This gives the limit (4) for the number of members in the representation, namely

$$m \leq r/\alpha + 1.$$

We should remark that choosing in this way, the requirement (20) will be satisfied automatically.

Applying (17) we can transform (23) to the following expression

$$|R_m(x)| \leq 2^{\alpha m} \pi^{-n/2} (\Gamma(m+1))^{-1} (|x| \sin\varphi)^{-(\alpha m+n)} \times$$

$$\times \sum_{\ell,j} (-1)^{\ell} \Gamma(\ell + (\alpha m+n)/2)(\Gamma(\ell - \alpha m/2))^{-1} \lambda_{2\ell,j}^{(m-1)} Y_{2\ell,j}(\xi)$$

The series we have got in the right side forms a function belonging to $L_2(S^{n-1})$ and depending on α and $\mu(\xi)$, therefore it is not difficult to derive the inequality:

$$\{ \int_{S^{n-1}} (R_m(|x|\xi))^2 d\xi \}^{1/2} \leq C_1(m) |x|^{\alpha m+n}.$$

Now the first summand I_1 is left to count:

$$I_1 = (2\pi)^{-n} \lim_{\varepsilon \to 0} \{ \int_0^{\infty} \exp(-\varepsilon|t|e^{-i\varphi})|t|^{n-1} e^{-i\varphi n} \times$$

$$\times \int_{S_+^{n-1}} \exp(-i(\tau,\xi)|t||x| e^{-i\varphi}) d\tau\, d|t| + \int_0^{\infty} \exp(-\varepsilon|t|e^{i\varphi})|t|^{n-1} e^{i\varphi n} \times$$

$$\times \int_{S_-^{n-1}} \exp(-i(\tau,\xi)|t||x| e^{i\varphi}) d\tau\, d|t| \}.$$

The further calculations can analogously be carried out as we did it in the lemmas 6 and 7. So we leave the detailed calculation and present only the final result:

$$I_1 = \pi^{-(n+1)/2} \lim_{\varepsilon \to 0} {}_2F_1\left(\frac{n+1}{2}, \frac{n}{2}; \frac{n}{2}; -(|x|/\varepsilon)^2 \right) \varepsilon^{-n}.$$

The known equality

$$(1+z)^{a} = {}_2F_1(-a, b; b; -z)$$

gives us a further expression of I_1 $(x \neq 0)$:

$$I_1 = \pi^{-(n+1)/2} \lim_{\varepsilon \to 0} \varepsilon \left(|x|^2 + \varepsilon^2\right)^{-(n+1)/2} = 0.$$

To complete the proof we note, that it is necessary to require for the existence of exact members in decomposition (i.e. $m \geqslant 2$) that

$$r \geqslant d.$$

REMARK 5. The method, suggested above, enables us to get a similar decomposition for the derivatives of the density $(D^N p)(x)$ (cf. (2)):

$$(D^N p)(x) = \sum_{k=1}^{m-1} 2^{dk+|N|} \pi^{-n/2} (\Gamma(k+1))^{-1} \tilde{\mu}_k(\xi) |x|^{-(dk+n+|N|)} + \tilde{R}_m(x),$$

where

$$\tilde{\mu}_k(\xi) = \sum_{l,j} (-1)^{l+|N|} \Gamma((l+dk+n+|N|)/2)(\Gamma((l-dk-|N|)/2))^{-1} \tilde{g}^k_{lj} Y_{lj}(\xi),$$

$$\tilde{g}^k_{lj} = \int_{S^{n-1}} \tau^N g^k(\tau) Y_{lj}(\tau)\, d\tau,$$

and

$$\|\tilde{R}_m(x)\|_1 \leqslant \tilde{c}(m) |x|^{-(dm+n+|N|)},$$

$$2 \leqslant m \leqslant 1 + [(r-|N|)/d], \qquad r \geqslant d + |N|.$$

Here $|N| = \sum_{M=1}^{n} i_M$ is the lenght of the multi-index.

THE PROOF OF THE COROLLARY 1. The lemma 2 gives us the possibility to carry the results of the theorem on to the case of Hölder spaces on the spheres. The only thing we need is to control accurately the order of smoothness of the function $\mu_k(\xi)$. Respecting the lemmas 3 and 4, from (21) and (22) we have $\mu_k(\xi) \in L_2^{r-d(k-1)}(S^{n-1})$. Exactly the same way like we proved the theorem, one can deduce the upper bound for m and the estimation of the remainder $R_m(x)$.

THE COROLLARY 2 can simply be proved integrating on the observed domain the formula (2).

In conclusion the author is grateful to V.M.Zolotarev and Yu.S. Hohlov for their attention to his investigation.

Steklov Mathematical Institute
Academy of Sciences of the USSR
Vavilov st. 42, 117333
Moscow, USSR

REFERENCES

1. Agranovich M.S. Elliptical simgular integro-differential Operators. Usp.Mat.Nauk, 20, 1965, N 5(125), 3-120 (in Russian).
2. Gradshteyn I.S., Ryzhik I.M. Tables of Integrals, Series and Products. M., Nauka, 1971 (in Russian).
3. Zolotarev V.M. One-dimensional stable distributions. Isdat Nauka, M., 1983 (in Russian).
4. Kratzer A, Franz W. Transceddental Functions. M., 1963 (in Russian).
5. Mikhlin S.G. Multidimensional singular integrals ans integral equations. M., 1962, (in Russian).
6. Nikolski S.M. Approximation of functions of several variables and embedding theorems. M., Nauka, 1977 (in Russian).
7. Nikolski S.M. On theorems of embedding; continuation and approximation of differentiable functions of several variables. Usp.Mat. Nauk, 16, 1961, N 5(101), 63-114 (in Russian).
8. Samko S.G. Generelized Riesz potentials and hypersingular integrals

with homogeneous characteristics, their symbol and inversion. Tr. Mat. Inst. Steklova, 156, 1980, 157-222 (in Russian).

9. Samko S.G. Hypersingular integrals and their applications. Rostov, 1984 (in Russian).

10. Slobodetzki L.N. Generalized Sobolev spaces and their applications to boundary value problems for partial differential equations. Leningrad, Gos. Ped. Inst., Uch. Zap. 197, 1958, 54-112 (in Russian).

11. Strichartz R.S. Multipliers on fractional Sobolev spaces. J.Math. Mech., 19, 1967, N 9, 1031-1060.

12. Arkhipov S.V. The density expansions of strictly stable distributions, to appear.

LIMITING BEHAVIOUR OF THE SUM OF I.I.D. RANDOM VARIABLES AND ITS TERMS OF GREATEST MODULI IN THE CASE OF LOGARITHMIC TYPE TALL FUNCTION

I.Factorovich

Let $X_1, X_2, \ldots$ be i.i.d. random variables and $F(x)$ be their common distribution function having slowly varying tall function $f(x) := 1 - F(x) + F(-x)$:

$$f(cx)/f(x) \underset{x \to \infty}{\longrightarrow} 1, \qquad c > 0,$$

and let $S_n := \sum_{i=1}^{n} X_i$; $X_n^{(k)}$ be the k-th largest in modulus of $\{X_1, X_2, \ldots, X_n\}$, $S_n^{(k)} := S_n - \sum_{i=1}^{k} X_n^{(i)}$. Darling [1] showed that in the case of positive X_i and $m = 1$:

$$E|S_n/X_n^{(1)} - 1|^m \underset{n \to \infty}{\longrightarrow} 0. \tag{1}$$

This was extended to the general case by Arov and Bobrov [2]. In the present paper the rates of convergences having form (1) and some of its generalizations are studied. It is unlikely to evaluate such a rate without any analytical information about asymptotic behaviour of f. So in this paper we assume that f belongs to the logarithmic type of tale functions.

DEFINITION. We say that the tale function $f(x) = 1 - F(x) + F(-x)$ belongs to the logarithmic type iff it equals $\varphi(\log x)$ for any $x > 0$ and some regularly varying function φ of a negative index $(-\alpha)$:

$$\varphi(cx)/\varphi(x) \underset{x \to \infty}{\longrightarrow} c^{-\alpha}, \qquad c > 0.$$

But this property of f is not sufficient to obtain a relatively simple expression for asymptotical behaviour of $E|S_n^{(1)}/X_n^{1}|^m$ and so we suppose that there exists the derivative $\varphi'(x):=\frac{d}{dx}\varphi(x)$ and that $(-\varphi')$ is a regular varying function. This supposition however is not necessary for the results formulated below being true. It is possible to show, e.g., that the behaviour of $F(x)$ is any fixed bounded interval does not influence asymptotic behaviour of $E|S_n^{(1)}/X_n^{(1)}|^m$ (we adopt $S_n^{(1)}/X_n^{(1)}=0$ if $X_n^{(1)}(=S_n^{(1)})=0$). So we follow Darling [1] and some more recent works of other authors who prefer rather clearness of explanation then the highest possible generality.

In addition to study of the limiting behaviour of $E|S_n^{(1)}/X_n^{(1)}|$ it is interesting to obtain asymptotic formulas for $E|S_n^{(\ell)}/X_n^{(k)}|^m$, $E|X_n^{(\ell)}/X_n^{(k)}|^m$ etc. It is accomplished below.

The well-known results of the theory of regular varying functions [3] are used in the present paper. So let us introduce the following notation for short. $RV_\alpha^\infty(RV_\alpha^0)$ denotes the class of regular varying at ∞ (at 0) functions of index α.

The following theorem first of all expresses more precisely the established in [2] dominant role of $X_n^{(k)}$ in the sum $\sum_{i=k}^{n} X_n^{(i)}$ when n tends to ∞.

THEOREM. Let the tail function $f(x)=1-F(x)+F(-x)$ belongs to logarithmic type:

$$f(x) = \varphi(\log x), \qquad x>0,$$

where $\varphi\in RV_{-\alpha}^\infty$ for some $\alpha>0$; $\varphi(-\infty)=1$;
there exists $\varphi'(y):=\frac{d}{dy}\varphi(y)$ for $y\in(-\infty,\infty)$;
$(-\varphi')\in RV_{-\alpha-1}^\infty$.

Then for natural m, $\ell\geqslant k$ and $n\to\infty$:

$$E|S_n^{(\ell)}/X_n^{(k)}|^m \sim$$

$$\sim\frac{(\alpha/m)^{\ell-k+1}}{(k-1)!}\Gamma\left(\ell+1+\frac{\ell-k+1}{\alpha}\right)\cdot n^{-\frac{\ell-k+1}{\alpha}} \Big/ \chi^{\ell-k+1}(n^{-1}), \tag{2}$$

$$E|X_n^{(\ell+1)}/X_n^{(k)}|^m \sim E|S_n^{(\ell)}/X_n^{(k)}|^m \tag{3}$$

where $\mathcal{L}(x) := x^{1/\alpha}\varphi^{-1}(x)$, $\mathcal{L}$ is a slowly varying function, $\varphi^{-1}(x) := \sup\{y: \varphi(y) \leqslant x\}$.

NOTE 1. The conditions of φ' existence and $(-\varphi') \in RV_{-\alpha-1}^{\infty}$ yield $\varphi \in RV_{\alpha}^{\infty}$. This is a corollary from the well-known integral criterion of regular variation [3, 4] .

NOTE 2. The assumption $\varphi(-\infty) = 1$ may be neglected if we adopt $X_n^{(\ell+1)}/X_n^{(k)} = S_n^{(\ell)}/X_n^{(k)} = 0$ in the case of $X_n^{(k)} = 0,\ \ell \geqslant k$.

PROOF. Let us consider at first the case of $F(0) = 0$. Without loss of generality one may suppose

$$X_i = f^{-1}(Y_i) = \exp \varphi^{-1}(Y_i),$$

where Y_i are independent uniformly distributed on (0,1) random variables, $\varphi^{-1}(x) = \sup\{y: \varphi(y) \leqslant x\}$. For natural $\ell \geqslant k$ the following equality holds:

$$E_n^{k,\ell} := E|S_n^{(\ell)}/X_n^{(k)}| = \frac{n!}{(k-1)!(\ell-k-1)!(n-\ell)!}\, E\{S_n^{(\ell)}/X_n^{(k)} \cdot \mathbb{1}_A\},$$

where $\mathbb{1}_A$ is the indicator function of the event

$$A := \{Y_1, Y_2, \ldots, Y_{k-1} \leqslant Y_k \leqslant Y_{k+1}, Y_{k+2}, \ldots, Y_{\ell-1} \leqslant Y_\ell \leqslant Y_{\ell+1}, \ldots, Y_n\}.$$

Therefore

$$E_n^{k,\ell} = \frac{n!}{(k-1)!(\ell-k-1)!(n-\ell)!} \times$$

$$\times \int\limits_{\substack{0 \leqslant y_1, \ldots, y_{k-1} \leqslant y_k \leqslant y_{k+1}, \ldots \\ y_{\ell-1} \leqslant y_\ell \leqslant y_{\ell+1}, \ldots, y_n \leqslant 1}} \prod_{i=1}^{n} dF(y_i)\, \frac{\sum_{i=\ell+1}^{n} f^{-1}(y_i)}{f^{-1}(y_k)} =$$

$$\frac{n!(n-\ell)}{(k-1)!(\ell-k-1)!(n-\ell)!}\int\limits_{0\le y_k\le y_\ell\le y_n} dy_k\cdot dy_\ell\cdot dy_n\cdot y_k^{k-1}(y_\ell-y_k)^{\ell-k-1}(1-y_\ell)^{n-\ell-1}\times$$

$$\times\frac{f^{-1}(y_n)}{f^{-1}(y_k)}.$$

Let us denote $\lambda := y_\ell$, $\varkappa := y_k$, $\nu := y_n$,

$$C^n_{k,\ell} := \frac{n!}{(k-1)!(\ell-k-1)!(n-\ell-1)!}.$$

Then

$$E^{k,\ell}_n = C^n_{k,\ell}\int_0^1 d\lambda(1-\lambda)^{n-\ell-1}\int_0^\lambda d\varkappa(\lambda-\varkappa)^{\ell-k-1}\varkappa^{k-1}\frac{1}{f^{-1}(\varkappa)}\int_\lambda^1 d\nu f^{-1}(\nu) =$$

$$= C^n_{k,\ell}\int_0^1 d\lambda(1-\lambda)^{n-\ell-1}\int_0^\lambda d\varkappa(\lambda-\varkappa)^{\ell-k-1}\cdot\varkappa^{k-1}\cdot\frac{f^{-1}(\lambda)}{f^{-1}(\varkappa)}\cdot\frac{1}{f^{-1}(\lambda)}\int_0^{f^{-1}(\lambda)}\alpha\, dF(\alpha).$$

Let us consider separately $\xi(x) = x^{-1}\int_0^x \alpha\, dF(\alpha) = x^{-1}\int_0^x \alpha\, p(\alpha)\, d\alpha$,

where p is the density of the distribution F. The function p belongs to RV^∞_{-1} because of

$$p(x) = -\varphi'(\log x)\cdot x^{-1}, \quad x>0,$$
$$(-\varphi')\in RV^\infty_{-1-\alpha}, \quad \log\in RV^\infty_0.$$

$E^{k,\ell}_n - I_n$ is divided into two summands $J_1(n,\theta)$ and $J_2(n,\theta)$ having the following forms:

$$J_1(n,\theta) := C^n_{k,\ell}\int_\theta^1 d\lambda\,[(1-\lambda)^{n-\ell-1}\xi(f^{-1}(\lambda))\,\eta(\lambda)],$$

$$J_2(n,\theta) := C^n_{k,\ell}\int_0^\theta d\lambda\,[(1-\lambda)^{n-\ell-1}\xi(f^{-1}(\lambda))\,\eta(\lambda) -$$

$$-e^{-(n-l-1)\lambda}\lambda^{l+(l-k+1)\alpha^{-1}}/\mathcal{L}^{l-k+1}(\lambda)\,\alpha^{l-k+1}(l-k-1)!].$$

Note that the nonincreasing of f^{-1} yields

$$\xi(f^{-1}) = \frac{1}{f^{-1}(\lambda)}\int_0^{f^{-1}(\lambda)} x\,dF(x) = \int_\lambda^1 \frac{f^{-1}(z)}{f^{-1}(\lambda)}\,dz \leqslant 1-\lambda,$$

$$\eta(\lambda) \leqslant \int_0^\lambda d\varkappa\,(\lambda-\varkappa)^{l-k-1}\varkappa^{k-1} = \lambda^{l-1}\,\frac{(k-1)!\,(l-k-1)!}{(l-1)!}.$$

Hence

$$J_1(n,\theta) \leqslant \frac{n!}{(n-l-1)!\,(l-1)!}\int_0^1 d\lambda\,(1-\lambda)^{n-l}\lambda^{l-1} <$$

$$< \frac{n!}{(n-l-1)!\,(l-1)!}\,\theta^{n-l}\int_\theta^1 d\lambda\cdot\lambda^{l-1} =$$

$$= \frac{n!}{(n-l-1)!\,l!}\,\theta^{n-l}(1-\theta)^l \underset{n\to\infty}{\sim} \frac{1}{l!}\left(\frac{1-\theta}{\theta}\right)^l\cdot\theta^n\cdot n^{l+1}.$$

Let us fix now an arbitrary $\varepsilon\in(0,1)$ and assume that $\theta>0$ is so small that

$$\left|\frac{\xi(f^{-1}(\lambda))\,\eta(\lambda)}{\alpha^{l-k+1}\lambda^{l+(l-k+1)\alpha^{-1}}/\mathcal{L}^{l-k+1}(\lambda)\,(l-k+1)!} - 1\right| < \varepsilon$$

for $0<\lambda<\theta$. In addition to this we need the following simply verifiable inequality

$$e^{-my} - (1-y)^m \leqslant m\cdot y^2/2\cdot e^{-(m-1)y}$$

where $0<y\leqslant 2$ and m is a natural number. Let us denote

$$\nu_n(\lambda) := \xi(f^{-1}(\lambda))\cdot\eta(\lambda),$$

$$\mu_n(\lambda) := (\ell-k+1)!\, \alpha^{\ell-k+1} \lambda^{\ell+(\ell-k+1)\alpha^{-1}} / \mathcal{L}^{\ell-k+1}(\lambda).$$

and begin evaluating $|J_2(n,\theta)|$:

$$|J_2(n,\theta)| = | C^n_{k,\ell} \int_0^\theta [(1-\lambda)^{n-\ell-1} - e^{-(n-\ell-1)\lambda}] d\lambda +$$

$$+ C^n_{k,\ell} \int_0^\theta \mu_n(\lambda)[(1-\lambda)^{n-\ell-1} - e^{-(n-\ell-1)\lambda}] d\lambda +$$

$$+ C^n_{k,\ell} \int_0^\theta e^{-(n-\ell-1)\lambda} [\nu_n(\lambda) - \mu_n(\lambda)] d\lambda | \leqslant$$

$$\leqslant (1+\varepsilon) C^n_{k,\ell} \int_0^\theta (n-\ell-1)\cdot\lambda^2/2 \cdot e^{-(n-\ell-2)\lambda} \mu_n(\lambda) +$$

$$+ \varepsilon C^n_{k,\ell} \int_0^\theta e^{-(n-\ell-1)\lambda} \mu_n(\lambda)\, d\lambda = (\varepsilon+1) C^n_{k,\ell} \cdot J_3(n) + \varepsilon I_n,$$

In accordence with the integral criterion of regular variation (theorem 2.1 in [3] and theorem 1 of § 9, Chapter in [4]) $p \in RV^{\infty}_{-1}$ is equivalent to $J(x) \sim x\, p(x)$, $x \to \infty$.

Hence for $y \to 0$:

$$\xi(f^{-1}(y)) \sim -f^{-1}(y)\cdot f'(f^{-1}(y)) = -\frac{f^{-1}(y)}{\frac{d}{dy} f^{-1}(y)} =$$

$$= -1/\frac{d}{dy}\log f^{-1}(y) = -1/\frac{d}{dy}\varphi^{-1}(y).$$

Furthermore the function φ^{-1} belongs to $RV^{0}_{-1/\alpha}$ [3] and by using the integral regular variation criterion one can obtain

$$-\frac{d}{dy}\varphi^{-1}(y) \underset{y\to 0}{\sim} \frac{\varphi^{-1}(y)}{\alpha y}.$$

Therefore

$$\xi(f^{-1}(y)) \underset{y\to 0}{\sim} \frac{\alpha y}{\varphi^{-1}(y)} = \alpha y^{1+1/\alpha} / \mathcal{X}(y)$$

where $\mathcal{X} \in RV_0^0$.

Now let us study the asymptotic behaviour of

$$\eta(\lambda) := \int_0^\lambda d\varkappa\,(\lambda-\varkappa)^{\ell-k+1}\,\varkappa^{k-1}\,\frac{f^{-1}(\lambda)}{f^{-1}(\varkappa)}$$

for $\lambda \to 0$. Taking into account $f^{-1}(\lambda)/f^{-1}(\varkappa) = \exp\{-(\varphi^{-1}(\varkappa) - \varphi^{-1}(\lambda))\}$ we may change the variable $c := \varphi^{-1}(\varkappa) - \varphi^{-1}(\lambda)$:

$$\eta(\lambda) = \int_0^\infty dc\{[\varphi'(c+\varphi^{-1}(\lambda))][\lambda - \varphi(c+\varphi^{-1}(\lambda))]^{\ell-k}\cdot\lambda^{k-1}\cdot\varphi^{k-1}(c+\varphi^{-1}(\lambda))\,e^{-c}\} =$$

$$= [-\varphi'(\varphi^{-1}(\lambda)]^{\ell-k}\,\lambda^{k-1}\int_0^\infty dc\left\{\frac{\varphi'(c+\varphi^{-1}(\lambda))}{\varphi'(\varphi^{-1}(\lambda))}\cdot\left[\frac{\varphi(\varphi^{-1}(\lambda)) - \varphi(c+\varphi^{-1}(\lambda))}{-\varphi'(\varphi^{-1}(\lambda))\,c}\right]^{\ell-k-1}\times\right.$$

$$\left.\times\left[\frac{\varphi(c+\varphi^{-1}(\lambda))}{\varphi(\varphi^{-1}(\lambda))}\right]^{k-1}\cdot c^{\ell-k-1}\cdot e^{-c}\right\}.$$

Let us denote the last integral by $I_{k,\ell}$ and take notice of the function written in braces converging to $c^{\ell-k-1}\cdot e^{-c}$ because of $\varphi \in RV_{-\alpha}^\infty$, $(-\varphi') \in RV_{-1-\alpha}^\infty$ and

$$\varphi(\varphi^{-1}(\lambda)) - \varphi(c+\varphi^{-1}(\lambda)) = -\int_{\varphi^{-1}(\lambda)}^{c+\varphi^{-1}(\lambda)} \varphi'(x)\,dx \underset{\lambda\to 0}{\sim} -\varphi'(\varphi^{-1}(\lambda))\cdot c$$

(it follows from $(-\varphi') \in RV_{-\alpha-1}^\infty$).

Furthermore the expression written in braces is positive for sufsiciently small λ and does not exceed the function

$$(\sup_{c\geq 0}[-\varphi'(c+\varphi^{-1}(\lambda))]/(-\varphi'(\varphi^{-1}(\lambda)))\cdot c^{\ell-k-1}\cdot e^{-c},$$

where the ratio tends to 1 for $\lambda > 0$ [3] . Consequently,

$$I_{k,\ell} \xrightarrow[\lambda \to 0]{} \int_0^{\infty} c^{\ell-k-1} \cdot e^{-c} dc = (\ell-k-1)!$$

and

$$\eta(\lambda) \underset{\lambda \to 0}{\sim} (\ell-k-1)! \, [-\varphi'(\varphi^{-1}(\lambda))]^{\ell-k} \cdot \lambda^{k-1}.$$

Now, taking into account $-\varphi'(\varphi^{-1}(\lambda)) = -1/\frac{d}{d\lambda}\varphi^{-1}(\lambda) = \xi(f^{-1}(\lambda))$,

one can obtain for $\lambda \to 0$:

$$\eta(\lambda) \sim (\ell-k-1)! \cdot \alpha^{\ell-k} \cdot \lambda^{\ell-1+(\ell-k)\alpha^{-1}} / \mathcal{L}^{\ell-k}(\lambda).$$

Studying the asymptotic behaviour of

$$E_n^{k,\ell} = C_{k,\ell}^n \int_0^1 d\lambda \cdot (1-\lambda)^{n-\ell-1} \cdot \xi(f^{-1}(\lambda)) \cdot \eta(\lambda)$$

one can approximate the integrand by the expression

$$(\ell-k-1)! \cdot \alpha^{\ell-k+1} \cdot e^{-(n-\ell-1)} \cdot \lambda^{\ell+(\ell-k+1)\alpha^{-1}} / \mathcal{L}^{\ell-k+1}(\lambda)$$

for $\lambda < \theta$ and by 0 for $\lambda \geq \theta$ where $0 < \theta < 1$:

$$I_n := C_{k,\ell}^n (\ell-k-1)! \cdot \alpha^{\ell-k+1} \int_0^{\theta} e^{-(n-\ell-1)\lambda} \cdot \lambda^{\ell+(\ell-k+1)\alpha^{-1}} / \mathcal{L}^{\ell-k+1}(\lambda) \, d\lambda =$$

$$= \frac{n!(n-\ell-1)^{-[\ell+1+(\ell-k+1)\alpha^{-1}]}}{(k-1)!(n-\ell-1)!} \cdot \alpha^{\ell-k+1} \int_0^{(n+\ell-1)\theta} e^{-z} z^{\ell+(\ell-k+1)\alpha^{-1}} / \mathcal{L}^{\ell-k+1}\left(\frac{z}{n-\ell-1}\right) dz.$$

Using another variable changing $w := 1/z$ and theorems 2.6 and 2.7 of [3] one can realize that the last integral is asymptotically equivalent to

$$\left[\mathcal{L}^{\ell-k+1}((n-\ell-1)^{-1})\right]^{-1}\int_0^{(n-\ell-1)\theta} e^{-x} x^{\ell+(\ell-k+1)\alpha^{-1}} dx \underset{n\to\infty}{\sim} \Gamma(\ell+1+(\ell-k+1)\alpha^{-1}/\mathcal{L}^{\ell-k+1}(n^{-1}).$$

Therefore

$$I_n \underset{n\to\infty}{\sim} \frac{\alpha^{\ell-k+1}}{(k-1)!}\Gamma(\ell+1+\alpha^{-1}(\ell-k+1)).n^{-(\ell-k+1)\alpha^{-1}})/\mathcal{L}^{\ell-k+1}(n^{-1}).$$

Let us prove now that for $n\to\infty$

$$|E_n^{k,\ell}-I_n|=o(I_n),$$

where the penultimate integral is denoted by $J_3(n)$. The asymptotic behaviour of I_n is already known and the limiting behaviour of $C^n_{k,\ell}\cdot J_3(n)$ is obtained in the same way and it shows that $C^n_{k,\ell}\cdot J_3(n) = o(I_n)$. Joining up the inequalities for $J_1(n,\theta)$ and $J_2(n,\theta)$ one can conclude that for $n\to\infty$:

$$|E_n^{k,\ell} - I_n| \leqslant o(I_n) + \varepsilon I_n.$$

Since ε is arbitrary fixed we can now consider (2) to be proved for $F(0)=0$ and $m=1$. Then assume that $F(0)\geqslant 0$. Note that (2) is now proved for random variables $Z_i:=|X_i|$, $i=1,2,\dots$, $Z_n^{(i)}:=|X_n^{(i)}|$,

$$\Sigma_n^{(\ell)} := \sum_{i=1}^{n} Z_i - \sum_{i=1}^{\ell} Z_n^{(i)}.$$

Hence

$$E|\Sigma_n^{(\ell)}/Z_n^{(k)}| = o(E|\Sigma_n^{(\ell-1)}/Z_n^{(k)}|)$$

for $\ell>k\geqslant 1$, $n\to\infty$. Therefore

$$E|X_n^{(\ell)}/X_n^{(k)}| = E|Z_n^{(\ell)}/Z_n^{(k)}| \sim E|\Sigma_n^{(\ell-1)}/Z_n^{(k)}| \geqslant E|S_n^{(\ell-1)}/X_n^{(k)}| \geqslant$$

$$\geq E|X_n^{(l)}/X^{(k)}| - E|(\Sigma_n^{(l-1)} - Z_n^{(l)})/X_n^{(k)}| \underset{n\to\infty}{\sim} E|X_n^{(l)}/X_n^{(k)}|,$$

which yields (3) and (2) for $m=1$. The theorem can be proved by the same method without essential complications for any natural m. Meanwhile in this proof the polynomial espansion of $\left(\sum_{i=l+1}^{n} f^{-1}(y_i)\right)^m$ leads finally to the relation

$$E|S_n^{(l)}/X_n^{(k)}| \underset{n\to\infty}{\sim}$$

$$\underset{n\to\infty}{\sim} \frac{m!}{(k-1)!\, m^{l-k}} \sum_{r=1}^{m} (r!)^{-1} \left[\sum_{\substack{m_1+m_2+\ldots+m_r=m \\ m_i\geq 1,\ i=1,2,\ldots,r}} \frac{1}{\prod_{i=1}^{r} m_i! \cdot \prod_{i=1}^{r} m_i} \right] \times$$

$$\times \alpha^{l-k+r}\, \Gamma(l+r+\alpha^{-1}\cdot(l-k+r)\cdot n^{-(l-k+r)\alpha^{-1}} / \mathcal{L}^{l-k+r}(n^{-1}),$$

where the right-hand part of (2) is the asymptotically dominating term of the sum. The other feature of the proof for $m\geq 2$ is application of induction by m for obtaining the asymptotical relation

$$E|\Sigma_n^{(l-1)}/Z_n^{(k)}|^m \underset{n\to\infty}{\sim} E|Z_n^{(l)}/Z_n^{(k)}|^m.$$

The induction is based on the following equality:

$$E|\Sigma_n^{(l-1)}/Z_n^{(k)}|^m = E(\Sigma_n^{(l)}/Z_n^{(k)}) +$$

$$+ E(Z_n^{(l)}/Z_n^{(k)})^m + \sum_{r=1}^{m-1} \frac{m!}{r!\,(m-r)!}\, E(\Sigma_n^{(l)}/Z_n^{(k)})^m.$$

ACKNOWLEDGEMENTS. The author is grateful to Professor V.M.Zolotarev for drawing attention to the problems and valuable suggestions and also to E.Omey for useful discussions.

The All-Union Scientific Research Institute
for Water Protection (VNIIVO)
-, Bakulin St., 310888, Kharkov, USSR

REFERENCES

1. Darling D.A. The role of the maximum term in the sum of independent random variables. TransAm.Math.Soc., 1952, 73, 95-107.
2. Arov D.Z., Bobrov A.A. The extrem terms of a sample and their role in the sum of independent variables. Theory Probab.Appl., 1960, 5, 377-396.
3. Seneta E. Regular varying functions. Lecture Notes in Math., 508, Springer, Berlin, 1976.
4. Feller W. An introduction to probability theory and its applications. John Wiley, New York, 1971.

ON THE ADAPTIVE ESTIMATION OF CHANGE POINTS

Ts.G.Hahubia

The paper deals with the change point estimation in a finite sequence of independent observations where it is a priori known that a change has occurred. The asymptotic distribution deviating from a normal one is obtained for a properly normalized maximum likelihood estimator of the change point in a conventional model, i.e. in the case when the distribution form before the change and after it is known and these distributions are contiguous. Further, parametric and semi-parametric models of this problem are considered. An adaptive estimation technique is proposed, i.e. the obtained estimators have same limit distribution as in a conventional model.

1. Conventional model.

Let a sequence of independent observations

$$x_1, \ldots, x_\tau, \; x_{\tau+1}, \ldots, x_n \qquad (1)$$

be given. The values $x_1, \ldots, x_\tau$ are known to be identically distributed with the density $f(x)$ and $x_{\tau+1}, \ldots, x_n$ have the density $g(x)$, $f(x) \neq g(x)$. Suppose $f(x)$ and $g(x) \neq 0$ for all $x \in \mathbb{R}^1$. One can naturally assume that for $n \to \infty$ we also have $\tau \to \infty$. Put $\rho = (\tau/n) \in (0,1)$ and consider a likelihood function

$$p_n(X, \rho) = \prod_{1 \le i \le n\rho} f(x_i) \prod_{n\rho < i \le n} g(x_i) \qquad (2)$$

where $X = (x_1, \ldots, x_n)$. The maximum likelihood estimator of the change point ρ is the point when $\sup\limits_{\rho \in [a, b]} p_n(X; \rho)$ is attained where

$[a, b] \subset (0,1)$ and $p_n(X;\rho)$ have the form of (2).

Let

$$g(x) = g_n(x) = f(x) + \delta_n b_n(x), \tag{3}$$

where $\delta_n > 0$, $\delta_n \to 0$ as $n \to \infty$ and $b_n(x) \to b(x) \neq 0$, $|b(x)| < C$ almost for every $x \in \mathbb{R}^1$. The following theorem is true.

THEOREM 1. Let $\hat{\rho}_n$ be a maximum likelihood estimator of the change point $\rho \in (0,1)$. If $f(x)$ and $b_n(x)$ are continuous functions almost everywhere in $\mathbb{R}^1$, $\int (b_n^2/f)(x)dx = 1$, $\int (b_n^2/g_n)(x)dx = 1$ and $n\varepsilon_n\delta_n^2 \to 1$ as $n \to \infty$ where $\varepsilon_n \to 0$ so that $n\varepsilon_n \to \infty$, then uniformly w. r. t. $\rho \in [a, b] \subset (0,1)$ the value $\varepsilon_n^{-1}(\hat{\rho}_n - \rho)$ converges in distribution to τ, which is the moment when the process

$$\xi(t) = \begin{cases} w_1(t) - t/2, & t \geq 0, \\ w_2(-t) + t/2, & t < 0 \end{cases} \tag{4}$$

attains its maximum, where $w_1(t)$ and $w_2(t)$, $t \geq 0$ are independent Wiener processes. The distribution function of the moment τ has the form $F_\tau(t) = P\{\tau \leq t\} =$

$$= \begin{cases} \Phi(\sqrt{t}/2) - (t/2)\,\Phi(-\sqrt{t}/2) + k_3(t/4), & t \geq 0, \\ \\ 1 - \Phi(\sqrt{|t|}/2) - (t/2)\,\Phi(-\sqrt{|t|}/2) - k_3(|t|/4), & t < 0 \end{cases} \tag{5}$$

where $\Phi(t)$ is a function of the standard normal distribution, $k_3(t)$ is the density of χ^2-distribution with three degrees of freedom.

The theorem is proved by Lemma 1. which is a generalization of Theorem 10.1 [1, p.146] for the case when the function of the likelihood ratio with probability 1 is a random process with trajectories from $\mathcal{D}(-\infty, \infty)$ -space, with Skorokhod's metric [2] of functions defined in $\mathbb{R}^1$, which are right-continuous without second-type discontinuities. In order to state Lemma 1, following the terminology given in [1], consider a family of models

$$\mathcal{E}_\varepsilon = \{\mathcal{X}^{(\varepsilon)}, \mathcal{U}^{(\varepsilon)}, P_\theta^{(\varepsilon)}, \quad \theta\in\Theta\} \qquad \Theta\subseteq \mathbb{R}^1 \tag{6}$$

generalized by the observations of X^ε where ε is a real parameter. We are interested in the estimation of the parameter θ when $\varepsilon\to 0$.

Suppose that the probability measures $P_\theta^{(\varepsilon)}$ are absolutely continuous with respect to some countably finite measure $\mu^{(\varepsilon)}$ on $\mathcal{U}^{(\varepsilon)}$ and a family of models (6) corresponds to the likelihood function $p_\varepsilon(X^\varepsilon;\theta) = dP_\theta^{(\varepsilon)}/d\mu^{(\varepsilon)}$. We denote by θ the true parameter values and consider the function of the likelihood ratio

$$Z_{\varepsilon,\theta}(t) = p_\varepsilon(X^\varepsilon;\ \theta+\varphi(\varepsilon)t)/p_\varepsilon(X^\varepsilon;\theta) \tag{7}$$

where $\varphi(\varepsilon)$ is some normalizing factor and $\varphi(\varepsilon)\to 0$ as $\varepsilon\to 0$. $Z_{\varepsilon,\theta}(t)$ is a random process defined for $t\in\{\varphi^{-1}(\varepsilon)(\Theta-\theta)\}$.

LEMMA 1. Let the parametric space Θ be an open one in $\mathbb{R}^1$; the likelihood ratio function $Z_{\varepsilon,\theta}(t)$ satisfies the following conditions:

1) for every $\theta\in\Theta$ the trajectories of $Z_{\varepsilon,\theta}(t)$ belong to the space $\mathcal{D}(-\infty,\infty)$ with probability 1;

2) uniformly w.r.t. $\theta\in K$ where K is some compactum from Θ as $\varepsilon\to 0$ for t from any finite interval the processes $Z_{\varepsilon,\theta}(t)$ weakly converge to the processes whose trajectories are continuous functions on $\mathbb{R}^1$ with probability 1, which converge to zero at infinities;

3) for every $\theta\in K$ the limit processes $Z_\theta(t)$ attain their maximum at the unique point $\tau(\theta)$ with probability 1.

Then uniformly w.r.t. $\theta\in K$ the distribution of the normalized maximum likelihood estimator $\varphi^{-1}(\varepsilon)(\hat\theta_\varepsilon-\theta)$ converges to the distribution of $\tau(\theta)$ as $\varepsilon\to 0$.

Proofs of Theorem 1 and Lemma 1 are given in [3] .

2. Parametric model

Let in sequence (1) the values $x_1, \ldots, x_r$ be distributed with the density $f(x, \theta_1)$ and the remaining $x_{r+1}, \ldots, x_n$ have the density $f(x, \theta_2)$, $\theta_1 \neq \theta_2$. The values θ_1 and θ_2 are unknown, but they belong to some open parametric set $\Theta \subset \mathbb{R}^1$ and

$$\theta_2 = \theta_1 + \delta_n \tag{8}$$

where $\delta_n > 0$, $\delta_n \rightarrow 0$ as $n \longrightarrow \infty$.

For the density $f(x, \theta)$ consider the following regularity conditions:

I. The functions $f(x, \theta)$, $(\partial \ln f/\partial \theta)(x, \theta)$ are continuous in x and $(\partial^2 \ln f/\partial \theta^2)(x, \theta)$ is bounded in x and θ almost everywhere.

II . For all $\theta, \theta' \in \Theta$ the Fisher information

$$\int (\partial \ln f/\partial \theta)^2 (x, \theta) f(x, \theta') \, dx < \infty ;$$

III.

$$\int \left(\left(\frac{\partial f(x, \theta)}{\partial \theta} \right)^2 / f(x, \theta') \right) dx = 1, \quad \theta', \theta \in \Theta.$$

Let θ_1 and θ_2 be unknown true values of the nuisance parameters and using observations (1) we shall construct consistent asymptotically normal estimators for them $\hat{\theta}_{1\rho} = \hat{\theta}_{1\rho}(x_1, \ldots, x_r)$ and $\hat{\theta}_{2\rho} = \hat{\theta}_{2\rho}(x_{r+1}, \ldots, x_n)$ respectively, which can be represented in the following way:

$$\sqrt{[n\rho]}\,(\hat{\theta}_{1\rho} - \theta_1) = [n\rho]^{-1/2} \sum_{1 \leq i < n\rho} l(x_i, \theta_1) + O_P(n^{-1/2}),$$

$$\sqrt{[n(1-\rho)]}\,(\hat{\theta}_{2\rho} - \theta_2) = [n(1-\rho)]^{-1/2} \sum_{n\rho < i \leq n} l(x_i, \theta_2) + O_P(n^{-1/2}), \tag{9}$$

where for every $\theta_j \in \Theta$ the function $l(x, \theta_j)$ satisfies the conditions

$$\int l(x, \theta_j) f(x, \theta_k)\, dx = 0,$$

$$\int l^2(x, \theta_j) f(x, \theta_k)\, dx < \infty, \qquad k, j = 1, 2. \tag{10}$$

In the expression for the likelihood function (2) we substitute the estimators of the nuisance parameters $\hat{\theta}_\rho = (\hat{\theta}_{1\rho}, \hat{\theta}_{2\rho})$ and have

$$p_n(X; \rho, \hat{\theta}_\rho) = \prod_{1 \le i \le n\rho} f(x_i, \hat{\theta}_{1\rho}) \prod_{n\rho < i \le n} f(x_i, \hat{\theta}_{2\rho}). \tag{11}$$

The estimator $\hat{\rho}_n$ of the change point ρ can be defined by the relation

$$p_n(X; \hat{\rho}_n, \hat{\theta}_{\hat{\rho}_n}) = \sup_{\rho \in [a, b]} p_n(X; \rho, \hat{\theta}_\rho), \quad [a, b] \subset (0, 1). \tag{12}$$

THEOREM 2. Let $\hat{\rho}_n$ be a estimator of the change point ρ defined by (12) where $\hat{\theta}_\rho = (\hat{\theta}_{1\rho}, \hat{\theta}_{2\rho})$ have representation (9) under conditions (10). If the density $f(x, \theta)$ satisfies regularity conditions I, II, III and in (8) $n\varepsilon_n\delta_n^2 \to 1$ as $n \to \infty$ where $\varepsilon_n \to 0$ so that $n\varepsilon_n \to \infty$ then uniformly w.r.t. $\rho \in [a, b] \subset (0, 1)$ and $\theta \in K \subset \Theta$ where K is compact, the limit distribution of $\varepsilon_n^{-1}(\hat{\rho}_n - \rho)$ will be (5).

Before we prove the theorems we shall prove two lemmas.

LEMMA 2. Let conditions of Theorem 2 hold and $x_1, \ldots, x_{[n\varepsilon_n t]}$ be a sequence of independent random variables having the same distribution density $f(x, \theta_2)$, $x \in \mathbb{R}^1$, $\theta_2 \in \Theta$. Then for t from any finite interval $[0, T]$ the random process

$$\xi_{n\rho}(t; \rho) = \sum_{1 \le i \le n\varepsilon_n t} \ln\left(f(x_i, \hat{\theta}_{1(\rho + \varepsilon_n t)}) / f(x_i, \hat{\theta}_{2\rho})\right) \tag{13}$$

uniformly w.r.t. $\rho \in [a, b] \subset (0, 1)$ and $\theta_1, \theta_2 \in K \subset \Theta$ weakly converges to the process $w(t) - t/2$ where $w(t)$ is a Wiener process.

PROOF. Under the conditions of the Lemma with probability as close to 1 as desired, beginning with some $n > n_0$ the following decomposition

$$\xi_n(t;\rho) = \sum_{1\le i\le n\varepsilon_n t} \ln(f(x_i,\theta_1)/f(x_i,\theta_2)) + \tag{14}$$
$$+ A_n(t;\rho) + B_n(t;\rho) + R_n(t;\rho)$$

is valid for process (13) where $A_n(t;\rho)$, $B_n(t;\rho)$ and $R_n(t;\rho)$ represent a difference of the two following corresponding processes

$$A_n^{(k)}(t;\rho) = \sum_{1\le i\le n\varepsilon_n t} \frac{\partial \ln f}{\partial\theta}(x_i,\theta_k)(\hat\theta_{k\rho'} - \theta_k),$$

$$B_n^{(k)}(t;\rho) = \frac{1}{2}\sum_{1\le i\le n\varepsilon_n t} \frac{\partial^2 \ln f}{\partial\theta^2}(x_i,\theta_k)(\hat\theta_{k\rho'} - \theta_k)^2,$$

$$R_n^{(k)}(t;\rho) = \frac{1}{6}\sum_{1\le i\le n\varepsilon_n t} \left(\frac{\partial^2 \ln f}{\partial\theta^2}(x_i,\theta_k') - \frac{\partial^2 \ln f}{\partial\theta^2}(x,\theta_k)\right)(\hat\theta_{k\rho'} - \theta_k)^2$$

for $k=1$ and $k=2$ where $\rho'=\rho+\varepsilon_n t$ when $k=1$ and $\rho'=\rho$ for $k=2$ and θ_k' belongs to a close neighbourhood of θ_k.

For $t\in[0,T]$ uniformly w.r.t. $\rho\in[a,b]$ and $\theta_1,\theta_2\in K$ each of the six processes weakly converges to zero. Indeed, for the processes $B_n^{(k)}(t;\rho)$ and $R_n^{(k)}(t;\rho)$, $k=1,2$ this is true by virtue of the boundedness almost everywhere of $\partial^2\ln f/\partial\theta^2$, the asymptotic normality of value (9) and since $\varepsilon_n\to 0$ as $n\to\infty$. As for the processes $A_n^{(k)}(t;\rho)$, $k=1,2$ by (9) they can be represented as

$$A_n^{(k)}(t;\rho) = ([n\varepsilon_n]/[n\rho'])^{1/2}[n\varepsilon_n]^{-1/2}\sum_{1\le i\le n\varepsilon_n t}\frac{\partial \ln f}{\partial\theta}(x_i,\theta_k)\times \tag{15}$$
$$\times [n\rho']^{-1/2}\sum_{1\le i\le n\rho'} l(x_i,\theta_k) + O_P(1).$$

Consider the process

$$\zeta_n(t;\theta_k) = [n\varepsilon_n]^{-1/2} \sum_{1\le i\le n\varepsilon_n t} \frac{\partial \ln f}{\partial\theta}(x_i, \theta_k)$$

For $k=2$ by Donsker's theorem [2, p.190] on any finite interval $t\in[0,T]$ the process $\zeta_n(t;\theta_2)$ weakly converges to a Wiener process. For $k=1$ we should note that by (8) under the conditions of the lemma the decomposition

$$f(x,\theta_2) = f(x,\theta_1) + \delta_n \frac{\partial f}{\partial\theta}(x,\theta_1) + O(\delta_n^2) \tag{16}$$

holds. By virtue of condition III and decomposition (16) conditions of Corollary 6 of Theorem 4 in [4] are satisfies, so that for $t\in[0,T]$ the process $\zeta_n(t;\theta_1)$ weakly converges to a biased Wiener process $w(t)+ct$ where c is a finite constant.

Since for $n\to\infty$ the value

$$(\varepsilon_n/\rho')^{1/2}[n\rho']^{-1/2} \sum_{1\le i\le n\rho'} \ell(x_i,\theta_k)$$

converges in probability to zero and $\zeta_n(t;\theta_k)$ weakly converges to a finite process with probability 1, by Theorem 4.4 [2, p.43] process (15) weakly converges to zero uniformly w.r.t. $\rho\in[a,b]$ and $\theta_1,\theta_2\in K$ when $t\in[0,T]$.

Hence by (14) and decomposition (16) process (13) can be written as

$$\xi_n(t;\rho) = \sum_{1\le i\le n\varepsilon_n t} \ln\left(1-\delta_n\left(\frac{\partial f}{\partial\theta}(x_i,\theta_1)/f(x_i,\theta_2)\right) + O(\delta_n^2)\right) + O_p(1).$$

The lemma is proved by virtue of condition III and Corollary 6 of Theorem 2 in [4] .

LEMMA 3. Let conditions of Theorem 2 hold. Then using observations

(1) the constructed processes

$$\eta_n(t;\rho) = \sum_{1\le i\le n\rho} \ln\left(f(x_i, \hat{\theta}_{1(\rho+\varepsilon_n t)}) / f(x_i, \hat{\theta}_{1\rho})\right) \qquad (17)$$

and

$$\gamma_n(t;\rho) = \sum_{n\rho< i\le n} \ln\left(f(x_i, \hat{\theta}_{2(\rho+\varepsilon_n t)}) / f(x_i, \hat{\theta}_{2\rho})\right)$$

for t from any finite interval $[0,T]$ uniformly w.r.t. $\rho\in[a,b]\subset(0,1)$ and $\theta_1,\theta_2\in K\subset\Theta$ weakly converge to zero.

PROOF. We shall prove the lemma for the process $\eta_n(t;\rho)$. The proof for $\gamma_n(t;\rho)$ is similar. Both for process (13) and (17) the decomposition

$$\eta_n(t;\rho) = \alpha_n(t;\rho) + \beta_n(t;\rho) + \tau_n(t;\rho)$$

is valid where

$$\alpha_n(t;\rho) = \sum_{1\le i\le n\rho} \frac{\partial \ln f}{\partial\theta}(x_i,\theta_1)\left((\hat{\theta}_{1(\rho+\varepsilon_n t)} - \theta_1) - (\hat{\theta}_{1\rho} - \theta_1)\right),$$

$$\beta_n(t;\rho) = \sum_{1\le i\le n\rho} \frac{\partial^2 \ln f}{\partial\theta^2}(x_i,\theta_1)\left((\theta_{1(\rho+\varepsilon_n t)} - \theta_1)^2 - (\hat{\theta}_{1\rho} - \theta_1)^2\right),$$

$$\tau_n(t;\rho) = \frac{1}{6}\sum_{1\le i\le n\rho}\left(\frac{\partial^2 \ln f}{\partial\theta^2}(x_i,\theta_1') - \frac{\partial^2 \ln f}{\partial\theta^2}(x_i,\theta_1'')\right)\times$$
$$\times\left((\hat{\theta}_{1(\rho+\varepsilon_n t)} - \theta_1)^2 - (\hat{\theta}_{1\rho} - \theta_1)^2\right)$$

where θ_1' and θ_2'' belong to a close neighbourhood of θ_1 .

Since under the conditions of the lemma the values $[n\rho]^{-1/2}\times$ $\times \sum(\partial\ln f/\partial\theta)(x_i,\theta_1)$ and $[n\rho]^{-1/2}\sum(\partial^2 f/\partial\theta^2)(x_i,\theta)$ are asymptotically normal, in order to prove the weak convergence to zero of each of the three processes it is sufficient to show that the process

$$\varkappa_n = [n\varrho]^{-1/2}((\theta_{1(\varrho+\varepsilon_n t)} - \theta_1) - (\hat{\theta}_{1\varrho} - \theta_1))$$

weakly converges to zero. This assertion is true since $\varkappa_n$ can be represented in the following way

$$\varkappa_n = [n\varrho]^{-1/2} \sum_{1 \le i \le n\varrho} \ell(x_i, \theta_1)\left(\frac{[n\varrho]}{[n(\varrho+\varepsilon_n t)]} - 1\right) +$$

$$+\left(\frac{[n\varrho]}{[n(\varrho+\varepsilon_n t)]}\right)^{1/2}\left(\frac{[n\varepsilon_n]}{[n(\varrho+\varepsilon_n t)]}\right)^{1/2}[n\varepsilon_n]^{-1/2} \sum_{n\varrho < i \le n(\varrho+\varepsilon_n t)} \ell(x_i, \theta_1),$$

which follows from (9), (10) and after some transformations. This completes the proof of the lemma.

Now we can prove Theorem 2.

PROOF OF THEOREM 2. It is to be verifies whether the condition of lemma 1 are satisfied. The sequence of observations (1) forms a family of models (6) where $\varepsilon = 1/n$, $n \to \infty$, $\theta = \varrho \in (0,1)$ and $\theta_1, \theta_2 \in \Theta$ are nuisance parameters. Likelihood function (11) corresponds to this family of models. Let $\varepsilon_n > 0$ be a normalizing factor, then likelihood ratio function (7) will have the form

$$Z_{n\varrho}(t; \hat{\theta}_\varrho, \hat{\theta}_{\varrho+\varepsilon_n t}) = \exp(\xi_{n\varrho}(t; \hat{\theta}_\varrho, \hat{\theta}_{\varrho+\varepsilon_n t})) \tag{18}$$

where $\hat{\theta}_{\varrho'} = (\hat{\theta}_{1\varrho'}, \hat{\theta}_{2\varrho'})$ ($\varrho' = \varrho$ or $\varrho' = \varrho + \varepsilon_n t$) have representation (9) anf for $t > 0$

$$\xi_{n\varrho}(t; \hat{\theta}_\varrho, \hat{\theta}_{\varrho+\varepsilon_n t}) = \overset{+}{\xi}_{n\varrho}(t; \hat{\theta}_\varrho, \hat{\theta}_{\varrho+\varepsilon_n t}) =$$

$$= \sum_{n\varrho < i \le n(\varrho+\varepsilon_n t)} \ln(f(x_i, \hat{\theta}_{1(\varrho+\varepsilon_n t)})/f(x_i, \hat{\theta}_{2\varrho})) +$$

$$+ \sum_{1 \le i < n\varrho} \ln(f(x_i, \hat{\theta}_{1(\varrho+\varepsilon_n t)})/f(x_i, \hat{\theta}_{1\varrho})) +$$

$$+ \sum_{n(\varrho+\varepsilon_n t)<i\leq n} \ln(f(x_i, \hat{\theta}_{2(\varrho+\varepsilon_n t)})/f(x_i, \hat{\theta}_{2\varrho})).$$

For $t<0$

$$\xi_{n\varrho}(t; \hat{\theta}_\varrho, \hat{\theta}_{\varrho+\varepsilon_n t}) = \xi^-_{n\varrho}(t; \hat{\theta}_\varrho, \hat{\theta}_{\varrho+\varepsilon_n t}) =$$

$$= \sum_{n(\varrho+\varepsilon_n t)<i\leq n\varrho} \ln(f(x_i, \hat{\theta}_{2(\varrho+\varepsilon_n t)})/f(x_i, \hat{\theta}_{1\varrho})) +$$

$$+ \sum_{1\leq i\leq n(\varrho+\varepsilon_n t)} \ln(f(x_i, \hat{\theta}_{1(\varrho+\varepsilon_n t)})/f(x_i, \hat{\theta}_{1\varrho})) +$$

$$+ \sum_{n\varrho<i\leq n} \ln(f(x_i, \theta_{2(\varrho+\varepsilon_n t)})/f(x_i, \hat{\theta}_{2\varrho}))$$

and

$$\xi_{n\varrho}(0; \hat{\theta}_\varrho, \hat{\theta}_{\varrho+\varepsilon_n t}) = 0.$$

Hence, starting with some $n>n_0$ the trajectory of process (18) belongs to the space $\mathfrak{D}(-\infty, \infty)$ with probability 1. By Lemmas 2 and 3 for t from any finite interval $[0, T_1]$, $T_1>0$ the process $\xi^+_{n\varrho}(t; \hat{\theta}_\varrho, \hat{\theta}_{\varrho+\varepsilon_n t})$ weakly converges to the process $w_1(t) - t/2$ uniformly w.r.t. $\varrho\in[a, b]$ and $\theta_1, \theta_2 \in K$. Similarly, for t from any finite interval $[-T_2, 0]$ $T_2>0$ the process $\xi^-_{n\varrho}(t; \hat{\theta}_\varrho, \hat{\theta}_{\varrho+\varepsilon_n t})$ weakly converges to the process $w_2(-t) + t/2$ where $w_1(t)$ and $w_2(t)$, $t\geq 0$ are independent Wiener processes.

Hence, likelihood ratio process (18) weakly converges to the process $\exp \xi(t)$ uniformly w.r.t. $\varrho\in[a, b]$ and $\theta_1, \theta_2\in K$ for t from any finite interval $[-T_2, T_1]$ and, hence, on the whole axis $(-\infty, \infty)$ where $\xi(t)$ has the form of (4). Evidently, the trajectories of the limit process $\exp \xi(t)$ are continuous functions on $(-\infty, \infty)$ converging to zero at infinities and attaining the maximum at a unique point with probability 1. Hence by Lemma 1 the distribution of the normalized estimator $\varepsilon_n^{-1}(\hat{\rho}_n - \rho)$ of the change point ρ uniformly w.r.t. $\rho \in [a,b]$ and $\theta_1, \theta_2 \in K$ converges to the distribution of τ, which is the moment when process (4) attains its maximum, the distribution having the form of (5). The theorem is proved.

3. Semi-parametric model

Let in a conventional model the densities $f(x)$ and $g(x)$ be unknown, but (3) still hold for them. Using observation (1) for the unknown densities $f(x)$ and $g(x)$ we can construct kernel type estimators $\hat{f}_{n\rho}(x)$ and $\hat{g}_{n\rho}(x)$, correspondingly.

Let

$$\hat{f}_{n\rho}(x) = ([n\rho]h_n)^{-1} \sum_{1 \leq i \leq n\rho} K\left(\frac{x - x_i}{h_n}\right)$$
$$\hat{g}_{n\rho}(x) = ([n(1-\rho)]h_n)^{-1} \sum_{n\rho < i \leq n} K\left(\frac{x - x_i}{h_n}\right) \tag{19}$$

where $K(x)$ is some real Borel function defined in $\mathbb{R}^1$ and h_n is a sequence of positive values converging to zero as $n \to \infty$ so that $nh_n \to \infty$.

In the expression for the likelihood function (2) $f(x)$ and $g(x)$ are replaced by their estimators, so that we have

$$\hat{p}_n(X;\rho) = \prod_{1 \leq i \leq n\rho} \hat{f}_{n\rho}(x_i) \prod_{n\rho < i \leq n} \hat{g}_{n\rho}(x_i). \tag{20}$$

The estimator $\hat{\rho}_n$ for the change point ρ can be defined from the relation

$$\hat{p}_n(X, \hat{\rho}_n) = \sup_{\rho \in [a,b]} \hat{p}_n(X;\rho); \quad [a,b] \subset (0,1). \tag{21}$$

To make the statement of the theorem more evident we shall introduce two definitions.

DEFINITION 1. We say that the density $f(x)$ belongs to the class $\mathfrak{F}_s$ if it is positive, bounded and continuous together with its derivatives up to the s -th order and $d^s f(x)/d^s x \neq 0$ almost for every $x \in \mathbb{R}^1$.

DEFINITION 2. We say that the function $K(x)$, $x \in \mathbb{R}^1$ belongs to the class H_s (s is an even non-negative number) if $K(x) \neq 0$ almost everywhere, $K(x) = K(-x)$, $\int K(x)\,dx = 1$, $\int K^2(x)\,dx < \infty$, $\sup\limits_{x \in \mathbb{R}^1} |K(x)| < \infty$, $\int x^i K(x)\,dx \;\, 0$, $i = 1 \div s-1$, $\int x^s K(x)\,dx \neq 0$, $\int x^s |K(x)|\,dx < \infty$.

THEOREM 3. Let $\hat{\varrho}_n$ be an estimator of the change point ϱ defined by (21) where the density estimators $\hat{f}_{n\varrho}(x)$ and $\hat{g}_{n\varrho}(x)$ have the form of (19) with the kernel $K(x) \in H_s$ and $h_n = cn^{-1}(2s+1)^{-1}$ where $c > 0$ and it is bounded. If densities $f(x)$, $g(x) \in \mathfrak{F}_s$ and under the conditions of Theorem 1 $n^{2s/(2s+1)} \varepsilon_n \to \infty$ and $n^{s/2(2s+1)} \delta_n \to \infty$ then uniformly w.r.t. $\varrho \in [a, b] \subset (0, 1)$ the distribution of $\varepsilon_n^{-1} \times$ $\times (\hat{\varrho}_n - \varrho)$ converges to (5).

To prove Theorem 3 we need two lemmas.

LEMMA 4. Let conditions of Theorem 3 hold. Then the random process

$$\hat{\xi}_n(t;\varrho) = \sum_{n\varrho < i \leq n(\varrho + \varepsilon_n t)} \ln(\hat{f}_{n(\varrho+\varepsilon_n t)} / \hat{g}_{n\varrho})(x_i)$$

for t from any finite interval $[0, T]$ will weakly converge to the process $w(t) - t/2$ uniformly w.r.t. $\varrho \in [a, b] \subset [0, 1]$.

PROOF. The process $\hat{\xi}_n(t;\varrho)$ can be written as

$$\hat{\xi}_n(t;\varrho) = \sum_{n\varrho < i \leq n(\varrho+\varepsilon_n t)} \ln(f(x)/g(x)) + \hat{\eta}_{1n}(t;\varrho) + \hat{\eta}_{2n}(t;\varrho) \tag{22}$$

where

$$\hat{\eta}_{1n}(t;\rho) = \sum_{n\rho < i \leq n(\rho+\varepsilon_n t)} \ln\left(1 + (\hat{f}_{n(\rho+\varepsilon_n t)}(x_i) - f(x_i))/f(x_i)\right),$$

$$\hat{\eta}_{2n}(t;\rho) = \sum_{n\rho < i \leq n(\rho+\varepsilon_n t)} \ln\left(1 + (\hat{g}_{n\rho}(x_i) - g(x_i))/g(x_i)\right).$$

The processes $\hat{\eta}_{1n}(t;\rho)$ and $\hat{\eta}_{2n}(t;\rho)$ for $t \in [0,T]$ uniformly w.r.t. $\rho \in [a,b]$ weakly converge to zero. We shall prove it for $\hat{\eta}_{1n}(t;\rho)$. For $\hat{\eta}_{2n}(t;\rho)$ the proof is similar.

Under the conditions of the lemma the kernel estimators (19) according to [5] are consistent and converge with the rate

$$\hat{f}_n(x) - f(x) = O_P(n^{-s/(2s+1)}). \tag{23}$$

Therefore, since by the condition $n^{(s+1)(2s+1)^{-1}} \varepsilon_n t \to 0$ and, hence also for $n^{(2s+1)^{-1}} \varepsilon_n t \to 0$ the following decomposition is true

$$\hat{\eta}_{1n}(t;\rho) = \sum_{n\rho < i \leq n(\rho+\varepsilon_n t)} (\hat{f}_{n(\rho+\varepsilon_n t)}(x_i) - f(x_i))/f(x_i) + O_P(1).$$

By [5] uniformly w.r.t. $\rho \in a, b$ and $t \in 0, T$ we have

$$E\hat{\eta}_{1n}(t;\rho) = n\varepsilon_n t\, O(n^{-s/(2s+1)}) \to 0,$$

$$D\hat{\eta}_{1n}(t;\rho) = n^2 \varepsilon_n^2 t^2 O(n^{-2s/(2s+1)}) = O(n^{(s+1)(2s+1)^{-1}} \varepsilon_n)^2 \to 0$$

which proves that $\hat{\eta}_{1n}(t;\rho)$ weakly converges to zero.

Consequently (22) can be written as

$$\hat{\xi}_n(t;\rho) = \sum_{n\rho < i \leq n(\rho+\varepsilon_n t)} \ln(f(x)/g(x)) + O_P(1).$$

The lemma is proved by virtue of condition (3) and Corollary 6 of Theorem 2 in [4] .

LEMMA 5. Let conditions of Theorem 3 hold. Then the random processes

$$\hat{\zeta}_{1n}(t;\varrho) = \sum_{1\leq i\leq n\varrho} \ln(\hat{f}_{n(\varrho+\varepsilon_n t)}/\hat{f}_{n\varrho})(x_i),$$

$$\hat{\zeta}_{2n}(t;\varrho) = \sum_{n(\varrho+\varepsilon_n t)<i\leq n} \ln(\hat{g}_{n(\varrho+\varepsilon_n t)}/\hat{g}_{n\varrho})(x_i)$$

for t from any finite interval $[0,T]$ uniformly w.r.t. $\varrho\in[a,b]\subset \subset(0,1)$ weakly converge to zero.

PROOF. We prove it for the process $\hat{\zeta}_{1n}(t;\varrho)$. For $\hat{\zeta}_{2n}(t;\varrho)$ the proof will be similar.

With (19) in mind we can write

$$\hat{\zeta}_{1n}(t;\varrho) = \sum_{1\leq i\leq n\varrho} \ln\Big(1+\varepsilon_n t(\varrho+\varepsilon_n t)^{-1}\Big(\frac{1}{[n\varrho]}\sum_{1\leq j\leq n\varrho} h_n^{-1} K\Big(\frac{x_i-x_j}{h_n}\Big)\times$$

$$\times\Big(\frac{1}{[n\varepsilon_n t]}\sum_{n\varrho<j\leq n(\varrho+\varepsilon_n t)} h_n^{-1}K\Big(\frac{x_i-x_j}{h_n}\Big) - \frac{1}{[n\varrho]}\sum_{1<j\leq n\varrho} h_n^{-1}K\Big(\frac{x_i-x_j}{h_n}\Big)\Big)\Big)\Big).$$

Applying (23) we have

$$\hat{\zeta}_{1n}(t;\varrho) = \sum_{1\leq i\leq n\varrho} \ln\Big(1+\varepsilon_n t(\varrho+\varepsilon_n t)^{-1}\Big(f(x_i)+O_P([n\varrho]^{-s/(2s+1)})\Big)^{-1}\times$$

$$\times\Big(g(x_i)+O_P([n\varepsilon_n]^{-s/(2s+1)}) - f(x_i) - O_P([n\varrho]^{-s/(2s+1)})\Big)\Big).$$

By virtue of (3) after the decomposition we have

$$\hat{\zeta}_{1n}(t;\varrho) = \sum_{1\leq i\leq n\varrho} \varepsilon_n t(\varrho+\varepsilon_n t)^{-1}\delta_n b_n(x_i)(f(x_i))^{-1} + O_P(1).$$

Hence for $t \in [0, T]$ uniformly w.r.t. $\rho \in [a, b]$ we have

$$\mathbb{E}\, \hat{\zeta}_{1n}(t;\rho) = O(1),$$

$$\mathbb{D}\, \hat{\zeta}_{1n}(t;\rho) = O([n\rho]\, \varepsilon_n^2 t^2 (\rho + \varepsilon_n t)^{-2} \delta_n^2) = O(\varepsilon_n).$$

This completes the proof of the lemma.

Now we can prove the theorem.

PROOF OF THEOREM 3. Similar to the proof of Theorem 2, we study the asymptotic behaviour of the process

$$\hat{Z}_{n\rho}(t) = \hat{p}_n(X; \rho + \varepsilon_n t) / \hat{p}_n(X; \rho)$$

where $\hat{p}_n(X;\rho)$ has the form of (20). Evidently,

$$\hat{Z}_{n\rho}(t) = \exp \hat{\xi}_{n\rho}(t) \tag{24}$$

where

$$\hat{\xi}_{n\rho}(t) = \begin{cases} \hat{\xi}^{+}_{n\rho}(t), & t > 0, \\ \hat{\xi}^{-}_{n\rho}(t), & t < 0, \end{cases} \tag{25}$$

$$\hat{\xi}_{n\rho}(0) = 0$$

where

$$\hat{\xi}^{+}_{n\rho}(t) = \sum_{n\rho < i \le n(\rho+\varepsilon_n t)} \ln(\hat{f}_{n(\rho+\varepsilon_n t)} / \hat{g}_{n\rho})(x_i) +$$

$$+ \sum_{1 \le i \le n\rho} \ln(\hat{f}_{n(\rho+\varepsilon_n t)} / \hat{f}_{n\rho})(x_i) +$$

$$+ \sum_{n(\rho+\varepsilon_n t) < i \le n} \ln(\hat{g}_{n(\rho+\varepsilon_n t)} / \hat{g}_{n\rho})(x_i)$$

and

$$\hat{\xi}_{n\varrho}^{-}(t) = \sum_{n(\varrho+\varepsilon_n t)<i\leq n\varrho} \ln(\hat{g}_{n(\varrho+\varepsilon_n t)}/\hat{f}_{n\varrho})(x_i) +$$

$$+ \sum_{1\leq i\leq n(\varrho+\varepsilon_n t)} \ln(\hat{f}_{n(\varrho+\varepsilon_n t)}/\hat{f}_{n\varrho})(x_i) +$$

$$+ \sum_{n\varrho<i\leq n} \ln(\hat{g}_{n(\varrho+\varepsilon_n t)}/\hat{g}_{n\varrho})(x_i).$$

Consequently, by Lemmas 4 and 5 process (25) weakly converges to process (4) uniformly w.r.t. $\varrho\in[a,b]$ and for t from any finite interval $[-T_2, T_1]$, $T_1, T_2 > 0$. Since process (24) attains its maximum at the point $t = \varepsilon_n^{-1}(\hat{\varrho}_n - \varrho)$ where $\hat{\varrho}_n$ is the estimator of the change point ϱ defined by relation (21) and conditions of Lemma 1 are satisfied, the value $\varepsilon_n^{-1}(\hat{\varrho}_n - \varrho)$ weakly converges to τ, which is the moment when process (4) attains its maximum. This completes the proof of the theorem.

REMARK. In the case when for a finite series of independent observations it is a priori known that the change occurred exactly k times at the moments $1<\tau_1<\tau_2<\ldots<\tau_k<n$ under certain conditions it can be proved for the three models that normalized estimators $\varepsilon_{n1}^{-1}(\hat{\varrho}_{n1}-\varrho_1), \ldots, \varepsilon_{nk}^{-1}(\hat{\varrho}_{nk}-\varrho_k)$ of the change points $\varrho_i = (\tau_i/n)\in(0,1)$, $i = 1\div k$, are asymptotically independent and each of them has distribution (5) in the limit.

Department of Prob.Theory and Math. Statistics
Tbilisi A.Razmadze Math. Institute of the
Acad. of Science of the Georgian SSR
150 a Plekhanov ave., Tbilisi, 380012
USSR

REFERENCES

1. Ibragimov I.A., Khas'minskii R.E. Asymptotic estimation theory. M.

Nauka, 1979, 528 p. (in Russian).

2. Billingsley P. Convergence of probability measures.- J.Wiley & Sons Inc., New York-London-Sydney-Toronto.

3. Hahubia Ts.G. Limit theorem for maximum likelihood estimation of change points.- Teor. Veroyatn. Primen., 1986, v.XXXI, N 1, 152-155 (in Russian).

4. Liptser R.Sh., Shiryayev A.N. Functional limit theorem for semimartingales.- Teor. Veroyatn. Primen., 1980, v.XXV, N 4, 683-703 (in Russian).

5. Nadaraya E.A. On mean square estimator of some non-parametric distribution density estimators.- In: Teor. Veroyatn. Mat. Stat., v.10, Kiev, 1976, 116-128 (in Russian).

PRECISE UPPER BOUNDS FOR THE FUNCTIONALS DESCRIBING TUMOUR TREATMENT EFFICIENCY

L.G.Hanin, S.T.Rachev, R.E.Goot, A.Yu.Yakovlev

1. Introduction

Many attempts to increase the efficiency of cancer therapy has been performed so far, most of them based on various schemes of fractionating of the total dose of irradiation. Several mathematical models of fractionated irradiation [1, 2] were proposed as a theoretical ground for such trials. It is important however to evaluate the upper limit of therapeutical success that can be achieved via an optimal treatment scheme. The treatment efficiency for a given sequence of doses the tissue is exposed to may be measured by the difference between average survival probabilities for normal and neoplastic cells, the mathematical expectation being taken with respect to the distribution of the cellular radiosensitivity [3] .

Within the framework of the classical "hit and target" theory [4] the individual survival probability of a cell is expressed by well-known "hit" function (see Section 2) and depends on the individual sensitivity x , the maximal quantity of "hits" (lesions) the cell can bear without being killed (m) and the applied dose D . It is commonly believed that the sensitivity x of a cell may be viewed as a probability of one "hit" in the "target" related to the unit of dose and it depends primarily on physical characteristics of radiation and geometrical parameters of a cell and its "target". On the contrary, the number m depends largely on the biological properties of a cell. But it must be kept in mind that the both parameters $\varkappa$ and m actually participate the description of the resultant cell radiosensitivity.

It is well known (see [5, 6]) that the biological response of a cell to irradiation is determined crucially by intracellular reparation processes. Fortunately, in the "repair" modification of the "hit and target" model the survival probabilities belong to the class of "hit" functions. In this case $\varkappa$ denotes the sum of the sensitivities of a cell itself and of its reparation system while m is the critical quantity of unrepaired lesions.

It should be noted that the "hit" functions are not more than approximations to the true survival probabilities. It leads us to definition of the upper bounds of the therapeutic efficiency functional involving extension of the latter to some sets of functions of survival probability type possessing only the most characteristic features of the "hit" functions.

The authors are aware of substancial source of therapeutical gain that arises from studying the time development of the transient processes in kinetics of irradiated populations of normal and malignant cells and from optimal control over corresponding sensitivity disttibutions. This important topic, however, is beyond this contribution.

2. Basic assumptions and introductory formalism

In the sequel we need the following assumptions.

1. The intervals between the time instants the doses $D_1, \ldots, D_n$ are administered at are long enough for accomplishment of the transient processes of inactivation and recovery of damaged cells.

2. Normal and neoplastic cells differ in their sensitivity distributions only. Neither neoplastic nor normal cells possess any advantage in their reproduction after treatment. The radiosensitivity of a cell is inherited by its progeny. Thus the radiosensitivity dis-

tributions are not influenced by the cellular proliferation processes.

3. In the "hit and target" model the distributions $d\nu_0(x,m)$ and $d\nu_1(x,m)$ of normal and neoplastic cells in respect to their parameters x and m decompose into direct products of the distributions $d\mu_0(x)\times d\rho_0(m)$ and $d\mu_1(x)\times d\rho_1(m)$. The way of interpretation of the parameters x and m mentioned in the introduction renders this hypothesis probable.

Denote $g(x,D)$ the survival probability of a cell with sensitivity x exposed to the dose D. In the "multihit-one target" theory of irradiated cell survival

$$g(x,D) = f_m(xD),$$

where

$$f_m(t) = e^{-t}\sum_{k=0}^{m}\frac{t^k}{k!}, \qquad m\in Z_+,$$

and xD is the expected number of lesions. In a more general case when a cell is exposed to a sequence of doses $\vec{D}=(D_1,\ldots,D_n)$ the survival probability is expressed by the function

$$g(x,\vec{D}) = \prod_{i=1}^{n} g(x,D_i).$$

We consider $g(x,\vec{D})$ as a function with the following natural properties: it is nonincreasing with respect to each argument, the others being fixed; $g(0,\vec{D}) = g(x,\mathbb{0}) = 1$ for all x and $\vec{D}$; $g(x,\vec{D})\to 0$ as one of the arguments tends to infinity and the others are fixed.

Let μ_0 and μ_1 be the distributions of the radiosensitivities of normal and malignant cells respectively. The expected therapeutic efficiency for a given treatment scheme $\vec{D}$ is expressed by the functional

$$\Phi(g)=\int_0^{\infty} g(x,\vec{D})\,d\mu_0(x)-\int_0^{\infty} g(x,\vec{D})\,d\mu_1(x)=\int_0^{\infty}\prod_{i=1}^{n} g(x,D_i)\,d(\mu_0-\mu_1)(x),$$

while in the "hit and target" approximation it is equal to

$$\Phi=\int_{\mathbb{R}_+\times\mathbb{Z}_+}\prod_{i=1}^{n} f_m(xD_i)\,d(\nu_0-\nu_1)(x,m).$$

Let $\mathcal{F}$ be a class (possibly depending on $\vec{D}$) of nonincreasing functions f on $\mathbb{R}_+$ such that $f(0)=1$ and $\lim\limits_{x\to+\infty} f(x)=0$. The upper bound $\Phi_{\mathcal{F}}$ of the treatment efficiency functional is defined by the formula

$$\Phi_{\mathcal{F}}=\sup_{f\in\mathcal{F}}\Phi(f) \quad , \text{ where } \quad \Phi(f)=\int_0^{\infty} f(x)\,d(\mu_0-\mu_1)(x).$$

The symbols F_0 and F_1 are used hereafter for the distribution functions of measures μ_0 and μ_1 on $\mathbb{R}$. The indicator function of a set A is denoted χ_A . The notation δ_u is referred to the Dirac measure at a point u .

3. The precise upper bound for the class of absolutely continuous functions

We start with the broadest class W of all nonincreasing absolutely continuous functions f on $\mathbb{R}_+$ such that $f(0)=1$ and $\lim\limits_{x\to+\infty} f(x)=0$. Note that the derivative f' of a function $f\in W$ is defined almost everywhere (a.e.) with respect to Lebesgue measure, $f'\leq 0$ a.e. and $\int_0^{\infty} f'(x)\,dx=-1$.

The precise upper bound desired is established by

PROPOSITION 1. $\sup\limits_{f\in W}\Phi(f)=\sup\limits_{x\in\mathbb{R}_+}(F_0-F_1)(x).$

PROOF. Integrating by parts we have for all $f \in W$

$$\Phi(f) = \int_0^\infty f(x)\,d(\mu_0 - \mu_1)(x) = -\int_0^\infty f'(x)(F_0 - F_1)(x)\,dx. \tag{1}$$

It follows immediately from (1) that

$$\sup_{f \in W} \Phi(f) \leqslant \sup_{x \in \mathbb{R}_+} (F_0 - F_1)(x).$$

To prove the inverse inequality denote $M = \sup_{x \in \mathbb{R}_+} (F_0 - F_1)(x)$ and put $E_n = \{x \in \mathbb{R}_+ : (F_0 - F_1)(x) \geqslant M - \frac{1}{n}\}$, $n \in \mathbb{N}$. Suppose $M > 0$, the case $M = 0$ being trivial. There exists such $N \in \mathbb{N}$ that $0 < \operatorname{mes} E_n < \infty$ for all n, $n \geqslant N$. Define the functions

$$f_n(x) = 1 - \frac{1}{\operatorname{mes} E_n} \int_0^x \chi_{E_n}(t)\,dt, \qquad n \geqslant N. \tag{2}$$

The inequalities

$$\Phi(f_n) = \frac{1}{\operatorname{mes} E_n} \int_{E_n} (F_0 - F_1)(x)\,dx \geqslant M - \frac{1}{n}, \quad n \geqslant N,$$

imply

$$\sup_{f \in W} \Phi(f) \geqslant M.$$

The proof is completed.

Introduce the set $E = \bigcap_{n \in \mathbb{N}} E_n$. In the case when $\operatorname{mes} E > 0$ the supremum of the functional Φ is attained at the function $f^* \in W$,

$$f^*(x) = 1 - \frac{1}{\operatorname{mes} E} \int_0^x \chi_E(t)\,dt.$$

On the contrary, if $\operatorname{mes} E = 0$ then such function does not exist but we can choose a sequence $\{f_n\} \subset W$ (consisting of the functions (2), for example) with the property $\Phi(f_n) \longrightarrow \Phi_W$.

It is the special case when there is the unique point $x_0 \in \mathbb{R}_+$

such that

$$\sup_{x \in \mathbb{R}_+} (F_0 - F_1)(x) = (F_0 - F_1)(x_0)$$

that is of the most practical interest. In this case $E = \{x_0\}$ and

$$\Phi_W = \Phi(f_0), \qquad \text{where} \quad f_0(x) = \begin{cases} 1, & 0 \leqslant x \leqslant x_0, \\ 0, & x > x_0 \end{cases}$$

(the function f_0 being not in W, of course). If the function $F_0 - F_1$ is continuous at the point x_0 the value $f_0(x_0)$ may be chosen arbitrarily. Suppose the latter is equal to 1/2 and denote the corresponding function $\tilde{f}_0$. It is worth noting that the function $\tilde{f}_0$ can be approximated by the "hit" functions in the following sense: if m and D tend to infinity in a way that $\frac{m}{D} = x_0$ then

$$f_m(xD) \longrightarrow \tilde{f}_0(x) \qquad \text{for all} \quad x \in \mathbb{R}_+ .$$

The fact that $\tilde{f}_0$ is the cell response to irradiation indicates the deterministic type of the cellular survival process i.e. the cells with sensitivity less than x_0 survive with probability 1 while the cells whose sensitivity exceeds x_0 die with probability 1. This phenomenon corresponds to the process of interphase death of cells exposed to high doses of irradiation. The value of the treatment efficiency functionsl for a tissue with deterministic response to irradiation and with fixed m, m being big enough, would be quite close to the upper bound Φ_W if one applies the dose $D_0 = \frac{m}{x_0}$.

4. The precise upper bound for the class of Lipschitz functions

It is natural to consider the real dependence of survival probability of a cell on its radiosensitivity as the function with bounded intensity. The latter can be identified with the (least) Lipschitz constant of the function $g(x, \vec{D})$ with respect to x. This observation leads us to consideration of the bound

$$\Phi_{L_M} = \sup_{f \in L_M} \Phi(f), \tag{3}$$

where L_M for $M > 0$ is the set of all nonincreasing functions f on $\mathbb{R}_+$ such that $f(0) = 1$, $\lim_{x \to +\infty} f(x) = 0$ and $|f(x) - f(y)| \leq M|x-y|$ for all $x, y \in \mathbb{R}_+$.

For the whole class Lip M of all Lipschitz functions f satisfying the inequality

$$|f(x) - f(y)| \leq M|x - y|, \qquad x, y \in \mathbb{R}_+,$$

the bound

$$\Phi_{\mathrm{Lip}M} = \sup_{f \in \mathrm{Lip}M} |\Phi(f)| \tag{3'}$$

is known as the Kantorovich metric and has the following explicit form

$$\Phi_{\mathrm{Lip}M} = M \int_0^\infty |F_0(t) - F_1(t)|\, dt.$$

Therefore one may write

$$\Phi_{L_M} \leq \Phi_{\mathrm{Lip}M}$$

and since the supremum in (3') is attained at the optimal function $f = f_{opt}$ with the derivative

$$f'_{opt}(x) = M \,\mathrm{sign}\, [F_0(x) - F_1(x)], \qquad x \in \mathbb{R}_+,$$

then $\Phi_{L_M} = \Phi_{\mathrm{Lip}M}$ if f_{opt} or $-f_{opt}$ belongs to L_M. But generally neither f_{opt} nor $-f_{opt}$ belongs to L_M and it is worth looking for another estimate in this class.

Remind the following definition.

Let $(X, \mathfrak{A}, \mu)$ be a measure space with nonnegative measure μ. The measure μ is called nonatomic if for every set $A \in \mathfrak{A}$ such that $\mu A > 0$ there exists a set $B \in \mathfrak{A}$ with the properties $B \subset A$ and $0 < \mu B < \mu A$.

The precise formula for the bound (3) is based on the following result.

LEMMA. Let $(X, \mathcal{A}, \mu)$ be a measure space with nonatomic measure μ, such that $\mu X = +\infty$, and F is a measurable real-valued function on X. For $a>0$ and $b>0$ define the set $G_{a,b} = \{g: 0 \leq g \leq a$ a.e. and $\int_X g\,d\mu = b\}$. Denote $c = \sup\{x: \mu(\{F \geq x\}) \geq \frac{b}{a}\}$.

1. If $\mu(\{F \geq c\}) \geq \frac{b}{a}$ then

$$\sup_{g \in G_{a,b}} \int_X gF\,d\mu = a \int_E F\,d\mu \tag{4.1}$$

for a set $E \in \mathcal{A}$ such that $\mu E = \frac{b}{a}$ and $\{F > c\} \subset E \subset \{F \geq c\}$.

2. If $\mu(\{F \geq c\}) < \frac{b}{a}$ then

$$\sup_{g \in G_{a,b}} \int_X gF\,d\mu = a \int_{\{F \geq c\}} F\,d\mu + c(b - a\mu(\{F \geq c\})). \tag{4.2}$$

PROOF. At first let us consider the case $\mu(\{F \geq c\}) \geq \frac{b}{a}$. The definition of c implies the inequality $\mu(\{F > c\}) \leq \frac{b}{a}$. It is easy to see that for a given set $A \in \mathcal{A}$ the function $B \mapsto \mu B$, $B \in \mathcal{A}$, $B \subset A$, takes all intermediate values between 0 and μA, this fact being the consequence of the assumption that μ is a nonatomic measure. Hence we can choose such $E \in \mathcal{A}$ that

$$\mu E = \frac{b}{a} \quad \text{and} \quad \{F > c\} \subset E \subset \{F \geq c\}. \tag{5}$$

We claim that $\int_X gF\,d\mu \leq a \int_E F\,d\mu$ for all $g \in G_{a,b}$. To prove it take $g \in G_{a,b}$. Via (5) we have

$$\int_X gF\,d\mu = \int_E gF\,d\mu + \int_{X \setminus E} gF\,d\mu \leq \int_E gF\,d\mu + c \int_{X \setminus E} g\,d\mu =$$

$$= \int_E gF\,d\mu + c\left(b - \int_E g\,d\mu\right) = \int_E gF\,d\mu + c \int_E (a-g)\,d\mu \leq$$

$$\leqslant \int_E gF\,d\mu + \int_E (a-g)F\,d\mu = a\int_E F\,d\mu.$$

Since the function $g = a\chi_E$ belongs to $G_{a,b}$ and $\int_X a\chi_E F\,d\mu = a\int_E F\,d\mu$, the statement of the lemma is, for the case under study, established.

Let now $\mu(\{F \geqslant c\}) < \frac{b}{a}$. Denote $E = \{F \geqslant c\}$. Repeating the first three transitions in the above estimates we have for all $g \in G_{a,b}$

$$\int_X gF\,d\mu \leqslant \int_E gF\,d\mu + c\left(b - \int_E g\,d\mu\right) = \int_E g(F-c)\,d\mu + cb \leqslant$$
$$\leqslant a\int_E (F-c)\,d\mu + cb = a\int_E F\,d\mu + c(b - a\mu E).$$

Thus

$$\sup_{g\in G_{a,b}} \int_X gF\,d\mu \leqslant a\int_{\{F\geqslant c\}} F\,d\mu + c(b - a\mu(\{F\geqslant c\})).$$

To obtain the inverse inequality take such a sequence $\{c_n\}_{n\in\mathbb{N}}$ that $c_n < c_{n+1}$ for all n and $c_n \to c$ as $n \to \infty$.

We will show that $\mu(\{F \geqslant c_n\}) = +\infty$ for all n. In fact, suppose the latter statement fails for some $n = n_0$. The definition of c implies $\mu(\{F\geqslant c_n\}) \geqslant \frac{b}{a}$ for all n. Since $\{F \geqslant c\} = \bigcap_{n\geqslant n_0}\{F\geqslant c_n\}$, $\{F\geqslant c_{n+1}\} \subset \{F\geqslant c_n\}$ for all n, and $\mu(\{F\geqslant c_{n_0}\}) < +\infty$ we have via continuity of the measure the inequality $\mu(\{F\geqslant c\}) \geqslant \frac{b}{a}$, which contradicts the assumption stated above.

Since the measure μ is nonatomic we can choose for each n a set $E_n \in \mathfrak{A}$ with the properties: $E_n \subset \{c_n \leqslant F < c\}$, $\mu E_n = \frac{b}{a} - \mu(\{F\geqslant c\})$. Set $g_n = a\chi_{E\cup E_n} \in G_{a,b}$ and observe that

$$\int_X g_n F\,d\mu = a\int_E F\,d\mu + a\int_{E_n} F\,d\mu \geqslant a\int_E F\,d\mu + ac_n\mu E_n =$$

$$= a\int_E F\,d\mu + c_n(b - a\mu E) \geqslant a\int_E F\,d\mu + c(b - a\mu E) - (c - c_n)b.$$

Hence

$$\sup_{g\in G_{a,b}} \int_X gF\,d\mu \geqslant a\int_{\{F\geqslant c\}} F\,d\mu + c(b - a\mu(\{F\geqslant c\})).$$

Thus formula (4.2) is also valid.

Our lemma is proved.

REMARK. Though the set E in the formula (4.1) is not, in general, determined uniquely by the conditions (5) the value of $\int_E F\,d\mu$ does not depend on the particular choice of the set E.

Now we are in a position to obtain the formula for the upper bound (3).

PROPOSITION 2. Denote $c = \sup\{x: mes(\{F_0 - F_1 \geqslant x\}) \geqslant M^{-1}\}$.

1. If $mes(\{F_0 \geqslant F_1\}) \geqslant M^{-1}$ then

$$\Phi_{L_M} = M\int_E (F_0 - F_1)(x)\,dx, \tag{6.1}$$

where $mes\,E = M^{-1}$ and $\{F > c\} \subset E \subset \{F \geqslant c\}$.

2. If $mes(\{F_0 \geqslant F_1\}) < M^{-1}$ then

$$\Phi_{L_M} = M\int_{\{F_0 > F_1\}} (F_0 - F_1)(x)\,dx. \tag{6.2}$$

PROOF. Observe that the set of all functions $-f'$ for $f\in L_M$ coinsides with the set $G_{M,1}$ (see lemma where $(X, \mathfrak{A}, \mu)$ is $\mathbb{R}_+$ with the Lebesgue measure). Suppose $mes(\{F_0 \geqslant F_1\}) < M^{-1}$. Then $c = 0$ since $\lim_{x\to+\infty}(F_0 - F_1)(x) = 0$. Using (1) and (5.1) with $F = F_0 - F_1$ we obtain (6.2). The formula (6.1) is derived straightforwardly from (4.1) by the same argument.

The proposition is proved.

REMARK 1. It follows from the proof of the lemma that in the case when $mes(\{F_0 - F_1\}) \geqslant M^{-1}$ the supremum of the functional Φ over L_M is attained at the function

$$f^*(x) = 1 - (\text{mes}\, E)^{-1} \int_0^x \chi_E(t)\,dt.$$

In the case when $\text{mes}(\{F_0 \geq F_1\}) < M^{-1}$ there is no such function in L_M but we can choose a sequence of functions $\{f_n\} \subset L_M$ such that $\Phi(f_n) \to \Phi_{L_M}$. For example,

$$f_n(x) = 1 - (\text{mes}\, H_n)^{-1} \int_0^x \chi_{H_n}(t)\,dt, \qquad n \in \mathbb{N},$$

where $H_n = \{F_0 \geq F_1\} \cup E_n, \quad E_n \subset \{F_0 < F_1\}, \quad \text{mes}\, E_n = M^{-1} - \text{mes}(\{F_0 \geq F_1\})$ and $\inf E_n \to +\infty$.

REMARK 2. The value of $\int_E (F_0 - F_1)(x)\,dx$ in (6.1) does not depend on the choice of the set E provided the latter is not defined uniquely.

The functional presented by the righthand side of (6.1) and (6.2) is worth studying for itself. Let F be a measurable function on $\mathbb{R}$ such that $\lim_{x \to \pm\infty} F(x) = 0$. For $\tau > 0$ we set

$$c_\tau = \sup\{x : \text{mes}(\{F \geq x\}) \geq \tau\} \tag{7}$$

and define

$$\Psi_\tau(F) = \tau^{-1} \int_{E_\tau} (x)\,dx,$$

where $\text{mes}\, E_\tau = \tau$, $\{F > c_\tau\} \subset E_\tau \subset \{F \geq c_\tau\}$ if $\text{mes}(\{F \geq 0\}) \geq \tau$ and $E_\tau = \{F > 0\}$ if $\text{mes}\{F \geq 0\} < \tau$.

An important property of the functional Ψ_τ is contained in

PROPOSITION 3. The function $\Psi_\tau(F)$ for a given F is nonincreasing with respect to τ.

PROOF. Note that

$$\{F > c_\tau\} \subset E_\tau \subset \{F \geq c_\tau\} \qquad \text{for all} \quad \tau > 0. \tag{8}$$

Take $\tau_2 < \tau_1$ and denote $c_i = c_{\tau_i}$, $E_i = E_{\tau_i}$, $i=1,2$. It follows from the definition (7) that $c_2 \geq c_1$. If $c_1 = c_2 = 0$ then we can put $E_1 =$

$= E_2 = \{F > 0\}$ which renderes the inequality $\Psi_{\tau_1}(F) \leqslant \Psi_{\tau_2}(F)$ trivial. If $c_1 = c_2 = c > 0$ then by (8) $mes(\{F > c\}) \leqslant \tau_2 < \tau_1 \leqslant mes(\{F \geqslant c\})$ and therefore we can choose the sets E_1 and E_2 in a way that $E_2 \subset E_1$. If at last $c_2 > c_1$ then, again by (8), $E_2 \subset \{F \geqslant c_2\} \subset \{F > c_1\} \subset E_1$. Thus we can assume without loss of generality that $E_2 \subset E_1$ and $mes E_2 = \tau_2$. Hence

$$\Psi_{\tau_1}(F) = \tau_1^{-1} \int_{E_1} F(x)\,dx = \tau_1^{-1}\Big(\int_{E_2} F(x)\,dx + \int_{E_1 \setminus E_2} F(x)\,dx\Big) \leqslant$$

$$\leqslant \tau_1^{-1}\Big(\int_{E_2} F(x)\,dx + c_2\, mes(E_1 \setminus E_2)\Big) < \tau_1^{-1}\Big(\int_{E_2} F(x)\,dx + \tau_2^{-1} mes(E_1 \setminus E_2) \int_{E_2} F(x)\,dx\Big) =$$

$$= \tau_2^{-1} \int_{E_2} F(x)\,dx = \Psi_{\tau_2}(F).$$

The proof is completed.

REMARK 1. The proposition 3 is supplied designedly with the direct proof in order to reveal the intrinsic causes. The fact itself that the function $\tau \longmapsto \Psi_\tau(F)$ is nonincreasing can be deduced "free of charge" from the formula

$$\Psi_\tau(F) = \sup_{g \in G_{\tau^{-1},1}} \int_{-\infty}^{+\infty} g(x) F(x)\,dx$$

(see lemma) and the inclusions $G_{p,1} \subset G_{q,1}$, $p < q$.

REMARK 2. The functionals Ψ_τ give rise to the family $\{\xi_\tau\}_{\tau > 0}$ of metrics defined on the set of all probability distributions on $\mathbb{R}$ in the following way

$$\xi_\tau(\mu_0, \mu_1) = \max\{\Psi_\tau(F_0 - F_1),\ \Psi_\tau(F_1 - F_0)\},\quad \tau > 0.$$

These metrics "soften" the uniform metric $\rho(\mu_0, \mu_1) = \sup_{x \in \mathbb{R}} |(F_0 - F_1)(x)|$ which appeares to be their limit case:

$$\lim_{\tau \to 0+} \xi_\tau(\mu_0, \mu_1) = \rho(\mu_0, \mu_1).$$

REMARK 3. In the special case when $F_0(x) \geqslant F_1(x)$ for all $x \in \mathbb{R}_+$ and the distributions μ_0, μ_1 on $\mathbb{R}_+$ have finite mean values $\bar{\mu}_0, \bar{\mu}_1$ we obtain for $r \geqslant 1$ the estimate

$$\xi_r(\mu_0, \mu_1) \leqslant \xi_1(\mu_0, \mu_1) = \int_{E_1} (F_0 - F_1)(x)\, dx = \int_{E_1} (\bar{F}_1 - \bar{F}_0)(x)\, dx \leqslant$$
$$\leqslant \int_{\mathbb{R}_+} (\bar{F}_1 - \bar{F}_0)(x)\, dx = \bar{\mu}_1 - \bar{\mu}_0,$$

where $\bar{F}_i = 1 - F_i, \quad i = 0, 1.$

The "hit and target" hypothesis enables explicit expression for the Lipschitz constant M. To make sure of this take the "m-hit" function $f_m(t) = e^{-t} \sum_{k=0}^{m} \frac{t^k}{k!}$ with the derivative $f_m'(t) = -e^{-t} \frac{t^m}{m!}$ and denote $a_m = \sup_{t \in \mathbb{R}_+} |f_m'(t)|$. Here the value m is assumed to be non-random. We obtain without any difficulty that $a_0 = 1$ and $a_m = |f_m'(m)| = e^{-m} \frac{m^m}{m!}$ for $m \geqslant 1$. The sequence $\{a_m\}_{m \in \mathbb{Z}_+}$ is decreasing and by Stirling's formula

$$\lim_{m \to \infty} \sqrt{2\pi m}\, a_m = 1.$$

Thus the Lipschitz constant of the survival probability function

$$g_m(x, D) = e^{-xD} \sum_{k=0}^{m} \frac{(xD)^k}{k!}$$

is $M = a_m D$. Similarly in the "vector" case the Lipschitz constant of the function

$$g_m(x, \vec{D}) = \prod_{i=1}^{n} g_m(x, D_i)$$

is $M = a_m D$, where $D = \sum_{i=1}^{n} D_i$ is the total dose. In this case the Lipschitz constant M will be the least one if (and only if) $D_1 = D_2 = \ldots = D_n$.

It follows from the proposition 3 that the maximum value of the Lipschitz bound for the populations with fixed difference $F_0 - F_1$ and exposed to the same total dose is achieved for $m = 1$.

Note that $\Phi_{L_M} \leqslant \Phi_W$ since $L_M \subset W$.

5. The estimate of the treatment efficiency functional in the "hit and target" model for the case of single exposure

Let $\rho_0 = \sum_{m=0}^{\infty} \alpha_m^0 \delta_m$ and $\rho_1 = \sum_{m=0}^{\infty} \alpha_m^1 \delta_m$ be the distributions of normal and neoplastic cells with respect to the critical value of unrepaired lesions. We use designations R_0 and R_1 for the corresponding distribution functions. Denote $\Delta(x, D)$ the difference between survival probabilities of normal and neoplastic cells with the sensitivity x exposed to the dose D,

$$\Delta(x,D) = \sum_{m=0}^{\infty} f_m(x\,D)\,\alpha_m^0 - \sum_{m=0}^{\infty} f_m(x\,D)\,\alpha_m^1 = \varphi(x\,D), \tag{9}$$

where

$$\varphi(t) = \sum_{m=0}^{\infty} f_m(t)(\alpha_m^0 - \alpha_m^1).$$

Then we have for $t \geqslant 0$

$$\varphi(t) = \sum_{m=0}^{\infty} \Big(e^{-t} \sum_{k=0}^{m} \frac{t^k}{k!}\Big)(\alpha_m^0 - \alpha_m^1) = e^{-t} \sum_{k=0}^{\infty} \sum_{m=k}^{\infty} \frac{t^k}{k!} (\alpha_m^0 - \alpha_m^1) =$$

$$= e^{-t} \sum_{k=0}^{\infty} \frac{t^{k+1}}{(k+1)!} \sum_{\ell=0}^{k} (\alpha_\ell^1 - \alpha_\ell^0) = e^{-t} \sum_{k=0}^{\infty} \frac{t^{k+1}}{(k+1)!} (R_1(k) - R_0(k)) \leqslant$$

$$\leqslant e^{-t} \sum_{\{k:\, R_1(k) > R_0(k)\}} \frac{t^{k+1}}{(k+1)!} (R_1(k) - R_0(k)) \leqslant e^{-t} \Big(\sup_{n \in \mathbb{N}} \frac{t^n}{n!}\Big) \int_{\{R_1 > R_0\}} (R_1 - R_0)(t)\,dt.$$

It is easy to see that

$$\sup_{n \in \mathbb{N}} \frac{t^n}{n!} = \frac{t^{[t]}}{[t]!}, \qquad t \geqslant 0,$$

where $[t]$ is 1 for $t\in[0,1)$ and the largest integer $\leq t$ for $t\geq 1$. Introduce the function

$$h(t) = e^{-t}\,\frac{t^{[t]}}{[t]!}, \qquad t\geq 0.$$

Then

$$\Delta(x,D) \leq h(xD) \int_{\{R_1>R_0\}} (R_1 - R_0)(t)\,dt. \tag{10}$$

Notice that (10) turns into equality if and only if $\rho_0=\delta_n$, $\rho_1=\delta_{n-1}$ and $[xD]=n$ for some $n\in\mathbb{N}$.

Point out also that the inequality (10) holds if the "hit" functions f_m in (9) are replaced by more general response functions $g_m(xD)$ of survival probability type such that

$$0\leq g_{m+1}(t) - g_m(t) \leq h(t), \qquad m\in\mathbb{Z}_+,\ t\geq 0. \tag{11}$$

We aim in this section to evaluate the bound

$$\Phi_{\mathfrak{F}} = \sup_{\{g_m\}\in\mathfrak{F}} \Phi(\{g_m\}),$$

where

$$\Phi(\{g_m\}) = \int_{\mathbb{R}_+\times\mathbb{Z}_+} g_m(xD)\,d(\mu_0\times\rho_0 - \mu_1\times\rho_1)(x,m)$$

and $\mathfrak{F}$ is the set of all sequences $\{g_m\}_{m\in\mathbb{Z}_+}$ of the functions $g_m\in L_{a_m}$ satisfying (11).

The functional Φ splits into two parts:

$$\Phi = \Phi_1 + \Phi_2,$$

where

$$\Phi_1(\{g_m\}) = \sum_{m=0}^{\infty} (\alpha_m^0 - \alpha_m^1) \int_0^{\infty} g_m(xD)\,d\mu_0(x),$$

$$\Phi_2(\{g_m\}) = \sum_{m=0}^{\infty} \alpha_m^1 \int_0^{\infty} g_m(xD)\,d(\mu_0 - \mu_1)(x).$$

Combining (10) with the equality $\sup_{t\in\mathbb{R}_+} h(t) = e^{-1}$ we obtain the estimate

$$\Phi_1(\{g_m\}) \leq \int_0^\infty h(xD)\, d\mu_0(x) \cdot \int_{\{R_1 > R_0\}} (R_1 - R_0)(t)\, dt \leq e^{-1} \int_{\{R_1 > R_0\}} (R_1 - R_0)(t)\, dt.$$

Taking into account the results of the preceding section we find that

$$\Phi_2(\{g_m\}) \leq \sup_m \int_0^\infty g_m(xD)\, d(\mu_0 - \mu_1)(x) \leq \sup_m \Phi_{L_{a_m D}} = \Phi_{L_D} = \Psi_{D^{-1}}(F_0 - F_1).$$

Finally we have

$$\Phi_{\mathcal{F}} \leq e^{-1} \int_{\{R_1 > R_0\}} (R_1 - R_0)(t)\, dt + \Psi_{D^{-1}}(F_0 - F_1). \tag{12}$$

The estimate (12) coincides with the Lipschitz bound for the populations of normal and malignant cells which are equally distributed with respect to m and with the bound (10) for the populations with the sensitivity $x = D^{-1}$. Thus it is sharp in the sense indicated above.

6. Numerical example

To compare the "real" efficiency of irradiation with its theoretical bound Φ_{L_M} gamma distribution was chosen as a suitable approximation to the measures $d\mu_0(x)$ and $d\mu_1(x)$. So the mean values $\bar{x}_0$ and $\bar{x}_1$ together with the corresponding coefficients of variation v_0, v_1 describe completely the radiosensitivities of normal and neoplastic cells.

TABLE 1. The values of $\Phi = \Phi_{L_M}$ and $S = S(D)$ for $D = D_{opt}$.

Variant N°	$m = 1$	$m = 3$	$m = 4$	$m = 19$
1.	Φ =0.499 S =0.341	Φ =0.511 S =0.406	Φ =0.564 S =0.455	Φ =0.752 S =0.694

	(D_{opt} =7)	(D_{opt} =10)	(D_{opt} =14)	(D_{opt} =70)
2.	Φ =0.517	Φ =0.542	Φ =0.551	Φ =0.658
	S =0.359	S =0.417	S =0.457	S =0.625
	(D_{opt} =8)	(D_{opt} =12)	(D_{opt} =15)	(D_{opt} =73)
3.	Φ =0.389	Φ =0.436	Φ =0.482	Φ =0.574
	S =0.284	S =0.334	S =0.370	S =0.537
	(D_{opt} =6)	(D_{opt} =9)	(D_{opt} =13)	(D_{opt} =68)
4.	Φ =0.136	Φ =0.138	Φ =0.161	Φ =0.182
	S =0.069	S =0.086	S =0.098	S =0.163
	(D_{opt} =10)	(D_{opt} =14)	(D_{opt} =17)	(D_{opt} =76)
5.	Φ =0.903	Φ =0.924	Φ =0.956	Φ =0.992
	S =0.689	S =0.779	S =0.835	S =0.981
	(D_{opt} =8)	(D_{opt} =12)	(D_{opt} =17)	(D_{opt} =87)

The critical values of unrepaired lesions m were assumed to be non-random and the function $f_m(xD)$ served the purposes of modelling the "real" response of a cell to single irradiation.

The following sets of parameters were used.

Variant 1: $\bar{x}_0=0.2$, $v_0=0.25$, $\bar{x}_1=0.4$, $v_1=0.25$

Variant 2: $\bar{x}_0=0.2$, $v_0=0.5$, $\bar{x}_1=0.4$, $v_1=0.25$

Variant 3: $\bar{x}_0=0.2$, $v_0=0.25$, $\bar{x}_1=0.4$, $v_1=0.5$

Variant 4: $\bar{x}_0=0.4$, $v_0=0.5$, $\bar{x}_1=0.4$, $v_1=0.25$

Variant 5: $\bar{x}_0=0.1$, $v_0=0.25$, $\bar{x}_1=0.5$, $v_1=0.25$

The optimal dose D_{opt} for every set of parameters was specified by means of the condition

$$\int_0^\infty f_m(xD)\, d(\mu_0-\mu_1)(x) \to max$$

and the values of Φ_{L_M} and the optimal "real" efficiency

$$S(D_{opt}) = \int_0^\infty f_m(xD_{opt})\, d(\mu_0-\mu_1)(x)$$

were computed.

Shown in Table 1 are the results of the computations. These data reveal rather small differences between the values of Φ_{L_M} and $S(D_{opt})$.

Hanin L.G., Goot R.E., Yakovlev A.Yu.
Department of Biomathematics
Central Research Institute of
Roentgenology and Radiology
Leningradskaja 70/4
Pesochnij -2
Leningrad 188646, USSR

Rachev S.T.
Institute of Mathematics
Bulgarian Akademy of Sciences
P.O.Box 373
1090 Sofia, Bulgaria

REFERENCES

1. Swan G.W. Optimization of human cancer radiotherapy. Berlin-Heidelberg-New York: Springer-Verlag, 1981.
2. Ivanov V.K. Mathematical modelling and optimization of cancer radiotherapy. Moscow: Energoatomizdat, 1986 (in Russian).
3. Rachev S.T., Yakovlev A.Yu. Theoretical bounds for the tumor treatment efficacy.- Syst.Anal.Model.Simul. (to appear).
4. Kapul'tcevich Yu.G. Quantitative regularities of cell radiation injury. Moscow: Atomizdat, 1964 (in Russian).
5. Alper T. Keynote address: survival curve models. In: Radiation biology in cancer research. New York: Raven Press, 1980, 3-18.
6. Goodhead D.T. Models of radiation inactivation and mutagenesis. In: Radiation biology in cancer research. New York: Raven Press, 1980, 231-247.

A MULTIVARIATE ANALOG OF THE CRAMÊR THEOREM ON COMPONENTS OF THE GAUSSIAN DISTRIBUTIONS

A.M.Kagan

1. Introduction

In 1936 Cramér proved his now famous theorem that began the arithmetic of probability distributions: If the sum $X+Y$ of independent random variables (r.v.'s) X, Y has a Gaussian distribution then X and Y are also Gaussian. The Cramér theorem can obviously be formulated in the following equivalent way. Let $X_1, X_2, \ldots, X_N$ be independent r.v.'s and $L = a_1X_1 + a_2X_2 + \ldots + a_NX_N$ be a linear form. If L has a Gaussian distribution then the r.v.'s X_j with $a_j \neq 0$ are also Gaussian.

With the help of the Cramér-Wold principle, the straightforward multivariate generalization of the Cramér theorem is easily obtained. Namely let $X_1, X_2, \ldots, X_N$ be random vectors (r.vec.'s) with the values in $\mathbb{R}^m$ and $a_1, a_2, \ldots, a_N$ be scalar coefficients. If a r.vec. $L = a_1X_1 + a_2X_2 + \ldots + a_NX_N$ has an m -dimensional Gaussian distribution then the r.vec.'s X_j with $a_j \neq 0$ are necessarily Gaussian.

In this paper we shall deal with a_n absolutely different multivariate version of the Cramér theorem. Let

$$L_j = a_{j1}X_1 + a_{j2}X_2 + \ldots + a_{jN}X_N, \quad j = 1, 2, \ldots, m \quad (1)$$

be m linear forms of independent r.v.'s. Denote by P the joint distribution of the r.vec. $(L_1, L_2, \ldots, L_m)$. From the Cramér theorem it follows immediately that if P is a Gaussian distribution in $\mathbb{R}^m$ then those r.v.'s X_j are Gaussian for which $a_{1j}^2 + a_{2j}^2 + \ldots + a_{mj}^2 > 0$.

It turns out that rather a large class of distributions in $\mathbb{R}^m$ exists we denote this class EPP (EPP means"exponential of pseudopolynomial") such that if $P \in EPP$ then the r.v.'s X_j entering all the forms (1) (i.e. corresponding to those j's for which $(a_{1j}$ $a_{2j} \ldots a_{mj} \neq 0$) are Gaussian.

All Gaussian distributions in $\mathbb{R}^m$ belong to EPP; however, in case of $m > 1$ they form only a part of EPP. When $m = 1$ EPP coincides with the class of all Gaussian distributions so that the Cramér theorem formally is put in the setup of our main result (Theorem 1). The proof of Theorem 1 covers only the case of $m \geqslant 2$ and is essentially based upon the Cramér and Marcinkiewicz [2] theorems (see also [3, Ch.'s 2,3]).

The structure of EPP is hinted at by that of a class of distributions arising in a natural generalization of the Darmois-Skitovitch theorem to the case of several linear forms [4]. The main result of [4] turns out to be a special case of Theorem 1. Thus, if one considers the latter as a multivariate analog of the Cramér theorem then one has to admit that the multivariate Cramér theorem is stronger than the multivariate Darmois-Skitovitch theorem. By the way, the proof of the (original) Darmois-Skitovitch theorem essentially makes use of the Cramér theorem.

In Section 2 the class EPP of distributions in $\mathbb{R}^m$ is introduced; in Section 3 the main result is formulated and proved; Section 4 contains a refinement of the main result.

2. The class EPP of distributions in $\mathbb{R}^m$.

Let $k \geqslant 0$ be an integer, $Q_{j\ell}(u_1, u_2, \ldots, u_{m-1})$, $j = 1, 2, \ldots, m$; $\ell = 0, 1, \ldots, k$ be continuous functions.

DEFINITION 1. Any function $Q(t_1, t_2, \ldots, t_m)$ of the form

$$Q(t_1, t_2, \ldots, t_m) = \sum_{j=1}^{m} \sum_{\ell=0}^{k} t_j^{\ell} Q_{j\ell}(t_1, \ldots, t_{j-1}, t_{j+1}, \ldots, t_m) \quad (2)$$

is called a pseudopolynomial.

Any polynomial is certainly a pseudopolynomial.

Let $\xi = (\xi_1, \xi_2, \dots, \xi_m)$ be a r.vec. with the values in $\mathbb{R}^m$, P its distribution, $f(t_1, t_2, \dots, t_m)$ the characteristic function (ch.f.) of the r.vec. ξ,

$$f(t_1, t_2, \dots, t_m) = E \exp i(t_1\xi_1 + t_2\xi_2 + \dots + t_m\xi_m), \quad t = (t_1, \dots, t_m) \in \mathbb{R}^m.$$

DEFINITION 2. A distribution P belongs to the class EPP if its ch.f. has the following representation

$$f(t_1, t_2, \dots, t_m) = \exp Q(t_1, t_2, \dots, t_m), \quad |t| < \varepsilon, \tag{3}$$

for some $\varepsilon > 0$ and some pseudopolynomial Q.

To see how the marginal (one-dimensional) distributions of a r.vec. $\xi \in$ EPP look like, let us set $t_2 = \dots = t_m = 0$. The ch.f. f_1 of the first component ξ_1 becomes

$$f_1(t) = a_k t^k + \dots + a_0 + q(t)$$

with $a_k = Q_{1k}(0, 0, \dots, 0), \dots, \quad a_0 = Q_{10}(0, 0, \dots, 0),$

$$q(t) = \sum_{j=2}^{m} Q_{j0}(t, 0, \dots, 0).$$

Hence the marginal distributions are arbitrary enough and are not reduced at all to the Gaussian ones.

The problem of discribing all those pseudopolynomials $Q(t_1, t_2, \dots, t_m)$ for which $\exp Q(t_1, t_2, \dots, t_m)$ is the ch.f. of a distribution in $\mathbb{R}^m$ seems rather difficult, though very interesting.

In connection with a generalization of the Darmois-Skitovitch theorem a special subclass of EPP was studied in [4]; this subclass (denoted $D_{m,m-1}$ in [4]) consists of all the distributions P in $\mathbb{R}^m$ whose ch.f.'s can be represented in the form (3) with special pseudo-polynomials

$$Q(t_1, t_2, \dots, t_m) = \sum_{j=1}^{m} Q_{j0}(t_1, \dots, t_{j-1}, t_{j+1}, \dots, t_m)$$

so that the ch.f.'s themselves are of the form

$$f(t_1 t_2, \dots, t_m) = \prod_{j=1}^{m} R_j(t_1, t_2, \dots, t_{j-1}, t_{j+1}, \dots, t_m), \quad |t| < \varepsilon. \tag{4}$$

The ch.f.'s of the infinitely divisible distributions belonging to $D_{m,m-1}$ are easily described in terms of the Levy spectral measures (see [4]).

3. Multivariate version of the Cramér theorem.

THEOREM 1. If the joint distribution P of the linear forms (1) belongs to the class EPP then the X_j 's corresponding to those j 's for which $a_{1j}\, a_{2j} \dots a_{mj} \neq 0$ are necessarily Gaussian.

For $m = 1$ Theorem 1 becomes the classical Cramér theorem, if one takes into account the Marcinkiewicz theorem. Hence, in the proof we may and shall assume $m \geqslant 2$.

PROOF OF THEOREM 1. Let us numerate the r.v.'s $X_1, X_2, \dots, X_N$ in such a way that for some n, $1 \leqslant n \leqslant N$,

$$\begin{gathered} a_{11}\, a_{21} \dots a_{m1} \neq 0, \dots, \quad a_{1n}\, a_{2n} \dots a_{mn} \neq 0, \\ a_{1,n+1}\, a_{2,n+1} \dots a_{m,n+1} = \dots = a_{1N}\, a_{2N} \dots a_{mN} = 0. \end{gathered} \tag{5}$$

The ch.f. of the r.vec. $(L_1, L_2, \dots, L_m)$ is

$$f(t) = f(t_1, t_2, \dots, t_m) = \prod_{j=1}^{N} f_j((a_j, t)), \quad t \in \mathbb{R}^m,$$

where $f_j(t) = E \exp itX_j$, $a_j = (a_{1j}, a_{2j}, \dots, a_{mj})$, $j = 1, 2, \dots, N$ and $(\cdot, \cdot)$ denotes the standard scalar product in $\mathbb{R}^m$.

By setting $\psi_j(t) = \log f_j(t), \quad |t| < \varepsilon, \quad \varepsilon > 0,$ sufficiently small one gets from the condition $P \in$ EPP:

$$\sum_{1}^{n} \psi_j((a_j, t)) + \sum_{n+1}^{N} \psi_j((a_j, t)) =$$

$$= \sum_{j=1}^{m} \sum_{l=0}^{k} t_j^{l} Q_{jl}(t_1, \dots, t_{j+1}, t_{j+1}, \dots, t_m). \tag{6}$$

Each addend of the second sum on the left hand side of (6) is degenerate in the same way as one of the functions

$$Q_{10}(t_2, t_3, \dots, t_m), \quad Q_{20}(t_1, t_3, \dots, t_m), \dots, \quad Q_{m0}(t_1, t_2, \dots, t_{m-1}).$$

That is why transferring the sum $\sum_{n+1}^{N}$ into the right hand side of (6) will result only in altering the functions $Q_{10}, Q_{20}, \dots, Q_{m0}$. We preserve the old notations for the new functions and turn to studying the principal functional equation:

$$\sum_{1}^{n} \psi_j((a_j, t)) = \sum_{j=1}^{m} \sum_{l=0}^{k} t_j^{l} Q_{jl}(t_1, \dots, t_{j-1}, t_{j+1}, \dots, t_m), \quad |t| < \varepsilon. \tag{7}$$

LEMMA 1. Let $a_1, a_2, \dots, a_n$ be pairwise non-colinear vectors in $\mathbb{R}^m$. Then continuous solutions $\psi_1, \dots, \psi_n$ of (7) are necessarily polynomials of degree $\leq n + (k+1)m - 2$ in a neighbourhood of zero.

PROOF OF LEMMA 1. Acting in the same way as in the proof of Lemma 1 in [4] let us take a vector $v^{(1)} \in \mathbb{R}^m$ orthogonal to a_n but not to any of the vectors $a_1, \dots a_{n-1}$. Assuming $|v^{(1)}|$ sufficiently small let us replace in (7) t with $t + v^{(1)}$ and then subtract from the resulting equation the original one. On replacing t with $t + v^{(1)}$ the general structure of the right hand side of (7) remains; only the functions Q_{jl} will change. However, what is important is the property of independence of Q_{jl} of the argument t_j which obviously survives.

Thus, one comes to

$$\sum_{1}^{n-1} \psi_j^{(1)}((a_j,t)) = \sum_{j=1}^{m} \sum_{l=0}^{k} t_j^l Q_{jl}(t_1,\ldots,t_{j-1},t_{j+1},\ldots,t_m), \quad |t|<\varepsilon,$$

where

$$\psi_j^{(1)}(u) = \psi_j(u+(a_j,v^{(1)})) - \psi_j(u)$$

and $Q_{jl}^{(1)}$, $j=1,2,\ldots,m;\ l=0,1,\ldots,k$ are continuous functions.

On eliminating in the same way the function $\psi_{n-1}^{(1)}$, then $\psi_{n-2}^{(2)}$ and so on, one comes after $(n-1)$ steps to the equation

$$\psi_1^{(n-1)}((a_1,t)) = \sum_{j=1}^{m} \sum_{l=0}^{k} t_j^l Q_{jl}^{(n-1)}(t_1,\ldots,t_{j-1},t_{j+1},\ldots,t_m), \quad |t|<\varepsilon, \tag{8}$$

where

$$\psi_1^{(n-1)}(u) = \psi_1^{(n-2)}(u+(a_1,v^{(n-1)})) - \psi_1^{(n-2)}(u)$$

and the vector $v^{(n-1)}$ is non-orthogonal to a_1.

LEMMA 2. Is a continuous function $\psi(t)$ satisfies for $|t|<\varepsilon$, $\varepsilon>0$ the equation

$$\psi(a_1t_1+a_2t_2+\ldots+a_mt_m) = \sum_{j=1}^{m} \sum_{l=0}^{k} t_j^l Q_{jl}(t_1,\ldots,t_{j-1},t_{j+1},\ldots,t_m) \tag{9}$$

where $a_1 a_2 \ldots a_m \neq 0$ and $Q_{jl}(u_1,\ldots,u_{m-1})$, $j=1,2,\ldots,m;$ $l=0,1,\ldots,k$ are arbitrary functions then $\psi(t)$ is a polynomial of degree $\leq (k+1)m-1$ in a neighbourhood of zero.

PROOF OF LEMMA 2. First replace in (9) t_1 with $t_1+a_1^{-1}h$, $|h|$

being sufficiently small, and subtract from the obtained equation the initial one. We get

$$\psi^{(1)}(a_1t + a_2t_2+\dots+a_mt_m) =$$
$$=\sum_{\ell=0}^{k-1} t_1^{\ell} Q_{1\ell}^{(1)}(t_2,\dots,t_m) + \sum_{j=2}^{m}\sum_{\ell=0}^{k} t_j^{\ell} Q_{j\ell}^{(1)}(t_1,\dots,t_{j-1},t_{j+1},\dots,t_m)$$

for some $Q_{j\ell}^{(1)}$. Acting in the same way $(k-1)$ times more and then passing, in turn, to the arguments $t_2,\dots,t_m$ we obtain after mk steps the following equation for the mk-th difference of the function $\psi(t)$:

$$\psi^{(mk)}(a_1t_1+a_2t_2+\dots+a_mt_m) =$$

$$= \sum_{j=1}^{m} q_j(t_1,\dots,t_{j-1}, t_{j+1},\dots,t_m), \quad |t|<\varepsilon. \tag{10}$$

The equation (10) is easily investigated (see [4]); its solution $\psi^{(mk)}(t)$ is necessarily a polynomial of degree $\leqslant m-1$ for $|t|<\varepsilon$, $\varepsilon>0$ sufficiently small. Hence, $\psi(t)$ is a polynomial of degree $\leqslant(k+1)m-1$ for $|t|<\varepsilon$. Lemma 2 is proved.

Returning now to the proof of Lemma 1 we conclude that $\psi_j(n)$, $j=1,2,\dots,n$ are polynomials of degree $\leqslant(k+1)m-1+(n-1)=n+(k+1)m-2$.

To complete the proof of Theorem 1 we first obtain from (7) by virtue of Lemma 1 (under the additional condition of pairwise non-colinearity of $a_1,a_2,\dots,a_n$) that

$$f_j(t)=\exp P_j(t), \quad |t|<\varepsilon, \quad j=1,2,\dots,n,$$

P_j being polynomials of degree $\leqslant n+(k+1)m-2$. It follows immediately from the Marcinkiewicz theorem that the r.v.'s $X_1,X_2,\dots,X_n$ are Gaussian.

In the general case we divide all the vectors $a_1, a_2, \dots, a_n$ into $(q+1)$ groups in such a way that within each group the vectors are colinear to each other but the vectors from different groups are not. We may always assume that the groups are

$$(a_1, a_2, \dots, a_{i_1}), (a_{i_1+1}, \dots, a_{i_2}), \dots, (a_{i_q+1}, \dots, a_n).$$

By virtue of what is said above all the sums

$$X_1 + \dots + X_{i_1}, \quad X_{i_1+1} + \dots + X_{i_2}, \dots, X_{i_q+1} + \dots + X_n$$

are Gaussian. From the (classical) Cramér theorem one concludes that all the r.v.'s $X_1, X_2, \dots, X_n$ are also Gaussian. Theorem 1 is proved.

4. A refinement of the main result.

Let $r_2 \geqslant 1, \dots, r_m \geqslant 1$ be integers, $r_2 + \dots + r_m = r$. Assume that

$$E|X_j|^{2r} < \infty \qquad j = 1, 2, \dots, N. \tag{11}$$

Then the ch.f. of the joint distribution P of the linear forms (1) has the following derivative of the order $2r$:

$$\frac{\partial^{2r} \log f(t_1, t_2, \dots, t_m)}{\partial t_2^{2r_2} \dots \partial t_m^{2r_m}}.$$

THEOREM 2. If the r.v.'s $X_1, X_2, \dots, X_N$ satisfy the condition (11) and the distribution P is such that

$$\left. \frac{\partial^{2r} \log f(t_1, t_2, \dots, t_m)}{\partial t_2^{2r_2} \dots \partial t_m^{2r_m}} \right|_{\substack{t_2 = 0 \\ \dots \\ t_m = 0}} = Q(t_1), \quad |t_j| < \varepsilon, \tag{12}$$

for some $\varepsilon > 0$, Q being a polynomial, then the r.v.'s X_j corresponding to those j 's for which $a_{1j} a_{2j} \dots a_{mj} \neq 0$ are Gaussian.

Theorem 2 is proved exactly in the same way as Theorem 3 in [4] .

Let now $P \in$ EPP and

$$Q_{jl} \equiv 0 \qquad \text{for} \quad l \geqslant 2r_j, \quad j = 2, \dots, m.$$

Assume that there exist the derivatives

$$\frac{\partial^{2r} Q_{jl}}{\partial t_2^{2r_2} \dots \partial t_m^{2r_m}}, \quad j = 1, 2, \dots, m; \ l = 0, 1, \dots, k$$

for $t_2 = 0, \dots, t_m = 0$. Then the ch.f. $f(t_1, t_2, \dots, t_m)$ of the distribution P satisfies the condition (12).

Thus, within the class of sufficiently smooth ch.f.'s Theorem 2 is stronger than Theorem 1; however, the latter imposes no apriori conditions on the ch.f.

The claim of Theorem 2 remains true if on the right hand side of (12) one replaces the polynomial Q with an entire function of the exponential type (cf. [5] , Theorem 2).

Leningrad Branch of

Steklov Mathematical Institute

191011, USSR, Leningrad, Fontanka 27

REFERENCES

1. Cramér H. Über eine Eigenschaft der normalen Verteilungsfunction.- Math.Z., 1936, B.41, N 2, 405-414.
2. Marcinkiewicz J. Sur une propriété de la loi de Gauss.- Math.Z., 1938, B.44, 632-638.

3. Linnik Yu.V., Ostrowskii I.V. Decomposition of random variables and vectors (in Russian).M., Nauka, 1972, 480 p.

4. Kagan A.M. New classes of dependent random variables and a generalization of the Darmois-Skitovitch theorem to the case of several forms (in Russian).- Teor. Veroyatn. Primen., 1988, 33, N 2.

5. Kagan A.M. A class of two-dimensional distributions arising in connection with the Cramer and Darmois-Skitovitch theorems (in Russian).- Teor. Veroyatn Primen., 1987, 32, N 2, 349-351.

A REFINEMENT OF LUKACS THEOREMS

F.M.Kagan

1. Let $x_1, x_2, \ldots, x_n,\ n \geq 2$ be an independent sample from the population with a distribution function (d.f.) $F(x)$, and

$$\bar{x} = \frac{1}{n}\sum_{1}^{n} x_i, \quad s^2 = \frac{1}{n}\sum_{1}^{n}(x_i - \bar{x})^2.$$

In 1942 Lukacs [1] proved that if

$$\int x^2 dF < \infty \tag{1}$$

then the relation

$$E(s^2 | \bar{x}) = \text{const} \tag{2}$$

is characteristic for the Gaussian d.f. $F(x)$. In [2] he proved that under the same condition (1) the relation

$$E(s^2 | \bar{x}) = c_0 + c_1\bar{x}, \qquad c_1 \neq 0 \tag{3}$$

holds iff $F(x)$ belongs to the family of Poissonian d.f.'s with shifts, i.e.

$$P\{x_i = a + kb\} = \frac{\lambda^k}{k!}e^{-\lambda}, \quad k = 0, 1, 2, \ldots .$$

The parameters a and b are determined by the constants c_0, c_1; $\lambda > 0$ plays the role of the parameter of the family.

Another theorem also due to Lukacs [3] developing the well known Marcinkiewicz theorem [4], combined with the idea of [5] allows us to refine the results of [1, 2].

2. Introduce the characteristic functions (ch.f.'s)

$$f(t) = \mathrm{E} \exp it x_1, \quad \varphi(t,\tau) = \mathrm{E} \exp i(nt\bar{x} + n\tau s^2), \quad t \in \mathbb{R}^1, \ \tau \in \mathbb{R}^1$$

and let ℓ be a vector in $\mathbb{R}^2$.

THEOREM. The relation

$$\frac{d}{d\ell} \log \varphi(t,\tau)\Big|_{\tau=0} = Q(t), \qquad |t| < \varepsilon \tag{4}$$

where $\varepsilon > 0$ and Q is a polynomial holds iff $F(x)$ is the convolution (may be degenerate) of a Gaussian and a Poissonian distributions.

Before proving the theorem note that the condition (4) is more general than (2) and (3) so that the theorem refined the results of [1, 2].

In fact, let $\varphi(t,\tau)$ be the ch.f. of a random vector (ξ, η) with $\mathrm{E}|\eta| < \infty$. Suppose that

$$\mathrm{E}(\eta \mid \xi) = c_0 + c_1 \xi \tag{5}$$

for some c_0, c_1. Multiplying both parts of (5) by $\exp it\xi$ and taking the mathematical expeclations gives

$$-i \frac{\partial \varphi(t,\tau)}{\partial \tau}\Big|_{\tau=0} = c_0 \varphi(t,0) - c_1 i \frac{\partial \varphi(t,\tau)}{\partial t}\Big|_{\tau=0},$$

whence

$$\frac{\partial \log \varphi(t,\tau)}{\partial \tau}\Big|_{\tau=0} - c_1 \frac{\partial \log \varphi(t,\tau)}{\partial t}\Big|_{\tau=0} = c_0 i \tag{6}$$

for $|t| < \varepsilon$ where $\varepsilon > 0$ is such that $\varphi(t,\tau) \neq 0$ for $|t| < \varepsilon, |\tau| < \varepsilon$.

If now to take the vector ℓ with the components $\left(\frac{1}{\sqrt{1+c_1^2}}, \frac{-c_1}{\sqrt{1+c_1^2}}\right)$ then (6) becomes (4) with $Q(t) = \mathrm{const}$.

3. Turning to the proof of the theorem we note first of all that

$$\frac{\partial\varphi(t,0)}{\partial t} = (f^n(t))' = n f^{n-1}(t) f'(t), \tag{7}$$

$$\frac{\partial\varphi(t,0)}{\partial\tau} = i\,E\{\sum_1^n (x_k - \bar{x})^2 \exp it \sum_1^n x_k\} =$$

$$= i\,E\{(\sum_1^n x_k^2 - n\bar{x}^2) \exp it \sum_1^n x_k\} =$$

$$= i\{-n f''(t) f^{n-1}(t) + \frac{1}{n}(f^n(t))''\} =$$

$$= i\{-n f''(t) f^{n-1}(t) + (n-1) f^{n-2}(t)[f'(t)]^2 + f''(t) f^{n-1}(t)\} =$$

$$= (1-n) i \{f''(t) f^{n-1}(t) - [f'(t)]^2 f^{n-2}(t)\}. \tag{8}$$

If the vector ℓ has components γ_1, γ_2 then on taking into account (7) and (8) one immediately gets from (4)

$$\gamma_1 n f'(t) f^{n-1}(t) + \gamma_2 (1-n) i \{f''(t) f^{n-1}(t) - [f'(t)]^2 f^{n-2}(t)\} =$$

$$= f^n(t) Q(t), \qquad |t| < \varepsilon. \tag{9}$$

From (9) it follows that for an $\varepsilon_1 > 0$

$$A g''(t) + B g'(t) = Q(t), \qquad |t| < \varepsilon_1, \tag{10}$$

where $g(t) = \log f(t)$, $A = \gamma_2 (1-n) i$, $B = \gamma_1 n$.

If $AB = 0$ then $f(t) = \exp Q_1(t)$, Q_1 being a polynomial, so that according to the Marcinkiewicz theorem $f(t)$ is the ch.f. of a Gaussian distribution.

Let now $AB \neq 0$. The general solution of (10) is of the form

$$g(t) = -\frac{A}{B} \exp(-\frac{A}{B} t) + Q_2(t),$$

Q_2 being a polynomial. Since $f(t)$ is a ch.f. one gets

$$f(t) = \exp\{\lambda(e^{i\Delta t} - 1) + Q_3(t)\} \tag{11}$$

where $\lambda > 0$, Δ is real and Q_3 is a polynomial.

From a result due to Luckacs [3] (see also [6 , Theorem 7.35]; for stronger results see [7, 8]) one concludes from (11) that the degree of Q_3 is $\leqslant 2$ so that $f(t)$ is the ch.f. of the convolution of a Gaussian and a Poissonian distributions.

Straightforward calculations show that if $f(t)$ is of the form (11) then the ch.f. $\varphi(t, \tau)$ satisfies the relation (4). The theorem is proved.

Dept. of Applied Mathematics and Mechanics, Tashkent University
Tashkent, Vuzgorodok 4
USSR

REFERENCES

1. Lukacs E. A characterization of the normal distribution. Ann.Math. Stat., 1942, 32, N 1, 91-93.
2. Lukacs E. Characterization problems for discrete distributions.- In: Proc.Internat. Symp. on Classical and Contagions Distributions, Montreal, 1963, 65-74.
3. Lukacs E. Some extensions of a theorem of Marcinkiewicz. Pac.J. Math., 1959, 8, N 3, 487-501.
4. Marzinliewicz J. Sur une propriété de la loi de Gauss. Math.Z., 1938, B.44, 612-618.
5. Kagan A.M. A class of two-dimensional distributions arising in the connection with the Darmois-Skitocitch and Cramér theorems (in Russian). Teor. Veroyatn. Primen., 1987, 32, N 2, 349-351.
6. Lukacs E. Characteristic functions (2nd ed.) Griffin, London, 1970.

7. Ostrowskii I.V. On entire functions satisfying certain special ineqialities connected with the theory of characteristic functions of probability distributions (in Russian). Uch.Zap. Mat.-Mech. Facult. i Kharkov. Mat. Obshchestva, 1963, 29, 145-168.

8. Zimoglyad V.V. On a class of functions with the "ridge" property. (in Russian). Tr.Phys.-Tech. Inst. Nizkich Temperatur Akad. Nauk Ukr. SSR, 1969, 1, 172-190.

ON THE CONNECTION OF RENYI'S THEOREM AND RENEWAL THEORY

V.V.Kalashnikov, S.Yu.Vsekhsvyatskii

1. Introduction

Let $\{X_i\}_{i\geq 1}$ be a sequence of nonnegative independent identically distributed random variables (i.i.d.r.v.'s), $EX_1 = 1$, $F(x) = Pr(X_1 \leq x)$. Let ν - be a geometrically distributed r.v., independent from $\{X_i\}$, $Pr(\nu = k) = q(1-q)^{k-1}$, $0<q<1$, $k > 1$. It is well known (Renyi' theorem) that r.v. $S(q) = \sum_{i=1}^{\nu} X_i$ converges to the exponentially distributed r.v. U, $Pr(U \leq x) = 1 - e^{-x}$. Convergence takes place both in case $X_i \xrightarrow{d} U$ and $q \to 0$ ($\xrightarrow{d}$ means convergence in distribution).

In Kalashnikov, Vsekhsvyatskii [2] estimates of the following form were derived:

$$d(S(q), U) \leq \varepsilon(q) B(F), \tag{1.1}$$

where $\varepsilon(q) \to 0$, $B(F)$ - a functional having distribution function (d.f.) $F(x)$ as an argument, d - a probabilistic metric. Main attention in our paper [2] was paid to the case $d = \zeta_1$, $(\zeta_1(X,Y) = \int_0^\infty |Pr(X \leq x) - Pr(Y \leq x)| \, dx$ - mean metric), and $d = \rho$, $(\rho(X,Y) = \sup_x |Pr(X \leq x) - Pr(Y \leq x)|$ - uniform metric). In the first case $B(F) \to 0$ when $X_1 \xrightarrow{d} U$ and the right hand of the estimate (1.1) has correct order of convergence to 0. In the case of uniform metric such property of the estimate (1.1) was obtained only under conditions of appropriate smoothness of d.f. $F(x)$. In general case function $\varepsilon(q)$ had correct order of convergence but $B(F)$ was limited below by some positive constant. In section 5 of this paper we present an estimate in uniform metric where $\varepsilon(q)\underset{q\to 0}{\longrightarrow} 0$, $B(F)\to 0$ when $X_1 \xrightarrow{d} U$.

The main purpose of this paper is to obtain nonuniform estimates of the following form

$$\varepsilon_1(q,x) \le \Pr(S(q)>x) \le \varepsilon_2(q,x), \tag{1.2}$$

where $\varepsilon_i(q,x)\underset{x\to\infty}{\longrightarrow} 0$, $i=1,2$ and $\varepsilon_1(q,x)-\varepsilon_2(q,x)\to 0$ when $q\to 0$. Such estimates are presented in sections 2 and 3 as well as some uniform estimates. In section 4 we present uniform and nonuniform estimates of renewal functions. These estimates are interesting and important by themselves and they also can be used in inequalities in sections 2 and 3.

We would like to mention very interesting application of presented theory. If we consider the first occurence time in the regenerative process then its distribution will be very much alike the distribution of r.v. $S(q)$ and we can use all obtained estimates in this case. It is really important because such scheme arises in many models in queueing, realibility theory and so on. For more information see [2].

2. Lower estimate $\varepsilon_1(q,x)$.

Let $S_0=0$, $S_n=X_1+\ldots+X_n$, $n\ge 1$ - be a renewal process generated by a sequence $\{X_i\}_{i\ge 1}$; $N(x)=\sup\{n: S_n\le x\}$ - number of renewal epochs on $[0,x]$; $H(x)=EN(x)$ - renewal function; $\delta_H(x)=H(x)-x$. Let us denote $q'=-\ln(1-q)$, $m_s=EX_1^s$, $s>1$. We can obtain the following representation of the distribution function to be estimated just from the definition of the variable $S(q)$

$$\Pr(S(q)>x) = Ee^{-q'N(x/q)}. \tag{2.1}$$

A lower estimate is implied easily by Jensen's inequality:

$$Ee^{-q'N(x/q)} \ge \exp\{-q'H(x/q)\} = \exp\{-q'\delta_H(x/q) - xq'/q\}. \tag{2.2}$$

So we can choose the following quantity as $\varepsilon_1(q, x)$

$$\varepsilon_1(q, x) = \exp\{-q'\delta_H(x/q) - q'x/q\}, \tag{2.3}$$

where we can use different estimates of $\delta_H(x)$. For example, if $\delta_H = \sup_x |H(x) - x|$ then the following inequalities are valid

$$\delta_H \leqslant m_2, \tag{2.4}$$

$$\delta_H(x) \leqslant 2/m_0 [1 + x^{2-s} m_s/2], \quad 1 < s \leqslant 2, \tag{2.5}$$

where m_0 is median of d.f. $F(x)$. The above relations do not demand any information about $F(x)$ except existence of m_2 or m_s. We can also use some particular estimates if we have additional information about d.f. $F(x)$. For example, if F is an aging distribution then $\delta_H \leqslant 0$. We present several new estimates of $\delta_H(x)$ and δ_H in the section 5.

3. Upper estimates $\varepsilon_2(q, x)$.

In order to obtain $\varepsilon_2(q, x)$ we need the following notations. Let $\{\tilde{X}_i\}$ be an auxiliary sequence of i.i.d.r.v.'s and $\tilde{F}(x) = \Pr(\tilde{X}_1 \leqslant x) \geqslant F(x)$. We shall use all notation introduced for sequence $\{X_i\}$ for $\{\tilde{X}_i\}$ too but with tilde. Additional restrictions on d.f. $\tilde{F}(x)$ will be imposed when needed. If we can find estimates

$$\varepsilon'(q, x) \geqslant \Pr(S(q) > x) - \Pr(\tilde{S}(q) > x) \tag{3.1}$$

and

$$\varepsilon''(q, x) \geqslant \Pr(\tilde{S}(q) > x), \tag{3.2}$$

then we can choose

$$\varepsilon_2(q,x) = \varepsilon'(q,x) + \varepsilon''(q,x). \tag{3.3}$$

THEOREM 3.1. Let there exists a number $p>0$ such that

$$(1-q)\,\mathbb{E}\exp(p\tilde{X}_1) \leqslant 1. \tag{3.4}$$

Then the following estimate is valid:

$$\Pr(\tilde{S}(q) > x) \leqslant \varepsilon''(q,x) = (1-q)^{-1}\exp(-px/q). \tag{3.5}$$

PROOF. Let us consider two-dimensional Markov process $\{\xi_n\}$ where $\xi_n = (\tilde{S}_n, n)$ is the state of this process at the time n . Let $\mathbb{A}$ be the generating operator of $\{\xi_n\}$. If number $x>0$ is fixed then the quantity $\tau = \tilde{N}(x) + 1$ is stopping time for $\{\xi_n\}$. Let us introduce nonnegative trial function

$$V(\xi_n) = (1-q)^n \exp(p\tilde{S}_n).$$

From (3.4) we obtain

$$\mathbb{A}V(n,S_n) = (1-q)^n \exp(p\tilde{S}_n)\,[(1-q)\mathbb{E}\exp(p\tilde{X}_{n+1}) - 1] \leqslant 0.$$

So we have

$$\mathbb{E}\,V(\xi_n) = V(\xi_0) + \mathbb{E}\sum_{j<\tau}\mathbb{A}V(\xi_j) \leqslant V(\xi_0) = 1. \tag{3.6}$$

From the other hand,

$$\mathbb{E}V(\xi_n) = \mathbb{E}[(1-q)^{\tilde{N}(x)+1}\exp\{p(x+\gamma(x))\}] \geqslant$$

$$\geqslant (1-q)^{-1}\exp(px)\Pr(\tilde{S}(q) \geqslant qx), \tag{3.7}$$

where $\gamma(x) = \tilde{S}_{\tilde{N}(x)+1} - x$ is an excess of the renewal process $\{\tilde{S}_n\}$. From equations (3.6) and (3.7) we derive estimate (3.5).

We shall show further that one can choose $p = q + O(q)$. Using (3.5) it will give us the needed upper estimate. Let us consider several cases which lead to different ways of choosing p.

A. Let for some $\lambda > 0$ the relation $\mathbb{E}\exp(\lambda X_1) = m_\lambda < \infty$ holds. In this case we put $\tilde{F} = F$ and, respectively, $\varepsilon'(q, x) = 0$. For every $0 < q < 1$ there exists such quantity $p = p(q) > 0$, $p \leq \lambda$, that

$$\mathbb{E}\exp(pX_1) = (1-q)^{-1}. \tag{3.8}$$

Just this value of p we put into relation (3.5). We can estimate p easily in terms of moments of r.v. X_1. For this purpose let us denote $b(\lambda) = m_\lambda - 1 - \lambda - \frac{\lambda}{2} m_2 \geqslant 0$. Then

$$\mathbb{E}\exp(pX_1) \leqslant 1 + p + \frac{p^2}{2} m_2 + p^3 b(\lambda)/\lambda^3.$$

Let us choose $p = p_1$ as solution of equation

$$p + p^2 m_2/2 + p^3 b(\lambda)/\lambda^3 = q/(1-q) \tag{3.9}$$

For such a choice estimate (3.5) remains valid. Finally, if we consider $q < [\lambda^3/b(\lambda)]^{1/2}/\{1 + [\lambda^3/b(\lambda)]^{1/2}\}$ then equality (3.9) implies that

$$p_1 = a(q)[1 - \tfrac{1}{2} a(q) m_2], \tag{3.10}$$

where

$$a(q) = (1-q)^{-1}[1 - q^2(1-q)^{-2} b(\lambda)\lambda^{-3}]. \tag{3.11}$$

Hence, in this case

$$P_1 = q + q^2(1 - m_2/2) + o(q^2). \tag{3.12}$$

Here and further we shall use functions like $o(q^2)$ only to simplify formulaes. At the same time, we must stress that all obtained estimates (2.3) and (3.5) can be formulated without using such functions.

From inequalities (2.3), (3.5) and equality (3.12) we can obtain the following estimates of convergence rate:

(a) Uniform estimate

$$\Delta_1(q) = \sup_x (\varepsilon''(q,x) - \varepsilon_1(q,x)) \leq$$

$$\leq \begin{cases} \frac{1}{2} q (m_2 - 1) \exp(-x_0), & \text{if} \quad m_2 \geq 1 + 2(1 + \delta'_H), \\ (1-q)^{-1}(q'\delta_H + q), & \text{in other case,} \end{cases} \tag{3.13}$$

where

$$x_0 = 1 - 2(1 + \delta_H)(m_2 - 1)^{-1}. \tag{3.14}$$

(b) Nonuniform estimate

$$\Delta_1(q, x) = \varepsilon''(q, x) - \varepsilon_1(q, x) \leq$$

$$\leq \exp(-p_1 x/q) \{ (1-q)^{-1}(q'\delta_H + q) + [q(m_2 - 1)/2 + o(q)]\, x \}. \tag{3.15}$$

It is not natural in this situation to consider convergence of function $\Pr(S(q) > x)$ to e^{-x} when $q \to 0$. Instead of this we consider the difference between $\Pr(S(q) > x)$ and the function

$$a_1(q,x) = \frac{1}{2}(\varepsilon_1(q,x) + \varepsilon''(q,x)) = \frac{1}{2}\{\exp(-q'\delta_H(x/q))\times$$

$$\times \exp(-x q'/q) + (1-q)^{-1}\exp(-x p_1/q)\}, \tag{3.16}$$

which naturally converges to e^{-x} when $q \to 0$. It follows from (3.13) - (3.16) that

$$|Pr(S(q)>x) - a_1(q,x)| \leq \frac{1}{2}\Delta_1(q,x), \tag{3.17}$$

$$\sup_x |Pr(S(q)>x) - a_1(q,x)| \leq \frac{1}{2}\Delta_1(q). \tag{3.18}$$

We can consider function $a_1'(q,x) = \min(1, a_1(q,x))$ instead of $a_1(q,x)$ which is monotone nonincreasing and limited from above by number 1. For this function estimates (3.17) and (3.18) stay valid.

Using inequality $\delta_H \leq m_2$ we can obtain that

$$\sup_x |Pr(S(q)>x) - a_1(q,x)| \leq q(m_2+1)/2 + o(q). \tag{3.19}$$

B. Let for some $s>1$ there exists moment $m_s = EX_1^s < \infty$. Let us put

$$\tilde{F}(x) = \begin{cases} F(x), & x < a/q, \\ 1, & x > a/q, \end{cases} \tag{3.20}$$

in inequality (3.1) where the value $a \geq 1$ will be chosen later. We have

$$\varepsilon'(q,x) = Pr(S(q)>x) - Pr(\tilde{S}(q)>x) =$$

$$= q \sum_{n=1}^{\infty} (1-q)^{n-1} [\Pr(qX_1 + \ldots + qX_n > x) - \Pr(q\tilde{X}_1 + \ldots + q\tilde{X}_n > x)] =$$

$$= q \sum_{n=1}^{\infty} (1-q)^{n-1} [\Pr(qX_1 > x) - \Pr(q\tilde{X}_1 > x)] *$$

$$* \sum_{j=0}^{n-1} \Pr^{*j}(qX_1 \leqslant x) * \Pr^{*(n-1-j)}(q\tilde{X}_1 \leqslant x). \qquad (3.21)$$

Using (3.20) we obtain from (3.21) that

$$\varepsilon'(q, x) = 0, \quad \text{if} \quad x \leqslant a.$$

If $x > a$ then

$$\Pr(qX_1 > x) - \Pr(q\tilde{X}_1 > x) = \Pr(qX_1 > x) \leqslant q^s m_s x^{-s}$$

and

$$\sum_{j=0}^{n-1} \Pr^{*j}(qX_1 \leqslant x) * \Pr^{*(n-1-j)}(q\tilde{X}_1 \leqslant x) \leqslant n.$$

So we see that the following relation is valid

$$\varepsilon'(q, x) \leqslant \begin{cases} 0, & x \leqslant a, \\ q^{s-1} m^s a^{-s}, & x > a. \end{cases} \qquad (3.22)$$

To obtain nonuniform estimate $\varepsilon_1(q, x) \xrightarrow[x \to \infty]{} 0$ we use the following inequality (for proof see [4] (3.22)):

$$\varepsilon'(q, x) \leqslant e q^{s-1} m_s x^{-s} B_s(q, x), \qquad (3.23)$$

where

$$B_s(q,x) = [1-s(x-1)^{-1}\ln x - (1-q)[q+(e-1)(q/s)^s m_s] \times$$

$$\times [s(x-1)^{-1}\ln x + (s(x-1)^{-1}\ln x)^2 q^\alpha m_{\alpha+1}]]^{-2}, \qquad \alpha = \min(1, s-1).$$

Let us note that $B_s(q,x) \to 1$ when $q \to 0$ or $x \to \infty$.

Now we would like to estimate probability $Pr(\tilde{S}(q) > x)$ (see (3.2)) using theorem 3.1. If $1 < s \leqslant 2$ we have

$$\mathbb{E}\exp(p\tilde{X}_1) \leqslant 1 + p + \mathbb{E}(p^2\tilde{X}_1^2)\exp(ap/q)/2 \leqslant 1 + p +$$

$$+ p^2 a^{2-s} m_s \exp(ap/q) q^{s-2}/2. \tag{3.24}$$

It follows from inequalities (3.24) and (3.4) that we can choose

$$p = p_s = q(1-q)^{-1}[1 - a^{2-s} m^s q^{s-1} (2(1-q))^{-1} \exp(a(1-q))] \tag{3.25}$$

in relation (3.5). In other words, when $1 < s < 2$

$$p_s = q - a^{2-s} m_s q^s e^\alpha/2 + o(q^s), \tag{3.26}$$

and when $s = 2$

$$p_2 = q + q^2(1 - m_2 e^\alpha/2) + o(q^2). \tag{3.27}$$

So we have from (3.5), (3.26), (3.27) that

$$\varepsilon''(q,x) = \begin{cases} (1-q)^{-1}\exp\{[-1 + a^{2-s} m_s q^{s-1} e^\alpha/2 + o(q^{s-1})]x\}, \\ \\ (1-q)^{-1}\exp\{[-1 + q(1 - m_2 e^\alpha/2) + o(q)]x\}. \end{cases} \tag{3.28}$$

Nonuniform estimate in case $1 < s < 2$ has the following form:

$$\varepsilon_2(q,x) - \varepsilon_1(q,x) \leqslant q\exp(-x(1-q^{s-1}m_s e))\{1+\delta_H(x)+xm_2 e/$$

$$/2 + o(1)\} + q m_s x^{-s} B_s(q,x). \qquad (3.29)$$

In case $s = 2$

$$\varepsilon_2(q,x) - \varepsilon_1(q,x) \leqslant q\exp(-x(1-q(m_2 e - 1))\{1+\delta_H + xm_2 e/$$

$$/2 + o(1)\} + q m_2 x^{-2} B_2(q,x). \qquad (3.30)$$

Similarly, when $s > 2$, the following estimate is valid

$$\mathbb{E}\exp(p\tilde{X}_1) \leqslant 1 + p + p^2 m_2/2 + (p^3 m_3)\exp(ap/q)/6.$$

This estimate leads to possibility of the following choice of $p = p_s$:

$$p_s = q(1-q)^{-1}\{1 - q(1-q)^{-1}m_2/2 - q^2(1-q)^{-2}m_3\exp(\frac{q}{1-q})/6\} \qquad (3.31)$$

or

$$p_s = q + q^2(1 - m_2/2) + o(q^2). \qquad (3.32)$$

So, when $s > 2$

$$\varepsilon''(q,x) \leqslant (1-q)^{-1}\exp\{[-1 + q(m_2 - 1) + o(q)]x\}. \qquad (3.33)$$

We can obtain from (3.5), (3.22), (3.33) that when $s > 2$

$$\varepsilon_2(q,x) - \varepsilon_1(q,x) = \varepsilon'(q,x) + \varepsilon''(q,x) - \varepsilon_1(q,x) \leqslant$$

$$\leq \begin{cases} q e^{-x_0}(1+\delta_H + x_0 m_2/2) + o(q), & x \leq a, \\ q[m_2 a^{-2} + e^{-\alpha}(m_2 a/2 - 1 + \delta_H)] + o(q), & x > a, \end{cases} \tag{3.34}$$

where $x_0 = max[0, \frac{2}{m_2}(m_2/2 - \delta_H - 1)]$.

Putting in (3.34) $a = m_2$, we find that

$$\sup_x (\varepsilon_2(q,x) - \varepsilon_1(q,x)) \leq q \exp(-x_0)(1+\delta_H + x_0 m_2/2) + o(q). \tag{3.35}$$

In case $s = 2$ we can obtain the similar estimate putting $a = 1$

$$\sup_x (\varepsilon_2(q,x) - \varepsilon_1(q,x)) \leq q(e\exp(-x_0)(1+\delta_H) + m_2/2)) + o(q), \tag{3.36}$$

where $x_0 = max[0, 1 - \frac{2}{m_2 e}(\delta_H + 1)]$.

And finally, if $a_2(q,x) = [\varepsilon_2(q,x) + \varepsilon_1(q,x)]/2$ then

$$\sup_x |P_r(S(q) > x) - a_2(q,x)| \leq q(1+\delta_H)/2 \leq q(1+m_2)/2. \tag{3.37}$$

Nonuniform estimate in case $s > 2$ have the following form:

$$\varepsilon_2(q,x) - \varepsilon_1(q,x) \leq q \exp(-x(1-q(m_2/2-1))\{1+\delta_H + x m_2 e/$$
$$/2 + o(1)\} + q m_s x^{-s} B_s(q,x). \tag{3.38}$$

4. Estimates in renewal theory

We shall denote $f(x)$ a density of d.f. $F(x)$ if such exists. Let us denote also $\tilde{F}(x) = \int_0^x [1-F(t)]\,dt$, $\tilde{f}(t) = 1 - F(t)$,

$$h(x) = \sum_{k>0} f^{*k}(x).$$

In this section we shall obtain different estimates of renewal function $H(x)$ and renewal density $h(x)$.

THEOREM 4.1. The following two-sided estimates are valid:

$$\rho(F, \tilde{F}) \leqslant \sup_x |h(x) - 1| \leqslant (\sigma(F, \tilde{F})/2 + \sup_x |f(x) - \tilde{f}(x)|)(1 - \sigma(F, \tilde{F})/2)^{-1}, \tag{4.1}$$

$$\varkappa_1(F, \tilde{F}) \leqslant \int_0^\infty |d(H(x) - x)| \leqslant (\varkappa_1(F, \tilde{F}) + 2\rho(F, \tilde{F}))(1 - \sigma(F, \tilde{F}))^{-1}, \tag{4.2}$$

$$\sup_x \int_0^x [F(t) - \tilde{F}(t)]\,dt \leqslant \sup_x |H(x) - x| \leqslant \frac{1}{2}[EX^2 \sigma(F, \tilde{F}) + \varkappa_1(F, \tilde{F})] \tag{4.3}$$

where $\sigma(F, G) = \int_0^\infty d\,|F(x) - G(x)|$.

THEOREM 4.2. If $\rho(F, \tilde{F}) \leq \varepsilon$ and $EX^{2+\tau} < \infty$ for some $\tau > 0$ then

$$\sup_x |H(x) - x| \leqslant 2\varepsilon + \varepsilon^{\tau/(1+\tau)} [EX^{2+\tau}]^{1/(1+\tau)} [2 + (T-1)^{-1} \times (2+\tau)^{-1}] (1+\tau)^{-1} (H(1) + 1), \tag{4.4}$$

where $T = \varepsilon^{-\tau/(1+\tau)} (EX^{2+\tau})^{1/(1+\tau)} + 1$.

PROOF OF THE THEOREM 4.1. We shall choose for the proof upper estimate (4.1) and lower estimate (4.3) because all upper and all lower estimates in telations (4.1) - (4.3) are proved similarly. The upper estimate (4.1) has sense only if density $f(x)$ is bounded. But in this case renewal density is bounded on every compact set. Using this fact, we can obtain:

$$\sup_x |h(x)-1| = \sup_x |(f(x)-\tilde{f}(x)) \times [1+H(x)]| \leq \sup_x |f(x)-\tilde{f}(x)|$$

$$+ \sup_x \left|\int_0^x [f(x-u)-\tilde{f}(x-u)] h(u)\, du\right| \leq \sup_x |f(x)-\tilde{f}(x)| + \sup_x \sup_{0\leq u\leq x} h(u) \times$$

$$\times\, \sigma(F,\tilde{F})/2 \leq \sup_x |f(x)-\tilde{f}(x)| + \sup_x |h(x)-1| \times \sigma(F,\tilde{F})/2 + \sigma(F,\tilde{F})/2 .$$

The proof of the validness of upper estimate (4.1) is completed.

To prove lower estimate in (4.3) it is sufficient to note that

$$\sup_x |H(x)-x| = \sup_x \left|\sum_{n=1}^{\infty} F^{*n}(x) - x\right| \geq \sup_x \left|\tilde{F} * \sum_{n=1}^{\infty} F^{*n}(x) - \tilde{F} * x\right| =$$

$$= \sup_x |x - \tilde{F}(x) - \tilde{F} * x| = \sup_x \left|\int_0^x [F(t)-\tilde{F}(t)]\, dt\right|.$$

PROOF OF THE THEOREM 4.2. At first let us note that

$$\sup_x |H(x)-x| \leq \rho(F,\tilde{F}) + \sup_x \int_0^x |F(x-y)-\tilde{F}(x-y)|\, dH(y). \tag{4.5}$$

Now we divide interval $[0,\infty)$, onto semiintervals $[1,2), \ldots, [n, n+1), \ldots$ and denote the k -th semiinterval as I_k . Let $M_k = \sup\{|F(x) - \tilde{F}(x)| :\ x \in I_k\}$ and $x_k^* \in [k-1, k]$ be such a point that

$$M_k = \lim_{x \to x_k^*,\ x \in I_k} |F(x) - \tilde{F}(x)|.$$

Let us construct two piece-wise constant functions $F'(t)$ and $\tilde{F}'(t)$ such that

$$F'(t) = \lim_{x \to x_k^*,\ x \in I_k} F(x) \quad ,\text{if} \quad t \in I_k, \quad k = 1, 2, \ldots,$$

$$\tilde{F}'(t) = \lim_{x \to x_k^*,\ x \in I_k} \tilde{F}(x) \quad ,\text{if} \quad t \in I_k, \quad k = 1, 2, \ldots$$

and estimate integral in the right hand side of inequality (4.5) by upper integral sum

$$\sup_x | H(x) - x | \leqslant \rho(F, \tilde{F}) + \sum_{x > k} \mathcal{M}_{[x]-k}[H(k+1) - H(k)] \leqslant$$

$$\leqslant \rho(F, \tilde{F}) + [H(1) + 1] \sup_x \sum_{x > k} \mathcal{M}_{[x]-k} \leqslant \rho(F, \tilde{F}) +$$

$$+ [H(1) + 1] \sum_{k \geqslant 0} \mathcal{M}_k = \rho(F, \tilde{F}) + [H(1) + 1] \varkappa_1(F', \tilde{F}'). \tag{4.6}$$

It is easy to see that for any $T \geqslant 1$

$$\varkappa_1(F', \tilde{F}') \leqslant T\rho(F, \tilde{F}) + \int_{T-1}^{\infty} [1 - F(x)]dx + \int_{T-1}^{\infty} [1 - \tilde{F}(x)]\, dx.$$

Using Chebyshev's inequality, we obtain

$$\varkappa_1(F', \tilde{F}') \leqslant T\rho(F, F') + (EX^{2+\tau})(T-1)^{-(1+\tau)}(1+\tau)^{-1} +$$

$$+ (EX^{2+\tau})(T-1)^{-\tau}(1+\tau)^{-1}(2+\tau)^{-1}.$$

We obtain estimate (4.4) by putting $T = 1 + [EX^{2+\tau}]^{1/(1+\tau)} \varepsilon^{1/(1+\tau)}$ in previous inequality; that completes the proof of theorem 4.2.

Now we turn to nonuniform estimates of renewal functions.

THEOREM 4.3. The following estimates are valid:

$$\sup_x |h(x)-1|\, x^{r} \leqslant (1-\sigma(F,\tilde F))^{-2}\, [\nu_r(F,\tilde F)\, [\rho(F,\tilde F) +$$

$$+ \sup_x |f(x)-\tilde f(x)|] + (1-\sigma(F,\tilde F))\, [\rho_r(F,\tilde F) +$$

$$+ \sup_x |x^{r}(f(x)-\tilde f(x))|]] \equiv \varepsilon_h^{r}(F,\tilde F), \tag{4.7}$$

$$\sup_x |H(x)-x-K|\, x^{r} \leqslant (1-\sigma(F,\tilde F))^{-1}\, [\, \sup_x |x^{r} \int_x^{\infty} [F(y)-$$

$$-\tilde F(y)]dy| + \nu_r(F,\tilde F)\, [3EX^{2}/2+1] + \rho_r(F,\tilde F)\times$$

$$\times [EX^{2}+2]] \equiv \varepsilon_H^{r}(F,\tilde F), \tag{4.8}$$

where $0<\alpha\leqslant 1$, $K=EX^{2}/2-1$, $\rho_r(F,G) = \sup_x |x^{r}[F(x) - G(x)]|$, $\nu_r(F,G) = \int_0^{\infty} x^{r} |d[F(x)-G(x)]|$.

COROLLARY. The following estimates of the rates of convergence are valid:

$$|h(x)-1| \leqslant \varepsilon_h^{r}(F,\tilde F)\, x^{-r}, \tag{4.9}$$

$$|H(x)-x-K| \leqslant \varepsilon_H^{r}(F,\tilde F)\, x^{-r}. \tag{4.10}$$

Turn to the problem of the order of convergence rate. The value of $\varepsilon_h^{r}(F,\tilde F)$ is limited if $EX^{1+r}<\infty$. If so, we see from (4.7) that $h(x)\to 1$ with convergence rate x^{-r}. Similarly, $H(x)$ converges to $x+K$ if $\varepsilon_h^{r}(F,\tilde F)$ is bounded and it happens only if $EX^{2+r}<\infty$.

In this case the rate of convergence is also x^{-r}. It is easy to see that this orders are correct.

PROOF OF THE THEOREM 4.3. Estimate (4.7) can be obtained as follows

$$\sup_x |h(x)-1|x^r \leq \sup_x |x^r(f(x)-\tilde{f}(x))| + \sup_x |x^r(F(x)-\tilde{F}(x))| +$$

$$+ \sup_x |x^r \int_0^x [f(x-y)-\tilde{f}(x-y)][h(y)-1]dy| \leq \sup_x |x^r(f(x)-\tilde{f}(x))| +$$

$$+ \rho_r(F,\tilde{F}) + \sigma(F,\tilde{F}) \sup_x x^r|h(x)-1| + \sup_x |h(x)-1| \times$$

$$\times \sup_x |\int_0^x [f(x-y)-\tilde{f}(x-y)](x^r-y^r)dy| \leq \sup_x |x^r(f(x)-\tilde{f}(x))| +$$

$$+ \rho_r(F,\tilde{F}) + \sigma(F,\tilde{F}) \sup_x x^r|h(x)-1| + \vartheta_r(F,\tilde{F}) \sup_x |h(x)-1|.$$

We complete the proof if we put upper estimate (4.1) in the last item.

When prooving the estimate (4.8) we shall use inequality $\sup_x |H(x)-x| \leq EX^2$ [3] (although there can be used any of the estimates (4.3), (4.4)):

$$\sup_x |H(x)-x-K|x^r = \sup_x |[F(x)-\tilde{F}(x)] * [H(x)+1] - K|x^r \leq$$

$$\leq \sup_x |[F(x)-\tilde{F}(x)]|x^r + \sup_x |x^r \int_0^\infty [F(x-y)-\tilde{F}(x-y)]d[H(y)-y]| +$$

$$+ \sup_x |x^r [\int_0^x [F(x-y)-\tilde{F}(x-y)]dy - K]| \leq \rho_r(F,\tilde{F}) + \sup_x |x^r [\int_x^\infty [F(y)-\tilde{F}(y)]dy +$$

$$+|K| \rho_r(F,\tilde{F}) + \sup_x |\int_0^x (x^r-y^r)[H(x-y)-(x-y)-K]d[F(y)-\tilde{F}(y)]| +$$

$$+ \sup_x \left| \int_0^x y^r [H(x-y)-(x-y)-K] d[F(y)-\tilde{F}(y)] \right| \leq [EX^2/2+2]\, \varrho_r(F,\tilde{F}) +$$

$$+ \sup_x \left| x^r \int_0^x [F(y)-\tilde{F}(y)]\, dy \right| + [3EX^2/2+1]\, \nu_r(F,\tilde{F}) +$$

$$+ \sup_x x^r |H(x)-x-K| \times \sigma(F,\tilde{F}).$$

We obtain estimate (4.8) by transferring the last item to the left hand side. So the proof of the theorem 4.3 is completed.

5. Estimates of convergence of $S(q)$ in terms of uniform metric

THEOREM 5.1. If r.v. $S(q)$ has density function limited by number $\bar{p}$ then for $1<s\leq 2$ the following estimate is valid:

$$\varrho(S(q),U) \leq q^{s-1} \max(1,\bar{p})\, \zeta_s(X,U) + q(\bar{p}+1)\, \zeta_1(X,U) + q\varrho(X,U), \quad (5.1)$$

where $\zeta_s(X,Y) = \sup\{|Eg(X)-Eg(Y)| : |g'(x)-g'(y)| \leq |x-y|^{s-1},\ x,y \in \mathbb{R}\}$.

We must note that the value of $\bar{p}$ in estimate (5.1) can be estimated using (4.1) and the fact that $\bar{p} \leq \sup_x h(x)$:

$$\bar{p} \leq \sup_x h(x) \leq 1 + (\sigma(F,\tilde{F})/2 + \sup_x |f(x) - \tilde{f}(x)|) \times$$

$$\times (1-\sigma(F,\tilde{F})/2)^{-1}.$$

The next assertion does not demand any restrictions on "smoothness" of $F(x)$.

THEOREM 5.2. For $1<s\leq 2$ the following estimate is valid:

$$\varrho(S(q),U) \leq (1-\zeta_1(X,U))^{-1} [q^{s-1} \zeta_s(X,U)[1+2\zeta_1(X,U) +$$

$$+ q\zeta_1(X,U)[1+2\zeta_1(X,U)] + q(H(1)+1)[2\varrho(X,U) + 2\varrho^{(s-1)/s}(X,U) \times$$

$$\times[\mathrm{E}X^{s}]^{1/s}/s + \exp(-\rho^{-1/s}(X,U)[\mathrm{E}X^{s}]^{1/s}))]. \tag{5.2}$$

Estimates (5.1) and (5.2) are non-trivial if $\mathrm{E}X^{s} < \infty$. This condition leads to q^{s-1} as an order of convergence rate; this order can not be improved.

Before proving theorems 5.1, 5.2 we formulate the following lemma which is proved in [2] :

LEMMA 5.1. Let X, Y, U, W be independent nonnegative r.v.'s, $\Pr(U \leqslant x) = 1 - e^{-x}$, the r.v. W has a density function $p_W(x) \leqslant \bar{p}$ for all x. Then

$$\rho(X+W,\ Y+W) \leqslant \bar{p}\, \zeta_1(X,Y),$$

$$\zeta_1(X+U,\ Y+U) \leqslant 2\zeta_s(X,Y), \qquad 1 < s \leqslant 2,$$

$$\rho(X+U+W,\ Y+U+W) \leqslant \max(1,\bar{p})\, \zeta_s(X,Y), \quad 1 < s \leqslant 2.$$

PROOF OF THEOREMS 5.1, 5.2. Let us denote $A(x) = \Pr(X \leqslant x)$, $A_q(x) = \Pr(qX \leqslant x) = A(x/q)$, $E(x) = \Pr(U \leqslant x)$, $E_q(x) = \Pr(qU \leqslant x) = 1 - e^{-x/q}$, $R_q(x) = \Pr(S(q) \leqslant x)$. We can write

$$\Pr(S(q) \leqslant x) - \Pr(U \leqslant x) = \sum_{n=1}^{\infty} q(1-q)^{n-1}(A_q^{*n}(x) - E_q^{*n}(x)) =$$

$$= \sum_{n=1}^{\infty} q(1-q)^{n-1}(A_q(x) - E_q(x)) * (A_q^{*(n-1)}(x) + A_q^{*(n-2)} * E_q(x) +$$

$$+ A_q^{*(n-3)} * E_q^{*2}(x) + \ldots + A_q * E_q^{*(n-2)}(x) + E_q^{*(n-1)}(x)) =$$

$$+ (A_q(x) - E_q(x)) * (q + (1-q)E(x) + (1-q)R_q(x) +$$

$$+ (1-q)^2 (\sum_{n=1}^{\infty} (1-q)^{n-1} E_q^{*n}(x)) * (\sum_{n=1}^{\infty} q(1-q)^{n-1} A_q^{*n}(x))) =$$

$$= (\mathcal{A}_q(x) - E_q(x)) * (q + (1-q)E(x) + (1-q)R_q(x) + q^{-1}(1-q)^2 E * R_q(x)),$$

hence

$$\rho(S(q),U) \leq q\rho(X,U) + q\zeta_1(X,U) + \rho(qX + S(q),\ qU + S(q)) +$$
$$+ q^{-1}\rho(qX + U_1 + S(q),\ qU + U_1 S(q)). \tag{5.3}$$

If density of $S(q)$ is less than $\bar{p}$ then we can immediately obtain the statement of theorem 5.1 from (5.3) using lemma 5.1.

If not, the term before the last in the right hand side of inequality (5.3) can be estimated in the same way as we have used in deriving of estimate (4.4)

$$\rho(qX + S(q),\ qU + S(q)) = q \sup_x \Big| \int_0^{qx} (\mathcal{A}(x-y) - E(x-y)) \times$$
$$\times d\sum_{n=1}^{\infty} \mathcal{A}^{*n}(y)(1-q)^{n-1} \Big| \leq q(H(1)+1)\{\rho(X,U) + 2\rho^{(s-1)/s}(X,U) \times$$
$$\times [EX^s]^{1/s}/s + \exp(-\rho^{-1/s}(X,U)[EX^s]^{1/s})\}. \tag{5.4}$$

The following inequalities estimate the last item in the right hand side of (5.3) using lemma 1

$$\rho(qX + U_1 + S(q),\ qU + U_1 + S(q)) \leq \rho(qX + U_1 + U_2,\ qU + U_1 + U_2) +$$
$$+ \sup_x |(E_q - \mathcal{A}_q) * (R_q - E) * E(x)| \leq q^s \zeta_s(X,Y) + \sup \Big| \int_0^x (R_q - E)(x-y) \times$$
$$\times (E_q - \mathcal{A}_q)(y)\,dy \Big| + \sup_x \Big| \int_0^x (R_q - E)(x-y) \int_0^y (E_q - \mathcal{A}_q)(u) e^{-(y-u)}\,du\,dy \Big| \leq$$
$$\leq q^s \zeta_s(X,U) + q\zeta_1(X,U)(\rho(S(q),U) + \zeta_1(S(q),U)), \tag{5.5}$$

where U, U_1, U_2 are independent and have the same d.f. $1-e^{-x}$. Putting estimates (5.4) and (5.5) in (5.3) we complete the proof of the theorem 5.2.

Kalashnikov V.V.
Institute for System Studies,
117312, Prospect 60 let Oktjybrjy,9
Moscow, USSR

Vsekhsvyatskii S.Yu.
Institute of Informatics
Problems,
117900, GSP-1, Vavilova
30/6,
Moscow, USSR

REFERENCES

1. Kalashnikov V.V. Estimates of the rate of convergence in Renyi theorem. Srability problems for stoch. mod. Moscow. Inst. for System Studies, 1983, (in Russian).
2. Kalashnikov V.V., Vsekhsvyatskii S.Yu. Metric estimates of the first occurrence time in regenerative processes. Lect. Notes in Math., v.1155, 1985, Springer-Verlag: Berlin, 193-208.
3. Daley D.J. Tight bounds for the renewal function of a random walk. Ann. Probab., v.B, N 3, 1980, 615-621.
4. Kalashnikov V.V., Vsekhsvyatskii S.Yu. Estimates in Renay's theorem in terms of renewal theorem. Theor. Veroyatn. Primen., N 1, 1988 (in Russian).

ON THE PRODUCTS OF A RANDOM NUMBER OF RANDOM VARIABLES IN CONNECTION WITH A PROBLEM FROM MATHEMATICAL ECONOMICS

L.B.Klebanov, J.A.Melamed, S.T.Rachev

Let $X_1, \ldots, X_n, \ldots$ be a sequence of independent identically distributed random variables (i.i.d. r.v.'s) which take positive values with probability one. Assume that ν_p is a random variable which is independent of this sequence and which has the geometric distribution

$$P\{\nu_p = k\} = p(1-p)^{k-1}, \qquad k = 1, 2, \ldots .$$

The purpose of this paper is to study the asymptotic distribution of the product $\prod_{j=1}^{\nu_p} X_j$ and to give an interpretation of the corresponding limit theorem in the terms of mathematical economics.

THEOREM 1. Consider the above mentioned r.v.'s $X_1, \ldots, X_n, \ldots, \nu_p$. Assume that the logarithmic moment of the r.v. X_1 exists, and also

$$E \ln X_1 = \gamma \neq 0.$$

Denote

$$Z_p = \prod_{j=1}^{\nu_p} X_j^p .$$

Then the r.v. Z_p has a limit distribution

$$F(x) = \lim_{p \to 0} P\{Z_p < x\},$$

which under $\gamma > 0$ is of the form

$$F(x) = \begin{cases} 1 - x^{-1/\gamma} & \text{for} \quad x \geqslant 1, \\ 0 & \text{for} \quad x < 1, \end{cases} \tag{1}$$

and under $\gamma < 0$

$$F(x) = \begin{cases} 0 & \text{for} \quad x < 0, \\ x^{-1/\gamma} & \text{for} \quad 0 < x \leqslant 1, \\ 1 & \text{for} \quad x > 1. \end{cases} \tag{2}$$

THEOREM 2. Consider r.v.'s $X_1, \ldots, X_n, \ldots, \nu_p$ which satisfy the conditions stated before Theorem 1. Assume that

$$E \ln X_1 = 0, \qquad \sigma^2 = E \ln^2 X_1 < \infty .$$

Put

$$Z_p' = \prod_{j=1}^{\nu_p} X_j^{p^{1/2}} .$$

Then the r.v. Z_p' has a limit distribution

$$F(x) = \lim_{p \to 0} P\{Z_p' < x\}$$

such that

$$F(x) = \begin{cases} 0 & \text{for} \quad x \leqslant 0, \\ \frac{1}{2} x^{\sqrt{2}/\sigma} & \text{for} \quad 0 < x < 1, \\ \frac{1}{2}\left(2 - x^{-\sqrt{2}/\sigma}\right) & \text{for} \quad x \geqslant 1. \end{cases} \tag{3}$$

Now let us consider the interpretation of Theorem 1 in the terms of economics. Assume that there is some output (business) in which we invest a unit of the capital at the initial moment $t = 0$. At the moment of time $t = 1$ we get a sum of capital $X_1 > 0$ (the nature of the r.v. X_1 depends on the nature of the output and that of the market). If the whole sum of capital remains in the business, then to the moment of time $t=2$ the sum of our capital becomes $X_1 \cdot X_2$, where the r.v. X_2 is independent of X_1 and has the same distribution as X_1 (provided that conditions of the output and of the market are invariable). Using the same argument further on, we find that to the moment of time $t=n$ the sum of capital is equal to $\prod_{j=1}^{n} X_j$, and also r.v.'s $X_1, X_2, \ldots, X_n$ are iid. From the economical sense it is clear that $X_j > 0$ $(j=1,\ldots,n)$. Now assume that there can happen the change of output or of the market conditions which makes further investment of capital in the business non-profitable.

We assume that the probability of this unfavorable event is the same for each moment of time $t=k$ and equals to p. Then the time till the appearance of the unfavorable event is a random variable ν_p with the geometric distribution $P\{\nu_p = k\} = p(1-p)^{k-1}$ $(k=1,2,\ldots)$. The sum of capital to the moment of appearance of the unfavorable event constitutes the value $\prod_{j=1}^{\nu_p} X_j$. Since the average time till the appearance of the unfavorable event is equal to $E\nu_p = \frac{1}{p}$, the "average annual sum of capital" is $Z_p = (\prod_{j=1}^{\nu_p} X_j)^p = \prod_{j=1}^{\nu_p} X_j^p$. The smallness of the value of p (i.e. $p \to 0$) follows from the fact that the unfavorable event happens rarely. In this case Theorem 1 shows that (under $\gamma \neq 0$) the r.v. Z_p is distributed approximately according to the Pareto law. In addition, if $\gamma > 0$, the business is profitable, and if $\gamma < 0$, the business is a failure.

One must pay attention to the following facts:

a) The Jensen's inequality implies that

$$\gamma = E \ln X_1 \leq \ln E X_1$$

with equality sign only if the r.v. X_1 is degenerate. Hence, if $EX_1 > 1$, it does not yet mean that the business is profitable, since it may be $\gamma < 0$.

b) The Pareto distribution has a mode equal to 1. Therefore in the case $\gamma > 0$ the producers with a sum of capital in the intervals $[x, x+\Delta x]$, $x > 1$ (where $\Delta x > 0$ is fixed), will ccur less frequently than those with a sum of capital in the interval $[1, 1+\Delta x]$. On the other hand, the mean value of the Pareto distribution increases with the increase of γ and under $\gamma \geqslant 1$ the mean becomes infinite. Hence, one can see that the main sum of capital is concentrated in the hands of a small group of producers.

c) The Pareto distribution has a heavy tail under $\gamma \geqslant \frac{1}{2}$. Therefore under summation of a large number of i.i.d. r.v.'s with the Pareto distribution, the limit distribution is stable. Thus the total income from a large number of outputs (with $\gamma \geqslant \frac{1}{2}$ and with the Pareto distribution) has an approximately stable distribution.

Remark that one can similarly interpret cases $\gamma < 0$ and $\gamma = 0$.

Consider now the described output process with $\gamma > 0$ and assume that a group of k producers behaves in the following way. Their incomes $X_1^{(1)}, X_1^{(2)}, \ldots, X_1^{(k)}$ ($X_1^{(j)}$ is an income of the j -th producer to the moment $t=1$) to the moment $t=1$ are added and then divided in equal parts. Next the producers invest the values

$\frac{1}{k}\sum_{j=1}^{k} X_1^{(j)}$ in the business, divide in equal parts the summarized income obtained to the moment $t=2$ and so on.

The unfavorable event for one of producers is unfavorable for the whole group. Then the value

$$\gamma_k = E\ln\left(\frac{1}{k}\sum_{j=1}^{k} X_1^{(j)}\right)$$

determines the form of the limit Pareto distribution. However, by virtue of the Jensen's inequality we have for $k>1$,

$$\gamma_k < \frac{1}{k}\sum_{j=1}^{k} E \ln X_1^{(j)} = E \ln X_1^{(1)} = \gamma.$$

Thus, if we denote by $F_k(x)$ the limit distribution of the normalized sum of capital for a group of k producers, and by $F(x)$ the one for a single producer, then for any $x>1$ we have

$$1 - F_k(x) < 1 - F(x),$$

i.e. the probability of exceeding the capital $x>1$ by a group of producers is strictly less than such probability for a single producer. In other words, equalization of income in the way stated above (the Russian term for it is "uravnilovka") brings damage.

Remark that the Pareto distribution possesses characteristic properties which convey its "balanced" nature. Namelly, the following assertions hold.

THEOREM 3. Let $X_1, X_2, \dots, X_n, \dots$ be a sequence of i.i.d. positive r.v.'s and denote by $F(x)$ a distribution function of the r.v. X_1. Assume that ν_p $(p \in (0,1))$ is a r.v. with geometric distribution and ν_p is independent of the sequence $\{X_n, n \geq 1\}$. The r.v.'s X_1 and $\prod_{j=1}^{\nu_p} X_j^{\sqrt{p}}$ are identically distributed iff $F(x)$ is of the form (3).

THEOREM 4. Let the r.v.'s $X_1, \dots, X_n, \dots, \nu_p$ be the same as in Theorem 3. Assume that $E|\ln X_1|^{\delta} < \infty$ for some $\delta > 0$. The r.v.'s X_1 and $\prod_{j=1}^{\nu_p} X_j^{p}$ are identically distributed iff $F(x)$ is of the form (1) or (2).

Let us clarify one more limiting property of the Pareto distribution associated with the maximums of a random number of r.v.'s.

THEOREM 5. Let the r. v.' s $X_1, \dots, X_n, \dots, \nu_p$ be the same as in Theorem 3. Assume that $E \ln X_1 = 1$ (one can achieve it by scale), and $1-F(x) \sim \lambda/x$ as $x \to \infty$. Denote

$$\bigvee_{j=1}^{\nu_p} X_j = \max\{X_1, X_2, \dots, X_{\nu_p}\}.$$

Then the limit distribution of the r.v. $p\bigvee_{j=1}^{\nu_p}(X_j-1)+1$ as $p\to 0$ is the Pareto distribution (1) with $\gamma=1$.

THEOREM 6. Let the assumptions of Theorem 5 hold. The r.v.'s $p\bigvee_{j=1}^{\nu_p}(X_j-1)+1$ and X_1 are identically distributed iff the r.v. X_1 has the Pareto distribution (1) with the parameter $\gamma=1$.

We do not give proofs of the stated theorems in detail. But let us remark that Theorem 1 follows from the well-known theorem for the sums due to Rényi [1] , Theorems 2 and 5 can be obtained with the help of B.V.Gnedenko's transfer theorems [2] , and Theorems 3, 4, 6 can be proved, for example, by using the method of intensively monotone operators [3] .

PROOF OF THEOREM 1. We have

$$\log Z_p = p\sum_{j=1}^{\nu_p}\log X_j .$$

Suppose that $\gamma = E\log X_1 > 0$. From Renyi's theorem [1] we obtain that the distribution of $p\sum_{j=1}^{\nu_p}\log X_j$ tends (as $p\to 0$) to the exponential distribution with parameter $1/\gamma$. Hence, the distribution of Z_p tends to the Pareto-distribution (1).

The case $\gamma<0$ may be reduced to the case $\gamma>0$ with the help of transformations $u_j=1/X_j,\ \nu_p=1/Z_p$.

Proof of Theorem 2 is similar to the proof of Theorem 1. But instead Renyi's theorem we need use corresponding result in [2] or theorem 2.4.2 in [3] .

PROOF OF THEOREM 3. Set $Y_j=\log X_j$. Suppose that $\varphi(t)$ is the characteristic function (c.f.) of Y_1 . The condition of identical distribution of X_1 and $\prod_{j=1}^{\nu_p} X_j^{\sqrt{p}}$ is equivalent to the following

$$\varphi(t) = p\varphi(p^{1/2}t)/[1-(1-p)\varphi(p^{1/2}t)].$$

It is easily seen that the function

$$\psi(t) = \exp\{1 - 1/\varphi(t)\}$$

is c.f. and

$$\psi(t) = [\psi(p^{1/2}t)]^{1/p}. \qquad (4)$$

To obtain the result we need only use theorem 2.1.1 in [3] .

Proof of Theorem 4 is similar to the proof of Theorem 3. We need only use theorem 2.3.1 instead theorem 2.1.1.

To obtain proofs of Theorems 5 and 6 we need replace theorems 2.4.2 and 2.3.1 by their analogies (see [2] and Chapter 3 in [3]).

Leningrad Civil Engineering Institute
II Krasnoarmeyskaya 4, Leningrad
198005, USSR
Institute of Mathematics
Bulgaria, 1090 Sofia, P.O.B.373

Mathematical Institute of
the Georgian Academy of
Sciences, Plekhanov Ave.,
150A, Tbilisi-12,
380012 USSR

REFERENCES

1. Rényi A. Posson-folyamat egy jemllemzëse.- Magyar tud. akad. Mat. Kutató int.közl., 1956, v.1, 4, 519-527.

2. Gnedenko B.V. On limit theorems for a random number of random variables.- In: Probability Theory and Mathematical Statistic. Fourth USSR-Japan Symposium Proceedings, 1982. Lect Notes Math., 1983, v.1021, 167-176.

3. Kakosyan A.V., Klebanov L.B., Melamed J.A. Characterization of distributions by the method of intensively monotone operators.- Lect. Notes Math., 1984, v.1088, 175 p.

THE ASYMPTOTIC DISTRIBUTIONS OF RANDOM SUMS

V.Yu.Korolev

1. Introduction

Let random variables (r.v.'s) $\{\xi_j\}_{j\geq 1}$ be independent. Put $S_n=\xi_1+\dots+\xi_n$. Consider the sequence of constants $\{a_n\}_{n\geq 1}, \{b_n\}_{n\geq 1}$ such that $a_n\in\mathbb{R}^1$, $b_n>0$, $\lim_{n\to\infty} b_n=\infty$ and

$$\frac{S_n-a_n}{b_n} \Rightarrow \xi \tag{1}$$

as $n\to\infty$. Here ξ is a r.v. with distribution function (d.f.) H and characteristic function (ch.f.) h. Symbol $\Rightarrow$ denotes convergence in distribution. It is well-known that H is an infinitely divisible d f belonging to the class L described by P.Levy.

Let ν be a positive integer r.v. with distribution depending on some, say, location parameter $\theta\in(0,\infty)$. Suppose that for each $\theta\in(0,\infty)$ r.v.'s ν and $\{\xi_j\}_j$ are independent. Our basic assumption is that

$$\nu\to\infty \tag{2}$$

in probability as $\theta\to\infty$. We shall study the asymptotic properties of "growing" random sums S_ν as $\theta\to\infty$. It is easy to see that any d.f. may be limiting for the d.f. of S_ν without additional restrictions. However the appropriate norming and centering narrows the class of limiting distributions. If nonrandom sums of r.v.'s are considered it does not matter whether the sums themselves or the separate summands are centered. But if the number of the summands in the sum is random then the centering of the sums and the centering of summands lead to different limiting distributions. It is clear that when the summands are centered by constants the random sum itself is centered by r.v. Moreover, random sums may be normed both by constants and by r.v.'s. We shall consider these situations after a brief preliminary historical commentary.

The study of the asymptotic properties of random sums normed by constants and centered by r.v.'s in most cases can be reduced to the consideration of random sums in the scheme of series. Asymptotic theory of random sums in the scheme of series was created by B.V.Gnedenko and his followers [1, 2, 3] . Some estimates of the accuracy of the approximation of the random sums of centered identically distributed independent r.v.'s by the scale mixtures of stable laws which turn out to be limiting in this case can be found in [4] .

In 1948 H.Robbins [5, 6] described a class of limiting distributions for random sums of noncentered r.v.'s normed by constants in the situation when the summands are identically distributed and have finite variances. Robbins class consists of location mixtures of normal laws. Later Robbins' results were generalized by Z.Rychlik and D. Szynal [7, 8] for nonidentically distributed summands. Dozens of papers are devoted to the description of the rate of convergence of d.f.'s of random sums to Robbins' mixtures. Main references can be found in [9, 10] . Except for the paper by D.Szász [11] on the convergence of random sums to a degenerate r.v., however, only a particular case was considered when the summands are supposed to have a finite variance and Lindenberg condition holds implying the normality of r.v. ξ . That's why the class of the asymptotic distributions of random sums of noncentered r.v.'s normed by constants has not yet been described exhaustively.

2. The asymptotic distributions of random sums normed by constants

Taking into account what we're said in the introduction we shall not consider random sums of centered summands. Introduce the functions $a(\theta): (0,\infty) \to \mathbb{R}^1$, $b(\theta): (0,\infty) \to (0,\infty)$, $d(\theta): (0,\infty) \to (0,\infty)$ such that $b(\theta) \to \infty$ and $d(\theta) \to \infty$ as $\theta \to \infty$. We shall use the following notation:

$$f_n(t) = \mathbb{E}\exp\{it(S_n - a_n)/b_n\},$$

$$f^{(\theta)}(t) = \mathbb{E}\exp\{it(S_\nu - a(\theta))/d(\theta)\},$$

$$\tilde{w}^{(\theta)}(t) = \mathbb{E}\exp\{it(a_\nu - a(\theta))/d(\theta)\},$$

$$r^{(\theta)}(t) = \tilde{w}^{(\theta)}(t)h(tb(\theta)/d(\theta)).$$

If $\tilde{W}_\theta$ is the d.f. corresponding to ch.f. $\tilde{w}^{(\theta)}$ then it is easy to see that ch.f. $r^{(\theta)}$ corresponds to d.f.

$$R_\theta(x) \equiv \tilde{W}_\theta(x) * H(xd(\theta)/b(\theta)).$$

The subsequent reasoning will depend on the behaviour of the function $b(\theta)/d(\theta)$.

THEOREM 1. Let (1) and (2) hold and besides that

$$\lim_{\theta\to\infty} b(\theta)/d(\theta) = 0. \tag{3}$$

If

$$\frac{b_\nu - b(\theta)}{d(\theta)} \Longrightarrow 0 \tag{4}$$

as $\theta \to \infty$ then for each $t \in \mathbb{R}^1$

$$\lim_{\theta\to\infty} |f^{(\theta)}(t) - \tilde{w}^{(\theta)}(t)| = 0. \tag{5}$$

PROOF. (3) and (4) imply

$$b_\nu / d(\theta) \Longrightarrow 0 \tag{6}$$

as $\theta \to \infty$. Denote $N_1 = N_1(\theta, \delta) = \{n: b_n \leqslant \delta b(\theta)\}$ for some $\delta > 0$. Fix an arbitrary $t \in \mathbb{R}^1$. Then we have

$$|f^{(\theta)}(t)-\tilde{w}^{(\theta)}(t)| = |\sum_{n=1}^{\infty} P(\nu=n)\exp\{it(\frac{a_n-a(\theta)}{d(\theta)})\}[f_n(tb_n/d(\theta))-1]| \leqslant$$

$$\leqslant \sum_{n=1}^{\infty} P(\nu=n)|f_n(tb_n/d(\theta))-1| \leqslant \sum_{n\in N_1} P(\nu=n)|f_n(tb/d(\theta))-1| + P(\nu\notin N_1). \quad (7)$$

If (1) hold then the family of ch.f.'s $\{f_n(t)\}_{n\geqslant 1}$ is equicontinuous in $t=0$ [12, p.206]. Therefore whatever $\varepsilon>0$ is considered, $\delta=\delta(t,\varepsilon)$ can be chosen to provide

$$|f_n(tb_n/d(\theta))-1)| \leqslant \sup_n \sup_{|\tau|<|t|\delta} |f_n(\tau)-1| < \varepsilon \quad (8)$$

for $n\in N_1(\theta,\delta)$. Since (6) holds, $\delta=\delta(t,\varepsilon)$ is given $\theta_0=\theta_0(\delta)$ can be chosen to provide

$$P(b_\nu/d(\theta)>\delta)<\varepsilon \quad (9)$$

for all $\theta\geqslant\theta_0$. Thus (7), (8) and (9) imply that

$$|f^{(\theta)}(t)-\tilde{w}^{(\theta)}(t)|<2\varepsilon$$

for $\theta\geqslant\theta_0$. Therefore the arbitrariness of ε establishes (5). The proof is over.

THEOREM 2. Let (1) and (2) hold and besides that

$$0<c_0\equiv\inf_\theta b(\theta)/d(\theta)\leqslant\sup_\theta b(\theta)/d(\theta)\equiv c_1<\infty. \quad (10)$$

Then (4) implies

$$\lim_{\theta\to\infty}|f^{(\theta)}(t)-r^{(\theta)}(t)|=0 \quad (11)$$

for each $t\in R^1$.

PROOF. Since

$$r^{(\theta)}(t)=h(tb(\theta)/d(\theta))\sum_{n=1}^{\infty}P(\nu=n)\exp\{it(a_n-a(\theta))/d(\theta)\}$$

then denoting $N_2 = N_2(\theta,\delta) = \{n: |b_n - b(\theta)| \leq \delta d(\theta)\}$ for some $\delta > 0$ we have

$$|f^{(\theta)}(t) - r^{(\theta)}(t)| = |\sum_{n=1}^{\infty} P(\nu = n)\exp\{it(a_n - a(\theta))/d(\theta)\}[f_n(tb_n/d(\theta)) -$$

$$-(h(tb(\theta)/d(\theta))]| \leq \sum_{n=1}^{\infty} P(\nu = n)|f_n(tb_n/d(\theta)) - h(tb(\theta)/d(\theta))| \leq$$

$$\leq \sum_{n\in N_2} P(\nu = n)|f_n(tb_n/d(\theta)) - h(tb(\theta)/d(\theta))| + P(\nu \notin N_2) \equiv$$

$$\equiv I_1(t,\theta,\delta) + I_2(t,\theta,\delta).$$

Fix an arbitrary $t \in \mathbb{R}^1$. Consider $I_1(t,\theta,\delta)$. We have

$$|f_n(tb_n/d(\theta)) - h(tb(\theta)/d(\theta))| \leq$$

$$\leq |f_n(tb_n/d(\theta)) - h(tb_n/d(\theta))| + |h(tb_n/d(\theta)) - h(tb(\theta)/d(\theta))| \equiv$$

$$\equiv J_{n1}(t,\theta) + J_{n2}(t,\theta).$$

Since $h(t)$ being a ch.f. in uniformly continuous, whatever $\varepsilon > 0$ is considered $\delta_0 = \delta_0(t,\varepsilon) \in (0, c_0)$ can be chosen to provide

$$J_{n2}(t,\theta) \leq \sup_{n\in N_2(\theta,\delta_0)} |h(tb_n/d(\theta)) - h(tb(\theta)/d(\theta))| \leq$$

$$\leq \sup_{t_1,t_2:\ |t_1-t_2|<|t|\delta_0} |h(t_1) - h(t_2)| < \varepsilon \tag{12}$$

for $n \in N_2(\theta,\delta_0)$. (1) implies the uniform convergence of f_n to h on every finite interval [12, p.204, 205] . Therefore for any $\varepsilon > 0$ we can choose $n_1 = n_1(t,\varepsilon,\delta_0,c_1)$ such that

$$J_{n1}(t,\theta) \leq \sup_{n\in N_2(\theta,\delta_0)} |f_n(tb_n/d(\theta)) - h(tb_n/d(\theta))| \leq$$

$$\leq \sup_{|\tau|\leq|t|(c_1+\delta_0)} |f_n(\tau) - h(\tau)| < \varepsilon \tag{13}$$

for all $n \geqslant n_1$, $n \in N_2(\theta, \delta_0)$. (10) guarantees that $\inf N_2(\theta, \delta) \to \infty$ as $\theta \to \infty$ whatever $\delta \in (0, c_0)$ is considered. Therefore we can choose θ_1 to provide first

$$[n_1, \infty) \cap N_2(\theta, \delta_0) = N_2(\theta, \delta_0), \quad \theta \geqslant \theta_1,$$

and second, since (4) holds,

$$I_2(t, \theta, \delta_0) < \varepsilon, \quad \theta \geqslant \theta_1. \tag{14}$$

From (12) and (13) we obtain

$$I_1(t, \theta, \delta_0) \leqslant \sum_{n \in N_2} P(\nu = n)[J_{n1}(t, \theta) + J_{n2}(t, \theta)] < 2\varepsilon$$

which together with (14) implies

$$|f^{(\theta)}(t) - r^{(\theta)}(t)| < 3\varepsilon$$

if only $\theta \geqslant \theta_1$. Arbitrariness of ε proved (11). The proof is over.

Theorem 2 states that the d.f. approximating $P(S_\nu - a \leqslant x d)$ for some a and d when the d.f. of r.v. $(b_\nu - b)/d$ is in some sense close to $\chi\ (x \geqslant 0)$ should be a convolution of a d.f. from class L and the d.f. of a linear transformation of the r.v. a_ν. Here and further $\chi(A)$ stands for the indicator function of the set A.

REMARK 1. Since the function $\psi(x) \equiv |x|^\beta$, $\beta > 0$, is monotonous and continuous when $x \geqslant 0$, condition (4) may be replaced by sometimes more easily verified condition

$$\frac{b_\nu^\beta - b^\beta(\theta)}{d^\beta(\theta)} \Longrightarrow 0 \tag{15}$$

as $\theta \to \infty$ for some $\beta > 0$. Note that (15) with $\beta = 2$ was the condition used in [5 - 9].

It turns out that under some rather general suppositions (15) holds when r.v. a_ν if approproately centered and normed by constants has a limiting distribution as $\theta \to \infty$. Consider a function $c(\theta): (0, \infty) \to (0, \infty)$. Let W_θ be the d.f. of r.v. $(a_\nu - a(\theta))/c(\theta)$. Suppose that

$$\lim_{\theta\to\infty} W_\theta(x) = W(x) \tag{16}$$

in each point of continuity of some proper d.f. $W(x)$. Denote $\overline{W}(x) = W(x) - W(-x-0)$, $\overline{W}_\theta(x) = W_\theta(x) - W_\theta(-x-0)$, $x \geq 0$. It is clear that (16) implies

$$\lim_{\theta\to\infty} \overline{W}_\theta(x) = \overline{W}(x)$$

if x is a point of continuity of $\overline{W}(x)$. We shall need the following "proportionality" condition. Denote

$$k_\beta(\theta) = \inf_n |(a_n - a(\theta))/(b_n^\beta - b^\beta(\theta))|$$

and suppose that

$$\lim_{\theta\to\infty} k_\beta(\theta)\, d^{\beta-1}(\theta) = \infty. \tag{17}$$

Finally, suppose that the limits

$$\gamma_1 = \lim_{\theta\to\infty}\{\gamma_1(\theta) \equiv c(\theta)/d(\theta)\} \qquad \text{and} \qquad \gamma_2 = \lim_{\theta\to\infty}\{\gamma_2(\theta) \equiv b(\theta)/d(\theta)\}$$

exist.

THEOREM 3. Let $\gamma_1 < \infty$ and (1), (2) and (17) hold. Then (16) implies

$$(S_\nu - a(\theta))/d(\theta) \Rightarrow \zeta \tag{18}$$

as $\theta \to \infty$, where ζ us a r.v. with d.f. $R(x) \equiv W(\gamma_1^{-1}x) * H(\gamma_2 x)$.

PROOF. Using the definitions of $k_\beta(\theta)$ and $\gamma_1(\theta)$ we have for any $\delta > 0$

$$P\left(\left|\frac{b_\nu^\beta - b^\beta(\theta)}{d^\beta(\theta)}\right| > \delta\right) = P\left(|a_\nu - a(\theta)| > \delta d^\beta(\theta) \left|\frac{a_\nu - a(\theta)}{b_\nu^\beta - b^\beta(\theta)}\right|\right) \leq$$

$$\leq P\left(\frac{|a_\nu - a(\theta)|}{c(\theta)} > \delta \gamma_1^{-1}(\theta)\, d^{\beta-1}(\theta)\, k_\beta(\theta)\right) =$$

$$= 1 - \overline{W}_\theta(\delta\gamma_1^{-1}(\theta) d^{\beta-1}(\theta) k_\beta(\theta)).$$

Therefore (16) and (17) imply (15). Now (18) appears to be a simple consequence of theorems 1 and 2.

REMARK 2. The results of [5 - 8] are the particular cases of theorems 1 - 3. Indeed, if as in [6] the summands are identically distributed, $E\xi_1 = m$, $D\xi_1 = \sigma^2 < \infty$ then obviously $a_n = nm$, $b_n^2 = n\sigma^2$. Now if we put $a(\theta) = mE\nu (= ES_\nu)$, $b^2(\theta) = \sigma^2 E\nu$, $c^2(\theta) = m^2 D\nu$, $d^2(\theta) = b^2(\theta) + c^2(\theta)$ $(= DS_\nu)$ then (17) holds automatically with $\beta = 2$ since $d(\theta)$ is supposed to tend to infinity as $\theta \to \infty$. Note that we don't put additional restrictions on W whiles in [6] $W(x)$ was supposed to be strictly positive for all finite x.

Now we shall get some estimates of the accuracy of the approximation in theorem 2. The estimate

$$\sup_x |P(S_n - a_n \le b_n x) - H(x)| \le \Delta_n \tag{19}$$

will be supposed to be given where $1 \ge \Delta_n \ge \Delta_{n+1}, n \ge 1$. For some $\varepsilon \in (0,1)$ let $l_\theta(\varepsilon)$ be the lower bound of ε-quantiles of r. v. ν. Put $M = \sup_x |x| H'(x)$. M is finite if H' is continuous.

THEOREM 4. Suppose that H' is continuous and (10) holds. Then for any $\delta \in (0,1)$ and $\beta > 0$

$$\sup_x |P(S_\nu - a(\theta) \le x d(\theta)) - R_\theta(x)| \le \sup\{\Delta_n : b_n \ge (1-\delta) b(\theta)\} +$$

$$+ Q(\beta,\delta) c_0^{-\beta} \delta^{-1} \max\{1, \delta M (1-\delta)^{-1}\} E \min\{\delta c_0^\beta, |b_\nu^\beta - b^\beta(\theta)| / d^\beta(\theta)\} \tag{20}$$

where $Q(\beta,\delta) = \chi(\beta \ge 1) + \max\{\beta^{-1}, \delta[(1+\delta)^\beta - 1]^{-1}\} \chi(0 < \beta < 1)$.

PROOF. Denote $N_3 = N_3(\theta,\delta) = \{n : |b_n - b(\theta)| \le \delta b(\theta)\}$, $x = x d(\theta) + a(\theta) - a_n$. Since

$$R_\theta(x) = \sum_{n=1}^{\infty} P(\nu = n) H(x_n / b(\theta))$$

then

$$\sup_x |P(S_\nu - a(\theta) \leq x\, d(\theta)) - R_\theta(x)| \leq$$

$$\leq \sum_{n=1}^{\infty} P(\nu = n) \sup_x |P((S_n - a_n)/b_n \leq x_n/b_n) - H(x_n/b(\theta))| =$$

$$= \sum_{n \in N_3} P(\nu = n) \sup_x |P((S_n - a_n)/b_n \leq x_n/b_n) - H(x_n/b(\theta))| +$$

$$+ \sum_{n \notin N_3} P(\nu = n) \sup_x |P((S_n - a_n)/b_n \leq x_n/b_n) - H(x_n/b(\theta))| \equiv A_1 + A_2. \qquad (21)$$

It is evident that

$$A_2 \leq P(|b_\nu - b(\theta)| > \delta b(\theta)). \qquad (22)$$

Further we have

$$A_1 \leq \sum_{n \in N_3} P(\nu = n) \sup_x |P((S_n - a_n)/b_n \leq x_n/b_n) - H(x_n/b_n)| +$$

$$+ \sum_{n \in N_3} P(\nu = n) \sup_x |H(x_n/b_n) - H(x_n/b(\theta))| \equiv A_{11} + A_{12}. \qquad (23)$$

According to Lagrange's formula for each $n \in N_3(\theta, \delta)$ and some $\omega_n \in (0, 1)$ we obtain

$$|H(x_n/b_n) - H(x_n/b(\theta))| = |x_n/b_n||1 - b_n/b(\theta)|\, H'(x_n/b_n(b_n/b(\theta) +$$

$$+ \omega_n(1 - b_n/b(\theta)))) \leq |1 - b_n/b(\theta)||b_n/b(\theta) + \omega_n(1 - b_n/b(\theta))|^{-1} \sup_y |y|\, H'(y) \leq$$

$$\leq M(1-\delta)^{-1}|1 - b_n/b(\theta)|$$

because

$$b_n/b(\theta) + \omega_n(1 - b_n/b(\theta)) \geq 1 - \delta$$

if $n \in N_3(\theta, \delta)$ and $\omega \in (0, 1)$. Therefore

$$A_{12} \leq M(1-\delta)^{-1} E|b_\nu - b(\theta)|/b(\theta)\, \chi(\nu \in N_3). \qquad (24)$$

Unification of (22) and (23) leads to

$$A_{12}+A_2 \leqslant \delta^{-1} \max\{1, \delta M(1-\delta)^{-1}\} E \min\{\delta, |b_\nu - b(\theta)|/b(\theta)\}. \tag{25}$$

It is quite easy to verify that for any $\delta>0$, $\beta>0$

$$\min\{\delta, |b_n - b(\theta)|/b(\theta)\} \leqslant Q(\delta,\beta)\min\{\delta, |b_n^\beta - b^\beta(\theta)|/b^\beta(\theta)\} \leqslant$$

$$\leqslant c_0^{-\beta} Q(\delta,\beta) \min\{\delta c_0^\beta, |b_n^\beta - b^\beta(\theta)|/d^\beta(\theta)\}.$$

That's why if we continue (25) we get

$$A_{12}+A_2 \leqslant c_0^{-\beta} Q(\delta,\beta)\delta^{-1} \max\{1, \delta M(1-\delta)^{-1}\} E \min\{\delta c_0^\beta, |b_\nu^\beta - b^\beta(\theta)|/d^\beta(\theta)\}. \tag{26}$$

Applying (19) we obtain

$$A_{11} \leqslant E\,\Delta_\nu\, \chi(\nu \in N_3) \leqslant \sup\{\Delta_n : b_n \geqslant (1-\delta) b(\theta)\}. \tag{27}$$

Now (20) follows from (21), (23), (26) and (27). The proof is over.

REMARK 3. Almost all the representations of Δ_n are of the form

$$\Delta_n = K_n / L(b_n)$$

where K_n depends on the distributions of $\{\xi_j\}_{j=1}^n$ and a positive function $L(\cdot)$ defined on the positive semiaxis is nondecreasing. For example, if $\{\xi_j\}_{j\geq 1}$ are identically distributed with d.f. F of r.v. ξ_1 belonging to the domain of normal attraction of a stable law G_α with the exponent $\alpha \in (0,2]$ then

$$\Delta_n = c_\alpha \max\{\rho_\varkappa, \rho_\varkappa^{1/(1+\varkappa)}\} n^{-(\varkappa-\alpha)/\alpha} \tag{28}$$

where c_α is a positive constant depending only on α, $\varkappa = 1+[\alpha]$ (here $[x]$ denotes the integral part of x), and for $p \geqslant 0$

$$\rho_p = \int_{-\infty}^{\infty} |x|^p |d(F(x) - G_\alpha(x))|,$$

see [13] . In this case $b_n = c n^{1/\alpha}$, $c>0$, and we can choose $b(\theta) = c\theta^{1/\alpha}$. The appropriate choice of $d(\theta)$ and slight modification of the above reasoning will lead us to the following estimate. For any

$\delta \in (0,1)$

$$\sup_x |P(S_\nu - a(\theta) \leqslant x d(\theta)) - R_\theta(x)| \leqslant c_\alpha \max\{\rho_\varkappa, \rho_\varkappa^{1/(1+\varkappa)}\}((1-\delta)^\alpha \times$$
$$\times \theta)^{-(\varkappa-\alpha)/\alpha} + Q(\alpha,\delta)\delta^{-1} \max\{1, \delta M(1-\delta)^{-1}\} \mathrm{E} \min\{\delta, |\nu/\theta - 1|\}.$$

REMARK 4. Theorem 4 provides the condition under which d.f. of r.v. $(S_\nu - a(\theta))/d(\theta)$ may be approximated by a location mixture of class L distributions if (1) and (2) hold and the density H' is continuous everywhere. These conditions prove to be formally weaker than (15) or (4). Indeed, (15) is equivalent to

$$\lim_{\theta\to\infty} \mathrm{E}\Psi((b_\nu^\beta - b^\beta(\theta))/d^\beta(\theta)) = 0 \tag{29}$$

for every bounded continuous function Ψ, whiles if (1) and (2) hold, the right-hand side of (20) tends to zero if (29) holds for the only function $\Psi(x) \equiv \Psi_t(x) = \min\{t, |x|\}$ where t is a positive number.

3. The asymptotic distributions of random sums normed by R.V.'s

The situation is much more simple if the random sums are normed by r.v.'s. Let $A(\theta): (0,\infty) \to \mathbb{R}^1$. Denote

$$f_1^{(\theta)}(t) = \mathrm{E}\exp\{it(S_\nu - a(\theta))/b_\nu\}, \qquad f_2^{(\theta)}(t) = \mathrm{E}\exp\{it(S_\nu/b_\nu - A(\theta))\},$$

$$f_3^{(\theta)}(t) = \mathrm{E}\exp\{it(S_\nu - a_\nu)/b_\nu\}, \qquad v_1^{(\theta)}(t) = \mathrm{E}\exp\{it(a_\nu - a(\theta))/b_\nu\},$$

$$v_2^{(\theta)}(t) = \mathrm{E}\exp\{it(a_\nu/b_\nu - A(\theta)\}.$$

THEOREM 5. Let (1) and (2) hold. Then for each $t \in \mathbb{R}^1$

$$\lim_{\theta\to\infty} |f_1^{(\theta)}(t) - v_1^{(\theta)}(t)h(t)| = 0, \tag{30}$$

$$\lim_{\theta\to\infty} |f_2^{(\theta)}(t) - v_2^{(\theta)}(t)h(t)| = 0, \tag{31}$$

$$\lim_{\theta\to\infty} |f_3^{(\theta)}(t) - h(t)| = 0. \tag{32}$$

PROOF. We shall produce the proof of (30). (31) and (32) are proved almost identically. By the law of total probability

$$f_1^{(\theta)}(t) = \sum_{n=1}^{\infty} P(\nu=n)\exp\{it(a_n - a(\theta))/b_n\} f_n(t),$$

$$v_1^{(\theta)}(t)h(t) = \sum_{n=1}^{\infty} P(\nu=n)\exp\{it(a_n - a(\theta))/b_n\} h(t).$$

Since (1) holds given $\varepsilon>0$ we can choose $n_2 = n_2(\varepsilon)$ to provide

$$|f_n(t) - h(t)| < \varepsilon$$

for all $n \geq n_2$. Therefore

$$|f_1^{(\theta)}(t) - v_1^{(\theta)}(t)h(t)| = |\sum_{n=1}^{\infty} P(\nu=n)\exp\{it(a_n - a(\theta))/b_n\}[f_n(t) - h(t)]| \leq$$

$$\leq \sum_{n=1}^{\infty} P(\nu=n)|f_n(t) - h(t)| \leq P(\nu\leq n_2)+\varepsilon.$$

Since (2) holds given $\varepsilon>0$ we can choose $\theta_2 = \theta_2(\varepsilon, n)$ to provide $P(\nu\leq n_2)<\varepsilon$ for $\theta \geq \theta_2$. Thus for the mentioned θ

$$|f_1^{(\theta)}(t) - v_1^{(\theta)}(t)h(t)| < 2\varepsilon$$

and arbitrariness of ε proves (30). The proof is over.

Let $F_{\theta,i}$ be the d.f. corresponding to ch.f. $f_i^{(\theta)}$, $i = 1,2,3$, and $V_{\theta,j}$ be the d.f. corresponding to ch.f. $v_j^{(\theta)}$, $j=1,2$. Denote

$$\Delta_{\theta,i} = \sup_x |F_{\theta,i}(x) - (H * V_{\theta,i})(x)|, \quad i = 1,2,$$

$$\Delta_{\theta,3} = \sup_x |F_{\theta,3}(x) - H(x)|.$$

THEOREM 6. For any $\varepsilon \in (0, 1)$

$$\Delta_{\theta,i} \leq E\Delta_\nu \leq \varepsilon + \Delta_{\ell_\theta(\varepsilon)}, \qquad i = 1, 2, 3. \tag{33}$$

The proof is quite obvious.

REMARK 5. Usually the evaluation of $\mathbb{E}\Delta_\nu$ is rather difficult so the right inequality (33) gives an estimate of $\Delta_{\theta,i}$ sufficient for practical purposes. Moreover, if we treat ε as a decreasing function of θ we may get some consistent estimates. For example, consider the case of identically distributed summands with (28) holding. Given $\delta > 0$ let $\varepsilon(\theta)$ be the solution of the equation

$$\varepsilon = \delta c_\alpha \max\{\rho_\varkappa, \rho_\varkappa^{1/(1-\varkappa)}\}(\ell_\theta(\varepsilon))^{-(\varkappa-\alpha)/\alpha}. \tag{34}$$

Then with the help of (33) we get

$$\Delta_{\theta,i} \leq (1+\delta) c_\alpha \max\{\rho_\varkappa, \rho_\varkappa^{1/(1-\varkappa)}\}(\ell_\theta(\varepsilon(\theta)))^{-(\varkappa-\alpha)/\alpha}$$

However to solve (34) is not a much more simple problem than to evaluate $\mathbb{E}\Delta_\nu$.

ACKNOWLEDGEMENT. The author wishes to thank professor V.M.Kruglov for stimulating discussions of the problems touched upon in this paper.

Dept. Of Computing Math. and Cybernetics
Moscow State University
Moscow, Leninskir Gory, USSR

REFERENCES

1. Gnedenko B.V., Fahim H. On a transfer theorem.- Dokl.Akad. Nauk SSSR, 1969, 187, N 1, 15-17 (in Russian).
2. Szász D. On the classes of limiting distributions for sums of a random number of independent identically distributed random variables.- Theor. Veroyatn. Primen., 1972, 17, N 3, 424-439 (in Russian).
3. Szász D. Limit theorems for the distributions of the sums of a

random number of random variables.- Ann.Math.Stat., 1972, 43, N 6, 1902-1913.

4. Sakalauskas V. On the limiting behaviour of sums of a random number of independent random variables.- Litov. Mat.Sb., 1985, 25, N 2, 164-176 (in Russian).
5. Robbins H. On the asymptotic distribution of the sum of random number of random variables.- Proc. Nat. Acad. Sci. USA, 1948, 34, 162-163.
6. Robbins H. The asymptotic distribution of the sum of random number of random variables.- Bull.Amer.Math.Soc., 1948, 54, N 12, 1151-1161.
7. Rychlik Z., Szynal D. On the limit behaviour of the sums of a random number of independent random variables.- Bull.Acad. pol. sci., ser. Sci, Math., ohys., astron., 1972, 20, N 5, 401-406.
8. Rychlik Z., Szynal D. On the limit behaviour of the sums of a random number of independent random variables.- Collog. Math., 1973, 28, N 1, 147-159.
9. Korolev V.Yu. Approximation of distributions of the sums of a random number of independent random variables by mixtures of normal laws.- Theor. Veroyatn. Primen., 1988, 33, to appear (in Russian).
10. Korolev V.Yu. Nonuniform estimates of the accuracy of approximation of distributions of the sums of a random number of independent random variables by mixtures of normal laws.- Theor. Veroyatn. Primen., 1989, 34, to appear (in Russian).
11. Szász D. Stability and law of large numbers for sums of a random number of random variables.- Acta Sci. Math., 1972, 33, 269-274.
12. Loéve M. Probability theory. 1962 (Russian edition).
13. Mitalauskas A.A. A remainder term estimate in the integral limit theorem in the case of convergence to a stable law.- Litov.Mat.Sb., 1971, 11, N 3, 627-639.

NORMAL AND DEGENERATE CONVERGENCES OF RANDOM SUMS

V.M.Kruglov

Introduction.

The concept of relative stability of the sums of independent positive random variables introduced by A.Ya.Khintchin turned out to be bound up with the central limit theorem. The description of this interconnection found by D.A.Raikov and investigated in detail by B.V.Gnedenko can be found in [1] , § 28.

In this paper we show that this interconnection still remains when the usual sums are replaced by the random sums of independent random variables (r.v.'s). We describe the mentioned interconnection with the help of classical results conbined with the two criteria of convergence of random sums distributions to normal and degenerate distribution functions (d.f.'s) stated below. When degenerate convergence is studied we consider the random sums of nonnegative summand which is enough for our purpose and these are the sums the relative stability has to do with.

Let for each $n = 1, 2, \ldots$ r.v.'s ν_n, ξ_{nk}, $k = 1, 2, \ldots$, be independent ν_n being nonnegative integer. The basic objects of our interest are the sums $S_0^{(n)} = 0$, $S_k^{(n)} = \xi_{n1} + \ldots + \xi_{nk}$ and the random sums $S_{\nu_k}^{(n)}$.

The statements presented below are based upon the supposition that,

$$P - \lim_{n \to \infty} \nu_n = \infty. \tag{1}$$

Here and further P -lim means the limit in the sense of convergence in probability. The other supposition is the random analoque of the uniform negligility condition:

$$P\text{-}\lim_{n\to\infty} \sup_{1\leq k\leq \nu_n} P(|\xi_{nk}| \geq \varepsilon) = 0 \tag{2}$$

for each $\varepsilon > 0$. For any t, $0 < t < 1$, let $\ell_n(t)$ denote the lower bound of t -quantiles of the random variable ν_n . Note that $\ell_n(t)$ is a nonnegative integer and the sequence $\{\ell_n(t)\}$ tends to infinity. (1) and (2) imply that for any t, $0 < t < 1$, and $\varepsilon > 0$

$$\lim_{n\to\infty} \sup_{1\leq k\leq \ell_n(t)} P(|\xi_{nk}| \geq \varepsilon) = 0. \tag{3}$$

For the sake of brevity we shall say that the sequence of r.v.'s convergences weakly to a r.v. if the corresponding sequence of d.f.'s convergences to the d.f. of the limiting r.v. in Levy's metric. It is well known that the convergence of the sequence of r.v.'s to a constant in probability is equivalent to the weak convergence of this sequence to the same constant. In the latter case for the sake of convenience we shall sometimes speak of convergence in probability and sometimes of the weak convergence having in mind one and the same sequence of r.v.'s. The sign $\Longrightarrow$ will be settled to denote the convergence of d.f.'s in Levy's metric.

Zolotarev's centers. It is quite easy to show that arbitrary d.f. can be limiting for the sequence of d.f.'s of random sums (see, for example, [5]). The class of limiting d.f.'s considerably diminishes if the summands are centered in an appropriate way. In this paper we shall use the centering constants introduced and studied by V.M.Zolotarev [2] , Chapter 3.

The center (more exactly, v -center) of a r.v. ξ with characteristic function f is the number $C(v,\xi) = v^{-1}\,\mathrm{Im}\ln f(v)$ where $v > 0$ is chosen in such a way that $f(v) \neq 0$.

Now we list some necessary properties of ϑ -centers.

1. If $P(\xi = a) = 1$ then $C(v, \xi) = a$.

2. If $\xi = \xi_1 + \ldots + \xi_n$ is a sum of independent r.v.'s then

$$C(v, \xi) = \sum_{k=1}^{n} C(v, \xi_k).$$

3. If the sequence of r.v.'s $\{\xi_n\}$ converges weakly to a r.v. ξ whose characteristic function does not turn into zero then

$$\lim_{n \to \infty} C(v, \xi_n) = C(v, \xi).$$

4. Let for each $n = 1, 2, \ldots$ r.v.'s ξ_n and η_n be independent and $C(v, \xi_n) = 0$. If the sequence $\{\xi_n + \eta_n\}$ is weakly compact and the characteristic function of any r.v. limiting for this sequence does not turn into zero then the sequence $\{\xi_n\}$ is also weakly compact.

As an example we mention that the center of a normal r.v. is equal to its expectation. We shall use this fact later.

The results.

Here we formulate our theorems providing some of them with brief commentaries. Let F_{nk} denote the d.f. of ξ_{nk} and $\tau > 0$ be a fixed number. Put

$$a_{nk}(\tau) = \int_{|x|<\tau} x \, dF_{nk}, \qquad \sigma^2_{nk}(\tau) = \int_{|x|<\tau} x^2 \, dF_{nk} - \Big(\int_{|x|<\tau} x \, dF_{nk} \Big)^2.$$

THEOREM 1. Suppose that $C(v, \xi_{nk}) = 0$ for some $v > 0$ and all $n, k = 1, 2, \ldots$. Then

$$P(S^{(n)}_{\nu_n} < x) \Longrightarrow \Phi_{\sigma^2}(x) = (2\pi\sigma^2)^{-1/2} \int_{-\infty}^{x} \exp\{-u^2/(2\sigma^2)\} \, du \qquad (4)$$

as $n \to \infty$ and simultaneously (2) hold iff for any $\varepsilon > 0$ and some $\tau > 0$

$$P\text{-}\lim_{n\to\infty} \sum_{k=1}^{\nu_n} P(|\xi_{nk}| \geq \varepsilon) = 0, \tag{5}$$

$$P\text{-}\lim_{n\to\infty} \sum_{k=1}^{\nu_n} \sigma_{nk}^2(\tau) = \sigma^2. \tag{6}$$

Possibly theorem 1 may be more convenient for applications reformulated in a following manner.

THEOREM 2. Suppose that $C(\vartheta, \xi_{nk}) = 0$ for some $\vartheta > 0$ and all $n, k = 1, 2, \ldots$. Then (2) and (4) hold simultaneously iff for almost all $t \in [0, 1]$ with respect to Lebesgue measure

$$P(S^{(n)}_{l_n(t)} < x) \Longrightarrow \Phi_{\sigma^2}(x) \tag{7}$$

as $n \to \infty$ and (3) hold simultaneously.

If the expectations of r.v.'s ξ_{nk} are finite then they are just the most convenient centering constants. This fact is illustrated by the following theorem.

THEOREM 3. Suppose that ξ_{nk} have zero expectations and finite variances $D\xi_{nk}$ satisfying the following condition

$$P\text{-}\lim_{n\to\infty} \sum_{k=1}^{\nu_n} D\xi_{nk} = \sigma^2. \tag{8}$$

Then (4) and

$$P\text{-}\lim_{n\to\infty} \sup_{1\leq k\leq \nu_n} D\xi_{nk} = 0 \tag{9}$$

hold simultaneously iff for any $\varepsilon > 0$

$$P\text{-}\lim_{n\to\infty} \sum_{k=1}^{\nu_n} \int_{|x|>\varepsilon} x^2\, dF_{nk} = 0. \tag{10}$$

The next theorem dwells upon the relative stability mentioned above. This theorem is an analoque of a classical one [1] , § 28.

THEOREM 4. Suppose that $\xi_{nk} \geq 0$ for all $n, k = 1, 2, \ldots$. Then

$$P(S_{\nu_n}^{(n)} < x) \Longrightarrow E(x - \sigma^2) = \begin{cases} 0, & x \leq \sigma^2, \\ 1, & x > \sigma^2, \end{cases} \tag{11}$$

as $n \to \infty$ and (2) hold simultaneously iff for each $\varepsilon > 0$ and some $\tau > 0$

$$\begin{gathered} P\text{-}\lim_{n\to\infty} \sum_{k=1}^{\nu_n} P(\xi_{nk} \geq \varepsilon) = 0, \\ P\text{-}\lim_{n\to\infty} \sum_{k=1}^{\nu_n} \int_0^{\tau} x\, dF_{nk} = \sigma^2. \end{gathered} \tag{12}$$

The next two theorems link relative stability with the central limit theorem for random sums. These theorems are analoques of the theorems of D.A.Raikov and B.V.Gnedenko mentioned in the introduction.

THEOREM 5. Let the conditions of theorem 3 hold. Then (4) and (9) hold simultaneously iff

$$P\text{-}\lim_{n\to\infty} \sum_{k=1}^{\nu_n} \xi_{nk}^2 = \sigma^2. \tag{13}$$

THEOREM 6. Suppose that (2) holds and $C(v, \xi_{nk}) = 0$ for some $v > 0$ and all $n, k = 1, 2, \ldots$. Then (4) holds iff for some $\tau > 0$

$$P\text{-}\lim_{n\to\infty} \sum_{k=1}^{\nu_n} (\xi_{nk} - a_{nk}(\tau))^2 = \sigma^2. \tag{14}$$

PROOF OF THE THEOREMS. We give the proof of theorem 1 in detail. The proofs of other theorems will be presented in an abridged way since their main motives will be exposed the proof of theorem 1 and besides that they will for the most part be reduced to combining classical theorems.

PROOF OF THEOREM 1. Necessity. According to theorem 2 of [5] there exist a subsequence $\mathcal{N}$ of natural numbers, a sequence of step functions $m_n(t),\ t\in[0,1]$, and a measurable stochastic process $\chi(t)$, $t\in[0,1]$, with independent increments such that for almost all $t\in[0,1]$ with respect to Lebesque measure the sequence of r.v.'s $\{S^{(n)}_{\ell_n(t)} - m_n(t)\}$ converges weakly to $\chi(t)$ as $n\to\infty,\ n\in\mathcal{N}$. Using the properties of ϑ-centers we get that the sequence $\{C(\vartheta, S^{(n)}_{\ell_n(t)} - m_n(t)) = -m_n(t)\}$ converges to $C(\vartheta, \chi(t))$ as $n\to\infty$, $n\in\mathcal{N}$. Therefore for the mentioned $t\in[0,1]$

$$P(S^{(n)}_{\ell_n(t)} < x) \Rightarrow P(\bar{\chi}(t) < x) = F_t(x),\quad n\to\infty,\quad n\in\mathcal{N}, \tag{15}$$

where $\bar{\chi}(t) = \chi(t) - C(\vartheta, \chi(t))$. Note that F_t is an infinitely divisible d.f. Repeating the proof of the cited theorem 2 of [5] we obtain

$$P(S^{(n)}_{\nu_n} < x) \Rightarrow P(\bar{\chi}(w) < x),\quad n\to\infty,\quad n\in\mathcal{N}, \tag{16}$$

where w is a r.v., uniformly distributed on $[0,1]$ and independent of $\bar{\chi}(t),\ t\in[0,1]$.

Now we shall show that for almost all $t\in[0,1]$ with respect to Lebesgue measure the random variable $\bar{\xi}(t)$ has the normal d.f. $\Phi_{\sigma^2}(x)$. To achieve this aim we define r.v.'s $\bar{\xi}_{nk}$ in such a way that, first, ν_n, ξ_{nk} and $\bar{\xi}_{nk}$, $k=1,2,\ldots$, are independent and, second, ξ_{nk} and $\bar{\xi}_{nk}$ are identically distributed. We construct the sum of differences $Z_k^{(n)} = (\xi_{n1} - \bar{\xi}_{n1}) + \ldots + (\xi_{nk} - \bar{\xi}_{nk})$ which is a symmetric r.v. Using the law of total probability and Levy's inequality [3], p.261, for the sums of symmetric r.v.'s we get

$$P(|Z_{\nu_n}^{(n)}| > x) = \sum_{r=1}^{\infty} P(\nu_n = r) P(|Z_r^{(n)}| > x) \geqslant$$

$$\geqslant \frac{1}{2} \sum_{r=l_n(t)}^{\infty} P(\nu_n = r) P(|Z_{l_n(t)}^{(n)}| > x) \geqslant \frac{1}{2}(1-t) P(|Z_{l_n(t)}^{(n)}| > x).$$

Let Ψ_t denote the convolution of $F_t(x)$ and $1 - F_t(-x+0)$. Putting $n \to \infty$, $n \in N$, in the previous inequality we have

$$\frac{1}{2}(1-t)[\Psi_t(-x) + 1 - \Psi_t(x)] \leqslant 2[\Phi_{\sigma^2}(-\tfrac{x}{2}) + 1 - \Phi_{\sigma^2}(\tfrac{x}{2})] \quad (17)$$

in each point where Ψ_t is continuous, since

$$P(|Z_{\nu_n}^{(n)}| > x) \leqslant 2\, P(|S_{\nu_n}^{(n)}| > \tfrac{x}{2})$$

and by the assumption (4) holds. (17) implies the finiteness of the integral

$$\int_{-\infty}^{\infty} \exp\{\alpha |x| \ln(1 + |x|)\}\, d\Psi_t(x)$$

for any $\alpha > 0$, and as a consequence, as it was proved in [4], the normality of the covolution $\Psi_t(x)$ and according to Cramer's theorem the normality of $F_t(x)$ itself. Thus we proved that $\bar{\xi}(t)$ is a normal r.v. with variance equal to $\sigma_t^2 \geqslant 0$. The expectation of $\bar{\xi}(t)$ equals the center $C(v, \bar{\xi}(t)) = 0$.

Since (4) and (16) hold the characteristic functions corresponding to d.f.'s $P(\bar{\jmath}(w) < x)$ and $\Phi_{\sigma^2}(x)$ coinside, i.e.

$$\int_0^1 \exp\{-\tfrac{1}{2}\sigma_t^2 u^2\}dt = \exp\{-\tfrac{1}{2}\sigma^2 u^2\}.$$

Taking a limit as $u \to 0$ after m -fold differentation of this identity we get

$$\int_0^1 (\sigma_t/\sigma)^{2m} dt = 1.$$

Evident reasoning connected with taking a limit as $m \to \infty$ leads us to $\sigma_t^2 = \sigma^2$ for almost all $t \in [0, 1]$. According to the theorem [3] , p.329, (15) is equivalent to the following three conditions: for almost all $t \in [0, 1]$

$$\sum_{k=1}^{l_n(t)} P(|\xi_{nk}| \geq \varepsilon) \to 0, \tag{18}$$

$$\sum_{k=1}^{l_n(t)} \sigma_{nk}^2(\tau) \to \sigma^2, \tag{19}$$

$$\sum_{k=1}^{l_n(t)} a_{nk}(\tau) \to 0, \tag{20}$$

as $n \to \infty$, $n \in \mathcal{N}$.

Now let's show that (5), (6) hold if the limit is taken as $n \to \infty$, $n \in \mathcal{N}$. We shall prove (6) since (5) can be proved the same way. For any $\delta > 0$ and $t \in (0, 1)$ we have

$$P(\sum_{k=1}^{\nu_n} \sigma_{nk}^2(\tau) > \sigma^2 + \delta) = \sum_{r=1}^{\infty} P(\nu_n = r)\, P(\sum_{k=1}^{r} \sigma_{nk}^2(\tau) > \sigma^2 + \delta) \leq$$

$$\leq \sum_{r=1}^{l_n(t)} P(\nu_n = r)\, P\Big(\sum_{k=1}^{r} \sigma_{nk}^2(r) > \sigma^2 + \delta\Big) + 1 - t \leq$$

$$\leq t\, P\Big(\sum_{k=1}^{l_n(t)} \sigma_{nk}^2(r) > \sigma^2 + \delta\Big) + 1 - t.$$

By analogy

$$P\Big(\sum_{k=1}^{\nu_n} \sigma_{nk}^2(r) < \sigma^2 - \delta\Big) \leq$$

$$\leq t + \sum_{r=l_n(t)}^{\infty} P(\nu_n = r)\, P\Big(\sum_{k=1}^{r} \sigma_{nk}^2(r) < \sigma^2 - \delta\Big) \leq$$

$$\leq t + (1-t)\, P\Big(\sum_{k=1}^{l_n(t)} \sigma_{nk}^2(r) < \sigma^2 - \delta\Big).$$

In the first series of inequalities t, $0<t<1$, can be chosen arbitrarily close to 1 and in the second series it can be chosen arbitrarily small. In both cases t can be chosen to suffice (19). Taking a limit as $n \to \infty$, $n \in W$, leads to (6).

Now sum up what we have done. If (4) holds then there exists a subsequence of indices W such that (5), (6) hold as $n \to \infty$, $n \in W$. Now take an arbitrary subsequence W_0 of natural numbers. Repeating the above reasoning we find the subsequence $W \subset W_0$ such that (5), (6) hold as $n \to \infty$, $n \in W \subset W_0$. Thus we proved that each of the two sequences of random variables in (5), (6) is compact in probability. All the convergent subsequences (of each of the two mentioned sequences) have the common limit. Therefore (5), (6) hold.

Sufficiency. (2) follows from (5). For any $t \in (0, 1)$ and $\delta > 0$ we have

$$P\Big(\sum_{k=1}^{\nu_n} \sigma_{nk}^2(r) > \sigma^2 + \delta\Big) \geq (1-t)\, P\Big(\sum_{k=1}^{l_n(t)} \sigma_{nk}^2(r) > \sigma^2 + \delta\Big),$$

$$P\left(\sum_{k=1}^{\nu_n} \sigma_{nk}^2(\tau) < \sigma^2 - \delta\right) \geq t\, P\left(\sum_{k=1}^{l_n(t)} \sigma_{nk}^2(\tau) < \sigma^2 - \delta\right).$$

These inequalities and (6) imply (19) as $n \to \infty$. By analogy we can see that (18) also holds as $n \to \infty$. By theorem [1], p.136, conditions (18) and (19) and the third property of the centres imply (20) as $n \to \infty$. By theorem [3], p.329, conditions (18), (19) and (20) imply (7) which as it was shown in [5] quarantees (4). The proof is over.

PROOF OF THEOREM 2. (2) and (7) are equivalent to (18), (19) as $n \to \infty$ for almost all $t \in [0, 1]$ with respect to Lebesgue measure. When we proved theorem 1 we made sure that (18), (19) are equivalent to conditions of theorem 1. Theorem 2 is proved.

PROOF OF THEOREM 3. If (1) holds then (8) and (9) are equivalent to

$$\lim_{n \to \infty} \sum_{k=1}^{l_n(t)} D\xi_{nk} = \sigma^2,$$

$$\lim_{n \to \infty} \max_{1 \leq k \leq l_n(t)} D\xi_{nk} = 0 \tag{21}$$

for each $t \in (0, 1)$ respectively. The sequence of sums $\{S_{l_n(t)}^{(n)}\}$ is weakly compact since their variances are bounded and expectations are equal to zero.

Necessity. Construct values $Z_k^{(n)}$ as it was done in the proof of theorem 1. Using the same reasoning we can show that the r.v.'s being weak limits of the subsequences $\{Z_{l_n(t)}^{(n)}\}$ have normal d.f.'s. Therefore if ξ is a weak limit of some subsequence $\{S_{l_n(t)}^{(n)}\}$, $n \in N$, then is also has a normal d.f. The first relation (21) implies the expectation of ξ to be the limit of expectations of sums $S_{l_n(t)}^{(n)}$

as $n \to \infty$, $n \in \mathcal{N}$. Therefore it equals zero. Taking (21) into account, with the help of theorem [3] , p.309, we see that ξ has d.f. $\Phi_{\sigma^2}(x)$. Since ξ is an arbitrary weak limit of the sequence of sums, the sequence of d.f.'s of sums $S^{(n)}_{\ell_n(t)}$ converges to $\Phi_{\sigma^2}(x)$ in Levy's metric. The mentioned theorem [3] , p.309, gives

$$\lim_{n \to \infty} \sum_{k=1}^{\ell_n(t)} \int_{|x|>\varepsilon} x^2 dF_{nk} = 0. \tag{22}$$

If (1) holds then (10) is equivalent to (22) for all $t \in (0, 1)$.

Sufficiency. (10) implies (22) for all $t \in (0, 1)$ which together with (21) give (7) which in its turn quarantees (4). The proof is over.

PROOF OF THEOREM 4. Using the law of total probability for any $t \in (0, 1)$ and $\delta > 0$ we have

$$P(S^{(n)}_{\nu_n} > \sigma^2 + \delta) \geqslant (1-t)\, P(S^{(n)}_{\ell_n(t)} > \sigma^2 + \delta),$$

$$P(S^{(n)}_{\nu_n} < \sigma^2 - \delta) \geqslant t\, P(S^{(n)}_{\ell_n(t)} < \sigma^2 - \delta),$$

$$P(S^{(n)}_{\nu_n} > \sigma^2 + \delta) \leqslant t\, P(S^{(n)}_{\ell_n(t)} > \sigma^2 + \delta) + 1 - t,$$

$$P(S^{(n)}_{\nu_n} < \sigma^2 - \delta) \leqslant t + (1-t)\, P(S^{(n)}_{\ell_n(t)} < \sigma^2 - \delta).$$

From these inequalities we obtain the equivalence of (11) and

$$P - \lim_{n \to \infty} S^{(n)}_{\ell_n(t)} = \sigma^2 \tag{23}$$

for each $t \in (0, 1)$. If (1) hold then these letter conditions are equivalent to the conditions (12). The proof is over.

PROOF OF THEOREM 5. Proving theorem 3 we showed that (4), (8) and

(9) are equivalent to (21) and (22) for each $t \in (0,1)$. In its turn this is equivalent to (21) and

$$\lim_{n\to\infty} P(S^{(n)}_{\ell_n(t)} < x) = \Phi_{\sigma^2}(x) \tag{24}$$

for each $t \in (0,1)$. If conditions (21) hold then by Raikov's theorem [1], p. 152, (24) is equivalent to

$$P-\lim_{n\to\infty} \sum_{k=1}^{\ell_n(t)} \xi_{nk}^2 = \sigma^2 \tag{25}$$

for each $t \in (0,1)$. If (1) holds then (25) equivalent to (14). Theorem is proved.

PROOF OF THEOREM 6. It is analogous to that of theorem 5. All changes consist of replacing Raikov's theorem and theorem 3 by the Gnedenko' theorem [1], p.152, and theorem 2 respectively.

Dept. of Computing Math. and Cybernetics
Moscow State University
Leninskie Gory
Moscow, USSR

REFERENCES

1. Gnedenko B.V., Kolmogorov A.N. Limit Distributions for Sums of Independent Random Variables. Moscow, Leningrad, 1949, 264 p. (in Russian).
2. Zolotarev V.M. Modern Theory of Summation of Independent Random Variables.. Moscow, Nauka, 1988, 415 p. (in Russian).
3. Loéve M. Probability Theory. Izd. Inostr. Lit., Moscow, 1968, 719 p. (in Russian).

4. Kruglov V.M. A characterization of a class of infinitely divisible distributions in a Hilbert space.- Mat.Zametki, 1974, 16, N 5, 777-782 (in Russian).

5. Szász D. Limit theorems for the distributions of the sums of a random number of random variables.- Ann.Math.Stat., 1972, 43, N 66, 1902-1913.

NEW DUALITY THEOREMS FOR MARGINAL PROBLEMS

WITH SOME APPLICATIONS IN STOCHASTICS

V.L.Levin and S.T.Rachev

1. Introduction

In what follows S is a topological space, $\mathcal{B}(S)$ is the σ-algebra of its Borel subsets, $C(S)$ is the vector space of continuous real-valued functions on S and $C^b(S)$ is the vector subspace of $C(S)$ consisting of bounded functions. All topological spaces dealt with in this paper are assumed to be completely regular and homeomorphic with universally measurable subsets of some compact Hausdorff spaces. The class of all such spaces will be denoted by $\mathcal{L}$. This class has been already considered in [18] . It will be important that $\mathcal{L}$ includes Polish spaces (:= metrizable separable spaces that may be metrized in such a way that they become complete) and that the product space $S_1 \times S_2$ belongs to $\mathcal{L}$ provided S_1 and S_2 belong to $\mathcal{L}$. Talking about measures on a topological space, we always mean the Radon measures, i.e. finite inner regular Borel measures. (Recall that a finite nonnegative Borel measure P on S is called inner regular when the equality

$$P(B) = \sup\{P(K) : K \subset B,\ K \text{ compact}\}$$

holds for each $B \in \mathcal{B}(S)$. A (signed) measure is said to be inner regular if the elements of its Jordan decomposition are inner regular.) The vector space of all (signed) measures on S will be denoted by $V(S)$, the cone of nonnegative measures by $V_+(S)$ and the set of probability measures by $M(S)$.

Given a nonnegative measure P on the product space $S_1 \times S_2$ one can consider its marginals $\pi_1 P \in V_+(S_1)$, $\pi_2 P \in V_+(S_2)$ defined by

$$\pi_1 P(B_1) = P(B_1 \times S_2) \qquad \text{for any} \qquad B_1 \in \mathcal{B}(S_1),$$

$$\pi_2 P(B_2) = P(S_1 \times B_2) \qquad \text{for any} \qquad B_2 \in \mathcal{B}(S_2).$$

Obviously $\pi_1 P \in M(S_1)$, $\pi_2 P \in M(S_2)$ provided $P \in M(S_1 \times S_2)$.

The simplest extremal marginal problem is stated as follows. Given measures $P_1 \in V_+(S_1)$, $P_2 \in V_+(S_2)$ with $P_1(S_1) = P_2(S_2)$ and a function c on $S_1 \times S_2$, one has to minimize the functional on $V(S_1 \times S_2)$

$$c(P) := \int_{S_1 \times S_2} c(x, y)\, dP \tag{1.1}$$

subject to

$$\pi_1 P = P_1, \qquad \pi_2 P = P_2. \tag{1.2}$$

The dual problems consists in minimizing the functional on $C^b(S_1) \times C^b(S_2)$

$$P_1(u_1) - P_2(u_2) := \int_{S_1} u_1(x)\, dP_1 - \int_{S_2} u_2(y)\, dP_2 \tag{1.3}$$

subject to

$$u_1(x) - u_2(y) \leq c(x, y) \qquad \text{for any} \quad (x, y) \in S_1 \times S_2. \tag{1.4}$$

Denote by $C(c; P_1, P_2)$ and $D(c; P_1, P_2)$ the optimal values of extremal problems (1.1), (1.2) and (1.3), (1.4) respectively:

$$C(c; P_1, P_2) := \inf\{c(P) : P \in V_+(S_1 \times S_2),\ \pi_1 P = P_1,\ \pi_2 P = P_2\} \tag{1.5}$$

$$D(c; P_1, P_2) := \sup\{P_1(u_1) - P_2(u_2) : \quad (u_1, u_2) \in C^b(S_1) \times \tag{1.6}$$

$$\times C^{b}(S_2), \quad u_1(x)-u_2(y)\leqslant c(x,y) \qquad \forall\,(x,y)\in S_1\times S_2\}.$$

It is clear that

$$D(c;\, P_1, P_2)\leqslant C(c;\, P_1, P_2) \tag{1.7}$$

for any bounded below universally measurable function $c:\ S_1\times S_2 \to \mathbb{R}^1\cup\{+\infty\}$.

In the paper of Levin [18] a duality theorem is proved asserting that the equality

$$C(c;\, P_1, P_2) = D(c;\, P_1, P_2) \tag{1.8}$$

holds for $S_1, S_2 \in \mathcal{L}$ and a lower semi-continuous (l.s.c.) function c $S_1\times S_2 \to \mathbb{R}^1\ \cup\{+\infty\}$ which may be represented in form

$$c(x,y) = sup\{\, h(x,y):\ h\in H\} \qquad \forall (x,y)\in S_1\times S_2, \tag{1.9}$$

where

$$H\subset C^b(S_1)\otimes C^b(S_2) := \{\sum_{k=1}^{n} \varphi_k(x)\psi_k(y):\quad \varphi_k\in C^b(S_1),$$
$$\psi_k\in C^b(S_2), \quad k=1,\dots,n, \quad n=1,2,\dots\}.$$

For a case of compact S_1, S_2 see also [17] . (It is not difficult to see that c admits a representation (1.9) iff it has a l.s.c. extension to $\beta S_1\times\beta S_2$, or, what is the same, iff c is bounded below and l.s.c. on $S_1\times S_2$. The class of all such functions will be denoted further by $LSC(\beta S_1\times \beta S_2)$. Here βS stands for the Stone-Cech complactification of S .)

Earlier versions of this duality theorem for compact S_1, S_2 and continuous c are given in [13] , [16] together with two methods of solving the problems (1.1), (1.2) and (1.3), (1.4). Both methods are based on approximating these problems by means of finite-dimensional linear programs. Some specific results concerning numerical solution of the problem (1.1), (1.2) for $S_1 = S_2 = [0, 1]$ may be found in the paper of Anderson and Philpott [1].

Certain duality theorems are proved by Rachev [22], [23] for a case of $S_1 = S_2 = S$ where (S, d) is a separable metric space and the cost function c depends on $d(x, y)$ and has a specific form. In these theorems the dual problem (1.3), (1.4) is considered in spaces of Lipschitz functions $u_1(x)$, $u_2(y)$ instead of spaces $C^b(S_1)$, $C^b(S_2)$.

We have to mention also the paper of Kemperman [11] and especially those of Kellerer [9], [10] including some duality theorems for rather general spaces and cost functions.

For $S_1 = S_2 = S$ and $c = d$ being a metric on S the functional $C(d; P_1, P_2)$ on $M(S) \times M(S)$ coincides with the Kantorovich-Rubinstein distance

$$\varkappa_d(P_1, P_2) = \inf\{d(P): P \in V_+(S \times S),\ \pi_1 P - \pi_2 P = P_1 - P_2\}. \tag{1.10}$$

This distance is closely related with the mass transfer problem which consists in minimizing (1.1) subject to

$$P \in V_+(S \times S), \quad \pi_1 P - \pi_2 P = P_1 - P_2 .$$

The last problem is more general and much more difficult than (1.1), (1.2). Its dual problem is to maximize the functional $P_1(u) - P_2(u)$ on $C^b(S)$ subject to

$$u(x) - u(y) \leqslant c(x, y) \qquad \text{for any} \quad x, y \in S.$$

The duality theorem for the mass transfer problem was first proved by Kantorovich and Rubinstein [8] for a case of metric compact space (S, d) and the cost function $c = d$. Extensions of the duality theorem to arbitrary (nonmetrizable) compact spaces and nonnegative continuous cost functions $c(x, y)$ with $c(x, x) = 0$ are obtained in [13] - [16]. In the joint paper of Levin and Milyutin [20] the mass transfer problem is studied for arbitrary compact S and discontinuous cost functions $c: S\times S \to \mathbb{R}^1 \cup \{+\infty\}$. In this paper conditions on c are given that are necessary and sufficient for the duality theorem to hold. (Every continuous cost function satisfies these conditions.) Extensions of the last results to a more general class of spaces (including all Polish spaces) see in recent papers of one of the authors [18], [19]. Concerning applications of the Kantorovich-Rubinstein distance in various problems of stochastics see the survey [23].

In the present paper some new duality theorems are established for two extremal marginal problems. The first problem $\mathcal{P}_1$ is to minimize the functional (1.1) subject to (1.2) and the additional constraints of moment type

$$\int_{S_1\times S_2} f_k(x,y)\, dP \leq b_k, \qquad k = 1,\dots, m. \tag{1.11}$$

The second problem $\mathcal{P}_2$ deals with the case $S_1=S_2=S$ and is obtained from $\mathcal{P}_1$ by replacing of (1.2) with

$$\pi_1 P + \pi_2 P = P_*, \tag{1.12}$$

where P_* is a given measure in $V_+(S)$. An application of the problem $\mathcal{P}_2$ (without the constraints (1.11)) may be found in [24], where explicit solutions for it are given in case of $S=\mathbb{R}^1$ and of certain specific cost functions c (e.g. the function $c(x,y)=-|x-y|^p$, $p\geq 1$, may be taken).

The optimal values of these two problems are functionals depending on c, P_1, P_2, $b=(b_1,\dots,b_m)$ in case of $\mathcal{P}_1$ and on c, P_*, b in case of $\mathcal{P}_2$. We denote these functionals by $\bar{v}_1(c;P_1,P_2,b)$ and $\bar{v}_2(c;P_*,b)$ respectively. The dual problems $\mathcal{D}\mathcal{P}_1$ and $\mathcal{D}\mathcal{P}_2$ consist in finding the values

$$\underline{v}_1(c; P_1, P_2, b) := \sup\{P_1(u_1) - P_2(u_2) - \sum_{k=1}^{m} \lambda_k b_k : u_1 \in C^b(S_1),$$

$$u_2 \in C^b(S_2), \ \lambda = (\lambda_k) \in \mathbb{R}_+^m, \ u_1(x) - u_2(y) - \sum_{k=1}^{m} \lambda_k f_k(x, y) \leq c(x, y)\}$$

and

$$\underline{v}_2(c; P_*, b) = \sup\{P_*(u) - \sum_{k=1}^{m} \lambda_k b_k : u \in C^b(S), \ \lambda = (\lambda_k) \in \mathbb{R}_+^m,$$

$$u(x) + u(y) - \sum_{k=1}^{m} \lambda_k f_k(x, y) \leq c(x, y)\}.$$

The duality theorems assert that $\overline{v}_1 = \underline{v}_1$ and $\overline{v}_2 = \underline{v}_2$ under certain assumptions about c and f_k, $k = 1, \ldots, m$. Moreover, for certain f_k, $k = 1, \ldots, m$ conditions on c may be given that are necessary and sufficient for the duality relations $\overline{v}_1 = \underline{v}_1$ or $\overline{v}_2 = \underline{v}_2$ to be true (see below assertions II of theorems 1 and 4).

Duality theorem for $\mathcal{P}_1$ (Theorem 1) is contained in Section 2 together with certain related result (Theorem 2), and in Section 3 the duality theorem is stated for problem $\mathcal{P}_2$ (Theorem 3).

In Section 4 the Kantorovich-Rubinstein distance $\varkappa_d(P_1, P_2)$ is considered for $S = \mathbb{R}^m$,

$$d(x, y) = |x_1 - y_1| + \ldots + |x_m - y_m| \ , \quad x = (x_k), \ y = (y_k)$$

and distributuins $P_1, P_2 \in M(\mathbb{R}^m)$, having densities. Using duality approach we obtain two estimates of $\varkappa_d(P_1, P_2)$ improving an estimate given earlier by Zolotarev [28] . Particular cases are pointed out where these estimates turn into exact equalities giving thereby explicit formulae for $\varkappa_d(P_1, P_2)$ (Theorems 4 and 5).

In Section 5 a new approach is proposed to approximation problems of maxima scheme for m -dimensional (dependent) random vectors (rv's). Its essential feature consists in using of functionals $C(c;P_1,P_2)$ and $\bar{v}_1(c;P_1,P_2,b)$ (for certain specific cost functions c) in order to measure the deviation of rv's X,Y with distributions P_1, P_2 . We evaluate the rate of convergence: (i) for normalized maxima of rv's (Theorem 6), (ii) for random maxima of rv's (Theorems 7 and 8), and (iii) in discrete version of the Max -invariance principle (Theorem 9).

2. Duality theorem for $\mathcal{P}_1$

Suppose that S_1 and S_2 belong to $\mathcal{L}$ and that f_k, $k=1,\dots,m$, belong to $LSC(\beta S_1 + \beta S_2)$. Define

$$W := \bigcap_{k=1}^{m} \operatorname{dom} f_k,$$

where

$$\operatorname{dom} f_k := \{(x,y)\in S_1\times S_2 :\ f_k(x,y)<\infty\},\quad k=1,\dots,m.$$

Observe that if c and c' are two bounded below and universally measurable functions $S_1\times S_2 \to \mathbb{R}^1\cup\{+\infty\}$ coinciding on W then the equality

$$\bar{v}_1(c;P_1,P_2,b) = \underline{v}_1(c';P_1,P_2,b) \qquad \forall\,(P_1,P_2,b)\in V(S_1)\times V(S_2)\times \mathbb{R}^m \tag{2.1}$$

holds.

Indeed, if the constraints set for $\mathcal{P}_1$ is nonempty then any measure $P\in V_+(S_1\times S_2)$ satisfying (1.11) is concentrated on W , while otherwise both sides of (2.1) are equal to $+\infty$. Here the usual convention is assumed that $\bar{v}_1 = +\infty$ when the constraints set is empty (in particular, this case takes place when $(P_1, P_2)\notin V_+(S_1)\times$

$\times V_+(S_2))$.

Now we state the dual problem $\mathcal{DP}_1$. It consists in maximizing the functional

$$P_1(u_1) - P_2(u_2) - \sum_{k=1}^{m} \lambda_k b_k \tag{2.2}$$

on the space $C^b(S_1) \times C^b(S_2) \times \mathbb{R}^m$ subject to the constraints

$$u_1(x) - u_2(y) - \sum_{k=1}^{m} \lambda_k f_k(x,y) \leq c(x,y) \quad \forall (x, y) \in W, \tag{2.3}$$

$$\lambda_k \geq 0, \qquad k = 1, \ldots, m. \tag{2.4}$$

The optimal value of $\mathcal{DP}_1$ is denoted by $\underline{v}_1(c; P_1, P_2, b)$. We assume by definition that $\underline{v}_1 = -\infty$ provided the constraints set (2.3), (2.4) is empty.

Now we are in position to state the duality theorem (for a compact case see also [17]).

THEOREM 1. (I) Suppose that $c: S_1 \times S_2 \to \mathbb{R}^1 \cup \{+\infty\}$ is bounded below and universally measurable. Then the existence of a function $c' \in LSC(\beta S_1 + \beta S_2)$ coinciding with c on W is sufficient for the duality relation

$$\bar{v}_1(c; P_1, P_2, b) = \underline{v}_1(c; P_1, P_2, b) \qquad \forall (P_1, P_2, b) \in V(S_1) \times V(S_2) \times \mathbb{R}^m \tag{2.5}$$

to be true. If, in addition, for given (P_1, P_2, b) the constraints set for $\mathcal{P}_1$ is nonempty then the value $\bar{v}_1(c; P_1, P_2, b)$ is attained, i.e. some measure $P \in V_+(S_1 \times S_2)$ exists which is an optimal solution for $\mathcal{P}_1$.

(II) In case $f_k \in C^b(S_1) \bar{\otimes} C^b(S_2)$, $k = 1, \ldots, m$ the condition that $c \in LSC(\beta S_1 \times \beta S_2)$ in necessary and sufficient for (2.5) to be true.

(III) Let $P_1 \in M(S_1)$, $P_2 \in M(S_2)$ and $b = (b_1, \ldots, b_m) \in \mathbb{R}^m$ be fixed. In order that $\underline{v}_1(c; P_1, P_2, b) < +\infty$ for all $c \in C^b(S_1) \bar{\otimes} C^b(S_2)$ it is necessary and sufficient that

$$P_1(u_1) - P_2(u_2) \leq \sum_{k=1}^{m} \lambda_k b_k \tag{2.6}$$

holds whenever

$$u_1(x) - u_2(y) \leq \sum_{k=1}^{m} \lambda_k f_k(x, y), \quad \forall (x, y) \in W. \tag{2.7}$$

Here, $u_1 \in C^b(S_1)$, $u_2 \in C^b(S_2)$, λ_k, $k = 1, \ldots, m$ are nonnegative constants with $\lambda_1 + \ldots + \lambda_m = 1$ and $C^b(S_1) \bar{\otimes} C^b(S_2)$ denotes the subspace in $C^b(S_1 \times S_2)$ consisting of functions which can be extended to $\beta S_1 \times \beta S_2$ with preserving of continuity.

Denote by $\mathbb{T}$ the class of functions $c: S \times S \to \mathbb{R}^1 \cup \{+\infty\}$ which may be represented in form

$$c(x, y) = \sup_{u \in Q} [u(x) - u(y)] \qquad \forall x, y \in S$$

where Q is a nonempty subset in $C^b(S)$. Obviously, $\mathbb{T} \subset LSC(\beta S \times \beta S)$. The following theorem proves to be useful in some applications of Theorem 1.

THEOREM 2. Let $S \in \mathcal{L}$ and let functions $c: S \times S \to \mathbb{R}^1 \cup \{+\infty\}$ and $f_k: S \times S \to \mathbb{R}^1$, $k = 1, \ldots, m$ belong to $\mathbb{T}$. Then the equality

$$\underline{v}_1(c; P_1, P_2, b) = \underline{v}_1'(c; P_1 - P_2, b) \tag{2.8}$$

holds for all $(P_1, P_2, b) \in V(S) \times V(S) \times \mathbb{R}^m$, where $\underline{v}_1'(c; P_1 - P_2, b)$ stands for optimal value of the extremal problem $\mathcal{P}_1'$ consisting in maximizing the functional $(P_1 - P_2)(u) - \sum_{k=1}^{m} \lambda_k b_k$ on $C^b(S) \times \mathbb{R}^m$ subject to the constraints

$$u(x) - u(y) - \sum_{k=1}^{m} \lambda_k f_k(x,y) \leqslant c(x,y), \quad \forall (x,y) \in S \times S,$$

$$\lambda_k \geqslant 0, \qquad k = 1, \ldots, m.$$

3. Duality theorem for $\mathcal{P}_2$

First we formulate the dual problem $\mathcal{DP}_2$. It consists in maximizing the functional

$$P_*(u) - \sum_{k=1}^{m} \lambda_k b_k \tag{3.1}$$

on $C^b(S) \times \mathbb{R}^m$ subject to the constraints

$$u(x) + u(y) - \sum_{k=1}^{m} \lambda_k f_k(x,y) \leqslant c(x,y) \qquad \forall (x,y) \in W, \tag{3.2}$$

$$\lambda_k \geqslant 0, \qquad k = 1, \ldots, m. \tag{3.3}$$

Here it is assumed that $S \in \mathcal{L}$, $f_k \in LSC(\beta S \times \beta S)$, $k = 1, \ldots, m$, and $W = \bigcap_{k=1}^{m} \operatorname{dom} f_k$ (cf. Section 2).

The optimal value for $\mathcal{DP}_2$ is denoted by $\underline{v}_2(c; P_*, b)$. As usually, we assume that $\underline{v}_2(c; P_*, b) = -\infty$ if the constraints set (3.2) , (3.3) is empty.

When $W = S \times S$, a certain function $c_*: S \times S \to \mathbb{R}^1 \cup \{+\infty\}$ may be associated with the problem $\mathcal{P}_2$ as follows. Given a point $(x,y) \in S \times S$ we define $c_*(x,y)$ as the optimal value of the next finite-dimensional linear program: minimize the (generalized linear) function

$$l(x,y; \alpha_1, \alpha_2, \alpha_3) := \alpha_1 c(x,y) + \alpha_2 c(x,y) + \alpha_3 [c(x,x) + c(y,y)] \tag{3.4}$$

subject to the constraints

$$\alpha_1 \geq 0, \quad \alpha_2 \geq 0, \quad \alpha_3 \geq 0, \quad \alpha_1 + \alpha_2 + 2\alpha_3 = 1, \tag{3.5}$$

$$\alpha_1 f_k(x,y) + \alpha_2 f_k(y,x) + \alpha_3 [f_k(x,x) + f_k(y,y)] \leq f_k(x,y), \quad k = 1,\dots,m. \tag{3.6}$$

(We use the words "generalized linear" saying about the function (3.4) because its coefficients may be equal to $+\infty$.) For a given $(x,y) \in S \times S$ the constraints set (3.5), (3.6) is a convex polyhedron in $\mathbb{R}^3$ containing the point $(\alpha_1, \alpha_2, \alpha_3) = (1,0,0)$ and thereby nonempty. Then

$$c_*(x,y) = \min_{(\alpha_1,\alpha_2,\alpha_3)} \ell(x,y; \alpha_1, \alpha_2, \alpha_3), \tag{3.7}$$

where the minimum is taken over the (finite) set of extreme points of this constraints polyhedron. It follows that $c_* \in LSC(\beta S \times \beta S)$ provided $c \in LSC(\beta S \times \beta S)$.

Observe also that

$$\underline{v}_2(c; P_*, b) = \underline{v}_2(c_*; P_*, b), \quad \forall\, (P_*, b), \tag{3.8}$$

which follows easily from the fact that the constraints sets for these two problems coincide.

Now we are in position to formulate the duality theorem.

THEOREM 3. (I) Suppose that $c: S \times S \to \mathbb{R}^1 \cup \{+\infty\}$ is bounded below and universally measurable. Then the existence of a function $c' \in LSC(\beta S \times \beta S)$ coinciding with c on W is sufficient for the duality relation

$$\bar{v}_2(c; P_*, b) = \underline{v}_2(c; P_*, b) \quad \forall\, (P_*, b) \in V(S) \times \mathbb{R}^m \tag{3.9}$$

to be true. If, in addition, the constraints set (1.11), (1.12) is nonempty for given (P_*, b) then the value $\bar{v}_2(c; P_*, b)$ is attained, i.e. some measure $P \in V_+(S \times S)$ exists which is an optimal solution for $\mathcal{P}_2$.

(II) In case $f_k \in C^b(S)\bar{\otimes}C^b(S)$, $k = 1, \ldots, m$, the condition that $c_* \in LSC(\beta S \times \beta S)$ is necessary and sufficient for duality relation (3.9) to be true.

(III) Let $P_* \in V_+(S)$ and $b = (b_1, \ldots, b_m) \in \mathbb{R}^m$ be fixed. In order that $\underline{v}_2(c; P_*, b) < +\infty$ for all $c \in C^b(S)\bar{\otimes}C^b(S)$ it is necessary and sufficient that

$$P_*(u) \leqslant \sum_{k=1}^{m} \lambda_k b_k \tag{3.10}$$

holds, whenever

$$u(x) + u(y) \leq \sum_{k=1}^{m} \lambda_k f_k(x,y) \quad \forall (x,y) \in W. \tag{3.11}$$

Here $u \in C^b(S)$ and λ_k, $k = 1, \ldots, m$, are nonnegative constants with $\lambda_1 + \ldots + \lambda_m = 1$.

In the proofs of Theorems 1 and 3 the abstract duality theorem is essentially used from the paper [20].

4. Explicit representations of the Kantorovich-Rubinstein distance

As we have pointed out in Section 1, if (S, d) is a Polish space then the Kantorovich-Rubinstein distance $\varkappa_d(P_1, P_2)$, $P_1, P_2 \in M(S)$, coincides with $C(d; P_1, P_2)$ (see (1.5)) and admits the dual representation

$$\begin{aligned} \varkappa_d(P_1, P_2) = \sup\{|P_1(u) - P_2(u)| :\ & u \in C^b(S), \\ |u(x) - u(y)| \leqslant d(x,y) \quad & \forall\, x, y \in S\}. \end{aligned} \tag{4.1}$$

In this section we give in certain cases explicit representations of $\varkappa = \varkappa_d$ for $S = \mathbb{R}^m$ and $d(x,y) = \| x - y \|$ where

$$\|x\| := |x_1| + \ldots + |x_m| \quad \forall x = (x_1, \ldots, x_m) \in \mathbb{R}^m$$

(see also [23] , § 2.3). We suppose that $P_1, P_2 \in M(\mathbb{R}^m)$ have densities p_1 and p_2 respectively.

THEOREM 4. (I) The inequality

$$\varkappa(P_1, P_2) \leqslant \alpha_1(P_1, P_2) \tag{4.2}$$

holds with

$$\alpha_1(P_1, P_2) := \int_{\mathbb{R}^m} \|x\| \, \Big| \int_0^1 t^{-m-1} (p_1 - p_2)\left(\frac{x}{t}\right) dt \Big| \, dx.$$

(II) If

$$\int_{\mathbb{R}^m} \|x\| \, d(P_1 + P_2) < +\infty \tag{4.3}$$

and if a continuous function $g: \mathbb{R}^m \to \mathbb{R}^1$ exists with derivatives $\frac{\partial g}{\partial x_i}$, $i = 1, \ldots, m$ defined almost everywhere (a.e.) and satisfying

$$\frac{\partial g}{\partial x_i}(x) = \operatorname{sign}\left[x_i \int_0^1 t^{-m-1} (p_1 - p_2)\left(\frac{x}{t}\right) dt\right] \tag{4.4}$$

a.e., $i = 1, \ldots, m$

then (4.2) holds with the equality sign.

THEOREM 5. (I) The inequality

$$\varkappa(P_1, P_2) \leqslant \alpha_2(P_1, P_2) \tag{4.5}$$

holds with

$$\alpha_2(P_1, P_2) := \int_{-\infty}^{+\infty} \left| \int_{-\infty}^{t} q_1(x_{(1)})\, dx_1 \right| dt +$$

$$+ \sum_{i=2}^{m} \int_{\mathbb{R}^{i-1}} \left[\int_{-\infty}^{0} \left| \int_{-\infty}^{t} q_i(x_{(i)})\, dx_i \right| dt + \right.$$

$$\left. + \int_{0}^{\infty} \left| \int_{t}^{\infty} q_i(x_{(i)})\, dx_i \right| dt \right] dx_1 \ldots dx_{i-1} \qquad (4.6)$$

where

$$x_{(i)} := (x_1, \ldots, x_n),$$

$$q_i(x_{(i)}) := \int_{\mathbb{R}^{m-i}} (p_1 - p_2)(x_1, \ldots, x_m)\, dx_{i+1}, \ldots dx_m, \quad i = 1, \ldots, m-1,$$

$$q_m(x_{(m)}) := (p_1 - p_2)(x_1, \ldots, x_m).$$

(II) If (4.3) holds and if a continuous function $h: \mathbb{R}^m \to \mathbb{R}^1$ exists with derivatives h'_i, $i = 1, \ldots, m$, defined a.e. and satisfying the conditions

$$h'_1(t, 0, \ldots, 0) = \operatorname{sign}\,[F_{11}(t) - F_{21}(t)],$$

$$h'_2(x_1, t, 0, \ldots, 0) = \begin{cases} \operatorname{sign} \int_{-\infty}^{t} q_2(x_{(2)})\, dx_2 & \text{if } t \in (-\infty, 0],\ x_1 \in \mathbb{R}^1 \\ -\operatorname{sign} \int_{t}^{\infty} q_2(x_{(2)})\, dx_2 & \text{if } t \in (0, +\infty),\ x_1 \in \mathbb{R}^1, \end{cases}$$

. . . .

$$h'_m(x_1, \ldots, x_{m-1}, t) = \begin{cases} \operatorname{sign} \int_{-\infty}^{t} q_m(x_{(m)})\, dx_m & \text{if } t \in (-\infty, 0],\ x_1, \ldots, x_{m-1} \in \mathbb{R}^1 \\ -\operatorname{sign} \int_{t}^{\infty} q_m(x_{(m)})\, dx_m & \text{if } t \in (0, +\infty),\ x_1, \ldots, x_{m-1} \in \mathbb{R}^1, \end{cases}$$

then (4.5) holds with the equality sign. Here F_{j1} stands for the distribution function (df) of $\pi_i P_j$.

REMARK. It is well-known that for $m = 1$

$$\varkappa(P_1, P_2) = \int_{-\infty}^{\infty} | F_1(x) - F_2(x) | \, dx$$

where F_i stands for df of P_i $i = 1, 2$. In case $m > 1$ there are not many explicit results concerning the calculation of the Kantorovich-Rubinstein distance. Certain approach to this problem, different from our one, in proposed in recent paper of Rüschendorf [26] , where some further references may be found.

The estimates (4.2) and (4.5) are of interest by themselves. They give two improvements of the Zolotarev estimate [28] :

$$\varkappa(P_1, P_2) \leqslant \nu(P_1, P_2),$$

where

$$\nu(P_1, P_2) := \int_{\mathbb{R}^m} \|x\| \, | p_1(x) - p_2(x) | \, dx$$

is the first absolute pseudomoment. Indeed, one can easily check that

$$\alpha_i(P_1, P_2) \leqslant \nu(P_1, P_2), \qquad i = 1, 2.$$

In the next section we shall use the following metric in $M(\mathbb{R}^m)$ (the so-called difference pseudomoment of order $s > 0$):

$$\varkappa_s(P_1, P_2) := C(d_s; P_1, P_2), \qquad P_1, P_2 \in M(\mathbb{R}^m). \tag{4.7}$$

Here

$$d_s(x, y) := \| \bar{Q}_s(x) - \bar{Q}_s(y) \|, \qquad \bar{Q}_s : \mathbb{R}^m \to \mathbb{R}^m, \tag{4.8}$$

$$\bar{Q}_s(x) := (Q_s(x_1), \ldots, Q_s(x_m)), \qquad Q_s(t) := t \, |t|^{s-1} \tag{4.9}$$

Since

$$\varkappa_s(P_1, P_2) = \varkappa(P_1 \circ \bar{Q}_s^{-1}, P_2 \circ \bar{Q}_s^{-1}),$$

then by (4.2) and (4.5) we obtain the estimates

$$\varkappa_s(P_1, P_2) \leq d_i(P_1 \circ \bar{Q}_s^{-1}, P_2 \circ \bar{Q}_s^{-1}), \quad i = 1, 2, \tag{4.10}$$

which are better than the Zolotarev estimate (See Theorem 3 in [28])

$$\varkappa_s(P_1, P_2) \leq \vartheta(P_1 \circ \bar{Q}_s^{-1}, P_2 \circ \bar{Q}_s^{-1}).$$

5. Rate of convergence in maxima scheme

5.1. Normalized maxima

As is well-known, the scheme of maxima of independent variables is one of the basic in limit theorems of probability theory (see [5], [4] , [29] , [21]). The main purpose of this section is to describe a new approach to studying the rate of convergence in maxima scheme, which would fit both for independent and dependent random vectors. The essential feature of this approach consists in using the functionals $C(c; P_1, P_2)$ and $\bar{v}_1(c; P_1, P_2, b)$ for estimating the rate of convergence.

Let $\mathfrak{X}^m$ be the space of all m-dimensional rv's $X = (X^{(1)}, \ldots, X^{(m)})$ on a common probability space $(\Omega, \mathfrak{A}, \mathbb{P})$. In what follows, we assume that $(\Omega, \mathfrak{A}, \mathbb{P})$ has no atoms, and hence the space of all distributions P_{XY} of pairs $X, Y \in \mathfrak{X}^m$ coincides with $M(\mathbb{R}^{2m})$. In this case the functionals C and $\bar{v}_1$ may be rewritten in form

$$C(c; P_1, P_2) = \inf\{\mathbb{L}_c(X,Y) : X, Y \in \mathfrak{X}^m,\ \mathbb{P}_X = P_1,\ \mathbb{P}_Y = P_2\}, \tag{5.1}$$

$$\begin{aligned} \bar{v}_1(c; P_1, P_2, b) = \inf\{\mathbb{L}_c(X,Y) : X, Y \in \mathfrak{X}^m,\ & \mathbb{P}_X = P_1, \\ \mathbb{P}_Y = P_2,\ & E f_k(X,Y) \leq b_k,\ k = 1, \ldots, m_1\}, \end{aligned} \tag{5.2}$$

where

$$\mathbb{L}_c(X,Y) := \mathbb{E}\, c(X,Y). \tag{5.3}$$

We shall assume that

$$c(x,y) = c_{H,s}(x,y) := H(\|\bar{Q}_s(x) - \bar{Q}_s(y)\|), \qquad s \geq 1, \tag{5.4}$$

where $\bar{Q}_s : \mathbb{R}^m \to \mathbb{R}^m$ is defined by (4.9),

$$\|x\| := |x_1| + \ldots + |x_m| \qquad \forall\, x = (x_1, \ldots, x_m) \in \mathbb{R}^m$$

and H is a nondecreasing continuous function on $[0, +\infty)$ vanishing at zero (and only there) and satisfying the Orlicz's condition

$$K_H := \sup\{H(2t)/H(t) : t > 0\} < \infty. \tag{5.5}$$

We are going to examine the rate of convergence for normalized maxima of rv's in terms of $\mathbb{L}_c$, C and $\bar{v}_1$. Let

$$K(X,Y) := \inf\{\varepsilon > 0 : \mathbb{P}(\|X - Y\| > \varepsilon) < \varepsilon\} \tag{5.6}$$

be the Ky Fan metric (distance in probability) in $\mathfrak{X}^m$ and let

$$\pi(P_1, P_2) := \inf\{\varepsilon > 0 : P_1(A) \leq P_2(A^\varepsilon) + \varepsilon \qquad \forall\, A \in \mathcal{B}(\mathbb{R}^m)\}$$

(A^ε stands for ε -neighbourhood of A in $\mathbb{R}^m$) be the Lévy-Prokhorov distance in $M(\mathbb{R}^m)$. Denote

$$m_{H,s}(X) := \mathbb{E} H(\|\bar{Q}_s(X)\|) \qquad \forall\, X \in \mathfrak{X}^m.$$

The next lemma gives the necessary and sufficient conditions for $\mathbb{L}_c$-, C- and $\bar{v}_1$ -convergences.

LEMMA 1. Let $c(x,y)$ be given by (5.4), $X, X_n \in \mathfrak{X}^m$ and

$$m_{H,s}(X_n) + m_{H,s}(X) < +\infty. \tag{5.7}$$

(I) $\mathbb{L}_c(X_n, X) \to 0$ as $n \to \infty$ if and only if both $K(X_n, X) \to 0$ and

$$m_{H,s}(X_n) \longrightarrow m_{H,s}(X) \quad \text{as} \quad n \to \infty . \tag{5.8}$$

(II) Let X_n and X have distributions P_n and P respectively. Then $C(c; P_n, P) \to 0$ as $n \to \infty$ if and only if $\pi(P_n, P) \to 0$ as $n \to \infty$ and (5.8) holds.

(III) Consider $\bar{v}_1(c; P_n, P, b)$ for $s = 1$, $m_1 = 1$, $b = \varepsilon_n$ and $f_1(x, y) := I\{\|x - y\| > \varepsilon_n\}$, where $\varepsilon_n \to 0$ as $n \to \infty$. Then

$$\bar{v}_1(c; P_n, P, \varepsilon_n) \to 0 \quad \text{as} \quad n \to \infty$$

if and only if both

$$\lim_{n \to \infty} \sup \varepsilon_n^{-1} \pi(P_n, P) \leq 1 \tag{5.9}$$

and

$$\lim_{N \to \infty} \lim_{n \to \infty} \sup \int_{\mathbb{R}^m} H(\|x\|) I\{\|x\| > N\} \, dP_n = 0. \tag{5.10}$$

In the sequel we always assume that $\bar{v}_1$ is given as in Lemma 1.

Now we shall introduce the notion of max domain of attraction for a sequence of dependent rv's. This notion proves to be a natural extension of the usual definition of max domain of attraction for a sequence of independent rv's (see § 2.4 in [4]).

For a, b and $x \in \mathbb{R}^m$ we write $ax + b$ to denote the vector $(a_1 x_1 + b_1, \ldots, a_m x_m + b_m)$. Let $\mathbb{X} = \{X_1, X_2, \ldots\}$ be a sequence of dependent rv's $X_k = (X_k^{(1)}, \ldots, X_k^{(m)})$, $k = 1, 2, \ldots,$

$$\xi_n := (\xi_n^{(1)}, \ldots, \xi_n^{(m)}), \quad \xi_n^{(i)} := \max_{1 \leq k \leq n} X_k^{(i)}, \quad i = 1, \ldots, m. \tag{5.11}$$

For short we shall write

$$\xi_n := \bigvee_{k=1}^{n} X_k$$

and

$$x \vee y := (max(x_1, y_1), \ldots, max(x_m, y_m)) \qquad \text{for any } x, y \in \mathbb{R}^m.$$

In the sequel, $X \overset{d}{=} Y$ means $\mathbb{P}_X = \mathbb{P}_Y$.

We say that the sequence $\mathbb{X}$ belongs to the max $\mathbb{L}_c$ -domain of attraction of the rv Y if there exist two sequences of constant vectors $\{a_1, a_2, \ldots\}$, $\{b_1, b_2, \ldots\}$ and a sequence of i.i.d. rv's $\mathbf{Y} = \{Y_1, Y_2, \ldots\}$ such that

$$Y \overset{d}{=} Y_1 \overset{d}{=} a_n \bigvee_{k=1}^{n} Y_k + b_n \tag{5.12}$$

and

$$\mathbb{L}_c(\theta_n, \zeta_n) \to 0 \qquad \text{as} \qquad n \to \infty \tag{5.13}$$

where

$$\theta_n := a_n \xi_n + b_n, \qquad \zeta_n := a_n \bigvee_{k=1}^{n} Y_k + b_n.$$

We shall use also the definition of the max K -domain of attraction that is obtained from the above one by replacing $\mathbb{L}_c$ with K in (5.13).

If $\mathbb{X}$ consists of i.i.d. rv's and belongs to the max K -domain of attraction of Y then

$$\mathcal{K}(\mathbb{P}_{\theta_n}, \mathbb{P}_{\zeta_n}) = \mathcal{K}(\mathbb{P}_{a_n \xi_n + b_n}, \mathbb{P}_Y) \to 0 \qquad \text{as} \quad n \to \infty,$$

i.e.

$$\theta_n \xrightarrow{W} Y \qquad \text{as} \qquad n \to \infty \tag{5.14}$$

where $\xrightarrow{W}$ stands for the weak convergence. The relation (5.14) means precisely that $\mathbb{X}$ belongs to the max domain of attraction of Y in the usual sense (see § 2.4 in [4]). On the other hand, by the Skorohod-Dudley theorem (see [3] , Theorem 19.1) (5.14) implies

$$K(\theta_n, Y) \to 0 \qquad \text{as} \quad n \to \infty \tag{5.15}$$

for suitable chosen probability space $(\Omega, \mathcal{A}, \mathbb{P})$ and Y . Therefore, if c is given by (5.4), $m_{H,s}(\theta_n) \to m_{H,s}(Y)$ and (5.14) holds, then by Lemma 1, (I), one can find $(\Omega, \mathcal{A}, \mathbb{P})$ and Y so that $\mathbb{L}_c(\theta_n, Y) \to 0$. This is a reason to consider the above definition as a natural generalization of the notion of max domain of attraction to a case of dependent rv's.

The limit theorems on the convergences (5.13) and (5.15) can be easily reduced to a case $a_n = n^{-1}\mathbb{1} := (n^{-1}, \ldots, n^{-1})$, $b_n =: \mathbb{0} = (0, \ldots, 0)$ (cf. [29] , [21] , where the convergence (5.14) is examined for i.i.d. rv's). So, we assume that $\theta_n = n^{-1}\xi_n$ and $\xi_n = n^{-1}\bigvee_{k=1}^{n} Y_k$.

Denote by $\mathcal{C}$ the class of functions $c: \mathbb{R}^{2m} \to [0, +\infty)$ of the form (5.4) where H satisfies the inequality

$$H(t_1, t_2) \leqslant H(t_1)H(t_2) \qquad \text{for any} \quad t_1 > 0, \quad t_2 > 0. \tag{5.16}$$

THEOREM 6. (I) Let $c \in \mathcal{C}$ and $\mathbb{X}$ belongs to the max $\mathbb{L}_c$-domain of attraction of Y . Suppose that $\mathbb{Y} = \{Y_1, Y_2, \ldots\}$ is a sequence of i.i.d. rv's with $Y_i \stackrel{d}{=} Y$ and that (X_k, Y_k), $k = 1, 2, \ldots$ is a sequence of (in general, dependent) identically distributed pairs of rv's.Then

$$\mathbb{L}_c(\theta_n, \xi_n) \leqslant \alpha_n \mathbb{L}_c(X_1, Y_1) \tag{5.17}$$

where

$$\alpha_n := H(m)\, n\, H(n^{-s}). \tag{5.18}$$

(II) Under the same assumptions as in (I), but with X belonging to the max K-domain of attraction of Y (instead of $\mathbb{L}_c$-domain), the inequality

$$K(\theta_n,\zeta_n)\leq\varphi^{-1}(\alpha_n\mathbb{L}_c(X_1,Y_1)) \tag{5.19}$$

holds, where α_n is given by (5.18), φ^{-1} is the inverse function of

$$\varphi(t):=t_sH(t_s),\quad t_s:=(2m)^{1-s}t^s.$$

(III) If X consists of i.i.d. rv's then

$$C(c;\mathbb{P}_{\theta_n},\mathbb{P}_Y)\leq\alpha_n C(c;\mathbb{P}_{X_1},\mathbb{P}_Y), \tag{5.20}$$

$$\bar{v}_1(c;\mathbb{P}_{\theta_n},\mathbb{P}_Y,\mathscr{B})\leq\alpha_n\bar{v}_1(c;\mathbb{P}_{X_1},\mathbb{P}_Y,\mathscr{B}), \tag{5.21}$$

and

$$\mathfrak{K}(\mathbb{P}_{\theta_n},\mathbb{P}_Y)\leq\varphi^{-1}(\alpha_n C(c;\mathbb{P}_{X_1},\mathbb{P}_Y)), \tag{5.22}$$

where α_n is given by (5.18).

If, in addition to (5.5) and (5.16), the function H is convex, then $c(x,y)=H(\|\bar{Q}_s(x)-\bar{Q}_s(y)\|)$ belongs to the class $LSC(\beta R^m\times\beta R^m)$ In this case, by Theorem 1, the functional $\bar{v}_1$ in (5.21) may be replaced with $\underline{v}_1$. Analogously, if $H(t)=t$ then $C(c;\mathbb{P}_{X_1},\mathbb{P}_Y)=\varkappa_s(\mathbb{P}_{X_1},\mathbb{P}_Y)$ (see (4.7)) and in appropriate cases one can use (4.10) for estimating the right-hans side of (5.20) by the explicit functionals α_i (see Theorems 4 and 5).

5.2. Random maxima

Now we start to investigate the rate of convergence in Rényi Max-theorem. This theorem is an analog of the Rényi theorem for sums of i.i.d. random variables (see [6], [7] and references there).

LEMMA 2. (Rényi Max-Theorem). Let $\mathbb{X}=\{X_1,X_2,\ldots\}$ be a sequence of rv's and

$$M(q) := q \bigvee_{j=1}^{\nu(q)} X_j , \qquad 0<q<1. \tag{5.23}$$

Here $\nu(q)$ is a geometric random variable with distribution

$$\mathbb{P}\{\nu = k\} = (1-q)^{k-1} q, \qquad k = 1, 2, \ldots$$

and $\nu(q)$ is independent of $\mathbb{X}$.

(I) Suppose $\mathbb{X}$ consists of i.i.d. rv's with common df F. Then $F_{M(q)}(x)$ has a limit $K(x)<1$ as $q \to 0$ for any $x \in \mathbb{R}^m$ if and only if there exist the finite limit

$$\Psi(x) := \lim_{u\to\infty} \frac{1}{u} \frac{F(ux)}{1-F(ux)} . \tag{5.24}$$

In this case

$$K(x) = \frac{\Psi(x)}{1+\Psi(x)} .$$

(II) If $Y_1, Y_2, \ldots$ are i.i.d. rv's with common df K and if $\nu(q)$ is independent of $Y_1, Y_2, \ldots$, then

$$Y_1 \overset{d}{=} W(q) := q \bigvee_{i=1}^{\nu(q)} Y_i . \tag{5.25}$$

We shall estimate the rate of convergence in Rényi Max-Theorem using the metrics

$$\tau_s(X,Y) := \mathbb{L}_{d_s}(X,Y), \quad \varkappa_s(P_1, P_2) := C(d_s; P_1, P_2)$$

and the functional

$$\omega_s(P_1,P_2) := \bar{v}_1(d_s; P_1, P_2, b)$$

where $d_s(x,y) = \| \bar{Q}_s(x) - \bar{Q}_s(y) \|$ (see (4.7), (4.8) and (5.3)).

THEOREM 7. (I) Let $\mathbb{X} = \{X_1, X_2, \ldots\}$ be a sequence of dependent rv's, $\mathbb{Y} = \{Y_1, Y_2, \ldots\}$ a sequence of i.i.d. rv's with common df K, and let

$\nu(q)$ be independent of $\mathbb{X}, \mathbb{Y}$. Suppose the pairs (X_i, Y_i), $i=1,2,\ldots$, are identically distributed. Then

$$\tau_s(M(q), W(q)) \leq q^{s-1} \tau_s(X_1, Y_1) \tag{5.26}$$

(II) If, in addition, $\mathbb{X}$ consists of i.i.d. rv's, then

$$\varkappa_s(F_{M(q)}, K) \leq q^{s-1} \varkappa_s(F_{X_1}, K), \tag{5.27}$$

$$\omega_s(F_{M(q)}, K) \leq q^{s-1} \omega_s(F_{X_1}, K) \tag{5.28}$$

Now, one can derive from (5.26), (5.27) the following estimates

$$K(M(q), W(q)) \leq (2m)^{(s-1)/s} q^{(s-1)/2s} \tau^{1/2s}(X_1, Y_1),$$
$$\mathcal{K}(F_{M(q)}, K) \leq (2m)^{(s-1)/s} q^{(s-1)/2s} \varkappa_s^{1/2s}(F_{X_1}, K). \tag{5.29}$$

Moreover, using the universal inequalities

$$\tau(X', X'') := E\|X' - X''\| \leq (2m)^{(s-1)/s} \tau_s^{1/(2s)}(X', X''),$$
$$X', X'' \in \mathfrak{X}^m,$$
$$\varkappa(P', P'') \leq (2m)^{(s-1)/s} \varkappa_s^{1/s}(P', P''), \qquad P', P'' \in M(\mathbb{R}^m) \tag{5.30}$$

(see Theorem 4 of [28]) we obtain from Theorem 7 the estimates of the rate of convergence in the Rényi Max-Theorem in terms of τ and the Kantorovich-Rubinstein distance $\varkappa$,

$$\tau(M(q), W(q)) \leq (2m)^{(s-1)/s} q^{(s-1)/s} \tau_s^{1/s}(X_1, Y_1),$$

$$\varkappa(F_{M(q)}, K) \leq (2m)^{(s-1)/s} q^{(s-1)/s} \varkappa_s^{1/s}(F_{X_1}, K). \tag{5.31}$$

Comparing (5.31) with (5.27) we see that in (5.31) the power of q rises. Using a more refine method we shall show that

$$\varkappa(F_{M(q)}, K) = O(q^{s-1}) \quad \text{as} \quad q \to 0. \tag{5.32}$$

The main idea of the proof of (5.32) is based on the "convolution method" first proposed by Bergström [2] (see also [27] , [29] , [6] , [7]) for sums of i.i.d. rv's. Here we exploit the convolution method for maxima of i.i.d. rv's.

First of all, we need the following "smoothing" inequality.

LEMMA 3. (Max-smoothing inequality). Let X and Z be two (in general, dependent) rv's. Suppose Y is rv with df K , independent of X, Z . Let K_i, $i = 1, \dots, m$ be the marginals of K and assume that

$$A_s := \max_{1 \le i \le m} \sup_{x \ge 0} K_i(x) s^{-1} x^{1-s} < \infty. \tag{5.33}$$

Then

$$\tau(X \vee Y, Z \vee Y) \le A_s \tau_s(X, Z). \tag{5.34}$$

If, in addition, X, Y and Z are mutually independent, than

$$\varkappa(F_{X \vee Y}, F_{Z \vee Y}) \le A_s \varkappa_s(F_X, F_Z). \tag{5.35}$$

The next theorem establishes (5.32) for $s \in (1, 2]$.

THEOREM 8. Let $\mathbb{X} = \{X_1, X_2, \dots\}$ be a sequence of i.i.d. rv's, $\mathbb{Y} = \{Y_1, Y_2, \dots\}$ a sequence of i.i.d. rv's with common df K and $\nu(q)$ a geometric rv. Assume $\mathbb{X}, \mathbb{Y}$ and $\nu(q)$ are mutually independent. Then for any $q \in (0, 1)$

$$\varkappa(F_{M(q)}, K) \le 2q\varkappa + (1-q)^2 A_s q^{s-1} \varkappa_s \tag{5.36}$$

where

$$\varkappa := \varkappa(F_{X_1}, F_{Y_1}), \quad \varkappa_s := \varkappa_s(F_{X_1}, F_{Y_1})$$

Note that Theorem 8 is informative only if $\varkappa_s < \infty$ and $A_s < \infty$. However, these conditions are satisfied often enough and can be rather simply verified in concrete cases. There exists an example showing that at least for $s=2$ the estimate (5.36) is precise w.r.t. the order of q.

5.3. Invariance principle for maxima scheme

Now we shall consider the rate of convergence in invariance principle for maxima scheme. Let $\mathbb{X}=\{X_1, X_2, \dots\}$, $\mathbb{Y}=\{Y_1, Y_2, \dots\}$ be two sequences of dependent m -dimensional rv's. Define the stochastic processes

$$L_n(t) := n^{-1/\alpha} \bigvee_{j=1}^{[nt]} X_j, \qquad M_n(t) := n^{-1/\alpha} \bigvee_{j=1}^{[nt]} Y_j$$

where $\alpha > 0$ and $[nt]$ means the integer part of nt . Our goal is to estimate the deviation between L_n and M_n in terms of suitable "metric" functionals. For simplicity, we consider the discrete case $t = 1, 2, \dots, T$.

Let $\mathcal{J}_m$ be the space of functions $x(t) = (x_1(t), \dots, x_m(t))$, $x_i : \{1, \dots, T\} \to \mathbb{R}^1$. For any fixed $c \in \mathcal{C}$ define

$$D_c(x, y) := \max_{t=1,\dots,T} c(x(t), y(t)), \qquad x, y \in \mathcal{J}_m.$$

We shall estimate the closeness between L_n and M_n in terms of

$$\mathbb{L}_c(X,Y) := E\, D_c(X,Y)$$

and the Ky Fan distance

$$K(X,Y) := \inf\{\varepsilon > 0 : \mathbb{P}(\sup_{1 \le t \le T} \|X(t) - Y(t)\| > \varepsilon) < \varepsilon\}$$

in the space $\mathfrak{X}(\mathcal{J}_m)$ of random variables taking values in $\mathcal{J}_m$. Analogously, we define the functionals $C(c; P_1, P_2)$, $\bar{v}_1(c; P_1, P_2, 6)$ and the Lévy-Prokhorov distance $\pi(P_1, P_2)$ for $P_1, P_2 \in M(\mathcal{J}_m)$.

THEOREM 9. (I) Assume $c \in \mathcal{C}$, $\beta_n = H(n^{-s/\alpha})H(m)nT$ and let (X_k, Y_k), $k = 1, 2, \ldots$, be a sequence of (in general, dependent) identically distributed random pairs, $X_k, Y_k \in \mathfrak{X}^m$. Then

$$\mathbb{L}_c(L_n, M_n) \leq \beta_n \mathbb{L}_c(X_1, Y_1)$$

and

$$K(L_n, M_n) \leq \varphi^{-1}(\beta_n \mathbb{L}_c(X_1, Y_1))$$

where φ is defined as in Theorem 6.

(II) If $\mathbb{X}$ and $\mathbb{Y}$ have independent components then

$$C(c; \mathbb{P}_{L_n}, \mathbb{P}_{M_n}) \leq \beta_n C(c; \mathbb{P}_{X_1}, \mathbb{P}_{Y_1}),$$

$$\bar{v}_1(c; \mathbb{P}_{L_n}, \mathbb{P}_{M_n}, b) \leq \beta_n \bar{v}_1(c; \mathbb{P}_{X_1}, \mathbb{P}_{Y_1}, b),$$

and

$$\mathfrak{x}(\mathbb{P}_{L_n}, \mathbb{P}_{M_n}) \leq \varphi^{-1}(\beta_n C(c; \mathbb{P}_{X_1}, \mathbb{P}_{Y_1}))$$

It is easy to show that if $m = 1$, $Y_1, Y_2, \ldots$ are i.i.d. with $\mathbb{P}(Y_1 < x) = \exp(-x^{-\alpha})$, $x > 0$, and $\mathbb{X}$ consists of i.i.d. rv's X_i that belong to the max domain of attraction of Y_1, then

$$M_n(\cdot) = n^{-1/\alpha} \max(Y_1, \ldots, Y_{n(\cdot)})$$

has the same distribution as the weak limit $L(\cdot)$ of

$$L_n(\cdot) := n^{-1/\alpha} \max(X_1, \ldots, X_{n(\cdot)})$$

(see [12], [25]). Hence, in this special case we obtain

$$C(c; \mathbb{P}_{L_n}, \mathbb{P}_L) \leq \beta_n C(c; \mathbb{P}_{X_1}, \mathbb{P}_{Y_1}), \tag{5.37}$$

$$\bar{v}_1(c; \mathbb{P}_{L_n}, \mathbb{P}_L, b) \leq \beta_n \bar{v}_1(c; \mathbb{P}_{X_1}, \mathbb{P}_{Y_1}, b), \tag{5.38}$$

$$\mathfrak{x}(c; \mathbb{P}_{L_n}, \mathbb{P}_L) \leq \varphi^{-1}(\beta_n C(c; \mathbb{P}_{X_1}, \mathbb{P}_{Y_1})). \tag{5.39}$$

The relationship (5.39) gives us the rate of weak convergence of $\mathbb{L}_n$ to $\mathbb{L}$, while (5.37) and (5.38) guarantee weak convergence plus convergence of the moments

$$E \sup_{1\le t\le T} H(\|\bar{Q}_s(\mathbb{L}_n(t))\|) \to E \sup_{1\le t\le T} H(\|\bar{Q}_s(\mathbb{L}(t))\|)$$

as $n\to\infty$ (see Lemma 1 and [22]).

6. PROOFS

As is mentioned above, Theorem 1 is proved for compact spaces in [17] . In the general case the proof is similar. Also, the proof of Theorem 3 proceeds on the lines of that of Theorem 1. and so we omit it.

PROOF OF THEOREM 2. Obviously,

$$v_1(c; P_1, P_2, b) = \sup_{\lambda_k \ge 0} [-\sum_{k=1}^{m} \lambda_k b_k + \mathcal{D}(\sum_{k=1}^{m} \lambda_k f_k + c; P_1, P_2)],$$

where the functional $\mathcal{D}$ is defined in (1.6). Note that

$$\sum_{k=1}^{m} \lambda_k f_k + c \in T$$

for any $\lambda_k \ge 0, \quad k = 1, \ldots, m$. Now, the duality relation

$$C(\sum_{k=1}^{m} \lambda_k f_k + c; P_1, P_2) = \mathcal{D}(\sum_{k=1}^{m} \lambda_k f_k + c; P_1, P_2)$$

holds (see Theorem 1 in [18]), which together with the equality

$$\mathcal{B}(\sum_{k=1}^{m} \lambda_k f_k + c; P_1 - P_2) = C(\sum_{k=1}^{m} \lambda_k f_k + c; P_1, P_2)$$

(see Theorem 2 in [18]) yields

$$v_1(c; P_1, P_2, b) = \sup_{\lambda_k \geq 0} [- \sum_{k=1}^{m} \lambda_k b_k + \mathcal{B}(\sum_{k=1}^{m} \lambda_k f_k + c; P_1, P_2)],$$

Here $\mathcal{B}$ stands for optimal value of the dual problem for corresponding mass transfer problem. The proof of finished, because the last equality is equivalent to (2.8).

The proofs of Theorems 4 and 5 are straightforward.

PROOF OF THEOREM 6. (I) This follows easily using (5.4) and (5.16).

(II) By the Chebyshev inequality

$$L_c(X,Y) \geq H(K(\bar{Q}_s(X), \bar{Q}_s(Y))K(\bar{Q}_s(X), \bar{Q}_s(Y))$$

for any $X, Y \in \mathfrak{X}^m$. Next, by the inequality

$$\sum_{i=1}^{m} |x_i - y_i| \leq \{ \sum_{i=1}^{m} |Q_s(x_i) - Q_s(y_i)|(2m)^{s-1} \}^{1/s}$$

one has

$$K(\bar{Q}_s(X), \bar{Q}_s(Y)) \geq (2m)^{1-s} K^s(X,Y),$$

hence

$$L_c(X,Y) \geq \varphi(K(X,Y)) \qquad \text{for any } X, Y \in \mathfrak{X}^m.$$

Now (5.19) follows from this and (5.17).

(III) The inequalities (5.20) and (5.21) follow easily from (5.17) and definitions (5.1), (5.2), while (5.22) is a consequence of (5.19) and the Strassen theorem (see [3, Theorem 10.2]).

PROOF OF THEOREM 7. (I) One has

$$\tau_s(\mathcal{M}(q), W(q)) = \tau_s\Big(q\bigvee_{i=1}^{\nu(q)} X_i,\ q\bigvee_{i=1}^{\nu(q)} Y_i\Big) =$$

$$= \sum_{k=1}^{\infty}(1-q)^{k-1} q\,\tau_s\Big(q\bigvee_{i=1}^{k} X_i,\ q\bigvee_{i=1}^{k} Y_i\Big) \leqslant$$

$$\leqslant \sum_{k=1}^{\infty}(1-q)^{k-1} q^{1+s} k\,\tau_s(X_1, Y_1) = q^{s-1}\tau_s(X_1, Y_1).$$

(II) This follows easily from (5.25) and (5.26).

PROOF OF THEOREM 8. We use the following property of the geometric distribution (see Lemma 6 in [7]):

$$\nu(q) \overset{d}{=} 1 + \delta_1 + \delta_1\delta_2 + \ldots + \delta_1\delta_2\cdot\ldots\cdot\delta_n + \delta_1\delta_2\cdot\ldots\cdot\delta_{n+1}\nu(q), \qquad (6.1)$$

where $\delta_1, \delta_2, \ldots$ are i.i.d. random variables, $P(\delta_i = 0) = q$, $P(\delta_i = 1) = 1 - q$ and $\delta_1, \delta_2, \ldots$ do not depend on $\nu(q), \mathbb{X}$ and $\mathbb{Y}$. Since $\nu(q)$, $\mathbb{X}$ and $\mathbb{Y}$ are mutually independent and

$$Y_i \overset{d}{=} q \bigvee_{k=j+2}^{\nu(q)+j+2} Y_k \qquad \text{for any } i, j,$$

then, by (6.1) and the triangle inequality,

$$\varkappa(\mathcal{M}(q), W(q)) := \varkappa(F_{\mathcal{M}(q)}, K) =$$

$$= \varkappa(q(X_1 \vee \delta_1 X_2 \vee \delta_1\delta_2 X_3 \vee \ldots \vee \delta_1\ldots\delta_n X_{n+1} \vee \qquad (6.2)$$

$$\vee\delta_1 \ldots \delta_{n+1} \bigvee_{k=1}^{\nu(q)} X_k),\ q(Y_1 \vee \delta_1 Y_2 \vee \delta_1 \delta_2 Y_3 \vee \ldots \vee \delta_1 \ldots$$

$$\ldots \delta_n Y_{n+1} \vee \delta_1 \ldots \delta_{n+1} \bigvee_{k=n+2}^{\nu(q)+n+2} Y_k)) \leq \sum_{j=0}^{n} \mathcal{B}_j,$$

where $\varkappa(\mathbb{Z}, \mathbb{Z}')$ stands for $\varkappa(F_{\mathbb{Z}}, F_{\mathbb{Z}'})$.

$$\mathcal{B}_0 := \varkappa(q(X_1 \vee \delta_1 X_2 \vee \ldots \vee \delta_1 \ldots \delta_n X_{n+1} \vee \delta_1 \ldots \delta_{n+1} \bigvee_{k=1}^{\nu(q)} X_k),$$

$$q(Y_1 \vee \delta_1 X_2 \vee \delta_1 \delta_2 X_3 \vee \ldots \vee \delta_1 \ldots \delta_n X_{n+1} \vee \delta_1 \ldots \delta_{n+1} \bigvee_{k=n+2}^{\nu(q)+n+2} Y_k)),$$

$$\mathcal{B}_1 := \varkappa(q(Y_1 \vee \delta_1 X_2 \vee \delta_1 \delta_2 \bigvee_{k=3}^{\nu(q)+3} Y_k),\ q(Y_1 \vee \delta_1 Y_2 \vee \delta_1 \delta_2 \bigvee_{k=3}^{\nu(q)+3} Y_k)),$$

and for $j = 2, \ldots, n$

$$\mathcal{B}_j := \varkappa(q(Y_1 \vee \delta_1 X_2 \vee \ldots \vee \delta_1 \ldots \delta_{j-1} X_j \vee \delta_1 \ldots \delta_j X_{j+1} \vee$$

$$\vee \delta_1 \ldots \delta_{j+1} \bigvee_{k=j+2}^{\nu(q)+j+2} Y_k),\ q(Y_1 \vee \delta_1 X_2 \vee \ldots \vee \delta_1 \ldots \delta_{j-1} X_j \vee$$

$$\vee \delta_1 \ldots \delta_j Y_{j+1} \vee \delta_1 \ldots \delta_{j+1} \bigvee_{k=j+2}^{\nu(q)+j+2} Y_k)).$$

Let us estimate $\mathcal{B}_0$. By the inequality

$$E\|X \vee Y - Z \vee W\| \leq E\|X - Z\| + E\|Y - W\|$$

we have

$$\varkappa(X \vee Y, Z \vee W) \leq \varkappa(X, Z) + \varkappa(Y, W) \tag{6.3}$$

for any pairs (X, Y) and (Z, W) with independent components $X, Y, Z, W \in \mathcal{X}^m$. Then

$$\mathcal{B}_0 \leq P(\delta_1 = 0)\,\varkappa(qX_1, qY_1) + \sum_{j=1}^{n} P(\delta_1 = 1, \ldots, \delta_j = 1, \delta_{j+1} = 0) \times$$

$$\times\, \varkappa(qX_1, qY_1) + P(\delta_1 = 1, \ldots, \delta_{n+1} = 1)[\varkappa(qX_1, qY_1) +$$

$$+ \varkappa(q \bigvee_{k=1}^{\nu(q)} X_k,\; q \bigvee_{k=n+2}^{\nu(q)+n+2} Y_k)].$$

Since the pairs (X_i, Y_i), $i = 1, 2, \ldots,$ are identically distributed, then, by (6.3),

$$\varkappa(q \bigvee_{k=1}^{\nu(q)} X_k,\; q \bigvee_{k=n+2}^{\nu(q)+n+2} Y_k) = \varkappa(q \bigvee_{k=1}^{\nu(q)} X_k,\; q \bigvee_{k=1}^{\nu(q)} Y_k) \leq \varkappa.$$

Hence

$$\mathcal{B}_0 \leq (q + q^2 + (1-q)^{n+1})\,\varkappa. \qquad (6.4)$$

Analogously, for $j > 0$, $\mathcal{B}_j$ can be estimated as follows:

$$\mathcal{B}_j \leq (1-q)^j\,[q^2 \varkappa(X_{j+1}, Y_{j+1}) + (1-q)\varkappa(q\, X_{j+1} \vee$$

$$\vee\, q \bigvee_{k=j+2}^{\nu(q)+j+2} Y_k,\; q \bigvee_{k=j+1}^{\nu(q)+j+2} Y_k)].$$

Applying Lemma 3, one obtains

$$\varkappa(q X_{j+1} \vee q \bigvee_{k=j+2}^{\nu(q)+j+2} Y_k,\; q \bigvee_{k=j+1}^{\nu(q)+j+2} Y_k) \leq A_s \varkappa_s(q X_{j+1}, q Y_{j+1}) =$$

$$= A_s q^s \varkappa_s,$$

hence

$$\mathcal{B}_j \leqslant (1-q)^j [q^2 \varkappa + (1-q) q^s \mathcal{A}_s \varkappa_s].$$

This together with (6.2) and (6.4) proves (5.36).

The proof of Theorem 9 is analogous to that of Theorem 6.

Central Economical and
Mathematical Institute
Krasikov str. 32
117 418 Moscow, USSR

Department of Applied Mathematics
and Statistics
State University of New York
at Stony Brook
Stony Brook, NY 11794-3600, USA

and

Institute of Mathematics,
Sofia, P.O.Box 343, Bulgaria

REFERENCES

1. Anderson E.J., Philpott A.B. Duality and an algorithm for a class of continuous transportation problems. Math.OperRes. 9, 1984,222-231.
2. Bergström H. On the central limit theorem in the space $\mathbb{R}_k$, $k>1$, Scand. Aktuarietidskr. 28, 1945, 106-127.
3. Dudley R.M. Probability and metrics. Aarhus: Aarhus Univ., 1976.
4. Galambos J. The asymptotic theory of extreme order statistics. New York-Chichester.Brisbane-Toronto: Wiley 1978.
5. Gnedenko B.V. Sur la distribution limite du terme maximal d'une série aléatoire. Ann.Math. 1943, 44, 423-453.

6. Kalashnikov V.V. Estimates of the rate of convergence in Rényi theorem. In: Proc.Stability problems for stoch.mod.1983,p.48-57. Moscow: Inst. for System Studies, 1983 (in Russian).
7. Kalashnikov V.V., Vsekhsvyatski- S.Yu. Metric estimates of the first occurence time in regenerative processes. In: Proc. Stability problems for stoch. mod., 1984, 102-130. Lect. Notes Math. 1155, Berlin-Heidelberg- New York-Tokyo: Springer, 1985.
8. Kantorovich L.V., Rubinstein G.S. On a space of completely additive functions. Vestn.Leningr.Univ., 13:7, 52-59 (in Russian).
9. Kellerer H.G. Duality theorems and probability metrics. In: Proc. 7th Brasov Conf, 1982, 211-220, Bucuresti 1984.
10. Kellerer H.G. Duality theorems for marginal problems. Z. Wahrscheinlichkeitstheor. Verw. Geb., 67, 1984, 399-432.
11. Kemperman J.H.B. On the role of duality in the theory of moments. In: Proc. Semi-Infinite Programming and Applications, 1981, 63-92. Lect. Notes in Econ.Math.Syst. 215, Berlin-Heidelberg.New York-Tokyo: Springer, 1983.
12. Lamperti A. On extreme order statistics. Ann.Math.Stat. 35, 1964, 1728-1737.
13. Levin V.L. Duality and approximation in the mass transfer problem In: Math.Econ. and Funct. Analysis, Moscow: Nauka 1974, 94-108 (in Russian).
14. Levin V.L. On the problem of mass transfer. Soviet Math.Dokl. 1975, 16, 1349-1353.
15. Levin V.L. Duality theorems for the Monge-Kantorovich problem. Usp. Mat. Nauk, 32:3, 171-172 (in Russian).
16. Levin V.L. The Monge-Kantorovich mass transfer problem In: Methods of Funct. Analysis in Math. Econ. Moscow: Nauka, 1978, 23-55 (in Russian).
17. Levin V.L. Mass transfer problem, strong stochastic dominance and probability measures with given marginals on the product of two

compact spaces. Preprint of Central Econ. and Math.Inst. Moscow 1983, (in Russian).

18. Levin V.L. The problem of mass transfer in a topological space and probability measures having given marginal measures of the product of two spaces. Soviet Math.Dokl. 29, 1984, 623-843.
19. Levin V.L. Measurable selections of multivalued mappings and the mass transfer problem. Soviet Math.Dokl., 35, 1987, 178-183.
20. Levin V.L., Milyutin A.A. The problem of mass transfer with a discontinuous cost function and a mass statement of the duality problem for convex extremal problems. Russian Math.Surveys 34:3, 1979, 1.78.
21. Omey E., Rachev S.T. On the rate of convergence in extreme value theory. Theory Prob.Appl (to appear).
22. Rachev S.T. On a class of minimal functionals on a space of probability measures. Theory Prob.Appl. 29, 1984, 41-49.
23. Rachev S.T. The Monge-Kantorovich mass transfer problem and its stochastic applications. Theory Prob.Appl. 29, 1984, 647-676.
24. Rachev S.T. Extreme functionals in the space of probability measures. In: Proc.Stab. problems for stoch. models, 1984, 320-348. Lect. Notes Math., 1155, Berlin-Heidelberg.New York-Tokyo: Springer, 1985.
25. Rachev S.T. Extreme functionals in the space of probability measures. In: Proc. IV Vilnius Conf. On Probab. Theory and Math. Stat. 1985 (to appear), Utrecht: VNU Science Press BV, 1986.
26. Rüschendorf L. The Wasserstein distance and approximation theorems. Z. Wahrscheinlichkeitstheor. Verw.Geb., 70, 1985, 117-129.
27. Senatov V.V. Uniform estimates of the rate of convergence in the multi-dimensional central limit theorem. Theory Prob.Appl., 25, 1980, 745-759.
28. Zolotarev V.M. On pseudomoments. Theory Prob. Appl., 23, 1978, 269-278.

29. Zolotarev V.M., Rachev S.T. Rate of convergence in limit theorems for the max-scheme. In: Proc. Stability problems for stoch. model., 1984, 415-442. Lect.Notes Math.1155, Berlin-Heidelberg-New York-Tokyo: Springer, 1985.

STABLE RANDOM VECTORS IN HILBERT SPACE

A.D.Lisitsky

Introduction

Let H be a real separable Hilbert space with inner product $(.,.)$ The Fourier transform of a Borel probability measure Ω on H is a complex valued function defined on H by equality

$$\hat{\Omega}(x) = \int_H e^{i(x,s)} \Omega(ds).$$

DEFINITION 1. The Borel probability measure Ω on H is called stable if for every positive integer k there exist a positive constant a_k and a vector $b_k \in H$ such that

$$[\hat{\Omega}(x)]^k = \hat{\Omega}(a_k x) e^{i(x, b_k)}.$$

It is known (see [1]) that any stable probability measure Ω on H is Gaussian or there exist a constant α $(0<\alpha<2)$ a finit measure μ on $S_H = \{x \in H: \ \|x\| = 1\}$ and a vector $\gamma \in H$ such that

$$\hat{\Omega}(x) = \exp\left(i(x,\gamma) - \int_H |(x,s)|^\alpha \mu(ds) + i C(\alpha, x)\right) \qquad (1)$$

where

$$C(\alpha, x) = \begin{cases} \operatorname{tg} \frac{\pi}{2}\alpha \int\limits_{S_H} (x,s)\, |(x,s)|^{\alpha-1} \mu(ds), & \alpha \neq 1, \\ \\ \frac{2}{\pi} \int\limits_{S_H} (x,s) \ln |(x,s)|\, \mu(ds), & \alpha = 1. \end{cases}$$

Conversely, for every constant α, $0<\alpha<2$, for every finit measure μ and for every vector $\gamma \in H$ there exists stable measure Ω with Fourier transform expressed by (1). Constant α is called type of stable measure Ω . If Ω is Gaussian, we say that Ω is of type 2.

So, in common case, stable measure depends of three parameters: α $(0<\alpha\leq 2)$, μ (μ is finit measure on H_s) and γ $(\gamma \in H)$.

DEFINITION 2. Stable measure Ω on H is called strong stable, if function $\lambda(x) = -\ln \Omega(x)$ is homogeneous, i.e. there exist real constant α such that for any $a>0$

$$\lambda(ax) = a^{\alpha}\lambda(x)$$

(obviously α is type of stable measure Ω).

DEFINITION 3. If support of a measure on H don't lie into any own linear subspace of H then such measure is called non-degenerated.

Let X be a random vector in H . It is well known that X generates a Borel measure (distribution) Ω_X on H according to the rule:

$$\Omega_X(E) = P(X \in E)$$

for any Borel set $E \subset H$.

DEFINITION 4. If a measure Ω_X is non-degenerate strong stable measure of type α , then random vector X is said to be strong stable random vector (or strong stable vector) of type α.

DEFINITION 5. Random variables X and X_1 are said to be d-equal if X and X_1 have the same distribution. This fact we express as $X \stackrel{d}{=} X_1$. Moreover, if X and X_1 are functions of other random variables, then latter are proposed independent, if they stand in the same part of equality. For example, equality $YY_1 \stackrel{d}{=} Y_2Y_3$ means, that Y and Y_1 are independent, Y_2 and Y_3 are independent and distributions of YY_1 and Y_2Y_3 coincid.

In section 2 main theorem 1 will be proved. On the base of the theorem we will define uniform and strong uniform random vectors.

In section 3 theorem 2 will be proved that establishes some multiplicative relations among strong uniform random vectors. (Notice, that d-equalities (8) and (10) are generalizations of 1-dimensional d-equality 3.3.4 and 3.2.7 in [2].)

At last, in the small section 4 a criterion of uniformity of strong stable random vectors in terms of connected random variables will be proved.

2. Main theorem

THEOREM 1. Let $\Omega = \Omega(\alpha, \mu, \gamma)$ be non-degenerated strong stable probability measure of type α and $0<\beta<\alpha$, then there exist non-degenerated strong stable probability measure $\Omega_1 = \Omega_1(\beta, \mu_1, \gamma_1)$ of type β such that

$$[-\ln \Omega(x)]^{\alpha^{-1}} = [-\ln \Omega_1(x)]^{\beta^{-1}}.$$

Moreover, for any Borel set $E \subset S_H$

$$\mu_1(E) = c \int_{\frac{x}{\|x\|} \in E} \|x\|^{\beta} \Omega(dx)$$

where

$$c = \pi\left(2 \sin \frac{\alpha\beta}{2} \Gamma(\beta) \Gamma\left(1 - \frac{\beta}{\alpha}\right)\right)^{-1}.$$

PROOF. Denote

$$\lambda(x) = -\ln \hat{\Omega}(x),$$

$$r(x) = |\lambda(x)|^{\alpha^{-1}},$$

$$\theta(x) = -\frac{2}{\pi\alpha} \arg \lambda(x)$$

i.e. $\lambda(x) = r^{\alpha}(x) \exp\{-\frac{\pi i \alpha}{2} \theta(x)\}.$

LEMMA. Let Ω be strong stable measure on $\mathbb{H}$ of type α and $-1<\beta<\alpha$. Then

$$\int_H |(x,s)|^{\beta}\,\Omega(ds) = r^{\beta}(x)\Gamma(1-\tfrac{\beta}{\alpha})(\Gamma(1-\beta))^{-1}\cos(\tfrac{\pi\beta}{2}\theta(x))(\cos(\tfrac{\pi\beta}{2}))^{-1}, \tag{2}$$

$$\int_H |(x,s)|^{\beta-1}(x,s)\Omega(ds) = r^{\beta}(x)\Gamma(1-\tfrac{\beta}{\alpha})(\Gamma(1-\beta))^{-1}\sin(\tfrac{\pi\beta}{2}\theta(x))(\sin(\tfrac{\pi\beta}{2}))^{-1}, \tag{3}$$

$$\int_H (x,s)\ln|(x,s)|\,\Omega(ds) = \Gamma(1-\alpha^{-1})\,r(x)\sin(\tfrac{\pi\theta(x)}{2}), \tag{4}$$

$$\int_H [\ln|(x,s)| - \tfrac{\pi i}{2}\,\mathrm{sign}(x,s)]\,\Omega(ds)] =$$

$$= \ln r(x) - \tfrac{\pi i}{2}\theta(x) + \Gamma'(1)(1-\alpha^{-1}). \tag{5}$$

PROOF OF THE LEMMA. Equalities (2) and (3) follows from Theorem 2.6.4 in [2] , and from the fact that

$$\int_H |(x,s)|^{\beta}\,\Omega(ds) = \int_{\mathbb{R}^1} |y|^{\beta}\,\Omega_X(dy)$$

and

$$\int_H |(x,s)|^{\beta-1}(x,s)\,\Omega(ds) = \int_{\mathbb{R}^1} |y|^{\beta}\,\mathrm{sign}\,|y|\,\Omega_X(dy)$$

where Ω_X is stable measure on $\mathbb{R}_1$ of type α , and

$$\hat{\Omega}_X(t) = \exp(-\lambda(tx)).$$

For establishing of equality (4) one must differenciate equality (3) with respect to β and put $\beta = 1$.

For establishing of equality (5) one must differenciate equality

(2) with respect to β, subtract product of $\frac{\pi i}{2}$ by (3) and put in the result $\beta=0$.

Lemma is proved.

COROLLARY. In conditions of the lemma

$$\alpha^{-1}\ln[-\ln\hat{\Omega}(x)] = \Gamma'(1)(\alpha^{-1}-1) + \int_H [\ln|(x,s)| - \frac{\pi i}{2}\,\mathrm{sign}\,(x,s)]\,\Omega(ds). \quad (5')$$

Returning to the proof of theorem 1 we consider two cases: $\beta \neq 1$ and $\beta = 1$.

1. $\beta \neq 1$.

For any Borel set $E \subset S_H$ we denote

$$K_E = \{x \in H \setminus \{0\} : \frac{x}{\|x\|} \in E\}$$

and consider finit Borel measure μ_1 on S_H

$$\mu_1(E) = \int_{K_E} \|x\|^\beta \Omega(dx) \cdot \pi\left(2\sin\frac{\pi\beta}{2}\Gamma(\beta)\Gamma(1-\frac{\beta}{\alpha})\right)^{-1}.$$

According to (1) measure μ_1 defines a new stable measure Ω_1 on H of type β such that

$$-\ln\hat{\Omega}_1(x) = \int_{S_H} |(x,s)|^\beta \mu_1(ds) - i\,\mathrm{tg}\frac{\pi\beta}{2}\int_{S_H} |(x,s)|^{\beta-1}(x,s)\,\mu_1(ds) =$$

$$= \pi\left(2\Gamma(\beta)\Gamma(1-\frac{\beta}{\alpha})\sin\frac{\pi\beta}{2}\right)^{-1}\left(\int_H |(x,s)|^\beta\Omega(ds) - i\,\mathrm{tg}\frac{\pi\beta}{2}\int_H (x,s)|(x,s)|^{\beta-1}\Omega(ds)\right)$$

Lemma allows to calculate received integrals and produces

$$-\ln\hat{\Omega}_1(x) = [\lambda(x)]^{\beta/\alpha}.$$

Required measure is constructed.

2. $\beta = 1$.

Denote $c = \pi/(2\Gamma(1-\alpha^{-1}))$ and $\gamma = -\frac{2c}{\pi}\int_{S_H} s \ln\|s\|\Omega(ds)$. For any Borel set $E \subset S_H$ denote

$$\mu_1(E) = c\int_{K_E} \|x\|\Omega(dx).$$

Then according to (1) finit measure μ_1 defines a new stable measure on H of type 1 such that

$$-\ln\hat{\Omega}(x) = i(\gamma, x) + \int_{S_H} |(x,s)|\mu_1(ds) - \frac{2i}{\pi}\int_{S_H}(x,s)\ln|(x,s)|\mu_1(ds) =$$

$$= i(\gamma,x) + c\int_H |(x,s)|\,\Omega(ds) - \frac{2ic}{\pi}\int_{S_H}(x,s)\ln\left(\frac{|(x,s)|}{\|s\|}\right)\Omega(ds) =$$

$$= c\left(\int_H |(x,s)|\,\Omega(ds) - \frac{2i}{\pi}\int_H (x,s)\ln|(x,s)|\,\Omega(ds)\right).$$

Lemma allows again to calculate received integrals and produces

$$-\ln\hat{\Omega}_1(x) = [\lambda(x)]^{\alpha^{-1}}.$$

Proof of the theorem is finished.

3. Strong uniform stable random vectors and multiplicative relations

Theorem 1 allows us to give next definition.

DEFINITION 6. Two strong stable vectors X and Y of types α and β respectively are called uniform, if their distribution Fourier transforms $\hat{\Omega}_X$ and $\hat{\Omega}_Y$ satisfies the relation

$$[-\ln\hat{\Omega}_X(s)]^{\alpha^{-1}} = c[-\ln\Omega_Y(s)]^{\beta^{-1}} \tag{6}$$

where c is any real positive constant.

If in relation (6) constant c equals to 1 then such strong stable vectors are called strong uniform.

Obviously, that for any pair of uniform strong stable vectors X

and Y there exists a $c_1 > 0$ such that random vectors X and $c_1 Y$ are strong uniform strong stable vectors.

Denote also $Y(\alpha, \theta)$ a random variable in $\mathbb{R}^1$ such that

$$E \exp(itY(\alpha,\theta)) = \exp(-|t|^{\alpha} \exp(-\frac{\pi i \alpha\theta}{2} \operatorname{sign} t))$$

where

$$0 < \alpha < 2, \qquad |\theta| \leqslant \theta_{\alpha} = \min(1, \tfrac{2}{\alpha} - 1). \tag{7}$$

Let $Z(\alpha, \varrho)$ (where $\varrho = (\theta+1)/2$) be a truncation of random variable $Y(\alpha, \theta)$, i.e. random variable with distribution

$$P(Z(\alpha,\varrho) < t) = P(Y(\alpha,\theta) < t \mid Y(\alpha,\theta) \geqslant 0)$$

(their properties are reflected in § 3.1 in [2]).

At last, if Y is random variable in $\mathbb{R}^1$, then denote $Y^{(\nu)}$ (ν - any real constant) random variable $|Y|^{\nu} \operatorname{sign} Y$.

THEOREM 2. Let X and X_1 are strong uniform random vectors of types α and β respectively, then

a) if $\beta < \alpha$, then

$$X_1 \stackrel{d}{=} X Y^{(\alpha^{-1})}(\tfrac{\beta}{\alpha}, 1); \tag{8}$$

b) if ν and θ such that $0 < \nu < \min(\frac{2}{\alpha}, \frac{2}{\beta})$ and $|\theta| \leqslant \min(1, \frac{2}{\alpha\nu} - 1, \frac{2}{\beta\nu} - 1)$, then

$$X Y^{(\nu)}(\beta\nu, \theta) \stackrel{d}{=} X_1 Y^{(\nu)}(\alpha\nu, \theta), \tag{9}$$

$$X Z^{(\nu)}(\beta\nu, \varrho) \stackrel{d}{=} X_1 Z^{(\nu)}(\alpha\nu, \varrho). \tag{10}$$

PROOF. All three d -equalities are proved by the same method, which bases on the using of characteristic transform. We remind that the characteristic transform of random variable Y on $\mathbb{R}^1$ is a matrix

$$W(t,Y) = \begin{pmatrix} w_0(t,Y) & 0 \\ 0 & w_1(t,Y) \end{pmatrix}$$

where $w_k(t,Y) = E\,|Y|^t (\operatorname{sign} Y)^k$, $k = 0, 1$ (for our purpose it is sufficient that w_k exists for small $t > 0$).

$W(t,Y)$ corresponds to the only distribution, and if Y and Y_1 are independent random variables then

$$W(t, YY_1) = W(t,Y)\,W(t,Y_1).$$

The idea of proof will be shown on the proof of equality (9). Equalities (8) and (10) may be proved more simply.

For our purpose it is sufficient to establish that for every $s \in H$ the equality

$$(X,s)\,Y^{\nu}(\beta\nu,\theta) \stackrel{d}{=} (X_1,s)\,Y^{\nu}(\alpha\nu,\theta)$$

holds. And for establishing of the fact it is sufficient, using properties of characteristic transform, to show, that characteristic transform for left and right hand sides of the last equality are the same.

Let $0 < t < \min(\alpha/\nu,\ \beta/\nu,\ \alpha,\ \beta)$, then, using (11) we have

$$W(t,(X,s)\,Y^{\nu}(\beta\nu,\theta)) = W(t,(X,s))\,W(t,Y^{\nu}(\beta\nu,\theta)).$$

It is not difficult to see that

$$w_k(t,(X,s)) = \int_H |(x,s)|^t (\operatorname{sign}(X,s))^k\, \Omega_X(dx), \quad k = 0, 1.$$

Using the lemma we obtain

$$w_k(t,(X,s)) = \tau^t(s)\,\Gamma(1 - t\alpha^{-1})(\Gamma(1-t))^{-1} \cos[\tfrac{\pi}{2}(k - t\theta(s))]\left(\cos[\tfrac{\pi}{2}(k-t)]\right)^{-1}, \quad k = 0, 1.$$

$W(t, Y^{\nu}(\beta\nu,\theta))$ is computated using Theorem 2.6.4 in [2] :

$$w_k(t, Y^{\nu}(\beta\nu, \theta)) = \Gamma(1-t/\beta)(\Gamma(1-t\nu))^{-1}\cos\frac{\pi}{2}(k-\theta\nu t)(\cos\frac{\pi}{2}(k-\nu t))^{-1}, \quad k=0,1.$$

The same method gives

$$w_k(t, (X_1, s)) = \tau^t(s)\Gamma(1-t/\beta)(\Gamma(1-t))^{-1}\cos[\frac{\pi}{2}(k-t\theta(s))](\cos[\frac{\pi}{2}(k-t)])^{-1}, \quad k=0,1;$$

$$w_k(t, Y^{\nu}(\alpha\nu, \theta)) = \Gamma(1-t/\alpha)(\Gamma(1-t\nu))^{-1}\cos\frac{\pi}{2}(k-\theta\nu t)(\cos\frac{\pi}{2}(k-\nu t))^{-1}, \quad k=0,1.$$

and we obtain

$$W(t, (X,s)Y^{\nu}(\beta\nu, \theta)) = W(t, (X,s))W(t, Y^{\nu}(\beta\nu, \theta)) =$$

$$= W(t, (X_1, s))W(t, Y^{\nu}(\alpha\nu, \theta)) = W(t, (X_1, s)Y^{\nu}(\alpha\nu, \theta)).$$

The last equality enable us to conclude that (9) is true, and one can check that conditions (7) are fulfilled.

The same method gives the proof of (8) and (10). We must only take into account, that

$$w_k(t, Z(\alpha, \varrho)) = (\sin\pi\varrho t)(\varrho\sin\pi t)^{-1}\Gamma(1-t/\alpha)(\Gamma(1-t))^{-1}, \quad k=0,1.$$

(see § 3.1 in [2]).

Theorem 2 is proved.

4. Uniform criterion among strong stable random vectors

THEOREM 3. Two strong stable random vectors X and Y are uniform iff $\frac{X}{\|X\|} \stackrel{d}{=} \frac{Y}{\|Y\|}$

PROOF. Necessity. Paying attention to remark after definition 6 we can suggest that X and Y are strong uniform of types α and β respectively and $\beta < \alpha$. Then from theorem 2 we obtain

$$Y \stackrel{d}{=} XY^{1/\alpha}(\beta/\alpha, 1).$$

It is known (see [2]) that $Y(\beta/\alpha, 1) > 0$ with probability 1, consequently

$$\frac{Y}{\|Y\|} \stackrel{d}{=} \frac{XY^{1/\alpha}(\beta/\alpha, 1)}{\|XY^{1/\alpha}(\beta/\alpha, 1)\|} \stackrel{d}{=} \frac{X}{\|X\|}.$$

Necessity is proved.

Sufficiency. Let Ω_X and Ω_Y are distributions of X and Y respectively. Let μ_X and μ_Y are measures on S_H such that for any Borel set $E \subset S_H$

$$\mu_X(E) = P\left(\frac{X}{\|X\|} \in E\right), \qquad \mu_Y(E) = P\left(\frac{Y}{\|Y\|} \in E\right).$$

As it is suggested that $\mu_X = \mu_Y$, then using equality (5') we obtain

$$\alpha^{-1} \ln[-\ln \hat{\Omega}_X(x)] = \Gamma'(1)(\alpha^{-1} - 1) + \int_H [\ln|(x,s)| - \frac{\pi i}{2} \operatorname{sign}(x,s)] \times$$

$$\times \Omega_X(ds) = \Gamma'(1)(\alpha^{-1} - 1) + \int_{S_H} [\ln|(x,s)| - \frac{\pi i}{2} \operatorname{sign}(x,s)] \mu_X(ds) +$$

$$+ \int_H \ln\|s\| \Omega_X(ds) = \Gamma'(1)(\alpha^{-1} - 1) + \int_{S_H} [\ln|(x,s)| - \frac{\pi i}{2} \operatorname{sign}(x,s)] \mu_Y(ds) +$$

$$+ \int_H \ln\|s\| \Omega_X(ds) = \Gamma'(1)(\alpha^{-1} - 1) + \int_{S_H} [\ln|(x,s)| - \frac{\pi i}{2} \operatorname{sign}(x,s)] \Omega_Y(ds) +$$

$$+ \int_H \ln\|s\| \Omega_X(ds) - \int_H \ln\|s\| \Omega_Y(ds) = \beta^{-1} \ln[-\ln \hat{\Omega}_Y(x)] +$$

$$+ \int_H \ln\|s\| \Omega_X(ds) - \int_H \ln\|s\| \Omega_Y(ds)$$

$$\alpha^{-1} \ln[-\ln \hat{\Omega}_X(x)] = \beta^{-1} \ln[-\ln \hat{\Omega}_Y(x)] + c$$

where $c \in \mathbb{R}^1$. From the last equality we obtain

$$[-\ln \hat{\Omega}_X(x)]^{\alpha^{-1}} = e^c [-\ln \hat{\Omega}_Y(x)]^{\beta^{-1}}.$$

Consequently X and Y are uniform.

Theorem 3 is proved.

More detail consideration of properties of uniform vectors in n -dimensional space is suggested to give in following papers.

Department of Mathematics and Mechanics
Leningrad State University
Leningrad, USSR

REFERENCES

1. Kuelbs J. A representation theorem for symmetric stable processes and stable measures on H .- Z.Wahrscheinlichkeitstheor. Verw. Geb., 26, 1973, 259-271.
2. Zolotarev V.M. One-dimensional stable distributions. Moscow, 1983 (in Russian).

THE MEAN'S CONSISTENT ESTIMATION, IN THE CASE RANDOM PROCESSES, SATISFYING PARTIAL DIFFERENTIAL EQUATIONS

L.Márkus

Introduction

The topic, indicated in the title is one of the fundamental statistical problems of random processes. Although quite a number of works are devoted to this question (see [2] , [4] , [6]), there is a gap between the very general investigations of random fields and the concrete formulae and speed limits, known only in special cases. One of the reasons may be that the analogue of the Ito's formula, which is the common tool of these concrete investigations, has not been found for random fields yet. So, to narrow the gap, it may be useful to take the problem into consideration from other aspects, as well.

In this paper I consider the following system. Any source emits a non-random signal ϑ , which is in general a multivariate function. Sending the signal to the observer a noise ξ - meaning a random field - is added to it. This noise is described by the equation

$$L\xi = \eta$$

where, say, L is a linear partial differential operator, and η is a standard Gaussian white noise. We observe the process $\xi + \vartheta$ on monotonously increasing compact domains in $\mathbb{R}^d$. On the base of these observations we estimate the signal, which is the mean (expectation value) of the observed process. For the description of the system we use the methods developed by Yu.A.Rozanov [7] , [8] . It has already been proved to be an elegant tool for other estimations (e.g. of the operator's coefficients [3]). Here we find that the method of the least squares gives the best estimation over the observation-domains. Furthermore we give the condition of the consistence of this estimations.

It has been formerly known for $d=1$ (see [2]) that if the signal is constant, the noise is elementary Gaussian, and the observation-time grows to infinity, then we can consistently estimate the mean. Finally we show an analogous example for the multidimensional case with elliptic operator.

1. Some preliminary results

Let $T \subset \mathbb{R}^d$ be an open domain. All over this paper S or S_n $n=1,2,\ldots$ denote open precompact domains in $\mathbb{R}^d$ with their boundary $\Gamma = \partial S$ or $\Gamma_n = \partial S_n$, such that $\bar{S} = S \cup \Gamma \subset T$, $\bar{S}_n = S_n \cup \Gamma_n \subset T$. Let $D(T)$ denote the space of infinitely differentiable functions with compact support on T. We assume that $D'(T)$ is endowed with the usual topology. $D'(T)$ denotes the space of distributions (linear continuous functionals) defined on $D(T)$. Let $F \subset D'(T)$ with the $\langle , \rangle_F$ scalar product be a local Hilbert space [8]. Such spaces are e.g. $L_2(T)$ the space of the Lebesque square integrable functions on T, or $\overset{\circ}{W}{}_2^k(T)$ and $W_2^k(T)$ the usual Sobolev spaces [1]. Furthermore let $L: D(T) \rightarrow F$ be a local [8] (e.g. differential) linear continuous operator. Equation $\|\varphi\|_W^2 = \langle L\varphi, L\varphi \rangle_F$, $\varphi \in D(T)$ defines a seminorm on $D(T)$, and after factorization and completion we get the Hilbert space W. The operator L can be extended by the continuity to W, and - without loss of the generality - we assume that its range is F. The range of the adjoint operator L^* gives the Hilbert space X, the dual of W, which consists of distributions, $X \subset D'(T)$ (see [8]). Therefore it is not meaningless to speak about the support of an $x \in X$, and so we can suppose that X is a local Hilbert space. We note, if $L=P$ is a positive operator then we can identify $\mathbb{F}$ and $\mathbb{X}$ (cf. [8]).

It has been proved to be useful to regard the functions of $\mathbb{W}$ as functionals over $\mathbb{X}$, and similarly to define the generalized random process, as follows

DEFINITION 1.1. $\xi : \mathbb{X} \to \mathbb{H}$ is called a generalized random (or resp. Gaussian) process over any local Hilbert space $\mathbb{X}$, if it is a linear continuous operator from $\mathbb{X}$ to the Hilbert space of random variables with finite second moment (resp. with Gaussian distribution), denoted by $\mathbb{H}$.

As any Gaussian process uniquely determined by its mean and correlation operator [6] we can determine the standard Gaussian white noise η over $\mathbb{F}$ as a generalized Gaussian process with zero mean and unit correlation operator: $E\eta = 0$, $B_\eta = id_{\mathbb{F}}$.

We denote the value of any (random or deterministic) functional ξ at x by (x, ξ).

The following theorem is important for us (cf. [6] II. §3.2.2).

THEOREM 1.1. Generalized Gaussian processes with common correlation operator generate equivalent measures if and only if the differences of their means are continuous linear functionals in the correlation norm.

Let $\mathbb{X}_1, \mathbb{X}_2, \ldots$ be a sequence of monotonous-y increasing subspaces of $\mathbb{X}$, $\mathbb{X}_\infty = \bigcup_{i=1}^{\infty} \mathbb{X}_i$. Let $\xi_\vartheta = (x, \xi_\vartheta)$, $\vartheta \in \Theta$ be a family of generalized processes with common correlation operator B, parametrized by $\vartheta = \vartheta(x) = E(x, \xi_\vartheta)$. We assume that the measures, generated by the restrictions of ξ_ϑ onto $\mathbb{X}_n$ are equivalent. As theorem 1.1 shows, there exists an h^n_ϑ in the subspace $\mathbb{H}^n_\vartheta$, spanned by the variables (x, ξ_ϑ), $x \in \mathbb{X}_n$ in $\mathbb{H}$, such that

$$\vartheta(x) = \langle (x, \xi_\vartheta), h^n_\vartheta \rangle_B$$

holds, where $\langle , \rangle_B$ denotes the correlation scalar product. So the parameter ϑ can be regarded for every n as an element of $\overline{\Theta}^n$, the closure (completion) after factorization of Θ in the scalar product $\langle \vartheta_1, \vartheta_2 \rangle_n = \langle \overset{n}{h}_{\vartheta_1}, \overset{n}{h}_{\vartheta_2} \rangle_B$ (more details see [6] III.§ 2.4).

DEFINITION 1.2. We say, that an $\alpha: \Theta \to \mathbb{R}$ function is linearly admissible, if there exists an $n_\alpha < \infty$ such that $\alpha(\vartheta)$ has an unbiased linear estimator from $\mathbb{H}_\vartheta^{(n)}$.

We note that α is linearly admissible if and only if it can be extended to a linear continuous functional on $\bar{\Theta}^n$ for $n \geq n_\alpha$ ([6] III, § 2.4).

2. The space of the possible means

Having tried to apply this method to the problem mentioned in the introduction, we found that we have to enlarge the class of the considered functions. We can do this more clearly, if we suppose a little more about the space F. As it is known, the projections of the elements of $L_2(T)$ or $\overset{0}{W}{}_2^k(T)$ onto $L_2(S)$ or $\overset{0}{W}{}_2^k(S)$ coincide if and only if they coincide as distributions over $D(S)$. Analogously, we suppose about F, that if $f_1, f_2 \in F$, then

$$\langle g, f_1 \rangle_F = \langle g, f_2 \rangle_F \qquad g \in \overline{F(S)} = \overline{LD(S)} \Longleftrightarrow \tag{2.1}$$

$$\Longleftrightarrow \qquad (\varphi, f_1) = (\varphi, f_2) \qquad \varphi \in D(S).$$

It is easy to see, that (2.1) involves the relation

$$F(T \setminus S)^\perp = \overline{F(S)}. \tag{2.2}$$

DEFINITION 2.1. We call F_{loc} the space of all distributions $f \in D'(T)$ satisfying the condition that for every $S \subseteq T$ open precompact domain there exists such an $f_S \in F$, that $(\varphi, f) = (\varphi, f_S)$ holds for every $\varphi \in D(S)$.

For $F = L_2(T)$ we get $L_{2,loc}(T)$ the space of locally square integrable functions, or from both cases $F = \overset{0}{W}{}_2^k(T)$ and $F = W_2^k(T)$ we get the well-known local Sobolev space $W^k_{2,loc}(T)$ (see [1], Definition 1.8). Obviously $F \subset F_{loc}$.

Furthermore we remark that the definition is correct, without the assumption of the property (2.1), but if (2.1) holds, then f_S can uniquely be chosen from $\overline{F(S)}$. So the equation $p_S f = \|f_S\|_F$ $f_S \in \overline{F}(S)$ defines a semonorm on F_{loc}. The family of these semonorms generates a locally convex vector space topology, and so F_{loc} is a Frechet space. The convergence structure is given the following way: $f^{(n)} \xrightarrow{F_{loc}} f$ iff $\forall\ S \subset T: (\varphi, f_S^{(n)}) \to (\varphi, f_S)$ $\varphi \in D(S)$. It is easy to check that F or $LD(T)$ are dense in F_{loc}, and if $\overset{(i)}{f} \in F(S)$, $i = 0, 1, 2, \ldots$, then $f^{(i)} \to f^{(0)}$ in $F \Longleftrightarrow f^{(i)} \to f^{(0)}$ in F_{loc}.

Hence $LD(T)$ is dense in F_{loc}, after factorization and completion from $D(T)$ we get the space W_{loc}. The operator L can be extended to W_{loc} by the continuity, and it is an isometry between W_{loc} and F_{loc}, furthermore $W \subset W_{loc}$, and we have $LW = F$, for the extended L, too.

Set $X_0 = \{x \in X,$ suppx compact $\}$. Let $w \in W_{loc}$, $Lw = f$ be a fixed element. First we define the value (x, w) for an arbitrary $x \in X_0$ $x = L^* g$, and then give a characterization of W_{loc}.

DEFINITION 2.2. With the notations above let $(x, w) = (L^* g, w) = \langle g, f_S \rangle_F$, where $supp\, x \subset S$, and $f_S \in F$ is the same as in the definition 2.1.

LEMMA 2.1. By the definition 2.2 w is a well-defined linear functional on X_0 and it is continuous on every $X(\bar{S}) = X(S \cup \Gamma)$. On the other hand every linear functional, having this property, can be identified one to one with an element of W_{loc}.

PROOF. Let $S_1 \subset S_2 \subset T$, so that $supp\, x \subset S_1$, and denote f_{S_1}, f_{S_2} the elements of F connected with f by definition 2.1. So $(\varphi, f_{S_1} - f_{S_2}) = 0$ for every $\varphi \in D(S)$, meaning that $f_{S_1} - f_{S_2} \in F(T \backslash S)$

by (2.2). Thus, because of the locality we have $\langle g, f_{S_1} - f_{S_2} \rangle_F = \langle x, L^*(f_{S_1} - f_{S_2}) \rangle = 0$, showing that (x, w) is well-defined. The continuity on $X(\bar{S})$ is the obvious consequence of $(x, w) = \langle g, f_{S_1} \rangle_F$, when $\bar{S} \subset S_1$.

To prove the lemma's second part, first we note that for every $g \in \overline{F(S_1)}$ $(L^* g, w) = \langle g, f_{S_1} \rangle_F$ holds with an $f_{S_1} \in \overline{F(S_1)}$ because $L^* \overline{F(S_1)} = L^* F(T \setminus S_1)^{\perp} \subset X(S_1)$ (cf. [8]). As $\langle g, f_{S_1} - f_{S_2} \rangle = 0$ for $g \in F(S_1)$, from (2.1) we get the relation $(\varphi, f_{S_1}) = (\varphi, f_{S_2})$ $\varphi \in D(S_1)$, and so it is possible to define for every $\varphi \in D(T)$

$$(\varphi, f) = (\varphi, f_{S_1}) \qquad \text{, where } S_1 \supset \text{supp } \varphi.$$

Choosing a sequence $\varphi_i \to \varphi_0$ in $D(T)$ per definitionem there exists a compact set $G \subset T$ so, that $\text{supp } \varphi_i \in G$, $i = 0, 1, \ldots$. Thus $(\varphi_i, f) = (\varphi_i, f_{S_1})$ with an $S_1 \supset G$, showing that $f \in D'(T)$. Furthermore, obviously from its definition, $f \in F_{loc}$, and so $f = Lw$ $w \in W_{loc}$, that gives the needed correspondence.

To complete the proof we note, that for $(x, v) \neq (x, w)$ from the property (2.1) it follows, that there exists at least one $\varphi \in D(S)$, $(\varphi, Lv) \neq (\varphi, Lw)$ in the case of $S \supset \text{supp } x$, showing the difference of the corresponding elements from W_{loc}.

Now let us turn to the generalized random process ξ , satisfying the equation

$$L \xi = \eta \tag{2.3}$$

in the following sense (see [7] , [8]):

$$(L^* g, \xi) = (g, \eta) \qquad g \in F$$

where η is a standard Gaussian white noise over F . Taking into account the form of the correlation operator (see [8]), we can summarize the theorem 1.1 and the lemma 2.1 as follows.

THEOREM 2.1. The elements of W_{loc} are exactly those linear functionals of X , which are mean values of Gaussian processes, having common correlation operator, and generating equivalent with ξ on compact domains.

3. The statistical problem

The definitions and results of the previous two sections provided us the tools to consider the statistical problem. We would like to estimate an unknown element of a given closed subspace V of W_{loc}. For the estimation we obtain information, observing the process $(x, \xi_V) = (x, \xi_0 + v)$, $x \in X$, on $X(\bar{S}_n) = \{x \in X,\ supp\, x \subset \bar{S}_n\}$, where $\bar{S}_n \subset S_{n+1}$, $\bigcup_{n=1}^{\infty} S_n = T$, furthermore ξ_0 satisfies (2.3) with standard Gaussian white noise η.

As it follows from the relations $X(\bar{S}_1) \subseteq X(\bar{S}_2) \subseteq \ldots$, $E(x, \xi_V) = (x, v)$ and the theorem 2.1, we are in the situation, described in the first section. Obviously all the subspaces $\mathbb{H}_V^n$ are isometrical with $\mathbb{H}_0^n$. Equations

$$\langle x, y \rangle_B = E(x, \xi_0)(y, \xi_0) = (x, [L^*, L]^{-1} y) = \langle x, y \rangle \tag{3.1}$$

hold for every $x, y \in X(S_n)$ (see [5]), showing the isometry between $X(\bar{S}_n)$ and $\mathbb{H}_0^n$, and between $\overline{\bigcup_{n=1}^{\infty} X(\bar{S}_n)} = \bar{X}_0$ and $\mathbb{H}_0^{\infty}$.

We denote by X_n the subspace $X(\bar{S}_n) \ominus \{x \in X(S_n) : (x, v) = 0$ for $\forall\ v \in V\}$. Comparing with the first section V plays the role of Θ there. So, let V_n denote the subspaces, corresponding to $\overline{\Theta^{(n)}}$. From the mentioned isometry we get with this notation

$$X_n = L^* L V_n. \tag{3.2}$$

LEMMA 3.1. Every linearly admissible function $x(v)$ can be got for $n \geq n_x$ as a unique element $\hat{x}_n \in X_n$, $x(v) = (\hat{x}_n, v)$.

PROOF. The facts mentioned before show that V_n $n < \infty$ is a closed subspace of the dual space of $X(\bar{S}_n)$, and V_∞ is the one of $\bar{X}_0$.

As we noted it in 1., the linear admissibility of $x(v)$ is equivalent of its continuity on V_n, $n \geq n_x$. So it can continuously be extended to $X(\bar{S}_n)^*$. Thus it has the form $x(v) = (x, v)$ for some $x \in X(\bar{S}_n)$. But then it can also be got as $x(v) = (\hat{x}_n, v)$, where $\hat{x}_n$ is the unique projection onto X_n of all $x \in X(S_n)$: $x(v) = (x, v)$.

DEFINITION 3.1. We call the random variable $(\hat{x}_n, \xi_V)$ the estimation of the least squares of $x(v)$ on S_n (see [6] , III, § 2.3).

Hence the common correlation operator $B = (L^*L)^{-1}$, from (3.2) we immediately get $B\hat{x}_n \in V_n$. Applying now the theorem 5 of [6] , III, § 2.3, and taking into account the normality, we can state

THEOREM 3.1. The estimator of the least squares on S_n coincides with the efficients, unbiased, $\mathbb{H}_V^n$ measurable estimator.

Now let us consider those $v \in V$, for which the equation $(x, v) = \langle (x, \xi_V), h_V^\infty \rangle$ fulfills for every $x \in X_0$, with an $h_V^\infty \in \mathbb{H}_V^\infty$. Because of the isometry of $\mathbb{H}_V^\infty$, $\mathbb{H}_0^\infty$ and $\bar{X}_0$ there exists a $y \in \bar{X}_0$ that for every $x \in X_0$ $(x, v) = \langle x, y \rangle$. Consequently (x, v) is continuous on X_0 by the norm in X , so $(x, v) = (x, w)$ holds for every $x \in X_0$, with a $w \in W$, thus $v = w$ by the lemma 2.1. This way we have

LEMMA 3.2. The Hilbert space V_∞ can be identified with $V \cap W$.

Let $\mathbb{H}_V$ denote the closed subspace, spanned by the variables (x, ξ_V) for every $x \in X$. Now we fix a linearly admissible function $x(v)$, and construct on every observation-domain S_n the efficient, unbiased, $\mathbb{H}_V^n$ measurable estimators $(\hat{x}_n, \xi)$ of $x(v)$ by the method of the least squares. Summarizing the theorems 6 and 7 of [6] , III § 2.4 and the lemma 3.2, we get the following

THEOREM 3.2. The sequence of the random variables $(\hat{x}_n, \xi_V)$ converges in $\mathbb{H}_V$ to an estimator h_V, and this is the efficient, unbiased ξ_V -measurable estimator of the value $x(v)$. Consequently $x(v)$ can be strong-consistently estimated, when $x(v) = 0$ for every $v \in V \cap W$

and so $V \cap W = 0$ is necessary and sufficient for the estimation's strong-consistence for every linearly admissible function.

Finally we remark that in our case the values of all tze linearly admissible functions uniquely determine the parameter ϑ , so the last statement can be regarded as the condition of the consistent estimation of the parameter itself.

4. An example

Let the operator in the original system be a positive alliptic one with constant coefficients:

$$L = P = \sum_{|k| \leq p} a_k D^{2k}, \qquad a_k \in \mathbb{R}.$$

So $X = F$ and $P: X \to W$, where $W = \overset{0}{W}{}_2^p$, $X = \overset{0}{W}{}_2^{-p}$ with the equivalent scalar product $\langle u, v \rangle_W = \sum_{|k| \leq p} a_k \int_T D^k u \, D^k v \, dt$ and $\langle u, v \rangle_W = (u, Pv) = \langle Pu, Pv \rangle$. We have $W_{loc} = W^p_{2,loc}(T)$. The theorems 2.1, 3.2 and 8 in [6] III gives the following

COROLLARY 4.1. The Gaussian processes ξ_θ $\theta \in \Theta$, where $\xi_\theta - E\xi_\theta = \xi_0$ satisfies (3.1) with $L = P$, generate equivalent measures, iff $E\xi_\theta \in \overset{0}{W}{}_2^p(T)$, and on compact domains generate equivalent measures, iff $E\xi_\theta \in W^p_{2,loc}(T)$.

The analogue of this statement for elementary Gaussian processes $(d = 1)$ is one of the best-known consequence of Girsanov's theorem (see [2]).

Suppose that Γ_n are $p+1$ times differentiable and let $W(\Gamma)$ denote the space of the traces of elements from W on any smooth Γ . As it is known $W(\Gamma) = W_2^{p-1/2}(\Gamma)$. The following direct decomposition holds: $X(\bar{S}) = \overline{PD(S)} \oplus X(\Gamma)$ (see [8]). It can be verified, that $W(\Gamma)^* = X(\Gamma)$ by $(w_\Gamma, x) = (w, x)$, $w_\Gamma \in W(\Gamma)$: $w|_\Gamma = w_\Gamma$, $x \in X(\Gamma)$, and the corresponding norms are equivalent. Furthermore $v, w \in W$, $w|_\Gamma = v|_\Gamma \iff \pi_\Gamma P w = \pi_\Gamma P v$ where π_Γ is the projection onto $X(\Gamma)$. From the continuity $(w_\Gamma, x) = \langle x_\Gamma, x \rangle$ with a unique $x_\Gamma \in X(\Gamma)$.

DEFINITION 4.1. By the equation $P w_\Gamma = X_\Gamma$ $P: W(\Gamma) \to X(\Gamma)$ is a linear continuous operator.

From this definition one can get $\pi_\Gamma P w = P w|_\Gamma$ $w \in W_{loc}$.

Let now $V < W_{loc}$ be $V = \{\theta \cdot \chi_T,\ \theta \in \Theta,\ \chi(t) = 1,\ t \in T\}$. Taking into account the form of the correlation operator, we consider here the weak stacionary solutions of (3.1). The function $x(\theta \cdot \chi_T) = \theta$ is linearly admissible. Direct calculations show that

$$\hat{x}_n = a_0 [(a_0 \lambda(S_n) + (\chi_T \pi_\Gamma P \chi_T)]^{-1} (P\chi)_{S_n}$$

where λ is the d-dimensional Lebesgue measure, $(P\chi)_{S_n} \in \dot{W}_2^{-p}(T)$ is the image of the characteristic function of S_n. As $(\varphi, \chi_{S_n}) = \int_{S_n} \varphi(t)\, d\lambda(t)$ $\varphi \in D(S_n)$ the notation $(\pi_{S_n} P \chi_{S_n}, \xi) = \int_{S_n} \xi\, d\lambda$ is reasonable (π_{S_n} is the projection onto $\overline{PD(S_n)}$). We have $\pi_\Gamma P \chi_{S_n} = P \chi_\Gamma$, and it can formally be written in the integral form with μ_n, Lebesgue-measure on the hypersurface Γ_n [5]. So the estimation of θ on S_n by theorem 3.1 is

$$(\hat{x}_n, \xi) = [a_0 \lambda(S_n)]^{-1} [a_0 \int_{S_n} \xi\, d\lambda + \sum_{0<|k|\leq p} a_k \int_{\Gamma_n} D^{2k-1} \xi\, d\mu_n]$$

and this is a strong-consistent estimation if $\lambda(T) = \infty$ (cf. [2], 3.2, 4.2, [4], 5.4).

ACKNOWLEDGEMENT. I am deeply grateful to professor Yu.A.Rozanov, who posed the problem and payed a continuous attention to my work. I am also thankful to professor M.Arató, who turned my attention to more concrete investigations.

Moscow State University, Leninskie Gory, Moscow, USSR

REFERENCES

1. Agmon Sh. Lectures on elliptic boundary value problems, Van Nostrand, New York, 1965.

2. Arató M. Linear Stochastic Systems with Constant Coefficients. Springer, 1984.

3. Gorjainov V.B. On Theorems of Levy-Baxter type for stochastic elliptic equations. Probab.Theor. and Appl., in prepavation (in Russian).

4. Grenander U. Stochastic Processes and Statistical Inference, Almgvist & Wiksells, Stockholm, 1950.

5. Reed M., Simon B. Methods of Modern Mathematical Physics. v.2, Acad.Press, New York, 1979.

6. Rozanov Yu.A. Gaussian infinite dimensional distributions. Trudi MIAN SSSR, Nauka, Moscow, 1967 (in Russian).

7. Rozanov Yu.A. Markovian random fields and boundary value problems for stochastic partial-differential equations. Probab. Theor. and Appl. 32, 1987, 3-34 (in Russian).

8. Rozanov Yu.A. On some generalization of the Direchlet-problem. Mat.Sborn, 3, 1983 (in Russian).

LIMIT THEOREMS IN THE SET UP OF SUMMATION OF A RANDOM NUMBER OF INDEPENDENT IDENTICALLY DISTRIBUTED RANDOM VARIABLES

J.A.Melamed

1. Introduction

The interest of specialists in the questions concerning the limit behaviour of sums $\sum_{j=1}^{\nu} X_j$ of a random number of random variables increases in the last years. This interest is quite natural, since the class of problems the solution of which is reduced to the consideration of the asymptotics of such sums is wide enough. These are problems of economics, physics, queueing theory, realibility theory, mathematical statistics, etc.

The first series of papers on this topic (started with [1]) is associated with the study of conditions on the random summation ν and on the summands X_j, which guarantee the convergence of the distributions of sums $\sum_{j=1}^{\nu} X_j$ to the normal law, and with the determination of the rate of this convergence. The references to a number of papers of this series are given in [2] .

However, it was noted in [3] that tha range of application of the normal law under summation of a random number of independent identically distributed random variables (i.i.d.r.v.'s) is not too large. Therefore the papers by B.V.Gnedenko and his pupils (see [3] - [5]), in which the class of limit distributions of sums of a random number of i.i.d. r.v.'s is described, start a qualitatively new step in the mentioned topic. The rate of convergence of distributions of these sums to the limiting ones was studied in [2] .

The characteristic property of the class of limit distributions for sums of a geometric number of i.i.d.r.v.'s is given in [6] . The question of when the distribution of a sum $\sum_{j=1}^{\nu} X_j$ is positive i.i.d.r.v.'s belongs to the same type as the distribution of X_j and the examples of random summations ν under which this fact is true, are considered in [7] .

The analogies of infinitely divisible, stable and normal laws in the scheme of summation of a random number of r.v.'s are introduced in [8] - [10] where the analytical properties of these laws are studied too.

Under the geometric summation of i.i.d.r.v.'s the Laplace distribution plays the function of the normal one. It appears in this scheme as a limit distribution under summation of i.i.d.r.v.'s with zero mean and finite variance (see [3] , [11, Theorem 2.4.2]) and also it is an analogy of the Gaussian law under the description of the class of geometrically strictly stable laws (see [8]). The problems concerning the asymptotic behaviour of distributions of geometric sums of i.i.d. r.v.'s are studied in [12] , [13] .

The exponential distribution plays the function of the degenerate one under the geometric summation of i.i.d. r.v.'s. It was noted for the first time by Rényi (see [14] , [15, p.174]) that the exponential distribution appears as a limit one in this scheme (see also [16] , [11, Theorem 2.4.10]). The estimates of the rate of convergence in Rényi's theorem in different metrics are studied in [17] - [19] .

It is noted in [9] that the analogies of the Gaussian law exist not for every random summation. In the present paper the effect of the so-called quick convergence is studied, local limit theorems for density functions and theorems on large deviations are obtained for those schemes of summation of a random number of i.i.d. r.v.'s, in which the analogies of the Gaussian and the degenerate law exist. It is found that certain distinctions arise in the scheme under consideration in contrast to the usual summation scheme.

In [20] the necessary and sufficient conditions for a quick convergence in the uniform metric of the distributions of sums of non-random number of i.i.d. r.v.'s to the normal distribution are obtained. It is shown here that there is no quick convergence of distributions of sums of a random number of a summands to the analogy of the Gaussian or degenerate law in the uniform and some other frequently used metrics such as, for example, λ -metric, Levy-Prokhorov metric, mean metric, Levy metric. An example of two weak metrics, in which the quick convergence remains valid for the scheme under consideration is given in the paper.

It is shown that unlike the nonrandom summation scheme when considering local limit theorems for densities of sums of a random number of i.i.d. r.v.'s the convergence in the uniform metric is not preserved if the modulus of the characteristic function (ch.f.) of summands belongs not to the space L^1, but to L^z, $z>1$ (compare with [21, p.590]).

The necessary definitions, examples and the obtained results are stated in sections 2-5. The proofs of the results are given in section 6.

2. ν_p -strictly Gaussian and ν_p -degenerate distributions.

Let ν_p be a non-negative integer-valued r.v. depending on the parameter $p \in \Delta$, where Δ is a subset of the interval $(0, 1)$ for which 0 is a concentation point. Assume that $E\nu_p = 1/p$ and denote by $\Psi_p(z)$ the generating function of the r.v. ν_p. Assume that

$$\lim_{p\to 0} P\{p\nu_p < x\} = A(x), \tag{1}$$

where $A(x)$ is some distribution function (d.f.) and also

$$0 < \int_0^\infty x \, d\mathcal{A}(x) < \infty . \tag{2}$$

Remid (see [9]) that the r.v. ξ is termed ν_p-strictly Gaussian if its mathematical expectation $E\xi = 0$, it has a finite variance and ξ is identically distributed with the r.v. $p^{1/2} \sum_{j=1}^{\nu_p} \xi_j$ where $\xi_1, \ldots, \xi_n, \ldots$ are i.i.d. r.v.'s independent of ν_p and identically distributed with ξ.

The necessary and sufficient condition for the existence of the ν_p -strictly Gaussian r.v. was stated in [10] .

THEOREM ([10]). The ν_p -strictly Gaussian r.v. exists under the above mentioned assumptions iff for every $z \geqslant 0$ the generating function $\psi_p(z)$ allows the following representation

$$\psi_p(z) = \psi\left[\frac{1}{p} \psi^{-1}(z)\right] , \quad p \in \Delta, \tag{3}$$

where

$$\psi(\tau) = \int_0^\infty e^{-\tau x} \, d\mathcal{A}(x) , \quad \tau > 0, \tag{4}$$

and ψ^{-1} is a function inverse to ψ . If representation (3) holds, then the ch.f. of the ν_p -strictly Gaussian r.v. is of the form

$$\varphi(t) = \psi(at^2) , \quad a > 0.$$

We term the distribution law ν_p-strictly Gaussian, if the r.v. ξ with this distribution is ν_p -strictly Gaussian.

Consider the examples of the ν_p -strictly Gaussian distribution laws (see [7]).

1) If ν_p is a degenerate r.v., then $\psi(\tau) = e^{-\tau}$, $\tau > 0$, and $\varphi(t) = e^{-at^2}$, $a > 0$, is the ch.f. of a normal distri-

bution.

2) If ν_p is a geometric r.v. with

$$P\{\nu_p = k\} = p(1-p)^{k-1}, \qquad k=1,2,\ldots, \quad p\in\Delta, \tag{5}$$

then $\psi(\tau) = \frac{1}{1+\tau}$, $\tau > 0$ and $\varphi(t) = \frac{1}{1+at^2}$, $a>0$, is the ch.f. of a Laplace distribution.

3) If $\{\nu_{p,m}\}_{m=2}^{\infty}$ is a sequence of r.v.'s such that

$$P\{\nu_{p,m} = 1+km\} = \begin{cases} p^{1/m}, & k=0, \\ [(\prod_{j=0}^{k-1}(\frac{1}{m}+j))/k!]\, p^{1/m}(1-p)^k, & k=1,2,\ldots, \end{cases} \tag{6}$$

$p\in\Delta$ (it is evident that $\nu_{p,1}$ is a geometric r.v. from example 2)), that $\psi(\tau) = (1+m\tau)^{-1/m}$, $\tau > 0$, and the sequence of the corresponding ν_p -strictly Gaussian laws is given by the ch.f.'s of the form

$$\varphi_m(t) = (1+mat^2)^{-1/m}, \quad a>0, \quad m=2,3,\ldots.$$

Define the analogy of the degenerate law for a r.v. ν_p with a generating function satisfying (3).

We say that the distribution is ν_p -degenerate if its ch.f. is of the form $\psi(ibt)$, $b\in\mathbb{R}^1$ where ψ is defined by relation (4).

Under the geometric ν_p it is an exponential disttibution and for r.v.'s $\{\nu_{p,m}\}_{m=2}^{\infty}$ with distributions (6) it is a sequence of gamma-distributions with ch.f.'s $(1+imbt)^{-1/m}$, $m=2,3,\ldots$.

Below we shall consider the ν_p -strictly Gaussian law with zero mean and unit variance, the ch.f. of which

$$\Phi(t) = \psi\left[-\frac{1}{\psi'(0)}t^2\right]. \tag{7}$$

In the sequel we call this law $\mathscr{G}(0,1)$-law for brevity. Hence, $\mathscr{G}(0,1)$ -law in example 2) is a Laplace distribution with the density function

$$g(x) = \frac{1}{\sqrt{2}}\, e^{-\sqrt{2}\,|x|} \tag{8}$$

and the ch.f.

$$\varphi(t) = \left(1 + \frac{t^2}{2}\right)^{-1}, \tag{9}$$

and those in example 3) are the sequence of symmetrized gamma-distributions with density functions

$$g_m(x) = \begin{cases} \frac{1}{2}\left(\frac{2}{m}\right)^{1/(2m)} \Gamma^{-1}\left(\frac{1}{m}\right)(-x)^{\frac{1}{m}-1} \exp\left\{\left(\frac{2}{m}\right)^{1/2} x\right\}, & x < 0, \\ \frac{1}{2}\left(\frac{2}{m}\right)^{1\ (2m)} \Gamma^{-1}\left(\frac{1}{m}\right) x^{\frac{1}{m}-1} \exp\left\{-\left(\frac{2}{m}\right)^{1/2} x\right\}, & x > 0 \end{cases} \tag{10}$$

and ch.f.

$$\varphi_m(t) = \left(1 + m\,\frac{t^2}{2}\right)^{-1/m}, \tag{11}$$

$m = 2, 3, \ldots.$

In the sequel we call the ν_p -degenerate law with mean θ the ch.f. of which has the form

$$\Phi^*(t) = \psi\,[i\theta t / \psi'(0)], \tag{12}$$

$\mathbb{D}(\theta)$ -law for brevity. In example 2) it is an exponential distribution with the density

$$d(x) = \begin{cases} 0, & x < 0, \\ \frac{1}{\theta}\exp\left\{-\frac{x}{\theta}\right\}, & x > 0 \end{cases} \tag{13}$$

and the ch.f.

$$\varphi^*(t) = (1 - it\theta)^{-1}, \tag{14}$$

and in example 3) it is a sequence of gamma-distributions with densities

$$d_m(x) = \begin{cases} 0, & x < 0, \\ (m\theta)^{-1/m}\Gamma^{-1}(1/m)x^{1/m-1}\exp\{-x/(m\theta)\}, & x > 0 \end{cases} \tag{15}$$

and ch.f.'s

$$\varphi_m^*(t) = (1 - im\theta t)^{-1/m}, \tag{16}$$

$m = 2, 3, \ldots$.

In this paper we study the asymptotic behaviour of distributions of appropriately normalized sums of ν_p summands X_j, where $X_1, \ldots, X_n, \ldots$ are i.i.d. r.v.'s with a ch.f. $\vartheta(t)$. In what follows we assume that two conditions are fulfilled:

A) r.v.'s $\nu_p, X_1, \ldots, X_n, \ldots$ are jointly independent;

B) the generating function $\psi_p(z)$ of the r.v. ν_p satisfies (3) with ψ defined by (4).

Now we can pass to exact statements.

3. On the quick convergence under ν_p-summation.

We shall consider two kinds of sums of a random number of summands. In the sequel

$$S_p = \frac{1}{\sigma\sqrt{E\nu_p}} \sum_{j=1}^{\nu_p} X_j = p^{1/2}\sigma^{-1}\sum_{j=1}^{\nu_p} X_j \tag{17}$$

is a sum of i.i.d. r.v.'s with $EX_1 = 0$, $DX_1 = \sigma^2$, and

$$S_p^* = \frac{1}{E\nu_p} \sum_{j=1}^{\nu_p} X_j = p\sum_{j=1}^{\nu_p} X_j \tag{18}$$

is a sum of i.i.d. r.v.'s X_j with $EX_1 = \theta > 0$.

In what follows we denote by $\varphi_p(t)$ and $\varphi_p^*(t)$ the ch.f.'s of the sums S_p and S_p^*, respectively.

First we shall study the asymptotic behaviour of the distribution of the sum S_p as $p \to 0$.

THEOREM 1. Assume that conditions A), B), (1), (2) are fulfilled and, moreover, $EX_1 = 0$, $0 < \sigma^2 = EX_1^2 < \infty$ and

$$0 < \int_0^\infty x^2 \, dA(x) < \infty. \tag{19}$$

Then the distribution of sum (17) tends to a $\mathcal{G}(0,1)$ -distribution as $p \to 0$.

I.A.Ibragimov [20] found the conditions for a quick convergence to the normal law, consisting in that if not two but a larger number r of moments of summands X_j in the sum $n^{-1/2} \sum_{j=1}^{n} X_j$ of a determined number of i.i.d. r.v.'s coincide with the Gaussian ones, then the rate of convergence in the uniform metric of the d.f. of this sum to the d.f. of the normal law increases with the growth of r. Does a similar result hold in the scheme of summation of a random number of i.i.d. r.v.'s ?

We show that the answer to this question is negative if the convergence is studied in the uniform metric (m.) ρ, or in such frequently used metrics as Levy m.L., Levy-Frokhorov m. π, mean m. $\varkappa_1$, uniform m. for ch.f.'s f_0 distance in variation σ, λ-m.

Theorem 1 implies the convergence of distribution of the sum S_p of a geometric number ν_p of summands to the Laplace distribution (8) (compare with [3]). At the same time the following assertion is true.

THEOREM 2. Let $X_1, \ldots, X_n, \ldots$ be i.i.d. r.v.'s, r $(r > 2)$ first moments of which exist and coincide with the corresponding moments of the Laplace distributions (8), but $v(t) \neq \varphi(t)$, where the ch.f.

$\varphi(t)$ is of the form (5). Let ν_p be a discrete r.v. with geometrical distribution (5), independent of the X's. Then

$$\lambda(\varphi_p,\varphi)=\min_{T>0}\{\max[\tfrac{1}{2}\max_{|t|\leqslant T}|\varphi_p(t)-\varphi(t)|,1/T]\}\geqslant Cp \tag{20}$$

(here and below we denote by C with or without subscripts different positive constants).

Utilizing V.M.Zolotarev's results on the comparison of metrics (see [22]), we get from (20) the following assertion.

THEOREM 3. Let the r.v. ξ have Laplace distribution (8). Let the conditions of Theorem 2 be fulfilled. Then whatever be the number $r>2$ of coinciding moments of X_1 and ξ

$$\rho(S_p,\xi)\geqslant Cp^3, \tag{21}$$

$$L(S_p,\xi)\geqslant Cp^3, \tag{22}$$

$$\mathcal{T}(S_p,\xi)\geqslant Cp^2, \tag{23}$$

$$\varkappa_1(S_p,\xi)\geqslant Cp^2, \tag{24}$$

$$\sigma(S_p,\xi)\geqslant Cp^2, \tag{25}$$

$$\mathcal{F}_0(S_p,\xi)\geqslant Cp. \tag{26}$$

REMARK 1. The argument similar to that used in the proof of Theorems 2, 3 easily implies that there is no quick convergence results in the scheme of $\nu_{p,m}$-summation of i.i.d. r.v.'s, either, where $\nu_{p,m}(m\geqslant 2)$ is a discrete r.v. with distribution (6), if the convergence of distributions of sums $p^{1/2}\sum_{j=1}^{\nu_{p,m}}X_j$ to distribution (10) is considered in the same metrics as in Theorems 2, 3.

Now we shall investigate the question of quick convergence in ideal metrics. Consider the metric ζ_s (its definition and properties are stated in detail in [22]) and show that though the rate of convergence in it of the distribution of the sum S_p to the Laplace distribution depends on the number r of first moments of X_1 and ξ coinciding among themselves, but in order to have the imporvement of the rate of this convergence one must each time choose a new metric ζ_s with $s = r + a$, $0 < a \leqslant 1$

THEOREM 4. Let the conditions of Theorems 2, 3 be fulfilled and, moreover, $E|X_1|^{r+1} < \infty$. Consider ζ_s metric with $s = r + a$, $0 < a \leqslant 1$. Then there exist constants $C_1 > 0$ and $C_2 > 0$ such that

$$C_1 p^{s+1} \leqslant \zeta_s(S_p, \xi) \leqslant C_2 p^{\frac{s}{2}-1} . \tag{27}$$

REMARK 2. The result similar to (27) is valid in the above cited scheme of $\nu_{p,m}$-summation $(m \geqslant 2)$ of i.i.d. r.v.'s, too.

Now we give an example of two weak metrics (i.e. the convergence in these metrics is equivalent to the weak convergence of the d.f.'s), in which the result on the quick convergence is preserved under a consideration of the scheme od summation of a random number of i.i.d. r.v.'s, too. These metrics have the following form:

$$\mu(X,Y) = \mu(\varphi_X, \varphi_Y) = \sum_{k=0}^{\infty} 2^{-k} \sup_{k \leqslant |t| < k+1} |\varphi_X(t) - \varphi_Y(t)|, \tag{28}$$

$$\tilde{\mu}(X,Y) = \tilde{\mu}(\varphi_X, \varphi_Y) = \sup_{t \in \mathbb{R}^1} \{ |\varphi_X(t) - \varphi_Y(t)| e^{-|t|} \} \tag{29}$$

(here φ_X and φ_Y are ch.f.'s of X and Y, respectively).

Consider the question concerning the improvement of the convergence in these metrics of the distribution of the sum $p^{1/2} \sum_{j=1}^{\nu_p} X_j$ with ch.f. $\varphi(t)$ to $\mathcal{G}(0,1)$ - distribution with ch.f. (7).

THEOREM 5. Assume that the r.v.'s $\nu_p, X_1, \ldots, X_n, \ldots$ satisfy conditions A), B) and the d.f. $A(x)$, defined in (1), has $r+1$ first moments $0 < \mu_j = \int_0^\infty x^j dA(x) < \infty, \quad j = 1, 2, \dots, r+1$. If at least one of the relations

$$\mu(\varphi_p, \Phi) \leq C_r p^{\frac{r-1}{2}}, \tag{30}$$

$$\tilde{\mu}(\varphi_p, \Phi) \leq C_r p^{\frac{r-1}{2}} \tag{31}$$

holds, then the r.v. X_1 has $r-2$ moments when r is even and $r-1$ moment when r is odd, and also these moments coincide with the corresponding moments of $\mathcal{G}(0,1)$-distribution. The converse assertion is true, too.

If the r.v. X_1 has r first moments such as those of $\mathcal{G}(0,1)$, i.e.

$$\alpha_j(X_1) = E X_1^j = \alpha_j = \begin{cases} 0 & , \text{ if } \quad j = 2l-1 , \\ (2l-1)! \dfrac{\mu_l}{\mu_1^l} & , \text{ if } \quad j = 2l, \end{cases} \tag{*}$$

$j = 1, \dots, r$, and $E|X_1|^{r+1} < \infty$, then relations (30), (31) are fulfilled.

COROLLARY 1. Let $X_1, \dots, X_n, \dots$ be i.i.d. r.v.'s ν_p be one of the summations from examples 1) - 3) and $\Phi(t)$ be the ch.f. of ν_p - strictly Gaussian r.v. ξ from the corresponding example 1) - 3). Assume that condition A) is valid. Then if even one of relations (30), (31) holds, the r.v. X_1 has $r-2$ moments for even r and has $r-1$ moments for odd r, and also these moments coincide with the corresponding moments of the r.v. ξ. The converse assertion is true, too,. If $\alpha_j(X_1) = \alpha_j(\xi)$, $j = 1, \dots, r$, and $E|X_1|^{r+1} < \infty$, then relations (30), (31) are fulfilled.

Consider now the asymptotic behaviour of the distributions of sums S_p^*.

THEOREM 6. Let conditions A), B), (1), (2) be valid and $EX_1 = \theta > 0$.

Then the distribution of sum (18) tends to $\mathbb{D}(\theta)$ -distribution as $p \to 0$.

Evidently, Rényi's theorem follows from this assertion as a special case when ν_p is a geometric r.v. with distribution (5).

Now study the question of quick convergence. It is found that here, exactly as in the case of convergence to $\mathcal{G}(0,1)$ -law, the quick convergence to $\mathbb{D}(\theta)$ -law is missing in metrics $\rho, L, \pi, æ_1, \chi_0, \sigma, \lambda$, can be detected by a sequence of metrics ζ_s and is valid in metrics (28), (29).

State rigorously these results.

THEOREM 7. Let $X_1,\dots,X_n,\dots$ be i.i.d. r.v.'s with finite r first moments, coinciding with the corresponding moments of the r.v. η_m with distribution (15) (where $m \geq 1$ is an integer)., but $v(t) \not\equiv \varphi_m^*(t)$ where $\varphi_m^*(t)$ is the ch.f. from (16) $(m \geq 1)$. Let $\nu_{p,m}$ be a discrete r.v., independent of X 's with distribution (5) or (6). Denote by $\varphi_{p,m}^*(t)$ the ch.f. of the sum $S_{p,m}^* = p\sum_{j=1}^{\nu_{p,m}} X_j$ $(m \geq 1)$. Then $\lambda(\varphi_{p,m}^*, \varphi^*) \geq C_m p$, $\chi_0(S_{p,m}^*, \eta_m) \geq C_m p$, $\sigma(S_{p,m}^*, \eta_m) \geq C_m p^2$, $æ_1(S_{p,m}^*, \eta_m) \geq C_m p^2$, $\pi(S_{p,m}^*, \eta_m) \geq C_m p^2$, $L(S_{p,m}^*, \eta_m) \geq C_m p^3$, $\rho(S_{p,m}^*, \eta_m) \geq C_m p^3$.

There exist such constants $C_m^{(1)} > 0$, $C_m^{(2)} > 0$ that the relation

$$C_m^{(1)} p^{s+1} \leq \zeta_s(S_{p,m}^*, \eta_m) \leq C_m^{(2)} p^{s-1}$$

holds for the metric ζ_s, $s = r + a$, $0 < a \leq 1$.

THEOREM 8. Assume that the r.v.'s $\nu_p, X_1,\dots,X_n,\dots$ satisfy conditions A), B), and the d.f. $A(x)$, defined in (1), has $r+1$ first moments $0 < \mu_j = \int_0^\infty x_j \, dA(x) < \infty$, $j = 1,\dots,r+1$, if at least one of the relations

$$\mu(\varphi_p^*, \Phi^*) \leq C_r p^r, \quad \tilde{\mu}(\varphi_p^*, \Phi^*) \leq C_r p^r \tag{32}$$

(where Φ^* is the ch.f. of the form (12)) is valid, then the r.v. X_1 has r moments when r is even, and $r-1$ moment when r is odd, and also these moments coincide with the corresponding moments of $\mathbb{D}(\theta)$ -distribution. The converse assertion is also true. If X_1 has r first moments such as those of $\mathbb{D}(\theta)$, i.e. $\alpha_j(X_1)=(\mu_j/\mu_1^j)\times\theta^j$, $j=1,\dots,r$, and $E|X_1|^{r+1}<\infty$, then relations (32) are valid.

COROLLARY 2. Let $X_1,\dots,X_n,\dots$ be i.i.d. r.v.'s and ν_p be a discrete r.v. with distribution (5) or (6). Let $\Phi^*(t)$ be the ch.f. of ν_p -degenerate r.v. η from example 2 or 3, respectively. Then if at least one of relations (32) is valid the r.v. X_1 has r moments under even r and $r-1$ moment under odd r, and also these moments coincide with the corresponding moments of the r.v. η. The converse assertion is also true. If $\alpha_j(X_1)=\alpha_j(\eta)$, $j=1,\dots,r$, and $E|X_1|^{r+1}<\infty$, then relations (30) are valid.

4. Local limit theorems for densities under ν_p -summation.

In this section we consider the problem of convergence of density functions under ν_p -summation of i.i.d. r.v.'s. First we study conditions, under which the sum S_p has a density, which converges to the density of $\mathcal{G}(0,1)$ -distribution.

It is known (see, e.g., [21 , p.590]) that under summation of a non-random number n of i.i.d. r.v.'s X_j with $EX_1=0$ and $DX_1=\sigma^2<\infty$ the assumption $\int_{-\infty}^{\infty}|v(t)|^s dt<\infty$, where $v(t)$ is the ch.f. of summands and s is some number more or equal to 1, is sufficient for the existence of the density of the sum $\frac{1}{\sigma\sqrt{n}}\sum_{j=1}^{n}X_j$ which uniformly converges to the density of the normal law $\mathcal{N}(0,1)$. We show in the example below that the cited assumption does not guarantee the uniform convergence of densities in the scheme of ν_p -summation.

EXAMPLE. Let $X_1,\dots,X_n,\dots$ be i.i.d. r.v.'s having centered gamma-distribution with the density function

$$\ell(x) = \begin{cases} 0, & x \leqslant -\lambda, \\ \Gamma^{-1}(\lambda)(x+\lambda)^{\lambda-1}\exp\{-(x+\lambda)\}, & x > -\lambda, \end{cases}$$

where $1/2 < \lambda < 1$. It is obvious that $EX_1 = 0$, $DX_1 = \lambda$ and the ch. f. $v(t) = e^{-it\lambda}(1-it)^{-\lambda}$. It can be easily seen that although $\int_{-\infty}^{\infty} |v(t)|^s dt < \infty$ for any $s \geqslant 2$, but $\int_{-\infty}^{\infty} |v(t)| dt = \infty$. Let ν_p be a geometric r.v. with distribution (5), independent of X's. Then the density function of the sum $(p^{1/2}/\lambda)\sum_{j=1}^{\nu_p} X_j$

$$f_p(x) = \sum_{k=1}^{\infty} p(1-p)^{k-1}(\lambda/p)^{\frac{\lambda}{2}k}\Gamma^{-1}(k\lambda)(x+k\lambda)^{k\lambda-1}\exp\{-\sqrt{\lambda/p}(x+k\lambda)\}$$

has an infinite discontionuity at the point $x = -\lambda$, so that

$$\sup_{x\in\mathbb{R}^1} | f_p(x) - g(x)| = \infty$$

and there is no uniform convergence of $f_p(x)$ to the density function $g(x)$ of Laplace distribution (8).

State a sufficient condition for the uniform convergence of the density of the sum S_p to the density of $\mathcal{G}(0,1)$-law (7).

Let the function Ψ from (3) satisfy the following condition

C) there exists $a > 1/2$ such that for any $\delta \in (0,1)$

$$\psi[\frac{1}{p}\psi^{-1}(z)] \leqslant C p^a z, \qquad p \in \Delta$$

for every $0 < z \leqslant 1-\delta$.

THEOREM 9. Let the r.v. ξ have $\mathcal{G}(0,1)$-distribution with the ch.f. $\Phi(t)$ such that

$$\int_{-\infty}^{\infty} \Phi(t)\,dt < \infty. \tag{33}$$

Let assumptions A), B), C) hold and, moreover, $EX_1=0$, $0<DX_1=\sigma^2<\infty$ and the ch.f. $v(t)$ of X_1 be such that

$$\int_{-\infty}^{\infty}|v(t)|dt<\infty. \tag{34}$$

Then the r.v.'s ξ and (17) possess continuous and bounded densities $f(x)$ and $f_p(x)$, respectively, and also

$$\lim_{p\to 0}\ \sup_{x\in\mathbb{R}^1}|f_p(x)-f(x)|=0. \tag{35}$$

COROLLARY 3. Let ν_p be a geometric r.v. with distribution (5), independent of the i.i.d. r.v.'s $X_1,\ldots,X_n,\ldots,$ with $EX_1=0$, $0<DX_1=\sigma^2<\infty$. If the ch.f. $v(t)$ of X_1 is such that (34) is valid, then sum (17) has a continuous bounded density $f_p(x)$ which converges uniformly to the density of Laplace distribution (8).

Consider now the convergence in L^q of f_p to f.

THEOREM 10. Let $X_1,\ldots,X_n,\ldots$ be i.i.d. r.v.'s having a density function with $EX_1=0$, $0<\sigma^2=DX_1<\infty$ and

$$\int_{-\infty}^{\infty}|v(t)|^s dt<\infty \tag{36}$$

for some $s\in(1,2]$. Assume that A), B) and the following condition

D) there exists $a>1/(2s)$ such that for any $\delta\in(0,1]$ $\Psi[\frac{1}{p}\Psi^{-1}(x)]\leqslant Cp^a x$ for every $p\in\Delta$ and $0<x\leqslant 1-\delta$ hold.

Consider $\mathcal{G}(0,1)$-distribution with the density $f(x)$ and ch.f. (7) satisfying

$$\int_{-\infty}^{\infty}\Phi^s(t)dt<\infty. \tag{37}$$

Then $f\in L^q$ $(q=\frac{s}{s-1})$, sum (17) possesses a density function $f_p\in L^q$ and

$$\lim_{p\to 0}\int_{-\infty}^{\infty}|f_p(x)-f(x)|^q dx = 0. \tag{38}$$

COROLLARY 4. Let $\nu_{p,m}$ $(m=1,2,3)$ be a r.v. with distribution (5) if $m=1$ and (6) if $m=2,3$, independent of the r.v.'s $X_1,\ldots,X_n,\ldots$. Assume that X_1 has a density with $EX_1=0$, $0<DX_1=\sigma^2<\infty$ and ch.f. $v(t)$ satisfying (36) with $3/2<s\leqslant 2$. Then the r.v. $(p^{1/2}/\sigma)\sum_{j=1}^{\nu_{p,m}} X_j$ $(m=1,2,3)$ has a density function $f_{p,m}\in L^q$, $q=s/(s-1)$, and also

$$\lim_{p\to 0}\int_{-\infty}^{\infty}|f_{p,m}(x)-g_m(x)|^q dx = 0 \quad (m=1,2,3),$$

where $g_m(x)$ is the density function (8) under $m=1$ and (9) under $m=2,3$. If $1<s\leqslant 3/2$ the assertion of the corollary holds only for $f_{p,1}$ and $f_{p,2}$.

Now consider the problem of convergence of the density of the sum S_p^* to the density of $\mathbb{D}(\theta)$ -law.

THEOREM 11. Let $X_1,\ldots,X_n,\ldots$ be i.i.d. r.v.'s with a density function such that $EX_1=\theta>0$ and the ch.f. satisfying (36) under some $s\in(1,2]$. Assume that conditions A), B) and

E) there exists $d>1/s$ such that for whatever $\delta\in(0,1)$

$$\psi[\tfrac{1}{p}\psi^{-1}(z)]\leqslant Cp^d z \text{ for every } p\in\Delta \text{ and } 0<z\leqslant 1-\delta;$$

F) for every $b>0$, $t\in\mathbb{R}^1$

$$|\psi(-ibt)|\geqslant\psi(b|t|)$$

are fulfilled. Consider $\mathbb{D}(\theta)$ -distribution with the density $f^*(x)$ and ch.f. (12), satisfying (37). Then $f^*\in L^q$ $(q=s/(s-1))$, sum (18) possesses a density $f_p^*\in L^q$ and

$$\lim_{p\to 0}\int_{-\infty}^{\infty}|f_p^*(x)-f^*(x)|^q dx = 0. \tag{39}$$

COROLLARY 5. Let ν_p be a geometric r.v. with distribution (5), independent of i.i.d. r.v.'s $X_1, \ldots, X_n, \ldots$. Let X_1 have a density function with $EX_1 = \theta > 0$ and the ch.f. $v(t)$, satisfying (36) under some $s \in (1, 2]$. Then sum (18) has a density $f_p^* \in L^q$ $(q = s/(s-1))$ and

$$\lim_{p \to 0} \int_{-\infty}^{\infty} | f_p^*(x) - d(x) |^q dx = 0, \qquad (40)$$

where $d(x)$ is a density function of dictribution (13).

5. Theorems on large derivations in the scheme of ν_p -summation.

In this section we state rough estimates for large deviations of distributions of sums S_p or S_p^* from the distributions of $\mathscr{G}(0,1)$ or, respectively, $\mathbb{D}(\theta)$ -law.

THEOREM 12. Assume that conditions A), B) are valid and, moreover, $EX_1 = 0$, $0 < DX_1 = \sigma^2 < \infty$, $E|X_1|^3 < \infty$. Denote by $F_p(x)$ the d.f. of sum (17) and by $G(x)$ the d.f. of $\mathscr{G}(0, 1)$ -law with a finite third absolute moment. Let $\{a_p\}$ and $\{\delta_p\}$ be sets of positive numbers satisfying the following conditions:

(i) $a_p \to \infty$ as $p \to 0$; (ii) $\delta_p \to 0$ as $p \to 0$;

(iii) $\dfrac{1 - G(a_p \pm \delta_p)}{1 - G(a_p)} \to 1$ as $p \to 0$; (iv) $\dfrac{p^{1/2}}{\delta_p^3 (1 - G(a_p))} \to 0$ as $p \to 0$.

Then

$$\frac{1 - G(a_p + \delta_p)}{1 - G(a_p)} - C_1 \frac{p^{1/2}}{\delta_p^3 [1 - G(a_p)]} \leq \frac{1 - F(a_p)}{1 - G(a_p)} \leq \frac{1 - G(a_p - \delta_p)}{1 - G(a_p)} + C_2 \frac{p^{1/2}}{\delta_p^3 [1 - G(a_p)]}, \qquad (41)$$

$$\frac{G(-a_p - \delta_p)}{G(-a_p)} - C_3 \frac{p^{1/2}}{\delta_p^3 G(-a_p)} \leq \frac{F_p(-a_p)}{G(-a_p)} \leq \frac{G(-a_p + \delta_p)}{G(-a_p)} + C_4 \frac{p^{1/2}}{\delta_p^3 G(-a_p)}. \qquad (42)$$

COROLLARY 6. Let $G_m(x)$ be a d.f. of law (8) under $m=1$ and of law (10) under $m=2,3,\dots$, and $\nu_{p,m}$ $(m=1,2,\dots)$ be a r.v. with distribution (5) under $m=1$ and (6) under $m=2,3,\dots$ independent of a sequence of i.i.d. r.v.'s $X_1,\dots,X_n,\dots$ with $EX_1=0$, $0<DX_1=\sigma^2<\infty$, $E|X_1|^3<\infty$. Let $F_{p,m}$ be a d.f. of the sum $(p^{1/2}/\sigma)\sum_{j=1}^{\nu_{p,m}} X_j$ and $\{a_{p,m}\}$ be a set of real numbers such that for any fixed m $a_{p,m}\to 0$ as $p\to 0$, $0<a_{p,m}<\varepsilon_m \ln p^{-1}$, where $0<\varepsilon_m<\frac{1}{2}\left(\frac{m}{2}\right)^{\frac{1}{2}}$ and d_m satisfies the inequality $0<d_m<1/6-(\varepsilon_m/3)(2/m)^{\frac{1}{2}}$. Then

$$\left(1+\frac{p^{d_m}}{a_p}\right)^{\frac{1}{m}-1}\exp\left\{-\left(\frac{2}{m}\right)^{\frac{1}{2}}p^{d_m}\right\}-C_{1,m}\exp\left\{\left(\frac{2}{m}\right)^{\frac{1}{2}}a_p\right\}a_p^{1-\frac{1}{m}}p^{\frac{1}{2}-3d_m}\leqslant$$

$$\leqslant\frac{1-F_{p,m}(a_p)}{1-G_m(a_p)}\leqslant \tag{43}$$

$$\leqslant\left(1-\frac{p^{d_m}}{a_p}\right)^{\frac{1}{m}-1}\exp\left\{\left(\frac{2}{m}\right)^{\frac{1}{2}}p^{d_m}\right\}+C_{2,m}\exp\left\{\left(\frac{2}{m}\right)^{\frac{1}{2}}a_p\right\}a_p^{1-\frac{1}{m}}p^{\frac{1}{2}-3d_m},$$

$$\left(1+\frac{p^{d_m}}{a_p}\right)^{\frac{1}{m}-1}\exp\left\{-\left(\frac{2}{m}\right)^{\frac{1}{2}}p^{d_m}\right\}-C_{3,m}\exp\left\{\left(\frac{2}{m}\right)^{\frac{1}{2}}a_p\right\}a_p^{1-\frac{1}{m}}p^{\frac{1}{2}-3d_m}\leqslant$$

$$\leqslant\frac{F_{p,m}(-a_p)}{G_m(-a_p)}\leqslant \tag{44}$$

$$\left(1-\frac{p^{d_m}}{a_p}\right)^{\frac{1}{m}-1}\exp\left\{\left(\frac{2}{m}\right)^{\frac{1}{2}}p^{d_m}\right\}+C_{4,m}\exp\left\{\left(\frac{2}{m}\right)^{\frac{1}{2}}a_p\right\}a_p^{1-\frac{1}{m}}p^{\frac{1}{2}-3d_m},\quad m=1,2,\dots$$

THEOREM 13. Assume that conditions A), B) hold and, moreover, $EX_1=\theta>0$, $EX_1^2<\infty$. Denote by $F_p^*(x)$ the d.f. of sum (18) and by $\mathcal{D}(x)$ the d.f. of $\mathbf{D}(\theta)$-law with a finite second moment. Let $\{a_p\}$ and $\{\delta_p\}$ be sets of positive numbers, satisfying the following conditions:

(i) $a_p\to\infty$ as $p\to 0$; (ii) $\delta_p\to 0$ as $p\to 0$;

(iii) $\dfrac{1-\mathcal{D}(a_p\pm\delta_p)}{1-\mathcal{D}(a_p)}$ as $p\to 0$; (iv) $\dfrac{p}{\delta_p^2\,[1-\mathcal{D}(a_p)]}$ as $p\to 0$. Then

$$\frac{1-\mathcal{D}(a_p+\delta_p)}{1-\mathcal{D}(a_p)}-C_1\frac{p}{\delta_p^2[1-\mathcal{D}(a_p)]}\leqslant\frac{1-F_p^*(a_p)}{1-\mathcal{D}(a_p)}\leqslant\frac{1-\mathcal{D}(a_p-\delta_p)}{1-\mathcal{D}(a_p)}+C_2\frac{p}{\delta_p^2[1-\mathcal{D}(a_p)]}\ . \tag{45}$$

COROLLARY 7. Let $\nu_{p,m}$ be a r.v. with distribution (5) under $m=1$ and (6) under $m=2,3,\ldots$, independent of a sequence of i.i.d. r.v.'s $X_1,\ldots,X_n,\ldots$ with $EX_1=\theta>0$ and $EX_1^2<\infty$. Let $F_{p,m}^*$ be a d.f. of the $p\sum_{j=1}^{\nu_{p,m}}X_j$ and $D_m(n)$ be a d.f. of $\mathbb{D}(\theta)$ - law (13) under $m=1$ and (15) under $m=2,3,\ldots$. Let $\{a_{p,m}\}$ be a set of real numbers such that for any fixed m

(i) $a_{p,m}\to\infty$ as $p\to 0$; (ii) $0<a_{p,m}<\varepsilon_m\ln p^{-1}$,where $0<\varepsilon_m<m$, and $0<d_m<1/2-\varepsilon_m/(2m)$. Then

$$\left(1+\frac{p^{d_m}}{a_p}\right)^{\frac{1}{m}-1}\exp\left\{-\frac{p^{d_m}}{m}\right\}-C_{1,m}\,a_p^{1-\frac{1}{m}}\exp\left\{\frac{a_p}{m}\right\}p^{1-2d_m}\leqslant$$
$$\leqslant\frac{1-F_{p,m}^*(a_p)}{1-\mathcal{D}(a_p)}\leqslant \tag{46}$$
$$\leqslant\left(1-\frac{p^{d_m}}{a_p}\right)^{\frac{1}{m}-1}\exp\left\{\frac{p^{d_m}}{m}\right\}+C_{2,m}\,a_p^{1-\frac{1}{m}}\exp\left\{\frac{a_p}{m}\right\}p^{1-2d_m},\qquad m=1,2,\ldots.$$

6. Proofs of theorems.

PROOF OF THEOREM 1. Since the generating function of the r.v. ν_p $\Psi_p(z)=\sum_{k=1}^{\infty}z^kP\{\nu_p=k\}$, then the ch.f. of the sum S_p has the form

$$\varphi_p(t)=\sum_{k=1}^{\infty}\left[v\left(\frac{p^{1/2}}{6}t\right)\right]^kP\{\nu_p=k\}=\Psi_p\left(v\left(\frac{p^{1/2}}{6}t\right)\right). \tag{47}$$

By virtue of the assumptions of the theorem it follows from (1) that for any t

$$\varphi_p(t)=\Psi\Big[\frac{1}{p}\big(\psi^{-1}(v(\theta))+(\psi^{-1}(v(\tau)))'\big|_{\tau=0}\cdot\frac{p^{1/2}}{6}t+\frac{1}{2}(\psi^{-1}(v(\tau)))''\big|_{\tau=0}\cdot\frac{p}{2}t^2+$$

$$+ o(pt^2))] = \psi[-\frac{1}{2\psi'(0)} t^2 + o(t^2)] \xrightarrow[p\to 0]{} \psi[-\frac{t^2}{2\psi'(0)}]$$

(where $o(t^2) \to 0$ as $p \to 0$ for any fixed t). It is easily seen that the limit distribution has a zero mean and unit variance. The proof is complete.

PROOF OF THEOREM 2. The ch.f. of the $p^{1/2} \sum_{j=1}^{\nu_p} X_j$

$$\varphi_p(t) = \sum_{k=1}^{\infty} p(1-p)^{k-1} v^k(p^{1/2}t) = \frac{pv(p^{1/2}t)}{1-(1-p)v(p^{1/2}t)}.$$

Therefore

$$|\varphi_p(t) - \varphi(t)| = \frac{|v(p^{1/2}t) - (1+pt^2)^{-1}|\,(1+pt^2/2)}{|1-(1-p)v(p^{1/2}t)|\,(1+t^2/2)}.$$

Since $|1-(1-p)v|^{-1} \geqslant [1+(1-p)|v|]^{-1} \geqslant 1/2$, we have for $t = \delta/p^{1/2}$ with $\delta \neq 0$,

$$|\varphi_p(\delta/p^{1/2}) - \varphi(\delta/p^{1/2})| \geqslant \frac{|v(\delta)-\varphi(\delta)|\,|\varphi(\delta)|}{2[1+\delta^2/(2p)]} \geqslant \frac{1+\delta^2/2}{2+\delta^2}|v(\delta)-\varphi(\delta)|p \geqslant Cp.$$

Hence, under $0 < T < \delta/p^{1/2}$ $\max\{\frac{1}{2}\max_{|t|\leqslant T}|\varphi_p(t)-\varphi(t)|, \frac{1}{T}\} \geqslant p^{1/2}/\delta$, and under $T > \delta/p^{1/2}$ this maximum $\geqslant p$, which implies (20). The proof is complete.

PROOF OF THEOREM 3. It is shown in [22, p.191] that π, $\varkappa_1$ and ζ_0 metrics are connected with λ-metric by the following inequalities: $\lambda^2 \leqslant (1+\frac{\sqrt{3}}{2}\pi)$, $\lambda^2 < \varkappa_1$, $\lambda^2 \leqslant \frac{1}{2}\zeta_0$, which, with regard to (20), implies (23), (24), (25).

π and σ metrics are connected by the inequality $\pi \leqslant \sigma$ (see

[22, p.11]), which, with regard to (23), implies (25).

Now deduce relation (21). Denote by F_p and G the d.f.'s of the r.v.'s S_p and ξ, respectively. We have

$$\varkappa_1(S_p,\xi)=\int\limits_{|x|\leqslant T}|F_p(x)-G(x)|\,dx+\int\limits_{|x|>T}|F_p(x)-G(x)|\,dx.$$

Since X_1 has $r>2$ moments such as the corresponding ones of ξ, then $DX_1=1$ and direct calculation shows that the r.v. S_p has a finite second moment $(DS_p=1)$. Therefore (see, e.g. [23, p.35])

$$\int\limits_{|x|>T}|F_p(x)-G(x)|\,dx\leqslant\int\limits_{|x|>T}F_p(x)\,dx+\int\limits_{|x|>T}G(x)\,dx\leqslant$$

$$\leqslant T^{-2}[\int\limits_{|x|>T}x^2dF(x)+\int\limits_{|x|>T}x^2dG(x)|\leqslant CT^{-2},$$

whence

$$\varkappa_1(S_p,\xi)\leqslant\int\limits_{|x|\leqslant T}|F_p(x)-G_p(x)|\,dx+CT^{-2}\leqslant 2T\rho(S_p,\xi)+CT^{-2}.$$

Choose $T>0$ from the condition $T\rho(S_p,\xi)=T^{-2}$. Then $T=(\rho(S_p,\xi))^{-1/3}$ and $\varkappa_1(S_p,\xi)\leqslant C(\rho(S_p,\xi))^{2/3}$, which, with regard to (24) implies (21).

Relation (22) follows from (21) and the inequality $\rho(S_p,\xi)\leqslant(1+\sup_x g(x))L(\xi,S_p)$ (see [22, p.107]). The proof is complete.

PROOF OF THEOREM 4. By virtue of the assumptions of the theorem the metric ζ_s, $s=r+a$, $0<a\leqslant 1$, is finite. ζ_s and λ metrics are connected by the relation $\lambda^{s+1}\leqslant 2^{-a}\zeta_s$ (see [22, p.125]), whence, with regard to (20), we obtain the lower bound in (27). In order to obtain the upper bound, consider a sequence of i.i.d. r.v.'s $\xi,\xi_1,\dots,\xi_n,\dots$ independent of $\nu_p,X_1,\dots,X_n,\dots$. Then, with re-

gard to the definition of the ν_p -strictly Gaussian r.v. and to the properties of ζ_s metric, we have

$$\zeta_s(S_p, \xi) = \zeta_s(p^{1/2}\sum_{j=1}^{\nu_p}\xi_j, p^{1/2}\sum_{j=1}^{\nu_p}X_j) =$$

$$= \sum_{k=1}^{\infty} p(1-p)^{k-1}\zeta_s(p^{1/2}\sum_{j=1}^{k}X_j, p^{1/2}\sum_{j=1}^{k}\xi_j) =$$

$$= p^{s/2}\sum_{k=1}^{\infty} kp(1-p)^{k-1}\zeta_s(X_1,\xi_1) = p^{s/2-1}\zeta_s(X_1,\xi_1) \leqslant C_2 p^{s/2-1}.$$

The proof in complete.

PROOF OF THEOREM 5. It easily follows from the definition of the metrics μ and $\tilde{\mu}$ that each of relations (30), (31) implies

$$\sup_{|t|<1} |\varphi_p(t) - \Phi(t)| \leqslant C_r^* p^{\frac{r-1}{2}}. \tag{48}$$

Denote $R_p(t) = \varphi_p(t) - \Phi(t)$, then $\varphi_p(t) = \Phi(t) + R_p(t)$, where according to (48)

$$\sup_{|t|<1} |R_p(t)| \leqslant C_r^* p^{\frac{r-1}{2}}. \tag{49}$$

By virtue of its definition and the assumptions of the theorem $\varphi_p(t) = \Psi_p[v(p^{1/2}t)] = \psi[\frac{1}{p}\psi^{-1}(v(p^{1/2}t))]$, whence

$$v(p^{1/2}t) = \psi[p\psi^{-1}(\varphi_p(t))] = \psi[p\psi^{-1}(\Phi(t) + R_p(t))]. \tag{50}$$

We prove the first assertion of the theorem by induction. Let at least one of relations (30), (31) be valid with $r = 2$. Then, by virtue of the equality

$$\Phi(p^{1/2}t) = \psi[p\psi^{-1}(\Phi(t))], \tag{51}$$

relation (50) and the mean value theorem, we have,

$$v(p^{1/2}t) - 1 = [v(p^{1/2}t) - \Phi(p^{1/2}t)] + [\Phi(p^{1/2}t) - 1] =$$

$$= \psi[p\psi^{-1}(\Phi(t)+R_p(t))] - \psi[p\psi^{-1}(\Phi(t))] + \frac{1}{2}\Phi''(0)pt^2 + o(pt^2) =$$

$$= \frac{\psi'[p\psi^{-1}(u(t))]}{\psi'[\psi^{-1}(u(t))]} pR_p(t) + \frac{1}{2}\Phi''(0)pt^2 + o(pt^2) \tag{52}$$

(here and below $u(t)$ is between $\Phi(t)$ and $\Phi(t)+R_p(t)$). It follows from (52) and (49) with $r=2$ that for any $t\in(-1,1)$

$$\lim_{p\to 0} \frac{v(p^{1/2}t)-1}{p^{1/2}t} = 0,$$

i.e.

$$v'(0) = 0. \tag{53}$$

Assume that at least one of relations (30), (31) is valid with $r=3$. Then relations (49) with $r=3$, (52) and (53) imply that for any $t\in(-1,1)$

$$\lim_{p\to 0} \frac{v(p^{1/2}t)-1-v'(0)p^{1/2}t}{\frac{1}{2}pt^2} = \Phi''(0),$$

i.e.

$$v''(0) = \Phi''(0). \tag{54}$$

It follows from (53), (54), with regard to (x) that

$$EX_1 = 0, \qquad EX_1^2 = 1.$$

Assume that the direct assertion of the theorem is proved already for every natural $r \leq 2k-1$. Consider the case $r = 2k$. Then relations (50), (51), $EX_1^j = \alpha_j$, $j = 1,\dots,2k-2,$ and the mean value theorem imply

$$v(p^{1/2}t) - \sum_{l=0}^{2k-2} \frac{v^{(l)}(0)}{l!}(p^{1/2}t)^l =$$

$$= v(p^{1/2}t) - \Phi(p^{1/2}t) + \Phi(p^{1/2}t) - \sum_{l=0}^{2k-2} \frac{\Phi^{(l)}(0)}{l!} (p^{1/2}t)^l =$$

$$= \psi[p\psi^{-1}(\Phi(t) + R_p(t))] - \psi[p\psi^{-1}(\Phi(t))] + \frac{\Phi^{(2k)}(0)}{(2k)!}(pt^2)^k + o[(pt^2)^k] =$$

$$= \frac{\psi'[p\psi^{-1}(u(t))]}{\psi'[\psi^{-1}(u(t))]} pR_p(t) + \frac{\Phi^{(2k)}(0)}{(2k)!}(pt^2)^k + o[(pt^2)^k]. \tag{55}$$

Relations (55) and (49) with $r = 2k$ imply for any $t \in (-1, 1)$ that

$$\lim_{p \to 0} \frac{v(p^{1/2}t) - \sum_{l=0}^{2k-2} \frac{v^{(l)}(0)}{l!} (p^{1/2}t)^l}{(p^{1/2}t)^{2k-1}/(2k-1)!} = 0,$$

i.e.

$$v^{(2k-1)}(0) = 0. \tag{56}$$

Finally, let at least one of relations (30). (31) be valid with $r = 2k+1$. Relations (49) with $r = 2k+1$, (55) and (56) imply that for every $t \in (-1, 1)$

$$\lim_{p \to 0} \frac{v(p^{1/2}t) - \sum_{l=0}^{2k-1} \frac{v^{(l)}(0)}{l!} (p^{1/2}t)^l}{(p^{1/2}t)^{2k}/(2k)!} = \Phi^{(2k)}(0),$$

i.e.

$$v^{(2k)}(0) = \Phi^{(2k)}(0). \tag{57}$$

Relations (56), (57) imply coincidence of moments

$$EX_1^j = a_j, \quad j = 2k-1,\ 2k.$$

Now prove the converse assertion of the theorem. By virtue of the definition

$$\Phi(t) = \psi_p[\Phi(p^{1/2}t)] = \sum_{k=1}^{\infty} P\{\nu_p = k\} \Phi^k(p^{1/2}t). \tag{58}$$

According to (47), (32) and (24),

$$|\varphi_p(t)-\Phi(t)|=|\sum_{k=1}^{\infty}P\{\nu_p=k\}[v^k(p^{1/2}t)-\Phi^k(p^{1/2}t)]|\leq$$

$$\leq\sum_{k=1}^{\infty}P\{\nu_p=k\}\,|v(p^{1/2}t)-\Phi(p^{1/2}t)|\sum_{n=0}^{k-1}|v(p^{1/2}t)|^{k-n-1}\cdot|\Phi(p^{1/2}t)|^{n}\leq \tag{59}$$

$$\leq\sum_{k=1}^{\infty}k\,P\{\nu_p=k\}|v(p^{1/2}t)-\Phi(p^{1/2}t)|=\frac{1}{p}|\,v(p^{1/2}t)-\Phi(p^{1/2}t)|.$$

With regard to (*) and the finiteness of $(r+1)$ -st absolute moments of X_1 and the r.v. ξ with $\mathcal{G}(0,1)$ -distribution, we obtain that

$$|v(p^{1/2}t)-\Phi(p^{1/2}t)|\leq C|p^{1/2}t|^{r+1}. \tag{60}$$

Relations (59) and (60) imply that

$$|\varphi_p(t)-\Phi(t)|\leq Cp^{\frac{r-1}{2}}|t|^{r+1}. \tag{61}$$

It is obvious that the series $\sum_{k=0}^{\infty}2^{-k}(k+1)^{r+1}$ converges, hence (61) implies that

$$\mu(\varphi_p,\Phi)\leq\sum_{k=0}^{\infty}Cp^{\frac{r-1}{2}}2^{-k}(k+1)^{r+1}<C_r p^{\frac{r-1}{2}}.$$

Since $\sup_{t\in\mathbb{R}^1}|t|^{r+1}e^{-|t|}$ is finite, relation (61) implies

$$\tilde{\mu}(\varphi_p,\Phi)\leq Cp^{\frac{r-1}{2}}\sup_{t\in\mathbb{R}^1}|t|^{r+1}e^{-|t|}\leq C_r p^{\frac{r-1}{2}}.$$

The proof is complete.

PROOF OF THEOREM 6. The ch.f. of sum S_p^* has the form

$$\varphi_p^*(t)=\sum_{k=1}^{\infty}[v(pt)]^kP\{\nu_p=k\}=\psi_p(v(pt)). \tag{62}$$

By virtue of the conditions of the theorem, (62) implies that for any t

$$\varphi^*(t) = \Psi[\frac{1}{p}(\Psi^{-1}(1) + (\Psi^{-1}(v(\tau)))'|_{\tau=0}\, pt + o(pt)] =$$

$$= \psi[it\theta/\psi'(0) + o(t)] \underset{p\to 0}{\longrightarrow} \psi[it\theta/\psi'(0)]$$

The proof is complete.

The proof of Theorems 7, 8 is carried out quite similarly to the proof of Theorems 2 - 5. We omit the details.

PROOF OF THEOREM 9. By virtue of (47), (34) and the inequality $|v(\tau)|^k \leq |v(\tau)|, \quad k \geq 1$, we have that

$$\int_{-\infty}^{\infty} |\varphi_p(t)|\, dt < \sum_{k=1}^{\infty} P\{\nu_p = k\} \int_{-\infty}^{\infty} |v(\frac{p^{\frac{1}{2}}}{6} t)| dt = \frac{6}{p^{1/2}} \int_{-\infty}^{\infty} |v(t)|\, dt < \infty .$$

This relation implies that for any $p \in \Delta$ the sum S_p possesses a continuous and bounded density $f_p(x)$ which can be presented in the form

$$f_p(x) = \frac{1}{2\pi} \int_{-\infty}^{\infty} e^{-itx} \varphi_p(t)\, dt. \tag{63}$$

It follows from (33) that r.v. ξ also possesses a continuous and bounded density $f(x)$ such that

$$f(x) = \frac{1}{2\pi} \int_{-\infty}^{\infty} e^{-itx} \Phi(t)\, dt. \tag{64}$$

We obtain from (63) and (64) that

$$\sup_{x \in \mathbb{R}^1} |f_p(x) - f(x)| \leq \frac{1}{2\pi} \int_{-\infty}^{\infty} |\varphi_p(t) - \Phi(t)|\, dt . \tag{65}$$

Let us estimate the integral in the right-hand side of (65). We have

$$\int_{-\infty}^{\infty} |\varphi_p(t) - \Phi(t)|\,dt \leqslant \int_{|t|<C} |\varphi_p(t) - \Phi(t)|\,dt + \int_{C<|t|\leqslant \sigma p^{-1/2}\varepsilon} |\varphi_p(t)|\,dt +$$

$$+ \int_{|t|>\sigma p^{-1/2}\varepsilon} |\varphi_p(t)|\,dt + \int_{|t|>C} \Phi(t)\,dt = I_1 + I_2 + I_3 + I_4. \tag{66}$$

Consider each of the integrals I_j separately. By virtue of Theorem 1

$$I_1 \leq 2C \sup_{|t|\leqslant C} |\varphi_p(t) - \Phi(t)| \to 0 \quad \text{as} \quad p \to 0. \tag{67}$$

Since $|v(\frac{p^{1/2}}{\sigma}t)| \leqslant 1 - \frac{pt^2}{4}$ in the interval $|\frac{p^{1/2}}{\sigma}t| < \varepsilon$, where $\varepsilon > 0$ is sufficiently small (see, e. g. [25, p.21-22]), then the following sequence of inequalities is fulfilled for the values of t such that $C<|t|<\frac{\sigma}{p^{1/2}}\varepsilon$: $1 - \frac{pt^2}{4} < 1 + \frac{\sigma^2\varepsilon^2}{4}$, $\psi^{-1}(1 - \frac{pt^2}{4}) > \psi^{-1}(1 + \frac{\sigma^2\varepsilon^2}{4})$, $\psi[\frac{1}{p}\psi^{-1}(1 - \frac{pt^2}{4})] < \psi[\frac{1}{p}\psi^{-1}(1 + \frac{\sigma^2\varepsilon^2}{4})] < \psi[\frac{t^2}{\sigma^2\varepsilon^2}\psi^{-1}(1 + \frac{\sigma^2\varepsilon^2}{4})]$, whence we obtain by virtue of (47) and (3) that

$$|\varphi_p(t)| \leqslant \sum_{k=1}^{\infty} P\{\nu_p = k\} |v(p^{1/2}\sigma^{-1}t)|^k \leqslant \sum_{k=1}^{\infty} P\{\nu_p = k\} (1 - \tfrac{1}{4}pt^2)^k =$$

$$= \psi[\tfrac{1}{p}\psi^{-1}(1 - \tfrac{1}{4}pt^2)] \leqslant \psi[(\sigma\varepsilon)^{-2}\psi^{-1}(1 + \tfrac{1}{4}(\sigma\varepsilon)^2)\, t^2] = \psi(at^2). \tag{68}$$

It follows from (68) and (33) that

$$I_2 \leqslant \int_{C\leqslant|t|\leqslant\sigma p^{-1/2}\varepsilon} \psi(at^2)\,dt \leqslant \int_{|t|\geqslant C} \psi(at^2)\,dt \to 0 \quad \text{as} \quad C \to \infty \tag{69}$$

Taking into account that $v(t)$ is a ch.f. of an absolutely continuous distribution, it can be easily shown that for any $\varepsilon > 0$ there is $\delta \in (0, 1)$ such that for each t satisfying the inequality $|t| > \varepsilon$, the relation $|v(t)| \leq 1-\delta$ is valid. Hence, by virtue of (47) and (3) we have for t such that $|p^{1/2}\sigma^{-1}t| > \varepsilon$

$$|\varphi_p(t)| \leq \psi[\tfrac{1}{p}\psi^{-1}(|v(p^{1/2}\sigma^{-1}t)|] \leq Cp^{d}|v(p^{1/2}\sigma^{-1}t)|, \quad p\in\Delta, \tag{70}$$

whence, on account of (34), we obtain

$$I_3 \leq Cp^{a} \int_{|t|>\sigma p^{-1/2}\varepsilon} |v(p^{1/2}\sigma^{-1}t)|dt < Cp^{d-\frac{1}{2}} \int_{-\infty}^{\infty}|v(t)|dt \xrightarrow[p\to 0]{} 0 . \tag{71}$$

And, finally, by virtue of (33)

$$I_4 = \int_{|t|>C} |\Phi(t)|\,dt \to 0 \qquad \text{as} \qquad C\to\infty . \tag{72}$$

Setting in (66) first $p\to 0$ and then $C\to\infty$ and taking into account relations (65), (67), (69), (71), (72), we obtain (35). The proof is complete.

PROOF OF THEOREM 10. By virtue of (47), (37) and the inequality $|v(\tau)|^{k} \leq v(\tau)$, $k \geq 1$, we have that

$$\int_{-\infty}^{\infty}|\varphi_p(t)|^{s}dt < \sigma p^{-1/2}\int_{-\infty}^{\infty}|v(t)|^{s}dt < \infty$$

which implies for any $p\in\Delta$ the existence of a density function $f_p\in L^{q}$, $q=s/(s-1)$ (see [25, Chapter 4]) of S_p. It follows from (37) that $f\in L^{q}$. Hence, according to [25, Chapter 4]),

$$\int_{-\infty}^{\infty}|f_p(x)-f(x)|^{q}dx \leq (2\pi)^{1-q/2}\Big(\int_{-\infty}^{\infty}|\varphi_p(t)-\Phi(t)|^{s}dt\Big)^{\frac{1}{s-1}}, \quad q=\frac{s}{s-1} . \tag{73}$$

Estimate the integral in the right-hand side of (73). We have

$$\int_{-\infty}^{\infty}|\varphi_p(t)-\Phi(t)|^s dt = \int_{|t|\leq C}|\varphi_p(t)-\Phi(t)|^s dt + \int_{C<|t|\leq \sigma p^{-1/2}\varepsilon}|\varphi_p(t)|^s dt +$$

$$+ \int_{|t|>\sigma p^{-1/2}\varepsilon}|\varphi_p(t)|^s dt + \int_{|t|>C}\Phi^s(t)\,dt = I_1 + I_2 + I_3 + I_4 . \qquad (74)$$

Consider each of the integrals I_j , separately. On account of Theorem 1

$$I_1 \leq 2C \sup_{|t|\leq C}|\varphi_p(t)-\Phi(t)|^s \to 0 \qquad \text{as} \qquad p \to 0. \qquad (75)$$

By virtue of (68) we obtain in the interval $|p^{1/2}\sigma^{-1}t| < \varepsilon$, where $\varepsilon > 0$ is sufficiently small that $|\varphi_p(t)|^s \leq \psi^s(at^2)$. Hence, taking into account (36), we obtain that

$$I_2 \leq \int_{|t|\geq C}\psi^s(at^2)\,dt \to 0 \qquad \text{as} \qquad C \to \infty. \qquad (76)$$

Using the same argument as under the proof of Theorem 9 we arrive at an inequality of the form (70) with $a > (2s)^{-1}$, which is valid for t such that $|p^{1/2}\sigma^{-1}t| < \varepsilon$, whence, on account of (37), we come (similarly to the proof of (71)) to the relation

$$I_3 \leq Cp^{as-\frac{1}{2}}\int_{-\infty}^{\infty}|v(t)|^s dt \to 0 \qquad \text{as} \qquad p \to 0. \qquad (77)$$

Finally, by virtue of (36),

$$I_4 = \int_{|t|>C}\Phi^s(t)\,dt \to 0 \qquad \text{as} \qquad C \to \infty. \qquad (78)$$

Relation (38) follows from (73)-(78). The proof is complete.

Theorem 11 can be proved similarly to Theorem 10. We omit the details.

PROOF OF THEOREM 12. In the proof of this theorem we use some ideas of the method of characteristic operators (see, e.g. [21,p.311-324] and also the translator's appendix in [26]). Denote by $\mathbb{C}$ the space of continuous and bounded functions on $\mathbb{R}^1$ with the norm $\|u\| = \sup_{x\in\mathbb{R}^1} |u(x)|, \quad u\in \mathbb{C}$.

The characteristic operator of a r.v. Y with the d.f. F_Y is an integral operator $T_Y : \mathbb{C} \to \mathbb{C}$, operating by the formula

$$T_Y u(x) = E u(x+Y) = \int_{-\infty}^{\infty} u(x+y)\, dF_Y(y). \tag{79}$$

We need an estimating lemma proved in [21, p.314-315] , [26,p.176-177].

LEMMA ([21] , [26]). Let $\eta_1,\dots,\eta_n,\zeta_1,\dots,\zeta_n$ be independent in each group r.v.'s. Then

$$\|T_{\eta_1+\dots+\eta_n} u - T_{\zeta_1+\dots+\zeta_n} u\| \leq \sum_{k=1}^{n} \|T_{\eta_k} u - T_{\zeta_k} u\| , \qquad u\in\mathbb{C}.$$

Now pass to the proof of the theorem. Let $\xi_1,\dots,\xi_n,\dots$ be i.i.d. r.v.'s with d.f. $G(x)$, independent of the r.v. ν_p . Denote $\bar{S}_p = p^{1/2} \sum_{j=1}^{\nu_p} \xi_j$. Consider a function χ which is three times continuously differentiable and such that

$$0 \leq \chi(x) \leq 1, \quad x\in\mathbb{R}^1; \quad \chi(x) = 0 \quad \text{for } x\leq 0 \text{ and } \chi(x)=1 \text{ for } x \geq 1$$

Put $\chi_p(x) = \chi((x-a_p)/\delta_p)$,. Then it is easily seen that

$$P\{S_p > a_p\} \geq E\,\chi_p(S_p), \tag{80}$$

$$P\{\bar{S}_p > a_p+\delta_p\} \leq E\,\chi_p(S_p), \tag{81}$$

$$\sup_{x\in\mathbb{R}^1} |\chi_p'''(x)| \leq C/\delta_p^3. \tag{82}$$

Compare the values $E\chi_p(S_p)$ and $E\chi_p(\bar{S}_p)$. On account of the identical distribution of summands in each of the sums S_p and $\bar{S}_p$ we obtain from (79) and the Lemma that

$$|E f_p(S_p) - E f_p(\bar{S}_p)| = |\sum_{k=1}^{\infty} P\{\nu_p = k\}[E f_p(S_k) - E f_p(\bar{S}_k)] \leq$$

$$\leq \sum_{k=1}^{\infty} P\{\nu_p = k\} | T_{S_k} f_p(0) - T_{\bar{S}_k} f_p(0)| \leq \sum_{k=1}^{\infty} P\{\nu_p = k\} \| T_{S_k} f_p - T_{\bar{S}_k} f_p \| \leq$$

$$\leq \sum_{k=1}^{\infty} k P\{\nu_p = k\} \| T_{p^{1/2} X_1/\sigma} f_p - T_{p^{1/2} \xi_1} f_p \| = \tag{83}$$

$$= \frac{1}{p} \| T_{p^{1/2} X_1/\sigma} f_p - T_{p^{1/2} \xi_1} f_p \|.$$

But $T_{p^{1/2} X_1/\sigma} f_p(x) = E f_p(x + p^{1/2} X_1/\sigma) = E[f_p(x) + f_p'(x) p^{1/2} X_1/\sigma +$ $+ \frac{1}{2} f_p'' p X_1^2/\sigma^2 + \frac{1}{6} f_p'''(x + \theta_1 p^{1/2} X_1/\sigma) p^{3/2} \sigma^{-3} X_1^3$, where $0 < \theta_1 < 1$. A similar expression can be written for $T_{p^{1/2} \xi_1} f_p(x)$. Therefore on account of the assumptions on the moments of the r.v.'s X_1 and ξ_1 and inequality (82) we have

$$\| T_{p^{1/2} X_1/\sigma} f_p - T_{p^{1/2} \xi_1} f_p \| = \sup_{x \in \mathbb{R}^1} | \frac{1}{6} E[f_p'''(x + \theta_1 p^{1/2} \sigma^{-1} X_1) p^{3/2} \sigma^{-3} X_1^3 - \tag{84}$$

$$- f_p'''(x + \theta_2 p^{1/2} \xi_1) p^{3/2} \xi_1^3]| \leq \frac{p^{3/2}}{6} \sup_{x \in \mathbb{R}^1} | f_p'''(x)| [E|X_1|^3/\sigma^3 + E|\xi_1|^3] \leq$$

$$\leq (C/\delta_p^3)[E|X_1|^3/\sigma^3 + E|\xi_1|^3] p^{3/2}.$$

It follows from (83) and (84) that

$$|E f_p(S_p) - E f_p(\bar{S}_p)| \leq (C_1/\delta_p^3) p^{1/2}. \tag{85}$$

Relations (80), (81) and (85) imply

$$[1 - G(a_p + \delta_p)] - C_1 p^{1/2}/\delta_p^3 \leq 1 - F_p(a_p),$$

whence follows the left-hand side ineqiality in (41).

The right-hand side inequality in (41) is obtained by a similar argument while we utilize the function $\tilde{\mathcal{F}}_p(x) = \mathcal{F}\left(\frac{x - a_p + \delta_p}{\delta_p}\right)$ instead of $\mathcal{F}_p(x)$.

In order to obtain inequalities (42), one must consider instead of $\mathcal{F}_p(x)$ the functions $\mathcal{F}_p^*(x) = \mathcal{F}^*\left(\frac{x + a_p + \delta_p}{\delta_p}\right)$ and $\tilde{\mathcal{F}}_p^*(x) = \mathcal{F}^*\left(\frac{x + a_p}{\delta_p}\right)$, respectively, with $\mathcal{F}_p^*(x) = 1 - \mathcal{F}(x)$, and repeat the corresponding argument. The proof is complete.

In the proof of Corollaties 6 and 7 we use the following asymptotic relation

$$\int_a^\infty \frac{\theta^\lambda}{2\Gamma(\lambda)} x^{\lambda-1} e^{-\theta x} dx \sim \frac{\theta^{\lambda-1}}{2\Gamma(\lambda)} a^{\lambda-1} e^{-\theta a}, \quad a \to \infty,$$

in order to write down the asymptotics of the tails of distributions (10), and (15). We omit the details.

The proof of Theorem 13 is quite similar to that of Theorem 12 and therefore is omitted.

Mathematical Institute Georgian Academy of Science
380012, USSR, Tbilisi, Plekhanov avc. 150A

REFERENCES

1. Robbins H. The asymptotical distribution of the sum of a random number of random variables.- Bull.Am.Math.Soc., 1948, 54, 1151-1161.
2. Sakalauskas V. On limit behaviour of sums of a random number of independent random variables (in Russian).- Litov.Mat.Sb., 1985, 25, N 2, 164-176.
3. Gnedenko B.V. On limit theorems for a random number of random variables.- In: Probability Theory and Mathematical Statistics.Fourth USSR-Japan Symposium Proceedings, 1982, Lect.Notes Math., 1983, 1021, 167-176.
4. Gnedenko B.V., Fahim H. On a transfer theorem (in Russian).- Dokl. Akad. Nauk SSSR, 1969, 187, 15-17.
5. Gnedenko B.V., Gnedenko D.B. On Laplace and logistic distributions as the limit ones in probability theory (in Russian).- Serdica,1982, 229-234.
6. Gnedenko B.V., Janjić S. A characteristic property of one class of limit distributions.- Math.Nachr., 1983, 113, 145-149.
7. Janjić S. On random variables with the same distribution type as their random sum.- Publ. Inst.Math., Nouv.Ser. 1984, 35 (49), 161-166.
8. Klebanov L.B., Manijy G.M., Melamed J.A. V.M.Zolotarev's one problem and analogies of infinitely divisible and stable distributions in the scheme of summation of a random number of random variables (in Russian).- Teor. Veroyatn. Primen., 1984, 29, N 4, 757-760.
9. Klebanov L.B., Manijy G.M., Melamed J.A. Analogies of infinitely divisible and stable laws for sums of a random number of random variables (in Russian).- In: Abstracts of Papers of IV International Vilnius Conference on Probability Theory and Mathematical Statistics.

Vilnius, 1985, 2, 40-41.

10. Klebanov L.B., Melamed J.A. Analytical problems connected with the sums of a random number of random variables (in Russian).- In: Abstracts of Papers of XX School- Colloquium on Probability Theory and Mathematical Statistics, Tbilisi, Metsniereba, 1986, p.21.

11. Kakosyan A.V., Klebanov L.B., Melamed J.A. Characterization of distributions by the method of intersively monotone operators.- Lect.Notes Math., 1984, 1088, 175 p.

12. Melamed J.A. On local limit theorem for densities and large deviations in the scheme of summation of a random number of random variables (in Russian).- In: Problems of Stability for Stochastic Models, Proceedings of Seminar., M., VNIISI, 1987, 70-75.

13. Melamed J.A. Estimate of deviation of distribution of a sum of geometric number of random variables from Laplace distribution and local limit theorem in this scheme (in Russian).- In: Teor. Veroyatn. Mat. Stat. Collection of papers dedicated to the seventieth birtday anniversary of Prof. G.M.Manijy. Tr. Tbilisi Mat.,Inst. Razmadze, 1988 (in print).

14. Rényi A. Poisson-folyamat egy jemllemzese.- Magyar tud.akad.Mat. Kutató int. közl., 1956, 1, N 4, 519-527.

15. Gnedenko B.V., Kovalenko I.N. Introduction to the queuing theory (in Russian). M., Nauka, 1966, 432 p.

16. Kovalenko I.N. On a class of limit distributions for rarefied streams of homogeneous events (in Russian).- Litov. Mat.Sb.,1965, 5, N 4, 569-573.

17. Kalashnikov V.V. Estimate of rate of convergence in Rényi theorem. (in Russian).- In: Problems of Stability for Stochastic Models. Proceedings of Seminar. M., VNIISI, 1983, 48-56.

18. Kalashnikov V.V. Vsekhsvyatskii S.Yu. Metric estimates of the first occurence time in regenerative processes.- Lect.Notes Math., 1985, 1155, 102-130.

19. Vsekhsvyatskii S.Yu. Some new results in a theorem due to Rényi.- Lect.Notes Math., 1985, 1155, 391-400.

20. Ibragimov I.A. On the accuracy od approximation of distribution functions of sums of independent values by the normal distribution (in Russian).- Teor.Veroyatn. Primen., 1966, 11, N 4, 632-655.

21. Feller W. Am introduction to probability theory and its applications. V.2 (Russian translation). M, Mir, 1967, 415 p.

22. Zolotarev V.M. Modern theory of summation of independent random variables (in Russian). M., Nauka, 1986, 415 p.

23. Linnik Yu.V., Ostrovskii I.V. Decomposition of random variables and vectors (in Russian). M., Nauka, 1972, 479 p.

24. Petrov V.V. Sums of independent random variables (in Russian). M., Nauka, 1972, 414 p.

25. Titchmarsh E. An introduction to the theory of Fourier integrals (in Russian). M., L., Gostechizdat, 1948, 479 p.

26. Lamperti J. Probability (Russian translation). M., Nauka, 1973, 184 p.

SOME ASYMPTOTIC PROPERTIES OF THE STABLE LAWS

A.V.Nagaev, S.M.Shkolnik

1. Introduction and main results

Let $p(x;\alpha,\beta)$ be the density function of the standard stable law with the characteristic function written in the so-called form (B)

$$\varphi(t) = \exp(-|t|^{\alpha} \exp(i\frac{\pi}{2}\beta(2-\alpha)\,\mathrm{sign}\,t)), \tag{1}$$

where $1<\alpha<2$, $-1\leqslant\beta\leqslant 1$.

If α and β are fixed, $\beta\neq-1$, then

$$p(x;\alpha,\beta) = \frac{1}{\pi}\Gamma(\alpha+1)\sin\frac{\pi}{2}(2-\alpha)(1+\beta)x^{-(\alpha+1)}(1+o(1)), \tag{2}$$

$$p(-x;\alpha,\beta) = \frac{1}{\pi}\Gamma(\alpha+1)\sin\frac{\pi}{2}(2-\alpha)(1-\beta)x^{-(\alpha+1)}(1+o(1)) \tag{3}$$

as $x\to\infty$. If $\beta=-1$, then the representation (3) remains valid, whereas instead of (2) we have

$$p(x;\alpha,\beta) = g(x;\alpha)(1+o(1)), \tag{4}$$

where

$$g(x;\alpha) = (2\pi\alpha(\alpha-1))^{-1/2}(x/\alpha)^{(2-\alpha)/2(\alpha-1)}\exp(-(\alpha-1)(x/\alpha)^{\alpha/(\alpha-1)}).$$

The case $\beta=1$ is reduced to that of $\beta=-1$ with the help of the well-known equality

$$p(x;\alpha,-\beta) = p(-x;\alpha,\beta). \tag{5}$$

As to relations (1) - (5) see, say, [1] .

The purpose of this paper is to obtain the asymptotics of $p(x;\alpha,\beta)$ when $\beta \to -1$ and $x = x(\beta) \to \infty$.

In view of (2) and (4) we may expect that

$$p(x;\alpha,\beta) = g(x;\alpha)(1+o(1)) + \frac{1}{2}(1+\beta)(2-\alpha)\Gamma(\alpha+1)x^{-(\alpha+1)}(1+o(1)) \qquad (6)$$

as $\beta \to -1$ and $x \to \infty$. It means that for $x \to \infty$ and $x \leqslant (\alpha(\alpha-1)^{(1-\alpha)/\alpha} - \tau)(\ln \frac{1}{1+\beta})^{(\alpha-1)/\alpha}$, the relation (4) remains valid whereas for $x \geqslant (\alpha(\alpha-1)^{(1-\alpha)/\alpha} + \tau)(\ln \frac{1}{1+\beta})^{(\alpha-1)/\alpha}$

$$p(x;\alpha,\beta) = \frac{1}{2}(1+\beta)(2-\alpha)\Gamma(\alpha+1)x^{-(\alpha+1)}(1+o(1))$$

Here τ is an arbitrary small positive number.

So in fact we deal with the large deviations problem. The following theorem justifies our expectations mentioned above.

THEOREM. If α is fixed so that $1<\alpha<2$, and $\beta \to -1$, then (6) takes place.

This theorem can be used for the investigation of the Fisher information matrix. It will be demonstrated in other paper of the authors.

2. Some preliminary remarks

Asymptotic properties of the density function of the stable laws are studied usually with the help of the contour integration techniques applied directly to the inversion formula. In our case it is the most acceptable to realize an asymptotic analysis of the following representation for $p(x;\alpha,\beta)$ (see [1])

$$p(x;\alpha,\beta) = \frac{\alpha}{2(\alpha-1)} x^{(\alpha-1)^{-1}} \int_{\Psi}^{1} A(\varphi)\exp(-x^{\alpha/(\alpha-1)}A(\varphi))d\varphi, \qquad (7)$$

where $x > 0$, $\psi = \beta(2-\alpha)/\alpha$,

$$A(\varphi) = \frac{\cos\frac{\pi}{2}(\varphi(\alpha-1)-\alpha\psi)}{\cos\frac{\pi}{2}\varphi}\left(\frac{\sin\frac{\pi}{2}\alpha(\varphi-\psi)}{\cos\frac{\pi}{2}\varphi}\right)^{\alpha(1-\alpha)^{-1}}. \tag{8}$$

Before to prove the theorem it is reasonable to make some remarks. It is clear that the asymptotic properties of the integral

$$I = \int_{\psi}^{1} A(\varphi)\exp(-x^{\alpha(\alpha-1)^{-1}}A(\varphi))\,d\varphi. \tag{9}$$

are determined by the behaviour of the function $A(\varphi)$ in a neighbourhood of the point $\varphi = 1$, where this function reaches its minimum. The problem is complicated by the fact that $A(\varphi)$ depends on the varying parameter β and this dependance is not regular in the point $\varphi = 1$. It is easily seen that for any $\varphi \in (\psi, 1)$ the function $A(\varphi)$ poinwise converges to

$$A_0(\varphi) = \frac{\cos\frac{\pi}{2}(2-\alpha+(\alpha-1)\varphi)}{\cos\frac{\pi}{2}\varphi}\left(\frac{\sin\frac{\pi}{2}(2-\alpha+\alpha\varphi)}{\cos\frac{\pi}{2}\varphi}\right)^{\alpha(1-\alpha)^{-1}} \tag{10}$$

as $\Delta = 1+\beta \to 0$. At the same time $A(1) = A_0(1)$ if $\beta = -1$, and $A(1) = 0$ if $\beta \neq -1$, where

$$A_0(1) = (\alpha-1)\alpha^{\alpha(1-\alpha)^{-1}}.$$

Let ε, μ, η be sufficiently small positive numbers, and $\varkappa = x^{\alpha(\alpha-1)^{-1}}$. In the neighbourhood of the point $\varphi = 1$ one can select two infinitely small intervals

$$\Delta_1 = (1-\Delta\varepsilon, 1), \qquad \Delta_2 = (1-\Delta^{\frac{1}{2}-\eta}-\varkappa^{-\frac{1}{2}+\mu},\ 1-\Delta^{\frac{1}{2}-\eta}),$$

which give the general contribution into the principal term of the asymptotics of the integral (9). On Δ_1 the function $A(\varphi)$ can be approximated by the power function

$$(\Delta(2-\alpha))^{(1-\alpha)^{-1}}(1-\varphi)^{(\alpha-1)^{-1}},$$

whereas on Δ_2 by the quadratic function

$$A_0(1)+A_0''(1)(\varphi-\varphi_\Delta)^2,$$

where $\varphi_\Delta = 1-\Delta^{\frac{1}{2}-\eta}$. The integral over Δ_1 asymptotically behaves like $(2-\alpha)(\alpha-1)\Gamma(\alpha)\Delta z^{-\alpha}$ as $z\to\infty$. The integral over Δ_2 is comparable with $\Delta z^{-\alpha}$ for very slowly growing z only (more exactly, for $z\leqslant(1/A_0(1)+\tau)\ln\Delta^{-1}$, where τ is as before).

List a number of the almost evident properties of the function $A(\varphi)$ and its derivatives up to second order as $\Delta\to 0$. It is convient to denote $\lambda = 1-\varphi$. If $0\leqslant\lambda\leqslant\Delta\varepsilon_1^{-1}$, then

$$A(\varphi)=\left(\frac{\lambda}{\Delta}\right)^{(\alpha-1)^{-1}}\left(2-\alpha+\frac{\lambda}{\Delta}(\alpha-1)\right)\left(2-\alpha+\frac{\lambda}{\Delta}\alpha\right)^{\alpha(1-\alpha)^{-1}}(1+O(\Delta^2)) \tag{11}$$

for any fixed $\varepsilon_1>0$. Further,

$$A(\varphi_\Delta)=A_0(1)\left(1+\frac{\pi^2}{8}\alpha\,\Delta^{1-2\eta}+O(\Delta^{1+2\eta})\right). \tag{12}$$

If $\varphi\to 1$ so that $\varphi\leqslant\varphi_\Delta$, then

$$A(\varphi)=A_0(1)+o(1). \tag{13}$$

As to the properties of the derivative $A'(\varphi)$ it is easy to obtain

$$A'(\varphi_\Delta)=O(\Delta^{\frac{1}{2}-\eta}), \tag{14}$$

and for $\varphi\to 1$, $\varphi\leqslant\varphi_\Delta$,

$$A'(\varphi)=o(1). \tag{15}$$

Let us show that the function $A(\varphi)$ is monotone decreasing on the interval $(1-\varepsilon_2, 1-\Delta\varepsilon_1^{-1})$ for all sufficiently small Δ and any fixed small positive numbers ε_1 and ε_2. It is evident that

$$A'(\varphi) = -\frac{\pi}{2(\alpha-1)} A(\varphi)A_1(\varphi), \tag{16}$$

where

$$A_1(\varphi) = -\alpha^2 \operatorname{ctg}\frac{\pi}{2}(\Delta(2-\alpha)+\lambda\alpha) + \operatorname{ctg}\frac{\pi}{2}\lambda + (\alpha-1)^2\operatorname{ctg}\frac{\pi}{2}(\Delta(2-\alpha)+\lambda(\alpha-1)).$$

If $\varphi\to 1$ so that $\varphi\leqslant 1-\Delta\varepsilon_1^{-1}$, then the following representation takes place

$$A_1(\varphi) = \frac{2}{\pi\lambda}\left(1+\frac{\alpha-1}{1+\Delta\lambda^{-1}(2-\alpha)(\alpha-1)^{-1}} - \frac{\alpha}{1+\Delta\lambda^{-1}(2-\alpha)\alpha^{-1}}\right) + O(\lambda).$$

Hence, for sufficiently small Δ and $\varphi\in(1-\varepsilon_2, 1-\Delta\varepsilon_1^{-1})$ we have $A_1(\varphi) > 0$. In view of (16) we obtain $A'(\varphi) < 0$.

Finally, with the help of the evident equality

$$A''(\varphi) = A(\varphi)((\ln A(\varphi))'' + (A'(\varphi)A^{-1}(\varphi))^2)$$

It is easily shown that for $\varphi\to 1$, $\varphi\leqslant\varphi_\Delta$,

$$A''(\varphi) = \frac{\pi^2}{4}A_0(1) + o(1). \tag{17}$$

3. Proof of Theorem

Divide the interval $(\psi, 1)$ into six parts Δ_k, $1\leqslant k\leqslant 6$. The intervals Δ_1 and Δ_2 have been already determined. Further, put

$$\Delta_3 = (\varphi_\Delta, 1-\Delta\varepsilon_1^{-1}), \qquad \Delta_4 = (1-\Delta\varepsilon_1^{-1}, 1-\Delta\varepsilon),$$

$$\Delta_5 = (1-\varepsilon_2, \varphi_\Delta - \varkappa^{-1/2+\mu}), \qquad \Delta_6 = (\psi, 1-\varepsilon_2).$$

Denote by I_k the part of the integral I corresponding to Δ_k. Then

$$I = I_1 + \ldots + I_6. \tag{19}$$

We shall estimate I_k consequently using the properties of $A(\varphi)$ given above. Preliminary let us agree to denote by c any positive constant which does not depend on Δ and x, by θ - any variable such as $-1 \leq \theta \leq 1$. The denotion $\omega(\varepsilon)$ will be used to indicate any positive function with the property

$$\lim_{\varepsilon \to 0} \omega(\varepsilon) = 0.$$

According to (11), for $\varphi \in \Delta_1$ we have

$$(1-\omega(\varepsilon))\left(\frac{\lambda}{\Delta(2-\alpha)}\right)^{(\alpha-1)^{-1}} \leq A(\varphi) \leq (1+\omega(\varepsilon))\left(\frac{\lambda}{\Delta(2-\alpha)}\right)^{(\alpha-1)^{-1}}.$$

Hence, $I_- \leq I_1 \leq I_+$, where

$$I_\pm = (1 \pm \omega(\varepsilon)) \int_0^{\Delta\varepsilon} \left(\frac{\lambda}{\Delta(2-\alpha)}\right)^{(\alpha-1)^{-1}} \exp\left(-\varkappa(1 \pm \omega(\varepsilon))\left(\frac{\lambda}{\Delta(2-\alpha)}\right)^{(\alpha-1)^{-1}}\right) d\lambda.$$

It is easy to see that

$$I_\pm = (2-\alpha)(\alpha-1)\Gamma(\alpha)\,\Delta\varkappa^{-\alpha}(1+\theta\omega(\varepsilon)),$$

whence

$$I_1 = (2-\alpha)(\alpha-1)\Gamma(\alpha)\,\Delta\varkappa^{-\alpha}(1+\theta\omega(\varepsilon)). \tag{20}$$

Further, we have

$$I_2 = \exp(-\varkappa A(\varphi_\Delta)) \int_{\varphi_0}^{\varphi_\Delta} A(\varphi) \exp\Big(-\varkappa A'(\varphi_\Delta)(\varphi-\varphi_\Delta) - \frac{\varkappa}{2} A''(\xi)(\varphi-\varphi_\Delta)^2\Big) d\varphi, \tag{21}$$

where $\varphi_0 = \varphi_\Delta - \varkappa^{-\frac{1}{2}+\mu}$ and $\varphi_0 \leq \xi \leq \varphi_\Delta$. Using (12) - (14) we obtain

$$I_2 = A_0(1)\exp(-\varkappa A(\varphi_\Delta) + O(\varkappa \Delta^{1-2\eta}) +$$

$$+ O(\varkappa^{1/2+\mu} \Delta^{1/2-\eta})) \int_{\varphi_0}^{\varphi_\Delta} \exp(-\frac{\varkappa}{2} A''(\xi)(\varphi - \varphi_\Delta)^2) d\varphi (1 + o(1)),$$

whence in view of (17)

$$I_2 = 2(\pi A_0(1)\varkappa)^{-1/2} \exp(-\varkappa A_0(1) + O(\varkappa \Delta^{1-2\eta}) +$$

$$+ O(\varkappa^{1/2+\mu} \Delta^{1/2-\eta}))(1 + o(1)). \quad (22)$$

Taking into account that the function $A(\varphi)$ monotone decreases on Δ_3 we have

$$I_3 \leq \Delta^{1/2-\eta} A(\varphi_\Delta) \exp(-\varkappa A(1 - \Delta \varepsilon_1^{-1})).$$

From (11) and (12) we get

$$I_3 = O(\Delta^{1/2-\eta} \exp(-\varkappa A_0(1)(1 - \omega(\varepsilon_1))). \quad (23)$$

According to (11) we have

$$I_4 \leqslant \Delta M_1 \exp(-\varkappa M_2), \quad (24)$$

where

$$M_1 = M_1(\varepsilon, \varepsilon_1) = \sup_{\varphi \in \Delta_4} A(\varphi) < \infty$$

and

$$M_2 = M_2(\varepsilon, \varepsilon_1) = \inf_{\varphi \in \Delta_4} A(\varphi) > 0.$$

Since $A(\varphi)$ monotone decreases on Δ_5, it follows that

$$I_5 = O(\exp(-\varkappa A(\varphi_0))).$$

Taking into account that φ_0 serves as the left edge of Δ_2, from (12), (14), (17) and (21) we obtain

$$I_5 = O(\exp(-\varkappa A_0(1) - c\varkappa^{2\mu} + O(\varkappa\Delta^{1-2\eta}) + O(\varkappa^{1/2+\mu}\Delta^{1/2-\eta}))). \qquad (25)$$

Since $A(\varphi)$ pointwise converges to the continuous function $A_0(\varphi)$ on the interval $(\psi, 1)$ as $\Delta \to 0$, we get

$$\underline{\lim} \inf_{\varphi \in \Delta_6} A(\varphi) \geqslant A_0(1-\varepsilon_2/2) > A_0(1).$$

Choose $\rho \in (0,1)$ so as $\rho A_0(1-\varepsilon_2/2) > A_0(1)$. Then

$$I_6 = \int_{\psi}^{1-\varepsilon_2} A(\varphi)\exp(-(1-\rho)\varkappa A(\varphi) - \varkappa\rho A(\varphi))\,d\varphi \leqslant$$

$$\leqslant ((1-\rho)\varkappa)^{-1}\exp(-\varkappa\rho A_0(1-\varepsilon_2/2)). \qquad (26)$$

Thus, all integrals in (19) are estimated. It remains to compare those estimations only.

Suppose that $\varkappa \to \infty$ and $\varkappa \leqslant (1/A_0(1)+\tau)\ln\frac{1}{\Delta}$. For such $\varkappa$ the representation (22) may be put down in the form

$$I_2 = (\pi A_0(1)\varkappa)^{-1/2}\exp(-\varkappa A_0(1))(1+o(1)). \qquad (27)$$

From (23), (25) - (27) we obtain

$$I_3 = o(I_2), \qquad I_5 = o(I_2), \qquad I_6 = o(I_2). \qquad (28)$$

In view of (20) and (24) we have for any $\varepsilon > 0$ and arbitrary increasing $\varkappa$

$$I_1 + I_4 = (2-\alpha)(\alpha-1)\Gamma(\alpha)\Delta\varkappa^{-\alpha}(1+\theta\,\omega(\varepsilon)).$$

Since ε is arbitrary small, it follows that

$$I_1 + I_4 = (2-\alpha)(\alpha-1)\Gamma(\alpha)\Delta\varkappa^{-\alpha}(1+o(1)) \qquad (29)$$

as $\Delta \to 0$ and $\varkappa \to \infty$. From (7), (9), (19), (27) - (29) it follows

(6).

Suppose that $\varkappa \geqslant (1/A_0(1)+\tau)\ln\frac{1}{\Delta}$. In this case instead of (22) it is sufficient to have

$$I_2 = O(\varkappa^{-1/2+\mu}\exp(-\varkappa A(\varphi_\Delta))),$$

which is valid due to a monotonicity of $A(\varphi)$ on Δ_2. From (12) we get

$$A(\varphi_\Delta) > A_0(1)(1-\delta)$$

for any $\delta > 0$. Choose δ so as to have

$$M = (1/A_0(1)+\tau)A_0(1)(1-2\delta) > 1.$$

Then for $\varkappa \geqslant (1/A_0(1)+\tau)\ln\frac{1}{\Delta}$

$$I_2 = O(\varkappa^{-1/2+\mu}\exp(-\varkappa A_0(1)\delta - M\ln\tfrac{1}{\Delta})) = o(\Delta\varkappa^{-\alpha}). \tag{30}$$

Similarly if to choose ε_1 properly one can obtain from (23)

$$I_3 = o(\Delta\varkappa^{-\alpha}). \tag{31}$$

With the help of (25) for any $\delta > 0$ we have

$$I_5 = o(\exp(-\varkappa A_0(1)(1-\delta))).$$

Choosing δ as before we find

$$I_5 = o(\Delta\varkappa^{-\alpha}). \tag{32}$$

Finally in view of (26) the following representation

$$I_6 = o(\Delta\varkappa^{-\alpha}) \tag{33}$$

for $\varkappa \geqslant (1/A_0(1)+\tau)\ln\frac{1}{\Delta}$ becomes trivial. In order to reach (6) for $\varkappa \geqslant (1/A_0(1)+\tau)\ln\frac{1}{\Delta}$ it is sufficient to join (7), (9), (19), (29) - (33).

The theorem is proved.

Dept of Applied Math., Tashkent Motor-Highway Inst.,

Karl-Marx street, 32, Tashkent, 700047, USSR

REFERENCES

1. Zolotarev V.M. One-dimensional stable distributions.- Amer.Math. Soc., Providence-Rhole Island, 1986.

A CHI-SQUARE GOODNESS-OF-FIT TEST FOR EXPONENTIAL DISTRIBUTIONS OF THE FIRST ORDER

M.S.Nikulin, V.G.Voinov

1. Introduction

Being the most often used the classical Pearson chi-square test is a convenient test if a broad class of alternatives is of interest. This χ^2-test is easily computed and has approximately the χ^2_{r-1} distribution for rather small sample sizes, r being the number of grouping intervals. In 1928 R.A.Fisher proposed to use a chi-square statistic to verify the hypothesis that the distribution function belongs to the family of continuous functiond depending on unknown parameters. He showed that the limiting distribution of Pearson's statistic X^2 is in this case not χ^2_{r-1} and that its distribution depends on how unknown parameters are estimated. He also showed that Pearson's statistics will have the χ^2_{r-s-1} limiting distribution (s is the number of parameters to be estimated) only if one estimates unknown parameters by minimum chi-square estimators based on grouped data.

In the 1950's Chernoff, Lehmann (1954) and Watson (1958) showed that a formal using of Pearson's test estimating unknown parameters by ungrouped data leads to a substantial difference of a limiting distribution from the chi-square distribution even if one groups data correctly. This limiting distribution generally turns out to be dependent on unknown parameters making it impossible to tabulate quantiles. A correct way of utilizing the Pearson's test has been pointed out by Chibisov (1971).

Nikulin (1973 a) and b))and later Rao and Robson (1974) returned to the Pearson's problem and proposed a modified Pearson like test statistic. Nikulin (1973 a) and b)) established that frequencied of getting into grouping intervals are asymptotically normal if one uses the so-called objective way of grouping the data where ends of intervals are random obtained by the estimated distribution function of the null hypothesis. A quadratic form of these frequences, being constructed with the help of a generalized inverse of the asymptotic covariance matrix under the null hypothesis follows in the limit the chi-square distribution with $r-1$ degrees of freedom, the number of unknown parameters being unessential. A modified quadratic form turns out to be a sum of the classical Perason's quadratic form and squares of special linear combinations of frecuencies, the number of this additions being equal to the number of parameters under estimation. McCulloch (1985) recommended to use such statistics whenever ungrouped data are available, since they indicate a significant increase in power with respect to the Pearson-Fisher statistics.

An another way of constructing the chi-square like tests exploits the best minimum variance unbiased estimators (MVUEs) of the unknown probabilities. These estimators being expressed in terms of a sufficient statistic permit to eliminate all perturbations due to the replacement of unknown parameters by their estimators. This fact has been used the first time by Bol'shev and Mirvaliev (1978). They have constructed a chi-square test for verifying the hypothesis that the distribution function belongs to the Poisson, binomial and negative binomial distributions. Dzhaparidze and Nikulin (1979) used the MVUEs for testing the normality by the Kolmogorov and omega-square statistics.

This paper generalizes the results of Bol'shev and Mirvaliev for a wide class of exponential distributions of the first order.

Section 2 is devoted to the construction of all needed MVUEs. Section 3 is concerned with a chi-square goodness-of-fit test for modified power series distributions. In section 4 we study the case of continuous exponential distribution of the first order.

2. Some MVUEs for modified power series distributions

Let we need to test the hypothesis H_0 which states that i.i.d. discrete random variables $X_1, X_2, \ldots, X_n$ follow a modified power series distribution

$$P_\theta\{X_i = x\} = \begin{cases} \dfrac{a(x)\Psi^{x}(\theta)}{B(\theta)}, & x \in \mathfrak{X}, \quad \theta \in \Theta, \\ 0 & , \text{otherwise} \end{cases} \tag{1}$$

where $\mathfrak{X} = \{0, 1, 2, \ldots\}$, $\Theta = \{\theta: 0<\theta<\varrho\}$, ϱ being the convergence radius of a series $B(\theta) = \sum_{x \in \mathfrak{X}} a(x)\Psi^{x}(\theta)$, is nonnegative on $\mathfrak{X}$, $\Psi(\theta)$ is positive, bounded and differentiable function on Θ and $B(\theta)$ is rigorously positive on Θ. A modified power series distribution (1) having been introduced by Gupta (1977) is a natural generalization of a power series distribution with $\Psi(\theta) = \theta$ introduced by Noack (1950). Since

$$\Psi^{x}(\theta) = \exp\{x \ln \Psi(\theta)\},$$

we see that (1) defines an exponential discrete probability distribution of the first order. The family (1) evidently possesses the complete sufficient statistic $S = \sum_{i=1}^{n} X_i$ for parameter θ. Its probability distribution under H_0 is

$$P_\theta\{S = s\} = \begin{cases} \dfrac{b(s, n)\Psi^{s}(\theta)}{B^{n}(\theta)}, & s \in \mathfrak{X}, \\ 0 & , \text{otherwise} \end{cases}$$

where

$$b(s,n) = \sum_{x_1+\dots+x_n=s} \prod_{i=1}^{n} a(x_i), \quad x_i \in \mathcal{X}.$$

If function $a(x)$ is such that for
$a(\alpha) > 0$, $a(\beta) > 0$ and $a(x) \equiv 0$ for all $x > \beta$, $x \in \mathcal{X}$ then (1) is a double truncated modified power series distribution

$$P_\theta\{X=x\} = \begin{cases} \dfrac{a(x)\Psi^{x}(\theta)}{B(\theta,\alpha,\beta)}, & x \in \mathcal{X}_\alpha^\beta = \{\alpha, \alpha+1;\dots,\beta\}, \\ 0 & \text{, otherwise} \end{cases} \tag{2}$$

Clearly, the sample space of a sufficient statistic $S = \sum_{i=1}^{n} X_i$ is $\tau_\alpha^\beta = \{n\alpha, n\alpha+1, \dots, n\beta\}$ and

$$P_\theta\{S=s\} = \begin{cases} \dfrac{b(s,n,\alpha,\beta)\Psi^{s}(\theta)}{B^{n}(\theta,\alpha,\beta)}, & s \in \tau_\alpha^\beta, \\ 0 & \text{, otherwise} \end{cases}$$

where

$$b(s,n,\alpha,\beta) = \sum_{x_1+\dots+x_n=s} \prod_{i=1}^{n} a(x_i), \quad x_i \in \mathcal{X}_\alpha^\beta.$$

A direct verification shows that numbers $b(s,n,\alpha,\beta)$ follow the recurrency

$$b(s,n,\alpha,\beta) = \sum_{k=l(s)}^{L(s)} a(k)\, b(k, n-1, \alpha, \beta), \tag{3}$$

where $l(s) = max\{\alpha, s-(n-1)\beta\}$, $L(s) = min\{\beta, s-(n-1)\alpha\}$.

In the sequel we shall consider parameters α and β as being known.

For constructing the needed MVUEs we shall use a trivial generalization of the well-known results of Patil (1963) and Joshi and Park

(1974) which can be stated without proof as follows:

THEOREM 1. Based on a sample $X=(X_1,\ldots,X_n)$ from (2) the necessary and sufficient condition for T to be the MVUE of $g(\theta)$ is

$$W[g(\theta)B^n(\theta,\alpha,\beta)] \subseteq W[B^n(\theta,\alpha,\beta)],$$

where

$$W[G(\theta)] = \{r:\ r \in \mathfrak{X}_{\alpha}^{\beta},\ \gamma_r > 0\},$$

γ_r are coefficients of $\Psi^r(\theta)$ in a series expansion $G(\theta) = \sum \gamma_r \Psi^r(\theta)$. If exists the MVUE T of $g(\theta)$ being a function of $S=\sum_{i=1}^{n} X_i$ is

$$T = T(S) = \begin{cases} \dfrac{c(S,n,\alpha,\beta)}{b(S,n,\alpha,\beta)}, & S \in W[g(\theta)B^n(\theta,\alpha,\beta)], \\ 0 & \text{, otherwise} \end{cases}$$

where $c(s,n,\alpha,\beta)$ are coefficients of $\Psi^s(\theta)$ in a series expansion $g(\theta)B^n(\theta,\alpha,\beta) = \sum c(s,n,\alpha,\beta)\Psi^s(\theta)$.

In what follows we shall use notations of Patil (1963). Let $A^{(i)} = \{a_1^{(i)}, a_2^{(i)}, \ldots\}$, $i=1,2,\ldots,n$ be arbitrary subsets of a set of non-negative integers. A sum $A_n = \sum_{i=1}^{n} A^{(i)}$ of n given subsets is defined as a set of all integers of the form $\sum_{i=1}^{n} a_k^{(i)}$, where $a_k^{(i)} \in A^{(i)}$. If all $A^{(i)} = A$, $i=1,\ldots,n$ then their sum $A_n = \sum_{i=1}^{n} A^{(i)} = \sum_{i=1}^{n} A$ is denoted by $n[A]$. A set containing only element a is denoted by $\{a\}$.

Let us now construct MVUEs of probabilities $P_\theta\{X=x\}$ if $x \in \mathfrak{X}_{\alpha}^{\beta}$. In this case

$$g(\theta) = P_\theta\{X=x\} = \frac{a(x)\Psi^x(\theta)}{B(\theta,\alpha,\beta)}, \quad x \in \mathfrak{X}_{\alpha}^{\beta}$$

and

$$g(\theta)B^{n}(\theta,\alpha,\beta) = a(x)\Psi^{x}(\theta)B^{n-1}(\theta,\alpha,\beta) =$$

$$= a(x)\Psi^{x}(\theta)\Big(\sum_{x=n\alpha}^{n\beta} a(x)\Psi^{x}(\theta)\Big)^{n-1} = a(x)\sum_{s\in(n-1)[\mathcal{X}_{\alpha}^{\beta}]} b(s,n-1,\alpha,\beta)\Psi^{s+x}(\theta)$$

$$= \sum_{s\in(n-1)[\mathcal{X}_{\alpha}^{\beta}]+\{x\}} a(x)b(s-x,n-1,\alpha,\beta)\Psi^{s}(\theta).$$

It follows that

$$W[g(\theta)B^{n}(\theta,\alpha,\beta)] = (n-1)[\mathcal{X}_{\alpha}^{\beta}] + \{x\}.$$

Further, we have

$$B^{n}(\theta,\alpha,\beta) = \Big(\sum_{x\in\mathcal{X}_{\alpha}^{\beta}} a(x)\Psi^{x}(\theta)\Big)^{n} = \sum_{s\in n[\mathcal{X}_{\alpha}^{\beta}]} b(s,n,\alpha,\beta)\Psi^{s}(\theta),$$

and $W[B^{n}(\theta,\alpha,\beta)] = n[\mathcal{X}_{\alpha}^{\beta}]$.

Since $W[g(\theta)B^{n}(\theta,\alpha,\beta)] \subseteq W[B^{n}(\theta,\alpha,\beta)]$, it follows from the theorem 1 that the MVUE $\hat{P}_{\theta}(x)$ of $P_{\theta}\{X=x\}$ is

$$\hat{P}_{\theta}(x) = \begin{cases} \dfrac{a(x)b(S-x,n-1,\alpha,\beta)}{b(S,n,\alpha,\beta)}, & S\in(n-1)[\mathcal{X}_{\alpha}^{\beta}]+\{x\}, \\ 0, & \text{otherwise}, \end{cases}$$

or equivalently

$$\hat{P}_{\theta}(x) = \frac{a(x)b(S-x,n-1,\alpha,\beta)}{b(S,n,\alpha,\beta)}, \quad l(S)\leqslant x\leqslant L(S), \tag{4}$$

where $l(S) = max\{\alpha, S-(n-1)\beta\}$, $L(S) = min\{\beta, S-(n-1)\alpha\}$.

COROLLARY 1. The recurrency (3) is simply the condition normalizing estimated probabilities $\hat{P}_\theta(x)$ to unit.

By analogy one is able to show that the MVUE $\hat{P}_\theta(x_1, x_2)$ of the point probability distribution $P_\theta\{X_1 = x_1, X_2 = x_2\}$, $x_1, x_2 \in \mathcal{X}_\alpha^\beta$, is

$$\hat{P}_\theta(x_1, x_2) = \begin{cases} \dfrac{a(x_1)a(x_2)b(S - x_1 - x_2, n-2, \alpha, \beta)}{b(S, n, \alpha, \beta)}, & S \in (n-2)[\mathcal{X}_\alpha^\beta] + \{x_1\} + \{x_2\}, \\ 0 & \text{, otherwise} \end{cases}$$

or equivalently

$$\hat{P}_\theta(x_1, x_2) = \frac{a(x_1)\,a(x_2)\,b(S - x_1 - x_2, n-2, \alpha, \beta)}{b(S, n, \alpha, \beta)}, \tag{5}$$

if $\max\{\alpha, S-(n-2)\beta - x_1\} \leqslant x_2 \leqslant \min\{\beta, S-(n-2)\beta - x_1\}$, $\max\{\alpha, S-(n-1)\beta\} \leqslant x_1 \leqslant \min\{\beta, S-(n-1)\alpha\}$ and $\hat{P}_\theta(x_1, x_2) = 0$ otherwise.

This estimator is evidently invariant with respect to a transposition of x_1 and x_2.

Since

$$E_\theta X = \sum_{x \in \mathcal{X}_\alpha^\beta} x P_\theta\{X = x\},$$

the MVUE $\hat{E_\theta X}$ of $E_\theta X$ is of the form

$$\hat{E_\theta X} = \sum_{x \in \mathcal{X}_\alpha^\beta} x \hat{P}_\theta(x) =$$

$$= \sum_{x = l(S)}^{L(S)} \frac{x\, a(x)\, b(S-x, n-1, \alpha, \beta)}{b(S, n, \alpha, \beta)} = \frac{S}{n}, \tag{6}$$

where $l(S) = \max\{\alpha, S-(n-1)\beta\}$, $L(S) = \min\{\beta, S-(n-1)\alpha\}$.

Define now the MVUE $\hat{Var_\theta X}$ of the $Var_\theta X$. Evidently, $\hat{Var_\theta X} = \hat{E_\theta X^2} - (\hat{E_\theta X})^2$, where

$$\hat{E_\theta X^2} = \sum_{x \in \mathcal{X}_\alpha^\beta} x^2 \hat{P}_\theta(x) = \sum_{x=\ell(S)}^{L(S)} \frac{x^2 a(x) b(S-x, n-1, \alpha, \beta)}{b(S, n, \alpha, \beta)}.$$

The MVUE $(\hat{E_\theta X})^2$ of $(E_\theta X)^2 = (E_\theta X_1)(E_\theta X_2)$ is

$$(\hat{E_\theta X})^2 = \sum_{x_1, x_2 \in \mathcal{X}_\alpha^\beta} x_1 x_2 \hat{P}_\theta(x_1, x_2) =$$

$$= \sum_{x_1=\ell(S)}^{L(S)} x_1 a(x_1) \sum_{x_2=\ell(S,x_1)}^{L(S,x_1)} \frac{x_2 a(x_2) b(S-x_1-x_2, n-2, \alpha, \beta)}{b(S, n, \alpha, \beta)}, \tag{7}$$

where $\ell(S, x_1) = max\{\alpha, S-(n-2)\beta - x_1\}$, $L(S, x_1) = min\{\beta, S-(n-2)\alpha - x_1\}$.

In view of (6) we have

$$\frac{S-x_1}{n-1} = \sum_{x_2=\ell(S,x_1)}^{L(S,x_1)} \frac{x_2 a(x_2) b(S-x_2-x_1, n-2, \alpha, \beta)}{b(S-x_1, n-1, \alpha, \beta)}.$$

Substituting this result into (7) gives

$$(\hat{E_\theta X})^2 = \sum_{x_1=\ell(S)}^{L(S)} \frac{x_1 a(x_1)(S-x_1) b(S-x_1, n-1, \alpha, \beta)}{(n-1) b(S, n, \alpha, \beta)} =$$

$$= \frac{S}{(n-1)} \sum_{x_1=\ell(S)}^{L(S)} \frac{x_1 a(x_1) b(S-x_1, n-1, \alpha, \beta)}{b(S, n, \alpha, \beta)} -$$

$$- \frac{1}{(n-1)} \sum_{x_1=\ell(S)}^{L(S)} \frac{x_1^2 a(x_1) b(S-x_1, n-1, \alpha, \beta)}{b(S, n, \alpha, \beta)} =$$

$$= \frac{S^2}{n(n-1)} - \frac{1}{n-1} \sum_{x_1=\ell(S)}^{L(S)} \frac{x_1^2 a(x_1) b(S-x_1, n-1, \alpha, \beta)}{b(S, n, \alpha, \beta)},$$

where $\ell(S) = max\{\alpha, S-(n-1)\beta\}$, $L(S) = min\{\beta, S-(n-1)\alpha\}$.

Combining this expression with that for $\widehat{E_\theta X^2}$ we finally obtain

$$\mathrm{Var}_\theta X = \frac{n}{n-1} \sum_{x=\ell(S)}^{L(S)} \frac{x^2 a(x) b(S-x, n-1, \alpha, \beta)}{b(S, n, \alpha, \beta)} - \frac{S^2}{n(n-1)} . \tag{8}$$

3. A chi-square goodness-of-fit test for modified power series distributions

Let N_j be a number of observations $X_1, X_2, \ldots, X_n$ from (2) equal to j (j 0, 1, ..., S). For any given value of $S = s$ frequencies N_j satisfy the relations

$$N_0 + N_1 + N_2 + \ldots + N_s = n, \qquad N_1 + 2N_2 + \ldots + sN_s = s$$

and their mutual conditional distribution function is

$$P\{\bigcap_{i=0}^{s} (N_i = n_i) \mid S = s\} = \frac{n!}{b(s, n, \alpha, \beta)} \prod_{i=0}^{s} (n_i!)^{-1} [a(i)]^{n},$$

where $n_0 + n_1 + \ldots + n_s = n$ and $n_1 + 2n_2 + \ldots + sn_s = s$.

Define

$$\delta_j(X_i) = \begin{cases} 1, & \text{if } X_i = j \quad (i = 1, 2, \ldots, n; \ j = 1, 2, \ldots, s) \\ 0, & \text{otherwise.} \end{cases}$$

Clearly that

$$E_\theta \delta_j(X_i) = P_\theta\{X_i = j\} = p_j, \qquad E_\theta \delta_j^2(X_i) = p_j .$$

It can be easily verified that for $j = 0, 1, \ldots, s$

$$E_\theta N_j = \sum_{i=1}^{n} E_\theta \delta_j(X_i) = n p_j, \qquad E_\theta S = n E_\theta X,$$

$$\mathrm{Var}_\theta N_j = n p_j (1 - p_j), \qquad \mathrm{cov}(N_i, N_j) = -n p_i p_j, \quad (i \neq j)$$

$$\mathrm{cov}(N_j, S) = -n p_j (j - E_\theta X), \qquad \mathrm{Var}_\theta S = n \mathrm{Var}_\theta X .$$

In what follows we use the results of Park (1973). Let $\varphi_n(\vec{u}, v)$ denote characteristic function of a random vector $(N_0 - E_\theta N_0, \ldots, N_k - E_\theta N_k, S)^T$, i.e. for any fixed k, $0 \leq k \leq S$, $\varphi_n(\vec{u}, v) = E_\theta\{\exp[\sum_{j=0}^{k} i u_j (N_j - E_\theta N_j) + i v S]\}$. Let $\Psi_n(\vec{u}, s)$ denote a conditional characteristic function of a vector $(N_0 - E_\theta N_0, \ldots, N_k - E_\theta N_k)^T$ given $S = s$. Then

$$\Psi_n(\vec{u}, s) = (2\pi P_\theta\{S=s\})^{-1} \int_{-\pi}^{\pi} \varphi_n(\vec{u}, v) e^{-ivs} dv.$$

Using the same technique as in Park (1973), one is able to show that the following theorem holds:

THEOREM 2. If $n \to \infty$ such that $S \asymp n$ then

$$\Psi_n(n^{-1/2}\vec{u}, s) \longrightarrow \exp\{-\tfrac{1}{2} Q^*(\vec{u})\},$$

where $Q^*(\vec{u})$ is the quadratic form in $\vec{u}$ with covariance matrix given by

$$\Sigma_1 = \Sigma_{11} - \frac{1}{Var_\theta X} \Sigma_{12} \cdot \Sigma_{21},$$

Σ_{11}, Σ_{12} and Σ_{21} being defined by the partition of a $(k+2) \times (k+2)$ matrix

$$\Sigma = \begin{pmatrix} \Sigma_{11} & \Sigma_{12} \\ \Sigma_{21} & Var_\theta X \end{pmatrix} = \|\sigma_{ij}\|,$$

where $\sigma_{jj} = n^{-1} Var_\theta N_j = p_j(1-p_j)$, $\sigma_{ij} = n^{-1} cov(N_i, N_j) = -p_i p_j$ $(i \neq j)$, $\sigma_{j,k+1} = n^{-1} cov(N_j, S) = p_j(j - E_\theta X)$, $i, j = 0, 1, \ldots, k$ and $\sigma_{k+1,k+1} = n^{-1} Var_\theta S = Var_\theta X$.

The matrix Σ_{11} can be represented as $\Sigma_{11} = D - pp^T$, where

$$D = \begin{pmatrix} p_0 & 0 & \ldots & 0 \\ 0 & p_1 & \ldots & 0 \\ \cdot & \cdot & \cdots & \cdot \\ 0 & 0 & \ldots & p_k \end{pmatrix}, \quad \vec{p} = (p_0, \ldots, p_k)^T.$$

Denoting $\vec{p}^{(1)}$ a vector with components jp_j, $j=1,\ldots,k$, we have

$$\Sigma_{12}\Sigma_{21} = (\vec{p}E_\theta X - \vec{p}^{(1)})(\vec{p}E_\theta X - \vec{p}^{(1)})^T.$$

Hence, for $Var_\theta X > 0$

$$\Sigma_1 = D - \vec{p}\vec{p}^T - (\vec{p}E_\theta X - \vec{p}^{(1)})(\vec{p}E_\theta X - \vec{p}^{(1)})^T / Var_\theta X. \tag{9}$$

Let us take r nonnegative integers $k_1, k_2, \ldots, k_r$, $r \geq 2$, such that

$$0 \leq k_1 < k_2 < \ldots < k_r = s = N_1 + 2N_2 + \ldots + sN_s$$

and let

$$\vec{N}^{(c)} = (N_1^{(c)}, N_2^{(c)}, \ldots, N_r^{(c)})^T, \quad \vec{W}^{(c)} = (W_1^{(c)}, W_2^{(c)}, \ldots, W_r^{(c)})^T, \; c=0,1,$$

be vectors components of which are defined by the formulas

$$N_j^{(c)} = \sum_{i=k_{j-1}+1}^{k_j} i^c N_i, \quad W_j^{(c)} = \sum_{i=k_{j-1}+1}^{k_j} i^c W_i, \quad j=1,2,\ldots,r,$$

where $W_i = \hat{P}_\theta(i)$ are MVUEs (4) of probabilities $p_i = P_\theta\{X=i\}$ and $k_0 = -1$.

Using the above cited theorem 2 of Park (1973) and formula (9) the following trivial generalization of the well-known result of Bol'shev and Mirvaliev (1978) can be obtained:

THEOREM 3. If the number of observations $X_1, X_2, \ldots, X_n$ is infinitely increasing in such a way that $S \asymp n$ and bounds of grouping intervals $k_1, k_2, \ldots, k_{r-1}$ remain constant, then the conditional distribution function of the vector $\vec{Z} = n^{-1/2}(\vec{N}^{(0)} - n\vec{W}^{(0)})$ with the given value of $S=s$ is asymptotically normal with

$$E\{\vec{Z} \mid S=s\} = \mathbb{0}, \qquad E\{\vec{Z}\vec{Z}^T \mid S=s\} = B + o(1), \quad n \to \infty,$$

where

$$B = D^{(0)} - \vec{W}^{(0)}\vec{W}^{(0)T} - \delta^{-1}[n^{-1}S\vec{W}^{(0)} - \vec{W}^{(1)}][n^{-1}S\vec{W}^{(0)} - \vec{W}^{(1)}]^T,$$

$D^{(0)}$ is a diagonal matrix with elements $W_1^{(0)}, W_2^{(0)}, \dots, W_r^{(0)}$ on the main diagonal, $\mathbb{0} = (0, \dots, 0)^T$ and (see (8))

$$\delta = \lim_{\substack{n \to \infty \\ S \asymp n}} \frac{n}{n-1} \sum_{x=\ell(S)}^{L(S)} \frac{x^2 a(x) b(S-x, n-1, \alpha, \beta)}{b(S, n, \alpha, \beta)} - \frac{S^2}{n(n-1)},$$

the rank of B being $r-1$.

We have prepared now to construct a chi-square-type statistic for testing the hypothesis that i.i.d. random variables $X_1, \dots, X_n$ follow a double truncated modified power series distribution (2). Following Bol'shev (1969) and Nikulin (1973a) and b)), consider a quadratic form

$$Y^2 = \vec{Z}^T B^- \vec{Z},$$

where B^- is the generalized inverse of B. Using theorem 3 we conclude that for fixed $k_1, k_2, \dots, k_{r-1}$ and $n \to \infty$ such that $S \asymp n$ the limit distribution of Y^2 will be chi-square with $r-1$ degrees of freedom. Direct calculations show that

$$Y^2 = \sum_{i=1}^{r} \frac{(N_i^{(0)} - nW_i^{(0)})^2}{nW_i^{(0)}} - (n\mu)^{-1} \Big(\sum_{i=1}^{r} \frac{W_i^{(1)} N_i^{(0)}}{W_i^{(0)}} - S\Big)^2, \tag{10}$$

where

$$\mu = \delta + \left(\frac{S}{n}\right)^2 - \sum_{i=1}^{r} \frac{(W_i^{(1)})^2}{W_i^{(0)}}.$$

One such that Y^2 is the sum of Pearson's statistic and the square of the linear form of frequencies $N_i^{(0)}$.

EXAMPLE 1. Let $X_1, X_2, \dots, X_n$ be i.i.d. random variables from geomettic population

$$P_\theta\{X = x\} = \theta^x (1-\theta), \qquad x = 0, 1, \dots, \quad 0 < \theta < 1,$$

which belongs to the family (2) with $a(x) = 1$, $\Psi(\theta) = \theta$, $\alpha = 0$, $\beta = \infty$ and $B(\theta, \alpha, \beta) = B(\theta) = (1-\theta)^{-1}$. The sample spare of a sufficient statistic $S = \sum_{i=1}^{n} X_i$ is $\mathcal{T} = \{0, 1, \dots\}$ and

$$P_\theta\{S=s\} = \frac{b(s,n,\alpha,\beta)\,\theta^s}{B^n(\theta)}, \quad s\in\mathcal{T}.$$

From (3) we have

$$b(s,n,\alpha,\beta) = b(s,n) = \sum_{k=0}^{s} b(k, n-1).$$

This is th. recurrency for $b(s,n) = \binom{n+s-1}{s}$. Substituting $b(s,n)$ into (4) we obtain the MVUE $W_i = \hat{P}_\theta(i)$ of $p_i = P_\theta\{X=i\}$ as

$$W_i = \frac{\binom{n+S-i-2}{S-i}}{\binom{n+S-1}{S}}, \quad 0\leq i\leq S, \quad n>1. \tag{11}$$

Inserting $b(s,n)$ into (8) gives

$$\widehat{Var_\theta} X = \frac{n}{n+1}\sum_{x=0}^{S}\frac{x^2\binom{n+S-x-2}{S-x}}{\binom{n+S-1}{S}} - \frac{S^2}{n(n-1)} = \frac{(n+S)S}{(n+1)n}$$

and

$$\delta = \lim_{\substack{n\to\infty \\ S \asymp n}} \frac{(n+S)S}{(n+1)n} = \frac{S}{n} + \left(\frac{S}{n}\right)^2. \tag{12}$$

Using (8), (19)-(12) we obtain a chi-square test for verifying the hypothesis that $X_1, X_2, \ldots, X_n$ are sampled from the geometric distribution. This particular result has been obtained earlier by Bol'shev and Mirvaliev (1978).

REMARK 1. For Y^2 test to be applicable we cite here some results on a rule of grouping formulated in the Steklov Mathematical Institute (see Bol'shev and Mirvaliev (1978) and Greenwood and Nikulin (1987)).

a) Intervals $I_1, I_2, \ldots, I_r$ should be selected by using the goodness of fit tests one can find in Pollard (1979), Kallenberg, Oosterhoff and Schriever (1985), Oosterhoff (1985) and Drost (1987).

4. A case of continuous exponential distributions of the first order

Let we need to test the hypothesis H_0 which states that i.i.d. real valued random variables $X_1, X_2, \ldots, X_n$ follow a probability distribution function with a density

$$f(x;\theta) = \begin{cases} (B(\theta,\alpha,\beta))^{-1}\, \nu(x) \exp\{x\, Q(\theta)\}, & \alpha \leqslant x \leqslant \beta, \\ 0 & \text{, otherwise} \end{cases} \tag{13}$$

where $B(\theta,\alpha,\beta) > 0$, $\nu(x) > 0$ if $\alpha \leqslant x \leqslant \beta$ parameters α and β being known. The probability density function of a complete sufficient statistic $S = \sum_{i=1}^{n} X_i$ for a parameter θ will be

$$g(s;\theta) = \frac{b(s,n,\alpha,\beta)}{B^n(\theta,\alpha,\beta)} \exp\{s\, Q(\theta)\}, \quad n\alpha \leqslant S \leqslant n\beta.$$

It can be shown that functions $b(s,n,\alpha,\beta)$ follow the recurrence relation

$$b(s,n,\alpha,\beta) = \int_{l(s)}^{L(s)} \nu(x)\, b(s-x,\ n-1,\ \alpha,\ \beta)\, dx,$$

where $l(s) = \max\{\alpha,\ s-(n-1)\beta\}$, $L(s) = \min\{\beta,\ s-(n-1)\alpha\}$.

It is easily verified (see, for example, a technique proposed by Karakostas (1985)) that the MVUE $\hat{f}(x;\theta)$ of $f(x;\theta)$ is

$$\hat{f}(x;\theta) = \frac{\nu(x)\, b(S-x,\ n-1,\ \alpha,\ \beta)}{b(S,\ n,\ \alpha,\ \beta)}, \quad l(S) \leqslant x \leqslant L(S). \tag{14}$$

Using the same technique as in Section 2 we find

joint conditional distribution of $X_1, X_2, \ldots, X_n$ with a given $S = \sum_{i=1}^{n} X_i$ in such a way that probabilities

$$W_j^{(0)} = P\{X_i \in I_j \mid S = s\}$$

will be not small, i.e. for any preselected $\Delta > 0$ the following condition must be true

$$P\{\min(W_1^{(0)}, \ldots, W_r^{(0)})\} \geq \Delta\} \to 1,$$

if $n \to \infty$ such that $S \asymp n$.

b) If $n \leq 1000$, than it is recommended to take $\Delta = \frac{n}{1000}$. For $n > 1000$ one should choose $\Delta = 0{,}005$.

c) Let $W_M = \max\{W_0, W_1, \ldots, W_s\}$ and let $T(u,v) = W_u + W_{u+1} + \ldots + W_v$, where $0 \leq u \leq M \leq v \leq S$. One should choose u and v such that $T(u,v) > \Delta$, $T(u, v-1) < \Delta$ and $T(u+1, v) < \Delta$. Among all these $T(u,v)$ we should choose a sum $T(u^*, v^*)$ for which the difference $T(u,v) - \Delta$ is minimal. With these u^* and v^* we may construct the "central" interval of the grouping which will contain all frequences N_i with the index i, satisfying the condition $u^* \leq i \leq v^*$.

d) All other intervals are defined succesively. The interval closest to the "central" from the right is defined by the condition $v^* + 1 \leq i \leq z$, where z can be found from conditions $z > v^*$, $T(v^*+1, z-1) < \Delta$ and $T(v^*+1, z) \geq 0$. The interval to be searched is defined by $v^* + 1 \leq i \leq z$.

The interval located to the left from the "central" is determined by analogy. It is necessary to take into account that if a sum of all ungrouped probabilities is less than Δ, then remaining ungrouped points have be united with the preceding interval.

This grouping rule gives probabilities of getting into $I_1, I_2, \ldots, I_n$ which are almost equal, i.e. it gives almost equiprobable class-intervals.

An addition information on the choice of cells in chi-square

$$\widehat{Var}_\theta X = \frac{n}{n-1} \int_{\ell(S)}^{L(S)} \frac{x^2 \nu(x) b(S-x, n-1, \alpha, \beta)}{b(S, n, \alpha, \beta)} dx - \frac{S^2}{n(n-1)}. \tag{15}$$

Following Nikulin (1973) define a vector $\vec{p} = (p_1, p_2, \ldots, p_r)^T$ such that

$$p_1 + p_2 + \ldots + p_r = 1, \qquad p_i > 0,$$

and find quantiles $x_0, x_1, \ldots, x_{r-1}, x_r$ from the following conditions

$$\int_\alpha^{x_i} \hat{f}(x;\theta)\, dx = p_1 + p_2 + \ldots + p_i, \quad i = 1, 2, \ldots, r-1,$$

where $x_0 = \alpha$ and $x_r = \min\{\beta, S-(n-1)\alpha\}$.

Let $\vec{\nu} = (\nu_1, \nu_2, \ldots, \nu_r)^T$ be a vector of frequencies for $X_1, X_2, \ldots, X_n$ being into intervals $(x_0, x_1], (x_1, x_2], \ldots, (x_{r-1}, x_r]$. Clearly $E\vec{\nu} = E\{\nu | S=s\} = n\vec{p}$. Let B be a conditional covariance matrix of a vector $\vec{Z} = (n)^{-1/2}(\vec{\nu} - n\vec{p})$, $S=s$ given.

Using the results of Chibisov (1971), Moreover (1971) and Nikulin (1973) one is able to show that for $n \to \infty$ such that $S \asymp n$ the conditional distribution of $\vec{Z}$ is asymptotically normal with

$$E\{\vec{Z} | S=s\} = \mathbb{0}, \qquad E\{\vec{Z}\vec{Z}^T | S=s\} = B + o(1),$$

matrix B being the same as in Section 3, but one should replace W_i by p_i. Hence, a test statistic Y^2 for H_0 is defined by (10) where we must insert p_i instead of W_i and calculate $\delta = \lim_{\substack{n\to\infty \\ S \asymp n}} \widehat{Var}_\theta X$ by (15).

EXAMPLE 2. Let $X_1, X_2, \ldots, X_n$ be i.i.d. random variables with probability density function

$$f(x;\theta) = \begin{cases} \theta \exp\{-\theta(x-\alpha)\}, & x \geq \alpha, \\ 0, & \text{otherwise}, \end{cases}$$

which belongs to the family (13) with $\nu(x) \equiv 1$, $B(\theta, \alpha, \beta) = B(\theta, \alpha) =$

$= \theta^{-1}\exp(-\theta\alpha)$, $Q(\theta) \equiv -\theta$ and $\beta = \infty$, α being known. The probability density function of a complete sufficient statistic $S = \sum_{i=1}^{n} X_i$ for parameter θ is

$$g(s;\theta) = \begin{cases} (\Gamma(n))^{-1}\theta^{n}\exp(n\theta\alpha)\exp(-\theta s)(s-n\alpha)^{n-1}, & s \geq n\alpha, \\ 0, & \text{otherwise}. \end{cases}$$

i.e. $\ell(s, n, \alpha) = (\Gamma(n))^{-1}(s - n\alpha)^{n-1}$. From (14) and (15) it follows that

$$\hat{f}(x;\theta) = \frac{n-1}{(S-n\alpha)^{n-1}}\left(S - x - (n-1)\alpha\right)^{n-2}, \qquad \alpha \leq x \leq S - (n-1)\alpha$$

and

$$\widehat{Var_\theta X} = \frac{n\Gamma(n)}{(n-1)(S-n\alpha)^{n-1}} \int_{\alpha}^{S-(n-1)\alpha} \frac{x^2(S-x-(n-1)\alpha)^{n-2}}{\Gamma(n-1)}\, dx - \frac{S^2}{n(n-1)} =$$

$$= \frac{S^2}{n(n+1)} + \frac{n\alpha^2 - 2\alpha S}{n+1}.$$

If $n \to \infty$ such that $S \asymp n$ then

$$\delta = \lim \widehat{Var_\theta X} = \left(\frac{S}{n} - \alpha\right)^2. \tag{16}$$

Let we choose equiprobable cells, i.e. $p_1 = p_2 = \ldots = p_r = r^{-1}$. Then

$$\int_{\alpha}^{x_i} \hat{f}(x;\theta)\, dx = p_1 + \ldots + p_i = \frac{i}{r}.$$

Substituting into this equation MVUE $\hat{f}(x;\theta)$ gives

$$x_i = [S - (n-1)\alpha] - (S - n\alpha)\left(1 - \frac{i}{r}\right)^{(n-1)^{-1}}.$$

Using quantiles x_i find a vector of frequencies $\vec{\nu}$. From (10),(16) and taking into account that $W_i = r^{-1}$, $W_i^{(1)} = iW_i = \frac{i}{r}$, we obtain the test statistic Y^2 as follows

$$Y^2 = (n r)^{-1} \sum_{i=1}^{r} (r \nu_i - n)^2 + (n\beta)^{-1} (\sum_{i=1}^{r} i \nu_i - S)^2,$$

where $\beta = \left(\frac{S}{n} - d\right)^2 + \left(\frac{S}{n}\right)^2 - (r+1)(2r+1).$

REMARK 2. There is another way of using the test (10) in the case of continuity. Take real-valued constants $\ell_0, \ell_1, \ldots, \ell_{r-1}, \ell_r$, $r \geq 2$, such that

$$\alpha_0 = \ell_0 < \ell_1 < \ldots < \ell_{r-1} < \ell_r = \beta,$$

define N_i - number of observations X_i getting into i-th interval $(\ell_{i-1}, \ell_i]$ $i = 1, 2, \ldots, r$ and using (14), calculate the MVUEs

$$W_i = \int_{\ell_{i-1}}^{\ell_i} \hat{f}(x, \theta)\, dx.$$

of probabilities

$$p_i = \int_{\ell_{i-1}}^{\ell_i} f(x; \theta)\, dx.$$

Then utilize (10) with

$$\delta = \lim_{\substack{n \to \infty \\ S \sim n}} \widehat{Var_\theta} X.$$

The only difficulty in this procedure is to choose constants ℓ_i, $i = 1, 2, \ldots, r$, which night give nonempty and equiprobable intervals.

Steklov Mathematical Institute
Leningrad Department
Fontanka 27
Leningrad, 191011, USSR

High Energy Physic
Institute, Kazakh Academy
Sciences
Frunze, USSR

REFERENCES

1. Bol'shev L.N. Cluster analysis.- Bull.Int.Stat.Inst., 1969, 43, 411-425.

2. Bol'shev L.N., Mirvaliev M. Chi-square goodness-of.fit test for the

Poisson, binomial and negative binomial distributions.- Teor Veroyatn. Primen. 1978, 23, 461-474.

3. Chernoff H., Lehmann _.L. The use of maximum likelihood estimates in tests for goodness of fit.- Ann.Math.Stat., 1954, 25, 579-586.
4. Chibisov D.M. Certain chi-square type tests for continuous distributions.- Teor.Veroyatn.Primen., 1971, 16, 3-20.
5. Drost F.G. Asymptotics for generalized chi-square goodness-of-fit test.- Vrije Univ., de Boelelaan, Amsterdam, 1987.
6. Dzhaparidze K.O., Nikulin M.S. Probability distributions of the Kolmogorov and omega-square statistics for continuous distributions with shift and scale parameters.- Zap.Nauchn.Semin.Leningr.Otd.Mat. Inst. Steklova, 1978, 85, 46-74.
7. Greenwood P.E., Nikulin M.S. Some remarks on the application of chi-square type tests.- Zap.Nauchn.Semin.Leningr.Otd.Mat.Inst.Steklova, 1987, 158, 49-71.
8. Gupta R.C. Minimum variance unbased estimation in a modified power series distribution and some of its applications.- Commun.Statist. Theor.Meth., 1977, 6, 977-991.
9. Joshi S.W., Park C.J. Minimum variance unbased estimation for truncated power series distribution.- Sankhyá: 1974, A36, 305-314.
10. Kallenberg W.C.M., Oosterhoff J., Schriever B.F. The number of classes in chi-squared goodness-of-fit tests.- JASA, 1985, 80, 959-968.
11. Karakostas R.X. On minimum variance unbased estimators.- Am.Stat. 1985, 39, 303-305.
12. McCulloch C.E. Relationsships among some chi-square goodness-of-fit statistics.- Commun.Stat. Theor.Meth., 1985, 14,593-603.
13. Moore D. A chi-square statistic with random cell boundaries.- Ann. Math.Stat., 1971, 42, 147-156.
14. Nikulin M.S. Chi-square test for continuous distributions with shift and scale parameters.- Teor.Veroyatn.Primen., 1973, 18, 559-568.

15. Nikulin M.S. On the chi-square test for continuous distributions.- Teor.Veroyatn.Primen., 1973, 18, 675-679.

16. Noack A. A class of random variables with discrete distributions.- Ann.Math.Stat., 1950, 21, 127-132.

17. Oosterhoff J. The choice of cells in chi-square tests.- Statist. Neerl., 1985, 39, 115-128.

18. Park C.J. The distribution of requency of the geometrical distribution.- Sankhyá: 1973, A35, 106-111.

19. Patil G.P. Minimum variance unbased estimation and certain problems of additive number theory.- Ann.Math.Stat., 1963, 34, 1050-1056.

20. Pollard D. General chi-square goodness-of-fit tests with data-dependent cells.- Z.Wahrscheinlichkeitstheor. Verw.Geb., 1979, 50, 317-331.

21. Rao K., Robson D.S. A chi-squared statistic for goodness-of-fit tests within the exponential family.- Commun.Stat., 1973, 3, 1139-1153.

22. Watson G.S. On chi-square goodness-of-fit tests for continuous distributions.- J.R.Stat.Soc., 1958, B20, 44-61.

A CONDITIONAL WEAK LAW OF LARGE

NUMBERS

E.Nummelin

Let $\xi_1, \xi_2, \ldots$ be a sequence of i.i.d. $\mathbb{R}^d$-valued random variables with common Laplace transform

$$\varphi(t) = E\exp(\langle t, \xi_1 \rangle), \qquad t \in \mathbb{R}^d.$$

We assume that the (convex) function $\log\varphi$ is essentially smooth (see e.g. [6], p.251). We denote by s the entropy function

$$s(v) = \inf_t \{\log\varphi(t) - \langle t, v \rangle\}, \qquad v \in \mathbb{R}^d.$$

The symbol S stands for the closed convex hull of the support of the distribution of ξ_1.

Let $B \subset \mathbb{R}^d$ be a convex Borel set such that $m_0 \notin B$ and $\mathring{B} \cap \mathring{S} \neq \emptyset$. Then there exists a unique point, called the dominating point of B, $v_B \in \overline{B}$ such that

$$s(v_B) = \sup_t s.$$

Actually, $v_B \in \partial B \cap \mathring{S}$. Moreover there exists the large deviation limit

$$\lim_{n \to \infty} \frac{1}{n} \log P\{\frac{S_n}{n} \in B\} = s(v_B)$$

(see Ney [4] and [5]).

We shall prove the following conditional limit theorem. The proof is postponed to the end of the paper.

THEOREM. Suppose that $\log\varphi$ is essentially smooth and let $B \subset \mathbb{R}^d$ be a convex Borel set so that $\mathring{B} \cap \mathring{S} = \emptyset$ and $m_0 \notin B$. Then for all $\varepsilon > 0$ there is a constant $I(\varepsilon) > 0$ such that

$$P\{|\frac{S_n}{n} - v_B| > \varepsilon \mid \frac{S_n}{n} \in B\} \leq e^{-nI(\varepsilon)} \qquad \text{ultimately.}$$

According to this result the sample means having nearly maximum entropy are observed with probability ≈ 1 . These kind of maximum entropy principles are classical results in statistical mechanics. From the point of view of probability theory they belong naturally to problems within large deviation theory. A close result to ours is Ellis' [2] Theorem III.4.4. Our proof is somewhat similar to that of Ellis' theorem the main difference being that we do not need results from "level II " large derivation theory. This is achieved by using the idea of the dominating point of a convex set B.

In an important paper [1] Csiszár studies the conditional convergence of the empirical distributions under the condition that the empirical distribution is"observed" in a given convex family C of probability measures. In this abstract set-up Csiszár shows that the resulting limit distribution is of Boltzmann type corresponding to a "dominating point" of C (called I -projection by Csiszár). The notion of convergence by Csiszár is convergence in information. It is clear that one can deduce the result of our Theorem from Csiszár's results at least in the case where the random variables $\xi_1, \xi_2, \ldots$ are bounded. (In the general case this kind of implication does not seem so evident.)

In a forthcoming paper [3] we shall describe how the result of our Theorem can be used to derive the grand canonical distribution for Poisson random fields (hence, as a special case, for the ideal gas).

PROOF OF THE THEOREM. Consider

$$B^{(\varepsilon)} = B \cap \{v \in \mathbb{R}^d, \quad \|v - v_B\| > \varepsilon\},$$

where $\varepsilon > 0$ is fixed and small, and $\|\cdot\|$ stands for the maximum norm (equivalent to the Euclidean norm). Denote

$$B_i = B \cap \{v \in \mathbb{R}^d ;\ v_i - v_{B,i} > \varepsilon\}$$

and

$$B_{-i} = B \cap \{v \in \mathbb{R}^d :\ v_i - v_{B,i} < -\varepsilon\},$$

$i = 1, 2, \ldots, d$. Then $B^{(\varepsilon)} = \bigcup_i B_i$, a finite union of convex sets. To each nonempty B_i there exists $v_{B_i} \in \bar{B}_i$ so that $\sup_{B_i} s = s(v_{B_i})$ and $s(v_{B_i}) > s(v_B)$ (by the uniqueness of v_B). Then $\sup_{B^{(\varepsilon)}} s > s(v_B) = \sup_B s$, too. Moreover,

$$\limsup_{n\to\infty} \frac{1}{n} \log P\{\|S_n n^{-1} - v_B\| > \varepsilon \mid S_n n^{-1} \in B\} =$$

$$= \limsup_{n\to\infty} \frac{1}{n} \log[P\{S_n n^{-1} \in B^{(\varepsilon)}\} / P\{S_n n^{-1} \in B\}] \leq$$

$$\leq \limsup_{n\to\infty} \frac{1}{n} \log P\{S_n n^{-1} \in B^{(\varepsilon)}\} - \lim_{n\to\infty} \frac{1}{n} \log P\{S_n n^{-1} \in B\} \leq$$

$$\leq \sup_{B^{(\varepsilon)}} s - \sup_B s < 0.$$

ACKNOWLEDGEMENT. I would like to thank Tapani Lehtonen for useful discussions on the subject.

University of Helsinki,
Finland

REFERENCES

1. Csiszár I. Sanov property, generalized I-projection, and a conditional limit theorem. Ann.Probab., 12, 1984, 768-793.
2. Ellis R. Entropy, Large Deviations, and Statistical Mechanics. Springer, New York, 1985.
3. Lehtonen T. and Nummelin E. Boltzmann distributions as conditional

limits of empirical distributions. In preparation, 1988.

4. Ney P. Dominating points and the asymptotics of large derivations for random walk on $\mathbb{R}^d$. Ann.Probab., 11, 1983, 158-167.
5. Ney P. Convexity and large deviations. Ann.Probab., 12, 1984, 903-906.
6. Rackafellar R.T. Convex Analysis. Princeton Univ. Press, Princeton, 1970.

ON THE RATE OF CONVERGENCE FOR THE EXTREME VALUE IN THE CASE OF IFR-DISTRIBUTIONS

A.Obretenov

Let F be a distribution function (d.f.) for which $f(x)=F'(x)$ exists, $F(0+)=0$ and $F(x)<1$ for all $x \geqslant 0$. Suppose that $F(x) \in IFR$ i.e. the failure rate function $r(x)=f(x)(G(x))^{-1}$ is non-decreasing, $G(x)=1-F(x)$. Let $X_1, X_2, \ldots, X_n$ be independent random variables with common d.f. F and $Z_n = max(X_1, X_2, \ldots, X_n)$ It is shown in [2] that if $r(x)$ is monotonic then the limit relation

$$\lim R(x) r(x) = 1, \quad x \to \infty, \text{ where} \tag{1}$$

$$R(x) = \frac{1}{G(x)} \int_x^{\infty} G(y)\,dy,$$

is both necessary and sufficient for the existence of constants a_n and $b_n > 0$ such that

$$\lim_{n \to \infty} P(Z_n < a_n + b_n x) = \exp(-e^{-x}). \tag{2}$$

Following the common extrem value theory one can see that the constants a_n and b_n may be choosen from the equalities

$$G(a_n) = n^{-1}, \quad b_n = (r(a_n))^{-1}. \tag{3}$$

Note that when $F \in IFR$ then

Research partially supported by the Committee of science, Bulgarian conncil of ministers, under contract N 60/ 1987.

$$r(x) \leq (R(x))^{-1}.$$

The present paper deals with uniform rate of convergence and asymptotic expansions in (2). The rate of convergence problem in (2) is treated in [1], [4], [5], [6] and [7]. The basic assumption in these works is the knowlege of the asymptotic behaviour of the difference between the d.f. F and the limit d.f. Another restriction is that the case $a_n = \log n$ is treated only. We shall give a result which is not covered by the papers refered too.

THEOREM. If $F(x) \in IFR$, $f(x) = F'(x)$ and $c(a_n) = \sum_{k=1}^{\infty} (-1)^{k+1} [1 - r(a_n)R(a_n)]$, where $G(a_n) = n^{-1}$, then

$$P(Z_n < a_n + b_n x) - \exp(-e^{-x}) = -e^{-z}[\varepsilon_n(x) + \frac{z^2}{2n} + o(n^{-1})], \quad z = e^{-x}, \tag{4}$$

where $|\varepsilon_n(x)| \leq c(a_n)$, $x \geq 0$.

To prove the theorem we shall need the following Lemma.

LEMMA. Let $f(x)$ and $g(x)$ be real functions defined on $[0, \infty)$ and differentiable, $g(x)$ be nonincreasing and $g(\infty) = f(\infty) = 0$. If

$$f'(x)/g'(x) = a - c(x), \tag{5}$$

where $c(x) \geq 0$, a is a constant then

$$f(x)/g(x) = a - \theta(x)c(x), \qquad 0 \leq \theta(x) \leq 1. \tag{6}$$

PROOF. Integrating the equality

$$F'(x) = ag'(x) - g'(x)c(x)$$

over $[t, +\infty)$ we get

$$f(t) = a - (1/g(t)) \int_t^{\infty} c(x)\,dg(x). \tag{7}$$

Denote $\mathcal{J}(t) = -\int_t^{\infty} c(x)\,dg(x)$ and put $y = g(x)$. Applying the mean value theorem we obtain

$$\mathcal{J}(t) = \int_0^{g(t)} c(g^{-1}(y))\,dy = \eta(t)C(t), \tag{8}$$

where $0 \leqslant \eta(t) \leqslant g(t)$. In (8) $g^{-1}(y)$ is the inverse function of $g(x)$, which exists since $g(x)$ is a monotone function. Combining (7) and (8) we find (6).

Note that the Lemma is a precision of the l'Hospital rule.

PROOF OF THE THEOREM. Assume that for some constants a_n and b_n the relation (2) holds. Then according to Theorem 1 in [2] the limit (1) is true. Construct the family of distribution functions $F_t(x) = 1 - G_t(x)$, where $G_t(x) = G(t+x)/G(t)$, $x \geqslant 0$. It is obvious that $G_t(x) \in IFR$ for all fixed $t > 0$.

Let $m_1(t)$ and $m_2(t)$ be respectively the first and the second moments of $F_t(x)$. Denote

$$f(t) = \int_t^{\infty}\int_x^{\infty} G(u)\,du\,dx,$$

$$g(t) = [G(t)]^{-1}\left[\int_t^{\infty} G(u)\,du\right]^2.$$

One can easily find that

$$f'(x)/g'(x) = 1/[2 - r(x)R(x)] \tag{9}$$

Puting $q(x) = 1 - r(x)R(x)$ from (9) we have

$$f'(x)/g'(x) = 1 - c(x), \tag{10}$$

where $c(x) = \sum_{k=1}^{\infty} (-1)^{k+1} q(x)$ and $C(x) \geqslant 0$, since $0 \leqslant q(x) \leqslant 1$. The relation (10) in fact is (5) with $a = 1$. One can check that functions $f(x)$ and $g(x)$ satisfy the conditions of the Lemma. The fact that $g(x)$ is nonincreasing follows from well-known property of a IFR-distribution. Namely, if the d.f. F belongs to the class IFR then the distribution function $F_1(x) = 1 - \mu^{-1}\int_x^\infty G(u)\,du$ belongs to the same class. Here μ is the first moment of F. Therefore the failure rate for d.f. $F_1(x)$ which is $[R(x)]^{-1}$, is non-decreasing. But, $g(x) = R(x)\int_x^\infty G(u)\,du$ and obviously $g(x)$ is non-increasing. So, applying (6) we obtain

$$f(x)/g(x) = 1 - \theta(x)c(x). \tag{11}$$

It is easy to check that

$$m_2(t)/(2m_1^2(t)) = f(t)/g(t)$$

and the relation (11) is

$$1 - m_2(t)/(2m_1^2(t)) = \theta(t)\,c(t). \tag{12}$$

Further, since $m_1(t) = R(t)$ and if we choose a_n from the condition $G(a_n) = n^{-1}$, $t = a_n$ and $b_n = R(a_n)$ we get

$$G_t(m_1(t)x) = nG(a_n + b_n x). \tag{13}$$

It is shown in [3] that the inequality

$$|G(m_1(t)x) - e^{-x}| \leq 1 - m_2(t)/(2m_1^2(t)). \tag{14}$$

Holds uniformly in x. Taking in account (10) and (13), the inequality (14) may be written as

$$|nG(a_n + b_n x) - e^{-x}| \leq \theta(a_n)c(a_n). \tag{15}$$

Denote $y = G(a_n + b_n x)$. The inequality (15) shows that

$$ny = e^{-x} + \varepsilon_n(x) \quad \text{, where} \quad \varepsilon_n(x) \to 0 \quad \text{, if} \quad n \to \infty .$$

Now, after elementary calculations with the difference

$$\Delta_n(x) = (1-y)^n - \exp(-e^{-x})$$

we get

$$\Delta_n(x) = \exp n \lg(1 - n^{-1}(z + \varepsilon_n(x))) - e^{-z} =$$
$$= -e^{-z}[(2n)^{-1}(z+\varepsilon_n)^2 + \varepsilon_n(x) + O(n^{-2})] =$$
$$= -e^{-z}[\varepsilon_n(x) + (2n)^{-1} z^2 + o(n^{-1})], \tag{16}$$

where $z = e^{-x}$.

However, $P(Z_n < a_n + b_n x) = (1-y)^n$, so that equalities (15) and (16) yield (4) for $x \geqslant 0$. The estimate for $\varepsilon_n(x)$ is given by right hand side of (12).

The following example shows that the term $\varepsilon_n(x)$ in (4) plays a role

EXAMPLE. Let the common d.f. $F(x)$ be

$$F(X) = \begin{cases} ax, & 0 \leqslant x < b, \\ 1 - xe^{-x}, & x \geqslant b, \qquad a = 1 - b^{-1}, \end{cases}$$

where b is determined from $b(1 + e^{-b}) = 2, \quad b = 1{,}68\ldots.$

If $x \geqslant b$ then $G(x) = xe^{-x}$ and the constant a_n is determined by $a_n e^{-a_n} = n^{-1}$, so that $a_n \sim \log n$. The failure rate $r(x)$ is

$$r(x) = \begin{cases} a, & 0 \leqslant x < b \\ 1 - x^{-1}, & x \geqslant b. \end{cases}$$

Therefore $F \in IFR$. First let us calculate $q(a_n) = 1 - r(a_n)R(a_n)$.

We have

$$f(a_n) = F'(a_n) = n^{-1}(1-a_n^{-1}),$$

$$\int_{a_n}^{\infty} G(x)dx = n^{-1}(1+a_n^{-1}),$$

so that

$$r(a_n)R(a_n) = f(a_n)[G^2(a_n)]^{-1}\int_{a_n}^{\infty} G(x)dx = 1-a_n^{-2}$$

and finally $q(a_n) = a_n^{-2} \sim (\log n)^{-2}$.

Since $c(a_n) \sim q(a_n)$ then the term $\varepsilon_n(x)$ in (4) is prevailing in the asymptotic.

Note that in this example we have

$$\psi(e^{x})|F(x) - \exp(-e^{-x})| \to \infty \qquad , \text{ if } \quad x \to \infty,$$

where $\Psi(y) = y(\log y)^{-1}$ is regularly varying function with index 2. Although we can not use the estimate, which is given in [4] (Corollary 3.3). The reason is that a_n is not equal to $\log a_n$ (here $a_n = \log n + \log\log n$).

Institute of Mathematics

Sofia, P.O.B. 373,

Bulgaria 1090

References

1. Anderson C.W. Super-slowly varying functions in extreme value theory. J.R. Stat. Soc., 1978, B40, 197-202.
2. Galambos J., Obretenov A. Restricted Domains of Attraction of $\exp(-e^{-x})$: Stochastic proc and their appl. 1987 (to appear).

3. Obretenov A. Bound on Deviation from exponentiality for IFR-functions.- Math. and Education in Math., 1984, 408-411.

4. Omey E., Rachev S.T. On the Rate of Convergence in Extreme Value Theory.- Theor. Veroyatn. Primen., 1987.

5. Smith R.L. Uniform Rates of Convergence in Extreme Value Theory. Adv. Appl.Prob., 1982, 14, 600-622.

6. Zolotarev V.M. Foreword.- In: Lect. Notes in Math., 1983, 982.

7. Zolotarev V.M., Rachev S.T. Rate of Convergence in limit Theorems for the max-scheme.- Lect. Notes in Math., 1985, 1155, 415-442.

ON THE RATE OF CONVERGENCE IN EXTREME VALUE THEORY

E.Omey

1. Introduction.

Let $X_1, X_2, \ldots, X_n$ be independent random variables with common distribution function (d.f.) F and let $M_n = \bigvee_{i=1}^{n} X_i$. For many F there exist normalizing constants $a_n > 0$ and $b_n \in \mathbb{R}$ such that as $n \to \infty$,

$$P\{M_n \leq a_n x + b_n\} \to G(x) \tag{1.1}$$

where G is a non-degenerate d.f. When this happens G must be one of the following types: $\Phi_\alpha(x) = \exp(-x^{-\alpha})$ $(x \geq 0,\ \alpha > 0)$, $\Psi_\alpha(x) = \exp(-(-x^{-\alpha}))$ $(x \leq 0,\ \alpha > 0)$ or $\Lambda(x) = \exp(-\exp(-x))$ $(x \in \mathbb{R})$. Moreover necessary and sufficient conditions on F for (1.1) are known. As an example we mention

LEMMA 1.1. Suppose $F(x) < 1$ for $x \in \mathbb{R}$. Then F is in the max-domain of attraction of Φ_α if and only if $1 - F \in RV_{-\alpha}$ (i.e. $\lim_{t \to \infty} (1 - F(tx))/(1 - F(t)) = x^{-\alpha}$ for all $x > 0$). If so, in (1.1) we can take $a_n = \operatorname{Inf}\{x : 1 - F(x) \leq \frac{1}{n}\}$ and $b_n = 0$

In this paper we discuss rates of convergence in (1.1). Such rates are useful for judging how close G is as an approximation to the d.f. of the normalized maxima. The problem of estimating the rate of convergence in (1.1) is not new and has been studied by several authors, see [2], [3], [4]. In particular Smith [3] relates uniform rates to slow variation with remainder. On the other hand, Zolotarev [4] , Omey and Rachev [3] approach the problem by using a metric approach. In the present paper we combine these two approaches and so complement the known results.

2. Main results.

In the sequel we will be concerned with rates of convergence in (1.1) in the case where $G=\Phi_\alpha$ and $b_n=0$. Since our results are stated in terms of the uniform metric we also obtain some results for d.f. F in domain of attraction of Ψ_α or Λ . Our starting point is the following notion of connection between r.v. We say that the r.v. U and V are connected by r if $r(U) \overset{\mathcal{D}}{=} V$ for some strictly increasing function r . By using connected r.v. it will be possible to transform properties of partial maxima of V to those of U . Indeed if $r(U) \overset{\mathcal{D}}{=} V$ and if $U_1, U_2, \ldots, U_n$ are i.i.d. and if $V_1, V_2, \ldots, V_n$ are i.i.d. then

$$\bigvee_{i=1}^{n} V_i \overset{\mathcal{D}}{=} \bigvee r(U_i) = r(\bigvee_{i=1}^{n} U_i)\,!$$

Now let Y_α denote a r.v. with d.f. Φ_α and let $U_1,\ldots,U_n$ be i.i.d. For any strictly increasing function r we have (here and in the sequel $\rho(\cdot,\cdot)$ denotes the uniform metric)

$$\begin{aligned}\rho(\bigvee_{i=1}^{n} U_i/a_n, Y_\alpha) &= \rho(r(\bigvee_{i=1}^{n} U_i), r(a_n Y_\alpha)) \\ &= \rho(\bigvee_{i=1}^{n} V_i/b_n, r(a_n Y_\alpha)/b_n) \\ &\leq \rho(\bigvee_{i=1}^{n} V_i/b_n, Y_\beta) + \rho(r(a_n Y_\alpha)/b_n, Y_\beta) \\ &\doteq (\mathrm{I}) + (\mathrm{II})\end{aligned}$$

Our problem now consists of 2 parts:

(I) find a suitable class of r.v. V for which (I) can be estimates in the best possible way;

(II) find a suitable class of functions r for which (II) can be estimated in the best possible way.

As to (I) we can take $V \overset{\mathcal{D}}{=} Y_\beta$ or V "close" to Y_β. If $V \overset{\mathcal{D}}{=} Y_\beta$ then obviously $\bigvee_{i=1}^{n} V_i \overset{\mathcal{D}}{=} n^{1/\beta} Y_\beta$ holds and $(I) \equiv 0$ with $b_n = n^{1/\beta}$.

It remains to estimate (II). The next lemma shows that we should restrict r to be regularly varying.

LEMMA 2.1. If $\lim_{n\to\infty} \rho(r(a_n Y_\alpha) n^{-1/\beta}, Y_\beta) = 0$, then $r \in RV_{\alpha/\beta}$ and $r(a_n) \sim n^{1/\beta}$ $(n \to \infty)$.

PROOF. The condition of the lemma implies that for all $x \geqslant 0$,

$$\lim_{n\to\infty} P\{ r(a_n Y_\alpha) n^{-1/\beta} \leqslant x\} = \exp(-x^{-\beta}).$$

If r^c is the inverse function of r we obtain that for $x > 0$,

$$\lim_{n\to\infty} r^c(n^{1/\beta} x)/a_n = x^{\beta/\alpha}.$$

This implies that $a_n \sim r^c(n^{1/\beta})$ $(n \to \infty)$ and that $r^c \in RV_{\beta/\alpha}$.

For convenience we shall now assume that $\beta = 1$ and that $a_n = r^c(n)$. In this case (II) reduces to

$$\rho(r(a_n Y_\alpha)/n, Y_1) = \sup_{x\geqslant 0} | G(r(a_n x)/r(a_n)) - G(x^\alpha)| \tag{2.1}$$

where $G = \Phi_1$.

In order to estimate the rate of convergence to zero in (2.1 we shall consider $G\left(\frac{h(tx)}{h(t)}\right) - G(x^\alpha)$ where $h \in RV_\alpha$, $\alpha > 0$ and where h is bounded on bounded intervals of $\mathbb{R}_+$. Furthermore we shall assume that h satisfies one of the following conditions: for all $x>0$,

$$\limsup_{t\to\infty} \frac{h(t)}{t^{\alpha}p(t)} \left| \frac{h(tx)}{h(t)} - x^{\alpha} \right| < \infty, \tag{2.2}$$

$$\lim_{t\to\infty} \frac{h(t)}{t^{\alpha}p(t)} \left(\frac{h(tx)}{h(t)} - x^{\alpha} \right) = 0, \tag{2.3}$$

where $p(x)$ is 0 -regularly varying with

$$a\left(\frac{x}{y}\right)^{\gamma} \leqslant \frac{p(x)}{p(y)} \leqslant b\left(\frac{x}{y}\right)^{\eta}, \quad \eta<\infty, \quad \gamma>-\infty, \quad x \geqslant y \geqslant x_0 .$$

In some cases we shall assume $p \in RV_{\delta}$ and

$$\lim_{t\to\infty} \frac{h(t)}{t^{\alpha}p(t)} \left(\frac{h(tx)}{h(t)} - x^{\alpha} \right) = \lambda(x) \tag{2.4}$$

exists and is finite for all $x>0$. If we define $L(x) = h(x)x^{-\alpha}$ then each of (2.2) - (2.4) reduces to

$$\limsup_{t\to\infty} \frac{|L(tx) - L(t)|}{p(t)} < \infty, \tag{2.2'}$$

$$\lim_{t\to\infty} \frac{L(tx) \quad L(t)}{p(t)} = 0, \tag{2.3'}$$

$$\lim_{t\to\infty} \frac{L(tx) - L(t)}{p(t)} = x^{-\alpha}\lambda(x) = \mu(x). \tag{2.4'}$$

We first need the following result, the proof of which follows from the results of Bingham and Goldie [1] :

LEMMA 2.2. (i) If (2.2') holds, then for $x>0$ such that $tx \geqslant t_0$ we have $|L(tx) - L(t)| / p(t) \leqslant r(x)$, where

$$r(x) = \begin{cases} A & \text{if } \eta < 0, \\ A + B \log x & \text{if } \eta = 0, \\ Ax^{\eta} & \text{if } \eta > 0 \end{cases} \qquad \text{if} \quad x \geq 1, \ t \geq t_0,$$

$$r(x) = \begin{cases} Ax^{\delta} & \text{if } \eta < 0, \\ (A + B|\log x|)\, x^{\delta} & \text{if } \eta = 0, \\ Ax^{\delta-\eta} & \text{if } \eta > 0. \end{cases} \qquad \text{if} \quad x \leq 1, \ tx \geq t_0.$$

(ii) If (2.3') holds the result (i) holds with $r(x)$ replaced by $\varepsilon r(x)$.

(iii) If (2.4') holds, then

a) if $\delta > 0$, then $L(x) \sim Ap(x) \quad (x \to \infty)$,

b) if $\delta < 0$, then $L(x) \to B$ and $B - L(x) \sim Ap(x) \quad (x \to \infty)$,

c) if $\delta = 0$, then $L \in \Pi(p)$ and $\mu(x) = A \log x$.

Now we prove

THEOREm 2.3. (i) If (2.2) holds with $\alpha < \eta$, then

$$\lim_{t\to\infty} \sup \frac{h(t)}{t^{\alpha} p(t)} \sup_{x \geq 0} \left| G\left(\frac{h(tx)}{h(t)}\right) - G(x^{\alpha}) \right| < \infty.$$

(ii) If (2.3) holds with $\alpha > \eta$, then

$$\lim_{t\to\infty} \frac{h(t)}{t^{\alpha} p(t)} \sup_{x \geq 0} \left| G\left(\frac{h(tx)}{h(t)}\right) - G(x^{\alpha}) \right| = 0.$$

PROOF. Let $m = \min\left(x_{\alpha}, \dfrac{h(tx)}{h(t)}\right)$ and $M = \max\left(x^{\alpha}, \dfrac{h(tx)}{h(t)}\right)$ and use $G'(x) = G(x)\, x^{-2}$ to obtain

$$\left| G\left(\frac{h(tx)}{h(t)}\right) - G(x^{\alpha}) \right| = \int_m^M G'(s)\, ds \leq \frac{G(M)}{m^2}\, (M - m)$$

Hence

$$T := \frac{h(t)}{t^{\alpha} p(t)} \left| G\left(\frac{h(tx)}{h(t)}\right) - G(x^{\alpha}) \right| \leq \frac{G(\mathcal{M})}{m^2} x^{\alpha} \frac{|L(tx) - L(t)|}{p(t)} .$$

Now, since $h \in RV_{\alpha}$ we have $a\left(\frac{x}{y}\right)^{\alpha-\varepsilon} \leq \frac{h(x)}{h(y)} \leq b\left(\frac{x}{y}\right)^{\alpha+\varepsilon}$ for $x \geq y \geq x_0$.

Let us first assume that $\mathcal{M} = x^{\alpha}$, then

$$T \leq \frac{x^{\alpha} G(x^{\alpha})}{(h(tx)/h(t))^2} \quad \frac{|L(xt) - L(t)|}{p(t)} .$$

If $x \geq 1$, $t \geq t_0$ we have $ax^{\alpha-\varepsilon} \leq \frac{h(tx)}{h(t)}$ and hence

$$T \leq a' x^{-\alpha+2\varepsilon} G(x^{\alpha}) r(x).$$

Using Lemma 2.2 we obtain that T is bounded. On the other hand, if $x \leq 1$, $tx \geq t_0$, then $a' x^{\alpha+\varepsilon} \leq \frac{h(tx)}{h(t)}$ and we obtain

$$T \leq a'' x^{-\alpha-2\varepsilon} G(x^{\alpha}) r(x).$$

Using Lemma 2.2, the boundedness of $x^{a} G(x^{b})$ and the boundedness of $x|\log x|$ $(0 \leq x \leq 1)$, we obtain that T is bounded also in this case.

If, as a second case, $m = x^{\alpha}$, in a similar way we obtain that T is bounded for $x > 0$, $tx \geq t_0$. Finally, if $x \leq 1$, $tx \leq t_0$, $t \geq t_0$ we use the boundedness of h on $[0, t_0]$ to obtain that

$$T \leq h(t) t^{-\alpha} (p(t))^{-1} (G(b/h(t)) + G(x^{\alpha})) \leq$$

$$\leq h(t) t^{-\alpha} (p(t))^{-1} (G(b/h(t)) + G(b' t^{-\alpha})).$$

Since $G(1/t)$ converges to zero exponentially fast and since $h(t)/t^{\alpha} p(t)$ is bounded by a power of t we obtain that T converges to zero in this last case. Combining these estimates we obtain the proof of the theorem.

As a corollary we state

COROLLARY 2.4. Suppose $\mathcal{U}$ is a r.v. with $r(\mathcal{U}) = Y_1$. If r satisfies the hypothesis of Theorem 2.3, then as $n \to \infty$

$$\rho(\bigvee_{i=1}^{n} \mathcal{U}_i / a_n, Y_\alpha) = O(a_n^{\alpha} p(a_n)/n)$$

(resp. $O(a_n^{\alpha} p(a_n)/n)$) where $a_n = r^c(n)$.

PROOF. We have $\bigvee_{i=1}^{n} \mathcal{U}_i \stackrel{\mathcal{D}}{=} r^c(nY_1)$ so that

$$\rho(\bigvee_{i=1}^{n} \mathcal{U}_i / r^c(n), Y_\alpha) = \rho(r^c(nY_1)/r^c(n), Y_\alpha) =$$

$$= \rho(r(r^c(n)Y_\alpha)/r(r^c(n)), Y_1).$$

This is (2.1) with $a_n = r^c(n)$. Now apply Theorem 2.3.

Next suppose that (2.4) holds with $\delta \leq 0$ (otherwose $\frac{p(t)}{L(t)} \to \infty!$).

With $\mathcal{M}$ and m as in the proof of Theorem 2.3 some calculations show that

$$T^* := G\left(\frac{h(tx)}{h(t)}\right) - G(x^{\alpha}) - g(x^{\alpha})\left(\frac{h(tx)}{h(t)} - x^{\alpha}\right)$$

satisfies

$$|T^*| \leq \left(\frac{G(\mathcal{M})}{m^4} - \frac{2G(\mathcal{M})}{m^3}\right) \frac{(\mathcal{M} - m)^2}{2}$$

where $g(x) = G'(x) = G(x)x^{-2}$. Using similar calculations as in the proof of Theorem 2.3 the following result is easily established.

THEOREM 2.5. If (2.4) holds with $\delta \leq 0$, then

$$\limsup_{t \to \infty} h^2(t)/t^{2\alpha} p^2(t) \sup_{x \geq 0} |T^*| < \infty. \tag{2.5}$$

REMARK Also (2.5) holds of (2.2) or (2.3) holds.

Now assume (2.4) holds with $\delta<0$. Lemma 2.2 (iii) shows that $h(x) \sim dx^{\alpha}$ in this case and (2.5) can be replaced by

$$\sup_{x\geq 0} \left| G\left(\frac{h(tx)}{h(t)}\right) - G(x^{\alpha}) - g(x^{\alpha})\left(\frac{h(tx)}{h(t)} - x^{\alpha}\right)\right| = O(p^{2}(t)). \tag{2.6}$$

Moreover, $\mu(x)$ in (2.4') equals $\mu(x) = C(x^{\delta} - 1)$ for some constant C. Now we have

$$(g(x^{\alpha})/p(t))(h(tx)/h(t) - x^{\alpha}) - d^{-1} g(x^{\alpha}) x^{\alpha} C(x^{\delta} - 1) =$$

$$= g(x^{\alpha}) x^{\alpha} t^{\alpha} (d\, h(t))^{-1} (d - h(t) t^{-\alpha})(L(tx) - L(t))/p(t) +$$

$$+ d^{-1} g(x^{\alpha}) x^{\alpha} ((L(tx) - L(t))/p(t) - C(x^{\delta} - 1)) = (\mathrm{I}) + (\mathrm{II})$$

As to (I) we have $t^{\alpha}/h(t) \to 1/d$ and $d - h(t)t^{-\alpha} \sim e p(t)$ $(t \to \infty)$. Hence

$$(\mathrm{I}) \leq C^{e} g(x^{\alpha}) x^{\alpha} \frac{|L(tx) - L(t)|}{p(t)} p(t).$$

As in Theorem 2.3 we obtain that $|\mathrm{I}|/p(t)$ is bounded as long as $tx \geq t_0$. As to (II) we use $K(x) = L(x) - d$ to obtain

$$(\mathrm{II}) = d^{-1} g(x^{\alpha}) x^{\alpha} (K(tx)/p(t) - Cx^{\delta}) - d^{-1} g(x^{\alpha}) x^{\alpha} (K(t)/p(t) - C)$$

$$= (\mathrm{II}_A) + (\mathrm{II}_B).$$

Since $K(t)/p(t) \to C$ and $x^{\alpha} g(x^{\alpha})$ is bounded we obtain $(\mathrm{II}_B) = O(1)$. As to (II_A) we use the uniform convergence properties of regularly varying functions to obtain that also $(\mathrm{II}_A) = o(1)$ as $t \to \infty$. Using

(2.6) and the estimates for (I) and (II) we obtain that for $x \geq 1$, $t \geq t_0$ or $x \leq 1$, $tx \geq t_0$, $t \geq t_0$,

$$\left| \frac{1}{p(t)} \left[G\left(\frac{h(tx)}{h(t)} \right) - G(x^{\alpha}) \right] - \frac{1}{d} x^{\alpha} g(x^{\alpha}) C (x^{\delta} - 1) \right| \leq C p(t).$$

Finally for $x \leq 1$, $tx \leq t_0$, $t \geq t_0$ we have as before that

$$\frac{1}{p(t)} \left| G\left(\frac{h(tx)}{h(t)} \right) - G(x^{\alpha}) \right| = o(1)$$

and also that

$$x^{\alpha} g(x^{\alpha})(x^{\delta} - 1) = o(1).$$

We conclude in the following

COROLLARY 2.6. If (2.4) holds with $\delta < 0$, then

$$\lim_{t\to\infty} \sup_{x \geq 0} \left| \frac{1}{p(t)} \left(G\left(\frac{h(tx)}{h(t)} \right) - G(x^{\alpha}) \right) - \frac{1}{d} g(x^{\alpha}) x^{\alpha} C (x^{\delta} - 1) \right| = 0.$$

In terms of Corollary 2.4 this corollary shows that the following asymptotic expansion is valid, uniformly in $x > 0$:

$$P\{ \bigvee_{i=1}^{n} U_i / a_n \leq x \} = P\{ Y_{\alpha} \leq x \} + p(a_n) d^{-1} g(x^{\alpha}) x^{\alpha} C (x^{\delta} - 1) + o(p(a_n))$$

where $g(x) = (P\{ Y_1 \leq x \})'$.

For $\delta = 0$, a similar expansion can be obtained.

E.H.S.A.L. Stormstraat N 2,

1000 Brussel, Belgium

REFERENCES

1. Bingham N.H. and Goldic C.M., Extensions of regular variation I, II .

Proc.Lond.Math.Soc., 1982, 3, 44, 473-496; 477-534.

2. Omey E. and Rachev S.T. On the rate of convergence in extreme value theory, 1986, submitted.
3. Smith R.L. Uniform rates of convergence in extreme value theory. 1982, Adv.Appl.Prob., 14, 600-622.
4. Zolotarev V.M. Foreword, Stability Problems for Stochastic Models. 1983, Lect. Notes Math., 982, Springer-Verlag.

SOME PROPERTIES OF STOCHASTIC PROCESSES

WITH LINEAR REGRESSION

A.Plucinska

The aim of this paper is the investigation of the memory of stochastic processes with the linear regression. We investigate the cases when the number of conditions can be reduced.

1°. Introduction and formulation of the results

Let $\mathfrak{X} = \{X_t, t \geq 0\}$ be a real valued, zero-mean stochastic process with the finite second moment.

Let $t_1 < t_2 < \ldots, \mathbf{t}_n = (t_1, \ldots, t_n), \quad k_{ij} = K(t_i, t_j) = E(X_{t_i}, X_{t_j})$. We assume throughout the paper that the distributions are non-degenerate, i.e.

$$K^{(n)} = \det[k_{ij}]_{i,j=1}^{n} > 0, \qquad n = 1, 2, \ldots .$$

We denote

$$\mu_{in} = E(X_{t_i} \mid X_{t_j}, \ j = 1, \ldots, n, \ j \neq i), \quad \mu_n = \mu_{nn}.$$

We shall say that the regression is linear if for every i, n, $\mathbf{t}_n$ $(1 \leq i \leq n, \quad n > 1)$

$$\mu_{in} \text{ is a linear function of } X_{t_j}, \quad j = 1, \ldots, n, \ j \neq i \tag{1}$$

For $i = n$ condition (1) will be written in the following form

$$\mu_n = \sum_{j=1}^{n-1} c_{jn}(\mathbf{t}_n) X_{t_j}.$$

The linearity of the regression is an often used assumption. A review of papers based on the linearity of regression is given for example in [1] .

The aim of this paper is the investigation of the memory of stochastic processes with the linear regression.

We are going to prove the following propositions:

PROPOSITION 1. Let (1) holds. If there exists n such that for every t_n the conditional expectation μ_n does not depend on $X_{t_{n-1}}$, i.e.

$$c_{n-1,n}(t_n) \equiv 0 \tag{2}$$

then $K(t_1, t_2) = 0$ for $t_1 \neq t_2$. There is no real stochastic process with such the covariance function ($\mathfrak{X}$ can be a white noise).

PROPOSITION 2. Let (1) holds. If there exist r, n $(n \geq 3,\ r \leq n-2)$ such that for every t_n the conditional expectation μ_n does not depend on $X_{t_r}, X_{t_{n-2}}$ then for every $N \geq r+2$ the conditional expectation μ_N does not depend on $X_{t_r}, \ldots, X_{t_{N-2}}$.

PROPOSITION 3. Let $\mathfrak{X}$ be a Gaussian process. If for every t_3

$$\mu_3 = E(X_{t_3} | X_{t_1}, X_{t_2}) = E(X_{t_3} | X_{t_2}) \tag{3'}$$

then $\mathfrak{X}$ is a Gaussian Markov process.

If for every t_4

$$\mu_4 = E(X_{t_4} | X_{t_1}, X_{t_2}, X_{t_3}) = E(X_{t_4} | X_{t_1}, X_{t_3}) \tag{3''}$$

then all the n -dimensional distributions of $(X_{t_1}, \ldots, X_{t_n})$ can be determined by the three dimensional distributions of $(X_{t_1}, X_{t_{k-1}}, X_{t_k})$, $k = 3, \ldots, n$.

The similar problems concerning the memory of stochastic processes with the linear regression were considered in [2] . In [2] the considerations were based on some additional continuity assumptions.

2°. Auxiliary results

Let $K_{ij}^{(n)}$ be the cofactor of k_{ij} of the matrix $[k_{ij}]_{i,j=1}^{n}$ and $K_{ijrr}^{(n)}$ be the cofactor of k_{ij} of the matrix $[k_{pq}]_{\substack{p,q=1\\ p\neq r,\, q\neq r}}^{n}$
The following formula holds for these determinants:

$$K^{(n)}K_{ijrr}^{(n)} = K_{ij}^{(n)}K_{rr}^{(n)} - K_{ir}^{(n)}K_{jr}^{(n)} \tag{4}$$

We shall use the following Lemmas:

LEMMA 1 [2] . If (1) holds then the coefficients c_{jn} are given by the formulas

$$c_{jn} = K_{jn}^{(n)}\left(K^{(n-1)}\right)^{-1}, \quad j = 1,\dots,n, \ n>1. \tag{5}$$

LEMMA 2 [3] . If (1) holds and for given n there exists j such that for every t_n

$$c_{jn}(t_n) \equiv 0 \tag{6}$$

then for every t_{n+1}

$$c_{j,n+1}(t_{n+1}) \equiv c_{j+1,n+1}(t_{n+1}) \equiv 0. \tag{7}$$

3°. Proofs of Propositions

PROOF OF PROPOSITION 1. In virtue of assumption (2), lemma 2 and formula (5) we get

$$K_{n-1,n+1}^{(n+1)} = K_{n,n+1}^{(n+1)} = 0. \tag{8}$$

It follows from (4), (8) that for $i<n$

$$K^{(n+1)}K_{i,i,n,n+1}^{(n+1)} = -K_{in}^{(n+1)}K_{i,n+1}^{(n+1)}, \tag{9'}$$

$$K^{(n+1)} K^{(n+1)}_{i,n,n+1,n+1} = K^{(n+1)}_{in} K^{(n+1)}_{n+1,n+1}, \tag{9''}$$

$$K^{(n+1)} K^{(n+1)}_{i,n,n,n+1} = K^{(n+1)}_{i,n+1} K^{(n+1)}_{nn}. \tag{9'''}$$

It follows from assumption (2) and formula (5) that

$$K^{(n+1)}_{i,i,n,n+1} = 0. \tag{10}$$

By (9'), (10)

$$K^{(n+1)}_{in} K^{(n+1)}_{i,n+1} = 0.$$

Thus $K^{(n+1)}_{in} = 0$ or $K^{(n+1)}_{i,n+1} = 0$. If $K^{(n+1)}_{in} = 0$ then by (9'') $K^{(n+1)}_{i,n,n+1,n+1} = 0$. This last relation holds for all t_{n+1} then this relation is equivalent to

$$K^{(n)}_{in} = 0, \qquad i < n. \tag{11}$$

Analogically condition $K^{(n+1)}_{i,n+1} = 0$ by formula (9''') also implies (11).

It is obvious that

$$\sum_{i=1}^{n} K^{(n)}_{in} k_{ij} = 0 \qquad \text{for} \quad j \neq n. \tag{12}$$

Therefore in virtue of (11) and (12) we have

$$k_{nj} K^{(n)}_{nn} = k_{nj} K^{(n-1)} = 0.$$

In other words for every j, t_n $(t_j \neq t_n)$

$$k_{nj} = K(t_j, t_n) = 0. \qquad \text{G.E.D.}$$

PROOF OF PROPOSITION 2. First we are going to show that the assumption of Proposition 2 i.e. conditions

$$K_{rn}^{(n)} = K_{n-2,n}^{(n)} = 0 \tag{13}$$

imply

$$K_{r,n-1}^{(n-1)} = K_{n-3,n-1}^{(n-1)} = 0. \tag{14}$$

We can write formula (4) in the following forms:

$$K^{(n)} K_{r,n-2,n-2,n}^{(n)} = K_{rn}^{(n)} K_{n-2,n-2}^{(n)} - K_{n-2,n}^{(n)} K_{r,n-2}^{(n)}, \tag{15'}$$

$$K^{(n)} K_{r,r,n-2,n}^{(n)} = K_{n-2,n}^{(n)} K_{rr}^{(n)} - K_{r,n-2}^{(n)} K_{r,n-2}^{(n)}. \tag{15''}$$

The right hand sides of formulas (15') and (15'') in virtue of (13) are equal zero. Then (14) follows immediately from (15') and (15'').

In virtue of (13), (14) we get

$$K_{r,r+2}^{(r+2)} = 0. \tag{16}$$

It follows from (16) and Lemma 2 that for $i = r, \ldots, n-2$, $n = r+2, r+3, \ldots,$ $r = 1, 2, \ldots$ and every t_n we have

$$K_{in}^{(n)} = 0.$$

Proposition 2 is thus proved.

PROOF OF PROPOSITION 3, part I. We put in Proposition 2 $r = 1$. Then by Proposition 2 and formula (3) we have

$$\mu_n = E(X_{t_n} | X_{t_1}, \ldots, X_{t_{n-1}}) = E(X_{t_n} | X_{t_{n-1}}), \quad n > 1. \tag{17}$$

Now we are going to show that the conditional variance satisfies the relation

$$\mathrm{Var}(X_{t_n} \mid X_{t_1}, \ldots, X_{t_{n-1}}) = \mathrm{Var}(X_{t_n} \mid X_{t_{n-1}}). \tag{18}$$

It is well-known that for a Gaussian distribution

$$\mathrm{Var}(X_{t_n} \mid X_{t_1}, \ldots, X_{t_{n-1}}) = K^{(n)}(K^{(n-1)})^{-1}. \tag{19}$$

Formula (17) and Lemma 2 imply

$$c_{n-2,n} = c_{n-3,n-1} = \ldots = c_{1,3} = 0. \tag{20}$$

It follows from formula (4) for $i = j = n-2, r = n$ and condition $c_{n-2,n} = 0$ that

$$K^{(n)} K^{(n)}_{n-2,n-2,n,n} = K^{(n)}_{n-2,n-2} K^{(n)}_{nn}$$

thus

$$\mathrm{Var}(X_{t_n} \mid X_{t_j}, \; j = 1, \ldots, n-1) = K^{(n)}(K^{(n-1)})^{-1} =$$

$$= K^{(n)}_{n-2,n-2}(K^{(n)}_{n,n,n-2,n-2})^{-1} = \mathrm{Var}(X_{t_n} \mid X_{t_j}, \; j = 1, 2, \ldots, n-3, n-1).$$

We repeat the reasoning $n-2$ times, taking into account formulas (20) we get (18). It follows immediately from (17) and (18) that $\mathfrak{X}$ is a Markov process. Q.E.D

4°. Examples

EXAMPLE 1. We put in Proposition 2 successively $r = 1, r = 2$. Then we get the following statements:

If there exists n such that for every t_n the conditional expectation μ_n does not depend on $X_{t_1}, X_{t_{n-2}}$ then for every $N > 2$

$$\mu_N = E(X_{t_N} \mid X_{t_{N-1}}).$$

If there exists n such that for every t_n the conditional expectation μ_n does not depend on $X_{t_2}, X_{t_{n-2}}$ then for every $N > 3$

$$\mu_N = E(X_{t_N} \mid X_{t_1}, X_{t_{N-2}}, X_{t_{N-1}}).$$

In particular for $N=4$ we get (3'').

EXAMPLE 2. Now we are going to give an example of the covariance function K such that (3'') holds. Let

$$K(t_1, t_2) = a + bf(t_1) + cf(t_1)f(t_2) \tag{21}$$

$a \geq 0$, $b > 0$, $b + cf(0) > 0$, f - a non-negative, increasing function. It is easy to verify that (21) is a covariance function, the special case of (21) is the covariance function of the Brownian bridge, the Brownian motion. It is easy to compute that $K_{24}^{(4)} = 0$, i.e. $c_{24} = 0$. The conditional expectation is given by formula

Then by Proposition 2 $K_{rn}^{(n)} = 0$, $2 \leq r \leq n-2$, $n \geq 4$.

If moreover (1) holds then the conditional expectation is given by formula

$$E(X_{t_3} \mid X_{t_1}, X_{t_2}) =$$

$$= \frac{-ac\,(f(t_3) - f(t_2))X_{t_1} + ((a + bf(t_1))(b + cf(t_3)) - acf(t_1))X_{t_2}}{(a + bf(t_1))(b + cf(t_2)) - acf_1(t)}.$$

If $a = 0$ or $c = 0$ then $E(X_{t_3} \mid X_{t_1}, X_{t_2}) = E(X_{t_3} \mid X_{t_2})$.

EXAMPLE 3. The next example such that (3'') holds is the following. Let

$$K(t_1, t_2) = a + b(t_1 - t_2) \tag{22}$$

where $a > 0$, $b > 0$, $0 < t < 2a/b$. It is easy to compute that for $n > 2$

$$K^{(n)} = 2^{n-2} b^{n-1} (2a + b(t_1 - t_n))(t_n - t_{n-1}) \ldots (t_2 - t_1) > 0.$$

Therefore function (22) is positive definite. We can also prove that $K_{24}^{(4)} = 0$. Then by Proposition 2 $K_{rn}^{(n)} = 0$ for $2 \leq r \leq n-2$,

$n \geq 4$. If moreover (1) holds then the conditional expectation is given by formula

$$E(X_{t_3} | X_{t_1}, X_{t_2}) =$$

$$= \frac{t_3 - t_2}{2a + b(t_1 - t_2)} X_{t_1} + \frac{a + b(t_1 - t_2)}{a + b(t_1 - t_2)} X_{t_2}.$$

Warsaw Technical University
ul.Polna 54 m.14
00-644 Warszawa, Poland

REFERENCES

1. Hardin C. On the linearity of regression. Z.Wahrscheinlichkeitsteor. Verw.Geb. 61, 1982, 293-302.
2. Plucińska A. On a property of the memory of stochastic processes with the linear regression.- Bull.Polon.Acad. Sci., 1988 (in print).
3. Plucińska A. On a stochastic process determined by the conditional expectation and the conditional variance. Stochastics, 10, 1983, 115-129.

ON CHARACTERIZATION OF GENERALIZED LOGISTIC AND PARETO DISTRIBUTIONS

J.Pusz

1. Introduction

The aim of this paper is to give the complete characterization of p -dimensional distribution function F satisfying

$$F(x_1,\dots,x_p) = \left(1 - p + \sum_{k=1}^{p} F_k^{-\alpha}(x_k)\right)^{-1/\alpha}, \quad \alpha>0, \tag{1.1}$$

where $F_1,\dots,F_p$ are its marginal univariate distribution functions. The same characterization is also valid for tail distribution function G and its tail marginal univariate values G_k $(k = 1,\dots,p)$:

$$G(x_1,\dots,x_p) = \left(1 - p + \sum_{k=1}^{p} G_k^{-\alpha}(x_k)\right)^{-1/\alpha}. \tag{1.2}$$

Our characterization is a generalization of results obtained for multidimensional Pareto distribution by Jupp and Mardia [1] . One can show that p -dimensional logistic and Pareto distributions satisfy (1.1) and (1.2) respectively. To see this let

$$F(x_1,\dots,x_p) = P(X_1< x_1,\dots,X_p< x_p) = \left(1 + \sum_{k=1}^{p} e^{-x_k}\right)^{-1/\alpha} \tag{1.3}$$

for $x_k\in\mathbb{R}$, $(k=1,\dots,p)$ and $\alpha>0$ be logistic distribution function for p random variables $X_1,\dots,X_p$. For univariate marginal distributions $F_1,\dots,F_p$ we have:

$$F_k(x_k) = P(X_k < x_k) = (1 + e^{-x_k})^{-1/\alpha} \tag{1.4}$$

where $x_k \in \mathbb{R}$ $(k = 1, \ldots, p)$.

One can easily check that these satisfy (1.1).

If G is tail distribution function for Pareto distribution defined by Mardia [4] :

$$G(x_1, \ldots, x_p) = P(X_1 \geq x_1, \ldots, X_p \geq x_p) =$$

$$= (1 - p + \sum_{k=1}^{p} b_k^{-1} x_k)^{-1/\alpha} \tag{1.5}$$

where $x_k \geq b_k > 0$ $(k = 1, \ldots, p)$ then the tail distribution functions G_k $(k = 1, \ldots, p)$ are defined as:

$$G_k(x_k) = P(X_k \geq x_k) = (b_k^{-1} x_k)^{-1/\alpha} \tag{1.6}$$

for $x_k \geq b_k > 0$ $(k = 1, \ldots, p)$.

We see that (1.2) is satisfied in obvious manner. For these reasons we call F, G satisfying (1.1) and (1.2) a generalized logistic distribution and analogously a generalized Pareto distribution.

2. A characterization of generalized logistic and Pareto distributions

Let us consider the following situation. For given continuously differentiable univariate distribution functions $F_1, \ldots, F_p$ and $\alpha > 0$ we can define function H_α on $\mathbb{R}^p$:

$$H_\alpha(x_1, \ldots, x_p) := \begin{cases} (1 - p + \sum_{k=1}^{p} F_k^{-\alpha}(x_k))^{-1/\alpha} & \text{if } F_k(x_k) > 0 \text{ for all } k = 1, \ldots, p \\ 0 & \text{if } F_k(x_k) < 0 \text{ for some } k. \end{cases} \tag{2.1}$$

LEMMA. H_α is a p-dimensional differentiable distribution function for any $\alpha > 0$. Moreover H_α has $F_1, \ldots, F_p$ as its marginal univariate values.

PROOF. It is obvious that $0 \leqslant H_\alpha(x_1, \ldots, x_p) \leqslant 1$ and H_α is differentiable.

Let us define intervals (a_k, b_k), $-\infty \leqslant a_k < b_k \leqslant +\infty$ for each k such that

$$0 < F_k(x_k) < 1 \qquad \text{for} \quad x_k \in (a_k, b_k)$$

$$\text{and} \quad \lim_{x_k \to a_k} F_k(x_k) = 0 \;, \quad \lim_{x_k \to b_k} F_k(x_k) = 1 . \tag{2.2}$$

Then it is evident from (2.1) that

$$\lim_{x_k \to -\infty} H_\alpha(x_1, \ldots, x_k, \ldots, x_p) = 0 \qquad k = 1, \ldots, p$$

and

$$\lim_{\min(x_1, \ldots, x_p) \to +\infty} H_\alpha(x_1, \ldots, x_p) = 1.$$

To finish the proof that H_α is a distribution function we have to show that

$$\Delta^{1}_{h_1} \cdots \Delta^{p}_{h_p} H_\alpha(x_1, \ldots, x_p) \geqslant 0 \qquad \text{for} \quad x_k \in (a_k, b_k) \tag{2.3}$$

Where operator $\Delta^{k}_{h_k}$ is defined for $h_k \geqslant 0$ such that $x_k + h_k \leq b_k$ and

$$\Delta^{k}_{h_k} g(x_1, \ldots, x_p) := g(x_1, \ldots, x_k + h_k, \ldots, x_p) - g(x_1, \ldots, x_k, \ldots, x_p).$$

In our case we obtain

$$\Delta^{1}_{h_1} \cdots \Delta^{p}_{h_p} H_\alpha(x_1, \ldots, x_p) =$$

$$= \frac{\alpha^{-1}(\alpha^{-1}+1)\dots(\alpha^{-1}+p-1)}{\alpha^{-p}} H_\alpha^{-p}(x_1+\theta_1 h_1,\dots,x_p+\theta_p h_p)\times$$

$$\times \prod_{k=1}^{p} (h_k F_k^{-\alpha-1}(x_k+\theta_k h_k) F_k'(x_k+\theta_k h_k)) \geqslant 0$$

where $0<\theta_k<1 \quad (k=1,\dots,p)$.

Since

$$H_\alpha(\infty,\dots,\infty,x_k,\infty,\dots,\infty)=F_k(x_k), \qquad x_k\in\mathbb{R}$$

we see that F_k is marginal distribution function for $k=1,\dots,p$ and this ends the proof.

REMARK: Our lemma gives one parameter families of distribution functions with given marginal values. For $p=2$ and $F_k(x_k)=1-e^{-\lambda_k x_k}$, $x_k>0$ $(k=1,2)$ our construction gives the some distribution function as in Kimeldorf, Sampson [3] .

Now we can state our

THEOREM 1. Let $F_1,\dots F_p$ be univariate continuously differentiable distribution functions and $H_\alpha(x_1,\dots,x_p)$ - p-dimensional distribution function as in Lemma.

Let F be p-dimensional differentiable distribution function for $(X_1,\dots,X_p)$ random variable and $0<\alpha<1$. Then the following conditions are equivalent

i) F is a generalized logistic distribution with parameter α i.e.

$$F=H_\alpha,$$

ii) $$E(F_k^{-\alpha}(X_k)-F_k^{-\alpha}(x_k)\mid X_1<x_1,\dots,X_p<x_p)=\frac{\alpha}{1-\alpha}F^{-\alpha}(x_1,\dots,x_p)$$

for $x_k\in\mathbb{R} \quad (k=1,\dots,p)$.

PROOF. For any random variable X with distribution function F the existence of mean value $E(F^{-\alpha}(X))$ for all $\alpha\in(0,1)$ follows from Lemma 1.1.8 proven by Kagan, Linnik, Rao [2] .

i) $\Longrightarrow$ ii) If $F = H_\alpha$ for some $\alpha \in (0,1)$ then we have

$$E(F_k^{-\alpha}(X_k) - F_k^{-\alpha}(x_k) \mid X_1 < x_1, \ldots, X_p < x_p) =$$
$$= F^{-1}(x_1, \ldots, x_p) J_k(x_1, \ldots, x_p) - F_k^{-\alpha}(x_k) \tag{2.4}$$

where

$$J_k(x_1, \ldots, x_p) = \frac{\alpha^{-1}(\alpha^{-1}+1)\ldots(\alpha^{-1}+p-1)}{\alpha^{-p}} \int_{-\infty}^{x_1} \ldots \int_{-\infty}^{x_p} F_k^{-\alpha}(y_k) \times$$

$$\times \left(\prod_{i=1}^{p} (F_i^{-\alpha-1}(y_i) F_i'(y_i))\right)\left(1 - p + \sum_{i=1}^{p} F_i^{-\alpha}(y_i)\right)^{-(\alpha^{-1}+p)} dy_1 \ldots dy_k =$$

$$= \int_{-\infty}^{x_k} F_k^{-\alpha}(y_k) F_k^{-\alpha-1}(y_k) F_k'(y_k) \left(1 - p + \sum_{\substack{i=1 \\ i \neq k}}^{p} F_i^{-\alpha}(x_i) + F_k^{-\alpha}(y_k)\right)^{-(\alpha^{-1}+1)} dy_k =$$

$$= \int_{-\infty}^{x_k} F_k^{-\alpha-1}(y_k) F_k'(y_k) \left(1 - p + \sum_{\substack{i=1 \\ i \neq k}}^{p} F_i^{-\alpha}(x_i) + F_k^{-\alpha}(y_k)\right)^{-\alpha^{-1}} dy_k +$$

$$+ \left(1 - p + \sum_{\substack{i=1 \\ i \neq k}}^{p} F_i^{-\alpha}(x_i)\right) \int_{-\infty}^{x_k} F_k^{-\alpha-1}(y_k) F_k'(y_k) \left(1 - p + \sum_{\substack{i=1 \\ i \neq k}}^{p} F_i^{-\alpha}(x_i) + \right.$$

$$\left. + F_k^{-\alpha}(y_k)\right)^{-(\alpha^{-1}+1)} dy_k =$$

$$= (1-\alpha)^{-1}\left(1 - p + \sum_{i=1}^{p} F_i^{-\alpha}(x_i)\right)^{1-\alpha^{-1}} - \left(1 - p + \sum_{\substack{i=1 \\ i \neq k}}^{p} F_i^{-\alpha}(x_i)\right) \times$$

$$\times \left(1 - p + \sum_{i=1}^{p} F_i^{-\alpha}(x_i)\right)^{-\alpha^{-1}}$$

for $k = 1, \ldots, p$.

Now from (2.4) we have obtain

$$E(F_k^{-\alpha}(X_k) - F_k^{-\alpha}(x_k) \mid X_1 < x_1, \ldots, X_p < x_p) = \alpha(1-\alpha)^{-1} F^{-\alpha}(x_1, \ldots, x_p)$$

for all $k = 1, \ldots, p$.

ii) $\Longrightarrow$ i) We have to prove that F has to be H_α. We can rewrite condition ii) as

$$\int_{-\infty}^{x_1}\cdots\int_{-\infty}^{x_p}\left(F_k^{-\alpha}(y_k)-F_k^{-\alpha}(x_k)\right)dF(y_1,\ldots,y_p)=\alpha(1-\alpha)^{-1}F^{1-\alpha}(x_1,\ldots,x_p)$$

then after differentiating on x_k we get

$$\frac{\partial}{\partial x_k}F^{-\alpha}(x_1,\ldots,x_p)=\frac{d}{dx_k}F_k^{-\alpha}(x_k),\quad k=1,\ldots,p.$$

The solution of these equations is

$$F^{-\alpha}(x_1,\ldots,x_p)=\sum_{i=1}^{p}F_i^{-\alpha}(x_i)+c.$$

Since $\lim\limits_{\min(x_1,\ldots,x_p)\to\infty}F(x_1,\ldots,x_p)=1$ and $\lim\limits_{x_k\to\infty}F_k(x_k)=1$

we get $c=-p+1$ and this ends the proof.

Analogously we can prove characterization for generalized Pareto distribution:

THEOREM 2. Let $G_1,\ldots,G_p$ be univariate continuously differentiable tail distribution functions, and let G be p-dimensional tail distribution function for $(X_1,\ldots,X_p)$ random variable. If $0<\alpha<1$ then the following conditions are equivalent

i) G is generalized Pareto distribution function with parameter α, i.e.

$$G(x_1,\ldots,x_p)=\left(1-p+\sum_{k=1}^{p}G_k^{-\alpha}(x_k)\right)^{-\alpha^{-1}},$$

ii)

$$E\left(G_k^{-\alpha}(X_k)-G_k^{-\alpha}(x_k)\mid X_1\geqslant x_1,\ldots,X_p\geqslant x_p\right)=\alpha(1-\alpha)^{-1}G^{-\alpha}(x_1,\ldots x_p)$$

for all $x\in\mathbb{R}$ $(k=1,\ldots,p)$.

3. Examples

a) Theorem 1 gives a new characterization for p -dimensional distribution function to be p -dimensional logistic distribution with parameter $0 < \alpha < 1$. This holds if and only if

$$E(e^{-X_k} - e^{-x_k} \mid X_1 < x_1, \ldots, X_p < x_p) = \alpha(1-\alpha)^{-1}(1 + \sum_{k=1}^{p} e^{-x_k})$$

for $x_k \in \mathbb{R}$ ($k = 1, \ldots, p$).

b) Analogously for p -dimensional Pareto distribution (1.5) we obtain equivalent condition

$$E(b_k^{-1}(X_k - x_k) \mid X_1 \geqslant x_1, \ldots, X_p \geqslant x_p) = \alpha(1-\alpha)^{-1}(1 - p + \sum_{k=1}^{p} b_k^{-1} x_k)$$

as previously obtained by Jupp and Mardia (1982) $(0 < \alpha < 1)$.

c) If we take univariate Cauchy distribution functions for random variable X_k :

$$F_k(x_k) = \frac{1}{\pi} \operatorname{arctg} x_k + \frac{1}{2}, \qquad x_k \in \mathbb{R} \quad (k = 1, \ldots, p)$$

then

$$F_\alpha(x_1, \ldots, x_p) = (1 - p + \sum_{k=1}^{p} (\frac{1}{\pi} \operatorname{arctg} x_k + \frac{1}{2})^{-\alpha})^{-\alpha^{-1}}$$

is a p -dimensional distribution function with F_k as its marginal distribution values. It can be equivalently described as

$$E((\frac{1}{\pi} \operatorname{arctg} X_k + \frac{1}{2})^{-\alpha} - (\frac{1}{\pi} \operatorname{arctg} x_k + \frac{1}{2})^{-\alpha} \mid X_1 < x_1, \ldots, X_p < x_p) =$$
$$= \alpha(1-\alpha)^{-1}(1 - p + \sum_{k=1}^{p} (\frac{1}{\pi} \operatorname{arctg} x_k + \frac{1}{2})^{-\alpha}).$$

Our distribution function F_α is not a p -dimensional Cauchy distribution with marginal values F_k .

Instytut Matematyki
Politechnika Warszawaka
00-661 Warsaw, Poland

REFERENCES

1. Jupp P.E., Mardia K.V. A characterization of the multivariate Pareto distribution.- Ann.Stat., 10, N 3, 1982, 1021-1024.
2. Kagan A.M., Linnik J.V., Rao S.R. Characterization problems in mathematical statistics. Wiley, New York, 1973,
3. Kimeldorf G., Sampson A. Uniform representations of bivariate distributions. Commun. Stat., 4(3), 1975, 293-301.
4. Mardia K.V. Multivariate Pareto distributions. Ann.Math.Stat., 33, 1962, 1008-1015. Correction Ann. Math. Stat., 34, 1962, 1603.

LIMIT THEOREMS FOR POSITIVE DEFINITE
PROBABILITY DENSITIES

H.-J.Rossberg

1. Introduction

Positive definite (pos.def.) functions are well known in probability theory due to the following celebrated theorem.

THEOREM 1.1 (Bochner-Hincin). Let h be a continuous complex-valued function on R_1. Then it is the characterictic function (c.f.) of a distribution function (d.f.) iff it is pos.def. and $h(0)=1$.

But pos.def. probability densities (p.d.) were explicitely introduced not earlier than in [3], and it was only J.L.Teugels [6] who had treated a remarkable particular case before. In [3] we underlined that it is no restriction of generality to assume that pos.def.p.d. are continuous.

In the sequel we will need two fundamental lemmas.

The proofs are given in [3] : lemma 1.3 represents a reformulation of a result of Mathias [2] who wrote the first paper in which pos.def. functions are explecitely treated.

LEMMA 1.2. Let p be a pos.def.p.d. with c.f. f ; then there exists an adjoint pos.def.p.d. $\hat{p}$ with c.f. $\hat{f}$ such that

$$\hat{f} = \frac{p}{p_0}, \qquad f = \frac{\hat{p}}{\hat{p}_0}, \qquad 2\pi p_0 \hat{p}_0 = 1, \tag{1.1}$$

where $p_0 := p(0)$, $\hat{p}_0 := \hat{p}(0)$. Moreover, $\hat{\hat{p}} = p$.

LEMMA 1.3. The p.d. p is pos.def. iff its c.f. f is real, nonnegative, and integrable over R_1 (in short: $f \geq 0$, $f \in L_1$).

In the present paper (F_n) stands for a sequence of absolutely continuous d.f. with corresponding sequence (p_n), (f_n) of p.d. and c.f., resp. If the p_n, $n \geqslant 1$, are pos.def. then, of course, there exist the adjoint sequences $(\hat{F}_n)$, $(\hat{p}_n)$, $(\hat{f}_n)$ with obvious notations. Moreover, we have in analogy to (1.1)

$$\hat{f}_n = \frac{p_n}{p_{on}} , \qquad f_n = \frac{\hat{p}_n}{\hat{p}_{on}} , \qquad 2\pi p_{on} \hat{p}_{on} = 1 . \tag{1.2}$$

These relations enable us to state a number of peculiar limit theorems; in particular, we will prove two new CLT for p.d., see Sect.6.

If there is a d.f. F such that we have complete convergence of (F_n) to F we write, as usual, $F_n \xrightarrow{c} F$. Analogously, if p is a continuous p.d. and $p_n(x) \rightarrow p(x)$, $x \in R_1$ as $n \rightarrow \infty$, then we denote this convergence by

$$p_n \xrightarrow{c} p .$$

To close this introduction we remind the reader of the following fact which is an immediate consequence of the definition of positive definiteness.

PROPOSITION 1.4. Let there exist a function $\mathfrak{p}$ such that $\lim_{n \to \infty} p_n = p$ on the line; if p_n, $n \geqslant 1$, are pos.def., then so is $\mathfrak{p}$.

2. Weak convergence of adjoint d.f.

We write

$$\hat{p}(t) = \hat{p}_0 \int_{-\infty}^{\infty} e^{itx} dF(x),$$

integrate from 0 to $u > 0$, and interchange the order of integrations on the right. Thus we obtain

$$\hat{F}(u) - \frac{1}{2} = \hat{p}_0 \int_{-\infty}^{\infty} \frac{e^{iux} - 1}{ix} dF(x), \quad u > 0. \tag{2.1}$$

In analogy we get

$$\hat{F}_n(u) - \frac{1}{2} = \hat{p}_{on} \int_{-\infty}^{\infty} \frac{e^{iux} - 1}{ix} \, dF(x), \qquad u > 0, \tag{2.2}$$

for the sequences occuring in connection with (1.2). The integrand vanishes at infinity; thus we obtain the following statement (i) from the extended Helly-Bray theorem (Cor.2.2.6 of [3]); here $F_n \xrightarrow{w} \Psi$ denotes weak convergence to some monotone function Ψ.

PROPOSITION 2.1. Assume that the d.f. F_n, $n \geq 1$ possess pos.def. p.d. so that the relations (2.2) hold.

(i) If $F_n \xrightarrow{W} \Psi$ and $\hat{p}_{on} \rightarrow \rho$, $0 \leq \rho < \infty$, then there exists $\hat{\Psi}$ such that $\hat{F}_n \xrightarrow{w} \hat{\Psi}$.

(ii) If $F_n \xrightarrow{w} \Psi$ and $\Psi(\infty) - \Psi(-\infty) > 0$, then $(\hat{p}_{on})$ is bounded.

PROOF OF (ii). It suffices to show that $\mathcal{I}(u) := \int_{-\infty}^{\infty} \frac{\sin ux}{x} \, d\Psi(x)$ cannot vanish a.e. For this purpose we consider the integral

$$\int_0^t \mathcal{I}(u) \, du = \int_{-\infty}^{\infty} x^{-2} \int_0^{tx} \sin v \, dv \, d\Psi(x)$$

which cannot vanish by assumption. Thus the assertion follows.

3. Relative compactness

We remind the reader of the following concept.

DEFINITION 3.1. A sequence (F_n) of d.f. is called relatively compact if, for every weakly converging subsequence $(F_{n'})$, the limit function F has no defect, i.e. if $F_{n'} \xrightarrow{W} F$ implies that F is a d.f. so that we have $F_{n'} \xrightarrow{c} F$.

From [3] , Sect.3.3, we collect together several facts.

CRITERION 3.2. (i) The sequence (F_n) is relatively compact iff the corresponding sequence (f_n) of c.f. is equicontinuous on R_1 .

(ii) This property in its turn is granted iff

a) either $(\mathrm{Re}\, f_n)$ is equicontinuous at 0

b) or the function $\psi := \underline{\lim}\, \mathrm{Re} f_n$ is continuous at 0 .

PROPOSITION 3.3. Let the sequence (F_n) consist of d.f. with pos.def. p.d. p_n, $n \geq 1$.

(i) If (F_n) is relatively compact then the sequence (p_{on}) is bounded away from zero; further, the sequence $(\hat{p}_n)$ of adjoint p.d. is equicontinuous on R_1 .

(ii) If $(\hat{p}_n)$ is equicontinuous at 0 and $\hat{p}_{on} > c > 0$, $n \geq 1$, then (F_n) is relatively compact.

PROOF. (i) Let us assume that there is a subsequence (n') with $p_{on'} \to 0$; then $\hat{p}_{on'} \to \infty$ by (1.2). Now we select a further subsequence $(n'') \subset (n')$ such that $F_{n''} \xrightarrow{c} F$; it leads to an immediate contradiction in view of Prop. 2.1 (ii). Thus we obtain the first assertion,and from now on we may assume that $\hat{p}_{on} \leq C$, $n \geq 1$.

By Crit. 3.2 (i) the sequence (f_n) is equicontinuous on R_1 . Thus for any given $\varepsilon > 0$ there is $\delta(\varepsilon) > 0$ such that

$$\varepsilon > |f_n(t+h) - f_n(t)| = \hat{p}_{on}^{-1} |\hat{p}_n(t+h) - \hat{p}_n(t)| \geq C^{-1} |\hat{p}_n(t+h) - \hat{p}_n(t)| , \quad n \geq 1,$$

for all $|h| < \delta$ and all $t \in R_1$. This implies the second assertion

(ii) We write

$$1 - f_n(h) = \hat{p}_{on}^{-1} (\hat{p}_{on} - \hat{p}_n(h)) \leq c^{-1} (\hat{p}_{on} - \hat{p}_n(h)) ;$$

hence, by our assumption, (f_n) is equicontinuous at 0 . Accordingly, Crit. 3.2 (ii) a) shows that (f_n) is equicontinuous on R_1 whence the assertion follows by Crit. 3.2 (i). The proof is complete.

Finally, we consider a relative compact sequence (F_n) with pos. def. p.d. (p_n) such that (p_{on}) is bounded; we seek conditions guaranteeing that $(\hat{F}_n)$ is also relative compact. Anticipating Prop.

4.1 we see that all possible limit d.f. of (F_n) have pos.def. p.d. whose maxima way, of course, in general differ. The following result will be applied in the proof of Prop. 5.2.

PROPOSITION 3.4. Let the above sequence (F_n) be relatively compact and assume $p_{0n} \to \lambda$ where λ is the common maximum of all possible pos.def. limit p.d. Then $(\hat{F}_n)$ is also relative compact.

PROOF. Assume $F_{n'} \xrightarrow{c} F$ for some subsequence (n'). Then Prop. 4.1 tells us that F has a pos.def. p.d. p. By assumption $\lambda = p(0)$ so that Prop. 4.2 can be applied to (F_n) ; it yields $\hat{F}_{n'} \xrightarrow{c} \hat{F}$ which it was our intention to prove.

4. Application of the continuity theorem for c.f.

In view of (1.2) it is tempting to ask what consequences are implied by $F_n \xrightarrow{c} F$ on one hand and $p_n \xrightarrow{c} p$ on the other; for the notations cf. the end of Sect. 1.

PROPOSITION 4.1. Let the d.f. F_n be absolutely continuous with pos.def. p.d. p_n and assume

$$p_{0n} < C, \quad n \geq 1, \qquad \text{and} \qquad F_n \xrightarrow{c} F$$

for some d.f. F . Then F possesses also a pos.def. p.d. p .

PROOF. By assumption and L.1.3 we have for the corresponding c.f. $f_n \geq 0$, $f_n \in L_1$, and it is enough to show that $f \in L_1$ where f is the c.f. of F . In view of the Fourier inversion theorem and the connuity theorem this is immediate from

$$2\pi C > 2\pi p_{0n} \geq \int_{-a}^{a} f_n(t)\,dt \longrightarrow \int_{-a}^{a} f(t)\,dt, \qquad a > 0.$$

Formula (2.2) indicates that we need stronger suppositions to conclude $\hat{F}_n \xrightarrow{c} \hat{F}$.

PROPOSITION 4.2. Let the above assumptions be true so that the pos.

def. p.d. p of F exists. If, moreover, $p_{on} \to p_o = p(0)$ then $p_n \xrightarrow{c} p$ and for the adjoint objects we have

$$\hat{p}_n \xrightarrow{c} p, \qquad \hat{F}_n \xrightarrow{c} \hat{F}.$$

The convergences of (p_n) and $(\hat{p}_n)$ are uniform on the line.

PROOF. First of all, we apply the continuity theorem and get

$$f_n = \frac{\hat{p}_n}{\hat{p}_{on}} \longrightarrow f = \frac{\hat{p}}{\hat{p}_o} \tag{4.1}$$

uniformly on every $(-a, a)$. Moreover, our assumptions lead to $\hat{p}_{on} \longrightarrow \hat{p}_o$. Accordingly, the identity

$$\hat{p}_n - \hat{p} = \hat{p}_{on}(f_n - f) + (\hat{p}_{on} - \hat{p}_o)f \tag{4.2}$$

implies $\hat{p}_n \xrightarrow{c} \hat{p}$ uniformly on every $(-a, a)$. This permits us to write

$$\int\limits_{|x| \geq a} \hat{p}_n \, dx = 1 - \int_{-a}^{a} \hat{p}_n \, dx \longrightarrow 1 - \int_{-a}^{a} \hat{p} \, dx = \int\limits_{|x| \geq a} \hat{p} \, dx. \tag{4.3}$$

Now we introduce $\delta_n := \sup_x |p_n(x) - p(x)|$ and obtain from the Fourier inversion theorem and (1.2)

$$2\pi \delta_n \leq \int_{-\infty}^{\infty} |f_n(t) - f(t)| dt \leq$$

$$\leq \int_{-a}^{a} |\ldots| \, dt + \frac{1}{\hat{p}_{on}} \int\limits_{|t| \geq a} \hat{p}_n dt + \frac{1}{\hat{p}_o} \int\limits_{|t| \geq a} \hat{p} \, dt \tag{4.4}$$

for all $a > 0$. Combining this with (4.1) and (4.3) we get

$$\overline{\lim}\, \delta_n \leq \frac{1}{\pi \hat{p}_o} \int\limits_{|t| \geq a} \hat{p} \, dt, \qquad a > 0,$$

so that $p_n \xrightarrow{c} p$ uniformly on the line.

Now we may write

$$\hat{f}_n = \frac{p_n}{p_{on}} \longrightarrow \frac{p}{p_o} = \hat{f} \tag{4.5}$$

whence $\hat{F}_n \xrightarrow{c} \hat{F}$ follows. The convergence $\hat{p}_n \xrightarrow{c} \hat{p}$ is uniform on R_1 by an analogous reasoning. The proof is complete.

We will need the above result in the proof of Th. 5.3. Now we turn to assumptions concerning the convergence of (p_n). For the proof of Prop. 4.4 we need the following well-known fact, see e.g. [4], L.3.3.9.

LEMMA 4.3. Let the sequence (h_n) of functions be equicontinuous on $(-a, a)$ for some fixed $a \leqslant \infty$ and assume $h_n \xrightarrow{c} h$ pointwise on $(-a, a)$. Then h is continuous and the convergence is uniform in every finite interval contained in $(-a, a)$.

PROPOSITION 4.4. Let $\mathfrak{K} \neq 0$ be an arbitrary real function on R_1 continuous at 0 and let the p.d. p_n, $n \geqslant 1$, be pos.def. Then the assumption

$$p_n(x) \longrightarrow \mathfrak{K}(x), \qquad x \in R_1, \tag{4.6}$$

implies that there exists a d.f. $\hat{F}$ with a pos.def. p.d. $\hat{p}$ such that $\hat{F}_n \xrightarrow{c} \hat{F}$; moreover, $\hat{p}_n \xrightarrow{c} \hat{p}$ uniformly on the line. Further, $\mathfrak{K}$ is continuous and the assumed convergence (4.6) is uniform on every finite interval. Finally, there is a monotone function G such that $F_n \xrightarrow{w} G$ where the d.f. F_n correspond to $p_n, n \geqslant 1$.

PROOF. Clearly, $p_{0n} = p_n(0) \longrightarrow \mathfrak{K}(0) =: \mathfrak{K}_0$. By Prop. 1.4 $\mathfrak{K}$ is pos.def., and since we assumed $\mathfrak{K} \neq 0$ we have $\mathfrak{K}_0 > 0$. Accordingly,

$$\hat{f}_n = \frac{p_n}{p_{0n}} \longrightarrow \frac{\mathfrak{K}}{\mathfrak{K}_0} =: \hat{f} \geqslant 0$$

where $\hat{f}$ is continuous at 0 by assumption. Thus the continuity theorem tells us that $\hat{f}$ is a c.f. and that $\hat{F}_n \xrightarrow{c} \hat{F}$ where $\hat{F}$ corresponds to $\hat{f}$. The assertion on $\hat{p}_n \longrightarrow \hat{p}$ follows now from Prop.4.2. It is now also clear that $\mathfrak{K}$ is continuous.

We show that $\hat{f} \in L_1$ by writing

$$\frac{1+o(1)}{\pi_0} = \frac{1}{p_{0n}} = 2\pi\hat{p}_{0n} \geqslant \int_{-a}^{a}\hat{f}_n(t)dt \longrightarrow \int_{-a}^{a}\hat{f}(t)dt \tag{4.7}$$

for all $a > 0$. Hence $\hat{F}$ possesses a pos.def. p.d. $\hat{p}$ by L.1.3.

Next, we may apply Prop. 3.3 (i) to $(\hat{F}_n)$ so that (p_n) is equicontinuous on the line. Accordingly, L.4.3 tells us that the convergence (4.6) is uniform on every finite interval.

Since we know that $\hat{F}_n \xrightarrow{c} \hat{F}$, $p_{0n} \longrightarrow \pi_0 < \infty$ we may apply Prop. 2.1 (i) to obtain the very last assertion. The proof is now complete.

Using somewhat sharper assumptions we may even conclude $F_n \xrightarrow{c} F$. For this purpose we need the following special case of a useful theorem proved in [5] .

LEMMA 4.5. The complete convergence

$$p_n \xrightarrow{c} p \tag{4.8}$$

of p.d. (p_n) to the p.d. p implies $F_n \xrightarrow{c} F$ for the corresponding d.f.

COROLLARY TO PROP. 4.4 Let F be a d.f. with p.d. p and replace in Prop. 4.4 the assumption (4.6) by (4.8). Then $F_n \xrightarrow{c} F$ and the assumed convergence (4.8) is uniform on the line.

PROOF. The first assertion is immediate from L.4.5, the second from Prop. 4.2.

5. Restricted convergence of p.d.

The following is of interest in connection with a recent theory which constitutes a new branch of the summation theory of r.v. Here the notion of restricted convergence or briefly "r-convergence" of a sequence (F_n) of d.f. on an interval plays an essential role; it is the question under which conditions complete convergence of (F_n) can be derived from r-convergence.

The starting point was a conjecture of V.M.Zolotarev concerning a new version of the CLT; here the assumption of r-convergence on $\mathcal{J}=(-\infty, x_0)$ was made; see Sect. 6. The present state of this theory which was initiated at the Karl Marx university Leipzig is elaborated in [4].

In the present section we show that r-convergence of pos.def. p.d. on a finite interval can lead to far-reaching conclusions even if the d.f. p_n under consideration are no convolutions.

It is important for the following reasonings that there do exist c.f. f which are uniquely defined by their values attained on a finite interval $(-a, a)$; the most important ones are so-called analytic c.f. The standard normal c.f. shows that they can have the properties occurring in L.1.3 so that the corresponding p.d. are pos.def. In this context the following lemma is crucial for our purpose, see e.g. [4], Prop.3.4.5.

LEMMA 5.1. Let f be a c.f. which is uniquely defined by its restriction to some interval $(-a, a)$. If the c.f. $f_n(t) \longrightarrow f(t)$, $|t| < a$, then we have for the corresponding d.f. $F_n \xrightarrow{c} F$.

PROPOSITION 5.2. Let the p.d. p, p_n be pos.def. with adjoint p.d. $\hat{p}$, $\hat{p}_n$, $n \geq 1$, and assume the r-convergence

$$p_n(x) \longrightarrow p(x), \quad |x| < a, \tag{5.1}$$

for some fixed $a > 0$. Then both (F_n) and $(\hat{F}_n)$ are relatively compact and the convergence (5.1) is uniform. Further,

$$\overline{\lim} \sup_x |\hat{p}_n(x) - \hat{p}(x)| \leq 2 p_0 \int_{|t| \geq a} p \, dt. \tag{5.2}$$

PROOF. First of all, we note that $p_{0n} \rightarrow p_0$. Thus (5.1) yields

$$\frac{p_0(t)}{p_{0n}} = \hat{f}_n(t) \longrightarrow \hat{f}(t) = \frac{p(t)}{p_0}, \quad |t| < a. \tag{5.3}$$

Hence the function

$$\psi(t) := \underline{\lim}\, \mathrm{Re}\, \hat{f}_n(t) = \mathrm{Re}\, \hat{f}(t)\ , \quad |t| < a,$$

is continuous at 0. Accordingly, Crit.3.2(ii) tells us that $(\hat{F}_n)$ is relatively compact.

Now we see from Crit.3.2(i) that the sequence $(\hat{f}_n)$ is equicontinuous on $\mathbb{R}_1$. Putting $h_n = \hat{f}_n$ we can apply L.4.3 so that the convergence (5.3) is uniform. Now we write

$$p_n - p = p_0 p_n (p_0^{-1} - p_{0n}^{-1}) + p_0(\hat{f}_n - \hat{f}) \tag{5.4}$$

and see that the assumed convergence (5.1) is also uniform; note that $p_n \leq p_{0n} \longrightarrow p_0$.

Clearly, $\hat{p}_{0n} = (2\pi p_{0n})^{-1} \longrightarrow (2\pi p_0)^{-1} =: \lambda$. Since $(\hat{F}_n)$ is relatively compact there exists a subsequence $(\hat{F}_{n'})$ such that $\hat{F}_{n'} \xrightarrow{c} \hat{G}$ where $\hat{G}$ has a p.d. $\hat{g}$ by Prop. 4.1. From Prop. 4.2 it follows now that $\hat{p}_{n'} \xrightarrow{c} \hat{g}$ where $\hat{g}(0) = \lambda$. Thus we have exactly the situation assumed in Prop. 3.4, it only concerns $(\hat{F}_n)$ instead of (F_n) . Thus (F_n) is relatively compact.

Finally, we have to derive (5.2). For this purpose we write

$$\hat{p}_n(x) - \hat{p}(x) = \frac{1}{2\pi} \int_{-\infty}^{\infty} e^{itx} (\hat{f}_n(t) - \hat{f}(t))\, dt.$$

Since the convergence (5.3) is uniform we get

$$|\hat{p}_n(x) - \hat{p}(x)| \leq o(1) + (2\pi p_{0n})^{-1} \int_{|t| \geq a} p_n\, dt + (2\pi p_0)^{-1} \int_{|t| \geq a} p\, dt\ ; \tag{5.5}$$

now the uniformity of the convergence (5.1) makes it possible to argue like in connection with (4.3). Hence the right side of (5.5) tends to the right side of (5.2) whence the desired inequality follows.

Now we arrive at our main result of the present section; note that in view of (1.1) there do exist pos.def. p.d. which are uniquely defined by their values on $(-a, a)$.

THEOREM 5.3. Let the assumptions of Prop.5.2 be true. If, moreover, p is uniquely defined by its restriction to $(-a, a)$ then

$$p_n \xrightarrow{c} p, \qquad \hat{p}_n \xrightarrow{c} \hat{p}$$

uniformly on the line.

PROOF. By assumption, $\hat{f}$ is uniquely defined by its restriction to $(-a, a)$. Accordingly, L.5.1 applies to $\hat{f}, \hat{f}_n$ so that $\hat{f}_n \to \hat{f}$ follows whence we get $\hat{F}_n \xrightarrow{c} \hat{F}$. From (5.1) we also get $\hat{p}_{0n} \to \hat{p}_0$. Hence Prop. 4.2 applies to $(\hat{F}_n)$ and yields the desired statements.

6. The CLT for pos.def. p.d.

The proceeding results permit an application to the CLT for p.d. We consider i.i. d.r.v. X_k, $k \geq 1$, subject to the d.f. F with c.f. f. Further, we introduce the sums

$$S_n = b_n^{-1}(X_1 + \ldots + X_n - a_n), \qquad n \geq 1, \tag{6.1}$$

where $b_n > 0$ and $a_n \in R_1$, and write F_n for their d.f. Let Φ and p_Φ stand for the standardized normal d.f. and its p.d., resp. It was V.M.Zolotarev's conjecture that the restricted convergence $F_n(x) \to \Phi(x)$, $x \leq x_0$, implies $F_n \xrightarrow{c} \Phi$, and it proved to be perfectly true, see [4], Prop. 10.4.1.

Next, we remind the reader of two lemmas. The first is M.Riedel's generalization of the CLT just meationed, see [4], Sect. 10.4; the second is due to B.V.Gnedenko, see [1].

LEMMA 6.1. Let

$$\underline{F}(x) = \varliminf_{n\to\infty} F_n(x), \qquad \overline{F}(x) = \varlimsup_{n\to\infty} F_n(x), \qquad x \in R_1.$$

Then the assumption

$$\lim_{x\to-\infty} \frac{F(x)}{\Phi(x)} = \lim_{x\to-\infty} \frac{\bar{F}(x)}{\Phi(x)} = 1 \qquad (6.2)$$

implies $F_n \xrightarrow{c} F$.

Note that (6.1) is by far less than r-convergence since convergence of (F_n) is not assumed in any point.

LEMMA 6.2. Let F be absolutely continuous with a bounded p.d. p. If $F_n \xrightarrow{c} \Phi$ then we have for the corresponding p.d.

$$p_n \xrightarrow{c} p_\Phi$$

Since pos.def. p.d. are always bounded we can directly combine these lemmas; note that we may put $a_n = 0$ in view of the symmetry of p.

THEOREM 6.3. Assume that F has a pos.def. p.d. p and put $a_n = 0$, $n \geq 1$, in (6.1). Then (6.2) implies

$$p_n(x) = b_n p_n^{*n}(b_n x) \xrightarrow{c} p_\Phi(x), \quad x \in R_1, \qquad (6.3)$$

and the adjoint p.d.

$$\hat{p}_n(x) = c_n \hat{p}^n(x b_n^{-1}) b_n^{-1}, \qquad c_n^{-1} := 2\pi \hat{p}_0^n p^{*n}(0), \quad n \geq 1,$$

tend also to p_Φ. The convergences are uniform on the line.

PROOF. The above lemmas imply (6.3). The convergence of $(\hat{p}_n)$ is a consequence of Prop. 4.2; note that Φ is self-adjoint, i.e. $\hat{\Phi} = \Phi$. The explicite formula for $\hat{p}_n$ follows from the fact that the p.d. adjoint to the convolution $p_1 * p_2$ has the form $c\hat{p}_1 \hat{p}_2$, see [3]. This completes the proof.

Finally, we turn to a CLT involving r-convergence of p.d. on a finite interval; of course, we adhere to the above notations.

THEOREM 6.4. Let p be a pos.def. p.d. and assume the r-convergence

$$p_n(x) \longrightarrow p_\Phi(x), \qquad |x|<a,$$

for some fixed $a>0$. Then all assertions of Th. 6.3 hold true.

PROOF. In view of the remarks which we made in connection with L.5.1 it is clear that p_Φ is - in the set of pos.def p.d. - uniquely defined by its restriction to $(-a,a)$ since the c.f. $\hat{f}$ corresponding to p_Φ according to (1.1) is $\exp\{-t^2/2\}$ so that it is an analytic c.f. Thus the assertions follow Th. 5.3.

Sections of Mathematics
Karl Marx University
Leipzig, GDR

References

1. Gnedenko B.V., Kolmogorov A.N. Limit distributions for sums of independent random variables.- Addison Wesley, Reading, Mass.1954.
2. Mathias M. Über positive Fourier-Integrale.- Math.Z. 1923, 16, 103-125.
3. Rossberg H.-J. Positive definite probability densities.- Teor.Veroyatn.Primen., submitted.
4. Rossberg H.-J., Jesiak B., Siegel G. Analytic methods of probability theory. - Akademie-Verlag, Berlin 1985.
5. Scheffé H.A. Useful convergence theorem for probability distributions. - Ann.Math.Stat., 1947, 18, 434-438.
6. Teugels J.L. Probability densities which are their own characteristic functions. - Bull.Sci.Math.Belg. 1971, 23, 236-272.

ON THE ESTIMATE OF THE RATE OF CONVERGENCE

IN THE CENTRAL LIMIT THEOREM

IN HILBERT SPACE

V.V.Senatov

Let $X_1, X_2, \dots$ be independent identically distributed random variables taking values from Hilbert space l_2 such that $EX_1 = 0$, $E|X_1|^2 < \infty$. We'll use symbol $|\cdot|$ to denote all possible norms in hand. Let X_1 posses the distribution P, $(X_1 + \dots + X_n)n^{-1/2}$ posses the distribution P_n and let B be the covariance operator of X_1, and let H be normal law with zero mean and covariance operator B. Without losses in generality eigen vectors of B coincide with basis vectors e_i, $i = 1, 2, \dots$ in l_2 and eigen values $\sigma_1^2, \sigma_2^2, \dots$ are ordered as $\sigma_1^2 \geqslant \sigma_2^2 \geqslant \dots$.

Let $S(R, a) = \{x \in l_2, \ |x - a| \leqslant R\}$ be a sphere of radius R and centre a in l_2. We denote ζ_s ideal metrics introduced by V.M.Zolotarev. Let

$$\tau_R(P, H) = \max\{(1+R)\zeta_3^{1/3}(P, H),\ (1+R^3)\zeta_3(P, H),\ \mu(P, H)\},$$

where μ is the uniform distance computed over convex sets in l_2.

THEOREM. Let $\sigma_6 = 1$ then

$$\sup\{|P_n(S(R,a)) - H(S(R,a))| : \ a \in l_2\} \leqslant c\tau_R(P, H)\, n^{-1/2}.$$

Here and further we denote all absolute constants as c.

The condition $\sigma_6 = 1$ formally speaking isn't restrictive (s.f. [2] where it is shown that the separatness of σ_6 from zero is necessary to obtain estimates $O(n^{-1/2})$), but in essence, omitting information about $\sigma_1, \ldots, \sigma_5$ which can be much greater that 1 drives us to losses in precision of our estimates. We won't investigate this problem in details because the main aim of this paper is to show the method of proof based on using both the metrical approach and the composition method. We also won't regard the existence of derivatives, the way we change the integration order and so on because it can be done without any difficulties.

We denote E^k k-dimensional Euclidean space as well as subspace of l_2 born by basis vectors $e_1, \ldots, e_k$ in l_2. By $l_2 \ominus E^k$ we denote orthogonal complement of E^k. For any vector $x \in l_2$ let x' be it's projection on E^k and let x'' be it's projection on $l_2 \ominus E^k$. Let E^k_x be the notation of $E^k + x$. For any sphere $S(R,a)$ in l_2 for any point x we denote $u = a - x$ and introduce the function $r(x,R,a) = (R^2 - |u''|^2)^{1/2}$. Let $s(x,R,a)$ be the intercept of $S(R,a)$ and E^k_x. If $|u''| > R$ then the set $s(x,R,a)$ is empty otherwise $s(x,R,a) = \{y : y'' = x'',\ |y' - a'| \leqslant r(x,R,a)\}$. Denote as $s(r,a)$, $r \geqslant 0$, $a \in E^k$, the sphere in E^k of radius r centered in a. Denote as $\Phi^{x,\sigma}$ the normal law with mean x and covariance operator $\sigma^2 I'$, where I' is the unit operator in E^k. Let $\Phi^{\sigma} = \Phi^{0,\sigma}$, $\Phi = \Phi^1$, $\varphi^{\sigma}(t) = c\sigma^{-k} e^{-|t|^2/2\sigma^2}$ be the density (in E^k) of Φ^{σ}.

Let $\varepsilon(v)$, $v > 0$ be an infinitely differentiable function. We introduce function

$$f_\varepsilon(x,R,a) = \Phi^{x,\,\varepsilon(r(x,R,a))}(S(R,a)) =$$

$$= \Phi^{\varepsilon(r(x,R,a))}(s(r(x,R,a)),\ u'). \tag{1}$$

Note that for any $y \in l_2$

$$r(x+y, R, a+y) = r(x,R,a), \qquad f_\varepsilon(x+y, R, a+y) = f_\varepsilon(x,R,a).$$

Having functions in hand we'll sometimes partly omit their arguments in obvious cases. Dealing with sets like $\{x: g(x) \geqslant c\}$ where g is certain function we'll merely write $g(x) \geqslant c$.

LEMMA 1. For $r(x) > 0$ the action of the first derivative of function $f(x)$ on vector $h \in l_2$ has the form

$$f'(x)(h) = (u'', h'')\, r^{-2} \int_{s(r,u')} \varphi^{\varepsilon}(t)\{k - (t,t)\varepsilon^{-2} + (t,u')\varepsilon^{-2}\}\, dt +$$

$$+ \int_{s(r,u')} \varphi^{\varepsilon}(t)\,(t,u')\,\varepsilon^{-2}\, dt + \tag{2}$$

$$+ \left(\varepsilon'(r)\,\varepsilon^{-1}(r)\, r\right)(u'', h'')\, r^{-2} \int_{s(r,u')} \varphi^{\varepsilon}(t)\{(t,t)\varepsilon^{-2} - k\}\, dt.$$

We recall that in this formula

$$\varepsilon = \varepsilon(r(x, R, a)), \qquad r = r(x, R, a), \qquad u = a - x.$$

REMARK. The value of the righthand side of (2) won't after if we multiply it by -1 and substitute the integration over $s(r,u')$ by the integration by the complement $s(r, u')$.

Let $\varepsilon(v)$, $v > 0$, be an infinitely differentiable function. We introduce functional sets $\mathcal{E}_l = \mathcal{E}_l(\varepsilon)$, $l = 1, 2, \ldots$, as follows. The set $\mathcal{E}_1$ includes functions $g(v) \equiv 1$ and $g(v) = \frac{\varepsilon'(v)}{\varepsilon(v)}\, v$. The set $\mathcal{E}_l$, $l > 1$, includes all functions from $\mathcal{E}_{l-1}$ and functions $g(v) \times \frac{\varepsilon'(v)}{\varepsilon(v)}\, v$, $g'(v)\, v$, where $g \in \mathcal{E}_{l-1}$.

Further speaking about sums of certain variables with certain coefficients we'll omit mentioning these coefficients.

LEMMA 2. The action of the l-th derivative of function $f(x)$ on vectors $h_1, \ldots, h_l$ can be presented as the sum of functions like

$$g(r)\, V_{l,\varrho,\theta}\left(\frac{u''}{r}, \frac{h_1''}{r}, \ldots, \frac{h_l''}{r}\right) \int_{s(r,u')} \varphi^{\varepsilon}(t)\, U_{l,q,\lambda}\left(\frac{t}{\varepsilon}, \frac{u'}{\varepsilon}, \frac{h_1'}{\varepsilon}, \ldots, \frac{h_l'}{\varepsilon}\right) dt \tag{3}$$

where

$$g(r) \in \mathcal{E}_\ell(\varepsilon);$$

$$V_{\ell,\rho,\theta} = \prod_{i=1}^{\ell} (u''/r,\ h_i''/r)^{\alpha_i} \prod_{\substack{i,j=1,\\ i\le j}}^{\ell} (h_i''/r,\ h_j''/r)^{\beta_{ij}},$$

$$\sum_{i=1}^{\ell} \alpha_i + 2\sum_{\substack{i,j=1,\\ i\le j}}^{\ell} \beta_{ij} = \rho, \qquad \sum_{i=1}^{\ell} \alpha_i = \theta; \tag{4}$$

$$U_{\ell,q,\lambda} = (t/\varepsilon,\ t/\varepsilon)^{a} (t/\varepsilon,\ u'/\varepsilon)^{b} (u'/\varepsilon,\ u'/\varepsilon)^{c} \prod_{i=1}^{\ell} (t/\varepsilon,\ h_i'/\varepsilon)^{a_i} \times$$

$$\times \prod_{j=1}^{\ell} (u'/\varepsilon,\ h_j'/\varepsilon)^{b_j} \times \prod_{\substack{i,j=1\\ i\le j}}^{\ell} (h_i'/\varepsilon,\ h_j'/\varepsilon)^{c_{ij}}; \tag{5}$$

$$\sum_{i=1}^{\ell} a_i + \sum_{i=1}^{\ell} b_i + 2\sum_{\substack{i,j=1\\ i\le j}}^{\ell} c_{ij} = q; \quad b + 2c + \sum_{i=1}^{\ell} b_i = \lambda; \quad \rho + q = \ell; \quad \lambda \le \rho;$$

all powers in (4) and (5) being non-negative integer numbers. The absolute value of derivative $f^{(\ell)}$, $\ell \ge 1$, being unchangeable to substitution integration over $s(r, u')$ by integration over complement $s(r, u')$ in all expressions like (3).

LEMMA 3. If $\varepsilon(v) \equiv c$ then set $\mathcal{E}_\ell(\varepsilon)$ for any $\ell = 1, 2, \ldots$ contain only the two functions $g(v) \equiv 0$, $g(v) \equiv 1$. If $\varepsilon(v) = (c_1 v^{-\gamma} + c_2)^{1/2}$, $\gamma > 0$ then set $\mathcal{E}_\ell(\varepsilon)$ contains only function like

$$g(v) = \sum_{i=0}^{\ell} a_i (1 + c_2 c_1^{-1} v^{\gamma})^{-i},$$

where a_i are independent from c_1 and c_2.

Let $\xi(v)$ be infinitely differentiable function, $\xi(v) = 0$ as $v \le 0$, $\xi(v) = 1$ as $v \ge 1$, $0 \le \xi(v) \le 1$, $v \in (-\infty, \infty)$, and $|\xi^{(\ell)}(v)| \le c(\ell)$, $\ell = 1, 2, \ldots$. Introduce function

$$w(x) = w(x, R, a) = \xi((r(x,R,a) - \rho)/\rho)$$

where number ρ is such that $0 < \rho \leqslant R$.

LEMMA 4. The l -th derivative of function $w(x)$ can be presented as sum of functions like

$$W_{l,\theta}(x, h_1, \dots, h_l) = \xi^{(m)}((r-\rho)/\rho) \prod_{i=1}^{l} (u'', h_i'')^{\alpha_i} \times$$

$$\times \prod_{\substack{i,j=1, \\ i \leqslant j}}^{l} (h_i'', h_j'')^{\beta_{ij}} r^{-p} \rho^{-q},$$

where $m \leqslant l, \quad p \geqslant 1, \quad q \geqslant 1,$

$$\sum_{i=1}^{l} \alpha_i + 2 \sum_{\substack{i,j=1 \\ i \leqslant j}} \beta_{ij} = l, \qquad \sum_{i=1}^{l} \alpha_i = \theta,$$

$$p + q = l + \theta, \qquad \theta \leqslant l,$$

α_i, β_{ij} being non-negative integer numbers. The following estimate is valid for the norm of l-th derivative

$$|w^{(l)}(x)| \leqslant c(l) \left(\frac{R}{\rho}\right)^{l} \rho^{-l} \tag{6}$$

We'll use the following notations

$$A(\rho) = A(\rho, R, a) = \{x \in l_2, \ \rho \leqslant r(x, R, a) \leqslant 2\rho\},$$

$$A(\rho_1, \rho_2) = A(\rho_1, \rho_2, R, a) = \{x \in l_2, \ \rho_1 \leqslant r(x, R, a) \leqslant \rho_2\},$$

$$\mathring{A}(\rho) = \mathring{A}(\rho, R, a) = \{x \in l_2, \ r(x, R, a) \geqslant \rho\},$$

$$S(\varepsilon, R, a) = S(R+\varepsilon, a) \setminus S(R, a),$$

$$\hat{S}(\rho, a') = \{x \in l_2, \ |x' - a'| \leqslant \rho\},$$

$$F(h,\rho)=F(h,\rho,R,a)=\{x\in l_2,\ r(x)\leqslant |a'-x'|\leqslant r(x)+h,\quad x\in A(\rho)\},$$

$$G(h,\rho)=G(h,\rho,R,a)=\{x\in l_2,\ r(x)-h\leqslant |a'-x'|\leqslant r(x),\quad x\in A(\rho)\},$$

$F(h,\rho_1,\rho_2)$, $G(h,\rho_1,\rho_2)$ and $F^0(h,\rho)$, $G^0(h,\rho)$ will denote sets which differ from the sets $F(h,\rho)$, $G(h,\rho)$ by substitution in their definitions $A(\rho_1,\rho_2)$ instead of $A(\rho)$ and $A^0(\rho)$ instead $A(\rho)$. $\mathcal{J}_B(x)$ will be the indicator of set B .

Further, regarding spaces E^k we'll put $k=6$. For any distribution P we denote P' it's projection on E^6 . We'll often use the estimate

$$P_n(\hat{s}(\rho,a'))=P_n'(s(\rho,a'))\leqslant c\rho^6$$

which is valid for $\rho\geqslant\{\tau_R n^{-1/2}\}^{1/6}$ and follows from known finite-dimensional estimates (s.f. [3]) and the estimate of normal measure of cylinder $\hat{s}(\rho,a')$. For fixed n we'll denote P_j the distribution of $(X_1+\ldots+X_j)n^{-1/2}$, $\tilde{P}_j$ the one of $(X_1+\ldots+X_j)j^{-1/2}$ and the analogous notations will be used for normal laws.

LEMMA 5. For any sphere $S(R,a)$ and $n\geqslant 2$ there exist such absolute constants K and C that for $\rho\geqslant\{\tau_R n^{-\frac{1}{2}}\}^{\frac{1}{6}}$ and $h\geqslant K(1+\rho^{-4})\tau_R n^{-1/2}$

$$P_n(F(h,\rho))\leqslant C\max(h^5,\rho^5)h, \tag{7}$$

$$P_n(G(h,\rho))\leqslant C\max(h^5,\rho^5)h. \tag{8}$$

LEMMA 6. For any sphere $S(R,a)$ and $n\geqslant 2$ there exist such absolute constants K and C that for $\rho\geqslant\{\tau_R n^{-1/2}\}$ and $h\geqslant K\tau_R n^{-1/2}$

$$P_n(F^0(h,\rho))\leqslant Ch, \tag{9}$$

$$P_n(G^0(h,\rho))\leqslant Ch. \tag{10}$$

Let $S(R,a)$ be a certain sphere in ℓ_2. Put $\varepsilon_0 = c_0 \tau_R n^{-1/2}$ where c_0 is considerably large absolute constant and regard the function $f_\varepsilon(x,R,a)$ defined by (1), where $\varepsilon = \varepsilon(\tau) = \{(\varepsilon_0 \tau^{-\alpha})^2 + \varepsilon_0^2\}^{1/2}$, $4 < \alpha < 5$.

LEMMA 7. For $n \geq 2$

$$\int_{A^0(\rho_0)} |\chi_{S(R,a)}(x) - f_\varepsilon(x,R,a)| P_n(dx) \leq c\tau_R n^{-1/2},$$

$$\int_{A^0(\rho_0)} |\chi_{S(R,a)}(x) - f_\varepsilon(x,R,a)| H(dx) \leq c\tau_R n^{-1/2},$$

where $\rho_0 = \varepsilon_0^{1/6}$.

Proofs of these lemmas aren't very difficult but take a lot of space (especially those of lemmas 2, 5 and 6) so they are omited.

PROOF OF THEOREM. In this proof we we'll usually prefer the simplicity of presentation to the exactness of estimates. It won't influence the final result as we aren't estimating absolute constants. Let $S(R,a)$ be a certain sphere in ℓ_2. As earlier we put $\rho_0 = \varepsilon_0^{1/6}$, $\varepsilon_0 = c_0 \tau_R n^{-1/2}$. We consider ε_0 being less that any fixed constant otherwise the estimate of theorem is obvious. Without losses in generality $R \geq c\rho_0$, where C is large enough otherwise

$$P_n(S(R,a)) \leq P_n(\hat{S}(R,a')) = P_n'(S(R,a')) \leq c\rho_0^6 = c\varepsilon_0$$

and the same estimate is valid for $H(S(R,a))$, from where the assertion of Theorem follows.

Introduce the function

$$w(x) = w(x,R,a) = \begin{cases} 0, & \tau(x) \leq \rho, \\ \xi((\tau(x) - \rho_0)/\rho_0), & \rho \leq \tau(x) \leq 2\rho, \\ 1, & \tau(x) \geq 2\rho_0, \end{cases}$$

and use the es imate

$$|P_n(S(R,a)) - H(S(R,a))| \leq |\int \chi_{S(R,a)}(x)\, w(x)(P_n - H_n)(dx)| + |\int \chi_{S(R,a)}(x)(1 - w(x))(P_n - H_n)(dx)|. \tag{11}$$

The integrand in the second term is non-zero only if $r(x,R,a) \leq 2\rho_0$ and $|x'-a'|^2 \leq R^2 - |x''-a''|^2 = r^2(x,R,a)$, i.e. it is non-zero on $\hat{S}(2\rho_0, a')$. As we've just seen P_n- and H-measures of this cylinder are less than $c\varepsilon_0$, so the second term in the right-hand side of (11) isn't greater than $c\varepsilon_0$. From Lemma 7 it follows that the first term in the right-hand side of (11) isn't greater than

$$c\varepsilon_0 + |\int (wf_\varepsilon)(x,R,a)(P_n - H_n)(dx)|.$$

So

$$|P_n(S(R,a)) - H(S(R,a))| \leq c\varepsilon_0 + |\int (wf_\varepsilon)(x,R,a)(P_n - H_n)(dx)| = c\varepsilon_0 + |\mathcal{J}|.$$

Let n be sufficiently large number. It is easily seen that

$$P_n - H_n = \sum_{i,j,k=0}^{m} (P_1 - H_1)^{*3} * H_{i+j+k} * P_{n-(i+j+k)-3} + H_{m+1} * P_{n-3m-3} * (P_{m+1} - H_{m+1})^{*2} + H_{m+1} * P_{n-2m-2} * (P_{m+1} - H_{m+1}) + H_{m+1} * (P_{n-m-1} - H_{n-m-1})$$

for any $m \leq (n-3)/3$. So, $\mathcal{J}$ can be presented as sum of values

$$\mathcal{J}_{ijk} = \int (wf_\varepsilon)(x)(P_1 - H_1)^{*3} * H_{i+j+k} * P_{n-(i+j+k)-3}(dx),$$

$$\mathcal{J}^1 = \int (wf_\varepsilon)(x)\, H_{m+1} * P_{n-3m-3} * (P_{m+1} - H_{m+1})^{*2}(dx),$$

$$\mathcal{J}^2 = \int (wf_\varepsilon)(x)\, H_{m+1} * P_{n-2m-2} * (P_{m+1} - H_{m+1})(dx),$$

$$\mathcal{J}^3 = \int (wf_\varepsilon)(x)\, H_{m+1} * (P_{n-m-1} - H_{n-m-1})(dx).$$

It is easy to see that

$$\mathcal{J}_{ijk} = \int \{ \int (wf_\varepsilon)(x+y, R, a)(P_1 - H_1)^{*3} * \Phi_{i+j+k} * \\ * P_{n-(i+j+k)-3}(dx) \} \, Q_{i+j+k}(dy). \qquad (12)$$

Here and further we denote Q the normal distribution such that $H = \Phi * Q$. The fact of existence of Q is obvious, it is normal law in l_2 with zero sixth eigen value.

From the properties of functions f and r we see that inner integral in (12) equals

$$\hat{\mathcal{J}}_{ijk} = \int (wf_\varepsilon)(x, R, b)(P_1 - H_1)^{*3} * \Phi_{i+j+k} * P_{n-(i+j+k)-3}(dx)$$

where $b = a - y$. It is clear, that

$$\hat{\mathcal{J}}_{ijk} = \int \{ \int w(x+t) f_\varepsilon(x+t)\, \Phi_{i+j+k}(dt) \} (P_1 - H_1)^{*3} * P_{n-(i+j+k)-3}(dx).$$

As $w(x+t)$ doesn't depend from $t \in E_6$, the inner integral in this expression is the product $w(x, R, b)$ by

$$\int f_\varepsilon(x+t)\, \Phi_{i+j+k}(dt) =$$

$$= \int \Phi^{x+t,\varepsilon}(S(R, b))\, \Phi_{i+j+k}(dt) =$$

$$= \int \Phi^{\varepsilon}(S(R, b - x - t))\, \Phi_{i+j+k}(dt) =$$

$$= \int \{ \int \chi_{S(R, b-x-t)}(z)\, \Phi^{\varepsilon}(dz) \} \, \Phi_{i+j+k}(dt) =$$

$$= \int \{ \int \mathcal{F}_{S(R,b-x)}(z+t)\, \Phi^{\varepsilon}(dz) \} \, \Phi_{i+j+k}(dt) =$$

$$= \int \mathcal{F}_{S(R,b-x)}(t)\, \Phi^{\varepsilon_{ijk}}(dt) =$$

$$= \Phi^{x,\varepsilon_{ijk}}(S(R,b)) = f_{ijk}(x,R,b),$$

where $\varepsilon_{ijk}^2 = \varepsilon^2(\tau) + (i+j+k)/n$. Now we see that

$$\hat{\mathfrak{I}}_{ijk} = \int \{ \int g(x,R,b-z)\, P_{n-(i+j+k)-3}(dz) \} (P_1 - H_1)^{*3}(dx),$$

where $g(x,R,b-z) = w(x,R,b-z) f_{ijk}(x,R,b-z)$.

Now from the definition of ζ_3 metric it isn't difficult to obtain the estimate

$$|\hat{\mathfrak{I}}_{ijk}| \leqslant \zeta_3^3(P, H)\, n^{-9/2} \times$$

$$\times \sup\{ | \int g^{(9)}(x,R,b-z)(h_1,h_2,\dots,h_9)\, P_{n-(i+j+k)-3}(dz) | : x \in l_2, |h_l| \leqslant 1, l = 1,\dots,9 \} =$$

$$= \zeta_3^3\, n^{-9/2} \times$$

$$\times \sup\{ | \int g^{(9)}(z,R,x)(h_1,h_2,\dots,h_9)\, P_{n-(i+j+k)-3}(dz) : x \in l_2, |h_l| \leqslant 1, l = 1,\dots,9 \}.$$

Let us estimate the value of

$$\int | g^{(9)}(z,R,x)(h_1,\dots,h_9) |\, P_{n-(i+j+k)-3}(dz) \qquad (13)$$

for arbitrary $x \in l_2$. Mark that function $w(z) \equiv 1$ on the set $\mathring{A}(2\rho_0,R,x)$ and $g^{(9)}(z,R,x) = f^{(9)}(z,R,x)$.

Define numbers

$$r_{ijk} = (\varepsilon_0/\delta_{ijk})^{\alpha^{-1}},$$

where $\delta_{ijk} = (\varepsilon_0^2 + (i+j+k)/n)^{1/2}$. If $r < r_{ijk}$ then $\varepsilon_0/r^\alpha > \delta_{ijk}$ and if $r > r_{ijk}$ then $\varepsilon_0/r^\alpha < \delta_{ijk}$. Always $r_{ijk} \leqslant 1$. It easy to see that there exist such c that $r_{ijk} \geqslant 2\rho_0$ as

$$m \leqslant cn(\varepsilon_0^{1-(\alpha/6)})^2. \tag{14}$$

Further we suppose that m satisfies (14). Note that $\varepsilon_{ijk}(r) \leqslant cr$ for $z \in \overset{o}{A}(2\rho_0)$. If $r \leqslant r_{ijk}$ the same follows from the fact that

$$\varepsilon_{ijk}(r) = ((\varepsilon_0/r^\alpha)^2 + \delta_{ijk}^2)^{1/2} \leqslant \sqrt{2}\,\varepsilon_0 r^{-\alpha} \qquad \text{and} \qquad \varepsilon_0 r^{-\alpha} < r.$$

The latter inequality is valid for all $r > \varepsilon_0^{1/(1+\alpha)}$ and moreover is valid for all $r > 2\rho_0$ as $\alpha < 5$. If $r > r_{ijk}$ the inequality $\varepsilon_{ijk}(r) \leqslant cr$ follows from inequalities

$$\varepsilon_{ijk}(r) \leqslant \sqrt{2}\,\varepsilon_0 r_{ijk}^{-\alpha} \leqslant \sqrt{2}\,\varepsilon_0 r_{ijk}^{-(\alpha+1)} r \leqslant \sqrt{2}\,\varepsilon_0 \rho_0^{-(1+\alpha)} r \leqslant cr.$$

Note that $\overset{o}{A}(2\rho_0) = A(2\rho_0, r_{ijk}) \cup \overset{o}{A}(r_{ijk})$. Define numbers $r_\varkappa = \rho_0 2^\varkappa$, $\varkappa = 1, \ldots, N$, where N is the smallest integer such that $r_N \geqslant r_{ijk}$. Let's regard the integral (13) on the set $A(r_\varkappa)$, $\varkappa = 1, \ldots, N-1$. Put $\delta = \max\{\varepsilon_{ijk}(v):\ r_\varkappa \leqslant v \leqslant 2r_\varkappa\}$. It is obvious that $\varepsilon_0 r_\varkappa^{-\alpha} \leqslant \delta < c\varepsilon_0 r_\varkappa^{-\alpha}$. Introduce sets $F_\nu = \bar{F}_\nu \setminus \bar{F}_{\nu-1}$, $G_\nu = \bar{G}_\nu \setminus \bar{G}_{\nu-1}$, $\nu = 2, 3, \ldots$, $F_1 = \bar{F}_1$, $G_1 = \bar{G}_1$, $\bar{F}_\nu = F(\nu\delta, r_\varkappa, R, x)$, $\bar{G}_\nu = G(\nu\delta, r_\varkappa, R, x)$, $\nu = 1, 2, \ldots$. Function $f_{ijk}^{(9)}(z, R, x)(h_1, \ldots, h_9)$ is the sum of values like

$$w(r)\, V_{9,p,\theta}(u''/r) \int_{S(r,u')} \varphi^\varepsilon(t)\, U_{9,q,\lambda}(t/\varepsilon, u'/\varepsilon)\, dt, \tag{15}$$

where $\varepsilon = \varepsilon_{ijk}(r(z, R, x))$, $r = r(z, R, x) = (R^2 - |u''|^2)^{1/2}$, $u = x - z$, functions $w(r)$ are bounded with our choice of $\varepsilon_{ijk}(r)$. For $|h_\ell| \leqslant 1$, $\ell = 1, \ldots, 9$, the value

$$|V_{g,p,\theta}| \leqslant |u'' r^{-1}|^{\theta} r^{-p} \leqslant (R r^{-1})^{\theta} r^{-p} \leqslant (R r^{-1})^{g} r^{-p}$$

and

$$|U_{g,q,\lambda}| \leqslant |t\varepsilon^{-1}|^{\gamma} |u'\varepsilon^{-1}|^{\lambda} \varepsilon^{-q}.$$

Preserving the density $\varphi^{\varepsilon}(t)$ as $c\varphi^{2\varepsilon}(t)e^{-c|t/\varepsilon|^2}$ we see that each of the values like (15) is less than

$$c(Rr^{-1})^{g} r^{-p} \varepsilon^{-q} |u'\varepsilon^{-1}|^{\lambda} \int_{S(r,u')} \varphi^{2\varepsilon}(t)\,dt, \tag{16}$$

$p+q=g, \quad \lambda \leqslant p.$

On the sets F_{ν}

$$r + (\nu - 1)\delta \leqslant |u'| \leqslant r + \nu\delta$$

and

$$\int_{S(r,u')} \varphi^{2\varepsilon}(t)\,dt \leqslant c \min(1, (r\varepsilon^{-1})^{6}) \exp\{-c(|u'| - r)^2 \varepsilon^{-2}\}$$

so on these sets the value of (16) is less than

$$c(Rr^{-1})^{g} r^{-p} \varepsilon^{-q} (r + \nu\delta)^{\lambda} \varepsilon^{-\lambda} \exp\{-c\delta^2(\nu-1)^2\varepsilon^{-2}\} \leqslant$$

$$\leqslant c(Rr_{\varkappa}^{-1})^{g} \delta^{-g} \nu^{g} \exp\{-c(\nu-1)^2\}. \tag{17}$$

As the right-hand side of (17) is independent from p, q, λ, θ the very same estimate is valid for derivative $|f^{(g)}(x)|$. In the same manner regarding sets G_{ν} we from (15) with integration over $S(r,u')$ substituted by integration over complement of $S(r,u')$ obtain the estimate

$$|f^{(g)}(x)| \leqslant c(Rr_{\varkappa}^{-1})^{g} \delta^{-g} \exp(-c(\nu-1)^2).$$

From these estimates it follows that integral (13) over the set $A(r_{\varkappa})$ is less than

$$c(Rr_{\text{æ}}^{-1})^9 \delta^{-9} \{ \sum_{\nu=1}^{\infty} \nu^9 \exp(-c(\nu-1)^2) P_{n-(i+j+k)-3}(\bar{F}_\nu) +$$

$$+ \sum_{\nu=1}^{\infty} \exp(-c(\nu-1)^2) P_{n-(i+j+k)-3}(\bar{G}_\nu)\}.$$

For any $c \geqslant 1$

$$P_{n-(i+j+k)-3}(\bar{F}_\nu) =$$

$$= \tilde{P}_{n-(i+j+k)-3}((n(n-(i+j+k)-3)^{-1})^{1/2} F(\nu\delta, r_{\text{æ}}, R, x)) =$$

$$= \tilde{P}_{n-(i+j+k)-3}((n(n-(i+j+k)-3)^{-1})^{1/2} F(c\nu\delta, r_{\text{æ}}, R, x)).$$

It is not difficult to see that with our choice of n and m there esists such c that for sets $\{n(n-(i+j+k)-3)^{-1}\}^{1/2} F(c\nu\delta, r_{\text{æ}}, R, x)$ for any æ and ν the conditions of Lemma 5 will be satisfied and we achieve the estimate

$$P_{n-(i+j+k)-3}(\bar{F}_\nu) \leqslant c\nu^6 \max(\delta^5, r_{\text{æ}}^5)\delta \leqslant c\nu^6 r_{\text{æ}}^5 \delta.$$

The very same estimate is true for the sets $\bar{G}_\nu$.

Now it is obvious that integral (13) over the set $A(r_{\text{æ}})$ is less than

$$cR^9 r_{\text{æ}}^{-4} \delta^{-8} \leqslant cR^9 r_{\text{æ}}^{8\alpha-4} \varepsilon_0^{-8}. \tag{18}$$

Having summed the right-hand side parts of (18) by $\text{æ} = 1, \ldots, N-1$ and taking into consideration the fact that $8\alpha - 4 > 0$ we obtain for integral (13) over the set $A(2\rho_0, r_{ijk})$ the estimate

$$cR^9 r_{ijk}^{8\alpha-4} \varepsilon_0^{-8}.$$

Using Lemma 6 instead of Lemma 5 after analogous considerations dealing with the set $\overset{\circ}{A}(r_{ijk})$ we obtain that integral (13) over the set $\overset{\circ}{A}(r_{ijk})$ is less than

$$cR^9 r_{ijk}^{-9} \varepsilon_{ijk}^{-8}(r_{ijk}) \leq cR^9 r_{ijk}^{-9} \delta_{ijk}^{-8}.$$

Now let's evaluate integral (13) over the set $A(\rho_0)$. We have to regard this case separately because the nineth derivative of the function $g = wf_{ijk}$ includes the summand $(w^{(9)}f_{ijk})(z)$ which doesn't tend to zero on the sets G_ν as $\nu \to \infty$. Define sets F_ν and $\bar{F}_\nu$ like it was done above, let $A(\rho_0) = (A(\rho_0) \cap S(R, x)) \cup (\bigcup_{\nu=1}^{\infty} F_\nu)$.

On sets F_ν we again have for any $|h_l| \leq 1$, $l = 1, \ldots, 9$, the estimate

$$|g^{(9)}(z)| \leq c(Rr^{-1})^9 \varepsilon^{-9} \nu^9 \exp(-c(\nu - c)^2)$$

where $\varepsilon = \varepsilon_{ijk}(\rho_0)$. The very same estimate (with $\nu = 1$) is valid on the set $A(\rho_0) \cap S(R, x)$. Because of the inclusion

$$A(\rho_0) \cap S(R, x) \subset \hat{s}(2\rho_0, x'),$$

$$F_\nu \subset \hat{s}(\nu\varepsilon + 2\rho_0, x').$$

We get for integral (13) over the set $A(\rho_0)$ the estimate

$$c(R\rho_0^{-1})^9 \varepsilon^{-9} \rho_0^6 \leq cR^9 \varepsilon_0^{-\gamma},$$

where $\gamma = 9 - (3\alpha - 1)/2$.

Now we can assert, that

$$|\hat{\mathcal{I}}_{ijk}| \leq cR^9 \varkappa_3 n^{-9/2} \{\varepsilon_0^{-\gamma} + r_{ijk}^{8\alpha-4} \varepsilon_0^{-8} + r_{ijk}^{-9} \delta_{ijk}^{-8}\}.$$

From the definition of r_{ijk} we can see that

$$|\hat{\mathcal{I}}_{ijk}| \leq cR^9 \varkappa_3 n^{-9/2} \{\varepsilon_0^{-\gamma} + \varepsilon_0^{-4/\alpha} \delta_{ijk}^{(4-8\alpha)/\alpha} + \varepsilon_0^{-9/\alpha} \delta_{ijk}^{9/\alpha - 8}\} =$$

$$= \mathcal{I}'_{ijk} + \mathcal{I}''_{ijk} + \mathcal{I}'''_{ijk}.$$

Further

$$\sum_{i,j,k=0}^{m} \mathcal{I}'_{ijk} \leq (m+1)^3 n^{-3} \varepsilon_0^{-\gamma} (R^3 \varkappa_3 / n^{1/2})^3.$$

As $mn^{-1} \leq c(\varepsilon_0^{(6-\alpha)/\alpha})^2$, we obtain that

$$\sum_{i,j,k=0}^{m} \mathcal{J}'_{ijk} \leq c\varepsilon_0^{(6-\alpha)-\gamma} \varepsilon_0^2 R^3 \varkappa_3 n^{-1/2}. \tag{19}$$

But $2-\gamma+6-\alpha>0$ if $\alpha>3$, i.e. the right-hand side of (19) is less than $cR^3\varkappa_3 n^{-1/2}$.

It is easily seen that

$$\sum_{i,j,k=1}^{m} \mathcal{J}'''_{ijk} \leq cR^3\varkappa_3 n^{-1/2} R^6 \varkappa_3^2 \sum_{i,j,k=1}^{\infty} \tau_R^{-4/\alpha} (i+j+k+\tau^2)^{(2-4\alpha)/\alpha} \leq$$

$$\leq cR^3\varkappa_3 n^{-1/2} R^6 \varkappa_3^2 \tau_R^{-4/\alpha} (\tau_R^2)^{(2-4\alpha)/\alpha+3} = cR^3\varkappa_3 n^{-1/2} R^6 \varkappa_3^2 \tau_R^{-2},$$

if $(4\alpha-2)/\alpha-3>0.$

It is easily seen that

$$\sum_{i,j,k=1}^{m} \mathcal{J}'''_{ijk} \leq cR^3\varkappa_3 n^{-1/2} R^6 \varkappa_3^2 \tau_R^{-2}$$

if $1-9/2\alpha>0.$

If $\alpha>\frac{9}{2}$ then sums of $\mathcal{J}''_{ij0}$ and $\mathcal{J}'''_{ij0}$, $1\leq i,j\leq m$, can be evaluated as

$$cR^3\varkappa_3 n^{-1/2} R^6 \varkappa_3^2 \tau_R^{-4}.$$

The same estimate is true for sums of $\mathcal{J}''_{i0k}$, $\mathcal{J}'''_{i0k}$, $1\leq i,k\leq m$, $\mathcal{J}''_{0jk}$, $\mathcal{J}'''_{0jk}$, $1\leq j,k\leq m$.

Sums of $\mathcal{J}''_{i00}$, $\mathcal{J}'''_{i00}$, $1\leq i\leq m$, $\mathcal{J}''_{0j0}$, $\mathcal{J}'''_{0j0}$, $1\leq j\leq m$, $\mathcal{J}''_{00k}$, $\mathcal{J}'''_{00k}$, $1\leq k\leq m$ are evaluated as

$$cR^3\varkappa_3 n^{-1/2} R^6 \varkappa_3^2 \tau_R^{-6}.$$

Because of estimates $R^3\varkappa_3\leq\tau_R$, $R^3\varkappa_3\leq\tau_R^2$, $R^3\varkappa_3\leq\tau_R^3$ all the above estimates are less than $c\varepsilon_0$.

Mark, that

$$\mathcal{J}'''_{000} \leq cR^9 \varepsilon_0^{-8} \beta_3^3 n^{-9/2} \qquad \text{and} \qquad \mathcal{J}'''_{000} \leq cR^9 \varepsilon_0^{-8} \beta_3^3 n^{-9/2}$$

so their sum is less than

$$c(R\beta_3^{1/3} n^{-1/2})^9 \varepsilon_0^{-8} \leq c\varepsilon_0.$$

It means that

$$\sum_{i,j,k=0}^{m} |\mathcal{J}_{ijk}| \leq c\varepsilon_0,$$

if $9/2 < \alpha < 5$.

Let's regard the value

$$\mathcal{J}^3 = \int (wf_\varepsilon)(x)\; H_{m+1} * (P_{n-m-1} - H_{n-m-1})(dx)$$

with $m = cn(\varepsilon_0^{1-\alpha/6})^2$. Difference of measures $P_{n-m-1} - H_{n-m-1}$ can be written as

$$P_{n-m-2k-1} * [(P_k - H_k)^{*2} + 2H_k * (P_k - H_k)] +$$

$$+ H_{2k} * (P_{n-m-2k} - H_{n-m-2k-1}),$$

$k < (n-m-1)/2$. So $\mathcal{J}^3 = \mathcal{J}_1^3 + 2\mathcal{J}_2^3 + \mathcal{J}_3^3$, where

$$\mathcal{J}_1^3 = \int (wf_\varepsilon)(x) H_{m+1} * P_{n-m-2k-1} * (P_k - H_k)^{*2}(dx),$$

$$\mathcal{J}_2^3 = \int (wf_\varepsilon)(x) H_{m+1} * H_k * P_{n-m-2k-1} * (P_k - H_k)(dx),$$

$$\mathcal{J}_3^3 = \int (wf_\varepsilon)(x) H_{m+1} * H_{2k} * (P_{n-m-2k-1} - H_{n-m-2k-1})(dx).$$

Estimate of $\mathcal{J}_1^3$ is reduced to one of the integrals

$$\int |(wf_{\varepsilon_{m+1}})^{(6)}(x)|\, P_{n-m-2k-1}(dx), \tag{20}$$

where $\varepsilon_{m+1}^2 = (\varepsilon_0 r^{-\alpha})^2 + \varepsilon_0^2 + (m+1)n^{-1}$ and $\delta \leq \varepsilon_{m+1}(r) \leq c\delta$, $\delta = ((m+1)n^{-1})^{1/2} \geq c\,\varepsilon_0^{1-\alpha/6}$, if $w(x) \neq 0$.

Define numbers $r_i = \rho_0 2^i$, $i = 1, \dots, N$ where N is the minimal integer number such that $r_N \geq 1$. Like it was shown above, we can see that integral (20) over the set $A(r_i)$ is less than

$$c(Rr_i^{-1})^6 \delta^{-6} r_i^5 \delta.$$

From this estimate it follows that integral (20) over the set $A(2\rho_0, r_N)$ is less (if $|h_l| \leq 1,\ l = 1, \ldots, 6$) than

$$cR^6 \rho_0^{-1} \delta^5.$$

Integral (20) over the set $A^0(r_N)$ is less than $cR^6\delta^{-5}$, and the same integral over the set $A(\rho_0)$ is less than $cR^6\delta^{-6}$

It means that

$$|\mathfrak{I}_1^3| \leq cR^6\delta^{-6} \varkappa_3^2(P_k, H_k) \leq$$

$$\leq c\delta^{-6}(kn^{-1})^2(R^3 \varkappa_3 n^{-1/2})^2 = c(\rho_0\delta^{-1})^6(kn^{-1})^2 R^3 \varkappa_3 n^{1/2}.$$

Let us take $k = [n(\delta\rho_0^{-1})^3]$, then $|\mathfrak{I}_1^3| \leq c\varepsilon_0$.

Put $n' = n - m - 2k - 1 - 2p$, $p = [n/4]$ and regard

$$\mathfrak{I}_3^3 = \int (wf_\varepsilon)(x) H_{m+1} * H_{2k} * (P_{n'+2p} - H_{n'+2p})(dx) = I_1 + 2I_2 + I_3,$$

where

$$I_1 = \int (wf_\varepsilon)(x) H_{2k+m+1} * P_{n'} * (P_p - H_p)^{*2}(dx),$$

$$I_2 = \int (wf_\varepsilon)(x) H_{2k+m+p+1} * P_{n'} * (P_p - H_p)(dx),$$

$$I_3 = \int (wf_\varepsilon)(x) H_{2k+2p+m+1} * (P_{n'} - H_{n'})(dx).$$

Estimation of I_1 can be reduced to estimation of

$$\int |(wf_{\varepsilon_{2k+m+1}})^{(6)}(x)| P_{n'}(dx), \tag{21}$$

where $\varepsilon^2_{2k+m+1}(r) = (\varepsilon_0 r^{-d})^2 + \varepsilon_0^2 + (2k+m+1)n^{-1}$ and $c\delta_1 \leq \varepsilon_{2k+m+1}(r) \leq \leq c\delta_1$, $\delta_1 = (k/n)^{1/2}$, if $w(x) \neq 0$. Let $r_i = \rho 2^i$, $i = 1, \ldots, N$, where N is the minimal integer number such that $r_N \geq \delta_1$. On the sets $A(r_i)$, $i = 1, \ldots, N-1$, the inequality $r(x) \leq c\delta_1$ is true.

Regard on $A(r_i)$ the sets

$$F_j = \bar{F}_j \setminus \bar{F}_{j-1}, \qquad G_j = \bar{G}_j \setminus \bar{G}_{j-1}, \qquad j = 2,3,\dots, \qquad F_1 = \bar{F}_1,$$

$$G_1 = \bar{G}_1, \quad \bar{F}_j = F(j\delta_1, r_i), \quad \bar{G}_j = G(j\delta_1, r_i), \qquad j = 1,2,\dots .$$

Function $w(x) \equiv 1$ on the sets F_j and the absolute value of the derivative $|(wf)^{(6)}| = |f^{(6)}|$ is less than sum of terms like

$$c(Rr^{-1})^6 r^{-p} \delta_1^{-q} ((2r_i + j\delta_1)/\delta_1)^{\lambda} (r\delta_1^{-1})^6 \exp(-c(j-c)^3)$$

($|h_l| \leqslant 1,\ l = 1,\dots,6$). The coefficient $(r\delta_1^{-1})^6$ arises from the estimate

$$\int_{S(r,u')} \varphi^{2\varepsilon}(t)\,dt \leqslant c(r\varepsilon^{-1})^6 \exp\{-c(|u'| - r)^2 \varepsilon^{-2}\},$$

$\varepsilon = \varepsilon_{2k+m+1}$. The same estimate is true on sets G_j . Note that sets G_j are empty for all j beginning with certain number as $r \leqslant c\delta_1$. So, integral (21) over the set $A(r_i)$, $i = 1,\dots,N-1$, is less than $cR^6 r_i^{-6}$. So integral (21) over the set $A(2\varrho_0, r_N)$ is less than $cR^6 \varepsilon_0^{-1}$ and integral (21) over the set $A(\varrho_0)$ is also less than this value. Like above we can see that integral (21) over the set $A^0(r_N)$ is less than $cR^6 \delta_1^{-6}$.

Integral (21) over the whole space l_2 is less than $cR^6 \varepsilon_0^{-1}$ as $\delta_1 \geqslant c(\delta \varrho_0^{-1})^{3/2} = c(\varepsilon_0^{1-\alpha/6} \varepsilon_0^{-1/6})^{3/2} = c(\varepsilon_0^{(5-\alpha)/6})^{3/2} \geqslant c\varepsilon_0^{1/6} = c\varrho_0$. Consequently,

$$|I_1| \leqslant cR^6 \varepsilon_0^{-1} (\varkappa_3 n^{-1/2})^2 \leqslant c\varepsilon_0 .$$

Estimation of I_2 and I_3 isn't difficult because normal laws $H_{2k+m+p+1}$ and $H_{2k+2p+m+1}$ include heavy normal component Φ_p, $p = [n/4]$. Estimates

$$|\mathcal{J}^1| \leqslant c\varepsilon_0 \qquad \text{and} \qquad |\mathcal{J}^2| \leqslant c\varepsilon_0$$

are achieved in the same manner.

When proving the theorem we supposed that $n \geqslant c$. The assertion of the Theorem when $n \leqslant c$ is obvious, as $\tau_R \geqslant \mu$.

Baykal'skaya 43-10
Moscow 107589
USSR

REFERENCES

1. Zolotarev V.M. Modern theory of summing of independent random variables. M., Nauka, 1984, 416 p.
2. Senatov V.V. On the orders of the convergence rate in the central limit theorem in the Hilbert space.- In: Stability problems for stochastic models. M., The institute for systems stidies, 1984, 128-135.
3. Senatov V.V. Several uniform estimates of the rate of convergence in the multi-dimensional central limit theorem.- Teor.Verojatn Primen., 25, 1980, 557-770 (in Russian).
4. Götze F. Asymptotic expansion for bivariate von Mises functionals.- Z.Wahrscheinlichkeitstheor. verb.Geb., B50, 1979, H3, 333-335.
5. Yurinskii V.V. On the accuracy of Gaussian approximation for the probability of hitting a ball.- Teor. Verojatn. Primen., 27, 1982, 270-278 (in Russian).
6. Osipov L.V., Rotar' V.I. On multidimensional central limit theorem. Theor. Verojatn. Primen., 29, 1984, 366-373 (in Russian).
7. Nagaev S.V. Speed of convergence to the normal law in Hilbert space. Teor. Verojatn. Primen., 30, 1985, 19-32 (in Russian).

STABILITY OF DECOMPOSITION IN SEMIGROUPS OF FUNCTIONS REPRESENTABLE BY SERIES IN THE JACOBI POLYNOMIALS

I.P.Trukhina and G.P.Chistyakov

Let $P_k^{(\alpha,\beta)}(x)$ $(\alpha, \beta > -1;\ k = 0, 1, \dots)$ be Jacobi polynomials ([1] p.70) normalized by the relation $P_k^{(\alpha,\beta)}(1) = 1$. Gasper [2] proved that if the pair (α, β) belongs to the set

$$V = \{(\alpha,\beta):\ \alpha \geqslant \beta > -1,\quad u(u+5)(u+3)^2 \geqslant (u^2 - 7u - 24)v^2\},$$

where $u = \alpha + \beta + 1$, $v = \alpha - \beta$, then

$$P_n^{(\alpha,\beta)}(x) P_m^{(\alpha,\beta)}(x) = \sum_k g(k,n,m) P_k^{(\alpha,\beta)}(x), \quad g(k,n,m) \geqslant 0. \tag{1}$$

It will be assumed below that $(\alpha,\beta) \in V \setminus \{(-\frac{1}{2}, -\frac{1}{2})\}$.
Note that ([1] , p.175)

$$|P_k^{(\alpha,\beta)}(x)| \leqslant 1, \qquad x \in [-1, 1] \tag{2}$$

Denote by $\mathcal{P}_{\alpha,\beta}$ the set of functions $f(x)$ representable for $-1 \leqslant x \leqslant 1$ as

$$f(x) = \sum_{k=0}^{\infty} c_k P_k^{(\alpha,\beta)}(x), \qquad c_k \geqslant 0, \qquad \sum_{k=0}^{\infty} c_k = 1.$$

It follows from (1) that $\mathcal{P}_{\alpha,\beta}$ is a semogroup under multiplication.

The semogroup $\mathcal{P}_{\alpha,\beta}$ has been considered by Schoenberg [3] , Kennedy [4] , Singham [5] , and Schwartz [6] . Schoenberg [3] showed that when $\alpha = \beta = (n-2)/2$ ($n \geqslant 2$ is an integer), the semigroup $\mathcal{P}_{\alpha,\beta}$ is isomorphic to the semigroup of positive definite functions on the n-dimensional sphere. I.V.Ostrovski and I.P.Trukhina [7, 8] described the class $I_0(\mathcal{P}_{\alpha,\beta})$ of functions from $\mathcal{P}_{\alpha,\beta}$, having no indecomposable factors in $\mathcal{P}_{\alpha,\beta}$:

$$I_0(\mathcal{P}_{\alpha,\alpha}) = \{\exp(a(x-1) + b(x^2-1)) : \ a \geqslant 0, \ b \geqslant 0\},$$

$$I_0(\mathcal{P}_{\alpha,\beta}) = \{\exp(a(x-1)) : \ a \geqslant 0\}, \qquad \alpha \neq \beta.$$

Stability of decompositions of functions of the class $I_0(\mathcal{P}_{\alpha,\beta})$ was studied in [9] . Let us introduce, following V.M.Zolotarev [10], the characteristic of stability of decompositions of elements from $\mathcal{P}_{\alpha,\beta}$:

$$\beta_\rho^{(\alpha,\beta)}(\varepsilon,\varphi) = \sup_{\{f:\ \rho(f,\varphi)\leqslant\varepsilon\}} \ \sup_{f_1\in K_f} \ \inf_{\varphi_1\in K_\varphi} \rho(f_1,\varphi_1),$$

where $\rho(f,\varphi) = \max_{-1\leqslant x\leqslant 1} |f(x) - \varphi(x)|$ and K_f is the set of factors of the function $f(x) \in \mathcal{P}_{\alpha,\beta}$. In [9] the following results were obtained.

THEOREM 1. Valid are the inequalities $(m = 1, 2)$:

$$A_1[\ln\ln(\varepsilon^{-1})]/\ln(\varepsilon^{-1}) \leqslant \beta_\rho^{(\alpha,\beta)}(\varepsilon, \exp(a(x^m-1))) \leqslant$$
$$\leqslant A_2[\ln\ln(\varepsilon^{-1})]/\ln(\varepsilon^{-1}), \quad a>0.$$

THEOREM 2. Valid are the inequalities $(a>0, \ b>0)$:

$$A_3[\ln\ln(\varepsilon^{-1})]/\ln(\varepsilon^{-1}) \leqslant$$
$$\leqslant \beta_\rho^{(\alpha,\alpha)}(\varepsilon, \exp(a(x-1)+b(x^2-1))) \leqslant$$
$$\leqslant A_4\{[\ln\ln(\varepsilon^{-1})]/\ln(\varepsilon^{-1})\}^{1/4}.$$

Here and below A_i, B_i and C_i will denote positive quantities depending only on a, b, α, β.

Note that the upper estimate in Theorem 1 can also be obtained proceeding from results of [11] .

Theorem 1 gives estimates of the stability of decompositions of elements of the class $I_0(\mathcal{P}_{\alpha,\beta})$, $\alpha \neq \beta$ and of elements of a special form of the class $I_0(\mathcal{P}_{\alpha,\alpha})$, accurate to the order of magnitude. For elements of $I_0(\mathcal{P}_{\alpha,\alpha})$ of the general form, Theorem 2 gives bilateral estimates of the decomposition stability close to those accurate to the order of magnitude. In this paper we shall present order-of-magnitude accurate estimates of the stability of decompositions of elements of the general form of the class $I_0(\mathcal{P}_{\alpha,\alpha})$. We shall prove the following

THEOREM. The following inequalities are true $(a>0,\ b>0)$:

$$A_5\{[\ln\ln(\varepsilon^{-1})]/\ln(\varepsilon^{-1})\}^{2/5} \leq \beta_\rho^{(\alpha,\alpha)}(\varepsilon, \exp(a(x-1)+b(x^2-1))) \leq$$

$$\leq A_6\{[\ln\ln(\varepsilon^{-1})]/\ln(\varepsilon^{-1})\}^{2/5}.$$

It is sufficient to prove this theorem for small ε, $0<\varepsilon<$ $<\varepsilon_0(a, b, \alpha)$.

1. Proof of the upper estimate

We shall show that the upper estimate may be obtained by using the estimated stabilities of decompositions of lattice infinitely divisible distribution laws (i.d.d.l.) obtained in [11] .

Denote $(a>0,\ b>0)$

$$\varphi(x) = \exp\{a(x-1)+b(x^2-1)\} = \sum_{k=0}^{\infty} \alpha_k P_k^{(\alpha,\alpha)}(x).$$

Let

$$f(x) = \sum_{k=0}^{\infty} c_k P_k^{(\alpha,\alpha)}(x) \in \mathcal{P}_{\alpha,\alpha},$$

$$f_j(x) = \sum_{k=0}^{\infty} a_{kj} P_k^{(\alpha,\alpha)}(x) \in \mathcal{P}_{\alpha,\alpha}, \quad j = 1, 2,$$

$$f(x) = f_1(x) f_2(x).$$

And let the following inequality be true:

$$|f(x) - \varphi(x)| \leq \varepsilon, \quad -1 \leq x \leq 1.$$

Denote by $N = N(\varepsilon)$ the integer defined by the inequality $(N-1)^{N-1} \leq \varepsilon^{-1} \leq N^N$. Put $(j = 1, 2)$

$$f_j^*(x) = \sum_{k=0}^{N-1} a_{kj} P_k^{(\alpha,\alpha)}(x) \Big/ \sum_{k=0}^{N-1} a_{kj},$$

$$f^*(x) = f_1^*(x) f_2^*(x).$$

Evidently, $f_j^*(x), f^*(x) \in \mathcal{P}_{\alpha,\alpha}$. We shall need the following facts.

LEMMA 1.1. [1, p.105]. $P_k^{(\alpha,\alpha)} \cos(\theta)$ is a trigonometric cosine-polynomial of the order k with nonnegative coefficients.

LEMMA 1.2 [9]. For all $x \in [-1, 1]$

$$|f^*(x) - \varphi(x)| \leq B_1^N / N^{N/2}, \tag{1.1}$$

$$|f_j^*(x) - f_j(x)| \leq B_2^N / N^{N/2} \tag{1.2}$$

and the estimates

$$\alpha_k \leq B_3^k / k^{k/2} \tag{1.3}$$

are true.

It follows from Lemma 1.1 that the functions $f_j^*(\cos\theta)$ are characteristic functions (ch.f.) of the symmetric integer-valued d.l. F_{jN}, whose spectra $S(F_{jN})$ lie on the interval $[-N, N]$ and the function $\varphi(\cos\theta)$ is the ch.f. of the symmetric integer-valued i.d.d.l. F of the Yu.V.Linnik's class $\mathcal{L}$ (for the definition of the class $\mathcal{L}$, see

[12] , p.129). Below it will be convenient to denote, as usual, the ch. f.d.l. F_{jN}, F by $\varphi(\theta, F_{jN})$, $\varphi(\theta, F)$. Note that the function $\varphi(\theta, F)$ because of Lemma 1.1, may be represented as

$$\varphi(\theta, F) = \sum_{k=0}^{\infty} \alpha_k P_k^{(\alpha,\alpha)}(\cos\theta) = \sum_{l=0}^{\infty} \delta_l \cos l\theta,$$

where for the coefficients δ_l , as is easy to see,

$$\delta_l \leq \sum_{k=l}^{\infty} \alpha_k . \tag{1.4}$$

Show that

$$Var(F_{1N} * F_{2N} - F) \leq B_4^N / N^{N/2}. \tag{1.5}$$

Using (1.3) and (1.4) find that

$$1 - F(2N) + F(-2N) \leq \sum_{l=2N}^{\infty} \delta_l \leq B_5^N / N^{N/2}.$$

By means of (1.1), we obtain the fact that the moduli of the magnitudes of jumps of the function of bounded variation $F_{1N} * F_{2N} - F$ on the segment $[-2N, 2N]$ calculated as the Fourier coefficients of the function $\varphi(\theta, F_{1N})\varphi(\theta, F_{2N}) - \varphi(\theta, F)$ do not exceed $2B_1^N / N^{N/2}$ Hence, noting that $S(F_{1N} * F_{2N}) \subset [-2N, 2N]$ we arrive at (1.5).

Apply now one of the results proved in [11] , on the stability of decompositions of lattice i.d.d.l. of the class $\mathcal{L}$.

THEOREM 3. Let F be an integral i.d.d.l. with the ch.f. $\varphi(\theta, F) = \varphi(\cos\theta)$ and let for the d.l. F_j, $j = 1, 2$, the following inequality be fulfilled:

$$|(F_1 * F_2)(x) - F(x)| \leq \varepsilon, \qquad x \in \mathbb{R}^1.$$

Then, there are the d.l. $\Lambda_j \in K_f$ (K_f is the class of components of the d.l. F), such that

$$\mathrm{Var}(F_j-\Lambda_j)\leq B\{[\ln\ln(\varepsilon^{-1})]/\ln(\varepsilon^{-1})\}^{2/5},\quad j=1,2,$$

where $B>0$ depends only on the d.l. F.

From this theorem, with account of the estimate (1.5) we conclude that there are the d.l. $\Lambda_j\in K_f$ such that

$$\mathrm{Var}(F_{jN}-\Lambda_j)\leq B_6\,N^{-2/5},\quad j=1,2. \tag{1.6}$$

From (1.6) it follows that

$$|\varphi(\theta,F_{jN})-\varphi(\theta,\Lambda_j)|\leq B_6 N^{-2/5}. \tag{1.7}$$

Let us show that the ch.f. $\varphi(\theta,\Lambda_j)$ does not differ much from a ch.f. of the symmetric d.l. The ch.f. of the d.l. Λ_j is known to be

$$\varphi(\theta,\Lambda_j)=\exp\{i\beta_j\theta+\gamma_{-2j}(e^{-2i\theta}-1)+\gamma_{-1j}(e^{-i\theta}-1)+$$
$$+\gamma_{1j}(e^{i\theta}-1)+\gamma_{2j}(e^{2i\theta}-1)\},$$

where $\beta_j\in\mathbb{R}^1$, $0\leq\gamma_{\pm1j}\leq a/2$, $0\leq\gamma_{\pm2j}\leq b/4$. Since the ch.f. $\varphi(\theta,F_{jN})$ are real-valued, then (1.7) leads to the following inequality for all $\theta\in\mathbb{R}^1$:

$$|\sin(\beta_j\theta+(\gamma_{1j}-\gamma_{-1j})\sin\theta+(\gamma_{2j}-\gamma_{-2j})\sin2\theta)|\leq B_7 N^{-2/5}. \tag{1.8}$$

We shall show first that $\beta_j=0$, $j=1,2$. Let $\beta_j\neq0$. Then, under the sine sign in (1.8) there is a continuous function tending to ∞ as $\theta\to\infty$. Therefore, for a certain θ the left-hand side of (1.8) is equal to unity, which is impossible, by (1.8). If now $\gamma_{1j}-\gamma_{-1j}$ and $\gamma_{2j}-\gamma_{-2j}$ have like signs, then (1.8) leads for sufficiently small θ to

$$|\gamma_{1j}-\gamma_{-1j}|+|\gamma_{2j}-\gamma_{-2j}|\leq B_9\,N^{-2/5}. \tag{1.9}$$

If the signs of these parameters are opposite, then (1.9) follows from (1.8), if put $\theta = \pi + \psi$, where $\psi > 0$ is sufficiently small. Using (1.9) and the inequality $|e^z - 1| \leq |z| e^{|z|}$ find now

$$|\varphi(\theta, \Lambda_j) - \exp\{2\gamma_{1j}(\cos\theta - 1) + \\ + 2\gamma_{2j}(\cos 2\theta - 1)\}| \leq B_{10} N^{-2/5}. \quad (1.10)$$

Using (1.2), (1.7) and (1.10) find finally for $x \in [-1, 1]$

$$|f_j(x) - \exp\{2\gamma_{1j}(x - 1) + 4\gamma_{2j}(x^2 - 1)\}| \leq B_{11} N^{-2/5}.$$

Thus, the upper estimate is proved.

2. Proof of the lower estimate

To obtain the lower estimate, the authors developed further the method employed in [11] to prove the accuracy of estimates of stabilities of decompositions of lattice distributions on $\mathbb{R}^1$. To construct an example giving the lower estimate, introduce special form functions. Denote

$$\varphi_1(x) = \exp\{\frac{a}{2}(x - 1) - \gamma n^{-4/5}(x^2 - 1) + n^{-2}(x^4 - 1) + n^{-4}(x^6 - 1)\},$$

$$\varphi_2(x) = \exp\{\frac{a}{2}(x - 1) + (b + \gamma n^{-4/5})(x^2 - 1) - n^{-2}(x^4 - 1) - n^{-4}(x^6 - 1)\},$$

where $n \geq 1$, $0 < \gamma < 1$. Represent the functions $\varphi_j(x)$, $j = 1, 2$, as

$$\varphi_j(x) = \sum_{k=0}^{\infty} s_{kj} P_k^{(\alpha, \alpha)}(x),$$

$$s_{kj} = s_{kj}(a, b, n, \gamma, \alpha).$$

Show that sufficiently many coefficients s_{kj} are nonnegative.

LEMMA 2.1. For any $a > 0$ there exist the positive quantities k_0, n_0, d and γ, depending only on a and such that $s_{k1}(a, n,$

$\gamma, \alpha) \geqslant 0$, if $n \geqslant n_0$, $k_0 \leqslant k \leqslant dn^2$.

PROOF. The coefficients s_{kj} $(j=1,2)$ can be calculated as follows (see [1] , formulae (9.2.3) and (4.1.1)):

$$s_{kj} = -iH_1(k,\alpha)\int_{|y|=r} (y^2-1)^{\alpha} Q_k^{(\alpha,\alpha)}(y)\varphi_j(y)dy,$$

where $r>1$, $H_1(k,\alpha)$ is a positive quantity depending only on k and α ; and $Q_k^{(\alpha,\alpha)}(y)$ are Jacobi functions of the second kind that are expressed via the hypergeometrical function $F(A,B,C,z)$ by the formula ([1] , Eg. (4.61.5))

$$Q_k^{(\alpha,\alpha)}(y) = 2^{k+2\alpha}[\Gamma(k+\alpha+1)]^2[\Gamma(2k+2\alpha+2)]^{-1}(y-1)^{-k-\alpha-1} \times$$

$$\times (y+1)^{-\alpha} F(k+1, k+\alpha+1, 2k+2\alpha+2, 2/(1-y)).$$

By using the square transform formula ([13] , § 2.11, (2.8))

$$F(A,B,2B,z) = (1-z/2)^{-A} F\left(\frac{A}{2}, \frac{A+1}{2}, B+\frac{1}{2}, \frac{z^2}{(2-z)^2}\right),$$

find

$$s_{kj} = -iH_2(k,\alpha)\int_{|y|=r} \varphi_j(r) y^{-k-1} F(\lambda,\mu,\nu,y^{-2})dy,$$

where $\lambda=(k+1)/2$, $\mu=(k+2)/2$, $\nu=k+\alpha+3/2$, $H_2(k,\alpha)>0$.

Substituting in the latter integral $y=re^{i\theta}$, rewrite s_{kj} as

$$s_{kj} = H_2(k,\alpha)r^{-k}\varphi_j(r)\int_{-\pi}^{\pi} \varphi_j(re^{i\theta})(\varphi_j(r))^{-1}e^{-ik\theta}F(\lambda,\mu,\nu,r^{-2}e^{-2i\theta})d\theta =$$

$$= H_2(k,\alpha)r^{-k}\varphi_j(r)\int_{-\pi}^{\pi}\exp\{t_{kj}(r,\theta)\}F(\lambda,\mu,\nu,r^{-2}e^{-2i\theta})d\theta,$$

where

$$t_{k1}(r,\theta)=\frac{a}{2}r(\exp(i\theta)-1)-\gamma n^{-4/5}r^2(\exp(2i\theta)-1)+$$

$$+r^4n^{-2}(\exp(4i\theta)-1)+r^6n^{-4}(\exp(6i\theta)-1)-ik\theta;$$

$$t_{k2}(r,\theta)=\frac{a}{2}r(\exp(i\theta)-1)+(b+\gamma n^{-4/5})r^2(\exp(2i\theta)-1)-$$

$$-r^4n^{-2}(\exp(4i\theta)-1)-r^6n^{-4}(\exp(6i\theta)-1)-ik\theta.$$

Since the coefficients s_{kj} are real,

$$s_{kj}=H_2(k,\alpha)r^{-k}\varphi_j(r)\int_{-\pi}^{\pi}T_{kj}(r,\theta)\,d\theta, \tag{2.1}$$

where

$$T_{kj}(r,\theta)=\exp\{\operatorname{Re}t_{kj}(r,\theta)\}\times$$

$$\times\operatorname{Re}[\exp\{i\operatorname{Im}t_{kj}(r,\theta)\}F(\lambda,\mu,\nu,r^{-2}e^{-2i\theta})].$$

To estimate the coefficients s_{k1}, choose in a special way the quantity $r=r(k)$. Denote

$$\psi(r)=\frac{a}{2}r-2\gamma n^{-4/5}r^2+4r^4n^{-2}+6r^6n^{-4},\qquad r\geq 0.$$

Clearly, if n is sufficiently large $(n\geq n_1(a))$, then $\psi'(r)\geq 0$ (below we shall assume all restrictions on the parameter n, arising in the course of the proof, to be valid). Therefore, $\psi(r)$ is an increasing function, and for any $k\geq 0$ the equation $\psi(r)=k$ has a unique solution which we denote by $r(k)$. If n is sufficiently large

$(n \geq n_2(a))$, then $\psi(r) \geq 6r^6 n^{-4}$ and thus $r(k)$ does not exceed the root of the equation $6r^6 n^{-4} = k$ i.e. $r(k) \leq (kn^4/6)^{1/6}$. Thus, for any d, $0 < d < 6$, if $k \leq dn^2$ then $r(k) \leq n$. Then, we shall believe that $k \leq dn^2$, where the number $d = d(a)$ will be chosen to be sufficiently small in the proof. It is easy to check that the following lower estimates are valid for $r(k)$:

$$\begin{aligned} r(k) &\geq k C_1^{-1}, \text{ if } k < \psi(n^{2/3}), \\ r(k) &\geq (C_1 d)^{-1/4} k^{1/2}, \text{ if } \psi(n^{2/3}) \leq k \leq dn^2. \end{aligned} \qquad (2.2)$$

Obtain some auxiliary inequalities for the hypergeometrical function by using the representation ([13] , § 2.1, (2)):

$$F(A, B, C, z) = \sum_{m=0}^{\infty} (A)_m (B)_m ((C)_m m!)^{-1} z^m, \qquad |z| < 1.$$

As is easy to see, if $A, B, C > 0$ then

$$|F(A, B, C, z)| \leq F(A, B, C, |z|), \qquad (2.3)$$

$$\operatorname{Re} F(A, B, C, z) \geq 2 - F(A, B, C, |z|). \qquad (2.4)$$

If moreover $C \geq B$, then

$$F(A, B, C, |z|) \leq \sum_{m=0}^{\infty} (A)_m (m!)^{-1} |z|^m = (1 - |z|)^{-A}. \qquad (2.5)$$

Now let us estimate the integral in (2.1). Show that there are d and k_1 depending on a, such that if $k_1 \leq k \leq dn^2$, then

$$F(\lambda, \mu, \nu, r^{-2}(k)) \leq 3/2. \qquad (2.6)$$

From inequality (2.5), including (2.2), we find that:

if $k \leq \psi(n^{2/3})$ and k is sufficiently large $(k \geq k_1(a))$ then

$$F(\lambda, \mu, \nu, r^{-2}(k)) \leq (1 - r^{-2}(k))^{-(k+1)/2} \leq$$
$$\leq (1 - C_1^2 k^{-2})^{-(k+1)/2} \leq 3/2;$$

if $k \geq \psi(n^{2/3})$, k is sufficiently large, and $d = d(a)$ is sufficiently small, then

$$F(\lambda, \mu, \nu, r^{-2}(k)) \leq (1 - (C_1 d)^{1/2} k^{-1})^{-(k+1)/2} \leq 3/2.$$

Inequality (2.6) is proved. Below d will denote the now chosen $d(a)$.

Denote $g(r) = \frac{a}{2} r + r^4 n^{-2} + r^6 n^{-4}$, $r \geq 0$. To estimate the integral $\int_{-\pi}^{\pi} T_{k1}(r(k), \theta)\, d\theta$, let us represent it as the sum integrals with respect to the sets Γ_i $(0 \leq i \leq 5)$ where

$$\Gamma_0 = \{\theta: \ |\theta| \leq \theta_0\}, \qquad \theta_0 = [g(r(k))]^{-5/12},$$

$$\Gamma_1 = \{\theta: \ \theta_0 < |\theta| < \pi/6\},$$

$$\Gamma_2 = \{\theta: \ |\theta \pm \pi/2| \leq \pi/10\},$$

$$\Gamma_3 = \{\theta: \ |\theta \pm m\pi/3| \leq \pi/10; \ m = 1,2\},$$

$$\Gamma_4 = \{\theta: \ 9\pi/10 \leq |\theta| \leq \pi\}, \qquad \Gamma_5 = [-\pi, \pi] \setminus \bigcup_{i=0}^{4} \Gamma_i$$

We shall estimate the integral with respect to Γ_0 from below and the moduli of the integrals with respect to Γ_i, $i > 0$, from above.

Let us first consider the integral with respect to Γ_0. Estimate the lower bound of the quantity

$$\mathrm{Re}\,[\exp\{i\,\mathrm{Im}\,t_{k1}(r(k), \theta)\}\, F(\lambda, \mu, \nu, r^{-2}(k) e^{-2i\theta})] =$$

$$= \cos[\mathrm{Im}\, t_{k1}(r(k), \theta)]\, \mathrm{Re}\, F(\lambda, \mu, \nu, r^{-2}(k)\, e^{-2i\theta}) - \qquad (2.7)$$

$$- \sin[\operatorname{Im} t_{k1}(r(k),\theta)] \operatorname{Im} F(\lambda,\mu,\nu, e^{-2i\theta} r^{-2}(k)).$$

From (2.3) and (2.6) it follows that for $\theta \in [-\pi, \pi]$, $k_1 \leq k \leq dn^2$

$$|\operatorname{Im} F(\lambda,\mu,\nu, r^{-2}(k)e^{-2i\theta})| \leq 3/2. \tag{2.8}$$

From (2.4) and (2.6), we find $(\theta \in [-\pi, \pi],\ k_1 \leq k \leq dn^2)$:

$$\operatorname{Re} F(\lambda,\mu,\nu, r^{-2}(k)e^{-2i\theta}) \geq 1/2. \tag{2.9}$$

Estimate the quantity

$$\operatorname{Im} t_{k1}(r(k),\theta) = \frac{a}{2} r(k)\sin\theta - \gamma n^{-4/5} r^2(k)\sin 2\theta + \\ + r^4(k) n^{-2}\sin 4\theta + r^6(k) n^{-4}\sin 6\theta - k\theta.$$

Clearly, the function $\operatorname{Im} t_{k1}(r(k),\theta)$ and its second derivative are, for $\theta = 0$, equal to zero, because of oddness, and the first derivative is, for $\theta = 0$, equal to zero, by the definition of the parameter $r(k)$. Therefore, for a certain θ_1; $0 \leq \theta_1 \leq \theta$,

$$|\operatorname{Im} t_{k1}(r(k),\theta)| = \frac{1}{6}\left|\frac{d^3}{d\theta^3}\operatorname{Im} t_{k1}(r(k),\theta)\Big|_{\theta=\theta_1} \theta^3\right| \leq$$

$$\leq \frac{1}{6}\left(\frac{a}{2} r(k) + 2^3\gamma r^2(k) n^{-4/5} + 4^3 r^4(k) n^{-2} + 6^3 r^6(k) n^{-4}\right)\theta^3.$$

It is easy to check that for sufficiently large n $(n \geq n_3(a))$

$$\frac{1}{6}\left(\frac{a}{2} r + 2^3\gamma r^2 n^{-4/5} + 4^3 r^4 n^{-2} + 6^3 r^6 n^{-4}\right) \leq 36 g(r)$$

Therefore, for $\theta \in \Gamma_0$,

$$|\operatorname{Im} t_{k1}(r(k),\theta)| \leq 36\,[g(r(k))]^{-1/4}. \tag{2.10}$$

Note that if $k \to \infty$, then $r(k) \to \infty$, and therefore, $g(r(k)) \to \infty$.

From (2.8) - (2.10) it follows that the quantity in (2.7) is bounded from below by a positive constant C_2, if $\theta \in \Gamma_0$, $k_2 \leqslant k \leqslant dn^2$ ($k_2 = k_2(a)$).

Let us estimate $\mathrm{Re}\, t_{k1}(r, \theta)$ from below. By using the inequality $|\sin\varphi| \leqslant |\varphi|$, find

$$\mathrm{Re}\, t_{k1}(r,\theta) = -(\arcsin^2\frac{\theta}{2} - 2\gamma n^{-4/5} r^2 \sin^2\theta + $$
$$+ 2r^4 n^{-2} \sin^2 2\theta + 2r^6 n^{-4} \sin^2 3\theta) \geqslant$$
$$\geqslant -(ar\frac{\theta^2}{4} + 8r^4 n^{-2}\theta^2 + 18 r^6 n^{-4} \theta^2) \geqslant -18\, g(r)\,\theta^2.$$

From the above obtained estimates it follows that

$$\int_{\Gamma_0} T_{k1}(r(k), \theta)\, d\theta \geqslant$$
$$\geqslant C_2 \int_{\Gamma_0} \exp\{-18\, g(r(k))\,\theta^2\}\, d\theta \geqslant \tag{2.11}$$
$$\geqslant \frac{1}{6} C_2 \,[g(r(k))]^{-1/2}, \qquad k_2 \leqslant k \leqslant dn^2.$$

Let now $\theta \in \Gamma_1$. Then by using the inequality $|\sin\varphi| \geqslant (\frac{2}{\pi}|\varphi|)$, $|\varphi| \leqslant \pi/2$, we find

$$\mathrm{Re}\, t_{k1}(r,\theta) \leqslant -\theta^2(\frac{a}{\pi^2} r - 2\gamma n^{-4/5} r^2 + 32 r^4 \pi^{-2} n^{-4} +$$
$$+ 72 r^6 \pi^{-2} n^{-4}) \leqslant -g(r)\,\theta^2/5, \qquad n \geqslant n_4(a).$$

Therefore, using (2.3) and (2.6), we obtain

$$\left|\int_{\Gamma_1} T_{k1}(r(k), \theta)\, d\theta\right| \leqslant$$
$$\leqslant \frac{3}{2} \int_{\Gamma_1} \exp\{-g(r(k))\theta^2/5\}\, d\theta \leqslant$$

$$\leq [g(r(k))]^{-1/2} \sigma(k), \qquad k_1 \leq k \leq dn^2, \tag{2.12}$$

where $\sigma(k) \to 0$ as $k \to \infty$.

Show that

$$\operatorname{Re} t_{k1}(r,\theta) \leq -C_3 r, \qquad \theta \in \Gamma_i, \quad 2 \leq i \leq 5, \tag{2.13}$$

and therefore

$$\left| \int_{\Gamma_i} T_{k1}(r(k),\theta)\,d\theta \right| \leq C_4 \exp\{-C_3 r(k)\}, \qquad k_1 \leq k \leq dn^2. \tag{2.14}$$

If $\theta \in \Gamma_2$, then

$$\operatorname{Re} t_{k1}(r,\theta) \leq -ar\sin^2\frac{\pi}{5} + 2\gamma n^{-4/5} r^2 - 2r^6 n^{-4} \sin^2\frac{6\pi}{5}.$$

Therefore, (2.13) is true for $C_3 < a\sin^2\frac{\pi}{5}$ and sufficiently small $\gamma = \gamma(a)$ (below γ will denote the now chosen $\gamma(a)$).

The estimate (2.13) is true for $i = 3$, because the function $\operatorname{Re} t_{k1}(r,\theta)$ on the set Γ_3 is estimated similarly, with the only difference that on Γ_3 it is $\sin^2 2\theta$ that is bounded from below by a positive constant, rather that $\sin^2 3\theta$, as was the case on the set Γ_2.

For $i = 4$, inequality (2.13) follows from the fact that for $r < C_5 n^{4/5}$ the inequality $-\frac{1}{2} ar\sin^2\frac{\theta}{2} + 2\gamma n^{-4/5} r^2 \sin^2 2\theta \leq 0$ is true, and for $r > C_5 n^{4/5}$

$$2\gamma n^{-4/5} r^2 \sin^2\theta - 2r^4 n^{-2} \sin^2 2\theta =$$

$$= 2\sin^2\theta\,(\gamma n^{-4/5} r^2 - 4r^4 n^{-2} \cos^2\theta) \leq 0, \qquad n \geq n_6(a).$$

If $\theta \in \Gamma_5$, then the estimate (2.13) is the more valid, because on Γ_5, both $\sin^2 2\theta$ and $\sin^2 3\theta$ are bounded from below by a positive constant. Thus, (2.14) is proved.

Put $n_0 = \max_{1 \le i \le 6} n_i$ with consideration for the estimates (2.11), (2.12) and (2.14), we conclude that for the d and γ chosen in the course of the proof,

$$s_{k1} \geq H_2(k, \alpha) r^{-k} \varphi_1(r) [\int_{\Gamma_0} T_{k1}(r(k), \theta) d\theta -$$
$$-\sum_{i=1}^{5} \int_{\Gamma_i} |T_{k1}(r(k), \theta)| d\theta] \geq 0,$$

if $n \geq n_0$, $k_0 \le k \le dn^2$ ($k_0 = \max\{k_1, k_2\}$). The lemma is proved.

LEMMA 2.2. There exist the constants a_0, b_0, $n_0(a, b) > 0$ and the quantities k_0, $d > 0$ depending on them, such that if $a \le a_0$, $b \le b_0$, $n \geq n_0$, $k_0 \le k \le dn^2$, then $s_{k2}(a, b, n, \gamma, d) \geq 0$ for any γ, $0 < \gamma < 1$.

PROOF. The proof of Lemma 2.2 is similar to that of Lemma 2.1 but is subject to some simplifications. We shall show the main points of the proof. As is easy to see, there exists $\delta_0 = \delta_0(b) > 0$ such that for $r < \delta_0 n$ the function $\psi(r)$ increases. For $k \le \psi(\delta_0 n)$ we denote the only solution of the equation $\psi(r) = k$ by $r(k)$. Estimate $r(k)$ from above and below. For any sufficiently small δ, there is $d(\delta, b)$ such that $\psi(\delta n) \geq dn^2$ and therefore, if $k \le dn^2$, then $r(k) \le \delta n$ (subsequently the number $\delta = \delta(b)$ will be chosen to be sufficiently small). Now, it is clear that there are the constants a_0, b_0 and n_0 and the quantity k_1, depending on them, such that $r(k) \geq (a_0/2 + 2b_0 + 2n_0^{-4/5})^{-1/2} \sqrt{k}$, if $a \le a_0$, $b \le b_0$, $n \geq n_0$, $k_1 \le k \le \psi(\delta_0 n)$. As a result, we find the following, for the said a, b, n and k and taking into account (2.5):

$$F(\lambda, \mu, \nu, r^{-2}(k)) \le [1 - (a_0/2 + 2b_0 + 2n_0^{-4/5})/k]^{-(k+1)/2} \le \frac{3}{2}. \tag{2.15}$$

Denote $g(r)=\frac{a}{2}r+(b+\gamma n^{-4/5})r^2$. Define Γ_0 and Γ_1 as in the proof of Lemma 2.1 and set $\Gamma_2=\{\theta:\ \pi/6\leq|\theta|\leq\pi\}$. Similarly to Lemma 2.1 check that there are sufficiently small $\delta=\delta(b)$ and $d=d(b)$ such that

$$|\mathrm{Im}(t_{k2}(r,\theta)|\leq 2g(r)\theta^3,\qquad r=r(k)\leq\delta n;$$

$$|\mathrm{Im}\,t_{k2}(r(k),\theta)|\leq 2[g(r(k))]^{-1/4},\qquad k\leq dn^2,\qquad \theta\in\Gamma_0;$$

$$-2g(r)\theta^2\leq \mathrm{Re}\,t_{k2}(r,\theta)\leq -g(r)\theta^2/5,\qquad |\theta|\leq\pi/6,\qquad r\leq\delta n.$$

Hence and from (2.15), follow the inequalities

$$\int_{\Gamma_0}T_{k2}(r(k),\theta)\,d\theta\geq C_6[g(r(k))]^{-1/2},\qquad k_2\leq k\leq dn^2;\tag{2.16}$$

$$\left|\int_{\Gamma_1}T_{k2}(r(k),\theta)\,d\theta\right|\leq C_7\exp\{-[g(r(k))]^{1/6}/5\},\qquad k_1\leq k\leq dn^2.\tag{2.17}$$

It is easy to check that

$$\mathrm{Re}\,t_{k2}(r,\theta)=-ar\sin^2\frac{\theta}{2}-2r^2\sin^2\theta\,[b+\gamma n^{-4/5}-r^2n^{-2}4\cos^2\theta-$$

$$-r^4n^{-4}(3-4\sin^2\theta)^2]\leq -ar\sin^2\frac{\theta}{2}\leq -C_8r,\qquad r\leq\delta n,\qquad \theta\in\Gamma_2;$$

and therefore,

$$\left|\int_{\Gamma_2}T_{k2}(r(k),\theta)\,d\theta\right|\leq C_9\exp\{-C_8r(k)\},\qquad k_1\leq k\leq dn^2.\tag{2.18}$$

From (2.16) - (2.18) follows the statement of the lemma.

LEMMA 2.3. For any $k_0 > 0$, there is $n_0 = n_0(k_0, \alpha)$ such that $s_{kj} \geq 0$ for $k \leq k_0$, $n \geq n_0$ and arbitrary $a, b > 0$, $\rho \in (0, 1)$.

$$u_1(x) = \exp\{\tfrac{a}{2}(x-1)\} = \sum_{k=0}^{\infty} \alpha_{k1} P_k^{(\alpha,\alpha)}(x),$$

$$u_2(x) = \exp\{\tfrac{a}{2}(x-1) + b(x^2-1)\} = \sum_{k=0}^{\infty} \alpha_{k2} P_k^{(\alpha,\alpha)}(x).$$

Since $u_j(x) \in \mathcal{P}_{\alpha,\alpha}$ then $\alpha_{kj} \geq 0$ $(j = 1,2)$. Show that $\alpha_{kj} > 0$. In view of orthogonality of the Jacobi polynomials,

$$\alpha_{kj} = H_3(k,\alpha) \int_{-1}^{1} u_j(x) P_k^{(\alpha,\alpha)}(x)(1-x^2)^{\alpha} dx,$$
$$H_3(k,\alpha) > 0. \tag{2.19}$$

By using the Rodrigues formula ([13] , § 10.8, (10)) and integrating k times by parts, find

$$\alpha_{k1} = H_4(k,\alpha)\, a^k \int_{-1}^{1} u_1(x)(1-x^2)^{\alpha} dx,$$

$$H_4(k,\alpha) > 0.$$

This representation suggests that $\alpha_{k1} > 0$. Denote

$$u_3(x) = \exp\{b(x^2-1)\} = \sum_{k=0}^{\infty} \alpha_{k3} P_k^{(\alpha,\alpha)}(x), \quad \alpha_{k3} \geq 0.$$

Compare the coefficients of $P_k^{(\alpha,\alpha)}(x)$ in the left- and right-hand sides of the inequality $u_2(x) = u_1(x) u_3(x)$. Applying Eg.(1) we find that $\alpha_{k2} = \alpha_{k1} \alpha_{03} + \ldots$, where the dots stand for the sum of nonnegative terms $\alpha_{\ell 1} \alpha_{m3}\, g(k, \ell, m)$. Since $\alpha_{k1} > 0$ and, as follows from (2.19), $\alpha_{03} > 0$, then $\alpha_{k2} > 0.$

By using the inequality $|e^z - 1| \leq |z| e^{|z|}$, we obtain the estimate

$|\varphi_j(x) - u_j(x)| \leq C_{10}\, n^{-4/5}, \quad x \in [-1, 1].$

Writing the coefficients s_{kj} by a formula similar to (2.19) and using (2), we see that $|s_{kj} - \alpha_{kj}| \leq H_5(k, \alpha)\, n^{-4/5}$. Hence, because the coefficients α_{kj} are positive, we arrive at the statement of the lemma.

Put $a_1 = \min\{a, a_0\}$, $b_1 = \min\{b, b_0\}$. Denote by $\varphi_j(x)$ $(j = 1, 2)$ the functions defined similarly to $\varphi_j(x)$ with a_1 and b_1 substituted for a and b. The coefficients of their series expansion by the Jacobi polynomials will be also denoted by $s_{kj} = s_{kj}(a_1, b_1, n, \gamma, \alpha)$. Introduce the function

$$q_j(x) = \sum_{k=0}^{[dn^2]} s_{kj} P_k^{(\alpha, \alpha)}(x) \Big/ \sum_{k=0}^{[dn^2]} s_{kj}.$$

(In the definitions of the functions $\tilde{\varphi}_j(x)$ and $q_j(x)$ the parameter γ is defined by Lemma 2.1 and the parameter d by Lemmas 2.1 and 2.2.) From Lemmas 2.1 - 2.3 follows

LEMMA 2.4. There is a quantity n_0 depending on a, b and α such that $q_j(x) \in \mathcal{P}_{\alpha, \alpha}$ for $n \geq n_0$.

Denote

$$q_3(x) - \exp\{(a - a_0)^+(x - 1) + (b - b_0)^+(x^2 - 1)\},$$

where $v^+ = \max\{v, 0\}$.

LEMMA 2.5. The following estimate is true

$$F(x) \equiv |q_1(x) q_2(x) q_3(x) - \exp\{(a-1) + b(x^2 - 1)\}| \leq n^{-C_{11} n^2}, \qquad x \in [-1, 1].$$

PROOF. The inequality is valid

$$F(x) \leq |q_1(x) q_2(x) - \tilde{\varphi}_1(x) \tilde{\varphi}_2(x)| \leq$$
$$\leq C_{12}(|q_1(x) - \tilde{\varphi}_1(x)| + |q_2(x) - \tilde{\varphi}_2(x)|). \tag{2.20}$$

Setting $x = 1$ in the definitions of the functions $\tilde{\varphi}_j(x)$, find that $\sum_{k=0}^{\infty} s_{kj} = 1$. Then, using (2), we can easily see that

$$|q_j(x) - \tilde{\varphi}_j(x)| \leqslant 2 \sum_{k > dn^2} s_{kj}.$$

Similarly to inequality (4.3) of [9], we find now that $|s_{kj}| \leqslant \leqslant C_{13}^{k} k^{-k/6}$. Therefore,

$$|q_j(x) - \tilde{\varphi}_j(x)| \leqslant n^{-C_{14} n^2}. \tag{2.21}$$

By applying this inequality to (2.20), we arrive at the statement of the lemma.

LEMMA 2.6. For any a_2, b_2 $(0 \leqslant a_2 \leqslant a,\ 0 \leqslant b_2 \leqslant b)$ the estimate is true:

$$\max_{-1 \leqslant x \leqslant 1} |q_1(x) - \exp\{a_2(x-1) + b_2(x^2-1)\}| \geqslant C_{15} n^{-4/5}.$$

PROOF. Denote

$$G(x) = |\tilde{\varphi}_1(x) - \exp\{a_2(x-1) + b_2(x^2-1)\}|.$$

Write a_2 as $a_2 = a_1/2 + \delta$. Clearly, if $\delta > -\gamma n^{-4/5}$, then $G(0) \geqslant \geqslant C_{16} n^{-4/5}$ for sufficiently large n, and if $\delta \leqslant -\gamma n^{-4/5}$ then $G(1) \geqslant C_{17} n^{-4/5}$. Therefore, $\max_{-1 \leqslant x \leqslant 1} G(x) \geqslant C_{18} n^{-4/5}$.

Hence, in view of (2.21), we arrive at the statement of the lemma.

From Lemmas 2.4 - 2.6, there follows the lower estimate in the theorem under proof.

Kharkov Univ., Dzrzinskii sg.4,
Kharkov 310077
USSR

Physical and Technical Inst.of
low temperature Acad. of Sci.
Ukr.SSR,
Lenin av. 47, Kharkov 310162
USSR

REFERENCES

1. Szegö G. Orthogonal Polynomials. N.Y., N.Y.: Amer.Math.Soc., 1959.
2. Gasper G. Linearization of the product of Jacobi polynomials.II .- Can.J.Math., 1970, v.22, N 3, 582-593.
3. Schoenberg I.J. Positive definite functions on spheres.- Duke Math. J., 1942, v.9, 96-108.
4. Kennedy M. A stochastic process associated with the ultraspherical polynomials.- Proc.Roy. Irish Acad., Sect.A 1961, v.61, 89-100.
5. Bingham N.H. Positive definite functions on spheres.- Proc.Camb. Phil.Soc., 1973, v.73, 145-156.
6. Schwartz A. Generalized convolutions and positive definite functions associated with general orthogonal series.- Pacific J.Math., 1974, v.55, N 2, 565-582.
7. Ostrovski I.V. and Trukhina I.P. On the arithmetics of Schoenberg-Kennedy semigroups.- In: Matem. Fizika i Funkzionalny Analiz. Trudy Nauchn.sem. Kiev: Naukova Dumka, 1976, 11-19 (in Russian).
8. Trukhina I.P. On semigroups of functions representable by series in the Jacobi polynomials.- Dokl.Akad.Nauk Ukr.SSR, ser.A, 1977, N 1, 11-19 (in Russian).
9. Trukhina I.P. Estimation of the stability of decompositions in semigroups of functions representable by series in the Jacobi polynomials.- In: Problemy Ustoychivosti Stokh. Mod. Moscow: VNIISI, 1984, 139-155 (in Russian).
10. Zolotarev V.M. On the problem of the stability of the decomposition of the normal distribution into components.- Teor. Veroyatn. Primen. 1968, v.13, N 4, 738-742 (in Russian).
11. Chistyakov G.P. On the stability of the decomposition of lattice infinitely divisible distribution functions of the Linnik class $\mathcal{L}$.- In: Problemy Ustoychivosti Stokh. Mod., Moscow: VNIISI, 1986, 84-107 (in Russian).

12. Linnik Yu.V. and Ostrovski I.V. Decomposition of Random Variables and Vectors.- Moscow: Nauka, 1972 (in Russian): Providence, RI, Amer.Math.Soc., 1977.

13. Eateman H. and Erdelyi A. Higher Transcendental Functions.- Moscow: Nauka, 1974, v.1 & 2 (in Russian); N.Y.- Toronto, London, McGraw Hill Book Co., Inc., 1953.

A REGRESSIONAL CHARACTERIZATION OF THE POISSON DISTRIBUTION

J.Wesolowski

In this short note we present a result which may be treated as a Poisson version of the famous Kagan, Linnik, Rao (KLR) characterization of the normal law - see KLR Theorem in [1] . The other results in this line are Khatri, Rao characterizations of the gamma distribution - see Theorems 6.2.1 and 6.2.2 in [1] .

THEOREM. Let $X_1, \ldots, X_n$ be independent real-valued random variables with finite non-zero expectations $n \geq 3$. Then

$$E\left(\prod_{k=1}^{n} X_k \mid X_2 - X_1, \ldots, X_n - X_1\right) = \text{const} \tag{1}$$

a.e. iff $X_1, \ldots, X_n$ are Poisson random variables with the same scale parameter.

PROOF. It is well-known (see, for example, Lemma 1.1.1 in [1]) that (1) is equivalent to

$$E\left(\prod_{k=1}^{n} X_k \exp\left(i \sum_{k=2}^{n} t_k (X_k - X_1)\right)\right) = cE \exp\left(i \sum_{k=2}^{n} t_k (X_k - X_1)\right),$$

where $c = \prod_{k=1}^{n} EX_k$. Consequently (1) is fulfilled iff

$$EX_1 \exp\left(-iX_1 \sum_{k=2}^{n} t_k\right) \prod_{k=2}^{n} EX_k \exp(it_k X_k) =$$

$$= c\,\mathbb{E}\exp\Big(-iX_1\sum_{k=2}^{n}t_k\Big)\prod_{k=2}^{n}\mathbb{E}\exp(it_kX_k).$$

Then for suitable small $\varepsilon > 0$ we have

$$g_1\Big(-\sum_{k=2}^{n}t_k\Big)+\sum_{k=2}^{n}g_k(t_k)=\ln c \qquad (2)$$

for $|t_k|<\varepsilon, \quad k=2,\dots,n$, where

$$g_k(t)=\ln\big(\mathbb{E}X_k\exp(itX_k)(\mathbb{E}\exp(itX_k))^{-1}\big), \quad |t|<\varepsilon.$$

As the solutions of the equation (2) we obtain (see, for example, Lemma 1.5.1 in [1])

$$g_k(t)=at+b_k, \qquad |t|<\varepsilon, \quad k=1,\dots,n.$$

Hence

$$\mathbb{E}X_k\exp(itX_k)=c_k\exp(at)\,\mathbb{E}\exp(itX_k), \quad |t|<\varepsilon, \qquad (3)$$

where $c_k=\exp(b_k), \quad k=1,\dots,n$. It follows from the form of the equation (3) that we can differentiate it in respect to t for $|t|<\varepsilon$ Taking $t=0$ in (3) before and then after differentiation we get

$$c_k=\mathbb{E}X_k, \quad a=ib, \quad b=V(X_k)/\mathbb{E}X_k, \quad k\ 1,\dots,n.$$

Thus the equation (3) implies

$$f_k'(t)=ic_k\exp(ibt)f_k(t), \qquad |t|<\varepsilon, \qquad (4)$$

where f_k is the characteristic function of $X_k, \quad k=1,\dots,n$.

We solve the differential equation (4) and obtain

$$f_k(t)=\exp\Big(\frac{c_k}{b}(\exp(ibt)-1)\Big), \qquad |t|<\varepsilon, \quad k=1,\dots,n. \qquad (5)$$

Consequently, from the analytic extension principle (see, for example,

Corollary 1 to Lemma 1.2.1 in [1]) it follows that the formula (5) is valid for any real t , and thus $b^{-1}X_k$ has the Poisson distribution, $k=1,\dots,n$.

Now let us assume that $b^{-1}X_k$ is a Poisson random variables, $k=1,\dots,n$. Then

$$g_k(t) = ibt + \ln(\lambda_k b), \qquad k=1,\dots,n.$$

Hence the equation (2) is fulfilled for any real t_k, $k=2,\dots,n$ with $c = b^n \prod_{k=1}^{n} \lambda_k$. As the consequence we obtain (1).

Jacek Wesolowski, Institute of Mathematics,
Technical University of Warsaw, Plac Jedności
Robotniczej 1, 00-661 Warsaw, Poland

Reference

1. Kagan A.M., Linnik Yu.V., Rao C.R. Characterization Problems in Mathematical Statistics. Wiley, New York, 1973.

HITTING TIMES OF SINGLE POINTS FOR 1-DIMENSIONAL GENERALIZED DIFFUSION PROCESSES

Makoto Yamazato

1. PREPARATION. Let $\{Y(t)\}$ be one-dimensional Brownian motion and let $\ell(t,x)$ be its local time. Let $m(x)$ be a right continuous nondecreasing function on $[-\infty,\infty]$ into $[-\infty,\infty]$ with $m(-\infty) = -\infty$ and $m(\infty) = \infty$. Define a measure $m(dx)$ by

$$m(dx) = dm(x).$$

Let

$$\Phi(t) = \int_{\mathbb{R}} \ell(t,x)\, m(dx).$$

Define a strong Markov process $\{X(t)\}$ by $X(t) = Y(\Phi^{-1}(t))$, killed at $\{\ell_1, \ell_2\}$. It is called the generalized diffusion process corresponding to the function m ([4]). The measure m restricted to (ℓ_1, ℓ_2), where

$$(-1)^i \ell_i = \sup\{(-1)^i x > 0;\ (-1)^i m(x) < \infty\},\ i = 1, 2,$$

is called the speed measure of the process $\{X(t)\}$. Let $\tau_y = \inf\{t > 0;\ X(t) = y\}$. If $P_x(\tau_y < \infty) < \infty$. We say that $\mu(dt) = P_x(\tau_y \in dt)/P_x(\tau_y < \infty)$ is a conditional hitting time distribution of y starting at x. Let

$$H_{gd} = \{\mu \in P(\mathbb{R}_+)\ ;\text{there is a g.d.p. such that } \mu \text{ is its conditional hitting time distribution}\}.$$

Here, starting points and hitting points are allowed to be boundary points.

2. CHARACTERIZATION OF H_{gd}. Let $\mathbb{R}_+=[0,\infty)$ and let $P(\mathbb{R}_+)$ be the class of probability distributions on $\mathbb{R}_+$. We denote the Laplace transform of $\mu\in P(\mathbb{R}_+)$ by $L\mu(\lambda)=\int e^{-\lambda x}\mu(dx)$. Let CE be the smallest subclass of $P(\mathbb{R}_+)$, which contains exponential distributions and closed under convolution and weak convergence. A probability measure μ on $\mathbb{R}_+$ is a CE distribution if there are $\gamma\geq 0$, at most countable nondecreasing sequence of positive numbers $\{a_i\}_{i\geq 1}$ satisfying $\sum a_i^{-1}<\infty$ such that

$$L\mu(\lambda)=e^{-\gamma\lambda}\prod a_i(\lambda+a_i)^{-1}. \tag{1}$$

We call $\{a_i\}$, $i\geq 1$ parameter sequence of μ. We say that a probability measure μ is a ME distribution if there is a probability measure G on $(0,\infty]$ such that

$$\mu([0,x])=\int_{(0,\infty]}(1-e^{-xu})\,G(du) \qquad \text{for } x>0.$$

Let ME be the class of ME distributions. Let CME be the class of distributions $\mu=\mu_1*\mu_2$ with $\mu_1\in CE$ and $\mu_2\in ME$. Let BO be the smallest class of distributions on $\mathbb{R}_+$ which contains ME and closed under convolutions and weak limits. Kent [3] showed that $H_{gd}\subsetneq BO$. On the other hand, Keilson [2] showed that the first passage time distributions of nonnegative birth and death processes are contained in CME. Moreover, he showed that the number of exponential distributions arising in the convolution is finite. I [5] refined Keilson's result and gave the converse result. I also showed that $H_{gd}\subset CME$ by approximation.

It is known that for $\mu\in ME$, there are a unique nonnegative measure σ on $[0,\infty)$ with $\int_{[0,\infty)}(1+\xi)^{-1}\sigma(d\xi)<\infty$ and $c>0$ such that

$$L\mu(\lambda)^{-1} = c\lambda + \int_{[0,\infty)} (\lambda/(\lambda+\xi))\, \sigma(d\xi). \tag{2}$$

The following is the main result of this talk.

THEOREM 1. In order that a probability measure μ on $\mathbb{R}_+$ belongs to H_{gd} it necessary and sufficient that there are a nondegenerate CE distribution μ_1 and a ME distribution μ_2 such that

$$\mu = \mu_1 * \mu_2,$$

$\gamma = 0$, $\{a_i\}$ is strictly increasing in the representation (1) of the Laplace transform of μ_1 and that $\sigma(\{a_i\}) > 0$ for each i where the measure σ which is defined by

$$L\mu_2(\lambda)^{-1} = c\lambda + \int_{[0,\infty)} (\lambda/(\lambda+\xi))\, \sigma(d\xi).$$

REMARK 1. Any gamma distribution with parameter greater than one is not contained in H_{gd}.

REMARK 2. Let $\mu \in ME$. If μ has a point mass at 0, then μ is not contained in H_{gd}.

By these remarks, we get the following.

COROLLARY. $H_{gd} \subsetneq CME$.

3. TAIL BEHAVIOUR. In the sequel, we assume that $0 \in (\ell_1, \ell_2)$ and μ is the hitting time distribution of $b > 0$ starting at 0.

THEOREM 2. If one of the following two assumptions holds, then there is $c > 0$ such that $\mu([t,\infty)) = O(e^{-ct})$ as $t \to \infty$.

(i) $\ell_1 > -\infty$ and there is $C > 0$ such that $(x - \ell_1)\, m((x, 0]) \leq C$ for all $x \in (\ell_1, 0]$.

(ii) $\ell_1 = -\infty$ and there is $D > 0$ such that $|x|\, m((-\infty, x]) \leq D$ for all $x \in (-\infty, 0]$.

THEOREM 3. Let $0 < \alpha < 1$. Let $K(x)$ be a positive function slowly varying at infinity such that $x^{\alpha-1} K(x)$ is increasing.

If

$$m([-x,0]) \sim x^{\alpha^{-1}-1} K(x) \qquad \text{as} \quad x \to \infty,$$

then

$$\mu([t,\infty)) \sim b/\Gamma(1+\alpha)\{\alpha(1-\alpha)\}^{-\alpha} t^{\alpha} L_{\alpha}(t) \qquad \text{as} \quad t \to \infty,$$

where $t^{\alpha} L_{\alpha}(t)$ is the inverse of $x^{\alpha^{-1}} K(x)$.

4. OUTLINE OF THE PROOFS.

PROOF OF THEOREM 1. Let $m \in M$ and let $E_m = (\operatorname{supp} m)|_{(\ell_1, \ell_2)}$. Let $\{X(t)\}$ be a g.d.p. corresponding to m. Suppose $0 \in (\ell_1, \ell_2)$. Set $b = \sup E_m$. Let $\tau_b = \inf\{t>0;\ X(t) = b\}$. It is sufficient to consider the case $P_0\{\tau_b < \infty\} > 0$ and $\mu(dt) = P_x(\tau_y \in dt)/$ $/P_x(\tau_y < \infty)$.

Let $\Phi(x,\lambda)$ and $\Psi(x,\lambda)$ be continuous solutions of

$$\Phi(x,\lambda) = 1 + \lambda \int_{[0,x]} (x-y)\Phi(y,\lambda)\, m(dy) \qquad \text{for} \quad x>0$$

$$= 1 - \lambda \int_{[x,0]} (x-y)\Phi(y,\lambda)\, m(dy) \qquad \text{for} \quad x<0$$

and

$$\Psi(x,\lambda) = x + \lambda \int_{[0,x]} (x-y)\Psi(y,\lambda)\, m(dy) \qquad \text{for} \quad x>0$$

$$= x - \lambda \int_{[x,0]} (x-y)\Psi(y,\lambda)\, m(dy) \qquad \text{for} \quad x<0,$$

respectively. Let

$$h_1(\lambda) = -\lim_{x \to \ell_1} \Psi(x,\lambda)/\Phi(x,\lambda),$$

$$h_2(\lambda) = \lim_{x \to b} \Psi(x,\lambda)/\Phi(x,\lambda),$$

$$h(\lambda) = (h_1(\lambda)^{-1} + h_2(\lambda)^{-1})^{-1}.$$

Moreover, let

$$u_i(x,\lambda) = \Phi(x,\lambda) - (-1)^i h_i(\lambda)\Psi(x,\lambda).$$

Then, for $\lambda > 0$, u_1 is a positive increasing function of x, satisfying

$$u_1(\ell_1, \lambda) = 0 \qquad \text{if} \qquad \ell_1 > -\infty$$

and

$$u_1^+(\ell_1, \lambda) = 0 \qquad \text{if} \qquad \ell_1 = -\infty.$$

So the Laplace transform of μ is given by

$$E_0(e^{-\lambda\tau_b}) = u_1(0,\lambda)/u_1(b,\lambda) = u_1(b,\lambda)^{-1}.$$

$$= h(\lambda)/\Psi(b,\lambda).$$

Total mass is equal to $\ell_1/(\ell_1+b)$. Letting that $L\mu_1(\lambda) = b/\Psi(b,\lambda)$ and $L\mu_2(\lambda) = h(\lambda)(\ell_1+b)\,\ell_1^{-1}$, it is nor difficult to see that $\mu_1 \in CE$ and $\mu_2 \in ME$. Also, it is not difficult to show the necessary conditions in the theorem. Conversely, let

$$L\mu(\lambda) = \prod a_i(\lambda + a_i)^{-1}$$

with $0 < a_1 < a_2 < \ldots \leqslant \infty$, with $\sum a_i^{-1} < \infty$. By the assumption

$$L\mu_2(\lambda)^{-1} = c\lambda + \int_{[0,\infty)} (\lambda/(\lambda+\xi))\,\sigma(d\xi)$$

with $\int_{[0,\infty)} (1+\xi)^{-1}\sigma(d\xi) < \infty$, $\sigma(\{0\}) = 1$ and $c \geqslant 0$ and a_i are point masses of σ. So decompose σ so that $\sigma = \sigma_1 + \sigma_2$ where $\operatorname{supp}\sigma_2 = \{a_i\} \cup \{0\}$ and $\sigma_2(\{0\}) = 1$. Then there are measures $\tilde{\sigma}_1$ and $\tilde{\sigma}_2$ on $[0,\infty)$ such that

$$(c\lambda + \int_{[0,\infty)} (\lambda/(\lambda+\xi))\sigma_1(d\xi))^{-1} = \int_{[0,\infty)} (\lambda/(\lambda+\xi))\tilde{\sigma}_1(d\xi) = h_1(\lambda)$$

$$(\int_{[0,\infty)} (\lambda/(\lambda+\xi))\sigma_2(d\xi))^{-1} = \int_{[0,\infty)} (\lambda/(\lambda+\xi))\tilde{\sigma}_2(d\xi) = h_2(\lambda).$$

Note that $h_1(0)=\infty$, $h_2(0) = 1$ and $h_2(\lambda)$ is meromorphic. Therefore,

$$h_2(\lambda) = \prod a_i(\lambda + a_i)^{-1} / \prod b_i(\lambda + b_i)^{-1}$$

with $0 < b_1 < a_1 < b_2 < a_2 < \dots$. There is m_2 on $[0, 1]$. There is m_1 on $(-\infty, 0]$ corresponding to h_1.

PROOF OF THEOREM 2.

(ii) If $\ell_1 = -\infty$ and $|x|\, m((-\infty, x]) \leq D < \infty$ for all $x \in (-\infty, 0]$, then by Kac-Krein $\sigma_1(\{0\}) > 0$ and $\inf \operatorname{supp} \sigma$ on $(0,\infty) \geq 1/4D > 0$ where σ_1 is the spectral measure of h_1 . So $\lambda h_1(\lambda)$ is analytic at $\lambda = 0$ and $\lambda h_1(\lambda)$ at $\lambda = 0$ is positive. Hence $h(\lambda) = \lambda h_1(\lambda) h_2(\lambda)/\lambda(h_1(\lambda) + h_2(\lambda))$ is analytic at $\lambda = 0$. Hence applying the residue theorem to inversion formula for Laplace transform, we get the conclusion. We can prove the case (i) in the same way.

PROOF OF THEOREM 3. It is shown by Kasahara that if

$$m([-x, 0]) \sim x^{\alpha^{-1}-1} K(x) \qquad \text{as} \quad x \to \infty,$$

then

$$h_1(\lambda) \sim D_\alpha \lambda^{-\alpha} L_\alpha(\lambda^{-1}) \qquad \text{as} \quad \lambda \to 0$$

where $D_\alpha = \{\alpha(1-\alpha)\}^{-\alpha} \Gamma(1+\alpha)\Gamma(1-\alpha)^{-1}$. We have

$$L\mu(0) - L\mu(\lambda) = h(0)/\Psi(b,0) - h(\lambda)/\Psi(b,\lambda)$$

$$\sim b/D_\alpha \lambda^{1-\alpha} L_\alpha(\lambda^{-1}).$$

By Tauberian theorem, we have

$$\mu([t, \infty)) \sim bt^{-\alpha}/\Gamma(1+\alpha)D_\alpha L_\alpha(t)$$

$$= b/\{\alpha(1-\alpha)\}^{-\alpha}\Gamma(1+\alpha)t^{\alpha}L_\alpha(t) \qquad \text{as } t \to \infty.$$

REMARK. We can show that if

$$m([-x,0]) \sim (x - \ell_1)^{-\alpha^{-1}-1} K(x) \quad \text{as} \quad x \to \ell_1,$$

then

$$\mu([t,\infty)) \sim t^{-\alpha}\mathcal{N}(t) \qquad \text{as} \quad t \to \infty,$$

where $\mathcal{N}(t)$ is a function slowly varying at infinity.

In this case we can not apply Kasahara's result directely.

Nagoya Institute of Technology

Nagoya, Japan

REFERENCES

1. Kasahara Y. Spectral theory of generalized second order differential operators and its applications to Markov processes. Japan J. Math., 1, 1975, 67-84.

2. Keilson J. On the unimodality of passage time densities in birth-death processes. Statist. Neerlandica, 35, 1981, 49-55.

3. Kent J.T. Eigenvalue expansions for diffusion hitting times. Z. Wahrscheinlichkeitstheor. verw. Geb., 52, 1980, 309-319.

4. Kotani S. and Watanabe S. Krein's spectral theory of strings and generalized diffusion processes. Functional Analysis in Markov Processes (M. Fukushima, ed.), Lect. Notes Math., 923, 1982, 235-259, Springer, Berlin.Heidelberg-New York.

5. Yamazato M. Characterization of the class of upward first passage time distributions of nonnegative birth and death processes and related results, submitted.

PSEUDOTRAJECTORIES AND STABILITY PROBLEMS FOR STOCHASTIC DYNAMICAL SYSTEMS[1)]

to the memory of A.N.Kolmogorov

Rolando Rebolledo[2)]

Our aim is to present a theoretical framework to analyze the stability od stochastic dynamical systems. The key is the introduction of pseudotrajectories, a weak topology related to them and some convex functionals playing the role of entropy, pressure, and free energy.

The motovation for this choice come from the study of metastable systems as they appear in some stochastic models of particle dynamics. In fact as many researchers have remarked, some physical models behave as they were attaining a stable state during a long time and, suddently, they move to another state, the true stable one. There exist many attemps of description of this phenomenon, namely, from the stochastic processes point of view, we have the works of Ellis-Newman-Rosen [6] , Cassandro-Galves-Olivieri-Vares [3] , Galves-Olivieri-Vares [7] The first three authors, take as departure point the analysis of "conditioned" limit theorems for sums of dependent random variables occurring in statistical mechanics. The others, take a pathwise approach to metastability, studying the asymptotic behaviour of "temporal means" related to the process description of the system. In both cases topology involved still the "classical" one used in studying trajectories of stochastic processes, namely, Skorokhod's topology for the space $D([0,\infty[, E)$. The problem arising then is that one camot

1) Research supported by Fondecyt grant # 1080/86-87.

2) Universidad Católica de Chile. Facultad de Matemáticas. Casilla 6177. Santiago, CHILE.

have a common setting to analyze stability and unstability, in particular, metastability. In fact, as Cassandro-Galves-Olivieri-Vares proved, the convergence of some subsequences of rescaled temporal means doesn't take place in Skorokhod's topology.

In our approach we provide a method based in two main sources. The first one is the introduction of a wider space than the usual Skorokhod's $\mathbb{D}([0,\infty[,\mathbb{E})$, endowed with a weaker topology, the second aspect, is the introduction of a suitable family of convex functionals in order to have at our disposal the so called "Thermodynamics Formalism".

The plan of the paper is as follows. In paragraph one, we introduce the basic space and analyze topological questions. In paragraph two we obtain stability results, and in the third one, the Thermodynamics Formalism and metastability are studied.

§ 1. Pseudotrajectories and stochastic dynamical systems

We begin introducing some notations and the concept of pseudotrajectory as it was defined by Knight [8] and Dellacherie-Meyer [4].

Take $\mathbb{E}$ to be a locally compact space with countable basis (in particular we can take $\mathbb{E}=\mathbb{R}^d$, the time run over the interval $[0,\infty[$, endowed with Lebesgue measure $\lambda(dt):=dt$. Call the compactification of the product space $\mathbb{E}\times[0,\infty[$; its borelian σ-algebra is represented by $\mathcal{K}$ and $M(K)$ (respectively $M^+(K)$) denotes the space of Radon measures defined over $(K,\mathcal{K})$ (respectively the cone of positive measures). We endow the latter space with the vague (or weak *) topology. Given a borelian function x from $[0,\infty[$ in $\mathbb{E}$ define $g_x(t):=(x(t),t),\ 0\leq t<\infty$, and denote by a boldface character $\boldsymbol{x}$, the image measure of λ by g_x over K . Equivalently, using the symbol $\langle,\rangle$ to denote integration, we have for all continuous function u with compact support from K in $\mathbb{R}$:

$$\langle \mathcal{F}, u \rangle := \int_{[0,\infty[} u(x(t), t)\, \lambda(dt)$$

$\mathcal{F}$ is an element of $M^+(K)$, we call it the pseudotrajectory of the function x.

Pseudotrajectories of borelian dunctions form a subspace of We denote this space by Ω_p. Let Ω denote the set of all elements ω of $M^+(K)$ that can be written in the form $\omega(dx, dt) = \int \alpha_s(dx) \otimes \varepsilon_s(dt)\, ds$, where $\alpha_s(dx)$ is a probability measure over E and $\varepsilon_s(dt)$ is Dirac measure concentrated on s for every $s \geqslant 0$, thus their projection over $[0,\infty[$ is λ.

Over the set Ω the topology induced by $M^+(K)$ is equivalent to the weakest topology for which mappings $\mu \mapsto \langle \mu, f \otimes g \rangle$ are continuous when f varies over the set of bounded continuous functions from E in $\mathbb{R}$, and g run over the set of continuous functions with compact support from $\mathbb{R}$ in $\mathbb{R}$.

The following inclusions holds: $\Omega_p \subset \Omega \subset M^+(K)$, a measure μ from Ω belongs to Ω_p if an only if there exists a borelian function x from $[0,\infty[$ in E such that $\alpha_s(dx) = \varepsilon_{x(s)}(dx)$ for λ-almost all s in $[0,\infty[$.

Both Ω and Ω_p are Polish spaces, Ω is indeed convex, compact and metrizable since it is vaguely (w^*)-bounded and closed (cf. Dellacherie-Meyer [4]), Ω_p is equal to the set of all extremal points of Ω, thus in vurtue of Choquest's theorem, it is a $\mathcal{G}_\delta$-subset of Ω, therefore it is a Polish space.

Let us call Ω_D the set of pseudotrajectories relative to functions from the space $D([0,\infty[, E)$. This space is no more Polish, it is only Lusin (meyer-Zheng [9]).

Following Meyer and Zheng, we introduce a family of remarkable functionals over $M^+(K)$.

Let $\mathcal{U}, \mathcal{V}$ be two open sets of E, μ an element of $M^+(K)$. Take an arbitrary subdivision of $[0, t]$, where $0 \leq t \leq \infty$,

$$\tau: \quad 0 = t_0 < t_1 < \dots < t_n = t.$$

Define an integer $(\leq \infty)$, $n^{\mathcal{U},\mathcal{V}}(\mu, \tau, t)$ by the relation:

(1.1) $n^{\mathcal{U},\mathcal{V}}(\mu; \tau, t) \geq k$ if and only if there exist $t^{\mathcal{U}_j}, t^{\mathcal{V}_j}$, $j = 1, \dots, k$, in the partition τ, such that $0 < t^{\mathcal{U}_1} < t^{\mathcal{V}_1} < t^{\mathcal{U}_2} < < t^{\mathcal{V}_2} < \dots < t^{\mathcal{U}_k} < t^{\mathcal{V}_k} \leq t$ and the measure μ charges the sets $\mathcal{U} \times]t^{\mathcal{U}_j}, t^{\mathcal{U}_{j+1}}[$, $\mathcal{V} \times]t^{\mathcal{V}_j}, t^{\mathcal{V}_{j+1}}[$, $j = 1, \dots, k-1$.

$n^{\mathcal{U},\mathcal{V}}(\mu; \tau, t)$ is a lower semi-continuous functional over measures μ ; and the same is true for

(1.2) $$N^{\mathcal{U},\mathcal{V}}(\mu, t) := \sup_{\tau} n^{\mathcal{U},\mathcal{V}}(\mu; \tau, t),$$ where τ run over all partitions of $[0, t]$.

This last functional will be called flux indicator from $\mathcal{U}$ to $\mathcal{V}$ on the interval $[0, t]$ for μ . This is the analogous to the "number of upcrossings" of a real function through an interval $[u, v]$ of the real line, before t (take $\mathcal{U} :=]-\infty, u[$, $\mathcal{V} =]v, \infty[$).

$N^{\mathcal{U},\mathcal{V}}(\mu, \cdot)$ is a increasing right-continuous function defining a positive integer-valued measure over $[0, \infty]$. If $\mathcal{A}$ is a borelian set, $N^{\mathcal{U},\mathcal{V}}(\mu, \mathcal{A})$ is the flux from $\mathcal{U}$ to $\mathcal{V}$ on $\mathcal{A}$. We denote $N^{\mathcal{U},\mathcal{V}}(\mu) = N^{\mathcal{U},\mathcal{V}}(\mu, \infty) = N^{\mathcal{U},\mathcal{V}}(\mu, [0, \infty])$.

In order to give a characterozation of $\Omega_{\mathcal{D}}$, we define

(1.3) $\Delta_k(E) := \{\mu \in \Omega :$ there exists a compact E_0 of E such that $\mu(E_0 \times [0, \infty]) = 1$ and for all disjoint subsets $\mathcal{U}, \mathcal{V}$ of E, $N^{\mathcal{U},\mathcal{V}}(\mu) \leq k\}$, for every $k \in \mathbb{N}$.

All these sets are closed in $M^+(K)$ and the following theorem holds

1.4. THEOREM.

$$\Omega_D = \bigcup_{k=0}^{\infty} \Delta_k(E).$$

This is merely a modification of Meyer-Zheng [9] theorem. We send the reader to this reference for the proof (c.f. also Rebolledo [11]).

1.5. DEFINITIONS.

Take $\mathcal{F}$ to be the borelian σ-algebra over Ω. The identity mapping on Ω will be denoted by μ $(\mu(\omega) = \omega)$.

The canonical flow $\Theta = (\Theta_t, t \geq 0)$ is defined on Ω as follows. Given ω in Ω, $\Theta_t(\omega)$ is taken as the image measure of ω by the mapping $(x, s) \mapsto (x, (s-t)^+)$, where (x, s) run over K, $t \geq 0$. Thus, all Θ_t are continuous in the w^*-topology and therefore, they are $\mathcal{F}$-measurable.

We define then the canonical filtration as $\mathbb{F} = (\mathcal{F}_t; t \geq 0)$ where $\mathcal{F}_t = \sigma(\Theta_s; s \leq t)$, $t \geq 0$. The system $(\Omega, \mathcal{F}, \mathbb{F}, \Theta)$ will be called the (canonical) stochastic basis for dynamical systems.

Let us introduce also the family of Cesàro means of Θ as the measures

$$\sigma_T(\omega) = \frac{1}{T} \int_0^T \Theta_t(\omega)\, dt, \qquad T > 0,$$

where the integral means the measure defined by the equality

$$\langle \sigma_T(\omega), u \rangle = \frac{1}{T} \int \langle \Theta_t(\omega), u \rangle\, dt, \quad T > 0$$

for all u in $C_0(K)$, the space of all continuous functions with compact support from K to $\mathbb{R}$.

Denote by $\mathcal{M}(E)$ the space of probability measures on E (endowed with the corresponding borelian σ-algebra) with the weak topology.

In order to avoid ambiguities we define (say, we choose a version of) $\alpha_t(\omega, dx)$ as a cádlág mesasure-valued process by means of the following procedure

$$\alpha_t(\omega, f) := \lim_n n \langle \omega, f \otimes 1_{[t,\, t+1/n[} \rangle, \quad \text{for all } t \geq 0, \quad \text{and all } f \in C_b(E).$$

In this form, we call $\alpha_0(\omega, dx)$ the initial state conditional distribution. Associated with the process α, we define the internal history $F = (\mathcal{F}_t;\ t \geq 0)$ as the family of sigma-fields generated by this process, i.e. $\mathcal{F}_t = \sigma(\alpha_u;\ u \leq t),\ t \geq 0.$

A stochastic dynamical system is a continuous mapping $P: q \mapsto P_q$ defined on an open set $\mathcal{D}(P)$ of $\mathcal{M}(\mathcal{M}(E))$ with values in $\mathcal{M}(\Omega)$, such that for all $q \in \mathcal{D}(P)$, $P_q(\Omega_{\mathcal{D}}) = 1$ and $q(\mathcal{A}) = P_q(\alpha_0 \in \mathcal{A})$ (q is the distribution of the initial state), for each borelian set $\mathcal{A}$ of $\mathcal{M}(E)$.

Since we are interested in the stidy of stability from a "distributional" point of view, we are led to work with the distributions of the canonical flow under the dynamical system $P = (P_q;\ q \in \mathcal{D}(P))$. Thus, a new flow is introduced, this time over $\mathcal{M}(\Omega)$ -and denoted by the same symbols $\Theta_t(P_q)$ is the distribution under P_q of the element Θ_t of the flow.

In this framework, a perturbation of a dynamical system $P = (P_q;\ q \in \mathcal{D}(P))$ is a family $\mathcal{P} = (P^\varepsilon;\ \varepsilon > 0)$ of dynamical systems such that for every q in $\mathcal{D}(P)$, $(P_q^\varepsilon;\ \varepsilon > 0)$ converges to P_q in the sense of weak topology when ε goes to 0.

1.6. EXAMPLES.

1.6.1. Take a population where the individuals are represented as points in $\mathbb{R}^d$. At every time t , there is a set $I(t)$ of living individuals and we assume the state of the population is fully described by the collection $(x_i,\ i \in I(t))$ of states of living individuals. This example is considered by Dawson (1978). A good description of the evolution of the population is obtained with the following measure-valued process:

$$X_t(dx) = \sum_{i \in I(t)} \varepsilon_{x_i}(dx) \qquad \text{for all} \quad t \geqslant 0.$$

This measure-valued process is such that $X_t(\mathcal{A})$ represents the number of living individuals in the region $\mathcal{A}$ of the space at time t .

For this problem our model is constructed taking $\mathbb{E}$ as the space of point measures on $\mathbb{R}^d$ endowed with the weak topology. The dynamical system is given by the family of probability distributions of pseudotrajectories of the measure-valued process X; $D(P)$ being here a set of Dirac measures supported by points of $\mathbb{R}^d$.

(1.6.2). Take a system of diffusing particles with interaction and branching that is, the situation is similar to the latter: the individuals are particles of fixed mass ε describing, as long as they live, a diffusion mouvement characterized by the equations

$$d Z_i(t) = \alpha(X_t, Z_i(t))\, dt + \beta(X_t, Z_i(t))\, dW_i(t),$$

$$Y_t(dx) = \sum_{i \in I(t)} \varepsilon_{Z_i(t)}(dx) \qquad \text{for all} \quad t \geqslant 0.$$

Coefficients $\alpha(X_t, \cdot)$ and $\beta(X_t, \cdot)$ are vector-fields depending on the measure-valued process (X_t) ; processes W_i are independent copies of a Brownian motion on $\mathbb{R}^d$; i varies on $I(t)$ the set of living individuals at $t \in \mathbb{R}_+$. The motion is completely described giving the instantaneous rates of "living" and "dying". To construct pseudotrajectories we take again $\mathbb{E}$ as the space of point measures on $\mathbb{R}^d$ endowed with the weak topology. The dynamical system is defined by the family of probability distributions of pseudotrajectories of Y .

(1.6.3). Consider a classical example of dynamical system in $\mathbb{R}^d$ described by the ordinary differential equation:

$$dX(t) = b(X(t))\,dt,$$

$$X(0) = x \in \mathbb{R}^d.$$

The coefficient b is taken to be the gradient of a C^2-potential a , having two local minima (hyperbolic critical points), and such that $a(x) \pm \infty$ if $|x| \pm \infty$:

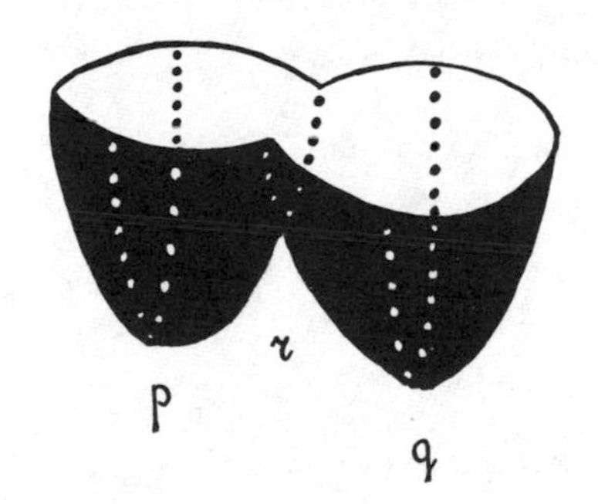

$$a(r) > a(p) > a(q); \qquad b = -\nabla^{a}$$

Fig. 1.

One assume further there exists $k > 0$, such that $|b(x)| \leq k(1 + |x|)$ on $\mathbb{R}^d$. This situation is well-known by specialists: the space $\mathbb{R}^d$ admits a decomposition $\mathbb{R}^d = D_p \cup W_r^s \cup D_q$ where D_p (resp. D_q) is the attraction domain of p (resp. q and W_r^s is the stable manifold of r).

Here the space E is simply $\mathbb{R}^d$. Call $X(x)$ the pseudotrajectory of the solution to the differential equation starting from x (initial distributions are of the form ε_x with x in $\mathbb{R}^d$); the dynamical system is defined by the family $P_x = \varepsilon_{X(x)}$ of probabilities, x in $\mathbb{R}^d$. Since $D(P)$ is a set of Dirac measures supported by points of $\mathbb{R}^d$, it can be partitioned in three remarkable subsets according to the decomposition of $\mathbb{R}^d$: $\{\varepsilon_x;\ x \text{ in } D_p\}$, $\{\varepsilon_x;\ x \text{ in } D_q\}$, $\{\varepsilon_x;\ x \text{ in } W_r^s\}$.

(1.6.4). Take the differential system (1.6.3) adding a random perturbation given by a "small noise":

$$dX(t) = b(X(t))\,dt + \varepsilon\, dW(t),$$

$$X(0) = x \in \mathbb{R}^d.$$

W represents the Wiener process on $\mathbb{R}^d$. This model has been studied by Galves, Olivieri and Vares [7]. Calling P_x^ε the probability distribution of solutions pseudotrajectory X_ε, we get an example of a perturbed dynamical system.

(1.7) We are now interested in the structure of invariant sets in Ω and in $\mathfrak{M}(\Omega)$.

Take the canonical desintegration $\omega(dx, dt) = \int \alpha_s(dx) \otimes \varepsilon_s(dt)\, ds$, of an element of Ω where $\alpha_s(dx)$ is a probability measure over $\mathbb{E}$ and $\varepsilon_s(dt)$ is Dirac measure concentrated on s for every $s \geqslant 0$ it is clear that probabilities $(\alpha_s(dx),\ s \geqslant 0)$ are not unique since we can modify them over Lebesgue-null sets of points $s \geqslant 0$, the representation of ω remaining unchanged. Nevertheless, the equivalence class-denoted $\omega(dx/s)$ of all $\alpha_s(dx)$ of the representation of ω is unique, for all $s \geqslant 0$. This is enough to introduce some remarkable subsets of Ω.

We say ω is a step measure if there exist a finite partition of $\mathbb{R}$ by intervals $J_1, \ldots, J_n$ (depending on ω and $\nu_1(\omega, dx)$, $\ldots$, $\nu_n(\omega, dx)$ in $\mathfrak{M}(\mathbb{E})$ such that

$$\sum_{k=0}^{n} \mathbb{1}_{J_k}(t)\, \nu_k(\omega, dx) \quad \text{is an element of the class } \omega(dx/t).$$

Then the desintegration of ω with respect to λ gives

$$\langle \omega, f \otimes g \rangle = \sum_{k=0}^{n} \langle \nu_k, f \rangle \int_{J_k} g(t)\, dt$$

when f varies over the set of bounded continuous functions from $\mathbb{E}$ in $\mathbb{R}$, and g run over the set of continuous functions with compact support from $\mathbb{R}$ in $\mathbb{R}$.

Let us denote by Σ the set of step measures.

(1.8). PROPOSITION.

For each element ω in Σ there exists $\tau(\omega)$ in $[0, \infty[$ such that for all $t \geq 0$ it holds $\Theta_{\tau(\omega)+t}(\omega) = \omega$.

PROOF. In fact, let J_n be the last interval of the partition of $[0, \infty[$ associated to the step measure ω. Take $\tau(\omega)$ as the infimum of J_n and to fix ideas, let us assume J_n to be closed to the left. Using the representation of ω we have $\omega(dx, du) = \int \alpha_s(dx) \otimes \varepsilon_s(du)\, ds$ and $\Theta_{\tau(\omega)+t}(\omega)(dx, du) = \int \alpha_{\tau(\omega)+t+s}(dx) \otimes \varepsilon_s(du)\, ds$, but $\alpha_s(dx) = \nu_n(dx)$ for λ-almost all s in $[\tau(\omega), \infty[= J_n$. Since $\nu_n(dx)$ doesn't depend on s, the equality of the proposition follows.

(1.9) COROLLARY.

The set $\mathbb{J}(\Omega)$ of all invariant elements of Ω under Θ is the subset of all ω in Σ of the form $\omega(dx, dt) = \nu(\omega, dx) \otimes \lambda(dt)$, where $\nu(\omega, dx)$ is a random element of $\mathfrak{M}(\mathbb{E})$.

By means of this corollary the characterization of invariant elements in $\mathfrak{M}(\Omega)$ follows.

(1.10) PROPOSITION.

A probability Q in $\mathfrak{M}(\Omega)$ is invariant if and only if $Q(\mathbb{J}) = 1$. Furthermore, the extremal points of the set $\mathbb{J}(\mathfrak{M}(\Omega))$ of invariant elements of $\mathfrak{M}(\Omega)$ are all probabilities of the form $Q = \varepsilon_\eta$, where

η run over $\mathbb{J}(\Omega)$.

PROOF. In fact, $\Theta_t(Q) = Q$ for all $t \geqslant 0$, if and only if $\int f(\Theta_t(\omega))\,Q(d\omega) = \int f(\omega)\,Q(d\omega)$, for all continuous and bounded function f and all $t \geqslant 0$. The latter is equivalent to $\Theta_t(\omega) = \omega$, Q -almost surely, i.e. $Q(\mathbb{J}(\Omega) = 1$ for all $t \geqslant 0$.

To prove the second assertion, let us call $\mathrm{Ext}(\mathbb{J}(\pi(\Omega)))$ the set of all extremal points of $\mathbb{J}(\pi(\Omega))$. Clearly $\{\varepsilon_\eta;\ \eta \in \mathbb{J}(\Omega)\}$ is included in $\mathrm{Ext}(\mathbb{J}(\pi(\Omega)))$. Reciprocally, assume Q to be extremal with a non-singleton support. This is then a non-empty compact with more than one element. Given a finite cover $(V_k;\ k = 1,\ldots,n)$ of it, there exists a collection $(f_k;\ k = 1,\ldots,n)$ of continuous functions of $\mathbb{J}(\Omega)$ in $[0,1]$ such that the support of f_k be included in V_k for all $1 \leqslant k \leqslant n$ and $\sum_k f_k(\omega) \leqslant 1$ for all ω in $\mathbb{J}(\Omega)$, the sum being equal to 1 over the support of Q. Define m_k to be the measure $f_k \cdot Q$ (indefined integral) and Q_k to be the probability $m_k/m_k(\Omega)$, $1 \leqslant k \leqslant n$. These probabilities give measure 1 to the set $\mathbb{J}(\Omega)$ now if we take $a_k = m_k(\Omega) > 0$, $1 \leqslant k \leqslant n$, we have $\sum_k a_k = 1$ and $Q = \sum_k a_k Q_k$, contradicting the extremality of Q. Thus the support of Q must be reduced to a single point.

§ 2. Stability

Consider a stochastic dynamical system $P = (P_q;\ q \in D(P))$, over the basis $(\Omega, \mathcal{F}, \mathbb{F}, \Theta)$. We say P_q is an equilibrium point of the system if it is invariant under the canonical flow. Our aim in this paragraph is to introduce a concept of stability for perturbed dynamical systems. Let us take a perturbation $\mathcal{P} = (P_q^\varepsilon;\ \varepsilon > 0,\ q \in D(P))$ of the system P.

(2.1) DEFINITION

The limit set (in the positive time) of q in $D(P)$, is the set of probabilities defined by the expressure

$L^+(q) = \{ Q \in \mathcal{K}(\Omega):$ there exist sequences $(\varepsilon(n)), (t(n))$, such that $\varepsilon(n) \downarrow 0$, $t(n) \uparrow \infty$, and $\Theta_{t(n)}(P_q^{\varepsilon(n)})$ converges weak to $Q\}$.

We denote by $L^+(\mathcal{P})$ the union of all $L^+(q)$, when q wun over $D(P)$.

(2.2) REMARK.

Clearly, $L^+(q) \neq \emptyset$ is and only if the family $\Theta_t(P_q^{\varepsilon})$; $\varepsilon > 0$, $t \geqslant 0$ is relatively weakly compact in $\mathcal{K}(\Omega)$.

(2.3) DEFINITIONS.

The system is stable if for every q in $D(P)$, the limit set $L^+(q)$ is non empty and every $Q \in L^+(q)$ is an equilibrium point.

A subset $\mathbb{Q}$ of $\mathcal{K}(\Omega)$ is an attractor if it contains $L^+(\mathcal{P})$ and this is non-empty. If $\{Q\}$ is an attractor we shall simplify saying that " Q is an attractor".

If the system is stable and $\mathbb{Q}$ is an attractor, we shall say that $\mathbb{Q}$ is asymptotically stable.

Finally, a question of notation. Limits "in t, ε " such as $\lim_{t,\varepsilon} f(t,\varepsilon)$ mean for us the limit of $f(t(\varepsilon),\varepsilon)$ along the filter of all functions $t(\varepsilon)$ from $]0,\infty[$ in $[0,\infty[$ such that $t(\varepsilon) \uparrow \infty$ when $\varepsilon \downarrow 0$. If function f doesn't depend on ε the above notation simply means "limit in t as $t \uparrow \infty$ ".

The following proposition is now inmediate.

(2.4) PROPOSITION.

The system is stable if and only if for all q in $D(P)$ the following condition holds

$$\limsup_{t,\varepsilon} \Theta_t(P_q^{\varepsilon})(\mathbb{J}(\Omega)) = 1.$$

PROOF. The set $\mathbf{J}(\Omega)$ is closed in the weakly compact space $\mathcal{M}(\Omega)$. Thus it is compact and the condition of the proposition is equivalent to both, weak compactness of $(\Theta_t(P_q^\varepsilon);\ \varepsilon>0,\ t\geq 0)$ and concentration of limit points on $\mathbf{J}(\Omega)$.

Now is natural to call a system unstable if it is not stable,i.e. if there exists q in $\mathcal{D}(P)$ -called unstable unitial point- such that

$$\lim \sup_{t,\varepsilon} \Theta_t(P_q^\varepsilon)(\mathbf{J}(\Omega)) < 1.$$

Denote by $\mathcal{D}_u(P)$ the set of unstable initial points and by $\mathcal{D}_s(P)$ the set of stable initial points, i.e. the set $\{q\in\mathcal{D}(P):\ \lim\sup_{t,\varepsilon}\Theta_t(P_q^\varepsilon)\times(\mathbf{J}(\Omega)) = 1\}$.

(2.5) EXAMPLES.

(2.5.1). Consider the classical dynamical system of example (1.6.3). Using the decomposition of $\mathbb{R}^d$, it is clear that for all $x\in\mathbb{R}^d$ $\lim\Theta_t(P_x) = \varepsilon_\eta$ where η run over the set $\mathbb{Q}$ of product measures $\varepsilon_p\otimes\lambda$, $\varepsilon_q\otimes\lambda$, $\varepsilon_r\otimes\lambda$, (depending on the position of the initial point x). Since $\Theta_t X(x)$ converges towards η, as t goes to ∞ . Then the system is stable and $\mathbb{Q}$ is an attractor.

(2.5.2). Given a Markov process with trajectories in $\mathcal{D}([0,\infty[,E)$ and with invariant measure ν , the associated dynamical system (P_x) satisfies $\lim\Theta_t(P_x) = \varepsilon_\eta$, where $\eta = \nu\otimes\lambda$. The system is stable and $\{\varepsilon_\eta\}$ is an attractor.

(2.5.3). As a typical case of unstable system, take a dynamical system with an attractor $\mathbb{Q} = \{Q_0, Q_1\} = \cup\{L^+(q);\ q\in\mathcal{D}(P)\}$, where Q_0 is invariant but $Q_1(\mathbf{J}(\Omega))<1$. This is the situation in example (1.6.4)*.

In order to classify unstability we introduce some remarkable functionals on dynamical systems.

§ 3. Functionals over dynamical systems

Assumptions and notations of previous paragraph still holding.

(3.1). DEFINITIONS.

For each $u \in C_0(K)$, we denote by $\mathcal{K}(u;q)$, $(q \in D(P))$ the pressure of the dynamical system defined by the expression

$$\mathcal{K}(u,q) := \limsup_{T,\varepsilon} \frac{1}{T} \log \int_\Omega \exp[-\int_0^T <\Theta_t(\omega), u> dt]\, P_q^\varepsilon(d\omega).$$

And the free energy of a probability Q at q is

$$e(Q,q) := \inf\{\mathcal{K}(u;q) + \int_\Omega <\omega, u> Q(d\omega); \quad u \in C_0(K)\}.$$

Now, introduce the limit

$$C(G;q) := \limsup_{T,\varepsilon} \frac{1}{T} \log P_q^\varepsilon(\sigma_T \in G) \quad \text{for all open set } G \text{ in } \Omega.$$

The barycenter of Q in $\mathcal{K}(\Omega)$, $b_Q = \int \omega\, Q(d\omega)$, is an element of the compact convex space Ω, (Bourbakk [2] , v.XIII, Chap.IV § 7). We define the entropy of Q as

$h(Q,q) = \inf\{C(G,q) : G$ is open in Ω and $b_Q \in \underline{G}\}$ (where the underline means closure).

Clearly $-\infty \leq h(Q;q) \leq 0$ and the following "Gibbs variational principle holds".

(3.2) THEOREM.

Under the hypothesis above, functionals $h(\bullet;q)$ and $e(\bullet;q)$ are upper semicontinuous; e is concave; $h \leq e$ and for all u in $C_0(K)$, the following equalities hold:

$$\mathfrak{K}(u; q) = \max\{e(Q; q) - \int \langle \omega, u \rangle Q(d\omega); \quad Q \in \mathfrak{K}(\Omega)\}$$

$$= \max\{h(Q; q) - \int \langle \omega, u \rangle Q(d\omega); \quad Q \in \mathfrak{K}(\Omega)\}.$$

PROOF. Let us fix a probability q in $\mathfrak{K}(E)$. Remark that $C(G,q)$ decreases with decreasing G (in the sense of inclusion). Given any real number a, call $\mathcal{G}(a)$ the family of all open sets G in Ω such that $C(G,q) > a$, ordered by inclusion.

Now since Ω is compact, so is $\mathfrak{K}(\Omega)$. Besides this, given $G \in \mathcal{G}(a)$, the set $\mathfrak{K}(\Omega/G) := \{Q \in \mathfrak{K}(\Omega):$ barycenter of Q is in $\underline{G}\}$ is closed. In fact, functions $Q \mapsto \int \langle \omega, u \rangle Q(d\omega)$ are continuous for each u in $C_0(K)$, then $Q \mapsto \int \omega Q(d\omega)$ is continuous from $\mathfrak{K}(\Omega)$ in Ω, by definition of the topology on Ω. That means that the intersection of all $\mathfrak{K}(\Omega/G)$, when G run over $\mathcal{G}(a)$, is closed, but such intersection is equal to $\{Q \in \mathfrak{K}(\Omega): h(Q,q) > a\}$. Thus $h(\cdot, q)$ is upper semicontinuous.

Using again the continuity argument on functions $Q \mapsto \int \langle \omega, u \rangle Q(d\omega)$ for each u in $C_0(K)$, it follows that $e(\cdot, q)$ is concave and upper semicontinuous as infimum (over $u \in C_0(K)$) od affine functions of the form $Q \mapsto \mathfrak{K}(u,q) + \int \langle \omega, u \rangle Q(d\omega)$.

Let us prove the inequality $h \leq e$. Take Q in $\mathfrak{K}(\Omega)$ and G an open set in Ω such that $b_Q \in \underline{G}$. Then

$$P_q^{\varepsilon}(\sigma_T \in G) \exp[-T \sup_{\omega \in \underline{G}} \langle \omega, u \rangle] \leq \int_G \exp[-\int_0^T \langle \Theta_t(\omega), u \rangle dt]\, P_q^{\varepsilon}(d\omega)$$

$$\leq E_q^{\varepsilon}(\exp[-\int_0^T \langle \Theta_t, u \rangle dt]).$$

Taking $\log$ dividing by $T>0$, and performing the "$\limsup$", yields

$$C(G,q) \leqslant \pi(u,q) + \sup\{<\omega,u>:\ \omega\in \underline{G}\}, \quad \text{for all } u\in C_0(K) \tag{3.2.1}$$

And $\inf\{\sup\{<\omega,u>:\ \omega\in \underline{G}\}:\ G$ open such that $b_Q \in \underline{G}\} = <b_Q, u>$, then

$$h(Q,q) \leqslant \pi(u,q) + \int <\omega,u>\, Q(d\omega), \quad \text{for all } u\in C_0(K). \tag{3.2.2}$$

Thus $h(q,q) \leqslant e(Q,q)$.

Finally, let us prove the "maximal" inequalities anounced in the Theorem.

Fix $u\in C_0(K)$ and $\eta>0$. Since Ω is compact, we can find a finite collection of open convex sets Ω_i, $i=1,\ldots,n$, covering Ω and such that $\sup\{|<\omega,u> - <\omega',u>|:\ \omega,\omega'\in \underline{\Omega}_i\} \leqslant \eta$. Remark that $C(G,q) \leqslant \sup\{h(Q,q):\ Q\in\pi(\Omega/G)\}$, then

$$\pi(u,q) \leqslant \limsup_{T,\varepsilon} \frac{1}{T}\log \sum_{i=1}^{n} P_q^{\varepsilon}(\sigma_T\in\Omega_i)\exp(-T\inf\{<\omega,u>:\ \omega\in\Omega_i\}).$$

Since for all $Q\in\pi(\Omega/\Omega_i)$, the barycenter b_Q is in $\underline{\Omega}_i$ we get

$$\leqslant \max_{1\leqslant i\leqslant n}\ [C(\Omega_i,q) - \inf\{<b_Q,u>;\ Q\in\pi(\Omega/\Omega_i)\}] + \eta$$

$$\leqslant \sup\{h(Q,q) - \int_{\Omega} <\omega,u>\, Q(d\omega):\ Q\in\pi(\Omega)\} + \eta$$

Thus,

$$\pi(u,q) \leqslant \sup\{h(Q,q) - \int <\omega,u>\, Q(d\omega):\ Q\in\pi(\Omega)\}. \tag{3.2.3}$$

But, by definition of the free energy we have for all u in $C_0(K)$:

$$\mathbf{e}(Q, q) - \int \langle \omega, u \rangle \, Q(d\omega) \leqslant \pi(u, q).$$

Using the inequality $h \leqslant e$ we finally have:

$$\sup\{h(Q, q) - \int \langle \omega, u \rangle Q(d\omega) : Q \in \pi(\Omega)\} \leqslant \tag{3.2.4}$$

$$\leqslant \sup\{e(Q, q) - \int \langle \omega, u \rangle Q(d\omega) : Q \in \pi(\Omega)\} \leqslant$$

$$\leqslant \pi(u, q) \leqslant$$

$$\leqslant \sup\{h(Q, q) - \int \langle \omega, u \rangle Q(d\omega) : Q \in \pi(\Omega)\}$$

which completes the proof of the theorem.

(3.3) REMARK.

From the construction of the entropy, it is clear that $h(Q, q)$ is maximum $(= 0 = \mathbf{e}(Q, q))$ if the family of dictributions $\mathbb{S}(q) = (\epsilon_T(P_q^{\varepsilon}))$ is relatively compact and Q is an element of the limit set $\mathbb{S}'(q)$. This is in particular the case when $L^+(q) \neq \phi$, and $Q \in L^+(q)$.

(3.4). COROLLARY.

For all stable system, the entropy arrains its maximum on $\mathbb{J}(\pi(\Omega))$.

More generally, if Q is an attractor set, then the entropy attains its maximum on Q.

Now the free energy $\mathbf{e}(Q, q)$ and the entropy $h(Q, q)$ will be $-\infty$ in particular whenever $\mathbb{S}(q)$ is not compact.

(3.5). DEFINITION.

Given an unstable dynamical stochastic system, we say it is metastable if there exist q in $D_u(P)$ for which the associated entropy functional $h(\bullet, q)$, attains its maximum on the set $\mathcal{E}$ of all probabilities Q supporting the set of step measures, i.e. $Q(\Sigma)=1$. In this case, every probability Q in $\mathcal{E}$ for which $h(Q,q)=0$ will be called a metastable iquilibrium point.

By remark (3.3), every unstable system for which $\mathcal{S}(q)=(\sigma_T(P_q^\varepsilon))$ is relatively compact and the limit set $\mathcal{S}'(q)$ has a non-empty intersection with $\mathcal{E}$, is metastable. Therefore we have the following criteria on metastability.

(3.6). PROPOSITION.

An unstable system is metastable if there exists $q \in D_u(P)$, such that for all family $(T(\varepsilon))$ going to ∞, there exists a subsequence $(T(n))$ and a random step measure ν such that for all finite collection $u_1, \dots, u_k$ in $C_0(K)$, the sequence of random variables $(\langle \sigma_{T(n)}, u_1\rangle, \dots, \langle \sigma_{T(n)}, u_k\rangle;\ n \in \mathbb{N})$ converge in $P_q^{\varepsilon(n)}$ -distribution to the vector $(\langle \nu, u_1\rangle, \dots, \langle \nu, u_k\rangle)$.

PROOF. Remark that every set of the form $W=\{\omega \in \Omega : \langle \omega, u_1\rangle \leqslant \alpha_1, \dots, \langle \omega, u_k\rangle \leqslant a_k\}$ is compact in Ω, for $u_1, \dots, u_k$ in $C_0(K)$, $a_1, \dots, a_k$ in $\mathbb{R}$. Denote by $\pi_{1,\dots,k}(\omega)$ the random vector $(\langle \omega, u_1\rangle, \dots, \langle \omega, u_k\rangle)$. Given $(T(\varepsilon))$, choose a subsequence by the hypothesis and call Q_n (resp. Q) the distribution of $\sigma_{T(n)}$ under $P_q^{\varepsilon(n)}$ (resp. the distribution of the random step measure ν over Ω). The convergence of dictributions $\pi_{1,\dots,k}(Q_n)$ towards $\pi_{1,\dots,k}(Q)$ imply tightness of (Q_n), first of all, since for all $\eta > 0$ we can choose a W-set such that $Q_n(W) \geqslant 1-\eta >$, for all n. Secondly, given any limit point Q' of (Q_n) we deduce that $\pi_{1,\dots,k}(Q) = \pi_{1,\dots,k}(Q')$; for all $u_1, \dots, u_k$ in $C_0(K)$, then $Q=Q'$ and the whole sequence (Q_n) converges towards Q.

Consequently, $\mathcal{S}(q)=(\sigma_T(P_q^\varepsilon))$ is relatively compact and $\mathcal{S}'(q)$ has a non-empty intersection with $\mathcal{E}$; thus, the system is metastable.

This method was used by Galves. A.-Olivieri E.- Vares M.E. [7] to prove metastability behaviour in the situation described in example (1.6.4).

An alternative method to prove the existence of a metastable equilibrium is given by the flux indicator (1.2) of measure-valued processes. In fact, in order to state relative compactness of $\mathbb{S}(q)$, it is sufficient to show that $(\mathbb{Z}^{T(\varepsilon)}(P_q^\varepsilon))$ is a tight family of distributions, where $\mathbb{Z}^{T(\varepsilon)}$ is the pseudotrajectory of the measure-valued process $Z^{T(\varepsilon)}$ defined by

$$Z_t^{T(\varepsilon)}(\omega) = \frac{1}{T(\varepsilon)} \int_t^{t+T(\varepsilon)} \varepsilon_{X(\omega)}\, ds$$

where X is the canonical process introduced in (1.5). As the reader can verify, the following relation holds

$$\langle \sigma_{T(\varepsilon)}(\omega),\ f \otimes g \rangle = \int_0^\infty \langle Z_t^{T(\varepsilon)},\ f \rangle g(t)\, dt = \langle \mathbb{Z}^{T(\varepsilon)},\ F_f \otimes g \rangle$$

where f is a bounded continuous function from E to $\mathbb{R}$; g is a real-valued continuous function with compact support defined on $[0, \infty[$ and F_f is the functional $\langle \cdot, f \rangle$.

Thus in order to study compactness of $(\mathbb{Z}^{T(\varepsilon)}(P_q^\varepsilon))$ it is possible to use Theorem (1.4). This was done in my papers [11] , [12] .

(3.5). PROPOSITION.

In order the system have a metastable behaviour it is sufficient that for one q in $D_u(P)$ there exist integers k and $j \geq k$, a partition of $[0, \infty[$ in non-empty intervals $(I(1), \ldots, I(j))$, such that

$$\limsup_{T,\varepsilon} P_q^\varepsilon (N^{\mathcal{U},\mathcal{V}}(\mathbb{Z}^{T(\varepsilon)}, I(i)) = 0, \quad i = 1,\dots,j$$

$$\text{and} \quad \mathbb{Z}^{T(\varepsilon)} \in \Delta_k(\mathfrak{X}(\mathbb{E})) - \Delta_0(\mathfrak{X}(\mathbb{E}))) = 1$$

for all disjoint open subsets $\mathcal{U}, \mathcal{V}$ of $\mathfrak{X}(\mathbb{E})$.

ACKNOWLEDGEMENTS.

The author wish to express his gratetude to the Academy of Sciences of the USSR, and to the organizers of the international Symposium on Stability Problems for Stochastic Models, Professors V.Zolotarev and V.Kalashnikov, for their kind hospitality.

REFERENCES

1. Bhatia N.P.-Szegö G.P. Stability Theory of Dynamical Systems. Springer-Verlag, Berlin-Heidelberg-New York, 1970.
2. Bourbaki N. Éléments de Mathématiques. Intégration. Chapitres 1,2,3 et 4 v. XIII Hermann, Paris, 1965.
3. Cassandro M.- Galves A.- Olivieri E.- Vares M.E. Metastable behaviour of stochastic dynamics pathwise approach. J.of Statist. Physics, 35, 1984, 603-634.
4. Dellacherie C.- Meyer P.A. Probabilités et potentiel, Chapitres 1 á IV, Hermann, Paris, 1975.
5. Dellacherie C.- Meyer P.A. Probabilités et potentiel. Chapitres IX á XI Théorie discrete du potentiel. Hermann, Paris, 1983.
6. Ellis R.S.-Newmann C.M.- Rosen J.S. Limits Theorems for Sums of Dependent Random Variables Occuring in Statistical Mechanics. II Conditioning, Multiple Phases and Metastability. Z. Wahkscheinlichkeitstheor. verb. Geb. 51, 1980, 153-169.
7. Galves A.- Olivieri E.-Vares M.E. Metastability for a class of dynamical systems subject to small random perturbations. Preprint

I.H.E.S., 1984.

8. Knight F. A predictive view of continuous time processes. Ann.of Probab., 3, 1975, 573-596.

9. Meyer P.A.- Zheng W.A. Tightness criteria for laws of semimartingales. Ann.I.H.P. v.20, N 4, 1984, 353-372.

10. Palis J.- Takens F. Homoclinic bifurcations and Hyperbolic Dynamics. IMPA, curso do 16 col. Brasileiro de Matematica, 1987.

11. Rebolledo R. Topologie taible et métastabilité. Séminaire de Prob. XXI, Lect. Notes Math., Springer-Verlag, 1987.

12. Rebolledo. Weakening the Skorokhod' Topology for Measure-valued processes. Teor. Veroyatn. Primen. N 1, 1987, 170-182.

3. Rebolledo R. Functionales Convexos sobre los Sistemas Dinámicos Estocástocos. Informe Téchnoco P.U.C./FM-87/5 To appear in Proceeding of the 16. Col. Brasileiro de Matematica, 1987.

14. Takahashi Y. Entropy Functional (free energy) for Dymanical Systems and their Random Perturbations. Taniguchi Symp. SA, Katata, North Holland ed., 437-467, 1982.

15. Vares M.E. Grandes desvios em processos markovianos. IMPA, curso do 15 Col. Brasileiro de Matemática, 1985.

Vol. 1232: P.C. Schuur, Asymptotic Analysis of Soliton Problems. VIII, 180 pages. 1986.

Vol. 1233: Stability Problems for Stochastic Models. Proceedings, 1985. Edited by V.V. Kalashnikov, B. Penkov and V.M. Zolotarev. VI, 223 pages. 1986.

Vol. 1234: Combinatoire énumérative. Proceedings, 1985. Edité par G. Labelle et P. Leroux. XIV, 387 pages. 1986.

Vol. 1235: Séminaire de Théorie du Potentiel, Paris, No. 8. Directeurs: M. Brelot, G. Choquet et J. Deny. Rédacteurs: F. Hirsch et G. Mokobodzki. III, 209 pages. 1987.

Vol. 1236: Stochastic Partial Differential Equations and Applications. Proceedings, 1985. Edited by G. Da Prato and L. Tubaro. V, 257 pages. 1987.

Vol. 1237: Rational Approximation and its Applications in Mathematics and Physics. Proceedings, 1985. Edited by J. Gilewicz, M. Pindor and W. Siemaszko. XII, 350 pages. 1987.

Vol. 1238: M. Holz, K.-P. Podewski and K. Steffens, Injective Choice Functions. VI, 183 pages. 1987.

Vol. 1239: P. Vojta, Diophantine Approximations and Value Distribution Theory. X, 132 pages. 1987.

Vol. 1240: Number Theory, New York 1984–85. Seminar. Edited by D.V. Chudnovsky, G.V. Chudnovsky, H. Cohn and M.B. Nathanson. V, 324 pages. 1987.

Vol. 1241: L. Gårding, Singularities in Linear Wave Propagation. III, 125 pages. 1987.

Vol. 1242: Functional Analysis II, with Contributions by J. Hoffmann-Jørgensen et al. Edited by S. Kurepa, H. Kraljević and D. Butković. VII, 432 pages. 1987.

Vol. 1243: Non Commutative Harmonic Analysis and Lie Groups. Proceedings, 1985. Edited by J. Carmona, P. Delorme and M. Vergne. V, 309 pages. 1987.

Vol. 1244: W. Müller, Manifolds with Cusps of Rank One. XI, 158 pages. 1987.

Vol. 1245: S. Rallis, L-Functions and the Oscillator Representation. XVI, 239 pages. 1987.

Vol. 1246: Hodge Theory. Proceedings, 1985. Edited by E. Cattani, F. Guillén, A. Kaplan and F. Puerta. VII, 175 pages. 1987.

Vol. 1247: Séminaire de Probabilités XXI. Proceedings. Edité par J. Azéma, P.A. Meyer et M. Yor. IV, 579 pages. 1987.

Vol. 1248: Nonlinear Semigroups, Partial Differential Equations and Attractors. Proceedings, 1985. Edited by T.L. Gill and W.W. Zachary. IX, 185 pages. 1987.

Vol. 1249: I. van den Berg, Nonstandard Asymptotic Analysis. IX, 187 pages. 1987.

Vol. 1250: Stochastic Processes – Mathematics and Physics II. Proceedings 1985. Edited by S. Albeverio, Ph. Blanchard and L. Streit. VI, 359 pages. 1987.

Vol. 1251: Differential Geometric Methods in Mathematical Physics. Proceedings, 1985. Edited by P.L. García and A. Pérez-Rendón. VII, 300 pages. 1987.

Vol. 1252: T. Kaise, Représentations de Weil et GL_2 Algèbres de division et GL_n. VII, 203 pages. 1987.

Vol. 1253: J. Fischer, An Approach to the Selberg Trace Formula via the Selberg Zeta-Function. III, 184 pages. 1987.

Vol. 1254: S. Gelbart, I. Piatetski-Shapiro, S. Rallis. Explicit Constructions of Automorphic L-Functions. VI, 152 pages. 1987.

Vol. 1255: Differential Geometry and Differential Equations. Proceedings, 1985. Edited by C. Gu, M. Berger and R.L. Bryant. XII, 243 pages. 1987.

Vol. 1256: Pseudo-Differential Operators. Proceedings, 1986. Edited by H.O. Cordes, B. Gramsch and H. Widom. X, 479 pages. 1987.

Vol. 1257: X. Wang, On the C*-Algebras of Foliations in the Plane. V, 165 pages. 1987.

Vol. 1258: J. Weidmann, Spectral Theory of Ordinary Differential Operators. VI, 303 pages. 1987.

Vol. 1259: F. Cano Torres, Desingularization Strategies for Three-Dimensional Vector Fields. IX, 189 pages. 1987.

Vol. 1260: N.H. Pavel, Nonlinear Evolution Operators and Semigroups. VI, 285 pages. 1987.

Vol. 1261: H. Abels, Finite Presentability of S-Arithmetic Groups. Compact Presentability of Solvable Groups. VI, 178 pages. 1987.

Vol. 1262: E. Hlawka (Hrsg.), Zahlentheoretische Analysis II. Seminar, 1984–86. V, 158 Seiten. 1987.

Vol. 1263: V.L. Hansen (Ed.), Differential Geometry. Proceedings, 1985. XI, 288 pages. 1987.

Vol. 1264: Wu Wen-tsün, Rational Homotopy Type. VIII, 219 pages. 1987.

Vol. 1265: W. Van Assche, Asymptotics for Orthogonal Polynomials. VI, 201 pages. 1987.

Vol. 1266: F. Ghione, C. Peskine, E. Sernesi (Eds.), Space Curves. Proceedings, 1985. VI, 272 pages. 1987.

Vol. 1267: J. Lindenstrauss, V.D. Milman (Eds.), Geometrical Aspects of Functional Analysis. Seminar. VII, 212 pages. 1987.

Vol. 1268: S.G. Krantz (Ed.), Complex Analysis. Seminar, 1986. VII, 195 pages. 1987.

Vol. 1269: M. Shiota, Nash Manifolds. VI, 223 pages. 1987.

Vol. 1270: C. Carasso, P.-A. Raviart, D. Serre (Eds.), Nonlinear Hyperbolic Problems. Proceedings, 1986. XV, 341 pages. 1987.

Vol. 1271: A.M. Cohen, W.H. Hesselink, W.L.J. van der Kallen, J.R. Strooker (Eds.), Algebraic Groups Utrecht 1986. Proceedings. XII, 284 pages. 1987.

Vol. 1272: M.S. Livšic, L.L. Waksman, Commuting Nonselfadjoin Operators in Hilbert Space. III, 115 pages. 1987.

Vol. 1273: G.-M. Greuel, G. Trautmann (Eds.), Singularities, Rep sentation of Algebras, and Vector Bundles. Proceedings, 1985. X 383 pages. 1987.

Vol. 1274: N. C. Phillips, Equivariant K-Theory and Freeness of G[illegible]p Actions on C*-Algebras. VIII, 371 pages. 1987.

Vol. 1275: C.A. Berenstein (Ed.), Complex Analysis I. Proceedings, 1985–86. XV, 331 pages. 1987.

Vol. 1276: C.A. Berenstein (Ed.), Complex Analysis II. Proceedings, 1985–86. IX, 320 pages. 1987.

Vol. 1277: C.A. Berenstein (Ed.), Complex Analysis III. Proceedings, 1985–86. X, 350 pages. 1987.

Vol. 1278: S.S. Koh (Ed.), Invariant Theory. Proceedings, 1985. V, 102 pages. 1987.

Vol. 1279: D. Ieşan, Saint-Venant's Problem. VIII, 162 Seiten. 1987.

Vol. 1280: E. Neher, Jordan Triple Systems by the Grid Approach. XII, 193 pages. 1987.

Vol. 1281: O.H. Kegel, F. Menegazzo, G. Zacher (Eds.), Group Theory. Proceedings, 1986. VII, 179 pages. 1987.

Vol. 1282: D.E. Handelman, Positive Polynomials, Convex Integral Polytopes, and a Random Walk Problem. XI, 136 pages. 1987.

Vol. 1283: S. Mardešić, J. Segal (Eds.), Geometric Topology and Shape Theory. Proceedings, 1986. V, 261 pages. 1987.

Vol. 1284: B.H. Matzat, Konstruktive Galoistheorie. X, 286 pages. 1987.

Vol. 1285: I.W. Knowles, Y. Saitō (Eds.), Differential Equations and Mathematical Physics. Proceedings, 1986. XVI, 499 pages. 1987.

Vol. 1286: H.R. Miller, D.C. Ravenel (Eds.), Algebraic Topology. Proceedings, 1986. VII, 341 pages. 1987.

Vol. 1287: E.B. Saff (Ed.), Approximation Theory, Tampa. Proceedings, 1985–1986. V, 228 pages. 1987.

Vol. 1288: Yu. L. Rodin, Generalized Analytic Functions on Riemann Surfaces. V, 128 pages, 1987.

Vol. 1289: Yu. I. Manin (Ed.), K-Theory, Arithmetic and Geometry. Seminar, 1984–1986. V, 399 pages. 1987.

Vol. 1290: G. Wüstholz (Ed.), Diophantine Approximation and Transcendence Theory. Seminar, 1985. V, 243 pages. 1987.

Vol. 1291: C. Mœglin, M.-F. Vignéras, J.-L. Waldspurger, Correspondances de Howe sur un Corps p-adique. VII, 163 pages. 1987

Vol. 1292: J.T. Baldwin (Ed.), Classification Theory. Proceedings, 1985. VI, 500 pages. 1987.

Vol. 1293: W. Ebeling, The Monodromy Groups of Isolated Singularities of Complete Intersections. XIV, 153 pages. 1987.

Vol. 1294: M. Queffélec, Substitution Dynamical Systems – Spectral Analysis. XIII, 240 pages. 1987.

Vol. 1295: P. Lelong, P. Dolbeault, H. Skoda (Réd.), Séminaire d'Analyse P. Lelong – P. Dolbeault – H. Skoda. Seminar, 1985/1986. VII, 283 pages. 1987.

Vol. 1296: M.-P. Malliavin (Ed.), Séminaire d'Algèbre Paul Dubreil et Marie-Paule Malliavin. Proceedings, 1986. IV, 324 pages. 1987.

Vol. 1297: Zhu Y.-l., Guo B.-y. (Eds.), Numerical Methods for Partial Differential Equations. Proceedings. XI, 244 pages. 1987.

Vol. 1298: J. Aguadé, R. Kane (Eds.), Algebraic Topology, Barcelona 1986. Proceedings. X, 255 pages. 1987.

Vol. 1299: S. Watanabe, Yu.V. Prokhorov (Eds.), Probability Theory and Mathematical Statistics. Proceedings, 1986. VIII, 589 pages. 1988.

Vol. 1300: G.B. Seligman, Constructions of Lie Algebras and their Modules. VI, 190 pages. 1988.

Vol. 1301: N. Schappacher, Periods of Hecke Characters. XV, 160 pages. 1988.

Vol. 1302: M. Cwikel, J. Peetre, Y. Sagher, H. Wallin (Eds.), Function Spaces and Applications. Proceedings, 1986. VI, 445 pages. 1988.

Vol. 1303: L. Accardi, W. von Waldenfels (Eds.), Quantum Probability and Applications III. Proceedings, 1987. VI, 373 pages. 1988.

Vol. 1304: F.Q. Gouvêa, Arithmetic of *p*-adic Modular Forms. VIII, 121 pages. 1988.

Vol. 1305: D.S. Lubinsky, E.B. Saff, Strong Asymptotics for Extremal Polynomials Associated with Weights on ℝ. VII, 153 pages. 1988.

Vol. 1306: S.S. Chern (Ed.), Partial Differential Equations. Proceedings, 1986. VI, 294 pages. 1988.

Vol. 1307: T. Murai, A Real Variable Method for the Cauchy Transform, and Analytic Capacity. VIII, 133 pages. 1988.

Vol. 1308: P. Imkeller, Two-Parameter Martingales and Their Quadratic Variation. IV, 177 pages. 1988.

Vol. 1309: B. Fiedler, Global Bifurcation of Periodic Solutions with Symmetry. VIII, 144 pages. 1988.

Vol. 1310: O.A. Laudal, G. Pfister, Local Moduli and Singularities. V, 117 pages. 1988.

Vol. 1311: A. Holme, R. Speiser (Eds.), Algebraic Geometry, Sundance 1986. Proceedings. VI, 320 pages. 1988.

Vol. 1312: N.A. Shirokov, Analytic Functions Smooth up to the Boundary. III, 213 pages. 1988.

Vol. 1313: F. Colonius, Optimal Periodic Control. VI, 177 pages. 1988.

Vol. 1314: A. Futaki, Kähler-Einstein Metrics and Integral Invariants. IV, 140 pages. 1988.

Vol. 1315: R.A. McCoy, I. Ntantu, Topological Properties of Spaces of Continuous Functions. IV, 124 pages. 1988.

Vol. 1316: H. Korezlioglu, A.S. Ustunel (Eds.), Stochastic Analysis and Related Topics. Proceedings, 1986. V, 371 pages. 1988.

Vol. 1317: J. Lindenstrauss, V.D. Milman (Eds.), Geometric Aspects of Functional Analysis. Seminar, 1986–87. VII, 289 pages. 1988.

Vol. 1318: Y. Felix (Ed.), Algebraic Topology – Rational Homotopy. Proceedings, 1986. VIII, 245 pages. 1988

Vol. 1319: M. Vuorinen, Conformal Geometry and Quasiregular Mappings. XIX, 209 pages. 1988.

Vol. 1320: H. Jürgensen, G. Lallement, H.J. Weinert (Eds.), Semigroups, Theory and Applications. Proceedings, 1986. X, 416 pages. 1988.

Vol. 1321: J. Azéma, P.A. Meyer, M. Yor (Eds.), Séminaire de Probabilités XXII. Proceedings. IV, 600 pages. 1988.

Vol. 1322: M. Métivier, S. Watanabe (Eds.), Stochastic Analysis. Proceedings, 1987. VII, 197 pages. 1988.

Vol. 1323: D.R. Anderson, H.J. Munkholm, Boundedly Controlled Topology. XII, 309 pages. 1988.

Vol. 1324: F. Cardoso, D.G. de Figueiredo, R. Iório, O. Lopes (Eds.), Partial Differential Equations. Proceedings, 1986. VIII, 433 pages. 1988.

Vol. 1325: A. Truman, I.M. Davies (Eds.), Stochastic Mechanics and Stochastic Processes. Proceedings, 1986. V, 220 pages. 1988.

Vol. 1326: P.S. Landweber (Ed.), Elliptic Curves and Modular Forms in Algebraic Topology. Proceedings, 1986. V, 224 pages. 1988.

Vol. 1327: W. Bruns, U. Vetter, Determinantal Rings. VII,236 pages. 1988.

Vol. 1328: J.L. Bueso, P. Jara, B. Torrecillas (Eds.), Ring Theory. Proceedings, 1986. IX, 331 pages. 1988.

Vol. 1329: M. Alfaro, J.S. Dehesa, F.J. Marcellan, J.L. Rubio de Francia, J. Vinuesa (Eds.): Orthogonal Polynomials and their Applications. Proceedings, 1986. XV, 334 pages. 1988.

Vol. 1330: A. Ambrosetti, F. Gori, R. Lucchetti (Eds.), Mathematical Economics. Montecatini Terme 1986. Seminar. VII, 137 pages. 1988.

Vol. 1331: R. Bamón, R. Labarca, J. Palis Jr. (Eds.), Dynamical Systems, Valparaiso 1986. Proceedings. VI, 250 pages. 1988.

Vol. 1332: E. Odell, H. Rosenthal (Eds.), Functional Analysis. Proceedings, 1986–87. V, 202 pages. 1988.

Vol. 1333: A.S. Kechris, D.A. Martin, J.R. Steel (Eds.), Cabal Seminar 81–85. Proceedings, 1981–85. V, 224 pages. 1988.

Vol. 1334: Yu.G. Borisovich, Yu. E. Gliklikh (Eds.), Global Analysis – Studies and Applications III. V, 331 pages. 1988.

Vol. 1335: F. Guillén, V. Navarro Aznar, P. Pascual-Gainza, F. Puerta, Hyperrésolutions cubiques et descente cohomologique. XII, 192 pages. 1988.

Vol. 1336: B. Helffer, Semi-Classical Analysis for the Schrödinger Operator and Applications. V, 107 pages. 1988.

Vol. 1337: E. Sernesi (Ed.), Theory of Moduli. Seminar, 1985. VIII, 232 pages. 1988.

Vol. 1338: A.B. Mingarelli, S.G. Halvorsen, Non-Oscillation Domains of Differential Equations with Two Parameters. XI, 109 pages. 1988.

Vol. 1339: T. Sunada (Ed.), Geometry and Analysis of Manifolds. Procedings, 1987. IX, 277 pages. 1988.

Vol. 1340: S. Hildebrandt, D.S. Kinderlehrer, M. Miranda (Eds.), Calculus of Variations and Partial Differential Equations. Proceedings, 1986. IX, 301 pages. 1988.

Vol. 1341: M. Dauge, Elliptic Boundary Value Problems on Corner Domains. VIII, 259 pages. 1988.

Vol. 1342: J.C. Alexander (Ed.), Dynamical Systems. Proceedings, 1986–87. VIII, 726 pages. 1988.

Vol. 1343: H. Ulrich, Fixed Point Theory of Parametrized Equivariant Maps. VII, 147 pages. 1988.

Vol. 1344: J. Král, J. Lukeš, J. Netuka, J. Veselý (Eds.), Potential Theory – Surveys and Problems. Proceedings, 1987. VIII, 271 pages. 1988.

Vol. 1345: X. Gomez-Mont, J. Seade, A. Verjovski (Eds.), Holomorphic Dynamics. Proceedings, 1986. VII, 321 pages. 1988.

Vol. 1346: O. Ya. Viro (Ed.), Topology and Geometry – Rohlin Seminar. XI, 581 pages. 1988.

Vol. 1347: C. Preston, Iterates of Piecewise Monotone Mappings on an Interval. V, 166 pages. 1988.

Vol. 1348: F. Borceux (Ed.), Categorical Algebra and its Applications. Proceedings, 1987. VIII, 375 pages. 1988.

Vol. 1349: E. Novak, Deterministic and Stochastic Error Bounds in Numerical Analysis. V, 113 pages. 1988.